IN THE
RUINS

By Kate Elliott

CROWN OF STARS

IN THE
RUINS

Volume Six of
CROWN OF STARS

Kate Elliott

www.orbitbooks.co.uk

ORBIT

First published in Great Britain in September 2005 by Orbit

Copyright © 2005 by Katrina Elliott

The moral right of the author has been asserted.

All characters and events in this publication, other than those clearly in the public domain, are fictitious and any resemblance to real persons, living or dead, is purely coincidental.

A CIP catalogue record for this book
is available from the British Library.

HARDBACK ISBN 1 84149 271 X
C FORMAT ISBN 1 84149 272 8

Printed and bound in Great Britain by
Clays Ltd, St Ives plc

Orbit
An imprint of
Time Warner Book Group UK
Brettenham House
Lancaster Place
London WC2E 7EN

www.orbitbooks.co.uk

AUTHOR'S NOTE

As all of my readers know, this has been a long and complicated series, with a long and complicated plot. Indeed, after a certain point in writing this series, there was simply no way to turn back.

In the two years it took me to write the final volume, I considered only the needs of the characters and the story in order to write as strong an ending as possible to CROWN OF STARS. I am satisfied that I did my best and, as much as I could, achieved the ending I envisioned.

However, at approximately 430,000 words, the manuscript I turned in to my publishers was simply too long to bind as a single volume. I was left with a choice. I could cut several hundred pages out of the book—and weaken the end of the series by leaving plot threads and characters' fates unresolved—or I could split the manuscript into two volumes, each of which would run about as long as PRINCE OF DOGS.

I spent a lot of time agonizing over length, wondering whether any book needs to be this long. In the end, however, I couldn't see a way to make the cuts without losing a significant amount of the story's impact, so I chose to make the split in order to preserve the story. This means that CROWN OF STARS will be published in seven volumes, rather than six.

In retrospect, I note that the number 'seven' echoes the mage's ladder, so perhaps in some way this was inevitable.

For those who welcome or are at least resigned to this development, thank you so much for your patience. For those who are understandably irritated by it, please accept my apologies. I had no idea what I was getting into when I started.

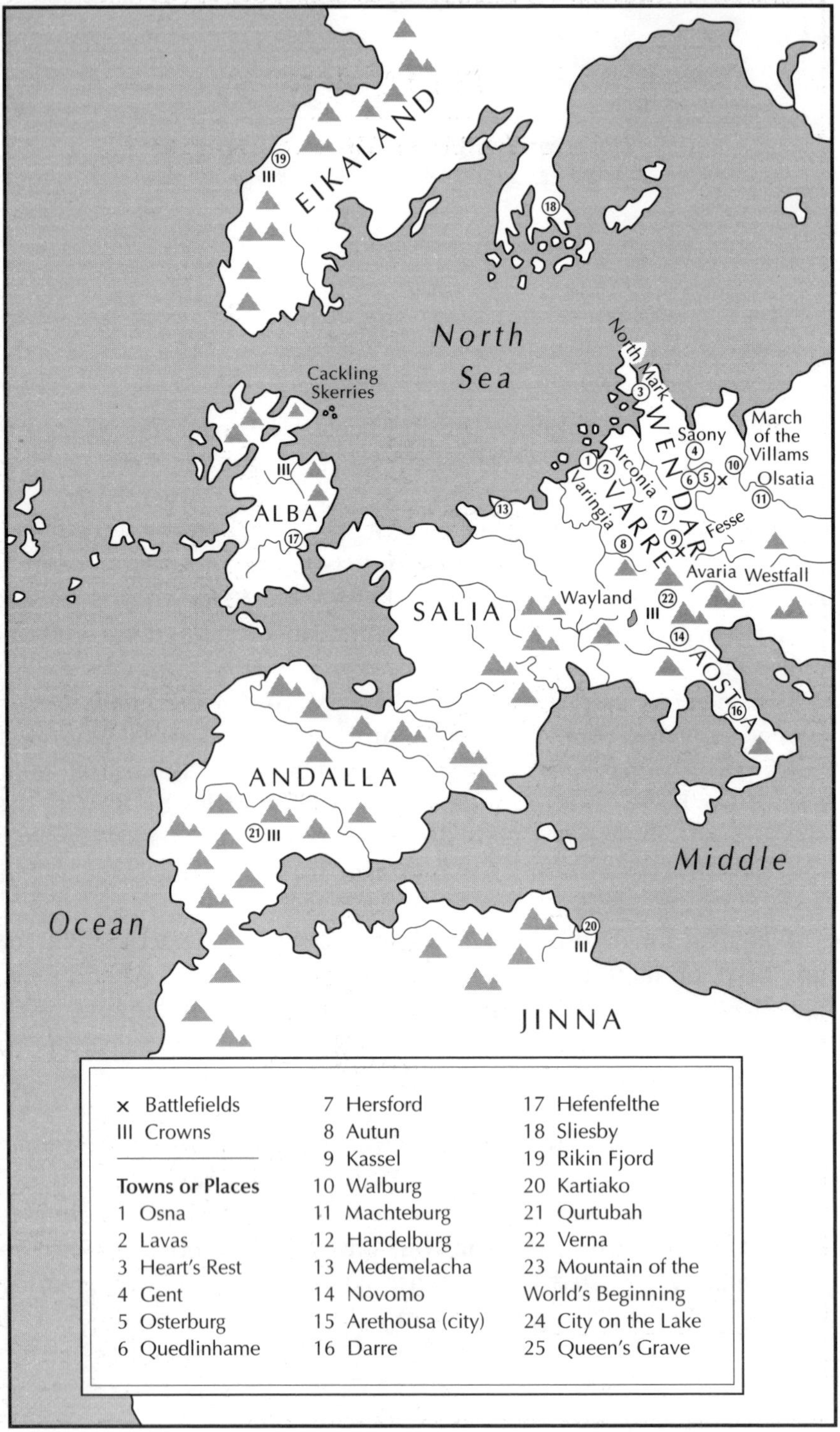

EIKALAND
North Sea
Cackling Skerries
ALBA
North Mark
WENDAR
Saony
March of the Villams
Olsatia
Arconia
Varingia
VARRE
Fesse
Avaria
Westfall
Wayland
SALIA
AOSTA
ANDALLA
Middle
Ocean
JINNA
× Battlefields
III Crowns
Towns or Places
1 Osna
2 Lavas
3 Heart's Rest
4 Gent
5 Osterburg
6 Quedlinhame
7 Hersford
8 Autun
9 Kassel
10 Walburg
11 Machteburg
12 Handelburg
13 Medemelacha
14 Novomo
15 Arethousa (city)
16 Darre
17 Hefenfelthe
18 Sliesby
19 Rikin Fjord
20 Kartiako
21 Qurtubah
22 Verna
23 Mountain of the World's Beginning
24 City on the Lake
25 Queen's Grave

NOVARIA

THE WORLD AFTER THE CATACLYSM

(steppe)

POLENIE

⑫

㉕ III
Austra ✕
Eastfall

Heretic's
Sea

UNGRIA

Dalmiaka ✕
III

ARETHOUSA ⑮

ASHIOI
㉓
㉔

JINNA

Sea

N

III

(desert)

Ocean

0   40   80   120   160

LEAGUES
(3 miles = 1 league)

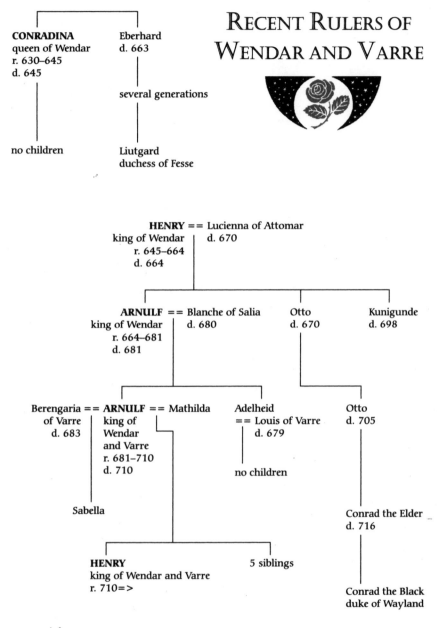

RECENT RULERS OF WENDAR AND VARRE

CONRADINA
queen of Wendar
r. 630–645
d. 645

no children

Eberhard
d. 663

several generations

Liutgard
duchess of Fesse

HENRY == Lucienna of Attomar
king of Wendar   d. 670
r. 645–664
d. 664

ARNULF == Blanche of Salia   Otto   Kunigunde
king of Wendar   d. 680   d. 670   d. 698
r. 664–681
d. 681

Berengaria == **ARNULF** == Mathilda   Adelheid   Otto
of Varre   king of   == Louis of Varre   d. 705
d. 683   Wendar   d. 679
             and Varre
             r. 681–710   no children
             d. 710

Sabella   Conrad the Elder
                                                             d. 716

HENRY   5 siblings
king of Wendar and Varre
r. 710=>   Conrad the Black
                                                             duke of Wayland

== married
r. reigned
d. died

CONTENTS

Part Three

ADVENTUS

Part Four

THE MOUNTAIN OF THE
WORLD'S BEGINNING

IN THE
RUINS

PROLOGUE

FEATHER Cloak was fertile, the only pregnant woman left among her people. Indeed, she was the only woman living who had quickened more than once. Therefore, she presided over the council of tribes because she had power the others did not possess, power that had been draining from the land during their exile. No one could explain this slow leaching, but they knew it presaged the death of both land and people. If anyone could save them, it must be the one in whom power still resided long after it had departed from the rest.

The Eagle Seat had yielded to her. In truth, it was now the only place she rested easily. Her older child was almost an adult in aspect and learning, but in the days when he had grown within her, he had not waxed so large. It seemed she would harvest a giant's spawn, although she happened to know that the sire of her budding child was Rain, who was no smaller or larger than any other man. He was a gentle soul of medium build, good-natured, a hard worker with clever hands, a skill for flint-knapping, and a well-omened name, and for all these reasons a much better choice for a father than arrogant warriors like Cat Mask and Lizard Mask who liked to shake their spears and strut before the women.

As they were doing now.

"We must gather in one place, farther inland where we'll be protected, and ready ourselves! Then we can act at once, and in numbers. We can strike before our enemy expects us!"

"Better to station ourselves in smaller groups, you fool! Spread out around the countryside. If one group is taken by surprise, the others will be able to harry the enemy and regroup when it is safe."

"If the enemy strikes first, if the enemy passes the White Road and

1

sets foot in our country, we are lost!" Cat Mask pounded the haft of the speaking staff repeatedly into the dirt to emphasize his point. As if his voice wasn't loud enough!

Lizard Mask had half a head of height over Cat Mask. He used it now, puffing up his chest and jutting out his chin, as he curled a hand around the haft above Cat Mask's hand. "If the enemy invades, how can we know where he will cross? If we're all in one place, we'll lose mobility. We'll lumber along as slowly as your mind works!"

"Feh! Your wish to be safe has made you frightened. We must be bold!"

"We must be cautious but clever, the thorn in their side."

"The arrow in their heart! One blow to cripple them, not a frenzy of meaningless stings that will only anger them but do no lasting damage."

The councillors were seated around the cavernous chamber, watching the two young warriors stamping and blowing in the center. The older women seemed amused and indulgent, while the younger women had settled into expressions of disgust or intent interest depending on their liking for belligerent male posturing. The older men stood with crossed arms and resigned expressions as they waited for the storm to die down; they had blustered in like manner in their own day and knew better than to intervene.

"A swarm of bees may bring down a wolf who angers them and disturbs their hive."

"A wolf may outrun them and stalk back at night when they sleep to rip their refuge to shreds for other animals to mangle and devour!"

Because men had the floor, it wasn't the place of women to speak, but Feather Cloak was not surprised when The Impatient One— Uapeani-kazonkansi-a-lari, daughter of Eldest Uncle—laughed.

"What fine phrases these are!" she cried. "Shall we acclaim the one who pierces us with the finest poetry?"

The two men flushed red. Faced with her mockery, they shifted their stances to join against her. In years past, The Impatient One had slept with both of them, and cast both aside, and whatever jealousy they nurtured each toward the other measured less than their resentment of her indifference.

"You argue over war," she went on, "but force of arms cannot win this battle."

"We must fight!" declared Cat Mask.

"Whether we choose to mass our forces or disperse them, we must be ready to fight," agreed Lizard Mask.

She snorted. "They are many and we are few. Beyond that, humankind are only one of the dangers we face. We may yet suffer grievous harm when the day comes—close now!"

As if to emphasize her point in the same way Cat Mask had rapped his spear against the ground, the land beneath shuddered. The vibration resembled a temblor but was instead the judder of the land as it called out like to like, seeking its home through the waves of aether that surrounded it. It shook right through Feather Cloak's body. Her womb clenched and relaxed in harmony with that rhythm. She wiped her brow with the back of a hand, knowing her time was close, just as the day they had so long awaited was close.

What was torn asunder would come back to its resting place, and the Ashioi, cursed and exiled, would come home.

Many spoke, all at once, now that The Impatient One had spoken out of turn. Peace. War. Appeasement. Negotiation. Each view had its adherents, but those who clamored for war shouted loudest.

"I will speak," Feather Cloak said. The rest, even The Impatient One, quieted. "Listen well. If we do not speak with one voice, we will surely perish. We no longer have leisure to argue. A decision must be made, so I will make it. Let it be done in this way: Let the people be gathered inland, where they may hope for the most safety. But let them assemble in thirteen groups, each apart from the others, so that if one falls into danger the others may yet escape. Cat Mask, you will split our warriors into two groups. The larger group will remain with you at a place of your choosing, where you can move and fight swiftly. Lizard Mask, you will order the rest into small groups that can patrol the borderlands to warn the rest of us if any hostile force passes our borders. The council will disperse with the others. I will remain here until the storm passes. White Feather will act as my midwife. For the rest, we must prepare to defend ourselves, but only after the storm can we know how we are situated and how many of us have survived. We will assemble again at that time to choose our course of action. I have spoken. Let none dispute my words."

She had only once before invoked her right to make a unilateral decision. No wise leader did so often. She sighed, doubly burdened, as the council acquiesced. Most left swiftly to carry out her orders. A few tarried, arguing in soft voices that nevertheless echoed and re-echoed in the cavern. Only Eldest Uncle remained silent where he sat, cross-legged, on the second terrace.

"You have offered no opinion, Uncle," she said.

"He has no opinion," replied his daughter, turning away from her conversation with her companion White Feather who, like her, was harsh but strong. "He has fallen in love with his grandson's naked mate, whom all men desire because she burns with the fire of the upper spheres."

Eldest Uncle sighed.

"Is this true?" asked Feather Cloak. "I admit I was surprised when you brought her before the council. She is dangerous, and in the way of such dangerous things, attractive and bright."

"She is young, and wanted teaching. If you women can think of nothing but sex, that is not my fault."

"My father and my son—both enslaved to her! What do you say, Feather Cloak?"

"I banished her, seeing what she was. Beyond the danger she poses to every earthly creature because of what she is, I saw no harm in her."

"You are a fool!"

Feather Cloak smiled, clasping her hands over her huge abdomen. "That may be. And maybe you are jealous."

Eldest Uncle chuckled.

The Impatient One glared.

"But I sit in the Eagle Seat. If you dispute my right to take this place, you will have to prove yourself more worthy than I am."

Like every adult among her people, Feather Cloak could use a bow and had learned to defend herself with knife and staff, but The Impatient One had relished the arts of war in which all adolescents trained. She was physically strong, with powerful limbs and a martial grace that could be used to protect, or to threaten, as she did now, tense and poised, a warrior ready to cast a spear at her enemy.

"I have walked the spheres! Do not mock my power."

"I do not mock you, Cousin. But I do not fear you either. Power is not wisdom. It is only power. Cat Mask and his warriors cannot protect us if he makes rash choices. We are weakened by our exile. We do not know what we may yet suffer. I counsel caution and readiness. You yourself spoke against using force of arms."

"Only because they are many, and we are few. We must strike swiftly with other means. The greatest and cruelest of their warriors can be overcome by sorcery. I have defeated even the wild beasts among them who would have torn me limb from limb."

"Beware," said Eldest Uncle quietly. "We have seen how much greater is suffering when sorcery is used for harm."

"You think we should surrender!"

"Do I? We must seek peace."

"Peace is surrender! Humankind will never offer us peace."

"How can you know this, Daughter?"

"I know them better than you do! I have lived among them. I bore a child to one of them." She looked defiantly at Feather Cloak. "They are not like us. They will never make peace with us. My son was raised as an outcast among them, and even so they seduced him to their ways."

"Better to have raised him in our ways," said Eldest Uncle, "instead of abandoning him there."

"So you would say! But it was decided to try the course of appeasement by birthing a child who would mix their blood and ours. That plan has failed!"

"Has it?"

"Do you believe otherwise? How can you know? You have not walked on Earth since the old days, and the old days are forgotten by humankind. They recall us only in stories, as an ancient enemy long banished and defeated. Or is it the memory of the Bright One that blinds you, so that you do not wish to war against them?"

"It is ill mannered for a daughter to speak so disrespectfully to her own sire," commented Feather Cloak. "Your words may carry truth, but your behavior gives us cause to doubt you."

"You *are* fools!" The Impatient One snapped her fingers, and one of the young warriors, loitering by the passageway that led out of the cavern, came to attention. "Still, it is possible—just possible—if they are not dead but only caught between the worlds. . . ." She grinned, leaped up the steps, and vanished into the darkness, the young man at her heels.

"Who is dead?" asked White Feather.

"*We* are caught between the worlds," said the elderly woman known as Green Skirt. "What mischief is she up to?"

"She'll try to get pregnant again," said White Feather. "She'll want the Eagle Seat. She'll wrest it from you, if she can."

Feather Cloak had weathered many trials in her life. They all had, who lived in exile. She smiled, feeling the familiar tug of weariness at her heart, leavened only by a memory of laughter she had once shared with The Impatient One when they were girls together. "In the old days," she said as the last of her council gathered around her, "we did not acclaim a leader solely on her fertility. It is a shame it has come to this." She patted her belly. Muscles tightened under her hand. The skin rippled as the child within rolled like one of the fabled merfolk underwater.

"How has the world changed?" she asked the others, marking each one with her gaze: Eldest Uncle, Green Skirt, the old warrior Skull Earrings, and White Feather, who would act as midwife. These were the ones she trusted most because they were honest, even and particularly when they did not agree. They were her spring, winter, autumn, and summer. "We do not know what we will find when we return to Earth, for none among us has walked in the other land as it is now. None except The Impatient One."

"Uapeani-kazonkansi-a-lari walked the spheres," said White Feather. "She risked her life so that she could learn what was necessary to cross over the aether and back onto Earth. We should not dismiss her words so lightly, just because she does not agree with her father."

Eldest Uncle chuckled.

Green Skirt had an older woman's distaste for nonsense. She lifted her chin sharply to show she disagreed. "That she refuses to listen to her elders is precisely what makes her opinion suspect. She is rash."

Skull Earrings crossed his arms. He had once been a bold, impetuous, impatient warrior like Cat Mask, but age, hunger, and despair had worn him down. He was like ancient gold, burnished to a soft gleam. "First, let us survive what is coming. We do not know what to expect, except what the Bright One told us. That our old enemies the Horse people and their human allies still live, and seek to exile us forevermore. If we survive, then we can send scouts to survey the lay of the land. If we do not survive, if we are cast adrift a second time, then we will certainly die. What can we do?"

"We can do nothing," said Eldest Uncle, "except take shelter and hope for the storm's winds to spare us."

"There must be something we can do!" cried White Feather. "Are we goats, to be herded at the shepherds's whim and slaughtered when it is time for meat?"

"Now—right now—we are helpless," said Eldest Uncle. "There is no shame in accepting this as truth, since it is so. I agree with my nephew." He gestured toward Skull Earrings.

The other man laughed. "After so many years, it is good we agree at last, Uncle!"

The old man smiled, but Feather Cloak saw that the gesture came only from the head, not his heart. "I will wait beside the clearing where the burning stone appears," he said.

"That is on the edge of the land," protested Feather Cloak. "The tides may wash over you. You will be at risk."

"As you are here, Feather Cloak."

"I cannot leave the Eagle Seat. I like you close at hand. It makes me feel more at peace."

He shrugged, knowing she was right, knowing that as leader she had no peace. The weight of the Eagle Seat was as heavy a burden as pregnancy. "Nevertheless, I must wait there, in case—"

White Feather snorted. "In case the Bright One reappears? Perhaps your daughter speaks the truth, Uncle. You have a young man's mind in an old man's body."

"That never changes!" he retorted, but he was not offended by her statement. The others laughed. "I am eldest. I will do as I wish in this. I will see what I will see. If the tides overwhelm me, so be it."

A contraction gripped Feather Cloak's womb. As if in echo, the earth trembled and shook on and on until she found herself breathing hard, hands clutching the eagle's wings.

White Feather knelt beside her. "You are close." She beckoned to Green Skirt, who nodded and hurried to the door to give a stream of directions to one of the warriors waiting there, a young woman wearing a fox mask tipped back onto her hair. The girl ran out to fetch water while White Feather emptied coals out of a hollow stick and coaxed a fire into flame. Skull Earrings fetched the birthing stool.

All this industry, and the intense grip of further contractions, distracted Feather Cloak. She had the merest impression of Eldest Uncle's brief farewell and the pair of young warriors who followed him. When she next looked around the chamber, all three were gone.

As the contractions came hard and with increasing frequency, she began no longer to be able to distinguish the forces shaking her body and those shaking the land. So many burdens; so much exhaustion; so great a trial to be faced. She had to let it go. It was beyond her control. All she could do was endure it. All she could do, between stabs of red-hot pain, was pray to Sharatanga, She-Who-Will-Not-Have-A-Husband.

"Guide us through this birth and this death. Give us your blessing."

Was that her voice or White Feather's? Was it Green Skirt speaking, as the green beads and little white skull masks clicked together each time the old woman moved? Did she herself mumble words, or only grunt and groan and curse as the pains of opening came and went?

She was vaguely sensible beyond her skin of the greater skin of the cosmos, that which wrapped Earth, opening as a flower opens to receive that which now returned to it: the exiled land. Vast forces moved within the deeps. The sea waters raged on the surface and winds howled, while in the caverns far beneath, rivers of fire shifted to create a new maze of pathways.

Earth is welcoming us home.

"Hush," said White Feather. "Hold your breath so you can push."

"Listen to what Feather Cloak says!" objected Green Skirt. "She can see where we cannot."

The pain of opening transformed her awareness as the child within pressed forward, ready to be born. It was not pain but inevitability that dragged her. Now the exiled land was drawn back to the place it had come from, where it had always belonged. Now the child would be born, because children must be born once they have begun that journey.

Four attended her: White Feather, Skull Earrings, Green Skirt, and the fox-masked young warrior, a serious girl who glared at everyone as she ran to and fro on whatever errands they gave her.

She knew this not because she paid attention to them, but because she knew all things. The vital soul that resides in the cosmos and imbues it and all things with life, even those that may seem dead, became visible to her. She saw the vibration of all things down to their smallest particle. She saw the reach of the heavens as they expanded in an infinite curve whose unknowable horizon confounded her. The exiled land was almost drained of this soul. Ruptured from its nurturing womb, it had waned as the tide of the sacred presence had ebbed. Now the vibrant net that entangled Earth swallowed them, and as the child in her belly was thrust out from its shelter, they were dragged in to the ancient nest in whose architecture still resided a memory of their place within it.

The slippery mass of a child dropped into White Feather's waiting hands.

She groaned, or perhaps it was the earth grinding at a register almost too low to be perceived.

"Another one!" cried Green Skirt in shock.

"Twice blessed! Twice cursed!" sang out White Feather, shoving the first infant into the waiting hands of Skull Earrings so she could catch the impatient second, now crowning.

Feather Cloak pushed as the world was born again, as the White Road flared into existence, a ribbon so bright that it shone, as Earth exploded beyond the borders of the Ashioi land. Firestorms raged and gales seared the land. Yet all this transpired at such a remote distance from the heart of the maelstrom that her awareness of the cosmos, too, faded, and she was after all weary. So weary.

"Two girls!" said Skull Earrings, cradling the first tenderly in his arms. "The gods have favored us!"

She slid down the long road of exhaustion and fell into sleep.

North of the land lies devastation so complete that the land steams. Has their return created such a wasteland that smoke and ruin are all she sees?

No. Beyond the scar lies land touched by fire, by wind, by raging seas, by great shifts in the earth itself, by tumult, but it is not dead.

She sees now what caused the land just beyond the White Road to be engulfed by molten rock. The Bright One walks in the wasteland. She created it with the power that resides within her, the curse she received from her mother's kin. She is naked and carries nothing except a bow layered with the magical essence of griffin bone. So bright it shines. . . .

She moaned and came awake, squinting against a light she did not recognize.

"Ah!" She shielded her eyes. "What is it?"

"He-Who-Burns!" cried Green Skirt. "That is the sun. See how his light shines!" She pointed at the roof of the cavern, where a yellow glare illuminated the spray of plant roots dangling from crumbling ridges of soil.

Skull Earrings stepped forward with White Feather beside him. "Here are your daughters," he said, displaying the dark babies.

White Feather nodded. "So small. So perfect!"

Weeping, she kissed them. "They will never know exile. We have come home."

PART ONE

THE TIDES OF DESTRUCTION

I
A VISION OF
THE END

1

WHEN the earth began to shake, his jailers abandoned him within the ruins of the old monastery, beside the roofless church and its stone tower. From his prison, in his cage in the back of the cart, he watched in a confused stupor as both horses and oxen bolted, spooked by the unnatural weather.

Along the shoreline of Osna Sound, the water receded far out past the line of the ebb tide, exposing seabed and a line of sharp rocks below the curve of the Dragonback Ridge. Above, the sky was a sheet of lightning that veiled the stars, but that light in the heavens was an uncanny thing because no thunder answered it. A stillness, more like an indrawn breath, settled over the country, and it hung there, waiting.

Soon.

The silence was broken with a roar as the ground jolted. The cart pitched over. The post to which Alain was chained snapped as it struck the ground. With a groan, the stone tower collapsed into a cloud of dust and grit that choked him as he sprawled, like the fish flopping in the exposed seabed, gasping for breath. Scattered by a rising wind, the storm of dirt quickly dissipated, but the ground had not finished shifting.

The Dragonback Ridge splintered with a deafening crack. Sheets of rock cascaded into the sound. Beneath the booming clatter of rock, the earth moved as the dragon woke. Its tail, lashing as it was freed from the soil, snapped trees. As its flank heaved up where once lay the high ridge, dirt avalanched seaward, obliterating the old shoreline. The creature lifted a claw and set it down, and the ground trembled beneath that tread. It raised its huge head to examine the heavens, then slewed around. Chained and caught, Alain could only stare as the head lowered down and down and paused at length before the cage to stare at him.

With one bite it could devour cart and man both. He struggled to his knees to face it, although it took all his strength to rise.

Its scales shone like gold. Its eyes had the luster of pearls. It was not untarnished from its waking: there was a cut in its belly, and from this a tear of bright, hot blood hissed, splashing over him. Its touch burned him to the heart, not with heat but with truth.

My heart is the Rose. Any heart is the Rose of Healing that knows compassion and lets it bloom.

It blinked, huffed a cloud of steam, reared its head up, and opened its vast wings. Their span shadowed the monastery grounds. It bunched its haunches, waited a breath, ten breaths, a hundred breaths, as if listening, as if it, too, were waiting.

A wind howled up out of the southwest, shattering trees as it came, and when it hit, the dragon launched itself. Alain fell, never sure if the gale or the weight of its draft had battered him down. Its shadow passed away. Beyond, the sea raged against the rocks. Above, the stars had gone out. All he could see of the sky was a swirling haze mixed of dust and ash and wind and bits of foliage, and the trailing sparks of a vast spell.

He heard still a roar of sound, building in volume, and before he understood what it was, a wave out of the sea swept over him. His chains held him under the water as he tumbled in its surf, fighting for the surface. And as he drowned, he saw in a vision the land unfolding before him. He saw as the spell tangled and collapsed in on itself. He saw the land of the Ashioi materialize out of the aether, back to the place it had come from long ago.

He saw what happened in the wake of that spell:

All down the western shoreline of the boot of Aosta, a ridge of volcanoes shakes into life. Lava streams out of the earth. Fields crack open, as the pit yawns beneath. An unstoppable tide of mud and ash slurry buries villages and the folk who live in them. There is no warning, no time to flee.

The waters of the Middle Sea that are displaced by the returning land speed outward in vast concentric rings. These waves deluge distant coastlines, drowning the shore.

All along the northern sea rivers run backward and ports are left dry as the land groans and shifts, rising no more than a finger's span as the weight settling in the south tilts the entire continent.

Temblors shake the land. The gale that blasted across the earth dissipates in wilderness among the dumb beasts. Deep in the earth, goblins race through ancient labyrinths, seeking their lost halls. Under the sea, the merfolk dive deep to escape the maelstrom. Out in the distant grasslands, the Horse people shelter in hollows in the land. The magic of the Holy One shields them from the worst even as it drains the life out of her.

All this he sees as he struggles in the waters. He sees, and he understands:

Those who were most harmed in ancient days ride out the storm with the least damage. It is humankind who suffer most. Perhaps Li'at'dano hoped or planned that in the end the weaving would harm those who were the greatest threat to her people: both the Cursed Ones, and her own human allies.

Perhaps the WiseMothers suspected that humankind would take the brunt of the backlash. Perhaps they had no choice except to do what they did, knowing that the belt was already twisted and the path already laid clear before their feet. They speak to him through rock and through water, although the salt sea almost drowns their voice.

It. Is. Done. You. Have. Saved. Us.

He gasps for breath but swallows water. The link between them is broken so sharply that it is as if it had never existed.

Caught in the riptide, he came clear of the water suddenly and flailed and gasped and choked and coughed as the tide hauled him toward the sea. The chain jerked him back to the ground. The cart, trapped in the fallen stones, had saved him, which had all this time imprisoned him. He lay there, too dazed to move.

At length daylight filtered into the haze of ash and dust that clouded the heavens. After a long time he realized that he was alive and that, impossibly, the world had survived. The great weaving that Adica had made so long ago with her compatriots was at long last finished. The spell had come all the way around and returned to where it began. The Lost Ones had returned from their exile.

He had seen both beginning and end, only of course the end was now a beginning.

After all, he was not alone in the ruins, as he had thought. The hounds came and with them came his foster father, Henri.

"Where are we going?" Alain asked him.

"Home, Son. We're going home."

2

BECAUSE the ridge had been obliterated by the dragon's waking, their way proved rough and strenuous as they walked toward home through a jumble of boulders, fallen trees, and tide-wracked debris. In the end Alain's legs failed him and his strength gave out. He could scarcely breathe. Once they reached a real path, Henri had to carry him, stopping at intervals to rest.

"You're nothing but bones and skin," Henri said one of those times. He sat, sweating, on a smooth beech tree, uprooted in last night's storm. Alain wheezed, curled up on the ground because he hadn't the strength to sit upright. The hounds nosed him fretfully. "You weigh no more than a child. I'll never forgive Lord Geoffrey for doing this to you. It's a sin to treat another human being so cruelly."

He was too weak to answer. The world seemed dim, but perhaps that was only because of clouds covering the sky.

Henri sighed. "You do stink, though, Son. Whew!" The affection in his voice made Alain's lips tremble, but he could not manage a smile. For so long he had endured. Now, safe, he thought he might at last die because he had been worn too thin. He wanted to go on, but he had nothing left.

"Here, now, you beasts, move aside."

Henri hoisted him effortlessly, shifted him onto his own back so Alain's head rested on Henri's shoulder, and kept walking. It seemed likely that they should have passed through Osna village, but apparently Henri kept to those woodland paths that took them around the village and onto the broad southern road. Many trees were

fallen. Branches littered the path. It was silent, not even bird call to
serenade them, and not a soul out on the roads the morning after.
Where the road forked, Henri veered to the right along a narrower
side path that wound through oak and silvery birch, maple and
beech. Long ago he had ridden down this path with Count Lavastine.
The memory seemed as a dream to him now, no more real than his
life with Adica. All gone, torn away by death.

Yet there was life here still. Some manner of person had husbanded these woods, cutting down trees for firewood and boat-
building in many spots but fostering quick-growing ash and
sparing half the slow-growing oaks in others. Coppice-cut willow,
hazel, and hawthorn flourished in various states of regrowth, some
freshly cut and others ready for felling again. Sorrow barked. Pigs
squealed away into the undergrowth.

"Who's there?" came a cry from ahead.

"I've found him!" cried Henri.

Alain hadn't the strength to raise his head, so, sidewise, he
watched the estate emerge as the path opened onto neatly-mown
hayfields and a tidy garden, recently harvested. Two corrals ringed
sheep and a pair of cows. Geese honked, and chickens scattered.
There was even a horse and a pony, riches for a free-holding family
without noble forebears. Folk had come out of the workshop and the
house to stand and stare, but it was the ones he knew best who ran
up the path to meet them. Julien was scarred and lean. Stancy was
pregnant; she ran forward with a child grasping her hand. Was that
third adult little Agnes, grown so comely and tall?

"That can't be Alain," said Julien. "That creature's nothing more
than skin pulled over bones."

"It's him," said Stancy. "Poor boy." She wiped away tears.

"Stink! Stink!" wailed the child, tugging to break free and run.
"He scares me."

"Hush!" Aunt Bel strode up to them, looked at him hard, and
frowned. "Stancy, kill a chicken and get a broth cooking. He'll not
be strong enough to eat solid food. Agnes, I'll want the big basin tub
for bathing him. Outside, though. Julien, haul water and tell Bruno
to heat it on the workshop fire. We'll need plenty. He can't be
chilled."

Like the chickens, they scattered but to more purpose.

"Dear God," said Aunt Bel. "That's a strong smell. We'll have to
wash him twice over before we bring him inside. I'll have the girls
make a good bed for him by the hearth. He'll be abed all winter, if

he survives at all. He looks more like a ghost than like our sweet lad."

"He can hear you."

"Can you hear me, boy?" she demanded. Because it was Aunt Bel asking, he fluttered his eyelids and got out a croak, not much more than a sigh. "It's a wonder he's still alive, abused like that." She made a clucking noise, quite disgusted. "It's a good thing you went after him, Henri."

"Don't let him die, Bel. I failed him once already."

"It's true you let your pride get the better of you. You were jealous."

The movement of Henri's shoulders, beneath Alain's chest, betrayed a reaction.

"Nay, there's nothing more to be said," retorted Bel. "Let it be, little brother. What's in the past is gone with the tide. Let him be. I'll nurse him myself. If he lives, then we can see."

A drop of moisture fell on Alain's dangling hand. At first, he thought it might be rain from those brooding clouds, but as they trudged down into the riot of the living, he realized that these were Henri's tears.

II
THE LUCK OF
THE KING

1

SANGLANT knew dawn came only because he could smell the sun's rising beyond the haze that concealed all horizons. Ash rained down on his army as they straggled through the scorched forest, dragging their wounded with them. Here and there fires burned in the treetops. Smoke rose, blending with the ash drifting over them. Limbs snapped and crashed to earth to create echoes within echoes as the devastated forest collapsed on itself.

They assembled in their tattered legions around the ancient fortress where Lady Wendilgard had met her death. Up on the height of half fallen walls, Captain Fulk posted sentries to watch over the wounded. The prince stood on the shattered ramp, once a causeway leading up into the fortress and now a series of broken stair steps littered with stones, weapons, and four dead men not yet dragged away. The last surviving troops who had heard the call to sheathe weapons and retreat emerged battered, bruised, and limping from the trees to take up places in the clearing. They were crammed shoulder to shoulder, weary and frightened, and all of them awaiting his command.

Perhaps two thousand troops remained to him, out of opposing armies which had each easily boasted twice that number. Of his personal guard, once numbering more than two hundred, some two score remained. Every man among them bore at least one wound, some minor and a few, no doubt, mortal. To his left waited Capi'ra and her centaurs, who had weathered the storm better than most, and a remnant of Quman soldiers. The winged riders had been hit hard in the field by the heavier numbers of Henry's army, but they had held their ground. It was largely due to their courage and will that he had saved as many of his troops as he had during that initial disastrous retreat when Henry's forces had overpowered him in the early part of the battle. Of the rest of his noble brethren who had marched with him from Wendar and the marchlands, he had only two surviving commanders: Lord Wichman and Captain Istvan, the Ungrian. Lord Druthmar was lost on the field, although no man living had seen him fall, and he had long since lost track of the rest of his captains and lords, who might still be huddling in the forest or lying among the dead.

Henry's army formed up to his right: Duchess Liutgard and her cavalry out of Fesse, Duke Burchard and his Avarians together with his daughter Wendilgard's remaining men, and others from Saony and the duchies of Varre. The terrible storm and the blast of burning wind had hit Henry's army as hard as his own.

Henry's army no longer.

Henry's corpse lay fixed over Fest's saddle. Sanglant held the reins.

"Your Majesty." Hathui bowed before him. "What now?"

"Where is Zuangua?" he asked, surveying the scene. "I see no Ashioi among our number."

"They did not follow us back this way, my lord prince . . ." Lewenhardt corrected himself. "Your Majesty." Like the others, the young archer was filthy, smeared with ash and dirt and blood. Ash pattered down, the sound of its steady rain audible even through the many noises of the army creaking into place, men weeping, men talking, horses in distress, a few dogs barking, and wagon wheels squeaking on the fine layer of ash and grit. "They went off into the trees toward the sea, along the old track they were following before. I don't know where they've gone."

"I do," Sanglant said. "They've abandoned us and gone home, for I'm thinking that their homeland must surely have returned from its long exile." It hurt to breathe. It hurt to think of Liath struggling among the living or lost to death. "Hathui, if we build a fire, can you seek Liath through the flames?"

"I can try, Your Majesty."

He nodded. She took two soldiers and trudged through the pall into the forest, where charcoal would be easy to gather. The trio passed a group of exhausted men stumbling out of the trees. The ash so covered every least thing that it was impossible to tell what lord or lady these soldiers had served before the night's cataclysm.

All his, now. Every one of them. With his dying breath, Henry had willed Wendar and Varre to his favorite child, his obedient son, the bastard, the one the king had long wished to succeed him despite all opposition.

"We cannot see into the future," Helmut Villam had once observed. That was a mercy granted to humankind, who would otherwise drown in a sea of unwanted knowledge filled with reversals, tragedies, unhoped-for rescues, and the endless contradictions of life.

He remembered the passion in his own voice that day by the river, below the palace of Werlida, when he had spoken so decidedly to his father the king. *"I don't want to be king. Or heir. Or emperor."*

And now, of course, he was. King, and heir to an empire he had never desired.

"What of your Aostan allies?" he asked his cousin Liutgard, nodding also at the old duke, Burchard.

The duchess shrugged, wiping ash off her lips with the back of one filthy hand. Her hair was streaked with ash, tangled and dirty; impossible to tell how fair it was under all the soot. "They fled west along the coast instead of following us," she said. "Their allegiance was to Adelheid, not to Henry. There are yet stragglers, and a few wandering confused among our troops. For the rest, those who live, I believe they will all fly home."

With a sigh, Sanglant rubbed his stinging eyes. "Has there been any report of the griffins?" he asked those standing nearest to him. Clustered behind Hathui were a dozen Eagles rescued from Henry's train.

In truth he needed no answer. If the gale had not killed the griffins outright, then it had surely blasted them far away. It seemed impossible for any creature in the air to have survived the storm.

Ai, God, he was so weary that he had begun to hear things, a strange rushing roar that nagged at his hearing until even the folk surrounding him heard as well. To the south, shouts of alarm rang out above the snap and crash of branches as though a second wind raked through the forest. Scouts left behind to stand sentry over the road tumbled into the clearing.

"The ocean! The ocean has risen!"

He gestured to Lewenhardt and Captain Fulk. Together they ran along the road into the trees, and before they had gone far they saw an astonishing sight. Water surged inland through the trees, losing depth quickly until it lapped and sighed around their boots. As they stared, it drained away, most into the ground but in a few stubborn rivulets back toward the sea, dragging twigs and leaves in its undertow. Sanglant knelt and brushed his fingers through a remnant pool as the roar of the receding waters faded. He touched the moisture to his lips, spat out the salty brine.

"This is seawater."

"That is not possible," said Captain Fulk. "No tide can rise so high. It's a league at least—more!—from here to the ocean!"

"Bring Fest. I'll need an escort of a hundred men. If there's any hope of capturing Queen Adelheid, we must seek her now. Bring Duke Burchard, since he knows the town and its defenses. Tell Duchess Liutgard to make an account of what provisions are left us, tend to the wounded, and ready the men for a long march. Bury the dead before they begin to rot."

"Even the emperor, Your Majesty?"

"No. We must prepare Henry for the journey north. See that his heart is removed from his body, and his flesh boiled until there is nothing left but bones."

The road through the forest had survived the conflagration, but it was muddy and streaked with debris. The wind gusted erratically and after one man was knocked out cold by a falling branch, they watched for limbs with each flurry. The trees were blackened and burned on the side facing the southeast. Desiccated leaves filtered down with the ever present ash fall. Light rose as the morning progressed, but the day remained hazy and dim and the heavens had a glowering sheen. Every sound was muffled by the constant hiss of ash and the layer of soot and mud blanketing the damp ground. It was cool, yet clammy, and the long walk exhausted them and their horses alike.

"Is it the end of the world, my lord pr— Your Majesty?" Lewenhardt whispered.

"If it is the end, then why are we not dead? Nay, Lewenhardt, it is as it seems. A terrible cataclysm has overtaken us. We may yet survive if we keep our wits about us, and if we hold together."

Duke Burchard drew the Circle of Unity at his chest, but said nothing. The old man seemed too stunned to speak. He was not alone in this. For every soldier who exclaimed out loud at the scorched forest and the marks of the recent flood there were four or five who gaped at the devastation as though they had, indeed, lost their wits.

"I dislike this, Your Majesty," said Fulk. "What if the sea returns?"

"We must see. Besides Queen Adelheid, we must seek out those who survived and hid until daybreak. Liutgard said many of the Aostans marched west along the coast. What of them?"

Pools of salty water filled the ruts in the road, and a gloomy vista awaited them when at last they emerged from the trees and gazed through the swirling ash that obscured the bay of Estriana, half a league away. The plain looked strangely scumbled, strewn with debris. He could not mark the field where the battle had been fought or the line of their retreat because branches and corpses and planks from wagons and all manner of flotsam lay tumbled everywhere. He saw no life at all in the distant town.

"You are sure?" he asked Duke Burchard. "You left Queen Adelheid behind in Estriana?"

The old man's voice was more like a croak. "So I did, Your Majesty. She held a reserve behind the walls in case of disaster. It was already agreed that she would remain in the tower rather than sortie out. She is a strategist, Your Majesty, not a soldier."

"So she is," agreed Sanglant, "if she yet lives. I walked right into the ambush she and Henry laid between them."

Burchard shook his head impatiently. "We saw well enough what trap Henry fell into. The daimone with which Presbyter Hugh ensorcelled him spoke his words and moved his limbs according to the presbyter's command. Henry did not speak. That plan was the queen's alone."

"She is a formidable opponent, then. What do we do with her now?"

Staring across the plain toward the Middle Sea, Burchard wept softly. "Perhaps bury her?"

The pall of dust hid the waters, which seemed, impossibly, at low tide, drawn far back across tidal flats.

"Ai, God!" cried Lewenhardt, who possessed the sharpest gaze among them, able to pierce the haze. "Look!"

The water was rising swiftly. It swelled at the mouth of the bay into a monstrous wave that crested into a wall of foaming white. The wave surged forward across the bay and smashed down onto the town and the shoreline, engulfing it and inundating the land. The water rose up and up, still climbing as it flooded the plain.

"Run!"

The others turned and fled. Sanglant could not bring himself to move. He could not *quite* believe, despite the evidence of his eyes, that the sea could rise so fast and run so far. The whiter crest that battered the town dissipated quickly, subsumed in the vast tidal swell that rolled inland across the plain. Fest snorted and shied, and he reined him in, turning in a complete circle before the horse settled, uneasy and in protest but holding fast.

"My lord prince!" cried Captain Fulk, returning in haste to rein up beside him. "We'll be drowned. You must come!"

The tide lapped to its highest extent a stone's toss from Fest, not even reaching the outlying trees of the forest, and sucked hissing and burbling back into the sea. All that lay strewn over the plain from the first surge rushed outward with it. Even the stone walls of Estriana toppled into the wave, all but the highest tower, which was protected by a double ring of walls that had taken the brunt of the impact.

His men, creeping back, wept to witness the sea's fury. As the wave receded, the ruins of the town emerged from the water. The stone walls were shattered at a dozen places. Seen through those gaps, the buildings looked like piles of sticks.

"Ai, God!" cried Duke Burchard. "Queen Adelheid must surely be dead! No one could have survived such a deluge!" He glanced at Sanglant and wiped his brow nervously. "Surely she had a reason for the terrible course she took, Your Majesty. Surely she did not wish to harm the king. She loved him. She is a good woman."

"Let us hope we do not have to make decisions as cruel as the one she felt herself forced to make," replied Sanglant.

"I think it most prudent if we retreat," said Fulk. "We have seen that these unnatural tides are not yet faded. Look how the water sucks back out again. What if a larger surge comes?"

"Look," said Lewenhardt. "Something is moving out there!"

Sanglant dismounted.

"Your Majesty!" protested Captain Fulk

"I'll walk. The footing looks too tricky for horses."

"Why go at all? If you're swept away—"

"I think we have time. The second wave did not approach until we had walked all the way from the old fort. If you have ever sat upon the sea's shore and watched the waves, Captain, you will have seen they have a rhythm of their own. These great waves need time to approach."

Fulk had stood firm through many terrible events when others quailed and faltered, and although the prospect of drowning clearly horrified him, he did not fail Sanglant now. "Very well. I'll come with you, Your Majesty."

Sanglant grinned and strode forward. The ground was not hopelessly muddy because the tide had come up and receded too swiftly to soak in, but damp ash made the ground slick and debris from the forest caught about their ankles and snagged in their leggings. It was not silent but uncannily still, with no sign of life but their own soft footsteps. The hissing fall of ash serenaded them. Maybe it would never stop raining down. Perhaps the heavens themselves had burned and now shed the soot of their destruction over the earth. The throttling gurgle of the sea faded in the distance as the tide receded back and back beyond the tidal flats, although it was difficult to see anything clearly through the haze. Now and again they caught the scent of rot.

They walked out onto the plain, glancing back at intervals to see the forest, farther away each time, and the troop clustered at the fringe of the trees, obscured by falling ash.

"Are you sure Lewenhardt saw anything, Your Majesty?" Fulk asked at last. "It could have been the wind. It's hard to see anything with all this cloud and ash."

"Hush." Sanglant held up a hand, and Fulk fell silent, not moving, chin lifted as he, too, strove to hear. But few men had the unnaturally keen hearing that Sanglant possessed, and Fulk could not hear the faint sounds of splashing. "It sounds like a fish flopping half out of water. There!"

A ditch had captured something living that now thrashed in a remnant of seawater. They came cautiously to the edge and stared down into a pit filled with a murky blend of mud, water, and scraps of vegetation. A corpse was fixed between the axles of a shattered wagon, face mercifully hidden by one wheel, legs gray where they stuck out of the scummy surface.

"Ai, God!" cried Fulk, stepping back in horror.

The tide had trapped a monster from the deeps. Sensing them, it heaved its body fully back into the water with a splash, but it had nowhere to hide. They could distinguish its huge tail sluicing back and forth. At last it reared up out of the mud defiantly, whipping its head side to side and spraying mud and flecks of grass and leaves everywhere. Its hair hissed and snapped at them, each strand like an eyeless eel seeking a meal out of the air. It had a man's torso, lean and powerful, shimmering with scales. It had a face, of a kind: flat eyes, slits where a nose should otherwise grow, a lipless mouth, and scaly hands webbed between its clawed fingers.

"It's a man-fish," whispered Fulk. "That kind we saw on the river!"

It was trapped and therefore doomed, washed in and stranded by the tide, but a fearsome beast nevertheless and therefore not worthy of mercy. Yet Sanglant frowned as Fulk drew his sword. The creature stared boldly at them. Sharp teeth gleamed as it opened its mouth. And spoke.

"Prinss Ssanglant. Cap'tin Fulk."

Fulk jumped backward. "How can this beast know our names!"

"Prinss Ssanglant," it repeated. The eels that were its hair hissed and writhed as though they, too, voiced a message, one he could not understand.

"Can you speak Wendish? What are you? What are you called?"

"*Gnat*," it seemed to say, yet it kept talking in a language he did not understand, although he had heard it before.

"That's Jinna."

"It's too garbled, Your Majesty. I can't tell."

"Can you speak Wendish?" he said slowly, because he knew no words of Jinna. He tried out the other languages he could stumble along in. "Can you speak Ungrian? Can you speak the tongue known to the Quman? Can you—"

"Liat'ano," it said, lifting a hand in pantomime to shade its flat eyes as would a man staring into the bright sun.

"Liathano! Do you speak of my wife, Liath?"

The creature hissed, as in agreement.

"What does this mean, my lord prince?" whispered Fulk. "How can such a monster know our names?"

"I don't know. How could such a creature have learned to speak Jinna?"

"Jinna!" The creature spoke again at length, but they could only shake their heads. Impatience burned at him like fire as he wondered what this creature knew and what it could tell him. Did Liath live, or was she dead? How did it recognize them?

"Are there any in our party who can speak the language of the Jinna?" asked Fulk.

"Only Liath," he said bitterly. "That's why she took those two

Jinna servants with her. She was the only one who could understand them."

"What do we do?"

"Drag it back to the sea. If it can speak, then it is no mute beast
but a thinking creature like us."

"What if it is our enemy? You see its teeth and claws. I heard the
stories the ship-master told us—that it eats human flesh."

"It is at our mercy." He shook his head. "It gives me hope that my
wife still lives. For that reason alone I can't kill it, or leave it to die,
as it surely will, stranded here."

It was, indeed, no mute beast. He gestured toward the sea. He
spoke his own name, and Liath's, and Fulk's, and gestured toward
the sea again, as the creature stared at them. When they clambered
down the crumbling bank and grabbed its arms, it did not fight
them. It was heavy, and strange, and difficult to drag although its
glistening tail slid easily over most obstacles. In the end, out of
breath and sloppy with mud and ash, they got it to what had once
been the shoreline. The sea had sucked well out into the bay, but
they dared not walk there among slick rocks knowing that the next
wave would come soon.

"Go with the Lord and Lady's grace," said Sanglant. "There is
nothing more we can do for you."

"Liat'ano," it said again, and pointed toward the sky and then
toward the ground.

"Does she live?" Sanglant asked, knowing that the pain in his
heart would never cease, not until he knew what fate had befallen
her and their daughter. He had lost so much, as they all had, but he
feared there was worse yet to come.

Lying there awkwardly on the ground, it glanced toward the sea,
then copied with eerie precision his earlier gesture. It waved toward
the forest, suggesting haste, and said a curt word, repeated twice,
something like *Go. Go.* It had the cadence of a warning. Surely it
could sense the tides of the sea better than he could. Fulk shifted
from one foot to the next, glancing from the creature to the sea and
back again.

"Ai, God!" swore Sanglant. "Come, Fulk."

They left, jogging across the plain. In places the tide had swept the
ground clear. Elsewhere, ditches, small ridges, or other obstacles had
caught debris in a wide swathe, corpses and branches and here and
there a weapon or wagon wheel tangled together and stinking as the
hours passed. Nothing moved on that plain. There was still no sign

of life among the broken walls of the town. No birds flew, and now and again lightning brightened the clouds, followed by a distant rumbling of thunder.

They heard the water rising before they reached the soldiers waiting for them at the edge of the forest, nervous as they listened and watched the glimmer of the sea. He turned as the rest of the troop hurried away along the road into the cover of the blasted trees. The water rose this time not in any distinguishable wave but as a great swell. He could not see the mer-creature. The light wasn't strong enough, and the shoreline was, in any case, too far away and the ground too uneven. Like the rest of them, it would survive the tide of destruction, or it would perish.

A dozen men waited at the verge, unwilling to depart without their prince. Without their *king*.

"She must still be alive," he said.

"Yes, Your Majesty," said Fulk.

Lewenhardt offered him reins. Sanglant mounted Fest and together the remnants of his once proud company rode into the trees.

2

"I looked through fire for those whose faces I know, Your Majesty, but I saw nothing."

Sanglant glanced toward his council members waiting on the ramp that led up into the ruined fortress. The army had settled down under the afternoon haze to lick its wounds, recover its strength, and assess its numbers and provisions. "The Seven Sleepers may have protected themselves from Eagle's Sight. We must act as if they still live. They remain a threat."

Hathui shrugged. "I saw flames and shadow. Flashes of things. An overturned wagon. Falling rocks. A horse killed by a falling branch. None of it made any sense, nor could I hold any one vision within the fire. And of Liath, I saw nothing."

"Ai, God!" He paced, kicking up ash, and spun to face her. "Seek her at nightfall, each night, and hope she seeks in turn."

"Nightfall is difficult to gauge with this cloud cover and ash fall,

Your Majesty. We might each seek the other every evening and never touch. The Eagle's Sight is a powerful gift, but a man butchering a deer has more accuracy and delicacy."

He laughed, more in pain than amusement. "The crowns have the same failing, do they not? Thus we are spared the weight of a power too great to combat by natural means. I no longer wonder—" He swept an arm wide to indicate the heavens and the shattered forest. "—why the church condemned sorcery. See what sorcery has wrought."

"Liath is a mathematicus, Your Majesty. Do you mean to put her aside because she knows the art of sorcery?"

He grinned. "I began as captain of the King's Dragons. I have always been a soldier. If a weapon is put in my hands, I use it. And anyway . . ."

And anyway. *I love her.*

He could not speak those words aloud. He was regnant now, but his position was by no means secure. He could show no weakness; he could *possess* no weakness, and if he did, if he loved unwisely, then he must conceal the nature of his desire or it would be used against him. In that way the Pechanek Quman had tried to dishonor him by tempting him with a woman's flesh. He had come close to falling.

"Seek her at nightfall, Hathui. Keep trying."

"Yes, Your Majesty."

He strode over to those who waited, climbed the ramp until he stood above them, and situated himself so all those gathered below or huddled within the ruined walls could hear. He raised a hand for silence, and they quieted, but it was never still. The hiss of falling ash, the crack of breaking branches in the forest, not as many now but sharp and startling each time the sound came, and the moans of the wounded ran beneath his words.

"Cousin," he said. "What accounting have you reached?"

Liutgard was an excellent administrator and a wise enough soldier that she let her captains fight her battles for her. When she was younger, her husband had carried her sword as a talisman in place of her, but since his death some years earlier she had shown a disturbing tendency to take to the field herself.

She beckoned her chief steward forward. That woman tallied their remaining forces and lines of command, about two thousand men and perhaps half that many horses remaining although strays were continually being roped in. They had salvaged provisions for about three weeks, if strictly rationed, but were low on fresh water and feed for the horses. There were not enough wagons to carry all the wounded though crude sledges could be built and the wounded placed upon those and dragged by healthy men.

"What now, Your Majesty?" Liutgard asked when her steward had finished.

"Yes, what now?" they asked, all the assembled nobles and captains, those who had survived.

He was at first silent, but at length he spoke. "If fire and ash and water have wreaked such havoc here, how badly has the rest of the land suffered?"

Lord Wichman laughed coarsely and shouted, "Surely we have survived the worst!"

"Hush! You fool!" said Liutgard to her cousin. "Do not tempt God! There may be worse yet to come. What do you mean to do, Your Majesty?"

The curse of foresight had spared him, as it spared all born of humankind. It was amazing that he had once said to his father: "*I don't want to be king with princes all biting at my heels and waiting for me to go down so they can rip out my throat. I want a grant of land, Liath as my wife, and peace.*" Such luxury was no longer in his grasp. If he did not lead, then this army would fall to pieces and much worse would indeed come to pass.

"We must move out, and swiftly. This land is too devastated to support an army."

"What of Queen Adelheid, Your Majesty?" demanded Burchard.

Sanglant laughed bitterly. "You and I both saw the ruins of Estriana. I think there are no survivors."

"Should we send scouts into the town?"

"How can we tell when another wave may overtake any of our scouts who go down to search? If we wait for the sea to subside completely, we will suffer losses ourselves from thirst and starvation. Nay, I pray you, Burchard, we have no choice. Queen Adelheid is living, or she is dead. If she is dead, there is no help for her. If she lives, those who have survived with her will lead her to safety. Our situation is too desperate."

Burchard bowed his head, but he did not protest. Liutgard nodded to show she approved.

"The Brinne Pass," he continued. "It's too late in the year to attempt the higher passes, but there's a chance at least that we can cross into the marchlands and thence west to Wendar."

"At last!" cried Liutgard. "Home!"

"Your Majesty," objected Burchard. "What about Darre? What about Henry's empire?"

"Without Wendar there is no empire. Imagine, if you will, how far the tide of this destruction may have spread. Look at it! We do not know how distantly the deadly winds have struck or what damage they leave in their wake. The people of Wendar have already suffered greatly. If there is no succor for them, they will turn to others who will offer them surety and order. We must secure what is ours first, our birthright. When that is safe, then we shall see if my father has an empire left to defend."

They knelt to display their obedience, all except Liutgard and Burchard.

"What of Henry's remains?" Liutgard asked.

"His bones and heart must go to Quedlinhame."

She sighed. He recalled her as so young and bright and spirited when they had grown up together in the king's schola. Now she looked as aged as he felt, scarred by Henry's ill-fated expedition into Aosta and by the events of the last two days. But she was too strong of spirit to dwell on what could not be changed. She beckoned to her steward and they spoke together before the duchess turned back to her cousin. "My steward has been overseeing the boiling, Your Majesty. She'll find a suitable chest, and a box for the heart."

"So be it. We'll camp here to tend our wounded and repair what we can in preparation for the journey to come. Drink sparingly. Fulk, send out scouts to search for water, and others to see if there is aught to be recovered from within the forest: wagons or armor, provisions, strays. Wounded. Anything. Bury the dead that you find, but we can leave them no monument and we can carry none of the dead home with us, none but my father. As soon as the king's remains are fit to move, we will leave."

As the rest dispersed to their night's bivouac, Hathui came up beside him. "What of Liath, Your Majesty? If she reached Dalmiaka, as she hoped, then she is south and east of us. We're leaving her behind."

"We cannot act unless we know she lives and exactly where she is."

"An expedition could be sent. I would go—"

"I haven't strength or provisions enough to split my forces."

"A small group only, Your Majesty. Ten or twelve at most surely—"

"To ride where?"

"We can guess where she *might* be. A scouting expedition only. I could find a dozen who would be brave enough—"

He gritted his teeth and she stammered to a halt, seeing his expression. "Do not pain me with these objections, Eagle. Liath is powerful enough to rescue herself."

"If she is injured?"

"Then I am too far away to help her. For God's sake, Hathui, do not forget my daughter! I have not! I do not know if Blessing lives, or is dead. If the Horse people kept their oath to us, or have killed her or enslaved her. I may never know. *But we must march north.* We must march now. I will not split up my army. No."

She met his gaze. She was a bold woman, and for that he respected her. "It is a terrible choice, Your Majesty."

"It is the choice that has to be made. We are two thousand here with at least a thousand horses, without enough water, feed, and food, in hostile country swept by untold damage, and with winter coming and mountains to be crossed. Our situation is dire. If we lose Wendar, we have lost everything. Liath will find us if she lives."

"I will pray, Your Majesty."

"So will we all."

III
AWAITING THE
FLOOD

1

SHE waited alone in a vast new world. For a long time she stood at the top of a ragged ridgeline, the earth smoking, hot in many places, and stared as the sun's rising illuminated the changed landscape. Devastation surrounded her. The extent of the destruction was staggering. What remained of the old land had been stripped to rock by the force of the explosion, or vaporized by the heat, or scalded clean by the blast of a gale. West and northwest as the wind blew, a cloud of ash obscured the horizon. East and northeast the ash fall wasn't as severe, but the ground had altered strangely, forming eerie ranks of hills one after the next, each with the same height and curve. In hollows, pools of muck stank like sulfur. Nothing moved. Nothing lived. Nothing that had once lived here existed even to decay. Right above her the sky had an odd look to it, which she recognized after long consideration as the natural blue sky.

Only to the south, most changed, had life escaped harm. Some magic, perhaps the embrace of the aether itself, had protected the Ashioi land from the backblast of the spell. Although it had suffered from drought during its exile, it appeared rich with its living bounty in contrast to the destruction around her. To the east, the sun struggled to break free of the ashy haze but could not; it glowered, an ominous red, as it climbed.

What to do?

The magnitude of the destruction so overwhelmed her that she could not even weep. It was as if half of her had been blasted clean away by the cataclysm, leaving her with no tears but rather a few practical questions that really had to be answered.

Clothes. Water. Food. Her lost companions. Sanglant and Blessing. The rest could wait.

Behind her the land looked impassable. Certainly she'd not find food or drink for many a league inland. There was no telling how far the storm had blown. She doubted she'd last long once night fell and the temperature dropped. It was late in the year. There had already been snow, now burned off for as far as she could see.

She shifted her grip on her bow and walked south toward the hills of the ancient land now returned. Ashioi country. She heard a faint horn call. From farther away, through the intense silence, a human cry shuddered, but it might have been a trick of the air. She saw nothing and no one. The heat of the ground chapped her feet, and as the morning passed her soles dried and cracked until they bled, leaving drops of blood as a trail in her wake. It was so hot, but heat had never troubled her. Thirst hit harder, and her feet hurt, and her skin stung from the ash. The spell had exhausted her. But if she stopped and could not get going again, then thirst, hunger, and weakness would defeat her, and no person born of humankind alone could negotiate this steaming landscape to rescue her, not until it cooled. And they would only attempt a rescue if they knew she was here, which they did not.

Sanglant was too far away to help her, if he even lived.

In time, the sun nosed up over the haze and reached zenith within that mote of clear sky directly above. The sun was so bright. Even the ground blinded her as she stumbled onto a ribbon of chalky white. She halted. She stood on a narrow road, bleeding onto its gritty surface. Behind there was nothing to see except empty wilderness and smoking pits. Ahead, the ground rose precipitously. Grass clung to the hill in patches. Here and there clefts and holes split the hillside like so many narrow cave mouths. At the height of the rise a ruined watchtower rose at the limit of a stand of pine trees.

She had been here before.

She had enough energy for a chuckle, then trudged upward, weary beyond measure. Unbelievably, he was there, waiting for her with a skin of water. He stepped out from behind the tumbled wall with a look of such surprise that she knew he had not, precisely, expected to see her.

"Liath!"

"Eldest Uncle! Ai, God! I've need of that water, if you've any to share."

"Plenty to share, as you will see." He smiled. "The young should know better than to parade in front of the old with that which can never be regained."

"I beg your pardon!" She guzzled water, but forced herself to stop before she drank the entire thing. She poured water on her hand and wiped her brow. Her fingers came away black with grime. She looked down at herself. "I'm cloaked in ash," she said, and it was true, but she was nevertheless naked even if smeary with soot. He was amused.

"Come with me." He gestured toward the trees.

"Where are we going?"

"To the river, where you can wash yourself. I'll see if I can weave a garment out of reeds."

The water gave her strength, but a second, more intangible force did so as well. She recalled clearly the last time she had walked through this grove of pine trees, just before she had ascended the mage's ladder into the heavens. Then, the air had been dry and the ground parched. Now she smelled water in the air. She felt it in the greening leaves and the rash of shoots lacing green trails along the ground. Its softness cooled her skin.

Yet, when they walked out from the shadow of the pines, the meadow that had once grown lush with cornflowers and peonies, lavender and dog roses, lay withered. On the path, drying petals crackled under their feet.

"Come." Eldest Uncle hastened forward, ignoring the dying clearing.

"This was once so bright. What happened to all the flowers?"

"The aether used to water this land, drawing moisture up from deep roots. Now that link is gone, and these flowers die. But the land will live. See there!"

See there! She hurried after him along what they had once called the flower trail, to the river. Where once a trickle had moistened the rocks, a current now flowed in full spate. Laughing, she splashed into the shallows and threw herself full length into the cold water. The shock stung. Her skin hurt, everywhere, but the water was like the kiss of God. She ducked her head under, and again, and a third time, and scrubbed her hair and scalp until the worst of the filth was gone, and afterward floated until her teeth chattered and her hands were blue. At last she fetched her bow and waded to the far shore. Eldest Uncle waited for her on a carpet of grass. Fresh shoots flourished along the river as far as she could see. The land that had once lain yellow and brown had turned with the onslaught of a false spring, although she knew that winter was yet to come.

"Ai, God!" She sat down beside him. Grass tickled her rump. Water dripped. "That felt good! I'm so tired."

She yawned, cradling her head on her bent knees, arms wrapped tight around her legs. The world slipped so easily away. She slid into a doze.

Started awake, hearing voices.

Eldest Uncle stood farther up the path, under the shade of trees, speaking with two masked warriors, one male and one female. She grabbed her bow, and recalled belatedly that she no longer had any arrows. That she needed no weapons. She *was* a weapon.

Memory struck, because she was vulnerable. She was only half awake, unable to fend off the visions. *The soldiers burned like torches. They screamed and screamed as their flesh melted off them . . .*

"Liath!"

I burned them. She was shaking.

Eldest Uncle knelt beside her. He did not touch her.

"Who are they?" she demanded, indicating the two young warriors with her glance. One wore a falcon mask and the other that of a buzzard, smooth and rufous and alert. She was shaking too hard to move. She felt sick to her stomach. "Must get up. . . . if Cat Mask . . ."

"These are not Cat Mask's warriors. They will not harm you."

Trust him, or do not trust him. "Why would you betray me?" she asked softly.

His smile had a bitter tinge, but he was not offended. "Why, indeed?"

She slumped forward, too weary to fight, and fell at once into a dreamless sleep.

2

SHE dreamed.

She walks through grass so tall she cannot see beyond it. The whisper of another creature's passage touches her ears, and she halts.

Grass bends, golden tops bowing and vanishing. Something big approaches.

She turns as the Horse shaman pushes through and pulls up short, seeing her. "Liathano! I have been looking for you!"

Other voices flood over them, and the grass and the centaur ripple like water stirred by a gusting wind.

"This one, again! If Cat Mask finds her, he'll kill her while she sleeps."

"Then we must be sure that Cat Mask does not find her. Will you tell him?"

"I will not!"

"You spoke against her before, White Feather."

"So I did. But now we are fallen safely back to Earth. It may be she had a hand in our homecoming, as she promised us. If that is the case, she does not deserve death. Although I think it best if one possessing such power does not bide long in our land."

Liath groaned and shook herself awake, startled to find a short mantle draped over her body. It covered her from shoulder to mid-thigh, and was woven out of a coarse brown thread. She sat up carefully, wrapping the cape around herself. She was sore everywhere. Her skin was rashy, and here and there marked with the imprint of a rock. Her neck ached, and she had a headache. Eldest Uncle offered her a pouch of water to drink. Sipping slowly, she surveyed her surroundings. There was noticeably more green than there had been when she'd fallen asleep. The trees seemed fuller, the ground moister. Even the distant meadow, seen across the flowing river, boasted a score of budding flowers, fresh growth that had sprouted while she slept. The light had changed; it was as dim as the gloom that presages a thunderstorm.

White Feather regarded her pensively, perhaps with distrust. Farther away, Falcon Mask and Buzzard Mask crouched on their haunches, watching her and then the river.

"How long did I sleep? Will it soon be nightfall?"

"Nightfall, indeed," agreed Eldest Uncle. "Nightfall of a new day. You slept through yesterday afternoon, an entire night, and most of this day."

She whistled, feeling as if she'd been punched in the stomach. "I'm still tired! Hungry and thirsty, too."

"Hunger is a pain we all share," said White Feather tartly. "But before I left the council hall, I heard a half dozen reports that the old fields are already sending up shoots. If we can survive the winter with what stores remain to us, we may hope for a plentiful harvest. Still. I would not see you fall into Cat Mask's hands because of weakness."

She offered Liath a square of dried berries and grains, and although it was tough to chew, it was edible and filling. Liath took her time as she ate, knowing how little food the Ashioi had. At least there was no shortage of water. The vegetation seemed to be growing unnaturally quickly, fertilized by the fading influence of the aether, as though all this potential had lain dormant for years, awaiting the flood. She nibbled. She knew she ought to save half for later, but she was so hungry she finished it all.

Like White Feather, Eldest Uncle looked away while she ate, to give her privacy or to restrain his own feelings of hunger.

"What now?" she asked him, getting his attention. "Am I in danger from Cat Mask? Will he come hunting me?"

"Only if he discovers you are here," said White Feather in her blunt way. "He fears an invasion of humankind."

Liath laughed bitterly. "Have you walked the land beyond the white path, north of here? Nothing lives there, nor can any living creature cross it."

"You crossed it."

"I created it."

White Feather touched the obsidian knife tucked into a sheath at her hip. "What do you mean?"

"I am born half of fire. The one you call Feather Cloak glimpsed the heart within me. That is why they called me 'Bright One.' " She wiped sweat from her brow. Although cloudy, it was hot. Even the breeze made her uncomfortable.

Eldest Uncle looked more at ease than she had ever seen him. He looked younger, an old man restored to vitality by his return to the world where he had been born. It was as if the waters flooded him as well, as if he were greening like the plants.

"Look!" cried Falcon Mask. She leaped to her feet. Far above, a pair of buzzards soared. She pushed her mask up to get a better look; she was crying, silently, with joy.

"A good omen," agreed Eldest Uncle. "You are not the only one who can cross. Others will come."

"Our enemies," said White Feather. "How is that a good omen?"

"Feather Cloak has birthed twin girls. What more powerful omen could there be?"

The older woman snorted. She had a stern face, no longer young. The white feather fastened to her topknot bobbed in the warm wind. "You are weak, Bright One. I make this promise to you in exchange for the promise you made to us, that you would see us safely home. Rest here to regain your strength and I will divert Cat Mask's attention from this place. After that, you must depart, or I will set Cat Mask and his warriors on you myself."

"Do not do that, I pray you," murmured Liath. "You do not understand. . . ." She was shaking again as memory gripped her hard. It was too much. She still heard their screams, the way the sound choked off when the fire burned away their voices. She squeezed her eyes shut and *willed* the memory to shut itself away behind a closed door.

"Whsst!" called Falcon Mask. "Gone now, into the trees. Yet there! Do you hear?"

From nearby came a raspy cry. At the unexpected sound, Liath opened her eyes.

"What is it?" demanded Buzzard Mask, pushing his mask up. He was as young as Falcon Mask. They might have been twins with their bronze faces, broad noses, and dark eyes.

"It's a tern," said Liath, recognizing the call. "It must have been blown inland. How far away is the sea?"

"I've forgotten," said Eldest Uncle.

"I've never seen the sea," said White Feather as the young warriors nodded to show that they, too, had never seen it. "I've only heard stories. How far the shore lies I do not know. I walked most of yesterday and all this morning to reach you, Uncle. Feather Cloak asks that you return. The warriors have moved out to explore the borderlands. There will be a council soon."

"What of my daughter?" asked Eldest Uncle.

White Feather shrugged. "She is stubborn."

"Ha! Tell me a truth I do not yet know."

"Feather Cloak thinks Kansi-a-lari has left the land. She cannot hear her footsteps on the earth. If she crossed the White Road, she would be invisible to us."

"How could she cross such devastation? It is a steaming wasteland."

"North of here," said Liath. "But what about the coasts? It might be possible to cross along the coast."

What had become of Gnat and Mosquito? No way to know, not unless she reached the sea, and even then she might never find them.

She barely had strength to rise and relieve herself in the privacy of the woods, barely managed afterward to stagger up the path with the mantle clutched around her torso and find her way to the remembered clearing that she had walked in so short, and so long, a time ago. Once, the burning stone had appeared here. The pallet of leaves and grass she had gathered days—nay, months or years—ago was scarcely disturbed. She collapsed onto it, under the shelter of a holm oak, and plunged into sleep.

Sanglant, riding on an unfamiliar horse. He is filthy and his expression is grim.

Fire burned in her heart, and in its flames she glimpsed Hathui and Hanna, looking for her, seeking, calling . . . but she was too exhausted to rouse.

Blessing shouts at a young man whose face seems familiar although Liath cannot name him, and he turns to face

a landscape of burning sand. A lion with the torso and face of a woman rears above her, raking with its claws as the girl screams, only it is not herself she sees but a young woman as dark of complexion as she is. A silver-haired man leaps into the fray, thrusting a burning torch between sphinx and bleeding girl. As he spins, panting, he sees her and cries out

"Liathano! Where are you?" The centaur shaman walks on the shore of a shallow river that snakes away through grassland

but the bright currents drag her away. She drowns, yet at the same time the aether feeds her as it feeds all that is elemental.

She stirred at intervals, sometimes finding food and drink waiting for her although she barely recalled eating and drinking; the threads of aether nourish her; it is all the food she needs. Other times she woke hoping to see the stars, but the haze never lifted and it was ungodly warm.

Thoughts emerged with unexpected clarity.

I should have looked for him at nightfall with Eagle's Sight.

Land displaces water of equal volume.

Did all the Seven Sleepers die, or did some survive?

If the thread that bound the Ashioi land to Earth is severed, then is the aetherical realm closed to us? Is the mage's ladder gone? Is my mother's home lost to me now? Where does the aether come from that is woven around the Earth? Is it constantly replenished or will it fade? Is there less of aether in the world now that the gateway is closed?

At nightfall, with Eagle's Sight, Hathui seeks in the fire, but sees only fragments, glimpses of fractured sight shot through with flames and shadow.

Sleep claimed her, and her thoughts, and what coiled in her heart and mind dissolved into dreams so finely spun that each filament frayed away into nothing, all a hazy white drift of ash spreading in all directions over pale dunes that had neither beginning nor end, only desolation

"Will she die? She's been like this since I left. That was five days ago!"

"I think she will not die. She's not wasting away. The substance that knits together the universe feeds her. It is invisible to us because it exists beyond our five senses. Remember that she walked the spheres and crossed through the burning stone, and what else after that I do not know, but we can imagine it was no easy task. Now she is paying the price."

"What if Cat Mask comes? He has gathered his warriors. He's made his peace with Lizard Mask, and they are making their plans, wondering when humankind will attack us."

"Cat Mask does not scare me, White Feather. Return to Feather Cloak. I will come when I can."

"Feather Cloak cannot delay the council any longer. If you do not walk back with me now, I will have to tell her you are not coming. The council will speak without your voice."

"I will not leave her until she is strong enough to fend for herself."

"Does no one look for her, Uncle? Has she no family?"

"She has her husband, but how can we know whether he lives or is dead? I have stood many mornings at the edge of the desolation to the north, beyond the White Road."

"A wasteland worthy of He-Who-Burns! It is a terrible sight."

"I do not know how far the destruction extends. I do not know who and what has survived or if they can even reach here, or will attempt it."

"Then perhaps we will have less fighting to do! It would serve humankind very well if their sorcery hurt themselves worst of all in the end."

"I am thinking we have all suffered, and will continue so. This weather makes me uneasy. We should see the sun."

"Should we? Does the sun often shine? It was always like this before."

"Because it was 'like this' when we journeyed in the aether, the land died. So will it now without rain and sun. These are not natural clouds. I remember what it was like when I was a young man. It was not like this. We saw both rain and sun."

"All this I will tell Feather Cloak. But if you will not accompany me, Eldest Uncle, then you must not complain if Cat Mask's views are accepted by the others simply because he talks the loudest and puffs up his manly chest."

A chuckle. "I trust you, White Feather, not to be dazzled by his words. Or his chest. Is there still no sign of my daughter?"

"A small sign. Scouting groups have walked the coastline and brought news of many strange things washed up on the shore. On the western coast about a day's walk from here, this green wing feather was found among the rocks. Do you recognize it?"

"Ah! Ah! Yes. It is the color of her eyes. This is surely the one I gave to her when she gained her woman's power. I cannot believe she would have discarded it so carelessly."

"Uh," said Liath, trying to rouse, but they did not hear her and she was so tired. How could anyone be so tired, all vitality drained from them?

"There were markings in the sand, too, but we could not interpret them. Something like this. . . ." A fine scritching eased her back into a dreamy haze. So soothing. So tired.

"I don't know. I would have to see it for myself. It looks like the track of a boat pulled up on shore."

"What is a boat? Oh, yes. A wagon that carries you over water. Where might she find a boat?"

"Perhaps it washed up on shore. . . ."

Water, like fire and air, is a veil through which distant sights can be glimpsed by those who do not fear to see. She dreamed.

Sanglant and a ragged army toil through a blasted countryside. He pauses beside a half dozen men in stained and ragged clothing who are digging a grave. They wear the badge of Fesse, its proud red eagle sigil visible despite the dirt.

"One of Liutgard's men?" he asks as they bend knees and kneel on the parched ground.

"Our sergeant, Your Majesty," says one. *"His wound went rotten, all black and with a nasty smell."*

His aspect is so grave, as if the cataclysm blasted him as well, right down to his soul.

"Will we see our homes again, Your Majesty?"

"This poor man will not. But the army will reach Wendar, although I fear our dead men and horses mark our trail for any who seek to follow us."

"It will be good to shake Aosta's dust from our feet! We came south over the high passes west of here, Your Majesty. How will we go home?"

"See!" He points toward a place she cannot see, not even in her dreams. "There are the mountains. We're close enough that you can see them even through the haze. That notch, there, marks the valley that will lead us up to the Brinne Pass. Once we have crossed, we will be in the marchlands."

"Your Majesty!" A man's urgent cry causes every soldier to stand nervously, awaiting a call to action against some as yet unseen foe. "See there!" A young man appears on a restive mare, a bow slung over his back and his hand extended as he indicates the cloudy heavens to the northeast. "The griffins!"

Shouts break out everywhere, some frightened and some triumphant, welcoming their return. A yelping call rings down from the sky as if in reply. Horses scream, and Sanglant reins in his gelding with a press of his knees. His lips part as he stares upward at a sight she cannot see, and yet she can feel the gleam of their presence, woven through with magic down to the bone. They fly overhead and on, continuing southeast.

"Where are they going, Your Majesty?" asks the young archer as all heads turn, following the course of that flight.

Sanglant shakes his head, eyes narrowed, and for an instant his shoulders slump, as though he has been defeated. "I don't know."

"Will they return?"

"I do not possess foreknowledge, Lewenhardt." Hearing his own words, thinking them, he smiles sharply and urges his mount forward on the path. "Best be grateful they survived the blast. Best to wonder why they fly toward the heart of the cataclysm."

She spins upward on the wind and finds herself aloft, flying with griffin wings. Her sight is as sharp as an eagle's.

Was she not an Eagle once? She learned the gift of sight and it inhabits her even in her dreams as she floats between dreaming and waking on the last fading swell of the aether as the aftershocks of the cataclysm rumble away into nothing. The breath of the heavens long spilled its respiration into the lower world through the thread that bound the exiled land to its root. Soon that road will be pinched closed.

Will the magic of Earth fade, no longer fertilized by that rich vitality? Aether is an element like the other four, woven through the very fabric of the cosmos. Surely some breath of aether remains on Earth.

Yet knowledge of the future is closed to her, because she is grounded here. It isn't even shadows seen beyond a translucent shroud; it is an impenetrable curtain. Only the elementals who breathe and respire in the pure aether can see forward and backward in time. Only God can know past, present, and future as if it is all one.

Did her mother know what fate awaited her? Did she go willingly into that darkness, or did she fight it?

Did she love my father anyway?

I'll never know.

The landscape skims past below, a blighted roll of dusty hills and tumbled forests. Now and again a village passes beneath her sight, roofs torn off, fences down, dead animals floating in briny pools. With each league as they move southeast the land's scars grow more noticeable. Trees are burned on one side, those that still stand. The ground is parched and bare. They have turned south and she smells the sea. Waves lap lazily against a battered shoreline. They pass over a ruined town whose stone walls have fallen into heaps. A cockroach scuttles along the stones. No. It is a person, small and fragile but somehow still alive. Then the town falls behind.

So close to the sea nothing moves except the wind through what remains of vegetation. Out in the water she sees the smooth back of a mercreature split the surface and slide beneath.

Is it Gnat, or Mosquito?

The griffin shrieks, and banks to the right in a wide circle. Below, marching along parallel to the shoreline, walk human figures. So many! Two thousand at least, or four or ten, impossible to count so many. It is a refugee host strung out in double or triple file and marching into the worst of the devastation. There are many children and old people among them. It seems there are more groups coming up from behind, all moving in the same direction.

She wants to cry out. She wants to warn them: "Turn back! This way lies ruin!" But she has no voice.

And then she truly sees them.

By face and feature they are Ashioi. Where have they come from? There were not so many children among the exiles as she sees in this

company. *The larger help the smaller. The warriors march in the van
and at the rear to guard the helpless, who are also the most precious.
They are well dressed in tunics and knee-length cloaks, their warriors in
fine armor and brightly painted masks.*

*The Ashioi she lived among, however briefly, were so poor that none
had more than a rag or worn skin to cover themselves with, not even the
warriors. That's why she sleeps beneath a covering woven of reeds. Eldest Uncle doesn't even have a spare tunic to gift her so that she might
not sleep, or wake, naked. All the animals died in exile, and toward the
end even the fields of flax withered.*

These are not the same people. Yet who else can they be?

*Ahead, the ground raises up to mark the blast zone. To the northeast
the earth steams, but along the shoreline the way remains barely passable because the sea has cooled the fire out of the depths. The earth lies
quiet. The Old Ones have withdrawn their power. All that is left is the
wasteland. On the strand a boat lies beached. A single figure rushes,
shouting, to greet the refugees.*

*Her sight tunnels. She fixes on her prey, and recognizes her:
Sanglant's mother, who is also Eldest Uncle's only daughter. Kansi-a-
lari runs forward, then stops short, staring at the man who leads the
rest. Her mouth drops open. She exclaims aloud, and he laughs, mocking her.*

*"So you are the one!" he says. "I met your son. But I did not believe
him. Greetings, Daughter."*

*"Daughter?" Her fierce expression clouds and her brows pinch to-
gether with confusion as she stares at the prince, who is certainly
younger than she is. "Why do you call me—"*

*"Look! Look up there!" Behind him, a warrior wearing a fox mask lifts
her bow, draws it deep, and looses an arrow.*

"Hai!" cried Liath, jerking upright, torn right out of sleep and
startling Eldest Uncle, who sat, as usual, bending and plaiting supple willow into a large basket.

"Ai, God!" she said a moment later in frustration, pulling the
mantle around her as Eldest Uncle chuckled. "Is there *nothing* I can
clothe myself with?"

"Indeed, Daughter, the women have concerned themselves mightily to please your modesty. See here."

Out of a second basket he lifted a folded square of cloth as though
it were more precious than gold. "In the vaults beneath the council
chamber the last treasure has been removed, oil and grain stored

against the final drought, bronze tools, cloth, and the scrolls sacred to He-Who-Burns."

The cloth was undyed although a trifle yellowed with age, and finely woven out of a thread whose softness she did not recognize. When she unfolded it, she discovered a sleeveless tunic that reached to her knees. She quickly slipped it on. It was shapeless, two rectangular blocks of cloth sewn together along the sides and shoulders, but functional enough to give her the confidence to test her legs. She tied the mantle on over it, then walked to the river to drink her fill. Berries ripened in dribs and drabs along the banks, and she ate until her fingers were stained purple although the berries tasted tart.

"I'm so hungry! Ugh! I'll give myself a stomachache with this."

"You're feeling better," said Eldest Uncle, who had followed her. She saw no sign of Falcon Mask and Buzzard Mask.

"Stronger, too. I dreamed . . ."

A horn's call sounded to the north.

"It wasn't a dream! Come quickly!"

While she slept, they had fixed a rope bridge over the rushing stream, three thick ropes strung taut between trees, with one for the feet and two above to hold on to. She got the hang of it quickly, balancing as she crossed with her bow slung over her back and Eldest Uncle behind her. The flower trail had bloomed in sickly patches of color, covered by a skin of ashy gray dust that coated leaves and stones. She shaded her eyes, then lowered her hand.

"There's no sun," said Eldest Uncle. "I remember sun from my youth, but we've seen the sun no more than two or three times while you slept and then only for a brief span."

"How long did I sleep?" They walked into the shade of the pine forest. Fallen needles squished under her feet. Before, everything had been so brittle. Now it seemed spongy.

"Ten nights. Eleven, perhaps. I lost count. The days are hazy, and the council argues."

"Look." She pointed to the watchtower. Falcon Mask perched on the uppermost wall, peering west.

Buzzard Mask saw them and came running. "Who are they?"

"Who are who?" Eldest Uncle replied.

Buzzard Mask had a youth's voice, not quite sure that it had broken. "There's an army coming along the White Road! They're not dressed like us, but many wear warrior masks."

Liath ran to the watchtower and clambered up beside Falcon

Mask. The young woman looked at her, surprised, then grinned and sidled to one side to make room. Young and bold, she did not fear heights, but for Liath it was dizzy-making to crouch up here with sheer wall and steep hillside plunging away below. Yet that giddy feeling was no worse than the sight of the desolation she had wrought, off to the north, the wasteland that was the aftermath of the eruption that had killed Anne and her people, most of them guilty of no greater crime than loyalty. What manner of man would refuse the summons of the skopos, after all? Yet Anne had not cared for their virtues, or their sins; they were pawns, nothing more, and pawns are sacrificed.

On the road, the lead group came into view beyond a straggle of trees, then was lost again behind foliage. Eldest Uncle spoke a word and crumpled to his knees. He would have fallen if Buzzard Mask hadn't leaped to his side to support him.

"What is it, Uncle? What ails you?"

"I am struck," he said to the youth. "I am hit."

"Get their attention," said Liath to Falcon Mask.

"There are so many! And more behind them! I've never seen so many people!" The young woman wavered. She was unsure, reluctant. "Is it safe?"

"They are your own people." She scrambled back down and knelt beside Eldest Uncle, who seemed too weak to rise. "Is it your heart?" she demanded, terrified that he would die right then.

"It is my heart." He wept silent tears as the procession reappeared on the White Road below them. It was strange to watch with the steep hillside and ragged forest on one side of the chalky ribbon of road and on the other the scarred, barren earth stretching north as far as she could see. These refugees were caught between two worlds, it seemed, as they had been for centuries.

She walked down the slope to meet them. Her hair was all tangles, and sweat and grit slimed her body.

I should have stopped to bathe.

Stepping onto the White Road, she faced their approach. The line of marchers wound away beyond a curve in the path, hidden behind trees and a distant ridgeline. They were the same people she had seen in her dream. The man leading them wore a crested helmet unlike the animal masks worn by the other warriors. He had a proud, handsome face, terribly familiar in a way she did not understand. As they neared and saw she did not mean to move, he raised a hand and halted and the others slowed to a halt behind him. He looked

Liath up and down while a fox-masked woman beside him glared, but it was Sanglant's mother, in the front, who spoke first.

"Liathano! Where is my father?"

Liath gestured.

"This one?" asked the handsome man. "This is your son's mate whom you spoke of?"

His gaze followed her gesture, and he looked toward the old man being helped down the steep slope by young Buzzard Mask. A cool wind out of the north rustled leaves. Out in the wasteland, dust funneled heavenward until, all at once, the wind's hand dropped it and a thousand million particles pattered to bare rock.

"Lost to me," he breathed. His spear clattered to the ground unheeded beside him, and he leaped forward like a hart and dashed up the hill, not many steps, after all. They were so close; they saw each other clearly. Liath ran after him, but when he stopped two paces from Eldest Uncle she stopped, too.

She stared, seeing it for the first time and understanding why the young man looked familiar. The daimones of the upper air can see forward and backward in time because time has no hold on them; they live above the middle world where time's yoke subjugates all living creatures. She had a moment's dislocation. For a moment, she saw as did her kinfolk: youth and age, what had been and what would become.

Eldest Uncle and the young warrior were the same man, but one was old and one was young.

Eldest Uncle covered his eyes and trembled. The other shook his head like a madman.

"Brother!"

"How can this be?"

It was only a whisper. Two whispers. She did not know which one spoke. Buzzard Mask released his hold on the old man, and the young one took a step toward the old one and as of one thought they embraced, holding tight, two creatures who in their hearts are one.

"Do you understand it yet?" asked Sanglant's mother. As she came up beside Liath, she indicated the men with a lift of her chin. She laughed, but not kindly, sensing Liath's bewilderment.

"Why do you dislike me so much?" Liath asked her.

"I don't know. I just do."

"How can you dislike someone you don't know?"

"I had to listen to my son talk on and on about you in the days we were together—you, and battle. Those are the only two things he's ever thought deeply about, if a man can be said to think deeply where his cock is concerned."

"You don't like your own son?"

"He's not what I wanted."

Liath smiled sharply, wishing she could intimidate others with clever words and the stiffening of her shoulders, as Sanglant could. "He's what he is, no more and no less than that. If you don't like it, you missed your chance to make him something else, didn't you? He is Henry's son, not yours."

"Born of humankind," said Kansi with a sneer.

"Look!" cried Falcon Mask from the wall. She had braced herself with one hand on the highest course of stone as she rose, balancing precariously with drops before and behind. She pointed at the heavens.

The two men released each other, stepping back from the embrace to stare as one at the cloudy sky. How strange it was to see a man both old and young, the same man, as if time had split him into two parts and in its circular discursion finally caught up with itself. There was a wink of light against the clouds as quickly gone.

"We saw two griffins," said the young man. "But our arrows scared them off."

Hope leaped in Liath's heart, but she said nothing.

Eldest Uncle rested a hand on the other one's shoulder, taking strength there, and gazed at the procession waiting on the White Road. "Who are these? Where have you all come from?"

"We were caught between the worlds in ancient days. Now you have returned, and we are released from the shadows."

"There are more of you?"

"I was with one group, but we met up with many others. There are more, still, coming this way."

"All those sent to the frontier before the end," said Eldest Uncle.

"What do you mean?" asked Sanglant's mother and Buzzard Mask at the same time.

"I must sit down," he said apologetically, but it was the young one who helped him up to the tower most solicitously, who sat beside him, staring intently at his face as though to memorize every wrinkle and crease.

"I never thought to see you again," said the young one. "I thought you were lost to me."

"I, too. I despaired, but then I lived." They had an easy way of touching, a hand placed carelessly on the other's knee or shoulder.

It was as though there was a misunderstanding between them and they had forgotten that normally there is an infinitesimal space between one body and the next, that which separates each solitary soul from another.

"You are old."

"I am eldest."

"Not bad looking, for an old man! Not like that warty, flabby old priest of a Serpent Skirt."

They laughed together, almost giggling, suddenly younger than their years, boys again. Brothers. Twins.

"Don't you see what this means?" demanded Sanglant's mother with fists on hips, looking disgusted as she watched them slap each other's arms. "More will come from the north! Cat Mask's army will grow. We need not fear our enemies any longer, not with such a force."

"Cat Mask's army?" asked the young one, turning away from his brother. "Who is Cat Mask? What has he to do with me?"

"Hsst! She-Who-Creates has much to answer for! Will you strut and preen like the rest of the young men and fight for command like so many pissing dogs?"

His eyes narrowed. "You are my daughter by blood. My niece. Do not speak so to your elders, young one!"

"You are younger than I am! I have a grown son! I can speak any way I please!"

"Evidently your daughter more than mine, Zuangua," said Eldest Uncle with a wheezy laugh. "Quick to temper, slow to wisdom. Both impatient. So I named her, remembering you."

Instead of answering, Zuangua rose and stared north, a gaze that swept the horizon. Now Liath saw the resemblance to his twin brother, to his niece, and to Sanglant. The lineaments of his face had the same curve and structure. She felt the warmth of a mild, woken desire, seeing him as an attractive man. Until he looked straight at her. His expression shifted, the tightening of lips, the merest wrinkling of the nose, but she felt his scorn, she knew that he recognized her interest and rejected it. Rejected *her*.

His sneer scalded. She wasn't used to indifference from men. She hadn't desired or sought their interest, truly, but she had become used to it. Even King Henry, the most powerful man she had ever met, had succumbed.

So I am repaid for my vanity, she thought, and was cheered enough to smile coldly back at him.

He turned away to address his brother. "We will return, all of us who were caught beyond the White Road when the spell was woven. We who were once shadows are made flesh again. We want revenge for what we suffered. We will return day by day, more coming each day until we are like the floodwaters rising. Once we are all come home, we will make an army and destroy humankind. Our old enemy."

"We are stronger than I thought!" murmured his niece. "Already more have joined the march than survived in exile!"

"It is not the right path," said Eldest Uncle.

"So you have always claimed, but see what they did to us." Zuangua gestured toward the barren wilderness. "This is what humankind made—a wasteland. You are old. Our people are diminished. Kansi said so herself, and if these rags are the best you have to wear, then I see it is true. The humans are many, but they are weak and the cataclysm has hurt them." He touched the stained cloth that bound his shoulder. "Their king gave this wound to me, but I killed him. He is dead and your grandson risen in his place."

Risen in his place.

Liath took a step back. The others did not notice, too intent on Zuangua's speech.

"He seeks an alliance. We did act in concert when his need was great, but now we must consider him a danger. We cannot trust humankind."

"We trusted them in the old days."

"A few. The others always fought us, and will do so again. They will never trust us."

"They won't," said Kansi. "They hate us. They fear us."

"Do you speak such words even of your son?" Eldest Uncle asked.

"His heart lies with his father. I do not know him."

"None of us know him. Better to learn what we can, scout the ground, before we act precipitously."

"Better to act before we are dead!" retorted Zuangua. "So your daughter has advised me."

"So." Eldest Uncle sighed and shut his eyes a moment. "The first arrow has pierced deepest. You will believe her, despite what anyone else has to say."

Liath had backed up four steps by now, one slow sweep at a time so as not to attract attention.

"Look!" cried Falcon Mask from up on the wall. "Is that an eagle?"

On the White Road, a hundred warriors raised their bows and each nocked an arrow.

"Let her go." Eldest Uncle caught Liath's gaze and lifted his chin in a gesture uncannily like that of his daughter. The message was unspoken: *Now!*

She bolted. Kansi leaped after her and got hold of the mantle's hem, but as Liath strained and Kansi tugged, Eldest Uncle shut his eyes and muttered words beneath his breath. The binding cord fell away and the mantle slipped off her shoulders into the Impatient One's clutching grip. Kansi stumbled as the tension was released. Liath ran.

"She is most dangerous of all—" cried Kansi.

Other voices called after her.

"That scrawny, filthy creature is a danger to us?"

"Not only a sorcerer, but . . . walked the spheres—"

"Let her go, Zuangua! I ask this of you, by the bond we shared in our mother's womb."

She stumbled over the White Road and tripped and banged her shin as she slipped over bare ground covered with ash and loose stone. The ground seemed to undulate of its own accord under her feet. Sharp edges sliced through her soles. Where her blood spattered on rock, it hissed, and the surface skin of rock gave way, cracking and steaming, as she leaped for a flat boulder whose surface remained solid. She smelled the sting of sorcery, a spell trying to slow and trap her: Ashioi magic, that manipulated the heart of things.

Liath sought her wings of flame, but the Earth bound her. She was trapped by the flesh she had inherited from her father.

"Hai! Hai!" shouted Zuangua far behind. "At will, archers! Do not let her escape!"

She had to turn back to face the attack. A score of arrows went up in flame, in a sheet that caught the next volley. But they would shoot again, and again. Arrows had felled her before. She had only one defense against arrow fire and she could not use it, not even to save her own life. Not again.

She would rather die than see another person melt from the inside out.

"I'll trap her!" cried Kansi. "The rock will eat her!"

A third volley vaulted into the air toward her and erupted into sparks and a shower of dark ash as she called fire into the shafts. The rock beneath her splintered with a resounding *snap*. The ground cracked open, and she fell.

The gust of wings and a sultry heat swept over her, and the golden griffin swooped down and took her shoulders in its claws.

With a jerk they lurched up, then down so she scraped her knees on rock, then up again, into the air. But not out of range.

More warriors had pressed forward on the road, spreading out at Zuangua's order to get a better shot. The griffin could not gain height easily. Liath was too heavy. But the beasts, too, were tacticians.

Shouts and screams erupted down the line of waiting Ashioi as the silver male skimmed low over the line of march from behind. That disruption was all it took for them to get out of range and the silver to bank high and head inland.

Held in the griffin's claws, knowing her weight was a burden, Liath dared not twist in the hope of seeing Eldest Uncle one last time. Her throat was dry and her heart ached. She feared that she would never see him again. What right had his brother and daughter to judge Sanglant out of their own anger at their ancient enemies and thus separate the old man from his only grandchild? Every right, they would say. But it made her angry that Eldest Uncle might never know his grandson or kiss the brow of his great grandchild, if Blessing still lived.

Nay, she knew it in her heart. She had seen true visions. Blessing had survived the cataclysm, just as Sanglant had.

"We will find her," she swore.

The pain of the griffin's grip tightening on her shoulders forced tears to her eyes, hot from pain, from anger, and from grief as they flew low over the wasteland and she saw it in all its hideous glory. A blasted wilderness of ash and stone and a skin of still smoking molten rock, cooling and hardening as the days passed. The channel deep into the earth was closed; the Old Ones had seen to that. But the devastation spread for leagues in all directions, and when at last she saw trees again, places where they hadn't been incinerated, they were blown down all in the same direction. Many trunks still stood, scorched on one side. As they rested and flew and rested and flew, the worst of the destruction eased and she saw vegetation growing again but never sun and rarely rain. Now and again lightning flared to the north. Once, she saw a ragged man herding a trio of sheep along a dusty path; amazingly, he did not look up when the griffin called, as if he had at last decided it was better not to know.

It's never better not to know.

The pain in her shoulders was bad, but enduring that pain brought her closer to her goal. What if she never knew what had happened to the others? If the griffins could not find Sanglant? If they never got Blessing back? Months, or at least weeks, had passed

since she and Sorgatani and Lady Bertha and their retinue had
stumbled into Anne's ambush. She might never know whether her
faithful companions had survived the storm. Hanna might be dead,
and poor Ivar lost forever in the wilderness that is distance, time,
and the events that drag us forward on an unwanted path. She had
so few that she counted as some manner of kin or companion that
she wept to think of losing any, and yet surely she had lost them
years ago, the day she crossed through the burning stone and ascended the mage's ladder. Sanglant was right: she had abandoned
them.

I had no choice.

It was getting dark. She was as ready for a rest from the vista of
desolation as the griffin was ready for a respite from the burden of
bearing her. The landing in a broad clearing was a tumble, and she
skinned one knee but didn't break anything. A stream's water, mercifully clear, slaked her thirst, but there was nothing to eat among
the withered plants. God, she was so hungry! She was so cold, and
her shoulders ached so badly. A claw had torn her skin above her
right breast. Blood leaked through the tunic, and it hurt to move her
arms to gather grass to press the wound dry.

For a while, as it got dark, she sat with eyes closed and tried to
breathe away the pain. The female crouched protectively over her,
letting her curl into the shelter of that soft throat and away from
the cutting wing feathers, for she had not even a mantle to cover
herself with. She dozed, although she had meant to gather sticks for
a fire. The griffin huffed and wheezed all night, and Liath slept erratically, waking at intervals to glance at the heavens, but she never
saw stars. It was very cold, but the griffin, like her, had fire woven
into its being, and that kept her alive, just as the pigs had once kept
her alive.

She smiled sleepily, remembering the pigs: Hib, Nib, Jib, Bib, Gib,
Rib, Tib, and the sow, Trotter. Silly names. It seemed so long ago. She
conjured Hugh in her mind, but he did not frighten her. All that fear
and pain was part of her now, woven into her bones and heart in
the same manner as her mother's substance. It did not make her less
than she was. The streaming waters cut a channel in the earth that
humankind named a river, and each winter and flooding spring that
channel might shift and alter, but the river remained itself.

She dreamed.

The aether had once been like a river, pouring from the heavens
into Earth along that deep channel linking Earth to Ashioi country

adrift in the heavens. But now that channel lies breached, buried, and broken, and the aether flows instead as a thousand rivulets, spreading everywhere, penetrating all things but as the barest trickle.

She walks along a stream of silver that flows through the grasslands, but there is no one waiting for her, only the remains of the Horse people's battered camp and a few hastily-dug graves.

Morning came with no sunrise, a lightening so diffuse that it wasn't clear it came from the east at all. It was quiet, not a breath of wind. A branch snapped, the sound so loud she scrambled to her feet just as the silver male called a challenge. A half dozen men appeared at the other side of the clearing, carrying staves and spears. They had the disreputable and desperate appearance of bandits. They stared at her for a long time, measuring what she offered and what danger she posed. She held her bow tight, but she had no arrows. Her quiver had burned away like all the rest, even her good friend, Lucian's sword.

At last, one stepped forward from the rest and placed his weapon on the ground. He spoke in a dialect of Dariyan, the local speech. She could follow the gist of it. "Are you angel or demon? Whence are you come?"

"I am as you see me," she answered boldly. "No more, and no less."

"Has God sent you? Can you help us?"

"What manner of help do you need?" They were desperate, certainly, but as she studied their callused hands and seamed, anxious faces, she realized they were farmers.

"We have lost our village," said the spokesman. "Our houses torn down by the wind. A lord with soldiers came by then, three days past. He took what stores we held by us. Now we have nothing to eat. We could not fight. They had weapons."

The spears were only sharpened sticks, and the staves were branches scavenged out of the forest. One had a shovel. Another carried a scythe.

"Be strong," she called, knowing how foolish the words sounded, but she had nothing to give them.

"Whuff!" coughed the female, rising, and the men scattered into the trees.

"Let's go." Better the pain in her shoulders than the knife of helplessness held to her throat. Whose army had stolen their grain? She hoped it was not Sanglant's.

It took the griffin two tries to get enough lift to get up over the trees, and if the clearing hadn't been so broad they wouldn't have accomplished it at all. They made less distance this day but still far more than she could have walked. As the afternoon waned, more a change in the composition of the light than anything, they came to earth on a wide hillside better suited for the griffin's size. The silver male had fallen behind and at length appeared with a deer in his claws.

She had nothing to cut with and so waited until she could pick up the scraps left by their ripping and tearing. She gathered twigs and fallen branches and stones and dug a fire pit with her hands as well as she could. To call fire into dry kindling took only a moment's concentration: seek fire deep within the parched sticks and—there!— flames licked up from the inner pile, neatly stacked in squares to give the fire air to feed on. The scraps of meat cooked quickly skewered on a stick, and she ate with juice dribbling down her chin.

The griffins settled away from the fire, too nervous to doze. She licked her fingers and studied the darkening sky. The cloud cover made it difficult to gauge sunset.

Sanglant. Blessing. Hanna. Sorgatani. Hathui. Ivar. Heribert. Li'at'- dano. Even Hugh. She sought them in the fire with her Eagle's Sight, but all she saw was a crackling blur of flames and shadow.

IV
TALES TO SCARE CHILDREN

1

"REFUGEES," said Fulk as he reined in beside Sanglant where the regnant rode in the vanguard of the army.

They had begun the climb into the foothills through dreary weather with scarcely a drop of rain and not a single glimpse of the sun. They had lost a hundred horses in the last ten days and still had the crossing over the mountains ahead of them with winter coming on. It had, at least, been unusually warm, but in the past two days the bite of winter had strengthened.

Fulk indicated a trail that led off the road into a hollow where some twoscore desperate travelers had taken shelter under wagons and canvas lean-tos against evening's approaching dark.

"I know this place," said Sanglant. "This is where we found those men with their throats cut, after the galla attacked us."

"Indeed, Your Majesty. I see no sign of the massacre now. It's a good camping spot. Do we stop here for the night? These folk may ask for food and water and we haven't any to spare."

"The Aostan lords are shortsighted," remarked Sanglant. "Every village we passed has already been looted. If there is no one to till the fields because the farmers have all died of starvation, if there is no seed grain, they will not be able to feed their war bands. So be it. We'll camp here."

Sanglant urged Fest forward and with Fulk, Hathui, and a dozen of his personal guard at his back he rode into the hollow. He feared no violence. They could not kill him, and in any case it was obvious that these ragged fugitives posed no danger to an armed man. They hadn't even posted a sentry, only thrown themselves to the ground in exhaustion.

Hearing horses and the noise of men's voices, the refugees staggered up, huddling in groups of two and three.

"Who are you?" he asked.

When they heard him speak, half fell to their knees and the rest wept.

"Is it possible?" asked one middle-aged man, creeping forward on his knees with arms outstretched in the manner of a supplicant. "You speak Wendish."

"We are Wendish," he began, but a woman in cleric's robes hissed sharply and tugged on the first man's sleeve.

"It is Prince Sanglant, Vindicadus. Look! There is the banner of Fesse!"

"Who are you?" he asked again, not dismounting.

The one called Vindicadus rose as others urged him forward. It was a strange group, only adults in their prime and youths. There was one suckling infant in arms, no young children, and no elderly. Under the dirt they were sturdily and even well clothed, and several by their robes he identified as clerics.

"We are Wendish folk, my lord. We are those from King Henry's progress who were left behind in Darre because we belong to the households of clerics and presbyters."

"Why are you here now?"

In their silence, their hesitation, their indrawn breaths, he heard an answer. Some looked away. Some sobbed. A pair of servants clung to the sides of a handcart on which a man lay curled, hands in fists, eyes shut. He was dressed in the torn and stained robes of a presbyter. There was blood in his hair, long dried to a stiff coppery coating.

"They attacked us, my lord," said the one called Vindicadus at last. "Because we were Wendish. They said we had angered God by our presumption. They said we had caused the storm of God's punishment. We are all that remains of those of Wendish birth and breeding who served in the palaces in Darre. Our companions were slaughtered that day, or died on the way. I pray you, my lord, do not abandon us."

"Who attacked you?"

"Everyone, my lord." He wept. "The Aostans. The people of Darre. The city took terrible damage in the winds and the tremors that followed. Fissures belch gas out of the earth. Toward the coast, fire and rock blasted up from the Abyss and destroyed everything it touched. At least three mountains spew fire all along the western coast. It is the end of the world, my lord. What else can it be?"

"True words," murmured Hathui.

"Will you help us, my lord? We are unknown to you, but many of us served in King Henry's schola."

"You are dressed in frater's garb. Are you such a one?"

"Nay, my lord. I am a lowly servingman from Austra, once bound to the service of Margrave Judith but later coming into the service of her magnanimous son, Presbyter Hugh."

Sanglant felt a kick up inside his ribs. Hathui looked at him sharply, as though he had given something away, and maybe he had. She knew Liath's history as well as he did. "You served Lord Hugh?"

"I did, my lord. Of his schola and retinue, six remain. The others are dead—" He choked on the word and for the space of five breaths could not go on. Sanglant waited, hearing the army toiling up the road just beyond the low ridge that separated the hollow from the main path. "They are dead." He was not an old man but he had seen better days; grief made him fragile. "The rest went north months ago with the presbyter."

"Hugh went north? When was this?"

"Months ago, my lord. In the month of . . . aye, let me see. It seems years ago. I don't recall now. It was late summer. Yes, that's right."

"Wise of him to avoid the disaster," muttered Sanglant.

"He might be dead, Your Majesty," said Hathui.

"So we can wish, but I must assume the worst." He glanced at her while the refugees waited. She raised an eyebrow, a gesture so slight that it shouldn't have hit him so hard. "Not just because of Liath! He is the one who seduced Adelheid to trust him. The one who ensorcelled my father. He is ambitious, and he has reached the end of his rope."

"Queen Adelheid was not a fool. She was ambitious in her own right. It might be she who seduced Hugh to dream of power beyond what he had otherwise hoped for."

He snorted. "Do you think so, Hathui?"

"Nay. Only that they found a ready ally, each in the other."

"Did he bed her?"

"I believe she was faithful to your father. She admired and re-spected Henry."

"I am glad to hear it. Although surely, if that is true, it makes her actions harder to understand."

"They have two children, Your Majesty. What mother does not seek advancement for her beloved children? Presbyter Hugh achieved his high position because of his mother's devoted affec-tion."

"True enough. Margrave Judith was no fool except in her love for him."

One of the clerics limped out of the crowd and whispered into Vindicadus' ear, then shoved him, pressuring him forward.

"My lord. I beg you. What news of the king? I know—we knew—you rebelled against him."

"My father is dead."

They cried out loud at that. He heard their whispers: *Murderer. Patricide.*

"Your Majesty," said Fulk in loud voice. "Here comes Duchess Liutgard."

Her mount picked its way down the slope. Her banner bearer rode to her left and her favored steward to her right. She gasped when she saw the refugees. Her face grew even whiter. Seven of them ran forward and flung themselves into the dirt before her, careful of the hooves of her horse, but she dismounted and tossed the reins to her steward before walking in amongst them and taking their hands, calling them by name.

"How has this happened? Why are you here?" she demanded.

They spoke all at once, words tumbling each over those of the others. ". . . blast of wind . . . rumblings, then a terrible quake . . . fire in the sky . . . glowing rock, flowing everywhere."

"Riots. A storming of the palace. Flight through the ruined streets.

"All is chaos, my lady," wept the eldest, who was not more than forty. "I am called Elsebet, a cleric in Emperor Henry's schola. We lost half of our number in the first day, and half again as many in our trek here. We dared not attempt the Julier Pass. This one, Brother Vindicadus, was once in the service of Presbyter Hugh and before him Margrave Judith. He knew of an eastern pass that was little traveled. You see what remains of the king's schola. We lost so many. Is it true? Is it true the regnant—the emperor—is dead?"

"Henry is dead," said Liutgard as she looked at Sanglant. "That we are any of us living now is due to my cousin, Sanglant. Henry named him as heir as he was dying. It was—" Her voice broke, but she went on. "It was the wish of his heart to see Prince Sanglant become regnant after him. Henry was not himself at the end, not for the last two or three years. He was ensorcelled by his queen and by Presbyter Hugh. It was Sanglant who freed him from their net. Hear me!" Her voice rang out above the murmurs. "It is true. I swear it on my mother's and father's graves. I swear it by the Hand of the Lord and Lady. Sanglant is regnant now over Wendar and Varre. He is the one we follow. He is leading us home."

"We'll set up camp here for the night," said Sanglant quietly to Fulk. "We must make room for these."

"We haven't enough to feed them, Your Majesty."

"We cannot abandon them. They are our countryfolk. If I cannot save them, then who will?"

Fulk nodded, and left to give the orders.

They settled down to camp in marching order as dusk crept over them. Every man and woman slept fully clothed and with weapons beside him, although many put off their mail. The horses were rubbed down, watered, and fed; it was their good luck to find an unpolluted stream close by. With Lewenhardt, Surly, and a limping Sibold in attendance, Sanglant walked down through the line of march, pausing to speak to many of the soldiers, and fetched up at last with the rear guard.

The centaurs, led by Capi'ra, had volunteered for this onerous task, and he supposed the sight of them alone might have deterred many a rash attack from behind.

"Anything?" he asked her after their greeting.

"The same as every day. We see signs of men following on our tracks, but they fade away. Fewer today. There are fewer folk living here, and if they would not attack us when they have greater numbers, then they will fear to attack us when they are only a handful."

He nodded. It was almost dark. Night came early now, not just because of the time of year. Even during the day the clouds obscured the sun. His skin ached for light. Everyone felt its lack.

"It is strange to walk among you," said Capi'ra after a silence. "Your kind are so reckless. I will be glad to return to my homeland." She snorted, a horsey sort of chuckle. "No offense meant to you, Sanglant. We are not easy here. The land looks wrong. It smells funny. The winds aren't the ones we know."

"Look!" he said, squinting. "I thought I saw a flash."

"Lightning?"

He beckoned. "Lewenhardt. Come forward. Do you see it?"

The archer rode forward and stared south into the dark sky. He began to shake his head, then stiffened. "Could it be?" he whispered, then shouted aloud. "The griffins! It is the griffins, Your Majesty!"

Sanglant rode forward past the rearmost line, head bent back to stare heavenward as the news was called down the line of march so men could control their horses. Dogs barked.

Lewenhardt came up beside him. "They're flying low. One has something . . . something in its grip . . . a deer, perhaps? If they've been hunting. . . . ?"

"Ai, God," breathed Sanglant.

Such a bolt of adrenaline slammed through him that he thought he would go blind. He slipped getting off Fest and stumbled running forward downslope as the griffins dipped low and lower still, Domina weighed down by the burden she carried. The precious burden brought all this way to him, the one who had decreed that they must move on and leave her, unsought and unfound, behind.

I am no better than she was. I did what I thought was necessary.

Domina stooped that last short drop and when Liath was a man's height from the ground the griffin released her and she tumbled, hitting hard. He fell to his knees beside her, wondering if she was alive or dead, but he knew she was living and not just because she laughed and cried and embraced him so tightly with her head pressed against his shoulder that when she pulled away he could see the impress of his mail on her cheek.

He was struck dumb.

"The Lord and Lady have blessed us," she said, wincing as she used him as a support to clamber to her feet. "The griffins found you."

He was paralyzed, still on his knees as she gritted her teeth and tested her shoulders, shrugged them up and down, drawing circles with her arms. Blood stained the pale cloth of her sleeveless shift, but any fool could see she wasn't badly hurt, only tired, thin, dirty, and very sore.

She stared at him, seeking into his heart. At last, she kissed him on the lips. She tasted salty, and a whiff of something like brimstone trailed off her body. He shut his eyes, savoring her touch, needing only to let all the flavors of triumph and horror and joy mix within him.

In time he found himself, his words, his strength.

"With you," he murmured, "anything."

He rose, holding her close although it was clear she was not going to fall.

"Is it true you are regnant now?" she asked.

"I am. How could you know?"

"I met Zuangua."

"Ah. What of your companions, the ones who departed with you through the crown?"

She shook her head. "I don't know. I lost them months ago." She shuddered. "It was a terrible thing, Sanglant. Terrible. Anne is dead."

Said in such a voice, raw with grief. He had no need to question. Anne was dead. Liath had done what needed doing, although the cost had been high. He felt a wild laugh rise, and swallowed his fear and sorrow and anger, because they had not yet come close to knowing the full weight of the storm or how far it had spread its wings.

"You'll tell me what I need to know," he said. "Come. I can get you a bit of food at least. You're too thin, my love."

"What of those we left behind?" she demanded, clinging to him so he couldn't take a step. "What of Blessing? Heribert? Where is Hanna? What about Ivar? And Sorgatani and Bertha? Are they all lost?"

"I don't know."

She let go of him to cover her face with her hands. He waited while she trembled, lost in a battle for which he carried no weapons, but at length as the night darkened and the griffins settled down with coughs, scratching in the dirt, and distantly a voice called for folk to lie back down and get some sleep by God . . . at length she sighed and lowered her hands.

"There," she said. "There. All done. Where are we going?"

"Home to Wendar." He took her hand as they walked up toward the army, who stared in astonishment. How could they not? He was their regnant now, and Liath would be their queen.

2

AT night, high in the Alfar Mountains, Liath stood beside a fire and told the story to several hundred listeners, who would in their turn pass the tale back to the rest of the army. Many more crowded up in the darkness, waiting in utter silence, but because she told the tale as a poet declaims into a shuttered hall, not as a captain shouts, her voice did not reach as far as his might have, pitched to pierce the clamor of battle.

Still, he could not tell the tale as she could. He left her to it while he sat in his father's chair, which, because it was the regnant's chair, was now his. The small chest containing Henry's ashes, bones, and heart sat on the ground to his left, pressed up against the legs of the chair. He did not like it to rest too far from him, day or night.

"My knowledge is incomplete," she began—as she would! "But this is what I know which is certain, as well as what I believe must be true based on the stories and experiences I have myself heard and seen. All this was hidden or forgotten for long years, for generations, a time beyond our imagining. It was forgotten or became legend long before the birth of the blessed Daisan, who brought Light to us all. This tale must come to light now. It should be known to as many people as possible, if we are to make sense of what we must do next."

He marked their audience. Closest sat the most noble of his companions, Duchess Liutgard, trembling Duke Burchard, Lord Wichman who was, for once, paying attention, and the other lords and a few ladies who had marched south with Henry or with him. Beyond them crowded the clerics of the king's schola, led by Sister Elsebet, and those church folk who rode in the retinue of one or the other noble. He noted that the man known as Vindicadus had found a place close enough to hear, although he had no noble patron who might speak up for him. Behind this rank stood the captains and stewards who ordered the army and farther back yet waited sergeants and soldiers and servants hoping to catch what they could.

All must hear, so that they would understand.

He had ordered this assembly. The tides of destruction they had experienced had made them wonder and had made them fear. Any explanation was better than none, no matter how strange it might sound even when it was the truth.

"Two thousand seven hundred and four years ago, the Horse people allied with seven sorcerers from seven human tribes against a common enemy, known to them as 'The Cursed Ones' or the Ashioi. They wove a spell of power using the music of the spheres. This is the sorcery we call 'the mathematica.' This spell they threaded through seven stone circles, which they called looms and we call crowns. This spell ripped the homeland of the Ashioi out of the Earth and cast it into the aether."

"What is the aether?" someone called.

"That part of the universe that lies within and beyond the upper spheres. It's one of the five elements. The others are air, water, fire, and earth. Aether is the most rarified and pure. Unlike the others, it is untainted by darkness. Beyond the upper spheres, so the scholars teach, exists only aether, nothing else." She hesitated and, hearing no further question, continued. "All the Ashioi were flung into the aether with their land, all except those who were not actually in their homeland at the time. These other Ashioi were pulled halfway but not completely out of the world. Their shades haunted the forests and trails of Earth for centuries as elves who shot poison darts at any person unlucky enough to stumble across them."

"Those are just tales told to scare children," said a voice from the crowd.

It was Vindicadus, once Hugh's servant. Sanglant had not expected to hear a challenge so soon.

Liath smiled, but her look was grim. "I have met shades while traveling through the deep forest. They are not tales. Their elfshot killed my horse. And drove off bandits."

Among the sergeants there came a flurry of movement. A white-haired man pushed forward into the ranks of the captains. "Let me speak!" he cried. "I have served with Prince Sanglant. He himself freed me and my four men from Salavii merchants who had captured us and meant to sell us into the east."

"What's your name?" asked Liath.

"This is Gotfrid," said Sanglant, before the old soldier could answer. "I recall you from Machteburg. What is it you have to say, Sergeant?"

"Just this." He surveyed the assembly with the hard gaze of a man who has seen enough that he no longer fears the disapproval of others. "I and my men—we survived the attack of Lost Ones. We saw our comrades fall beneath the sting of their darts. If you doubt the lady, then I pray you, answer me how I could have seen them as well. Two of my men are still with me. They will tell as well, if you ask, what they saw."

"What of the other two?" Sanglant asked, knowing the answer because he had already heard the tale.

The man gestured with his hand, a flick, as dismissal. His throat and chin tightened.

Folk murmured, but it was hard to tell who they believed.

"Is there anyone else here who wishes to speak about the existence of the Lost Ones?" asked Liath.

No one did. The heckler had vanished back into the crowd. Sanglant could, in a manner of speaking, smell that he still lingered, and he wondered what twisted loyalty held the man to Hugh of Austra. Liath was already going on.

"As centuries passed, the story of the great spell was lost until it became nothing more than legend. The Ashioi came to be known as the Aoi, the Lost Ones. The knowledge used to weave the spell was lost also, because, I believe, all seven of the sorcerers who wove it were killed in the backlash from the spell."

A murmur followed this statement, quickly stilled.

"Perhaps they left no apprentices to carry on their learning, although that would surprise me."

"Perhaps those who were left behind chose to forget," said Sister Elsebet. "What the church has condemned must be immoral."

"This was before the time of the blessed Daisan," said Liath. "They would not have been able to follow the rulings of the church."

"They might have known in their hearts that it was wrong," retorted the cleric.

Liath nodded amiably. "There are many possible answers. Perhaps their apprentices were too inexperienced, or too secretive, or too horrified to pass on the knowledge. Perhaps they were told not to. We'll never know, since we have no way of asking."

"I pray you, Lady Liathano," said Duchess Liutgard with a doubting smile, "how can you tell us this knowledge was lost when you stand here before us branded as a mathematicus yourself? The Holy Mother Anne boasted of her sorcery, and taught these arts openly in the skopal palace these last two or three years."

Liath nodded, echoing the other woman's formality. They did not know each other. Liutgard knew of Liath only as the Eagle who had stolen Henry's favorite child away from the glorious alliance Henry had promised him. Yet it seemed to Sanglant that Liath was deaf to whatever undertones sang through the nobles as they measured her. She was focused, simply and always, on understanding the truth.

"A good question, my lady. If you will allow me to unfold my argument, then the map will become clear to all, I hope."

Liutgard nodded. She was, Sanglant thought, not afraid to offer Liath a reasonable chance to explain herself.

"In time, certain half-Ashioi, half-human descendants of the original Ashioi built a powerful empire in the southern lands bordering the Middle Sea. They called it Dariya, and called themselves Dariyans. As it was sung by the poet,

> "Out of this people came one who ruled
> as emperor over men and elvish kind both."

"The Dariyan Empire soon ruled much of the northwestern continent and the lands along both the northern and southern shores of the Middle Sea. We are traveling on a road paved by this empire. Eventually, the Horse people—the Dariyans and historians call them the 'Bwr' which is derived, I think, from the word—"

She broke off, catching herself, and, as a rider shifts her mount's direction, got herself back on the main path.

"The Horse people became aware of the Dariyan Empire. They feared and hated the Dariyans because the Dariyans were descended in part from the hated Ashioi. In the early 200s, the Bwr invaded in a host and burned and pillaged the city of Dariya. It's likely that in the course of their invasion they contracted a plague that decimated their numbers. They retreated to the eastern steppe that was their ancient homeland to protect themselves against further incursions by humankind, although humankind had once been their chief allies."

Burchard coughed. "Are these Horse people you speak of not the same ones who ride with us, as our allies? Does this mean they are still our enemy? Or our friends?"

Liutgard's mouth tightened as she looked past Sanglant to the honor guard attending at his back. Her forces had taken the worst of the centaur assault. She had no reason to love the Horse people.

Sanglant glanced behind. Captain Fulk and Captain Istvan stood behind his chair, alert to the disposition of his most loyal forces.

Capi'ra and her sergeants waited in shadow, seeming at first glance like women mounted on horses, but he could hear their soft whickering commentary although he could not understand what they were saying. Beyond them rested the slumbering griffins with their wing feathers touched by the light of the camp's bonfire.

Smoke stung his face as the wind shifted. He fanned a hand to drive it away although in truth it made no difference.

"The Horse people are our allies, Burchard," he said.

"*Your* allies," said Liutgard.

"Mine," he agreed, "and thus, for the moment, yours, Cousin. I pray you, Liath, go on."

"I pray you!" cried a voice from the back, that damned servingman again. "You speak of the lives and empires of the heathen, yet you have not said one word about the blessed Daisan! Do you even believe in God?"

"Hush!" said someone else in the crowd.

"Let her speak!" cried another, the words echoed by a chorus of "let her speak" and "yes" and "shut your mouth."

"Else we'll be standing out here in the damned cold all night and freeze our hands to what they're scratching," finished a wit.

"Well," said Liath, raising her voice as the others dropped theirs. She slid easily into the silence. "All here have heard told the life of the blessed Daisan and his chief disciple, Thecla the Witnesser. This we know and believe, that the blessed Daisan revealed to all of humankind the truth of the Circle of Unity, of the Mother and Father of Life, and our belief in the Penitire." Her gaze had a peculiar way of going flat when she quoted from memory, as if she looked inward, not outward. " 'The blessed Daisan prayed in ecstacy for six days and on the seventh was translated up to the Chamber of Light to join God.' "

Her gaze sought the heckler, and perhaps it found him, because she paused for a moment with a fixed stare, then smiled just a little as a bully might, seeing his prey flinch. The man had by this time moved so that his body was hidden to Sanglant's line of sight.

"What matters to the story I tell you tonight is that the belief in the Circle of Unity and the Word of the blessed Daisan spread outward on the architecture of the old Dariyan Empire."

"More than that!" interposed Sister Elsebet indignantly.

"Ai, God! Spare us these interruptions! I'm still scratching!" cried the wit.

Sanglant sighed.

Sister Elsebet stepped forward and glared her audience into silence. "None of us can speak as if this war is ended."

"Which war is that?" asked Liath. "I thought I was speaking of a war."

Elsebet pounded her staff twice on the ground. "I will listen, but I will not remain silent on this matter. I pray you, Your Majesty!"

He was caught, and he knew it as well as the cleric did. "Go on, Sister. What is it you must say?"

"That the woman has knowledge of sorcery and history I can see, and perhaps respect. But the war that afflicts those of us who live within the Circle of Unity is never ending. It is impossible to speak of the blessed Daisan without speaking as well of those who have sought to corrupt his holy teachings."

"Have we time for this?" Sanglant asked Liath.

A foolish question. She was interested, and entertained. She could go on in this vein for hours. "You speak of heresy, Sister Elsebet, do you not?"

"As must we all! Alas!"

"Then I pray you, educate us."

Once offered, quickly taken. Sister Elsebet did not strike Sanglant as a fussy, troublesome woman, nor had he in their brief acquaintance been given any reason to believe she was one of Hugh's adherents.

"Go on," he said, giving her permission.

She came forward. Liath did not, in fact, make way or give up her own place standing on a conveniently situated rock that elevated her a bit above the rest, but she did drop her chin and, between one breath and the next, efface herself. The shift was astonishing. Sanglant had never seen her do such a thing before, as if she doused the radiance that made her blaze. Before, she must command the gaze; now, she was only a woman standing on a rock listening as a cleric spoke of the holy truth that sustained them.

"This is the truth! Heed me! Many heresies have troubled the church since the living body of the blessed Daisan was lifted up into the Chamber of Light. But in these dark days there are two we must guard against most assiduously.

"The first is known as the Redemptio. This is the belief that the blessed Daisan was martyred by the Empress Thaissania, She of the Mask. That only after his death by flaying and his supposed resurrection did he ascend to the Chamber of Light. This heresy was eventually squelched and forbidden. As it deserved!

"The second, and greater, heresy concerns the constitution of the blessed Daisan himself. The elders of the church ruled that the blessed Daisan was no different than any other human, claiming only a divine soul made up of pure light trapped in a mortal body admixed with darkness. The adherents of the greater heresy claim otherwise and declared that the blessed Daisan alone among humankind was half divine and half mortal. In the year 499, the Emperor of Arethousa turned his back on the skopos in Darre and abandoned the truth because of his belief in this half divinity. So was the holy word of the blessed Daisan wounded by the Enemy's sharp arrows."

She drew the Circle at her chest and turned to bow to Sanglant.

"How does this affect the tale?" he asked.

"Heresy must affect us all," retorted Sister Elsebet. "Right belief is what sustains us! It would be a greater tempest even than the one we suffered in Aosta should these heretical beliefs take hold and drown the foundation on which all our lives rest! On what we and the church mothers know to be true! Perhaps this tempest is not merely the playing out of an ancient sorcery but a warning sent to us by God!"

He looked at Liath.

She lifted her chin, squared her shoulders, made herself visible again, the center of attention. Yet this was not the charisma that allows a commander to lead men to their death in battle. This was, purely, control over the unnatural fire that burned within her.

"It may be, Sister Elsebet," she agreed without any evidence of insincerity. "Yet I know this. The land of the Ashioi returned to Earth because those who wove the sorcery in ancient days did not understand fully the consequence of what they did. The land returned because it could not do otherwise. It was bound as if in a great circle, necessarily returning to the place it started."

"Indeed," agreed the cleric stoutly. "For this same reason the church mothers have always disapproved of sorcery."

"Yes, so it was. Sorcery was restricted by the church in two separate rulings. Certain of the magical arts were allowed to be taught under the supervision of the church, but others were condemned, specifically those that related to foreseeing the future and controlling the weather as well as knowledge of the mathematical properties of the stars and planets. In truth, although this was unknown to the church councils that condemned them, these were the very arts used in ancient days to weave the spell that cast the Ashioi into exile."

Elsebet nodded, as if her point was now proven. She did not step aside. Liath kept talking.

" 'Between the Bwr invasion and the troubled church, the creaking edifice of the old empire at last collapsed.' "

"So wrote Taillefer's chronicler, Albert the Wise."

"Indeed he did, which is where I got the phrase. The last of those who believed in the Redemptio, in the east beyond Arethousa, vanished when the Jinna Empire conquered those lands in the name of their god."

"Fire worshipers!" muttered the wit.

"I hear they worship naked," said Wichman suddenly. "I'd like to see those Jinna women dancing around the flames!"

"Enough!" snapped Sanglant. "I pray you, go on."

"I pray you," Liath said, surveying the assembly, "I am nearly done."

"Which is what she said before," added the wit, and there was a smattering of chuckles.

She smiled and waited for quiet before she went on. "These Jinna conquered the southern shore of the Middle Sea as well. The lands around the old imperial capital fell into chaos for many decades, but at length various princedoms and duchies and counties arose. These folk called themselves Aosta. They called their capital Darre, and it was in Darre—once the capital of the Dariyan Empire—that one regnant or another pretended to rule Aosta."

This slighting comment was appreciated. A few distant soldiers cheered.

She acknowledge them with a lift of a hand. "Only in the northwestern kingdom of Salia did a ruler consolidate enough power to extend his reach. The Salian king, Taille, renamed himself the Emperor Taillefer and crowned himself with a seven-pointed crown that he called his 'crown of stars.' As part of his imperial policy, Taillefer sent missionaries for the Daisanite Church into the lands east of Salia. Heathen tribes embraced the Circle of Unity. Chieftains sent their own sons and daughters out into the more distant wilderness to convert yet more peoples. So came the Wendish into the Circle."

"This history of empire any good scholar knows," said Sister Elsebet. "That good woman, Sister Rosvita, was writing her history of the *Deeds of the Great Princes*. Yet she—she, too—" She faltered. She wept.

"A woman firm in her scholarship," said Liath. "I believe she would understand that it is necessary to see the tapestry as a whole in order to understand the consequence of the spell. If you will, I will go on.

"Taillefer's empire disintegrated after the emperor's death. At that time, King Arnulf the Elder of Wendar annexed lands formerly allied to Salia by marrying the heirs of Varre to his own children. When these heirs died without issue, he named himself king of Wendar and Varre. In time, the regnancy passed to Arnulf the Younger, and then to *his* son, Henry, the second of that name. So might we learn from Sister Rosvita, were she here to teach us!

"Henry married an Arethousan princess named Sophia. She bore him three children, Sapientia, Theophanu, and Ekkehard. The king struggled against his own older sister, Sabella, but he triumphed over her at Kassel, in the duchy of Fesse."

She nodded at Liutgard, who lifted a hand and touched her own brow, as if remembering those lost in that battle: brother against sister.

"Henry's own cousin Conrad, too, it seemed, chafed at being a duke, but his ambitions are as yet unknown. Some years after the death of Queen Sophia, Henry married Princess Sapientia to Prince Bayan, the younger brother of the Ungrian king, Geza. He hoped, it seemed, that this alliance would protect his eastern marchlands from marauders. Soon after, Henry married an Aostan princess of noble birth, called Adelheid, and traveled south to Aosta with the intention of having himself crowned Emperor and of driving all Jinna and Arethousan interlopers out of lands that ought to belong to the holy church and its imperial champion. And this he did, as you know, because you rode beside him. You triumphed, because he triumphed."

Those who had survived the expedition were still proud of seeing their king crowned as emperor. Sanglant saw the memory of victory in their expressions, but he also saw their grief.

"Many disturbances were rising in the lands beyond Wendar. They struck hard. From the east, the Quman barbarians led by their prince Bulkezu plundered the marchlands and Avaria. Some among you will remember his defeat."

This got cheers as well, and Sanglant heard his name rise out of the crowd. She waited, and went on when she could.

"In the north, the Eika savages raid along the coast, united under a single chieftain. Reports suggest that civil war plagues the kingdom of Salia. In Arethousa, there is always corruption and intrigue, as the poets and historians tell us. But this was not all. Strange creatures out of legend walked abroad. Across the lands people began to whisper that the end of the world was at hand."

"So it is!" called a voice from the crowd, and many cried out in agreement.

Liutgard rose unexpectedly, looking angry. "Was this, that we suffered, the end of the world? We are still alive, although many dear to us are dead. Henry is dead—may he rest at peace in the Chamber of Light. But the world is not ended."

Liath raised a hand to show that she had heard and understood her objection. "Earth still holds beneath us, although I think we may find much in the land has been altered. I pray you, Duchess Liutgard, hear what I have to say. How is it that the woman who called herself Anne and who ruled over you as skopos knew of the Ashioi? How did she know about the ancient spell which would come to fruition on that night, that one night, when the crown of stars crowned the heavens? At midnight on the cusp of the tenth and eleventh days of Octumbre, in the year 735, as we measure the years after the proclamation of the Holy Word. How is it she knew this?"

It was a sorry satisfaction for Sanglant to recall that he had warned Henry's court and no one had listened to him.

"After the death of Emperor Taillefer, his empire fell into disunion because there was no male heir. He left three daughters and a few bastard sons. One of these claimed the throne and was later killed by his rivals." She glanced at Sanglant. He nodded, having heard this story before. Its existence did not threaten his hold on the throne.

"Two of Taillefer's daughters were married to princes of the realm and they vanish from our history. But his daughter Tallia was placed in the church as a biscop. There she studied the ancient arts of the mathematici together with her most intimate and faithful servant, a woman named Clothilde. These two and their adepts discovered that the ancient story of the Ashioi was a true story. They discovered that within a few decades—well, almost a hundred years—there would be a second cataclysm. They thought they could prevent this cataclysm with a second weaving. They believed that the Ashioi, now in exile, were scheming to return to Earth and conquer humankind. But the truth is that it was the spell which was flawed. The land of the Ashioi was flung outward on such a path that it would inevitably come back to where it had begun. We have all ridden such trails, thinking we are going elsewhere only to end up where we started!"

She hoped for a chuckle but did not get one. Her audience listened intently, but they did not, necessarily, believe what she was saying. Sanglant could see in each posture the extent of their belief: Sister Elsebet with her head bent skeptically; Sergeant Gotfrid scratching his beard as if puzzled; a woman fitted with a steward's tabard staring raptly with mouth parted as she fingered the knot that tied her scarf beneath her chin.

"The other Salian clerics at that time believed that Biscop Tallia had gone too far in studying the malefic arts of black sorcery. The Council of Narvone was convened and all sorcery associated with the mathematici as well as malefici was placed under ban. As was Biscop Tallia. Yet she did not cease her efforts. In time she discovered what she had long sought: a child born to Queen Radegundis, the last wife of Taillefer. This infant was raised in the church and became a monk. Soon after his birth, Tallia died, leaving her handmaiden, Clothilde, to continue her work.

"Clothilde was patient. Late in life, Taillefer's son was tempted by a very young woman, a novice. On her he got a child. Afterward, he fled. But the child was taken from its mother and raised by Clothilde."

"What became of the father and mother?" asked Sister Elsebet, listening intently now, as if she had heard some portion of this story before.

"Taillefer's son? I think that he remained in the church. But the woman who gave birth to his child? I don't know. I know only that Anne was the granddaughter of Taillefer, the child of Taillefer and Radegundis' lost son. She was raised by Sister Clothilde as a mathematicus among a band of mathematici who called themselves the Seven Sleepers. They were asleep, they told themselves, waiting quietly until the time came to act. Anne was to be the agent of that act: to cast the Ashioi once and for all time away from Earth."

"Would it not have been better had she done so?" asked Liutgard. She gestured toward the ragged army gathered around. "Would it not have spared us this?"

Liath shook her head. "No. You saw what tides of destruction the spell wrought. That devastation would have rebounded on Earth tenfold had Anne's spell succeeded. It would have been far worse. Earth is not meant to be sundered from Earth. The ancient ones—our ancestors—meant to save themselves. But by their own act they doomed us. I think they were ignorant. They did not know. Yet we are left with the consequences nonetheless."

PART TWO

IN THE RUINS

V
SALVAGE

1

ANNA clawed awake from a terrible dream. She lay with eyes closed, aware of the rise and fall of her breathing, and let the threads of that awful nightmare fade. An endless trek across a wilderness of grass under the hammer of a brutal winter cold. A blizzard turning to flowers. Bulkezu's hand tightening on her throat. Blessing as limp as a corpse, wasting away, dying. Buried alive deep within an ancient tumulus. Worms crawling over and swallowing her body.

With each exhalation the images became more tattered until at last they dissolved into nothing, and with a sigh of relief she opened her eyes. It was still night. Clouds hid the stars. She couldn't see anything, not even her hand in front of her face.

Even a moonless night was never this dark.

Her heart thundered. She whimpered, afraid to move or speak lest speaking and moving reveal her nightmares as truth. If she wished hard enough, it would all go away and she would be back in Gent sitting cozy by the fire in Mistress Suzanne's weaving hall.

A voice mumbled a curse. Stone snapped on flint. A spark glittered, faded, then a second snap struck and its spark caught a wick. As light bled into their grave, memory returned in a rush.

Prince Sanglant's army had marched east in search of griffins and sorcerers. He had found them and much more besides, but Blessing had fallen ill with an aetherical sickness and had to be left behind, close to death. Six attendants stayed with her. In the hope that the spell woven by Princess Liathano through the stone crown would miraculously preserve Blessing in a kind of stasis, they had crawled into the grave mound between the stones. There they had waited until blue fire engulfed them and all sensation ceased.

Anna groaned and raised up on her elbows, staring around in shock. Brother Heribert had lit the lamp, and he, too, stared slack-jawed at their surroundings. Thiemo, Matto, the Kerayit healer, and the young Quman soldier still slept, each in his place in the ring around Princess Blessing. But the low, cramped chamber in which they had taken their place had vanished . . . and so had Blessing.

"Ai, God! Lord protect us! Lady have mercy!" Anna scrambled to her feet.

"What's happened?" As Heribert rose, he almost lost his footing as a temblor rumbled through the ground. The flame wavered. A web of blue fire shuddered into existence around them, hot and bright.

"Something's coming," said Heribert. "Can you feel it, Anna? It's like a weight descending. We're not safe here."

She stared at the high cavern in which they stood. Stalactites glittered under the net of fire. Thiemo snored softly, one hand cupped at his throat. Matto lay with mouth agape and eyes and hands fast shut. It was all true. They had crawled into the ancient burial chamber to protect Blessing and possibly to die, but they hadn't died and indeed they were no longer where they had started out. The burial chamber had been dirt; this place was stone. In the burial chamber there had barely been room to stand upright in the center; this place could hold a council of twoscore nobles *and* their horses. In the burial chamber there had been a single entrance, a tunnel that led to the outside. Here, at least four passageways left the chamber at different directions. They might be anywhere.

She, too, felt a stiffening in the air, a tension in the earth, like the breath of a huge monster about to lunge out of darkness onto its hapless prey.

"Come quickly!" Blessing's voice pierced the silence, although there was no sign of her in the chamber. "No! This way! You're so slow! I said *this* way!"

"What a brat!" said a second voice, laughing.

"I am *not* a brat! I'm not!"

"You are!"

"I'm not!"

Blessing's companion laughed merrily, and before Anna or Heribert could react two figures trotted into the cavern, the smaller grasping the larger by his wrist. Blessing dropped her grip and clapped her hands to crow in triumph.

"Look what I found, Brother Heribert! And not just that, but a pile of treasure!"

The earth shook violently. The net of blue fire sparked and dazzled, and began to pulse.

"Lord have mercy," said Heribert, staring at Blessing, who looked painfully thin but otherwise emphatically alive and vital. Anna didn't know whether to be giddy with joy or annoyed that Blessing after all hadn't changed one bit and probably hadn't a thought to spare for the sacrifice her attendants had made so willingly for her.

"I'm Berthold," said the youth, a nice-looking boy most likely a little younger than Anna, fifteen or sixteen or so. He wore a handsome pale blue tunic of an excellent weave trimmed with yellow embroidery, a hip-length cape lined with pale fox fur, and soft leather boots bound up with laces. He held calfskin gloves casually in one hand, and at his waist rode a sword in a richly tooled sheath bearing the mark of the silver tree.

"Lord have mercy," repeated Heribert, shifting his stunned gaze away from Blessing. "You must be Villam's son."

"So I am," said the lad, not one bit surprised at being recognized. A noble youth out of a house as important as Villam's expected to be known. "We crawled in here to explore but must have fallen asleep. The rest of my companions are still asleep. I could only wake up Jonas. He's trying to get the others awake. I don't know where this chamber came from!" He gestured toward the high ceiling, and the four sleeping men. "It wasn't here when we explored under the tumuli yesterday. How did you get here?"

The earth shook once again. The pulse of the light had begun to shift in pitch until Anna could actually hear a melodic rise and fall shot through with an unearthly harmony. The temperature was beginning to rise.

"I want to get out of here," said Blessing. "Something very very bad is about to happen." She turned on Berthold. He stood a head taller than she did, although he wasn't as tall as her father. "Help me wake them up!"

Berthold's expression twisted, eyes opening in mock horror, mouth opening to an "o" of pretend fear. "Of course, my lady!" He spoiled the moment by laughing again. "Who made you regnant?"

She stamped her foot. "My father is Prince Sanglant. I am the great granddaughter of the Emperor Taillefer. You have to do what I tell you to do!"

He snorted with amusement, glanced at Anna to estimate her station and importance, and nodded at Brother Heribert. "Who are you, Brother?"

"I am called Brother Heribert. I am a cleric in Prince Sanglant's schola."

"Is it true this brat is Prince Sanglant's daughter?"

"I'm not a brat!"

"She is indeed, my lord."

"How can she be the great granddaughter of Emperor Taillefer? Henry's forebears have no connection to that noble house."

Heribert hesitated just long enough for Berthold to go on, impatient as his thoughts skipped ahead.

"Prince Sanglant has a schola? How can he? He's the captain of the King's Dragons. I didn't even know he had a daughter this old, but I suppose it's no surprise given what everyone says about him and women. Heh! I wonder what Waltharia will have to say about that! She thought she walked that road first!"

"What road?" demanded Blessing.

Heribert flung up a hand as if to say, "stop." "I pray you, Lord Berthold. We must untangle these lineages later. Princess Blessing is right. We'd best flee." He wiped sweat from his brow. "I don't like being trapped in here."

"Nor do I," admitted the youth, looking around. "Although it is the most amazing thing! Who could have dug such caverns? You should see the treasure back there! Golden helms and mounds of emeralds and garnets! Jeweled belts. Necklaces. I told them not to pick anything up, but they would cram their sleeves—all but Jonas, he's the only one who listens to me—"

A temblor shook the earth so hard that Anna had trouble keeping her feet. The Kerayit healer moaned, fighting sleep but not quite able to wake. Thiemo and Matto didn't stir at all. The blue fire had become so bright she had to squint. The cavern shone, walls gleaming. The stone sweat as heat swelled. It was like being trapped inside a box that had been thrown onto a fire.

"No one is listening to me!" shrieked Blessing. She pounced on Thiemo and shook him. "Wake up! Wake up!"

Without warning, the Quman soldier leaped to his feet, knife in hand as he assessed his surroundings. Over the last months Heribert had picked up the rudiments of the Quman speech. He spoke now, and the young man nodded abruptly, lowered the knife, and knelt beside Matto, shaking him. The Kerayit healer opened her eyes and, with a grunt, scrambled to her feet. She pointed to the fiery blue net whose brightness by now made the light in the cavern almost unbearable.

"Sorcery," she said in halting Wendish. "Go now. Go quick."

"Do you know the way out?" asked Heribert.

"I don't," said Berthold. "It's all changed. It wasn't like this at all yesterday when we crawled in here—"

"I know how to go!" exclaimed Blessing.

"Take her," said Heribert to Anna. "We'll have to carry Thiemo and Matto if we can't wake them up."

"Do you really think she knows anything?" demanded Berthold, more in disbelief than in anger. He had begun, finally, to appear nervous.

"I do know! I do!"

"Have you a better plan?" asked Heribert in his mildest tone. "I haven't. One is as good as another. We'd best hurry."

Thunder shook the cavern, a stalactite shuddered loose from the ceiling, crashed to the floor, and shattered into stinging shards. Anna caught one on her cheek. Blood trickled down her skin.

"Lord Berthold!" A young man no older than Villam's son staggered out of a passageway. He shaded his eyes, brought up short by the blinding net of light. Another tremor shook them. A second stalactite cracked and fell, and the poor youth leaped aside and shouted out loud as he flung up his arms to protect himself. Dust and debris scattered.

"Where are the others?" demanded Berthold. He, too, was pale now. He, too, looked frightened.

"I can't wake them!" said poor Jonas, who had been crying. "I don't know what's wrong!"

"This way!" cried Blessing, who had run to a different passageway, one opposite the tunnel that Berthold's companion had just emerged from. "I said this way! We've got to hurry! The storm is coming. It will crush us if we're in here!"

She shot off a quick command in the Quman language, surprising both Heribert and Anna, who hadn't known she could speak any language other than Wendish. The Quman soldier got Matto under the arms and began dragging him.

"Here!" Galvanized, Anna ran forward and got hold of Matto's ankles, heaving him up, but after ten paces his limp weight was too much for her, and she wasn't weak.

"Help us, I pray you, Lord Berthold," said Heribert. "Let's carry these two free and come back for your companions."

Berthold hesitated, then fixed his mouth in a grim line and ran over to Thiemo. "He looks familiar," he mused, grabbing him under the arms. "Here, Jonas. Help me!"

The Kerayit healer came to Anna's rescue, taking Matto's ankles, and Anna after all had to pursue Blessing, who had already vanished up the passageway. The floor was seamless, swept clean of debris, pebbles, dirt. Threads of light pierced the stone itself, woven entirely through the underground labyrinth. With each tremor, with each pulse, tiny cracks fissured the stone. At any moment the entire place might splinter and collapse. This was not the fate she had expected. Panic lent her wings, and she raced on Blessing's trail and would have plunged to her death had Blessing not screamed out loud just in time for Anna to stumble to a stop beside the girl, at the edge of an abyss.

The passageway ended in a wide, deep hole. It was as if a giant had stuck a spear far down into the earth and drawn it up again, leaving this empty shaft behind. The net of light that illuminated the labyrinth did not penetrate into its depths. There was no way across, and no obvious way down or up.

"Look," said Blessing, pointing to the cliff face opposite them. "There's a ledge there, and a passageway."

"No way to reach it, Your Highness," said Anna, barely able to speak. She couldn't catch her breath. "We'll have to go back and find another route."

"Is, too!" Blessing ran to the edge where the walls of the passageway met the sheer curve of that huge shaft. She reached, she gripped, and between one breath and the next had clambered out along the wall toward the far side.

Fear strangled Anna's voice. She was helpless, terrified, still woozy. She still could not believe that she was awake and in this terrible predicament. Ai, God. If only she could wake up and find herself back in Gent! The earth shook, and although Anna shrieked out loud, Blessing did not fall; she had too good a grip; she was fearless, that girl. Impossible. Already halfway across, clinging like a lizard to the rock face.

"Anna? Anna! Ai, God!" Heribert came up behind her, not far ahead of the rest.

"I'll have to follow her." Without waiting for his reply, because if she waited she would lose her courage, she ran to the edge and brushed a hand over the rock wall, finding handholds and narrow brims easily. Someone had carved these here. They couldn't be natural, placed so cunningly and conveniently. She crept along the wall, knowing better than to look down. As long as she didn't look down, she could believe that the ground lay one step below. It was easier that way to move across the rock face. It was easier that way not to panic.

"Princess Blessing, come back!" cried Heribert.

"Won't!" Blessing leaped to the far ledge just as another tremor shook them. A rock fell from above, and Anna shut her eyes and held on, listening, but she never heard it strike bottom. She was by now breathing so hard that she was dizzy, and when she opened her eyes she saw that Blessing had disappeared into the far passageway.

"Go on, Anna!" shouted Heribert. "You've got to get her back! We can't carry the rest across this!"

She heard the others arrive, heard their shocked exclamations and the buzz of discussion, but she could not concentrate on them to pick out words. She had to pick a path across the face, one handhold and toehold at a time, and at last she swung onto the far ledge which by now resembled a grand broad field, it looked so inviting and safe although it wasn't more than an arm's span in width. She landed there, panting, sweating, mouth dry, just as a horrible grinding roar shuddered up from the depths. In the passageway behind Heribert and the others, dust roiled, punched outward by a tremendous rockfall back the way they had come.

"Go, Anna! Go!" shouted Heribert before the dust engulfed him.

Despite the brilliant web of sorcery, she could not see Thiemo and Matto through the haze. She saw the blur of movement, glimpsed a Quman bow case and a Kerayit headdress, heard voices yell and shriek, but nothing more. Nothing more.

Far away, down that dark passageway lying behind her, Blessing called out impatiently. "Come! Come! Hurry!"

She ducked down, banging her head once on stone before getting the hang of the low ceiling. It was dark as the grave. No net of sorcery wove light to guide her footsteps. Twice she stumbled and bruised herself, and the third time she tumbled to hands and knees and yelped in pain.

A warm hand fastened on her shoulder. "Hurry! Where are the others?"

"They can't cross, Your Highness." She coughed. Dust had scoured her lungs. Grit abraded her palms. "They can't carry Lord Thiemo and Matto across that wall. We've got to go back."

"I can't leave them behind!" cried Blessing, with a fury that caused her hand to tighten on Anna's shoulder until it hurt. She should have been weak after her illness, but she wasn't. "Papa says you never leave your companions behind. We have to rescue them."

"I think there was a rockfall." She coughed again. It hurt to cough. "We can't go back the way we came. Ai, God. What if they're all dead?"

The earth groaned and rumbled beneath them, around them, everywhere. They were trapped in a tomb and it was too late to save themselves. They would die here—

A body slammed into Anna, tripped over her, and went sprawling, knocking Blessing down.

"Highness!" Anna smelled the Kerayit healer, whose peculiar scent of sour milk and an unidentifiable musk always tickled her nose.

She sneezed. The others piled up behind them, trapped in the low tunnel. A cloud of dust blasted past them, choking the passage.

"Move! Move!" said Lord Berthold from out of the dust. "The whole place is collapsing."

Anna scrambled forward, grabbing Blessing's arm and pulling her along with her. They raced blind, tripping, stumbling, staggering, but the passage ran true, without turns or branches, until at length they stumbled onto stone steps, and climbed up them. Just as Anna realized that she could see through her stinging eyes, they emerged into a shallow cave carved out of a hillside by a massive collapse of dirt, as if half the side of the hill had fallen away. Dust puffed and billowed around them. Beyond, a sickly gray light bled color out of the air.

Anna crept to the opening. One by one the others joined her: Princess Blessing, Lord Berthold, his companion Jonas, the Kerayit healer, and last the young Quman soldier supporting Brother Heribert, who fell to his knees, hacking as though he meant to cough his lungs out. All of them wept blood from scrapes and cuts. All were covered with dust and dirt. Lord Berthold cursed and muttered, while Jonas tried to soothe him.

"They're dead! Dead! I abandoned them! Ai, God, I've no honor left! I ran for my life. Better to have died—"

"Look!" shouted Blessing, and at the same moment the Kerayit healer cried, "Down!"

They dropped to their knees, but Anna stared anyway. She couldn't stop staring. They looked out over a valley nestled between high peaks. Once the valley had boasted a fine rich forest along its slopes, but now the trees were tumbled and snapped, shorn down as though by a giant's scythe. A vast creature hung suspended in the air, stretched across the hazy sky. It was there only for an instant, a flash of gold scales, before the sound of its wings thundered and it vanished beyond the peaks. Snow and ice crashed from the summit in a distant avalanche. The boom echoed on and on and on.

A pall of dust shrouded the sky. It was dim, but not dark; twilight, but not day. Now and again lightning stabbed through the cloudy haze, unseen except as a ghostly glimmer, quickly gone. Once the noise of the avalanche faded, they heard no answering thunder. A monstrous orange-red glow rose along one horizon. Maybe it heralded the rising sun, but if so it was no sun she ever wanted to see.

"Is it day or night?" asked Anna.

No one answered her. Berthold wept with anger and shame, and his companion Jonas tried in vain to comfort him. The Kerayit and Quman cowered, covering their eyes and muttering prayers, each in their own language. Heribert wheezed, struggling to breathe. Even Blessing stood in shocked silence.

Something very bad had happened, just as Blessing had predicted.

As they stared, a light rain began to fall, hissing where it struck ground. It wasn't rain at all but hot ash, so fine that it drizzled like rain only to burn and sizzle where it touched the earth. The ashy rain darkened the sky until that orange-red glow faded and Anna could no longer see the snowy peaks beyond. Dirt spit on her from the roof of the overhang. A huge weight fell right on top of them. The impact shuddered through the hill, and the overhang crumbled in on itself as a second crash sent a shower of fine dirt and clods of earth and rocks spilling over them.

Anna grabbed Blessing's wrist and yanked her out into the ash fall. They ran, stumbling through loose dirt, sliding as the ground gave way underneath, coughing as ash burned their lungs. Only when they came to rest on ground that didn't shiver beneath their feet did they turn. They had sheltered beneath a mound atop which stood a stone crown, and both hill and stones had collapsed. Two of the great menhirs leaned crazily, not yet fallen. The others had crashed down. One had smashed onto the slope just above the overhang, causing it to give way.

"Must . . . get . . . out . . . of . . . the . . . rain," gasped Berthold.

"Where's Brother Heribert?" Blessing wrenched her arm free from Anna's grasp and floundered up through slippery dirt. "Brother Heribert! Brother Heribert!"

She found an arm sticking out of dark earth. The rest of him was buried.

Sliding and cursing, they struggled up along the unstable ground and with their hands dug him out and dragged him to firm ground. He was limp. He had already stopped breathing. The earth had choked him. Blessing howled in rage.

"No! No!" She flung herself down beside his body. "You aren't dead! I don't allow it!"

A numbness took hold of Anna. She no longer felt she was here, up to her knees in dirt and roots and crawling things and slimy, hot ash, but only watching herself and the others from a distance. Thiemo and Matto were gone. There was no possible way they could have survived the collapse within the tunnels, and even if they had somehow miraculously been spared, they had no way to climb free because the stone crown here was destroyed and thereby their path to the outside world.

As for the rest of them, they had traveled, all unknowing, a great distance. They could be anywhere. Any when, if what Hathui and the others predicted was true. If time ran both swiftly and slowly within the crowns.

They stood gasping and weeping in a desolation, no longer able to distinguish sky from mountain because of the shroud of ash. It was growing cold. A wind moaned down from veiled heights. A glimmer of light flashed around them. A breeze curled around Anna's shoulders before kicking up dirt in a line that led straight to Blessing, who was still sobbing and shouting by Heribert's body, slamming her fists into his chest over and over while the rest stood too stunned and overwhelmed to move.

For an instant Anna thought a pale shimmer of light illuminated the frater's slack face, pouring over him as water pours over rocks in a stream. Blessing shrieked and scrambled backward. Heribert's body jerked. His eyes snapped open. He sat up, folding forward and coughing dirt out of his mouth. He wiped dirt from his face and, wondering, shook it from his hands.

"Where?" he said hoarsely. "Where is he gone, the one I have been waiting for? His husk is here, but he is lost."

They all stared at him.

"You were dead," said Jonas.

"Was I?" he asked. He got his feet under him, slipped once, and Blessing dashed forward and helped him stand.

"I said you couldn't die! I did! I did! You're not dead. Are you?"

He covered his eyes with a hand. Blessing clung to his other arm, wiping her filthy face on his tattered sleeve.

"The rest are dead," said Berthold suddenly. "Ai, God."

"There was nothing you could have done," said Jonas desperately

Berthold shook his head. "I know!" he said bitterly, gesturing toward the fallen stones and sunken hill. "It was in God's hands, not ours. We'll die if we stay here. My lungs hurt. There's nothing to drink. This ash covers everything. I can't tell if it's day or evening or morning. I don't know where we are, but we must leave this valley and find a place of safety."

Brother Heribert turned, still awkward as he gained control of his limbs. He stared at Berthold for a while as if sorting through what possible meaning his words might have. Anna was still too numb to speak, but she did notice how very blue his eyes were, startlingly so in contrast to his pale, dirty face. She'd never noticed his eyes before.

"I know how to leave this valley," he said, his voice still hoarse, not really like Heribert's voice at all. "Follow me."

2

IVAR had never experienced rain like the downpour that drowned them now. If he turned his head up, he wouldn't be able to breathe. He and Erkanwulf huddled under the spreading boughs of an oak tree in the great forest called the Bretwald as the storm churned the path first to mud and then into a stream of boiling, frothing water. They had nowhere to shelter, no one to beg for help, and plenty of trouble keeping their mounts from bolting.

"Look there!" cried Erkanwulf, shaking as he pointed.

Out in the forest lights bobbed, weaving among trees obscured by the pounding rain and the curtain of night. The young soldier took a step forward, meaning to call out to them, but Ivar grabbed his cloak and yanked him back against the tree.

"Hush, you idiot! No natural fire can stay lit in this downpour! Don't you remember who attacked us before?"

"Ai, God! The Lost Ones! We're doomed."

"Hush!"

It was too late. The lights turned their way.

"Come on!" Ivar splashed out onto the path, jerked up hard when his horse refused to budge. He grabbed the reins with both hands and yanked and tugged and swore, but in an argument of weight, the horse won, and it refused to leave the shelter of the tree.

"What do we do?" gasped Erkanwulf.

"Abandon the horses."

"We can't!"

"Is it better to be dead?"

The lights wove a new pattern, circling in toward their prey, and he heard a shout, a very human shout, and then the most horrifying and peculiar and inhuman sound that had ever assailed him.

"What is that?" Erkanwulf whispered.

A beast's vast cry rolled over them. The sound made Ivar's heart freeze, and Erkanwulf's mount reared up, then slipped and staggered sideways, dragging Erkanwulf with it away down the slope.

The gale hit so hard and unexpectedly that Ivar actually was blown off his feet, and only his mount's stubborn footing saved him from washing away down the foaming canal of water that the path had suddenly become. Wind cracked through the forest, splintering trees everywhere. Trunks crashed to the ground, giants falling to earth. The noise was a hammer, its echo ringing on and on as he cowered on his knees under the oak tree. All he could do was pray. Boughs shaken loose tumbled everywhere. Leaves whipped him in the face.

A *crack* splintered through the howl of the wind. A huge branch split off the oak tree and plummeted to earth, striking Erkanwulf's horse on the head. The beast went down as if flattened. Erkanwulf slipped in the mud as the reins jerked taut, and somehow got caught under the horse's shoulder as the ground gave way.

Ivar crept over to Erkanwulf, but because of the slickness of the mud and the angle of the ground and the thick tangle of branches and leaves, he couldn't budge the horse. The poor animal was dead, killed instantly.

The gale roared past and faded, although the treetops still shook and danced. It was no beast after all, merely an unnatural blast of wind. The rain eased a little.

"Ah!" Erkanwulf managed something like a grin; his face was a smudge against the darkness. "It hurts!"

"Damn. Damn." It seemed everyone he traveled with ended up in worse trouble after knowing him!

"I should have known better," continued Erkanwulf through gritted teeth. "I had a cousin who was killed by a falling branch in a windstorm. Ah! Eh! Leave it be a moment!"

Ivar got to his feet and wiped moisture from his brow, trying to clear his sight. His hair was soaked. His leggings sagged and slid as the strips of cloth loosened, and his boots made a stropping sucking sound with each step as he came around the tree and peered into the darkness.

The lights were strung out not twenty paces from him. He shrieked because he was so surprised, and pressed the ring Baldwin had gifted him to his lips, praying.

"Who are you?" called a voice out of the night. It spoke Wendish.

"I'm just a messenger. No one who means any harm. My companion is hurt. I think his horse is dead. I can't shift it off him. I pray you. Help us. Or leave us alone."

The lights circled in like wary dogs and resolved into lanterns cunningly protected from the rain by caps of bronze and walls of a bubbly glass that made the flame within dance in weird distortions. Hooded figures carried the lanterns. There were four of them, whether men or shades he could not tell because they wore cloaks drawn tightly around their bodies. Most strangely, they were all barefoot.

"Have you any weapons?" their leader asked. "Throw them down, if you please. We don't mean to hurt you. We're not bandits, not like those we're hunting."

"I can't fight one against four!"

"If you won't throw down your weapons, we'll leave you here in peace, but we won't help your companion." There was a pause as the one who spoke raised his lantern higher to get a look at Erkanwulf and the two horses, one down, one holding still with head up and eyes rolling white. Erkanwulf had either fainted or was playing at it. "Good mounts. Pity about that one, but if it's dead or broke a leg, it'll make a good stew."

"Who are you?" Ivar didn't dare surrender his precious weapons to bandits.

"We're King Henry's men. We got a charter some years back to keep this road through the Bretwald free and clear. He made us free of service to any lord or lady. We've kept our word to him. That's why we were hunting bandits. There was a problem a month back. Honest folk got attacked. It's not a good time to travel."

"Aye, Martin," interjected one of his companions. "And no better to be standing out here in this rain and storm, you lackwit! What if that wind comes howling back and kills the rest of us like it killed that horse? This rain and storm are bad enough, but that gale was something out of the Abyss! I'm not waiting out here any longer! If there's just two of them, they're scarcely that mob of bandits what set on those merchant wagons, can they be?"

It was a woman who spoke, and a woman who set down her lantern with a grunt of disgust and walked over to the fallen horse's head and knelt beside it, pulling back one eye. "It's dead. Here, you!" She gestured impatiently to Ivar. "Come help me get your friend loose."

She was strong. Together, they shifted the shoulders of the horse enough for Erkanwulf to scoot free. When her hood fell back, Ivar saw she was young, with old scars on her face suffered in a battle or a burning.

"Ahow!" yelped Erkanwulf, but although bruised and in a great deal of pain he stood on his right leg and gingerly moved all the joints in his left one by one—hip, knee, ankle—even though his ankle hurt so badly he couldn't stand on it. The curve of the ground had kept the horse's full weight off him, and the dense cover of leaf litter and debris had offered enough cushion that he evidently hadn't broken anything.

The horse, however, was quite dead.

"If we leave it out here," said the one called Martin, "the wolves will eat it before we can get back to butcher it. There's a fair bit of riches in that horse!"

"It's my horse!" said Erkanwulf. "Given me by Princess Theophanu's steward!"

Martin had the confident bearing of a young man accustomed to working all day at things he was good at. "A princess' steward, eh? Is she one of King Henry's children? I can't recall them all. We'll put you up until your leg is better, and make a decent trade to you for what we take of it. We could use horsehair. No one in the village owns a horse. The froth meat'll go bad if it isn't used at once. And the wolves'll take it all if we don't get moving. We'll have to cut it up and hang it after."

Although he, too, was no older than Ivar, he acted as the leader, gesturing toward his other two companions. "Bruno, you take the injured one, put him on the horse, and lead them back to the village. Tell Nan we're coming, and then come back yourself with sacks or netting, whatever you can find. The cart. I'm sure Ulf and Balt will help you."

"I don't like to be separated from my comrade," said Ivar.

Martin shrugged. There wasn't threat in the gesture, just reality. The light on his face showed good health and clear eyes, and he had a way of examining Ivar that made Ivar want to grin, although he wasn't sure why. "We'll need your help here. Two to hold the lanterns and keep their eyes open for wolves, and two to cut. Uta and I will do the cutting, unless you've skill in that direction."

"I'm better with a sword."

"That's how it looks to me," agreed Martin. "It's why we approached you so cautiously. You're noble born, I'd wager, but I don't think this fellow is."

"Oof!" swore Erkanwulf, accidentally putting weight onto his left foot. "Ai! That hurts."

Ivar's mount had to be led aside and calmed, and when he was ready, Erkanwulf got a heave up into the saddle.

Bruno shied away from leading the horse. "It's so big! What if it steps on me?"

"I can ride this fellow well enough," said Erkanwulf to Ivar, although it was clear that pain was biting deep. "He and I get along just fine, you know. Let's go, I pray you."

Bruno led them away, a single lantern swinging to and fro in rain and darkness.

"You're not feared of bandits attacking them?" Ivar asked as they faded into the stormy night.

"Not in that direction. It's past here to the east where there's been trouble. Anyway, I don't know what to think. I've never stood a storm like this one. It's not natural. Only a fool would stay out in weather like this."

Ivar laughed, and Martin grinned, handing him the lantern.

The fourth in their group was a speechless lad whom Uta and Martin never referred to by name. While Ivar held the light as steady as he could, the others got to work, with the lad alternating between working and holding a light.

"Think we can hang it?" Uta asked.

"Don't trust those branches," said Martin, looking upward at the rattling mass of oak boughs. The wind kept steady and strong, and the rain beat over them. "Can we shift it up on its back?"

In the end they used rope to tie up its hindquarters a bit. Uta cut the hide from anus to throat, the insides of the legs and a circle above the fetlock, all done with surprising speed and gentleness. No intestines spilled. With Martin's help she peeled the hide off and finished the cut at the neck. The nameless lad set down his lantern and rolled the bloody hide up so it would be easy to carry.

"There!" said Uta, pointing down the road with her dripping knife.

A trio of lanterns approached, resolving into the youth called Bruno and three men, one trundling a handcart, one carrying a pair of baskets lined with canvas, and the third hauling a net and a hand-saw.

"What damage at home?" Martin asked.

"Roof tore off the new weaving shed," said one of the older men, "but all else held. Still, it'll be the Enemy's own work to clear up when it comes light again."

They looked Ivar over as if they thought he might have had a hand in the destruction, and then got to work. Blood melded with rain on the ground. The hot smell of intestines, finally freed by a deeper incision, cut through the chill night air and the scent of rain as they captured them in one of the baskets. They pulled out the precious inner meats. Working quick and dirty as the rain continued to fall, they dismantled the horse into manageable pieces.

"I'll be glad to get out of this," said Martin as they got everything loaded up and balanced. They were leaving nothing behind.

It was an oddly cheerful procession, although it was so cold and miserable. Ivar could not talk; he was too tired. The others laughed and joked as they squelched along, sticking frequently in mud, cursing and swearing as they dug out the wheels for the third time, stumbling and once losing the kidneys entirely when the nameless lad lost hold of his side of one basket. But Uta groped around in the underbrush and found them both, gleaming wetly, still warm. The carcass steamed in the cold air, its soul dissolving upward, if horses had souls. Had the scholars at Quedlinhame ever discussed such a question? Ivar could not remember. His old life seemed impossibly distant. All he knew now was that his feet were numb and his nose was running and there was an unfathomable amount of debris fallen just within the halo of the lanterns although fortunately no great trunk had fallen across the road.

A dozen folk waited for them at the gateway of a palisade dimly seen in the murky night. A cluster of buildings huddled within its safety, but it was too dark to note more than shapes scattered across a clearing. He was hustled into the blessed warmth of a long hall while his companions took the carcass elsewhere to hang. Erkanwulf sat on furs beside the hearth fire, talking to a wakeful child crouched beside him.

"Ma!" The child called to a woman who had led Ivar in from the gate. She pushed back her hood to reveal a face more handsome than pretty. She had an infant bundled against her chest in a sling. "He says he was at Gent! Just like Da!"

"You're out of Gent?" asked the woman in surprise.

"Nay," replied Erkanwulf, "I was only there one time, when there was a big battle. That was years ago. I was just a lad."

"My husband was a refugee out of Gent. Mayhap after that big battle you speak of, the one with the Dragons."

"They all died!" cried the child happily. "All those Dragons! All but one! That was the captain. Nothing can kill him!" he added confidingly to Erkanwulf. "He's a great warrior, the best who ever lived."

Ivar was too cold and wet even to work up a smoldering burn at the mention of Prince Sanglant, that most noble and attractive of creatures. It just didn't seem important.

Erkanwulf smiled at the child, then nodded at Ivar. "You're a sight, my lord cleric," he said with a mocking lift of his head.

The woman stopped dead, and turned to Ivar with her jaw dropping open. She had all her teeth and good, clean, healthy eyes. Her grip, when she caught his elbow, was uncomfortably strong. "Are you a churchman? We haven't had a deacon, or a frater even, out our way for years and years. We've been wanting. . . ."

Laughing, Martin and Bruno came into the hall, pausing in the dug-out entryway to take off their boots.

"Martin!" she called, and Martin looked up at the sound of her voice and grinned at her. What they shared, Ivar felt as a joyful presence, like the perfume of the first meadow flowers of spring, that penetrated even in this dank and fetid winter hall. The hall had stood up to the gale; the presence glimpsed in their shared gaze had withstood the storms of life. "This one is a cleric! Maybe he could give us God's blessing on our marriage."

"Surely we have God's blessing already," said Martin as the child ran over to him and leaped up into his arms, cuddling there.

"Hush!" She made a sign with her hands, and spat, and then

looked embarrassed. "Begging your pardon, my lord cleric. Old ways die hard. I mean nothing by it. But it's bad fortune to say what might attract the evil eye. Would you do it? We've nothing to offer but a place to sleep and something to eat and drink for as long as you must bide here until your companion is healed and you can go on. And these unnatural rains end. Can you speak God's blessing over us? We've been handfasted these six or seven summers but never had God's blessing spoken over us."

I can't.

But as she stared at him, eyes wide and a hopeful smile on her lips, he could not say "no" to her. He didn't know the words. He'd forgotten most things and learned little to begin with. He hadn't paid attention because he hadn't wanted to. He'd wanted everything else. Anything out of his reach had seemed so bright and ripe to him, like the perfect apple dangling from a branch too high to ever reach.

"I'll sing God's blessing over you," he said, "in the morning."

Ai! She was so happy as the rest stamped in and by lantern light stripped down to shifts and cozied into the pallets and platforms tucked up under the eaves that they slept on, all snugged together for warmth. They offered him an honored place close to the hearth, and he lay down beside Erkanwulf and the little lad, who had taken a liking to the rider, but although he closed his eyes, he could not sleep.

After a while Erkanwulf stirred, and whispered, "I've never heard you sing a blessing, not once in all this time. You're just a heretic, not a real churchman, aren't you?"

"Is there any harm in it?" Ivar murmured. "I served as a novice at Quedlinhame. It isn't as if a frater or cleric is likely to wander through here. Anyway, they've served us a good turn."

Erkanwulf grunted softly. "I suppose there's no harm in it. Funny, though. That one, called Martin, he came out of Gent years ago, so I hear. He was a lad then and he settled here and married a local girl. This is their boy." The child was snoring softly on the other side of Erkanwulf. "The wee lad has never heard of Autun or Lady Sabella or Biscop Constance, but he knows all about Gent and roads east." His voice got rough, or perhaps his leg was paining him. "What will we do? We've only one horse now. You know as well as I do that we've nothing but empty promises to carry back to Biscop Constance."

"Let me think. Something strange is abroad in the world, don't you suppose? That wind . . . it sounded liked the cry of a living soul.

Made me shiver right down through my skin. It made me think of a verse from the Holy Book, only I can't remember it right, something about the seas boiling and the wind tossing down trees."

Erkanwulf snorted. "Every deacon and cleric and frater I've ever met has a better memory than you, Lord Ivar, most noble cleric."

He spoke mockingly, but the words didn't sting. It was Erkanwulf's way to tease. A year ago, a month ago, Ivar would have stewed and simmered, turning those words over and over, but not now.

"The verses spoke of the end of the world," he said instead. "I feel we have been touched by a terrible, grand sword, a weapon wielded by God, or by those among humankind who don't fear what they should fear. Did you ever see trees fall so? Like sticks kicked over by a boy!"

"I did not. Never in my life, and I've stood in forests when the wind howled on winter nights. I thought I would piss myself, I was so scared."

Rain still drummed on the thatch roof of the hall, steady and ominous.

"That's right," agreed Ivar. "It wasn't natural. Nor were those shades we saw before either. We have to keep our eyes open and be ready to act. We have to get back to Biscop Constance no matter what. And go quickly, as soon as the weather breaks."

But in the morning, it rained. In the afternoon, it rained. All the next night, it rained. For five days it rained without letting up. The villagers kept busy with many tasks around the long hall and within the warren of huts and hovels and sheds they had erected within their log palisade. They ate the froth meat out of the horse in a series of soups that stretched the meat so that it would feed the two dozen or so folk across several days. Every evening as the light faded they gathered around the hearth fire and demanded Erkanwulf tell them the tale of Gent, or that Ivar regale them with the story of the ill-fated expedition east into the marchlands under the command of Princess Sapientia and Prince Bayan of Ungria.

"Look here, I pray you, my lord cleric," said Martin late on the sixth day after he'd come in from outside. He stank of smoke. He'd been curing horse meat. He rummaged in a chest and brought out a parchment tied with a strip of leather. This he rolled out on the table. Folk crowded around, whispering as they stared at the writing none of them could read. "It's our charter! From the king himself, may God bless him and his kin. Do you see the seal here?" He touched the wax seal reverentially. "We just heard it the once, read by that Eagle that rode through here, the one with a dark face. She had to take it away so it could get the king's seal. Another Eagle, a red-haired one like to you, rode through a year or so after and brought it back to us. But he couldn't read. Can you read it for us, so we can hear it again?"

How they all gazed at him with hopeful expressions! They were such a sturdy group, healthier than many because the forest provided so much, all but a steady supply of grain and salt which, they'd told him, they traded for. Even in lean years they could survive with less grain. They hadn't any horses, but three milk cows. They had forage for their goats and sheep as well as certain plants and tubers out of the forest that could be eaten by humankind in hard times even if they weren't tasty. They ate meat often, and they were proud of it, knowing that folk beyond the forest never fared so well.

He bent over the diploma. The lantern light made the pen strokes waver. He'd never read well nor did he like to, but the months in Queen's Grave and the unrelenting supervision of Biscop Constance had forced him to labor over Dariyan, the language used both by the church and by the king's schola for all decrees and capitularies.

They waited, so quiet that the sound of dripping rain off the outside eaves made him nervous. He kept expecting the rain to start up again. Luckily, it was not a long document. He stumbled through it without utterly shaming himself. King Henry's promise was straightforward: the foresters would be free of service to any lord or lady as long as they kept the king's road passable for himself and his servants and messengers and armies.

"The Eagle read it better," murmured Martin's wife to her husband, then blushed when Ivar looked at her.

"Eagles can't read," he said. "They learn the words in their head and repeat them back. That's what she must have done."

"Nay, she read it all right," said one of the older men. "I recall that well enough. She touched each word as she spoke it. How could she know which was which if she weren't reading? Strange looking girl, too, not any older than my Baltia here." He set a hand on the head of an adolescent girl perhaps sixteen or seventeen years of age. "I don't know if she were pretty, but she sure caught the eye."

"She was at Gent, too," said Martin. "She was the one what saved us, those of us who escaped."

"I know who you mean!" said Erkanwulf from his seat on the

bench. "We rode with her, Captain Ulric's band out of Autun, that is. She was riding with Count Lavastine's army, but she was a King's Eagle, after all. I'd wager it was the same one."

Ivar sat down, clenching his hands. He shut his eyes, and at once they fussed around him and Martin's wife, called Flora, brought him ale to drink to clear his head.

"I will never be free of her." He hadn't meant to say it out loud. He laughed, seeing them stare at him. Erkanwulf looked skeptical. Martin looked puzzled. Flora's mouth had turned up softly, and her gaze was gentle, as though she had guessed it all. She touched her young husband on the shoulder, and he started, glanced at her, and reading something in her expression—words weren't the only marks that could be read!—he rolled up the diploma and stashed it away in the chest beneath the community's other precious possessions.

"You said you'd give us your blessing, Lord Ivar," he said. "Will you do so?"

"I'll do so."

He rose. Old memories clung. They were a stink he would never be rid of. Liath had never been his, and she would never have chosen him. *She sure caught the eye.* He wasn't the only man to have thought so. But it no longer mattered. The world had changed in a way he did not yet understand.

"Stand before the hearth fire with clasped hands," he said to Martin and Flora. He'd never witnessed a commoner's wedding. Rarely did a deacon officiate in any case, since the law of bed and board made a marriage. He dredged for scraps of verse, God's blessings for fecundity, the wedding of church and humankind as bride and groom, the necessity of holding fast to faith.

"For healthful seasons, for the abundance of the fruits of the earth, and for peaceful times, let us pray. Have mercy upon us, now and ever, and unto ages of ages."

Flora wept. Martin sobbed. Their son skipped around them in glee while the baby waved its chubby arms. Balt and his daughter broke out a flute and a fiddle, and the others took the table down and cleared a space for dancing. Erkanwulf tested his healing ankle by spinning Uta round and round, and he came back, laughing, to sit and rest and grimace.

"Don't be so grim," he said to Ivar. "Standing there with your arms crossed and a frown like my grandmam's! Heh! She never smiled one day in her long life! My da used to say that a spell had been put on her when she was a young sprite that she'd drop dead if she was ever happy, so there you are. She was the oldest person I ever saw till the day she dropped dead."

The story teased a grin out of him. "Was she smiling?"

"She was not! It wasn't the curse that felled her. She got hit in the head by a piece of wood that flew free when one of my uncles was chopping up a log. A little like my poor horse, now I think on it."

"Erkanwulf! How can you speak so disrespectfully of the dead?"

"She was a mean old bitch. That's just how it was. No one was sorry to see her go except the dog."

Like me. But he shook himself. It was a lie he told himself, and he didn't know why. He had told himself that lie for years, ever after Hanna had chosen to go with Liath over him. But he had seen how false the lie was the day Sigfrid, Ermanrich, and Hathumod had cried to see him risk his life for Biscop Constance. He had seen how false it was the day Baldwin had given up his freedom for the rest of them. He had seen how false it was the day Baldwin wept, believing him dead. Maybe Hanna, and Liath, had scorned him, but there were others who needed him. Who were waiting for him.

He grabbed Erkanwulf's shoulder. "As soon as the road's clear enough that the horse isn't at risk, we'll go."

"If you wish," agreed Erkanwulf. "You've got a strange look on your face. Has an imp gotten into you?"

"It's time. We've got to act while we have the chance."

"Time for what?"

"Time for Captain Ulric and all the men loyal to him to choose whether to act, or to give way. Princess Theophanu can't help us. It's up to us to free Biscop Constance. There's only one way to do it."

3

A burning wind struck with such ferocity that every tent in camp was laid flat. A hail of stinging ash passed over them where they huddled under whatever shelter they could find. After all this, after the rumbling and groaning of earth faded, the terrible glare of lightning gave way to a sickly gleam that Hanna at long last identified as dawn. She crawled out from under the wagon into the cloudy light of a new day in which everything had changed. She had taken shelter with Aurea, Teuda, and poor, addled Petra with her perpetually vacant expression.

"Stay there," she whispered to the others. Their pale faces stared out at her.

"Do you see Sister Rosvita?" Aurea looked ready to scramble out, but Hanna waved her back.

"Stay there! You can't imagine—just stay there."

It was impossible to think such a day could ever dawn. It was impossible to imagine a world that resembled the one she surveyed now. The great traveling camp made up of the combined armies of King Geza of Ungria and Lady Eudokia of Arethousa looked like a field of rubbish. A few brave souls staggered to and fro uttering aimless cries into the dawning light. Clouds covered the sky. The air, especially to the south and west, was yellow because of a dragging haze that obscured her view in every direction beyond an arrow's shot. Only to the east was it vaguely lighter. A layer of ash covered everything, and it seemed most of the animals on which the army relied had fled. She had grit on her lips and in her eyes, and a skin of ash over every part of her body, even beneath her clothing, even under her eyelids.

"Hanna!'

She stumbled forward over a broken tent pole to grasp the arms of Sister Rosvita. "God be praised, Sister! Where are the others?"

"I have them all accounted for except Aurea, Teuda, and poor Sister Petra."

"They are with me. What of Mother Obligatia?"

"She lives." Rosvita shut her eyes as she exhaled, a sigh that seemed to shake the ground. Hanna found that she had tears in her eyes, knowing they had survived.

Thus far.

A bubble of canvas stretched and shifted like a living creature as Fortunatus emerged, wiping grime off his face. Beyond, not one tent remained standing. A body lay unmoving on the ground, but Hanna could not be sure the person was dead.

"I pray that was the worst of it," said Rosvita as she lowered her hand. "We must find water and food."

"We must decide what to do next, Sister. It will take days for this army to recover, if it ever does. There should be twice as many people. Are they all still hiding, or have they fled?"

Or died?

Rosvita glanced toward the collapsed tent in which she had sheltered. Fortunatus lifted up the heavy canvas as Ruoda and Gerwita crawled out. Gerwita, seeing the camp, burst into tears.

"We are faced with a difficult choice, Eagle. Do we flee on foot, knowing we may perish from hunger and thirst?" She gestured toward the hazy south and west. "I do not like the look of that. I would not turn my steps in that direction unless I had no other choice. But by traveling north and east we remain in Dalmiakan country, under the suzerainity of the Arethousan Empire. Yet in such circumstances, is it better to be a prisoner so we can be assured a bowl of gruel each day?"

"I don't think there are any assurances any longer, Sister. I pray you, let me scout the camp while you get the rest of our party ready to move out. Perhaps there is a bit of water or food you can find in the wreckage."

"Who will accompany you?"

"Alone, I may pass unnoticed in this chaos. I'll see what I can see. See what has become of kings and queens and noble generals."

Rosvita nodded grimly before kissing Hanna on either cheek. "Go carefully, Eagle. We will be ready when you return."

Hanna had lain all night on top of her staff and her bow and quiver. She had a bruise down her chest and abdomen from their pressure into her flesh, but she hadn't dared lose her weapons to the wind. She grabbed them now as Aurea crawled out from under the wagon and helped silent Petra emerge into the dusty air. She slung bow and quiver over her back and walked into the camp with her staff held firmly in her right hand, gaze flicking this way and that, but the people she saw crawling through the debris or standing with hands to their heads seemed too stunned to think of doing her harm.

A slender hound whimpered in the dirt; its hips were bloody, and though it kept trying to rise, it could not stand on its hind legs. A man scrabbled in the ruins of a wagon that had, somehow, completely overturned.

"Help me!" he said, to no one. "Help me!"

She came over and with her help he heaved up the heavy wagon, just enough so he could look underneath.

"No! No! No!" he cried in Arethousan, and he leaped back, releasing his hold on the wagon. The abrupt increase in weight caught her off guard. She barely released the slats and jumped back herself, scraping her fingers, as the wagon's bed crashed back onto the ground.

"Hey!" she called, but he ran off through the camp, still crying, "No! No!"

"Ai, God!" she swore, sucking on her fingers. She had picked up two splinters, one too deep to pry loose. "Oh, damn! Ouch!"

She wasn't eager to see what lay under the wagon, so she walked on through the ruins of the camp. As she neared the central compound, she saw more signs of life, soldiers hurrying about their tasks, some of them leading horses. A line of wagons was being drawn into position. A handsome bay so spooked that it shied at every shift and movement was being calmed by a stolid groom. Even here, the royal tents lay in heaps and mounds, fallen into ridges and valleys over whatever pallets and tables and benches sat inside. A rack of spears had toppled to spill all over. She glanced around to see if anyone was looking, bent, and snatched up one of the spears. No one stopped her. A gathering of some hundreds of people milled and swarmed in a clear spot beyond the collapsed tents. She edged forward into the crowd and wove and sidestepped her way far enough in that she could see what was going on.

Nothing good: A storm of nobles arguing. That didn't bode well. She used her hip to nudge her way past a weary soldier and her height to see over the heads of the shorter, stockier Arethousans. No one seemed to notice her in particular; the ash had turned her white-blonde hair as grimy as that of the rest.

"But you promised me!" Princess Sapientia was saying. She had weathered the night better than many. Her face was clean and she didn't have dark circles under her eyes.

King Geza had not fared so well. He was pacing, hands clenched, and his gaze touched his wife's figure only in glances. He was looking for something; Hanna wasn't sure what.

"I have five adult sons. Any one of them may believe this disaster is a sign from God for him to usurp my place."

"They would not have done so before, after you left?"

"No. My officials were in place. Who knows what has become of them? This was no natural storm. The priests will speak in many tongues, all arguing among themselves. The Arethousans will scold the Dariyans. The old women will creep from their huts and start scouting for a white stallion. I must go home and see to my kingdom lest it fall to pieces."

"This storm may not have touched Ungria! It's so far away."

Geza stopped for long enough to look at Sapientia with disgust. "Only a fool would not recognize this storm for what it is. As soon as my soldiers are ready, we march."

"But you promised me—!" She choked on the words. She could not get them out of her throat. "I married you!"

"Come with me, then. Once Ungria is safe—"

"What of my kingdom?" she exclaimed.

"By the blessed Name of God, woman! All that lies south of here is blasted, so the scouts say. To the west, toward Aosta—who can see for the smoke and fire? Do not be blind. I will not ride to Wendar. I turn my back on Aosta, just as God has."

"You promised me!"

Hanna wanted to shake her, but King Geza was faster, and less patient than Prince Bayan to be sure.

"Then I divorce you, Sapientia. Go on your way as you please."

"*Divorce* me?"

"I divorce you. Must I repeat myself? Ah! Captain! What news?"

"We're ready, Your Majesty."

"Then we go." He gestured. The captain shouted a command in Ungrian, and half the men milling around scattered so swiftly that Hanna felt spun in circles although she didn't move.

"But what about me?" cried Sapientia plaintively.

"I divorce you. It is done. Feh!" He strode off, talking in a low voice to his captain. He didn't even look back as the handsome bay was led up for him to ride.

Sapientia stood gasping, her hands opening and closing although she had nothing to grasp onto.

Hanna whistled under her breath and began to retreat out from the chuckling, staring crowd of Arethousans, softly, slowly, taking care not to draw attention to herself, just a quiet hound slinking off to do its business, nothing worth noticing. Off to the right she heard the shouts of men and the jangling of harness as a large troop moved out. Lord protect them! Geza had abandoned his bride and his allies without a moment's hesitation. She knew she had to get back to Sister Rosvita quickly. She knew what the answer was, now, to their predicament.

Move fast, and get out of the way.

"There!"

She spun, but it was too late. Sergeant Bysantius strode up with a dozen guards at his heels.

"Eagle! Come with us."

They had already surrounded her. She saw, around them and beyond them, the steady tidal flow of troops and servants toward a distant goal. Bysantius grabbed her elbow and towed her along with him.

"They're wanting you," he added.

"What about my companions?"

"They're not wanting your companions."

Lady Eudokia was seated on a stool under a torn awning fixed in place by four men holding up poles tied to each corner of blue silk. The fabric echoed the clear heavens they could no longer see. Her young nephew clung to her robes, face hidden in her lap. She sipped from a cup while Lord Alexandros spoke to a trio of captains, all of them pale with ash and looking as dour as any farmer who has just seen his field of rye marred by the black rot. Beyond, wagons rumbled into place in a line of march. A rank of mounted soldiers trotted past, heading for the front of the line, which was obscured by haze. The Arethousan army was moving out.

"Exalted Lady." Sergeant Bysantius dropped to both knees, bowed, and rose. He shoved Hanna forward. "The Eagle, as you requested."

She tripped over her feet and barely had time to right herself before the general whistled, listening to the report of one of his captains.

"Geza's gone already? Hsst! We'll leave a small rear guard behind to bring any who scattered in the night. Bring the horses!" He saw Hanna, but nodded toward the sergeant. "That was fast."

"I found her wandering, Your Excellency."

"She's too valuable to lose, as we agreed before. You'll be in charge of her, Bysantius. It will be your head if she escapes." He turned away and walked to his horse.

It was strange how easily she understood Arethousan now, as if the scent of camphor tossed into the flame to let the lady and the general see what she saw had at the same time opened her mind and let it steal words out of theirs.

"I pray you, Your Excellency," she cried, starting forward. "Exalted Lady. I pray you, my companions . . . I know where they are. If you'll just let me go and make sure they're with one of the wagons—"

He paused, turning back to frown at her. "You misunderstand us. We do not need your companions anymore. They are of no use to us because our circumstances have changed so greatly."

"Surely you don't mean to abandon them!"

He shrugged and walked away.

"Sergeant! Exalted Lady!"

Lady Eudokia sipped at her cup and ignored Hanna's cries.

"No offense," murmured Bysantius, gripped her arm, "but you'd do better to come quietly."

"I can't abandon them! They'll die!"

"It's out of your hands, Eagle. You are the prisoner of Lord Alexandros now."

She ripped her arm out of his grasp and bolted, but two of the guards tackled her. She went down hard, but kept fighting until they pinned all her limbs. They stripped her of her weapons, tied her hands and feet with rope, and threw her in the back of a wagon as it lurched past in the train of Lord Alexandros. Scraped, bloody, and bruised, she wept with fury, hating herself for her helplessness.

HANNA did not return. They waited for hours at the edge of camp, hoping not to be noticed, and indeed it was as if they had become invisible. No one paid them the least mind. There was no telling what hour of the day it was, or what service they ought to sing, because the clouds never lifted and the light kept its smoky, sullen glow, scarcely enough to read by.

At intervals they watched vague shapes that seemed to be troops moving in the distance, perhaps a line of march receding toward the northeast, but the haze obscured most movement beyond an arrow's shot. Their eyes stung and their noses ran from the constant irritation of falling ash and blowing grit. Yet the patter of ash fall eased by the time Fortunatus sighed and turned to Rosvita.

"What if she is not coming back, Sister? Should one of us go look for her?"

"We will not split up. What happens to one, happens to all."

"We have waited here long enough," said Mother Obligatia. They had set her litter across the wagon and shielded her with a canvas awning so that the ancient nun could ease up on her elbows and survey the scene. "Night will come and find us standing like dumb beasts in the field."

Rosvita smiled, feeling how stern her heart had become. Smiles meant something different here in the aftermath; they betokened not happiness or laughter but determination. "You are right. We must make a decision, or others will choose for us."

They had taken turns circling out from their position, venturing only to that point where they could still see back to the group as they searched in the wreckage for food and water. They had found five corpses, put one dreadfully injured dog out of its misery, and managed otherwise to collect a small store of provisions and, most importantly, a score of sacks and leather bottles filled variously with wine, sweetened vinegar, and a nasty-tasting liquid that stank of aniseed but was something they might be able to drink in dire need.

The wagon under which Aurea had sheltered was too heavy to drag, but Hilaria discovered a handcart in decent shape, needing only a small repair to the axle because it had tipped over and spilled its load of bundled herbs.

"Some peddler following the army," said Aurea as she helped the girls gather up what could be salvaged: lavender, mostly, sage, tufts of bay and basil, and feverwort. "A bag of chestnuts! Why would anyone abandon such treasures?"

"Perhaps the peddler is dead," said Ruoda sharply. Gerwita began to snivel.

"We'll stay together," said Rosvita, seeing that tempers would run high with exhaustion and fear driving them. "Take turns hauling the cart."

They set off with Rosvita in the lead beside Diocletia. Behind them, Fortunatus and Teuda carried Mother Obligatia's litter. Heriburg followed with the precious books slung over her back. Ruoda and Gerwita shepherded Petra, while Jerome and Jehan took turns pushing the cart. Tireless Hilaria paced up and down the line to spell those who needed a rest, and Aurea set herself as their rear guard. They had no particular destination but made their way through rippling lakes of torn and crumpled canvas, past discarded shoes and forgotten harness, an iron kettle, a red cap, and a broken leather strap affixed to a bronze Circle of Unity in the Arethousan style with crossed bars quartering the interior. The armies had left an eerie silence in their wake but for the wind grumbling through scraps of canvas and a dog snuffling at an overturned wagon, trying to dig its way in to something caught underneath.

But for the wind and the dog, nothing and no one moved in the haze. Those folk the armies had not taken with them had, evidently, fled the scene, fearing worse to come. It was difficult to imagine what could be worse than what they had suffered during the night.

"Look!" murmured Diocletia. "There's someone—there!"

A figure huddled in a clearing notable for the lack of debris on all sides except a single expanse of splotched canvas that had once been a grand tent and a scattering of spears tumbled on the ground. The creature crouched with its head buried in its dirty riding skirts and its arms wrapped around its knees, like a child.

Rosvita gestured for the others to halt. She ventured forward cautiously with Diocletia beside her. The nun paused to pick up a spear, and Hilaria and Aurea hurried up beside her to gather up the rest. They walked softly, but even so, the person seemed utterly lost not to have heard their approach. They halted a body's length from her—it was now obvious it was a woman—and Diocletia moved sideways so that if the woman was armed and dangerous she might not strike them both dead with one blow. How had it come to this, that a holy nun should think like a soldier, weighing tactics? Was this to be the fate of all humankind in the weeks and months to come?

"Friend," said Rosvita in Arethousan, as gently as she knew how. "We will not harm you."

At first, she gained no response. But at last that dark head stirred and a woman raised a tearstained face to stare at her with an expression of such hopelessness that Rosvita felt tears in her own eyes drawn out by that naked anguish.

She was stunned as she recognized the other woman. "Your Highness," she said in Wendish. "I am Sister Rosvita. Do you remember me? Where is King Geza?"

"I divorce you," said the princess, each word formed so precisely that it seemed she was repeating a phrase spoken by someone else. Her gaze was bleak, and her hands were dirty, as if she had been digging.

"Are you alone, Your Highness?"

Sapientia's laugh was that of a madwoman, quickly cut off. "A prince without a retinue is no prince!"

"We are your retinue, Your Highness."

Sapientia stared at her for a long time without answering. Rosvita began to doubt the princess had heard her.

Fortunatus crept up beside Rosvita and leaned to whisper in her ear. "There is no one left, Sister. She's been abandoned, just as we were." He sounded as shocked as she felt. "She is King Henry's daughter! What will we do?"

"We must take her with us."

A robed person swept past them and heedlessly knelt down within range of the princess. "Come, little lamb," she said in Dariyan. "You've strayed far, but we'll take care of you now."

It was Sister Petra. Her expression was calm, almost blank, but her voice had a soothing gentleness. If Princess Sapientia understood her coaxing, spoken as it was in Dariyan, she made no sign, but she allowed herself to be helped to stand, she allowed herself to be herded along without protest. She said not one word more as they made their way through the wreckage of the camp, always moving upslope and away from the distant ocean, until they came at long last to a pine wood whose sparse canopy gave them a measure of shelter as the light changed and became rather more dense. Night was coming on, although a glow remained in the sky, painting the heavens a deathly orange-red. They rigged up a serviceable shelter and dined sparingly on a stew of leeks and turnips flavored with a bay leaf and cooked over an open fire in the kettle they had found in the deserted camp.

"We are well set for a hike in the woods," said Fortunatus, attempting levity although there wasn't much to be had.

Rosvita smiled gratefully at him. They had a single spoon, which they passed around between them to eat out of the kettle. "We have provisions, and freedom. It is more than we had before."

"Best be grateful for each least blessing God grant us," agreed Mother Obligatia. She was so tiny and so frail that the power of her voice always amazed Rosvita. She was actually sitting up for the first time in many days, as if the terrible night had strengthened her.

Her words awoke someone else. Sapientia had let the spoon pass by without acknowledging that it, or anything, existed. She had walked in a trance, pressed along by the constant attentions of Sister Petra, whose entire being was focused on her helpless charge. The glow of the fire painted shadows on the princess' face, making of her a mask whose expression could not be fathomed because it was so empty. But the mask spoke.

"A prince without a retinue is no prince," she repeated.

Rosvita knelt beside her. "We are your retinue, Your Highness."

After a long silence, Sapientia turned her head and looked straight at the cleric, although Rosvita at first wasn't sure the princess knew who she was. Behind her, Jerome slurped at the spoon.

"You love my father, Sister Rosvita," Sapientia said.

"I love him and serve him, Your Highness."

"Do you love me, Sister?"

"Nay, child, not in the same way. I have known your father for a very long time. He has my heart, but you have my loyalty. I will not abandon you."

Sapientia slammed fists into the ground and again, and again. "Not like all the others! My father! Bayan! Sanglant! The Pechanek mothers! Geza! Every one of them deserted me!" The storm broke over her. She sobbed in great heaves, trembling all over. Petra stroked her shoulders, murmuring words that made no sense, and after a while the princess calmed.

Wind crackled through limbs. Among the trees a branch snapped and crashed down to the ground. Otherwise it was so quiet. Too quiet. They had seen no birds all day. No telltale rustling marked the comings and goings of the little nocturnal creatures who ought to be scuttling about their nightly rounds.

Sapientia's reaction was such a brief window, opened to show a light within and perhaps soon to be shut. Rosvita had to ask, although she feared the answer.

"Your Highness. Did you see Hanna? The Eagle who was with us?"

Sapientia did not raise her head. Her voice was hoarse and ugly. "She's dead."

"Ai, God," Rosvita whispered. "You saw her dead? You saw her body?"

Sapientia refused to answer, only stared at the ground.

"What will we do?" they asked, one by one, all but Mother Obligatia.

"I should never have let her go off alone!"

"Nay, Sister," said Mother Obligatia, scolding her. "The Eagle did what she had to do. That was her duty. She knew it was dangerous."

Guilt burned. Rosvita thought of Hanna as one of her charges, now that they had traveled so far together. She could not find any ease in her heart by prating about duty. She rose and paced around the fire, examining each one who had followed her so far: Mother Obligatia with her ancient sorrows and dangerous past; the abbess' three stout attendants in the persons of Diocletia, Hilaria, and the lay sister Teuda; poor Petra, now cooing and stroking the unresponsive Princess Sapientia; Rosvita's faithful servant Aurea, with her strong arm and steady head; that gaggle of young clerics who admired her far too well, timid Gerwita, stubborn Heriburg, clever Ruoda, and the two young men, Jerome and Jehan, still youths in so many ways. Last of all, she met the gaze of the one who was her secret strength: Brother Fortunatus. He nodded at her. He would never waver.

"We rest as well as we can, for we will need our strength. It seemed to me that the light was better in the east, but that way lies Arethousa. Unless tomorrow brings an unexpected change, we must try our luck to the northwest. We must try to reach Wendar. God help us."

God help me, she thought, as they made ready to rest on the cold ground, arranging cloaks and canvas and blankets over themselves, a jumble of treasures they had salvaged out of the camp. They had provisions to last for perhaps five days. *God help me, I pray you. I do not want to lose another one.*

Out in the forest, a twig snapped. All of them looked up, startled and anxious. They waited, but no further noise beyond that of the wind rattling in the boughs disturbed the evening silence.

"What if there are bandits, Sister Rosvita?" asked Gerwita. Her voice was so soft it almost vanished under the sound of the wind. "We have no weapons to defend ourselves. We can't use those spears."

The girl looked scared. The others stared at Rosvita, waiting for her answer.

She caught Fortunatus' gaze. He smiled bravely.

"We have our wits, child. Let us pray they are weapon enough."

VI
THE ENEMY'S HANDIWORK

1

"LOOK, Your Excellency. Can that be Darre?"

The soldier shifted impatiently as his comrade led Antonia's mule the last few paces to the top of the ridge. From this vantage point the plain of Dar could usually be seen in all its glorious expanse: the river, the towers rising on the palace rock, the domes of the two great cathedrals, the manifold streets as twisty as the Enemy's minions, the western hills that blocked the path to the sea, the thousand fields on which the ancient city had first taken root and grown into an empire.

Antonia's eyes hadn't stopped stinging since that awful night when the wind had torn the thatch off the cottage in which she sheltered, and ash had started to fall. She rubbed them now as they halted.

"God help us," added the soldier, voice choked. "The western hills are all on fire. And the plain of Dar—look!"

"I see nothing," said his companion.

It was a foul soup of air, like the congealed breath of the Enemy: smoke and brimstone, the stench of the Pit. For the space of one breath, a shift in the wind stripped the worst layer of haze off the land and she glimpsed the distant towers and walls of Darre before they were swallowed up again in the fog.

"We must descend," she said, and she heard the two guards whistle hard between teeth. They were frightened because they were weak, although they had guarded her faithfully enough on their journey. She had lost count of the days.

"Who knows what kind of creatures might be lurking down there in that smoke," said the taller one, called Focas. "They could have claws as long as my arm. They might rip us to pieces."

"God will protect us," said Antonia. "Have we not met dangers? Have we not survived?"

Pietro spoke less but said more that was to the point. "What if we can't breathe that fouled air?"

"We must go down," repeated Antonia. "We must reach Tivura, to see if the princesses have survived. As for the rest, I fear God have punished the wicked most decisively."

The soldiers looked at each other, a glance that excluded her, as they had always excluded her. They served her faithfully, it was true, but out of loyalty to Empress Adelheid. Still, no matter how irritating it was that they could not recognize her worth and God's favor, she endured it because she had to, because it was another test thrown in her path. God honored the righteous, but They did not always spare them trouble and ingratitude.

"The princesses," said Pietro. "That's what the empress would want."

Focas nodded. "The princesses," he agreed. "We must see if they can be rescued, if they are indeed trapped down there, although we must hope they are not. If their stewards have any wits about them at all, which I doubt, they would have fled to a safe place."

"No one can flee God's wrath," said Antonia sternly. "There are those who have done what they ought not." She gestured toward the hazy landscape below. "Thus are they rewarded with chastisement and death."

Focas rubbed his forehead, looking anxious.

Pietro hefted his spear. "No use waiting."

They started down the road, which was utterly deserted although the day wasn't far gone. It was difficult to measure the hours because the cloud cover never lifted and the light had a sameness to it that made noon seem like twilight and morning no different than afternoon. Ash squeaked under their feet. Pebbles rolled and crackled, and more than once Focas or Pietro slipped and, swearing, caught themselves before they fell. Fortunately, the mule was a sure-footed creature, stolid and companionable and not particularly stubborn.

As they descended, the light changed and deepened to a queer yellow fog that painted their skin the color of parchment. The hollows of their eyes darkened until the two soldiers looked like walking corpses as they strode along. Down and down they walked, as into the Pit. The world had emptied. They saw no one and no thing. Even the grass had withered into dry stalks. Now and again they crossed a stream running down from the circling heights, but a sour taste choked the water although they forced it down anyway. It sat heavily in parched stomachs. Antonia felt sick. Her head pounded and her throat burned. Each breath scraped as she wheezed along.

In time twilight faded to night. They set up camp off the road but not so far that they would lose sight of it and thus find themselves lost in the morning. The mule ate its lean dinner; they had only two days of grain left and certainly there was little enough to graze. They had bread and cheese and wine for themselves. The soldiers took turns on guard duty. She slept on her cloak under a canvas lean-to. She did not mind the hardship, although her old bones ached and her head never stopped hurting.

At dawn Pietro hissed. "Focas! Rouse you! Do you hear that?"

She rose and came to stand beside them, fingering the amulet at her chest.

She heard the jingle, too, and touched each man on the elbow. "Stand you as still as mice when the owl swoops. Say nothing."

They, too, wore amulets, as did the mule. She had woven them with her own hands out of wolfsbane and turnsole, and still nursed blisters on her palms and fingers.

The procession emerged out of the haze: a line of sobbing, hacking, coughing men and women coffled in a line and guarded by a crew of men who in another life might have been soldiers as honorable as the ones who stood on either side of her. The soldiers wore cloth tied over mouths and noses to protect themselves from the air. The prisoners had nothing but the rags on their backs. A few were naked. As they shuffled past, she counted them: eight, sixteen, thirty-two, sixty-four. Over one hundred in all, a remnant.

Although their guards were alert, looking from side to side and pointing here and there into the gloom, they marked no watchers, even those standing in plain sight a stone's throw off the road. As the last man, a brawny, swaggering fellow, faded from sight, Pietro let out a great sigh that was more of a hoarse choke, and touched his chest where the amulet lay.

"Lord be praised," he said.

Focas choked down a hysterical laugh. "Didn't you recognize him? That was Sergeant Hatto there walking last of all. Do you think those were slaves they were herding away?"

"Slaves now, whatever they were before." Pietro knelt, touched his hand to the dead earth, and kissed his fingers. "I pray you, Your Excellency, let us go swiftly."

"This land is a charnel house," said Focas. "I can smell it."

They walked again that day, and the stench of sulfur got worse. Antonia's headache got worse. Her eyes wept from the burning. In time, they saw off to either side glowing cracks spewing ghastly yellow smoke. It was as though the Earth itself was breaking apart. Once Pietro almost fainted when the wind caught him full on with a streamer of air off one of the fumaroles, but he staggered forward gasping and vomiting until he was out of danger. After that they were careful to keep cloth tied tightly across mouth and nose.

They walked as though in a tunnel, since they could see no great distance to any side. The haze clouded everything, making the world seem by one measure very small indeed and by another like a vast unknowable wasteland that could never be crossed but only suffered. Trudging on in this way they missed the crossroads where they might turn aside to Tivura and came at the end of the second day to the walls of Darre. In all that time they had seen not a single living creature except that one sad procession. No birds flew; no sheep blatted; no goats disturbed their rest, seeking scraps to eat. The mule was not faring well, but it had a strong sense of self-preservation and refused to fall behind. Even so, Antonia walked rather than rode for fear it might buckle and toss her to the ground. If she broke a leg, she, too, would be trapped in this purgatory.

That was what it was, of course. She recognized it as they saw the gaping gates rise out of the fog in front of them and beheld the tumbled ruins of the fairest and most magnificent city humankind had ever built. Had they unwittingly crossed through a stone crown into the world where galla roamed? Had Anne's magic brought down the destruction? Or had the Lost Ones returned with plague and fire to defeat their ancient enemies?

"We'll go to the palace, camp there tonight, and after take the road to Tivura."

"I don't like to go into the city," said Focas as Pietro stroked his beard. "It scares me. I don't mind saying so. It scares me."

"None will see us. I think the city deserted in any case."

Pietro hesitated. Even after all this time he did not trust her; he did not look to her as a servant ought to obey his master. Still, in the end he turned to Focas and said, breath whistling as he spoke, "The empress. She would want it, would she not?"

The empress. They were all Adelheid's faithful soldiers, every one of them.

Fuming, she followed them into the empty city. Twice, they saw dogs slink away around corners, tails tucked tight and heads down. Of dead folk there were none, but human bones they saw aplenty scattered across avenues and the open squares. Fallen apartment blocks and tumbled columns lay like dead beasts in the rubble. Each entryway was a dark mouth; each was silent. Wind swirled dust up from the streets to blend with the haze. Once, from far away, they heard a shout. Their footfalls scraped ominously, echoing off the walls. But they saw no one.

"How many days since that wind blasted us?" Focas whispered as they reached the paved ramp that led up to the two palaces built atop the central hill. "This happened then, don't you think? The storm brought destruction with it. I could smell it in the air, like it was diseased."

Pietro scratched his nose, then sneezed. "I wish we'd stayed with the empress. No telling if she lives, or is dead."

Close by, a dog growled, and both soldiers whirled, raising their spears, to be greeted by a heavier silence.

"Come," said Antonia. "It will be dark soon. Let's find shelter."

They made their way up the ramp past broken-down wagons abandoned in haste and in one case with the remains of a horse scattered around the traces where dogs had ripped it apart. Focas counted swords, and had reached the astounding total of fifty-five before they reached the top.

"Who would throw down their good iron swords like that?" he muttered to Pietro. The two men stood a stone's throw away from Antonia, but she overheard them nevertheless.

"Dead men. We'll be dead, too, if we don't get out of here. This is a fool's errand."

"Hush!"

From the top of the ramp they surveyed the city. Nothing moved but for a tumbling scrap, hard to say what it was but probably a bit of cloth, rolling down a distant avenue. The fog obscured even the towering walls and distant gates. Of church towers, she saw none. Perhaps they had all fallen. Off to the west in the hills bordering the sea, streaks of fire that marked red flowing rivers pierced the sullen haze despite the distance.

Surely even the Pit smelled sweeter and nourished more life!

Surely not. This was the Enemy's handiwork.

"Come," she said.

They ventured into the broad courtyard that fronted the twin palaces. The imperial palace had burned. It still stank of charred wood, a sharp scent overlying the reek of brimstone and decay. The skopos' palace had many more sections built entirely of stone, and these had survived with less damage.

"I had thought to examine the regnant's schola and library," said Antonia thoughtfully as they stood in the courtyard that separated the two palaces. "But it appears too dangerous to walk there."

She advanced nevertheless into an alcove where a sooty face peered at her out of the stone: a woman's visage wreathed with snakes that were also her hair. A viscous green puddle had collected in the basin below her open mouth, once a fountain where travelers might splash water on dusty faces before entering the great hall to meet the regnant. The mule strained toward the water. Pietro hauled it back.

"Perhaps there is something left in the barracks, if the rats haven't eaten it all up," said Antonia. "Go carefully, see what you can find. Seek grain and water for the beast, and provisions for ourselves. Also, a place to shelter for one night."

"Yes, Your Excellency. I'll go, and Focas will stay and attend you."

"Nay, best you go together. I will attempt the skopos' palace and meet you here by this fountain."

"If there are dogs, or madmen . . . ?"

She nodded. "Do as I command."

"Yes, Your Excellency."

Impertinent man! She crossed under the shadow of a vast arch and found, in the usual niche, a brace of lanterns that, amazingly, had not been tampered with, together with flint and scraps of linen. These she carried as she walked quietly along the old familiar corridors. It was utterly silent. In here, she could not even hear the wind. Now and again she glimpsed withered gardens through open windows and doors. The fountains, of course, had all stopped running. Dust scraped under her feet.

She almost did not recognize the double doors that led into the audience chamber. The gold leaf that had once covered the relief carved into those doors had been pried off and taken away by thieves or by faithful servants. Who could know? One door sat askew, having lost two hinges. She did not touch it but tugged on the other, which opened with a groan into the empty hall.

Her footfalls echoed softly as she walked. The ceiling arched high above, dimly perceived. The mural washed across the far wall, depicting the Translatus of the blessed Daisan, had splintered with a thousand cracks, and the Earth beneath his feet had vanished into a pile of fragments on the floor. Up on the dais, the skopos' chair was broken into pieces and all the gems pried out. A single amethyst had been left behind, dropped in haste, no doubt. She picked it up, turned it, but there wasn't light enough to catch the glints within. Still, in a pinch, it might serve her. She tucked it into the pocket sewn into her sleeve, then pushed past the curtain at the far right and came into the private sanctum of the skopos.

A room, whitewashed, with paintings of noble saints gracing the ceiling. There was a single table, a battered chest whose lock had been broken, and a shattered ceramic bowl at the foot of the bare pallet where, once, the skopos had rested. Anne had not scorned luxury, but neither had she coveted it.

The thieves had skipped over the single locked cupboard, sealed with an amulet. She studied it, careful not to touch its knot in any way: wolfsbane, which was poison to the skin, for invisibility, lavender for chastity and thereby to keep locks unbroken, and thistle for strength. Cunningly woven, certainly, but she recognized the pattern as one she had taught to certain of Anne's clerics. A brief murmured spell, a douse of oil over the dry herbs from the lamp's reservoir, and she snapped flint, got a spark, and set a scrap of linen burning. The amulet flared so brightly that she stepped back in surprise, shading her eyes. After so many days under a veiled sky, she had forgotten how brilliant light could be. The amulet vanished in a swirl of ash.

She used the point of her knife to cut the binding rope off the latch. Steam hissed along the blade and it glowed white hot, then spat sparks. The latch fell free, and the right side cabinet door swung open, moaning like the wail of the damned.

Anne had cared little for earthly things. This truth was never more in evidence than now. Anne had abandoned everything in her desire to destroy the Lost Ones. Everything.

She had left behind the holy vestments, the golden cup, although not the staff of her office. But there were other treasures as well: wrapped in a layer of greased leather and under that cushioned in lambskin was an ancient, degraded spear which Antonia recognized as the Holy Lance of St. Perpetua, once carried by Emperor Henry into battle. Henry would never have left such a holy relic behind; its protection was worth more than a thousand soldiers. But Henry, after all, had been ensorcelled; he hadn't needed or wanted such things; hadn't noticed they were missing, because the daimone had obeyed only what commands its master gave it, disregarding the rest.

He had even disregarded the most potent symbol of imperial power, which was bundled up so casually in plain linen that anyone might be excused for believing it was nothing important. How Anne had come to possess it Antonia did not know, but when she unwrapped it, she knew she had gained something important indeed:

Emperor Taillefer's seven-pointed golden crown, adorned with seven jewels—the crown of stars.

2

THEY reached the villa Tivura two days later, having lost their way twice because it was so difficult to navigate in the haze. The mule trudged on without complaint, but it was clearly ill; gunk wept from its eyes, and its breathing, like that of its human masters, was labored. Each breath she took scraped in Antonia's chest. If they did not leave the plain of Dar soon, they would all succumb to the foul air.

"Is this the right stream?" Pietro asked for the fourth time, breaking off to cough again. He hacked incessantly.

"We are on the right road. It rises." Speaking hurt, so Antonia spoke little.

The mule tugged at its reins, trying to get to the water. Focas knelt at the bank and scooped up water, tasting it. He spat it out, then wiped his lips. "Not as bad as before. It might be safe to let the poor beast drink. It doesn't taste of rotten eggs like it did downstream. It isn't warm."

The two soldiers looked at her. She nodded. "Let it drink, then, but not too much. I'll go ahead."

"Your Excellency!"

"I do not fear bandits."

"You should, Your Excellency!" exclaimed Focas. "Dogs, too. We had to beat off that pack last night. They smelled us."

She hesitated. She hated showing fear, but in truth the dogs had been starving and therefore dangerous. At last she settled down on the ground and waited while the mule drank and Pietro washed his hands and face in the streaming water. It seemed clear. Although the constant rain of dust out of the air had certainly fouled it, it didn't stink the way it had down by its confluence with the Greater Tivur, whose course led through Darre and thence south through rolling hills to the sea.

Those hills were on fire. At intervals the haze lightened, and since they were moving slowly upslope as they walked northeast, she caught glimpses of the red rim of fire that scorched the western horizon at all hours, easiest to see at night, of course, but visible during the daytime as well.

Her legs ached and her hip shot through with pain as she rose, but she closed her lips tightly as they moved on. In a hundred paces more the famous lady columns ghosted out of the fog: stone columns carved into the shapes of dour women, escorting them into the garden of the long-dead emperor who had built the most beautiful paradise known on Earth, so it was said. Some called it a replica in stone of the garden that grew at the entrance to the Chamber of Light, but Antonia knew better. The Dariyan emperors had scorned the truth. They had worshiped idols and demons. Therefore, everything they had built, while sturdy, was irrevocably tainted by the kiss of the Enemy.

Still, Empress Adelheid's grandfather had refurbished the domed hall, and one of her great-aunts had built stables where once the emperor had housed his guests. The stone ladies glowered at them, faces half obscured, but they were only stone and could not therefore impede their progress.

"Look!" said Pietro, and coughed. Coughed again. "A light!"

Focas looked at Pietro. Together, without exchanging words, they nodded. "I'll go ahead, Your Excellency. In case it's bandits."

Her chest hurt. She was too tired to complain. She just wanted to rest her feet. Focas strode ahead. Truly, it was remarkable how well he had held up. He was as strong as a bull, and far more tractable than his companion. His form faded into the haze, although by now they could see the curved facade of the grand court that greeted visitors. They paused where the paved road gave way to the broad forecourt. Turning, Antonia looked into the haze over the plain, but it was impossible to see anything. On clear days, one could see Darre away in the distance, surrounded by fields.

She choked, coughing. The mule wheezed.

"Hsst!" whispered Pietro. "Do you hear?"

"Where did the light go?" she asked, scanning the wide court and the semicircle of columns, but no lantern or torch burned now.

"Hsst! Look!"

Ghosts advanced out of the fog, wreathed in trailing haze, formless and faceless although about the height of men.

She was ready. She had always been ready, knowing how little surety there was in traveling with such a small party. She unsheathed her small knife and grabbed at the mule, pressing the point to one of the veins in the side of its neck. A trickle of blood flowed over her fingers as she spoke the words that would raise a galla. The air hummed. Where blood beaded on the mule's hide the haze coalesced as though forming a rope out of darkness. The tang of the iron forge drifted up from the earth.

"Your Excellency! See what I have found!" Focas strode into view, easy among the ghosts. "We have found what we sought! They have been sheltering here in the catacombs. This good captain says the princesses are alive and in his care."

Too late! The spell had gone too far and must be released or else rebound upon her. The stink of the forge gusted on the breeze. A shadow spilled into the ground beside the pooling blood. The mule brayed and jerked away from the knife, then collapsed as its blood pumped onto the ground.

"What—?" cried Focas, as the men behind him drew their weapons.

It was a small galla, appetite whetted by the taste of blood, but it would demand more before it could be dispatched. It would turn on her, or on anyone. Its substance thrummed in the air as it materialized into this plane. Its muttering words—*pain pain pain*—ghosted in the air like the sound of tolling bells. The air of this world burned it. It was angry, and trapped, and panicked. She had to act quickly.

She sealed the spell with a name.

"Pietro of Darre!" she whispered without hesitation.

"Your Excellency!" cried Focas, hanging back as the others cried out loud in fear. "What foul creature plagues us?"

"A traitor among us! One who does not serve the empress has brought a demon into our midst to murder the princesses!" She flung up her hands; her sleeves slid down her arms as she cried out. "St. Thecla save us! Matthias, Mark, Johanna, Lucia! Marian and Peter! Deliver us from evil! Seek the one whose spirit has fallen to the Enemy! Seek the one who would destroy us! Take him! Take him! Drive his soul into the Pit! And then begone!"

The shaft of darkness that formed the body of the galla in this world writhed like a chained soul seeking release. The stink choked her, but she kept her arms raised; she did not falter. The galla had the gift, or curse, of sight. They could see into the souls of every man and woman. The darkness lurched, spinning sideways.

Its bell voice rang dully. *"Pietro."*

Pietro screamed. He, and the darkness, vanished, and only his bones remained.

The galla had escaped back to its own sphere. That whiff of iron dissipated, subsumed in dust.

Men shouted and wept but gathered most pleasingly around her as sheep flock to the shepherd when they fear the assault of the wolf. Focas fell to his knees, sobbing. The mule struggled to its feet, but collapsed again.

"Your Excellency! I am Captain Falco."

"I know you, Captain Falco. You are the empress' most faithful captain."

He nodded, acknowledging what was to him not compliment or flattery but the breath that allowed him to exist. He appeared unshaken by Pietro's death, but it was difficult to judge.

"You have done well to guard the princesses. Where are they?"

"Safely in the catacombs, Your Excellency. What news of the empress?"

Always the empress! Yet there would be time to mold these soldiers to her will, and those who refused her could be disposed of, as God desired. The disobedient, after all, were doomed to the Pit.

"Alas, I do not know what has become of the empress. She sent me ahead but remained herself on the coast, in the town of Estriana. She had set an ambush for the northern prince, the rebel, the one who sought to kill his own father, the Emperor Henry."

"Patricide!" Falco was a stolid, competent soldier of medium height, with the broad shoulders of a man who has swung a sword and carried a shield since he was a lad. "I had heard the Wendish were barbarians. Now I know it to be true!"

In Antonia's opinion, the Wendish were simple, honorable folk in their own crude way, without more than a finger's weight of the capacity for greed, backstabbing, and treachery that thrived among the sophisticated Aostans. The southerners plundered and robbed each other, cut each other's throats, and whored with their own sons and daughters. Still, it was best not to mention that to Captain Falco, who might take offense even though it was only the truth. God would overwhelm the wicked and reward the righteous, and Antonia would see justice done while she was waiting for Them to act on Earth.

Focas crept forward and poked at the scatter of bones with the butt of his spear. "Can it be?" he croaked. "Can Pietro have been harboring a foul demon in his soul this entire time? I did not see it! I did not see it!"

"Hardship blinds us," she said kindly.

"It is well you are here to protect us," said Falco, but his tone was bland and his gaze without passion.

"Indeed," she agreed. "We must go swiftly. The land here is poisoned by the Enemy. It is best we move north in haste."

Still, he hesitated. "What if the empress comes seeking her daughters, Your Excellency? They are her treasure. She will not abandon them."

She nodded. "We must leave a few men behind. You pick them, Captain."

"It is likely that the men I leave behind will die."

"We will all die in time. That is God's will. They will only ascend sooner to the Chamber of Light, where the righteous find peace."

He frowned. In the silence, as he considered, some of his men coughed. The claws of the Enemy sank deep. So many had been infected with the taint that had gripped Pietro, and that she struggled against with every breath.

"Darre is lost, Captain. Best we move quickly before we are overtaken by the Enemy as that one was." She gestured toward the bones.

His frown deepened, and he stiffened, clenching his hands. "Very well, Your Excellency. It is past time we carry the princesses away. Both suffer from a grippe. I will leave Terence and Petrus, and this man of yours, Focas."

He was testing her, but she was equal to the challenge. "Very well. See that it is done, and that the rest make ready."

"Where do we go?"

"This question, indeed, I have pondered on my long journey. We met refugees who say the coast is awash and many towns destroyed. West, as we see, is all on fire. We must go north."

"Where?"

"There is one whose loyalty we can count on, who will shelter us. We must march north past Vennaci and take the road to Novomo."

VII
ON THE ROAD

1

A griffin's cough woke him. He sat up, instantly alert, but only with his second breath did he recall where he was and what he was missing.

"Liath!" he said sharply.

She was gone.

He jumped up, wrestled on his tunic, and pushed out past the tent flap.

"Your Majesty!"

"Where is—? Ah. Be at ease, Benedict. Sibold."

"Your Majesty." The soldiers nodded as Sanglant walked past them toward the campfire set beyond the ring of tents. He heard them whisper to each other.

"I win! Told you he wouldn't stay sleeping."

"You did not win! We didn't wager *whether*, but *when*."

Liath sat cross-legged beside the fire, hands open and relaxed on her thighs as she stared into the flame. Hathui paced behind her. The Eagle glanced up as Sanglant walked up and nodded, acknowledging him. He halted behind Liath to wait.

The last few nights had been really cold, the first hard winter chill since the warm nights and overcast days after the great storm. That chill made him uneasy in a way he could not explain. It hurt in his bones the way a coming change in the weather might make a man's joints ache, warning him of rain. The ground was cold and dry beneath his bare feet. It was, as always now, too cloudy to see stars or moon, but the heavens still bled an unnatural light, almost as bright as if there were a full but bloody moon.

"How long have you been out here?" he asked Hathui in a low voice.

"Too long, Your Majesty."

"Still nothing?"

"Nothing. If Liath cannot see within the flames, then I think no one can."

He and Hathui waited in companionable silence. Liath had a remarkable capacity to focus; she did not once shift, not even to brush the hair away from her cheek as the wind stirred it, which surely must distract her. He twitched, wanting to smooth back her hair, wanting to touch her. She seemed blind and deaf to their presence, although they stood just behind her. He could never be so close to her and ignore her so thoroughly. She was a roaring fire to him, a force impossible to shut out. The heat of her smote him, although he doubted anyone else noticed it. He was the one who burned.

"Isn't she cold?" he asked, but Hathui only shrugged, and because he couldn't stand not doing *something* he went back to the tent and fetched a cloak, which he draped over Liath's shoulders. She did not thank him; if she noticed the thick cloak at all, she gave no sign.

He paced. Twice Hathui added wood to the fire. Neither time did Liath alter her intent stare, as if the Eagle's movement and the hot lick of fresh flame did not register. After some time the darkness lightened, heralding dawn, and as a wind rose off the Alfar Mountains now south of them, she finally sighed and sat back, rubbing her eyes.

"Ai, God. No matter how deeply I search—" She looked up, then, and smiled, seeing him. "Aren't you cold?" she demanded. "You're practically naked!" She shuddered, drawing the cloak more tightly around her shoulders. "I'm freezing." She laughed. "Where did this come from?"

He shook his head, a little disgusted, if truth be known. Resigned. Amused. She was not the woman he had believed he married.

"What news?" he asked instead, offering her a hand.

She took it and let him pull her up, dusted off her tunic and leggings, and blew on her hands to warm them. Her fingers were red from cold. "It matters not how deeply I search. It's as if my Eagle's Sight has vanished. There are twenty Eagles with this army, yet none of us can see through the flames. We are blind."

"I am no blinder than I was before."

"True enough, my love, but I am blind, and I don't like it because I don't know what it means."

"What it means to be blind? Like those of us who are not as gifted as you?"

She looked sharply at him, hearing the pinch in his words. "That isn't what I meant at all! Eagle's Sight gives us an advantage, nothing more. It gives a sense of surety that perhaps makes one over-confident. It's as if a curtain has fallen across our vision, and we can catch only fragments and glimpses through a rip in the cloth. Was it the cataclysm that blinded us? Is it the haze and the clouds? Is it magic, woven by the Ashioi to cripple us? Was the Eagle's Sight woven into the great crown in ancient days, and is it clouded because the crowns are fallen? I don't know, and what I don't know I can't solve."

"Are the crowns fallen?"

She rubbed her eyes, yawned, and he caught her under the arm. She leaned against him, eyes shut.

"Anne is dead. That's all I know. Anne and everyone with her are gone." Her sigh shuddered through her body. "I felt those who wove the other crowns until the moment Anne died and the crown she wove was destroyed. I cannot say if the others survived the fire and the storm. They may have, or they may be dead, too."

"You don't think every person at the other crowns died, too?" asked Hathui. "You said that you . . . that you destroyed everything—all life—within a league of the crown where Anne was."

Liath pushed away from Sanglant, and when he reached for her, she shook her head, needing to stand alone. "I don't know if the fire reached through the weaving to touch the others. Without Eagle's Sight, I may never know. I am sorry for the sake of Meriam. I liked her."

"She treated me with respect," muttered Sanglant, "unlike the rest of them."

Her gaze flashed to him, and a smile lifted her lips. "It is true, my love, that they did not treat you as you deserved. Yet consider that they are likely dead now, while we have survived."

"I cannot regret their deaths, considering all we have suffered."

"Nay, that's not what I meant. Only that I never thought about what would happen afterward. Aren't we blind in that way, all of us? We march toward the gate, but it's the gate we see, not the land lying beyond. We can't see that landscape until the gate is opened and we've stepped through. Then it's too late to go back."

Around them, folk stirred as they rose and made ready to march. They had crossed the Brinne Pass in fifteen days. The northern air had invigorated the sullen and the exhausted, who could see how much closer they were to home. Certainly, less dust plagued them. In the early days it had filtered down constantly to coat hands and faces with a film of grit that they hadn't the leisure or water to wash off.

Soldiers rolled up blankets. Sentries called out a challenge to men trudging into camp with full buckets drawn from a nearby stream, while grooms led the horses to water in groups of twenty. As ragged and weary as his men looked, he knew the horses managed worst of all. The army was almost out of grain, a meager ration to begin with, and the grazing was poor. At least, here on the northern slopes of the mountains, the water was clear, unclouded by particles and ash. Yet it still hadn't rained, despite the clouds, and both villages they had passed as they came down out of the mountains had been deserted, houses and huts blown down by the great storm.

"I can't stop seeing them," she whispered. "The way they burned. I can't stop hearing them scream."

He knew better than to touch her when she was in this mood. "They were your enemies." He'd said the same thing a hundred times in the last fifteen days. "They would have killed you."

"I know. But I still feel unclean, as though I'm stained with the Enemy's handiwork."

He waited. As the light rose, the world came into view: hills, forest, wilting trees. Drought and lack of sun, unseasonable heat followed by this sudden cold winter blast, had taken their toll on the vegetation. To the north the land was too hilly to see far. The road twisted away past a ridgeline, lost to sight. To the south, on a clear day, they would have been able to see the mountain peaks, but there was yet a haze dusting the air, ever present. Even at midday the light lacked strength. It was uncanny. Indeed, it scared him more than anything else. He was no farmer, but he knew what farmers needed: rain, sun, and seasonable weather. After years of civil strife, invasion, drought, famine, and plague, he could not imagine that any Wendish noble or biscop held plentiful stores in reserve. They had already suffered hard times. How long would these clouds linger?

"Death in battle is not the worst we may see," he said at last. "Those deaths may be the most merciful ones, in the end."

She had shed a few tears, but she wiped them away. She examined him as she might study a manuscript, that look that devoured, so rarely turned on him! He did not understand her yet. He wasn't even sure what she thought of him. That she was willing to *love* him passionately he knew. Of the rest, of what lay beyond lust, he had to unfold piece by piece.

"I'll keep trying," she said, and it took him a moment to realize she meant that she would keep trying to find her Eagle's Sight. "The crowns, too. If they're all fallen, then we have no advantage over our enemies. But no disadvantage either as they have nothing we do not also possess. Unless there are those still who can see with Eagle's Sight while denying it to us."

"Do you think there might be?"

She looked at Hathui. Hathui shrugged, without expression. The two women trusted each other in a way that, annoyingly, excluded him.

"I don't think it likely any other person born of humankind has survived who can see if I cannot." Liath said the words without vanity or arrogance. "Eagle's Sight ran through the world on the river of aether. That element is bound into my being, so I should be more sensitive to its ebb and flow than most of my father's kinfolk. Yet it also seems likely to me that a sorcerer whose skills are honed to the finest pitch might be able to discern things I cannot. And I know nothing of those ancient ones who spoke to me, or the Ashioi, or the Horse people. They may still possess the sight, while we've gone blind. And anyway, I am so young, so ignorant, compared to someone like Li'at'dano—"

"See who comes," interrupted Hathui, lifting her chin.

The centaurs had proved hardiest of all his soldiers. Like goats, they seemed able to eat almost anything, although he had never seen any of the Horse people eat meat. Capi'ra's fine coat was discolored by streaks of grime, but she looked perfectly able to trample him on the spot if he gave offense.

He nodded, acknowledging her. She stamped once.

"It is time." She gestured toward the east. "We turn east and follow the hills on our own path. We come to northern plains of Ungria and from there east to home. Our alliance is finished. Now we leave."

"I am sorry to see you and your people go," he said, "but I know I cannot hold you here."

"That is right."

He smiled. She did not smile in reply, but neither did she frown. "What of the future?" he asked. "What of our alliance?"

"I report on all we witness to the council, as you would say. The ones who lead us will discuss all that happened. The strong minds will decide. We, the rest, will follow."

"What of our daughter?" asked Liath.

"I have not forget your daughter, Bright One. See who comes with me." She flicked a hand up.

There were some of the steppe-dwelling Kerayit among her dozen attendants, but to Sanglant's surprise the shaman, Gyasi, had also come, together with a pair of Quman captains. He hadn't noticed them at first because, not mounted, they weren't yet wearing their wings, and judged by facial features alone they did not look so very different from the Kerayit tribesmen.

The shaman and his companions knelt before Sanglant, tapped knuckles to foreheads as they acknowledged Liath's presence.

"We beg you, master," said Gyasi, "let us return with the Horse people to our homeland. I will be your messenger. I will seek news of your daughter. I will bring her back to you if she still lives. My clan owes her our service, for as long as she lives."

Liath looked away, wiping a tear off her cheek. "She lives," she muttered. "I saw her." She swung back to face Sanglant. "I should go."

"No. I grieve for Blessing as well. I fear for her. But it serves no purpose for you to travel east on a journey that could take years. I weep for my daughter. I miss her. But if you go, it will not bring her back more quickly. And if she is dead—"

"She is not dead!"

"She is not dead if our wills make it true, but we don't know. I trust Gyasi to find her and bring her home. Heribert is with her. That must be enough. There is too much at stake elsewhere, and I. Need. You."

She lifted a hand. She could not answer in any other way. It was not acquiescence, precisely. She was herself torn and indecisive.

"Take what supplies you need, Gyasi. You take as well my heart, for my daughter is precious to me."

Gyasi nodded. "She saved my life and that of my nephews, Majesty. This obligation I owe to her. I am not a man unless it is discharged."

Even so, even knowing he did what was necessary, he found that he, like Liath, could not speak because of sorrow and fear choking the words in his throat. He, too, lifted a hand. The gesture must speak where he would otherwise break down. So much loss; Blessing might be the least of it.

The shaman rose, but paused before he turned away. The centaurs and their attendants were already moving toward the pathless forest while Gyasi hummed a queer little tuneless melody under his breath. A twisting track opened between the trees, not quite seen, not quite felt, but present as mist rising from the hills at dawn. The fall of hooves, the rattle of harness, the soft conversations among men all vanished, bit by bit, as the party moved onto that path and vanished into the woodland. Behind Sanglant, the army made ready to leave, but men stopped in their tasks, hearing that uncanny music, and stared as the forest swallowed the centaurs and their companions. Last of all, Gyasi stepped onto the path, and the trees closed in behind him. At once, the forest appeared as an impenetrable tangle of fallen logs and stands of beech and fir grown among brambles and thickets of sedge and bilberry.

"Their path will be swift, I'd wager," murmured Hathui.

"Let us leave this behind," said Liath, more quaver than voice. "I will cry."

Every man and woman was eager to get moving, to reach home. To discover if home had weathered the storm. Many, like Liutgard and Burchard and what remained of their armies, had been away from Wendar for years, having marched south with Henry in his quest to restore Taillefer's fallen empire. That was all gone now.

So much else was gone, he thought, brooding as they rode at a steady pace along the road. Often they had to halt while those in the vanguard cleared the road. The storm had torn through this countryside, leaving debris everywhere. No one would lack firewood for burning this winter, had they any game to roast over the flames.

"You are quiet, Your Majesty," said Hathui having given up her attempts to get Liath to speak.

"What have we left?" he asked her. "What was once an alliance is now, again, only loyal Wendishmen and marchlanders."

"Isn't that for the best?"

"Is it? Did we not have strength in numbers? Did we not have strength because we reached across the old boundaries? My father was not foolish in thinking that empire would make him strong."

"It killed him."

Hathui's tone surprised him, but as he examined her face, he saw neither anger or resentment, only sadness.

"Did it? That he marched south to Aosta—perhaps. Yet any of us might die, on any day."

"Perhaps not you, Your Majesty."

The barb had a sharp hook. "That may be, yet I pray you consider that my father might have died in his bed, or fighting against his enemies in Wendar, as easily as he was captured by the queen's plots."

"Do not forget Hugh of Austra, Your Majesty."

Ah.

He glanced at Liath, but she seemed far removed from their conversation. She had light hands on her mount, a submissive mare who was content to follow where the rest led. She was far beyond him, a world away, judging by her frown and the unfocused nature of her gaze, not quite lighting on tree or earth or cloudy sky.

"I have not forgotten him, Hathui. Where he is now, I cannot say."

"Dead, I hope," muttered Hathui. "I saw him murder Villam with his own hands. I will never forgive him that, although my forgiveness is not a thing a man of his station cares about. If he lives, he will have found refuge. I hope he is dead."

"I would just like to know." He laughed. "Better to know that there's a man in the dark stalking you with a knife. Even if you can't see him. Yet what do you make of it, Hathui?"

"Of Hugh's plots and Queen Adelheid's treachery?"

"Nay. Of this new alliance."

"What alliance, Your Majesty?" She looked around, as if expecting a pack of wolves to lope out of the surrounding woods. As they moved down into the bowl of a valley, beech and silver fir gave way to spruce. The dense boughs of spruce had absorbed the heavy winds better than most trees. Although the road was darker, often shaded and dim, few broken branches and fallen trees blocked their path.

"That between the Quman and the Horse people."

"Is there one?" Liath had been listening, after all. She spoke as if the question had been addressed to her. "The Horse people are few, so they say. If they do not make allies of the Quman, they will end up fighting them. So they have done for generations, surely, with the aid of sorcery."

"So they have done, but it is not clear what will become of sorcery now, or how the balance of power will change with the return of my mother's people. If I were one of the leaders of the Horse people, I would seek allies. It may be they will seek an alliance with the Quman. It may even be they will seek an alliance with the Ashioi."

"The Horse people and the Ashioi were enemies."

"Long ago."

"I have met Zuangua, as have you, Sanglant. To him, to the many who lived in the shadows all that time, it is not long ago but yesterday. Even to the ones who were born in exile, it is within the living memory of your grandfather, who can tell the tale."

Sanglant had only the vaguest memory of his father's father, Arnulf the Younger, but Henry's mother, Queen Mathilda, had patted and cosseted her young grandson as affectionately as could so reserved a woman. All her love was held tight for Henry. She had admired Sanglant, but his birth had meant most to her, he suspected, because it gave Henry his claim to the regnancy.

So it was strange to think of having a grandfather, so old a man that he had seen the world almost three millennia ago. He could not grasp such an expanse of time. He had never been one to hoard grudges or dwell on the past. He refused to live in Bloodheart's hall forever, chained down with the dogs.

"That may be true," he replied, "but enemies can become allies if a greater threat rises."

"Who would that be?" demanded Hathui. "If the stories are true, humankind and the Horse people moved heaven and earth in truth to cast away the Ashioi. If I were one of the Lost Ones, I'm not sure I could forgive that. If I were one of the Horse people, I'm not sure I would expect to be forgiven."

He laughed. "We are not the Horse people. They are not like us. Li'at'dano said so herself. She said that humankind have driven them far into the east, and decimated their herds through disease and conflict."

"The Quman did that," said Hathui, "who hate and fear them."

"And others. But Capi'ra and her troop have seen the west, now. Wendish folk defeated the Quman. Anne and her sorcerers raised this great storm. If I were one who leads among the Horse people, then I would fear Wendar."

"There is another power that you neglect," said Liath suddenly. "Anne did not raise the storm. The ancient ones did. Li'at'dano did. The Ashioi land would have returned in any case. Anne meant to exile them again, to destroy them for all time. That she did not, that worse destruction did not overtake us all, is due to the voices from the north. There is power there we must not ignore."

"The Eika?" Hathui asked. "They are barbarians. One chieftain might strike and lay waste along the coast, but I recall how Count

Lavastine held them off with his local milites. A strong Wendish and Varren resistance will beat them back."

"Perhaps," said Sanglant. "It bears watching."

"There is so much we do not know," murmured Liath, "and it will be more difficult to learn now that we are blind."

2

WHEN they stopped at nightfall, Hanna left her guards while they argued over whether or not to set up a tent for the night, and staggered over to a trickling stream. In the midst of a crowd of hot, thirsty, complaining Arethousan soldiers she splashed water on her face and slurped down as much as she could hold in her cupped hands. Soon the water became murky from so many stamping through the shallows. A man slammed into her shoulder as he pushed forward toward the stream. He muttered a curse, looked at her once, then a second time, and called to his fellows.

"The Wendish bitch! See here! She's slipped her leash."

All at once a half dozen of them pressed back from the water to encircle her. She had overreached because her thirst had driven her forward rashly. She turned her wrists in toward her body to grip the chain, ready to use it as a weapon.

Sergeant Bysantius appeared beside her with a quirt. "Back! Back!" he cried as he slashed left and right, driving the soldiers away from her.

Her heart was still racing, and her mouth had gone dry, so she pretended to a calmness she did not feel as she sat back on her heels and wiped her forehead as well as she could with her wrists manacled. "I thank you, Sergeant."

He raised one eyebrow, then pointed behind her with the quirt. "I didn't come for you. See, there. General Lord Alexandros waters his horses."

They marched these days through dry, hilly countryside devoid of habitation. This stream poured out of a ravine. Except at this ford, its banks were too steep for horses to drink. Muttering, the soldiers headed back to camp.

"Up!" Sergeant Bysantius grabbed her elbow and pulled her up-right. "Out of the way."

She shook her arm out of his grasp before he could lead her away. The chain that bound her ankles allowed her to walk but not run, and she was unable to avoid the rush of horses brought to the stream by the general's grooms. Alexandros himself rode a chestnut mare with a pale gold coat. His entire string had chestnut coats, most pale and a few richly dark in shade. He pulled up, dismounted, and tossed his reins to a groom before walking over to Sergeant Bysantius.

"Sergeant, bring the Eagle to me at my tent."

"Yes, my lord general."

He strode away with a dozen men swarming in attendance.

"He has no need to crawl for a taste of water as the rest of us do," she said bitterly to the sergeant. "He has wine to drink while his soldiers go thirsty."

Bysantius scratched his cheek. "He has earned his rank and his privileges. He's no better born than half these men."

She laughed. "How can that be? He is a lord."

"A man who commands an army is likely to be addressed as 'lord,' I'm thinking. Even by those who were born under a canopy boasting the imperial star. Especially if they need the men and weapons he can bring to their cause."

"The exalted Lady Eudokia needs him in order to raise her nephew to become emperor?"

He shrugged. "A strong hand rules where weaker hands sow only chaos. Come."

She followed up along the dusty ground on the trail of the lord general, now vanished into the glut of wagons, horses, milling troops, and canvas tents that marked the camp. Every night the camp was set up in the exact same order, every tent sited in relation to the emperor's tent according to its inhabitants' rank, position, and importance to the royal child. This night, they had halted in the middle of what had once been a village.

Three brick hovels stood in the midst of a dozen ancient olive trees, but the tiny hamlet appeared abandoned, perhaps yesterday, perhaps one hundred years ago. In this dry country it was impossible to tell.

Bysantius paced himself so as not to get ahead of her. Over the last ten or so days she had accustomed herself to the chains so that she could walk without stumbling.

"I thank you," she repeated.

"For what kindness?" he asked, almost laughing.

"For saving me from whatever unkindness I might have suffered from those soldiers."

"The general wants you unharmed. You're no use to him dead."

She was, apparently, no use to him living, but she forbore to say it, knowing it foolish to remind her captors that they might be better off saving for their own men the bit of food they fed to her each day. "Is it true of all of you, that you serve the lord general and not the exalted lady?"

Now he did laugh. "The priests teach us that we serve God, is that not so? God served humankind by walking among us for a time so He could lead us into the Light."

"That is a heresy."

"Nay, you Darrens are the heretics. You say that the blessed Daisan was only a man like you and me." He spoke without heat. He was not, apparently, a man made passionate by religious matters.

"The deacons of my own land taught me that the blessed Daisan prayed for seven days and nights and was lifted up to the Chamber of Light by the Mother and Father of Life. You don't believe the tales of his martyrdom, do you?"

"No, not his martyrdom." Yet he frowned. "The blessed Daisan holds two natures within him, for how else could he have been translated into the Chamber of Light while still living? Still, folk do talk of this martyrdom, how his skin was flayed from his body."

"I've met more than one person in the west who whispers the heresy of the Redemption. I didn't know folk spoke of it here, too."

He slapped his quirt against his thigh and glanced first left, then right, as they made their way through camp. Exhausted, men sat on the ground or reclined on blankets or cloaks. "Anyone might hear. The Patriarch has spies among the troops."

If that were so, it must mean that the Patriarch feared the power of the heresy. Why spy out what you did not fear? Yet surely the heresy Ivar professed had come from somewhere. Why not from the east? It was the most likely story. Despite what Bysantius said, they were heretics here anyway with their talk of "two natures." Once that door was opened, as Deacon Fortensia used to say in Heart's Rest, any shameless layabout could creep in and pretend to be a holy saint.

"You ever put thought to what you've hope for, if the lord general grants you your freedom?" asked Bysantius as they approached the general's big tent, just now shuddering into place as soldiers and servants raised the canvas over the frame and staked it down.

"What I've hope for? I hope to go home! I serve the emperor, Henry."

"Scouts say the land is blasted west of here. That ash and dust and fire parch the air. I don't think the Wendish king has an empire left. You'd do better to stick it out in civilized country."

Her eyes burned. She wiped away tears as she struggled with dismay. "I hadn't heard those reports." In her own country, she would have. Eagles talked to each other and knew everything, as much as anyone could know. They knew almost as much as the regnant, because they were his eyes and ears.

"You're a prisoner," he replied, gaze bent on her, "but you might be otherwise."

"Otherwise?" She sniffed back her tears, hating to show weakness.

"I'd marry you, if you were willing."

"Marry me?" The incongruity of the comment dried her tears and her anger, then made her laugh. "Marry me?"

"You're strong, capable, smart. The exalted Lady Eudokia tells me you're still a virgin. You'd make a good wife. I like you. You haven't given up."

Now she burned but for other reasons. *How could the exalted lady know?*

"I haven't given up. I'm not accustomed to these chains yet."

His sidelong gaze was measuring, not angry. "It was fairly asked. I might hope for the same courtesy in an answer."

"I am still a prisoner. Ask me when I am free to leave or stay as I wish."

"Huh," he said, half of it a laugh and the rest nothing she could interpret. With his quirt he indicated the entrance to the general's tent. "Go in."

"You're not coming in?" she asked, and had to stop herself from grabbing his arm as at a lifeline. She could not bring herself to speak the thought that leaped into her mind: *Alone, I fear the general's anger, but if you were there I might hope for someone to protect me against it.*

He brushed a hand through his dark hair as would a man preening for a lover's visit. "Go in," he repeated, and lifted his quirt. "I've a few guards to speak to. They've gotten careless."

Careless about her.

He nodded, dismissing her, and walked away. General Lord Alexandros' guards moved their spears away from the entrance and let her pass. Inside, a servant unrolled a rug to cover the red-gray earth, but otherwise the general had dispensed with the opulent furnishings that had surrounded him before the great storm. No green silk draped the bare canvas walls. Chairs and rich couches were banished, replaced by a bench, a pallet, and a pitcher of water set in a copper basin, placed on a three-legged stool. He was sitting on the bench wiping dust off his face with a square of linen while a captain dressed in a red tabard gave his report. This man had an unusual accent and spoke at such a galloping pace that she had trouble understanding him.

". . . a day ahead of us . . . refugees . . . the city. They fled . . . the sea. These folk are the ones . . . the storm in the sky . . ."

The general glanced up, noted her, and beckoned to a servant. "A fire," he said softly to the man, who slipped out as the captain kept speaking.

". . . They fled to the hills . . . the sea . . . the city . . . they are lying . . . it is true . . . do you wish to speak to them?"

"No, not yet. If their story is true, we will meet others who tell the same tale. If it is false, then we will soon know. Put out a double sentry line. Stay on guard against bandits and thieves."

As the captain left, the servant returned with a brazier heaped with glowing coals. A second man walked behind him carrying a cloth sling filled with sticks. They set up a tripod on the dirt and cradled the brazier in it.

Alexandros gestured toward the brazier, but said nothing. She knelt in the dirt because she had not been given permission to touch the rug. One of the servants fed sticks to the coals. They blazed. She bent her attention to the flames, seeking within for those she knew: King Henry, Liath, Ivar, Prince Sanglant, Wolfhere, Sorgatani, Sister Rosvita and her retinue, Captain Thiadbold, and even her friends among the Lions, one by one.

She saw nothing in the flames except flickering shadows. Perhaps every soul she knew had died in the storm. Possibly Ingo, Folquin, Leo, and Stephen were well and truly dead, lost in the cataclysm or in a battle she did not yet know they had fought. Probably Rosvita and the other clerics had died of thirst and starvation or been slaughtered by bandits.

The entrance flap shifted. The movement of light across the

ground startled her so much that she sat back on her heels, blinking, to see a pair of servants carry in the litter on which Lady Eudokia traveled. A trio of eunuchs placed four stools on the rug and stepped back as the servants placed the litter on this foundation, well off the ground. The eunuchs bathed the lady's face and hands in water, then retreated.

"What news?" the lady asked Alexandros.

"As you see, no different than last night or the one before or every night before that. Either she lies, or she is telling the truth and has lost her Eagle's Sight."

"If so, is it a temporary blindness or a permanent one?"

He scratched his neck, grimacing, then rubbed his eyes as if he were exasperated. "What else do you know of this sorcery, Exalted Lady?"

"Nothing I have not already told you. Its secrets are not known to us. I will attempt the camphor again, but it is the last I possess."

"See!" He fixed his one-eyed gaze on Hanna. A knife held to her throat could not have frightened her more. How could a common-born man rise to be called a "lord"? Either he was in league with the Enemy, or the Arethousans were stranger than any folk she understood. That he was ruthless she knew; he had done nothing to succor Princess Sapientia; he had abandoned his other hostages without, apparently, a second thought. He drove his men forward at a difficult pace and left the stragglers behind.

"*See.*"

Lady Eudokia tossed three tiny twigs onto the fire. The choking scent of camphor filled Hanna's lungs and made her eyes water and her head pound. She saw flames, burning and burning, and although the smoke and incense made her eyes sting, she kept staring into the dance of fire.

Let them believe she was only a breath away from success.

"Nothing," said Lady Eudokia, but she sounded curious more than disgusted. "We may as well cavort naked with the fire worshipers as stare at these coals."

The general had not moved, but Hanna felt his presence as a threat. "Is she lying, Exalted Lady?"

"I think she is not lying. I see only flames."

"If we do not need her, then . . ."

"Let us not be hasty, General. You are thinking as a soldier in battle. Think rather that those who brought this storm down upon us may have survived. I do not know what powers they hold to themselves. If they have the ability to cloud Eagle's Sight, we must consider what is best for us. Hold the Eagle in reserve, in case matters change."

"What if it takes years?"

She lifted a hand in a lazy gesture of disinterest. "I have an aunt who has for twenty-eight years resided in the convent of St. Mary of Gesythan. It is better for the family that she remain alive than that she be killed. None leave that isolation once they are banished within. This one can be placed in the convent as well."

"She is a westerner and thus a heretic."

"True enough. She need not receive every comfort, as do the others."

He scratched his neck again, leaving a trail of rashy red. "A good enough plan. But I agree only on the condition that she remain in my custody until that time, and that I be granted leave to visit her there whenever I wish."

"If my nephew becomes emperor, General, then these are no obstacles."

He nodded. She clapped her hands, and the eunuchs wiped her face again before moving back so the servants could carry her away. As the tent flap closed behind her retinue, the general turned to the soldiers waiting respectfully behind him. He pointed. A captain dressed in a blue tabard came forward and began delivering his report, but Hanna was too dizzy with fear to catch more than scraps of phrases:

". . . may be the same bandits who shadow us . . . may be another group . . . scouts can never find them . . . nay, never a trace . . ."

She ought to memorize each utterance, to hoard them like the treasures they were. She was an Eagle. What she heard, she remembered. What she remembered, she could report to her regnant just as this man reported to his. But she could not concentrate because she could not banish from her mind a vision of whitewashed walls surrounding her, too high to be climbed and without any gate for escape.

A pair of servants trudged in bearing buckets of water. They set them down and busied themselves with the pitcher and basin. Her eyes were still stinging. As much as she swallowed, she could not get all her fear and frustration and anger down.

Is this all her life came to? Had she somehow angered God so much that she was to be passed from one hand to the next as a prisoner? The general might call her an Eagle, but she was no such thing. It would have been better to have stayed in Heart's Rest and marry Young Johan even with his smelly feet and braying, stupid laugh. A cow or goat was not precisely free, but at least it wasn't caged within narrow walls. She knew better than to let self-pity overwhelm her, but the temptation just for this moment was to fall and fall.

One servant poured water from pitcher into basin. Because the scent of water hit her hard, she looked at them. They were both middle-aged men, wiry and strong, with stern expressions. They were the kind of men who have risen far enough to receive a measure of comfort and security as retainers of a powerful lord. One was, indeed, handsome enough that she might have looked twice at him if he hadn't been old enough to be her father. Bysantius' unwanted but flattering proposal had woken old feelings in her. It wasn't so bad to be desired or at least respected. Ivar was lost to her. She had admired Captain Thiadbold, but held loyal to her Eagle's vows. Rufus had, momentarily, tempted her, but in the end she had chosen the easier path. She had held herself aloof. She had never succumbed.

Not as Liath had.

In a way, she was envious of Liath, who had embraced passion without looking back, despite the trouble it had brought her.

I am not so impulsive.

Yet it wasn't so. She had left Heart's Rest to follow Liath. She had walked without fear into the east. She had wandered in dreams into the distant grasslands seeking the Kerayit shaman who had named Hanna as her luck.

The good-looking servant winked at her, then rubbed at his dirty forehead with the stump of his right arm, cut off at the wrist and cleanly healed. The position of his arm concealed his mouth from his companion. His lips formed a word once, then a second time, soundless but obviously meant to be understood.

Patience.

She startled back. Had she imagined it? Was he speaking in Wendish?

He and the other servant, carrying the emptied buckets, walked out the door, keeping silence as a new captain droned on with his report. She heard, in the wake of their passing, a faint tinkling like that of tiny bells shaken by a breeze.

Five breaths later she knew, and was surprised it had taken her so long. He hadn't been wearing a churchman's robes but rather the simple garb of an Arethousan peasant. He had looked different, somehow; harder and keener and even, strange to say, more like a man who might want to be kissed, not a celibate churchman.

Yet he had loved once, and passionately. Like Liath, he had leaped and never regretted.

The rank perfume of the camphor faded, but air within the enclosed tent seemed to rush in a whirlpool around her as though stirred by daimone's wings. Why was Brother Breschius working as a servant in the camp of his enemy's army?

The wasp sting burned in her heart.

3

SANGLANT'S army bedded down in and around yet another deserted village. The signs of abandonment did not tell a clear tale: had all the inhabitants died? Had they only fled, hearing the approach of an unknown army? Or had they fled days ago in the wake of the storm? Had some other force driven them away or taken them prisoner?

In these distant marchland borderlands, empty wilderness stretched wide, and villages were without exception bounded by log palisades, which protected mostly against wild beasts both animal and human since a true army would make short work of such meager fortifications. This one had not burned, but the gates sat wide and the vanguard had marched in without seeing any living creature except for a pair of crows that fluttered away into the trees, cawing.

"I miss birdsong," Liath said. "Even in winter, there should be some about."

Sanglant was out on his evening round of the army. Hathui had gone with him, leaving her with a trio of Eagles who regarded her with wary interest. She did not feel easy with Sanglant's noble brethren and preferred the company of the messengers.

"Hanna spoke of you," said the redheaded one called Rufus.

"Hanna! When did you last speak with Hanna?"

"Months ago. More than that, perhaps. A year, or more. She came south with a message from Princess Theophanu. Hathui says that she and Hanna met on the road, in Avaria or Wayland—I'm not sure which—and that Hanna knew the truth of what had happened to the king but she never confided in me or anyone."

"Why not?"

"She was watchful. That's all I know. I liked her."

Liath propped her chin on a cupped fist and frowned at the Eagle. He was a likable, even-tempered young man who reminded her vaguely of Ivar but perhaps only because of his red hair. They looked nothing alike, and he did not have Ivar's inconvenient and ill-timed passions.

She sighed. Heart's Rest seemed impossibly distant. That interlude with Hanna and Ivar, innocent friends, could never have happened in a world as blighted as this one. How blind she had been in those days! Hanna's friendship was true enough, but Hanna had been struggling with her own obstacles, which Liath had blithely ignored. Ivar had never been her friend; she had pretended otherwise because his infatuation with her had made her uncomfortable.

Because he had seemed so callow, compared to Hugh. As much as she had hated Hugh, she had never truly stopped comparing Ivar to him, and found Ivar always wanting although he was honest and true.

"Hanna is my friend," she said at last, seeing that the others— Rufus, dark-haired Nan, and an older man all the other Eagles called Hasty because of his deliberate way of doing things but whose name was Radamir—watched her. "I wish we had news of her."

"I don't know if she survived the earthquake," said Rufus. "That one that collapsed St. Mark's. I heard a rumor that she and some of the king's schola crept away during the tumult. I was gone by then. She had been placed in Presbyter Hugh's retinue, but Duchess Liutgard was unhappy about it. He never allowed Hanna to make her full report to the king—that is, the emperor."

She questioned him further, but he hadn't much more to relate although it all emerged in greatest detail, since Eagles honed their ability to memorize and recollect.

"I pray she still lives," Rufus finished. "She is a good woman."

"If any can survive this, Hanna can."

Behind, a commotion signaled the approach of Sanglant and his entourage: the tread of footsteps, the babble of conversation, a chuckle, a muttered wager. It never let up. Tonight he spoke with his cousin, Liutgard, whom he seemed to trust, while that bastard

Wichman trailed behind making crude jokes to the Ungrian captain, Istvan, who bore his witticisms stolidly. A bevy of nobles swarmed around; a steward waited at his right hand; soldiers loitered beyond the firelight, never straying far.

He stood straight and held the centermost place among his retinue, with that astonishing ability to know where each of his attendants were without skipping from place to place like an anxious dog seeking a pat on the head. But she could see in his face and bearing that the journey and the obligations thrust upon him were exhausting him. He was strong, but even the strongest must rest.

Soldiers had already pitched the journeying tent in which they slept. Thank the Lord and Lady that it was too small to admit more than two people.

She caught Captain Fulk's attention, and he nodded at her and chivvied the king toward his pallet, separating him smoothly away from the others. Liath wasn't sure if Fulk liked her, or even respected her, but on this account, at least, they understood one another.

She took her leave of the Eagles and, as Sanglant's attendants made ready to sleep, dispersed to their own encampments, or settled in for guard duty, she crawled into the tent and pulled off her boots.

"You must come with me when I tour the army," he said impatiently. "You must be seen at my side, as my consort. As co-regnant."

"I pray you, give me time. I am not yet accustomed to it."

She doubted she would ever become accustomed to it. She needed peace, and silence, and the company of books, but she dared not tell him that, not now. Not yet.

He seemed about to say something, but did not, and stripped off the rest of his clothing instead. In general, unless attack was imminent, he preferred to sleep naked, and he was warm enough to protect her against the cold, which always debilitated her.

"I will never get used to cold," she said as she pulled off her shift and, shivering, pressed herself against him skin to skin while pulling furs and cloaks over them.

"Yet you burn!" he whispered, kissing her.

"Umm," she said.

But after a moment he lay back, and she rested her head on his shoulder and waited. She was getting to know him. At moments like this, he had something in his mind troubling him that he would at length spit out.

"Are you still angry with me?" he asked. "For forbidding you from going after Blessing?"

Guilt, like a hungry dog, will stare and stare. She had lived with its presence all day until it had become a dead weight in her stomach. His breathing was steady. Hers was not.

"Oh, love, had I insisted on going, I would have gone, and you could not have stopped me."

He caught in his breath as if slapped, but said nothing; then let it out again, and still said nothing.

She went on, because his silence hurt too much. "I abandoned her. In Verna, first, even though it wasn't my choice to leave. For the second time out on the steppes, when we left her behind knowing she was close to death. And now, this time, for the third. So many voices chase through my head. What use is such a long journey when there are others who can make it for me? Who are better able to endure the trek. Who can serve in this way, as I can serve in others."

He still made no answer except to stroke her arm, shoulder to elbow, shoulder to elbow, his way of pacing when he was lying down.

"I do not even know Blessing. I may never know her. That is the choice I face. That is the choice I made."

"I could have gone," he said angrily, hoarsely, but his voice always sounded like that. "Yet she is one child. Wendar and Varre and all who live there—all who survived the cataclysm—may fall into chaos. Without the order imposed by the regnancy, there will be war between nobles, between duchies and counties. That is the choice I made. It is the obligation I accepted, although I never sought it. How is your choice different?"

"I am not Henry's heir. I am not even Taillefer's great grandchild. I am the daughter of a minor noble house, nothing more."

"That strangely makes me think of Hugh of Austra, who would not have cared one whit for the daughter of a minor noble house, if that is all you were."

"Ah! That was a cruel blow."

"So it was intended to be. I grieve for Blessing. No one does more than I do. I admit I didn't always like my sweet girl, but I always loved her. *Love* her. If she is dead, Liath, if she already died, then we made the right choice."

"I saw her."

"You are blind in your Eagle's Sight. What was this vision, then? True, or false?"

"I believe it was true. I saw Blessing. I saw Li'at'dano. I think I saw Wolfhere. I saw a vision of you, when you took in the Wendish refugees who had fled Darre. Henry's schola, most of them."

"That's right," he admitted. "It might well have been a true vision."

"Or it might have been a dream. I might only have wanted to see her so badly. . . . It seemed so real. I saw her arguing with a youth, a young man—"

"Thiemo? Matto?"

"I never saw him before."

"Might it have been the past you saw?"

"Nay—she was the age she was when we left her." But not yet as old as in that terrible vision when she had seen Blessing held prisoner by Hugh. "It was the present, or the future. I'm sure of it. It means she lives."

"If that is so, and if Gyasi brings her back to us safe and alive, then we made the right choice."

"What if she dies because one of us did not go to her?"

"Then we will be responsible. How else can we judge? What else can we do? Each day I must choose, and some may die, and some live, because of decisions I make."

"Ah, God. It is no good task. So many are already dead."

"And yet more would be dead, if you had not confronted Anne and killed her. You know it is true."

"It is true," she said reluctantly, "but I feel no triumph in victory."

"That is because we gained no victory. All we managed was no defeat."

"I met a party of farmers in Aosta. After the griffins rescued me from Zuangua. These farmers had lost their homes to the windstorm. Passing troops had stolen what remained of their stores. No doubt it seemed fitting to that lord and his army to do so, for he must supply his own in order to fight."

"So he must, but he will not eat the next year if all those who farm for him die of starvation."

One of the knots plaguing her stomach relaxed. "I suppose that is only one tiny injustice among so many great ones. Yet it makes me think of words Hathui once said: 'The Lord and Lady love us all equally in Their hearts.' "

"That being so," he murmured in reply, "why did God make Wichman the son of a duchess and Fulk, who is in every way his superior as a man, the son of a minor steward without rank or standing except that which I give him? Why did I live when all my faithful Dragons died?"

"The church mothers have an answer to all these questions, else we would fall endlessly into the Pit for wondering."

"What is their answer?"

"I can quote chapter and verse, but in the end, their answers are all the same: Humankind cannot know the mind of God."

"As dogs cannot know the mind of their master, although they strive to be obedient?"

She laughed.

"I must acquire a pack of loyal hounds, who will sit at my feet and growl at the faithless and remind me of how untrustworthy courtiers can be. Poor things."

"The dogs, or the courtiers?"

"Do you remember my Eika dogs? What awful creatures they were, not dogs at all, truly. Yet I miss them in one way. I never had to guess their intentions. I could always trust them to go for my throat if they thought I was weakening."

She hesitated, and he felt the tension in her and turned to kiss her cheek. "Say it. Do not fear me, so that you think you must hold your tongue."

"Very well, then. Must you be king? With the dogs always circling around?"

"I must," he said, taking no offense at her question. "Alas that my father is dead. I wish it were otherwise."

"He has other children."

"They are not fit. Sapientia you know. Theophanu is capable, but she is too reserved and hasn't gained the love and support of those she would need to lead. Ekkehard is too light-minded. Henry's children by Adelheid are too young, and anyway they will receive little support in the north if Adelheid were to claim the Wendish throne for them. They may hope to inherit Aosta if they have survived the storm. Nay, let it be. Henry wished for this for many years. Now it has come to pass. I am his obedient son."

But because she lay so close against him, she felt his tears.

4

SOON the Arethousan army, in retreat, began to meet refugees on the road. As Hanna tramped along behind the wagon to which her new guards had tied her, she studied the folk huddled at the side of the track. Like most Arethousans, they were swarthy and short, with broad faces and handsome, dark eyes. The women displayed a voluptuous beauty that fear and poverty could not yet disguise. They carried bundles on their backs and sniveling children in their arms. Some pushed handcarts piled with belongings. Now and again she would see a man holding the halter of a donkey. More often a family had two or three scrawny goats tied together on a single lead. Once she saw a bloated corpse, but it wasn't obvious how the man had died.

They stood silently as the army passed. After a time she began to think they were like the mosaics seen in churches in Darre, figures with kohl-lined eyes and magnificent robes frozen forever against a backdrop of open woodland. Only once did she hear one speak.

"I pray you, I'll do anything for a piece of bread for me and my child." A skinny young woman clutched a slack-eyed, emaciated child to her hip as she twitched her rump awkwardly to attract the notice of the soldiers.

Bysantius strode forward before any man could step out of line. He slashed at her face with the quirt. She cried out and retreated up the slope through dry grass that crackled around her. A man emerged out of the woods from behind a stand of prickly juniper. He was tugging up the drawers under his tunic as he sauntered back to join the rest, but before he'd gone three steps a woman appeared.

"You never gave me what you promised!" she shouted.

He didn't even look back. "I took what you offered, whore!"

Men sniggered, but glanced nervously toward their sergeant.

Bysantius stuck his quirt into his belt and drew his knife before the soldier could step down onto the path. "Pay her what you promised."

The soldier—he was young and cocky—pulled up short, eyeing the knife. "I've nothing to pay her. I eat what the rest of us do, when it's handed out at night. I've no coin, as you ought to know, Sergeant. I'm to be paid with land."

"Then you're a thief."

The column staggered to a halt as soldiers poked and pulled at each other, turning to see the confrontation.

"Thieves are punished with death, by the lord general's order. Any man who takes without permission is a thief."

"Here, here," said the man, extracting a crust of bread from his sleeve, "no harm done." He turned, tossed the bread at the woman, and hurried back into line, his face red and the rest hooting at him. The woman scrabbled in the dirt and, scooping up the crust, ran away into the woods.

"Get on!" Bysantius added a few curses, sheathed his knife, and strode up the line brandishing his quirt.

Hanna, too, had stashed away a bit of her last night's meal, nothing more than a bit of dry cheese, the last cut off a round. She fished it out of her sleeve and hissed.

"Tss! Here, you!" The young woman with the child had been weeping, huddled on the hill. Hanna tossed the cheese at her, but the wagon jerked forward and she stumbled to her knees and then scrambled to get up before she was dragged, and by the time she got herself stable again, she had lost sight of mother and child.

She was, therefore, doubly hungry that night, but as she ate the thin gruel out of the pot she couldn't regret what she had done.

"Mind you," said Sergeant Bysantius, coming over to crouch beside her, "the infant will die a day later rather than sooner. You're just prolonging her misery."

"Perhaps not. You can't know what will happen. Why are all these refugees on the road?"

He scratched his neck. It was a mark of the general's respect for the sergeant that he had been given command of the rear guard, but the dry and dusty conditions, the constant kick of dust all day long, had caused his skin to rash. "Nothing good, I'm thinking," he said. "Nothing good."

Years ago she, Liath, Hathui, Manfred, and Wolfhere had ridden east into the rising sun, traveling toward Gent. On that ride she had seen streams of refugees fleeing the Eika invasion. They had come on carts and on foot, leading donkeys or carrying crates that confined squawking chickens. They had hauled children and chests and sacks of withered turnips or baskets filled with rye and barley. The road, damp with rain, had churned to mud under the crush of so much traffic. Yet, despite their desperation, those Wendish refugees had not had the despairing, hopeless look of Arethousa's wretched, fled from what every man and woman in the army referred to always and only as "the city."

For days, stories passed up and down the line, but in the end even these rumors and purported eyewitness accounts could not prepare them for their first sight of "the splendid daughter of the sea," the great capital city of the empire of Arethousa. Chained to the wagon, Hanna could not see as the vanguard of the army reached a distant rise. The entire unwieldy column staggered to a halt as the men in the front seized up and the ones behind pushed forward to clamor for news.

That news swept through them like wind. She leaned against the wagon's tailgate with eyes closed and let the rush pour over her. It was so good to rest.

". . . only the walls survived . . ."

"You're a fool to believe it. Have you seen?"

"Nay, but it's what they're all saying!"

"So did the refugees, poor cattle. Doesn't mean they're right. A giant wave! Tssh! Let's go—"

"Stay in line!" The sergeant's quirt struck, variously, wagons, flesh, and the dirt. "Stay in line! Don't break ranks!"

She opened her eyes. The soldiers leaned forward like hounds straining at their leashes, quivering, anxious, eager to race forward. But they held their ranks. A rider in the red tabard that marked the imperial scouts galloped back along the line of march and pulled up beside Bysantius.

"General Lord Alexandros desires your attendance at a council," said the man. "I'm to command the rear guard in your absence. He says to bring the Eagle."

The rider looked around, seeking her, but because days of dust had veiled her pale hair, he didn't mark her. He dismounted instead and handed the reins to Bysantius, who smiled grimly and shouted at the guards to unlock Hanna's leg irons.

Her new guards were called Big Niko and Little Niko by the other soldiers, although the two were the same height. They were phlegmatic fellows who made up in attention to detail what they lacked in conversation and wit. They untied her from the rope that tethered her to the wagon, then unshackled her ankles. It felt strange to walk without the chafing on her legs, without the weight, without the cubit's length of restriction clipping her stride. Bysantius swung onto the horse, then extended a hand to help her up behind him.

She disliked his closeness. He stank, but no doubt she did as well. Given the conditions in which they had marched, anyone would reek. That he didn't smell worse was remarkable. He was, without question, a powerfully built man. She tried holding onto the cantle, but as they started forward her awkward seat behind the saddle forced her to cling to his belt. Her head, shoulders, and breasts pressed against his back. Mercifully, he said nothing about the intimate nature of their position. He had enough to do to press forward along the line with soldiers calling to him for news at every step. Here, so close to the city, the way was broad, paved in the center with wide, dusty lanes to either side for additional traffic. What remained of forest sat far back from the road and then only to the south. North was clear-cut, the sloping land studded here and there with clusters of sad hovels now overrun with refugees. Folk stood in doorways, watching mutely as the army passed. If they owned livestock, their animals were well hidden. She heard not even one chicken's squawk or a goat's complaining bawl. Uncounted fresh graves lay in ranks behind each village and along the roadside.

The road led up a long incline and at length they reached the height of the rise where Lady Eudokia and the general had halted with their close companions. All faces were turned toward the east. Besides the shifting of feet and the occasional protest of a horse held on too tight a rein, there was no sound except for a soughing whisper that might be the surf.

Bysantius let out his breath all in a hissed sound. He was rigid. His broad shoulders hid half the view, but by craning her neck to peer past his back she saw a wash of cloudy sky that blended into the glitter of a distant sea and, beyond it, the contours of another land lying away across the narrow strait. Off to her right, slopes ran down to a coastal plain and the sea, but the crowd to her left concealed the sight they all stared at.

"Sergeant Bysantius!" General Lord Alexandros' voice cracked the silence.

The sergeant started, shaken out of his stupor. He turned parallel to the shore, and she saw everything.

The land beyond was a jumble of muted colors, a formless wilderness without trees or houses. The general waited just where the road began to pitch and wind away down toward a peninsula jutting out into the winter-gray sea waters. The promontory had a rounded gleam, ringed by pale stone and paler spume where water rolled up against the shore. The rugged lines of its heights and valleys confused her, while at her back she heard groans and tears from the folk gathered on the road. Many fell to their knees and beat their hands on the ground.

"What catastrophe has overcome us?" said the general, his voice little more than a scrape.

The curtains that screened the exalted lady's litter from the sun and prying eyes had been thrown back so Lady Eudokia could see the full sweep of the scene. Her lips were pressed tight, but she did not weep. Beside her, her nephew picked at his nose as he whistled tunelessly under his breath, scuffing his feet, knocking his knees together, and otherwise behaving as though he wished they could get moving before he died of boredom.

"Only sorcery could encompass so much destruction," she said. "But see. The walls are intact."

"In a manner of speaking." He wiped tears from his face. "A man's heart is intact when his beautiful mistress sends back the bracelets and baubles he has given her and takes up with another man, but he is ruined nevertheless."

"Men are slaves to their desires, it is true. He is ruined, but he is not dead, and in time he will forget her. This is a bad analogy, Lord General. Think rather—we must rebuild, because the one who rebuilds will rule those who are grateful for the restoration of what was lost."

"Arethousa was not built in a day, exalted lady."

"No use waiting, then. We must inventory what remains, and what manner of workforce we have at our disposal, and what stores survive to feed our army and the people. If God is merciful, this winter will be mild."

"If God is merciful, there will be rain, and the sun will emerge from behind these damned clouds! How can you not weep?"

"Tell me my tears will build a palace, and I will weep. Let us build and plan our revenge, even if it is my nephew's children who must lead our armies into war. We must act quickly in case any of my cousin's partisans have escaped. We must take control of the city while there are none to resist us."

This time the general almost did break down, but with an iron will he controlled his body, his expression, his voice, and his entire being. "That is not a city. That is a ruin. Ai, God. My dear wife."

The words sparked connections in her mind. What had bewildered her came clear. The peninsula was covered not by rocky terrain and fallen stones but by a vast city so huge that she had not recognized it for what it was. Its walls ringed the shoreline. Double walls made a skirt across the headland. What splendor these ruins might once have possessed she could only guess at. They were too big to comprehend, and the extent of the destruction staggered her because it made no sense. She traced the distant lines that marked the ground but could not measure palaces, churches, houses, or stables in the jumble. From this distance she saw nothing she could recognize as rooftops, no spectacular domes, only stair steps of tumbled stone in heaps and mounds that she had at first mistaken for natural formations.

Surely this was an ancient ruin. Not even the gale wind could have destroyed so much and on such a scale. It was difficult to grasp, much less hold onto, their grief. It all seemed so remote, no more than an idea they had all long clung to.

"A wave drowned all, so we have been told," said Lady Eudokia. "How can any wave be large enough to overwhelm the city? It must have been some other thing, a spell perhaps, rising out of Jinna lands. Rising off the sea."

"Look there!" said Bysantius, pointing.

A gauzy mist was rising off the strait. Wisps of fog wafted up out of the ruins as the breeze blew in off the sea. Fog rose every place there was water. It seemed the ruins were awash, because the mist thickened, poured upward, and advanced inland toward their position as a wall of white like a towering wave off the sea. It swallowed the ground, the view, the sky.

"God save us," muttered Bysantius, but he held his position.

General Lord Alexandros drew his sword.

"Leave off," snapped Lady Eudokia. "Put me down, you fools. Bring me my chest. Let me see what I can do to dispel this unnatural mist."

No natural mist moved in such a manner. Hanna twisted to look behind her. Men backed away, making signs against evil. Her ears popped, and the few dogs remaining among the army began barking. As the fog advanced on a strong wind off the sea, the beasts tucked tails between legs and ran. Their fear, like a shower of arrows, struck throughout the ranks.

"Hold fast!" cried the general.

"Shit!" swore Bysantius.

"You clumsy fools!" swore Lady Eudokia, her voice cracking with anger as one of her eunuchs lost his grip on the chest and it spilled to the ground.

The fog swept in. Between one breath and the next they drowned. Not in water, but in a veil of concealment so thick that she could no longer see the general or the exalted lady. Even the head of Bysantius' horse swam in and out of view. A tinkling of bells teased her ears, then faded.

Once, years ago, in the custody of Bulkezu, she had seen an opening and bolted, but he had caught her, of course. Of course. Yet why be ruled by fear, as were those bawling and shouting around her?

She saw her chance.

She pushed back over the mare's rump, slid down, and landed as Bysantius called out sharply.

"The prisoner! The Eagle!"

She dared not run for the sea, not knowing what had destroyed the city and what might still lurk under the waves or on the far shore. She ran south instead, knocked into soldiers before she saw them, shook loose and kept going before they realized what hit them. She tripped once, three times, ten, but her bruised shins and aching elbows goaded her on. This time she would escape. This time it would be different even if she died in the wilderness or was hacked to death by angry Arethousan farmers.

That thought gave her pause enough to come panting to a halt, adrift in the fog with a sparse grove of trees around her, gnarled and low like the ubiquitous olives. She heard the clamor of the army behind her, surging as would the ocean in a storm as waves strike higher rocks and disintegrate into spray.

"Form ranks! Form ranks!" cried Sergeant Bysantius, his voice ringing out of the fog. Yet she sensed no body near to hers. That he sounded close was a trick of the weather.

Maybe it wasn't so wise to wander alone, chained, and foreign in a land so notoriously unforgiving to strangers. *Beware Arethousans*, so went the saying. They were treacherous and deceiving, liars and heretics. But they had fed her, and the sergeant and her guards had kept her safe from those who would have been happy to assault her. She stumbled forward until she lurched into a tree, and sagged there with leaves and twigs tracing the contours of her back as she tried to catch her breath. The damp air chilled her lungs. She heard a nagging chimelike sound, as though her ears were ringing. As though her mind and heart were overwhelmed and dazzled. The choice seemed impossible: give up her freedom and live, or run and die.

"Hanna!"

The voice startled her into action. Despite knowing it was the wiser course, she could not sit quietly and be recaptured. Not again. She bolted, and slammed right into a body, oversetting him.

"Ah! Ow! I pray you, don't run, Hanna. Come with me."

That the words were Wendish was all that stopped her from scrambling away into the fog.

"Quickly." He grasped her arm with surprising strength. She could barely see his face, yet sound carried well in the fog by some trick of the wind. A horn belled. Men shouted, and she heard Bysantius' voice raised above the rest.

". . . the Eagle. I'll cut off your cocks myself if she escapes. . . ."

"Come," said her rescuer. "We must hurry. This way."

"Brother Breschius? How can it be?"

"Run now, answers later. Quiet. Easier for them to hear us than see us."

He slipped his hand down her arm until he held her wrist, then set off briskly into the forest with her stumbling behind. She had so many questions she thought she might burst, but the speed of their retreat and the single-minded intensity of his silence as he wove his way through the fog-shrouded trees without ever smacking into one kept her silent. Behind, she heard shouting and curses, the thrash of men cutting through underbrush. A hazy flicker of light marked torches.

"They're following us!"

"Hush. Do not fear. Listen to what is in your heart. If you do, you'll see the way as well as I do."

What was in her heart right now was a yammering like that of dogs racing after a terrified rabbit. Yet beneath the fear she listened for the sound of her feet slapping the ground, echoed by Breschius' surer tread and the constant singing of delicate bells. She listened for the susurration of leaves as the wind blew the mist in from the distant shore. A man's shout rose out of the background whispers, but faded as the frater took a sudden right-hand shift in direction. She had lost track of where they were going, knew only that they still jogged through the sparse forest she had observed from the road as they had walked this day. It was prickly; every shrub and tree stabbed at her. Thorns scraped her face, but they were softened by the weight of the fog, whose passage was silent. Fog could not be heard, only seen and tasted and smelled. Its clammy touch made her hands and face grow stiff with cold. Her tongue tasted the brine of the waters. Ghostly faces loomed out of the fog but were swept away before they touched her. She fell into them. She saw with their eyes what they had seen:

The sea rises without warning and inundates the coastlands and the shining city and its impregnable walls. A wall of water rages through the strait, pouring through to reach the Heretic's Sea beyond, but in the city that wave washes all the way into the hills before dissipating and spilling back into the strait. As suddenly as the sea swelled, it now empties until long stretches of shoreline are left bare to the sky, revealing mud-slicked rocks and here and there the remains of boats and ships foundered close to land. Indeed, a brave man—or a foolhardy one—cries out that he can walk across to the far shore, and he sets out with walking staff and a bundle of cheese and bread slung over his shoulder. Of those who have not already drowned, and they are many because the first wave is not the deepest, some grab up what possessions and children they can easily lay hands on and hasten for the hills, but others forage through the flooded streets and down to the glistening shoreline, seeking treasure.

All those who had not fled drowned when the second wave came, and then the third. Only afterward did the disturbance subside.

All along the coastal plain, remnants of this flood tide pooled within the fallen ruins of the city and in hollows and declivities in the land. No sun dried them out, and the earth was so saturated by water that it could not drink all that had swamped it. It was from these waters that the fog was called. Its essence could almost be tasted. What had been left behind could be bound to the will of one trained in weather magic and condensed by means of the sorcery she had learned from her teacher into a fog that would bewilder her enemy, the ones who held her luck hostage. This tempestari had sent her slave into the heart of the camp and bound him with spells so no one would discover him. Now he followed the torch of her power back to the place where she and her companions waited.

On all sides the fog concealed the land, but where Breschius walked, he walked as on a skein of silk teased out of the fog, a silvery path that led around every obstacle and wove around the contours of the landscape in a labyrinth that would confuse their pursuers. Hanna saw it now as clearly as he did. She no longer stumbled. He let go of her wrist, and together they settled into a swift walk which tired them less than running but still moved them swiftly away from the army.

She no longer heard shouts and calls but once she heard a dog's booming bark; once she heard a horse neigh; once she heard a woman's sobs.

"How far—?"

He raised a hand, and she stopped speaking. A silver bracelet ornamented with tiny bells gleamed at his wrist.

They walked what she judged to be about the distance from her mother's inn to Count Harl's hunting cottage, where if she left at dawn bearing a round of cheese destined for the count's table she would get there soon after midday. He gave her a leather bottle filled with sour-tasting water. She drank whenever her throat got too dry. The fog held steady for a long while, but gradually it thinned until the landscape emerged around them, insubstantial at first but gaining weight and texture.

Up here in the hills, Arethousa was a drier land by far than Heart's Rest. Wendar boasted lush forests grown thick with undergrowth. The density of foliage washed a hundred hues of green across the hillsides. Arethousa, by contrast, was a land of gold and brown. Even the leaves had a dusty pallor and were often waxy or more like thorns than leaves. The ground layer crackled beneath her feet where she stepped on straggling vines and runners. The grass was brittle, and its chaff irritated her nose as she kicked it up with each step.

The tree cover was sparse. Often they crossed out from under what passed for shade and into a meadow of pale grass or spiny thornbush, where they caught such light as gleamed from the veiled heavens. Once, pausing, she pointed toward a lightening in the cloud cover.

"Do you think the sun is breaking through?" she asked.

"Hurry," he said. "We're losing the thread as the fog dissipates. Come, Hanna."

It seemed to her that the frater's vision was more subtle than hers. Although mist drifted within the trees and in patches across open ground, she had lost sight of the pulsing thread of light that led them. Still, she was free, she was unharmed, and although she was ravenous and light-headed, on the whole she felt content. It was an odd feeling, really, one she had rarely experienced in the last several years. She felt at ease and untroubled. At long last, it seemed, she was walking in the right direction.

He followed a defile down along stony ground, whistling the familiar melody to the psalm "Do not hide Your face from me in my time of trouble." An animal trail led through a grove of oak trees, the only oaks she had seen for many days. They emerged into a clearing protected by high rock walls and cooled by the splash of a slender waterfall pouring off a cliff face. A scrape sounded behind them, and she turned to see a sentry, unseen until now, slip away into the trees back along the track.

A campsite had been laid out around a pool worn into the rock below the falls. Lean-tos woven out of branches and reeds substituted for canvas tents. A fire burned under an overhang. There were two dozen or more horses confined by a fence made of thorny bushes, and a score or more people at work or rest in whatever shade they could find. She smelled meat roasting. The scent so overpowered her—she hadn't eaten meat for months, and nothing more than a portion of gruel for days—that she staggered as the pain of hunger bit into her stomach. Breschius steadied her. Folk looked up, their faces pale beneath a layer of grime.

"Hanna!"

They reached her before she registered their identity. She was hugged and only then did she meet the gaze of Brother Fortunatus over young Gerwita's dark head as the novice wept to see her. Fortunatus smiled as Gerwita let Hanna go and stepped aside for Sister Rosvita to come forward.

"Hanna!" The cleric embraced her. "God be praised. We feared that you were dead, but the witch told us that you yet lived."

"The Arethousans took me prisoner," she said, astonished to find herself crying. "Oh, it is good to see you, Sister Rosvita. Are all of you here?"

"All of us, by the grace of God. And one more—" She looked back over her shoulder to a woman sitting alone on a rock beside the pool, as might an outcast.

"That's Princess Sapientia!"

"So it is."

"Ai, God! What happened to her retinue?"

"We're not sure. She rarely speaks, but it appears that King Geza divorced her and abandoned her."

"Yes, yes, of course. I saw him speak the words just before the Arethousans took me."

"For your Eagle's Sight?" Rosvita released her while the others clustered around, saying little but smiling like fools.

"For my Eagle's Sight," replied Hanna bitterly. "Which has abandoned me rather like King Geza abandoned Princess Sapientia. How came you here? Who are these others?"

She scanned the vale. In the shadows to the east she saw now a peculiar wagon built into a tiny house. Even veiled by shadows its colors gleamed. It alone of every object she had glimpsed in the last ten or twelve days was not coated with a layer of ashy dust. Either it had been washed clean, or the dust could find no purchase there. Sorcery works in strange ways.

"It's Sorgatani!"

Her tongue was dry. Her vision blurred, and she swayed as the exhaustion brought on by their long walk combined with a flash of anxiety to make her knees weak and her hands damp. She had yearned to meet this mysterious stranger again and yet she feared to meet one who had laid such a frightening obligation on Hanna's head. What did it mean to be the luck of a Kerayit shaman? It seemed she was about to find out.

"As for the others," said Rosvita, "there in that wagon resides the pagan sorcerer we are not allowed to see. This troop of soldiers is led by Lady Bertha, who is Margrave Judith's second daughter. They accompanied Prince Sanglant's wife to the shores of the Middle Sea to combat the Holy Mother Anne. It seems they emerged from the crown into the midst of Anne's camp and were set upon. In the battle, Liath was separated from the others and lost. The rest escaped. They have wandered these lands since the cataclysm, seeking news of Liath, if she yet lives."

These words flowed past Hanna, who heard little and comprehended less as she stared at the wagon and its bright patterned walls, where lion and antelope and horse figures loped into an unseen but understood vista beyond the sight of mortal kind, known only to those who have walked between the worlds and mounted the pole of the world tree into the heavens. The utterance of Liath's name acted as a hook and yanked her back to herself, a fish floundering out of water.

"Liath was here? What happened to her?"

"That you must ask the one you call Sorgatani. Fewer than half of Lady Bertha's soldiers survived the battle. Come, you are wanted."

A powerfully built woman strode up. She carried herself with the arrogance of noble birth, a thing so unconscious that Hanna knew at once this soldierly-looking female must be Margrave Judith's daughter. There was little resemblance between her and her mother, and even less to her beautiful half brother.

"This is the Eagle?"

"I am Hanna, my lady. I serve the Emperor Henry."

"Emperor! Well, I hope his quest for Taillefer's crown has served him well, but I fear he has only served the plots and plans of those who ensorcelled him."

"I fear so, my lady."

She beckoned, and a pair of soldiers showed Hanna to the stump of a tree hollowed and marked by ax blows, where an armorer plied his trade mending armor. Lady Bertha followed them and watched with interest as Hanna laid her chain across the log and leaned away, grimacing, as the men took turns hammering at the links until one shattered.

"You can manage with that for now," said the lady. "Go on, then. Sorgatani is anxious to see you."

"Yes, my lady. How did you know how to find me?"

"Hanna," said Breschius.

She followed him. Rather than leading her first to the isolated wagon, he took her aside to the rim of the pool, where a naturally stepped rock ledge gave access to the water just out of sight of the main camp.

"You must wash first," he said. "You can't come into her presence so dirty as you are. I'll get clean clothing for you."

"Where will any of you have clean clothing?" She gestured toward the camp. "It looks as rustic as the hideout of bandits."

"Wash," he said, and left her there.

She stripped and carried her filthy tunic and leggings into the water with her. It was cold enough, God knew, and the water more bracing than the chilly air, but nevertheless with her teeth chattering and her eyes stinging she endured it and scrubbed her hair and scalp with her fingers and rubbed down her skin as well as she could, crying and laughing together because it hurt to get clean. The shackles on her wrists and ankles had rubbed her skin raw in spots, but after the first sharp pain, the ice of the water numbed her injuries.

Breschius returned with a square of folded cloth draped across his left forearm, held in place with his stump pressing it down from above. He chimed when he walked. It seemed he wore anklet bells as well as the belled bracelet. He placed the clothing on the rock and sat with his back to her at the top of the stair-step ledge. His hair, cut short, was clean, and his clothing had been washed and mended. Even his hand was not as dirty as those of the soldiers she had seen working and loitering in camp.

"Were you with Liath?" she asked.

"I was. Sorgatani, Lady Bertha, and Her Highness Lady Liathano came from the uttermost east, passing through two crowns until we came to the shore of the Middle Sea. There we met the forces of the skopos. Many of our people were slain, but we escaped because . . . because the lady called fire."

The tremor in his voice gave her a sick feeling in the pit of her stomach. When she said nothing, not sure what to say, he went on.

"Although we were pursued, Sorgatani used her weather magic to conceal us. So we escaped to these hills. Here we have remained."

"Where is Liath?"

"Dead, perhaps. Living, perhaps. We do not know."

She heaved herself up onto the lowest ledge, shaking and trembling. "Ai, God, I pray she is not dead."

"Sorgatani does not think so. She believes she lives still, although we do not know where she is."

"Is that why you stayed here? Seeking her?"

"No."

She found a ragged but clean scrap of linen on the top of the pile and rubbed off as much of the water as the cloth could absorb. Despite the chill in the air, it was still warmer out of the water than in it. He remained silent, back still turned, as she shook out a silk robe that barely reached her knees although it had perhaps been meant for a shorter, stouter woman. Certainly it was broad enough for her shoulders and hips. It was a rich red, embroidered with golden dragons grappling with golden phoenixes.

"This is no Wendish tunic!"

"These are the clothes that belonged to one of her servants."

"Her slaves? I will wear no slave's robes, however rich they may appear!"

"You are no slave, Hanna. You are Sorgatani's luck. These are the only spare clothes we have until yours dry and can be repaired."

"What of the woman who wears these?"

"She is dead."

"Then who serves Sorgatani? I know it is said—what you told me once—ai, God! It seems so long ago! You told me that a Kerayit shaman can be seen by no person except her blood kinfolk along her mother's lineage, her slaves, her luck, and her pura, who is also her slave. How came you by these garments?" She had found, now, a cloth belt and a heavier wool tunic to throw over the silk underrobe. Beneath them came baggy linen drawers dyed a soft purple. The soft leather boots had to be fastened by garters to the broad belt, which was studded with gold plates embossed with the heads of griffins.

"Both her slaves died in our flight, alas, as did all nine of the Kerayit guardsmen who fought so that she might not be captured. Without any to serve her, Sorgatani would have perished as well, because of the geas laid upon her kind."

"Then who serves her?"

As quickly as she asked the question, she knew the answer. He did not turn, or shift at all, but his shoulders tightened and the angle of his head altered subtly and dangerously.

"You became her pura?" she asked, as shocked as she could be.

He chuckled. "Certainly she is beautiful, but alas, she made no such tempting offer. I accepted the chains that make me her slave."

"Do you not serve God, Brother? How can you serve both God and an earthly master?"

"Is it not a worthy service to save the life of another, even if she is a heathen? So I do believe. If I did not serve her, she would have died. No one else in Lady Bertha's troop was willing to take on the duty. In any case, without Sorgatani's protection, we would have been discovered and killed long ago, and we would not gain a steady supply of meat to feed ourselves."

"Are you content, Brother?"

"I am resigned, Hanna. God command me to serve. I have discovered that I am often surprised by the unexpected nature of that service."

She could not interpret his tone, and found that she did not want to think too hard about what he might have sacrificed and what it might mean that she was about to meet a woman who had claimed a relationship to her that Hanna did not remotely understand. "What of Sister Rosvita and her companions? Did Sorgatani find them, too?"

"In a manner of speaking. Following your trail, we fell upon them hiding in the woods and so took them in."

"Following my trail? That of the Arethousan army?"

"No, although truly it was not difficult to follow the army's dust cloud as it marched. You are Sorgatani's luck. Brought so close to you, how could she fail to know where you were? Thus were you found, and rescued. Come, are you ready?"

She sighed as she clasped her belt and smoothed a hand over the bumps and ridges made by the embroidery. Such fine cloth would only be worn by the most noble of princes, in the west, and yet the Kerayit clothed their slaves in this finery. "Yes. As ready as I will ever be."

Her hair was tangled and she had no comb, but it was cleaner than it had been before. Her stomach growled, and she willed away a flash of dizziness as the wind shifted to spill the fat smell of meat past them.

"Leave your old clothing," he said. "I'll see that it is cared for."

"I thank you."

She was aware of the camp as a scene unfolding beyond her reach. When they reached the wagon, she mounted the steps and touched the latch tentatively.

"Go on," said Breschius gently. "Don't set your foot on the threshold."

She slid open the door and stepped over the threshold, ducking so as not to hit her head. The Kerayit were either much shorter than Wendish folk, or they disdained to waste space simply to accommodate height.

She stumbled as she entered the interior, assaulted by its disproportion. The inside was larger than it had any right to be. She felt dizzy, but the fit passed as she pushed the door closed behind her and straightened up into a spacious, circular chamber richly furnished and eerily quiet. It had a round, felt roof, although definitely the wagon had conveyed no such thing on the outside. A central pole pierced the smoke hole, and the heavens, seen through that hole, shone with a silvery sheen shot through with flashes of light that might be distant lightning or sparks from a nearby fire.

"What manner of place is this?"

"This is where I live, Hanna. Be welcome here."

Sorgatani stepped out from the shadows. She was as beautiful as Hanna remembered from her dreams, if features molded so differently from those known in Wendish lands could be called beautiful. Hanna thought they could. She had not forgotten Bulkezu.

Sorgatani's black hair was braided and pinned up against her head, and she wore as a crown a net of delicate golden chains that fell past her shoulders to brush her robe of golden silk. The simple beauty of that fabric put the gaudy embroidery of Hanna's tunic to shame, and she had a sudden uncomfortable insight that what had seemed a rich garment to her inexperienced gaze might not be one in truth when compared to the fineness of Sorgatani's garb.

Hanna advanced cautiously to the central pole. There Sorgatani met her and extended both hands, palms up and open. She did not touch her. She kept a hand's breadth of distance between them, air that felt alive to Hanna's skin, as if it had the same breath and soul that animated all living things.

"We are met after long apart," said the Kerayit woman. "My luck has been taken prisoner by others, but now I have reclaimed you."

"I am not your slave!"

Sorgatani withdrew her hands. "Did I say you were? I forget you do not know the customs of the Kerayit."

"Forgive me. I do not mean to offend. Yet I must ask—is it true you traveled with Liath? Is she alive? Where did you first meet her?"

"Far east, in the grasslands, we met. I accompanied her because it was thought my sorcery could assist her, but it proved not to be true." She sighed. "I liked her."

That sigh, her expression, the slump of her shoulders: all these touched Hanna in a way no other claim could have. Impulsively she grasped Sorgatani's hands in hers. The other woman's hands were callused and her grip, like Hanna's, was strong. "She is my friend, too. If yours as well, then we are sisters, are we not? In friendship, at least."

Sorgatani's dark eyes widened, and her mouth opened, but only a gasp came out.

Hanna released her. "I beg pardon."

"No. None is needed. It is just—I am not accustomed to being touched."

"So Brother Breschius told me." Compassion spilled like light. "It must be difficult, living so alone."

"It's true I am lonely, Hanna." She smiled shyly. "When are you going to bring me my pura?"

"Ai, God! I'm not sure I'm fit for such a duty! There is much I do not know. I am the King's Eagle, but your luck as well. I do not know what it means. A man cannot serve two masters."

"You do not serve me! You are my luck, that is all."

Hanna set a palm to her forehead. "I'm dizzy. Is there any place I may sit down?" She began to move to the broad couch to the left of the door, but Sorgatani steered her to a similar couch set on the right side of the door. "Women don't sit or sleep on that side. Here." She seated her on an embroidered cushion, then clapped her hands.

The door slid open and Breschius entered, carrying a tray in one hand which he balanced adroitly with his stump. It contained a fine porcelain cup steaming with an aromatic brew and a bowl of leek-and-venison stew. He placed the tray on the bed and retreated to the opposite side, where he knelt on a layer of rugs.

"Eat." Sorgatani busied herself opening and shutting drawers in a tall chest standing beside the couch. At her back rested a saddle set on a wooden tree, decorated with silver ornaments and draped with a fine bridle.

Hanna tried not to wolf down her food, knowing it better to eat slowly to spare her stomach the shock of rich food. The tea eased the cold, as did the cozy warmth in the chamber, which emanated from a brazier. As she ate, she studied the furnishings: an altar containing a golden cup, a mirror, a handbell, and a flask. The couch, more like a boxed-in bed, behind Breschius was covered by a felt blanket displaying bright animals: a golden phoenix, a silver griffin, a red deer. No familiar sights greeted her, as would have been the case in any Wendish hall or house she'd had reason to bide in when she rode her messages for King Henry. In the land of the Kerayit, she was a stranger.

"I saw you in dreams, sometimes," she said at last, not knowing how to speak to one whose language she ought not to know; not knowing how to interpret the many things she saw that were unfamiliar to her. "I looked for you through fire, but these many days I have not been able to see you, or anyone."

Sorgatani turned. It was apparent she had been waiting for Hanna to speak, thus showing she was finished eating.

"Your Eagle's Sight, do you mean?" Sorgatani looked over at Breschius. The net that covered her hair chimed in an echo of his anklets and bracelet. Her earrings swayed, a dozen tiny silver fish swarming on the tide of her movement. "Liath spoke of this gift. She taught me its rudiments."

"She taught you!"

"Is it meant to be hoarded only to your chieftain's messengers?"

"So I always understood."

"Yet who taught them? Have you ever asked yourself that? And why?"

"Why were we taught? So that we might see and speak across distances, and thus communicate with each other and with the regnant. In this way the regnant gains strength."

"For what purpose? Nay, do not answer that question. All chieftains wish to be strong so they can vanquish those who stand against them. Yet before I learned to see through fire, I learned about the nature of the heavens and the mysteries of the crowns. For all my life I have been able to perceive beyond the veil of the world the gateway which we here in the middle world see as a burning stone. In its flames those with sight can see across long distances, and some can even hear and speak words. The Holy One, whose knowledge is ancient and terrible, can glimpse past and future."

"So it was when we crossed through the crowns! I saw down many passageways!"

"Just so."

Breschius fetched the tray and went out.

When he was gone, Sorgatani sat down on the bed beside Hanna and leaned closer to her. She smelled of a heavy, attractive musk, stronger than lavender. "But hear me, Hanna. For all my life, the burning stone was like a beacon. Yet when the Ashioi returned, its light faded. I can barely touch it, or sense it, barely see it. It's as if I have gone blind."

"Blind?" Sorgatani's scent distracted Hanna badly. She found it hard to think.

"I think Eagles trained themselves to see through the many gateways of the burning stone, although they did not know what they were doing. It flared so brightly that many could see through its passages."

"Do you think it was destroyed in the wake of the cataclysm?"

Sorgatani shook her head. "The burning stone is not an artifact of the great weaving. In ancient days, so it is told, the Holy One had the power to see and speak through the gateway. That was before the great weaving was set on the looms. But only she had the power to call the gate into being, so it is told. The great weaving fed the power of the burning stone because Earth and heavens were joined by the thread of the Ashioi land, cast out into the aether. Now, that thread is severed."

"So we are blind. What do we do now?"

"That is what you and I must decide."

Hanna winced. "Do you really think Liath survived?" she asked, not wanting to trust to hope.

Sorgatani glanced toward the pura's bed. A blanket was folded on the chest at the foot of the bed, but no one slept there. "Liath was alive up to the moment of the cataclysm. She was captured by the one called Anne, whom we fought. We would all have been killed, but Lady Bertha—a fine warrior!—broke us out of that camp. Afterward, my brave Kerayit raided their camp under cover of a fog I had raised, but they found no trace of her. So we waited nearby, concealed by my arts, because I felt that she was not dead but only biding her time. So she was. When that night came, when the Crown of Stars crowned the heavens, she brought to life rivers of molten fire out of the deep earth. We fled, because otherwise we would have died as did all of Anne's tribe. Every one of them. If Liath survived the deluge of fire, I do not know."

For a long time Hanna was silenced by the force of Sorgatani's tale. At last, she spoke.

"Why did you stay here in this country?"

"I stayed to find you, Hanna. I waited at my teacher's side long enough while you suffered under the Quman beast's whip. I would not allow it to happen again. I knew you were alive. When we found the holy women and their companions, we marked the trail of those who had taken you. So, here we are. What do we do now?"

Hanna let it go, at last, and sagged forward. Sorgatani caught her, and she lay her head against the Kerayit woman's silk-clad shoulder and rested there most comfortably. "I want to go home," she whispered. "But what will you do now?"

"I will go where my luck leads me, of course." She whistled sharply, a sound that made Hanna cover her right ear, which was nearest to Sorgatani's lips.

The door slid open. Breschius appeared, his figure limned by the fading light behind him.

"Let Lady Bertha know that tomorrow we turn our path north. We will cross the mountains and travel west to Wendar."

He vanished as he closed the door.

After a pause, Sorgatani asked: "What will we find in Wendar? What manner of place is it?"

"It will be as strange to you as this wagon is to me," she said, half laughing, half crying, and completely exhausted, too tired, indeed, to stand and seek out a place to rest. "As for what we will find there, I don't know. I think the world has changed utterly. I have seen such destruction that at first it made no sense to me. A vast city flattened as with a giant's hand. Refugees on the roads, many of them starving. Clouds of dust everywhere. How much worse may it be elsewhere? What if there is worse yet to come? I must seek out the regnant of Wendar, whoever that is now, and give my report. That I must do first. Afterward—"

"Afterward" was too vast a landscape to survey.

VIII
THE PHOENIX

1

THE estate Ivar and Erkanwulf rode into looked very different from Ivar's father's manor and compound. It had no significant palisade, only a set of corrals to keep livestock in and predators from the forest out, and there was a wooden tower set on a hillock just off the road to serve as a refuge in times of trouble. An enclosure surrounded a score of fruit trees. Several withered gardens lay in winter's sleep, protected by fences to keep out rabbits and other vermin. Four boys came running from the distant trees, each one holding a crude bow. Dogs barked. A barefoot child seated in the branches of one of the fruit trees stared at them but said no word. A trio of men loitering beside an empty byre greeted them with nods.

In Heart's Rest the village had grown up around a commons, and in addition lay a morning's walk from Count Harl's isolated manor. Here, in Varre, houses straggled along the road like disorderly soldiers. Fields stretched out in stripes behind them until they were overtaken by woods. A tiny church had been built where the path they rode crossed with a broad wagon track. The house of worship was ringed by a cemetery, itself disturbed by a dozen recently dug graves. Wattle-and-daub huts with roofs low to the ground lay scattered hither and yon, but Erkanwulf led them to the grandest house in the village, a two-storied stone house standing under the shadow of the three-storied wooden tower.

"Who lives here?" Ivar asked, admiring this massive stone structure and the single story addition built out behind it. There were also three sheds and a dozen leafless fruit trees.

"My mother."

Before they reached the stone house, the church bell rang twice. Ivar looked back to see that two of the men who had greeted them beside the byre had vanished.

"She's chatelaine for the steward here, my lord," Erkanwulf added. "It was the steward who asked Captain Ulric to take me into the militia. They're cousins twice removed on their mother's side."

It was cold, and even though it was near midday, the light had the faded glamour of late afternoon. They hadn't seen the sun for weeks, not since many days before the night of the great storm and their rescue by the villagers who lived deep within the Bretwald.

A woman came out of the farthest shed. Her hair was covered by a blue scarf and her hands were full of uncombed wool. "Erkanwulf!" She turned and fled back into the shed. As though her cry had woken the village, a stream of folk emerged from every hovel and out of sheds and fields to converge on the stone house.

It was a prosperous village. Ivar held his mount on a tight rein, preferring not to dismount in case there was trouble. He counted fully twoscore folk ranging in age from toddling babies to one old crone who supported her hobbling steps on a walking stick. There were older men, and lads, but no young men at all, not one.

Erkanwulf dismounted and tied his horse to a post before running down the path and into the arms of a fair-haired girl of perhaps sixteen or seventeen years of age. He grabbed her, spun her around, and kissed her on the cheek. Hand in hand they walked swiftly back to the stone house. His mother came out of the shed with her hands empty and a grim look in her eyes.

"Who is this?" cried the girl, breaking free of Erkanwulf's grip and walking boldly right up to Ivar's horse. She had no fear of the animal. She rummaged in the pocket tied to her dress and pulled out a wizened apple, which was delicately accepted by the beast.

"Too high for the likes of you," said Erkanwulf with a snort. "Unless you're wanting a noble bastard to bring to your wedding bed."

"You!" said the girl with a roll of her eyes. She grinned at Ivar. She was plump, healthy, very attractive, and well aware of her charms.

"And a monk besides," Erkanwulf added.

"As if that ever stopped a man!" She laughed. She had lovely blue eyes, deep enough to drown in, as the poets would say, and she fixed that gaze on Ivar so hard that he blushed.

"Hush, you, Daughter," said Erkanwulf's mother. "Don't embarrass me before this holy man. I beg your pardon, Your Excellency."

"No offense taken," Ivar said awkwardly.

The mother swung her gaze from the one to the other. It was difficult to say who blanched more, the sister or the brother. "What are you doing here, Erkanwulf? There came the lady's riders looking for you last autumn. We had a good deal of trouble because of your disobedience. Best you have a good reason for bringing her wrath down on us."

"What trouble?" He looked around the circle of villagers gathered and saw that their mood was sour, not welcoming.

When she did not answer, he said, "We can trust this man. I swear to you on my father's grave."

She held up a hand and folded down one digit for each offense. "Steward was taken back to Autun with both her son and daughter, as hostage for our good behavior. Bruno and Fritho were whipped for protesting. Your brother and four cousins took to the woods and hide there still, like common bandits, because the lady's riders said they'd hold them as hostage against your return. Goodwife Margaret's two grandsons were led off God know where, although they said they meant to make them grooms in the lady's stables." The crone bobbed her head vigorously. "How is Margaret to plow her fields now? You best make a good accounting for yourself, Son, for as bad as all that is," and now she folded in her thumb, and shook a fist at him, "we lost also our entire store of salted venison meant to husband us through to spring. They took it as tax, a fine levied against your desertion. New year is coming. Our stores grow thin. Much of what remains is rotting. What with this cold weather, too much rain all winter, and no sun for these many weeks, I fear more trouble to come. What do you say?"

"He came at my order," said Ivar, "and in the service of Biscop Constance."

Folk murmured. Some drew the circle at their breast while others made the sign to avert the evil eye.

"She's dead, may God have mercy on her," said Erkanwulf's mother.

"She's not dead but living in a monastery they call Queen's Grave."

"That's what they said. That she was interred in Queen's Grave."

"It's a place, not a graveyard," he said patiently, seeing that the villagers had lost a bit of the suspicion that closed their features. "It's a convent. She's alive. Lady Sabella deposed her, although she had no legal right to do so since Biscop Constance was given her place as both biscop and duke by the regnant himself."

"King Henry is Wendish," said one of the men who had greeted them so suspiciously by the byre. "As is the biscop. At least Lady Sabella is daughter of the old Varren royal family on her mother's side."

"She's a heretic," said Erkanwulf's mother. "Our deacon was taken away because she wouldn't profess."

"Was she? Has the truth come so far as out here to this place?" demanded Ivar.

"He's a heretic, too," observed Erkanwulf dryly, indicating Ivar.

"Hush, you," said his mother before turning her attention back to Ivar. "It's true enough, Your Excellency. The lady came riding by on her progress one fine day last spring."

"It was summer," interrupted Erkanwulf's sister. "I recall it because the borage was blooming and it was the same color as his eyes."

"Tssh! Hush, girl! We heard enough about all that back then. I beg pardon, Your Excellency. My children will rattle on. The lady prayed with us, and said if we professed the Redemption she'd send us salt and spices in the autumn. But none came. Because of your disobedience, Erkanwulf!"

"Still," said her daughter, with a dreamy smile, "I liked listening to what the lady's cleric had to say."

"Because of his blue eyes!" said the old crone with a wheezy laugh. "Ah, to be young!"

"I am surrounded by fools!" cried the chatelaine, but even her expression softened as she allowed herself a moment's recollection. "Yet it's true he was the handsomest man I've ever seen. More like an angel than a man, truly. And so soft-spoken, with a sorrow in his heart. Why, his good counsel softened even old Marius' heart and he patched up his ancient quarrel with his cousin William that they'd been nursing for twenty years."

"That was a miracle!" observed the crone wryly. "And he *was* handsome! Whsst!"

"You're the fools!" cried Erkanwulf, for whom this recital had become, evidently and all at once, too much to bear. "There can only be one young lord fitting *that* description, and he's no cleric. He's the lady's kept man, her concubine. She beds him every night, and parades him during the day like a holy saint wanting only a shower of light to transport him up to the Chamber of Light!"

"You're just jealous because Nan wouldn't roll you!" retorted his angry sister.

"At least she doesn't bed every man who comes asking!"

Everyone began talking at once, as many laughing as scolding, but his mother walked right over to him and slapped him. "You'll speak no such disrespectful words, young pup! Nor have you explained yourself yet! Steward put herself out for you because she liked you and thought well of you. Now look where it's gotten her! Speak up! The rest of you shut your mouths and listen!"

No captain could have controlled his unruly band of soldiers more efficiently. They quieted, coughed, crossed arms, shushed children, scuffed feet in the dirt, and waited for Erkanwulf to start.

Ivar forestalled him by raising a hand. "I'll speak."

"Begging your pardon," said the chatelaine hastily, as he'd known she would. He was a churchman, but in addition he sat mounted on a fine horse, and carried a sword.

"I escaped from Queen's Grave with the aid of Erkanwulf, here, and his captain."

"Hush!" muttered Erkanwulf. "I won't have him getting in trouble."

"He'll be in trouble soon enough," said Ivar

"What trouble?" demanded the chatelaine. "Are you speaking of Captain Ulric? He's a good man, local to these parts. I want you to make no trouble for him."

"You'll make no trouble for him if you'll bide quietly once we've left and say no word of our passing. We rode to Princess Theophanu—"

"That's one of the Wendish royals," said one of the old fellows wisely, and gained a clout on the backside from the crone.

"Hush, you! Let the brother speak!"

"Do you live better under the rule of Lady Sabella than you did under Biscop Constance?" he asked them.

One by one they frowned and considered until the chatelaine said, grudgingly, "Biscop Constance ruled fairly. If she promised a thing, then it was delivered. The lady's companions take what they wish when they want and tax us according to how the fit takes them."

"Who rules in Wendar and Varre?" he asked.

"Sabella's daughter rules in Varre," they agreed, "together with her husband, the Wayland duke, the one with burned skin. Conrad the Black."

"You'd accept the rule of Lady Tallia over that of the rightful regnant, King Henry?"

"What kind of kinship does Henry hold to us? It's his elder sister Sabella who is born out of the Varren royal house. Not Henry. He was born to a Wendish mother, nothing to do with us. He never came here anyway. Once or twice to Autun. That's all. It's nothing to do with us."

"I don't like that heresy," said the chatelaine.

Several others murmured agreement.

"The story of the Redemption sounded fair enough to me," said Erkanwulf's sister, then flushed. "And not just because of that cleric."

"This one is a heretic, too, so 'Wulf says," replied the crone. "So what's to choose between them? Is all the royals heretics now?"

"No, not all of them," said Ivar reluctantly, seeing by their expressions that he could not win this battle using his careful arguments. They were not Wendish. He was. In a way, he had already lost.

"I'd stand up for Duke Conrad," said the old man. "He's of good blood even with that foreign creature that gave birth to him, but the old duke, Conrad the Elder, was his father. Nay, I say enough with the Wendish. Let them plough their own fields and leave ours to us who are born out of Varren soil."

"So be it," said Ivar. "Come, Erkanwulf. We'd best ride now, while we've still light." He turned his attention to the chatelaine, who made no gesture to encourage them to stay. "I pray you, give us a loaf and cheese. If all goes well, and you aid us by keeping silence, we'll rid you of the Wendish now biding on Varren earth."

"What did you mean, back there?" Erkanwulf demanded as they rode out not long after. He was surly, having argued again with his sister and gotten only a perfunctory kiss from his mother. " 'Rid Varren soil of those from Wendar.' I thought we meant to aid Biscop Constance! I can't help that those fools back there don't see her for what she is—a finer steward by far than Lady Sabella!"

"No use arguing with them. They can't help us anyway. In truth, if many of you Varrens feel the same way, then we must act quickly.

I thought there might be many who hated Lady Sabella's rule. Those villagers by Queen's Grave were willing enough to help us."

"They have to feed and house the guards. At least two girls from that village was abused by the guards, if the story I heard is true. The folk there have no reason to love Lady Sabella. But as for others—what is one regnant to them, compared to another? They pay tithes either way, and live at the mercy of the weather and bandits and wolves and what measure of taxes the stewards take on behalf of the nobles each year."

"Surely they must have seen that Biscop Constance was a fair ruler?"

Erkanwulf shrugged. "How many winters did she rule in Autun? The local folk know only that some Wendish noble was set in place by the Wendish king. We Varrens have no reason to love the Wendish, my lord. That's an old grudge, for sure."

"Yet you and your captain and his men were willing to aid Biscop Constance in getting a messenger out."

"We took her measure, my lord, when we served her in Autun. We know her for what she is. But there's war in Salia now. Our borders are at risk. Captain Ulric may no longer be barracked in Autun. He may have been sent southwest to fight. Or he may refuse to help us now. Maybe he's done as much as he's willing to do to aid Biscop Constance. I don't know. Duke Conrad is fair to soldiers. He's a good man to fight for."

"Surely you know Captain Ulric well enough to know what's in his mind! He sent you to aid me, after all."

"We've been gone for months. Things have changed."

They rode in silence for a while along the path that cut through woods. Ash and sycamore swayed softly among oak and beech and hornbeam. It was cloudy, as always these days, and cold and dry. The rains of last autumn had evidently poured all their moisture into the earth in the space of a month or so of incessant rain. Over the winter there had been little snow, although the clouds never lifted, and in time the roads had dried enough for Ivar and Erkanwulf to set off again from their refuge in the Bretwald.

"I didn't like leaving," said Erkanwulf after a while.

"What? Your village? They didn't treat you very nicely."

"Nay, not them. You see why I left! No, I liked that steading in the Bretwald. They were good, decent, kind people. That's the kind of place I'd like to settle down, not that I'm likely to."

"What do you mean? Settle in Bretwald?"

Erkanwulf was about the same age as Ivar, not as tall, and lanky in the way of a young man who never quite got enough food as he could eat growing up. He was tough—Ivar knew that—but he shrugged like a man defeated. "If I leave Captain Ulric's company, I'll have to go back to my village and let my mother make a marriage for me. Who else would have me? I'd be an outlaw if I left the place I'm bound to by birth."

"They took in strangers in the Bretwald."

"That's true. Refugees from Gent. I liked it there, with no lord holding a sword over their head and telling them what to do."

"Until bandits realize how wide that road is, and attack them who have no lord to defend them."

"They'd need more hands, then, wouldn't they? A man who had some experience fighting would be of use to them." Erkanwulf brooded as they moved through the woods. No birds sang. Except for the murmuring wind and the soft fall of their horses' hooves, there was no sound at all. The quiet made Ivar nervous. He hadn't felt quite right since that terrible night when wind and rain had battered them and killed Erkanwulf's horse. They had commandeered the old nag Erkanwulf rode from a village whose name Ivar had already forgotten. Those folk hadn't greeted them kindly, but they'd offered them shelter and given up the old mare in exchange for some of Princess Theophanu's coin. Those villagers didn't love the Wendish either, and with King Henry gone so long from his usual progress around the countryside, they saw no reason not to turn their hearts toward the old stories of Varren queens and kings who had once ruled these lands without any Wendish overlord telling them what to do.

A long time ago, so it seemed, he had been young and thoughtless. He smiled, thinking back on it. Perhaps not so long ago. But so much had happened. He had been thrown headlong into a world whose contours were more complicated than he had ever imagined as the neglected youngest child of the old count up in Heart's Rest.

"For all I know, my father is dead by now, and my brother Gero become count in his place."

Erkanwulf glanced at him, his expression unreadable. "What has that to do with us? My lord?"

"Nay, nothing. I just thought of it. I just thought how the world is changed, as you said yourself. Not just because of that storm or Biscop Constance's imprisonment, or any of those things, but because I left my father's estate and journeyed farther than I ever expected to go. I can't be that youth that I once was. When I think of how I was then . . . I don't know. It's just different now. We've chosen our path. We can't go back."

"Huh. True enough words."

"What do you think we'll find in Autun?" Ivar asked.

Erkanwulf only sighed. "I hope we find what we're looking for. Whatever that may be."

2

IT snowed the morning they crossed the river on the ferry and moved into a straggle of woodland near the southern gate of Autun. They stumbled over two corpses half hidden under branches and mostly decomposed. Skulls leered at them, so they moved on. In the ruins of an old cottage abandoned among the trees, they stabled the horses with fodder and water, tying their thread-worn blankets over the animals' backs. After that, they trudged overland to the city walls. No pristine stretches of fresh white snow blanketed the fields. It was all a muddy gray.

They passed several clusters of huts and cottages, shutters closed and doors shut against the cold. No one was about. Once they heard a goat's bleat; once a child's weary wailing dogged them before fading into the distance.

Erkanwulf led them first along the river and thence to a postern gate. They approached cautiously, hoods cast up over their faces. Ivar hung back as Erkanwulf strode forward to confront the two men hanging about on guard.

A conversation ensued; he knew them. After a moment he beckoned Ivar forward and without further conversation they were hustled past the gates and into the alleys of the city. Autun was a vast metropolis; Sigfrid had told him that perhaps ten thousand people lived there, cheek by jowl, but Ivar wasn't sure he believed it. That was an awful lot of people, too many to comprehend. Even Prince Bayan and Princess Sapientia's combined armies hadn't numbered more than ten or fifteen centuries of soldiers in addition to auxiliaries and militia.

On this late winter afternoon, few braved the streets. In one square a trio of beggars huddled by a public fountain, hands and faces wrapped in rags to protect themselves from the bitter cold. The tiny child's face was thin from hunger, and he scooted forward on his rump, like a cripple without use of his legs, to catch the copper coin Ivar tossed to them.

"Bless you, Brother!" the mother croaked, surprised.

"Where the phoenix flies, there is hope of salvation," he said to her.

Her face lit. "Truth rises with the phoenix!" she answered triumphantly. "Bless you! Bless you!"

Unnerved, he hurried after Erkanwulf, who had not waited.

"We're trying to come in quietly," scolded the young soldier when Ivar caught up to him. "Don't leave a trail."

"They were hungry."

"Everyone is hungry! A coin will gain them bread today, if there's any to be had, but nothing tomorrow."

"God enjoin us to ease suffering where we can. What is that she said about the phoenix?"

"Hush."

They hurried across a broader avenue and stood in the narrow alley waiting for a score of mounted soldiers wearing the stallion of Wayland to pass before they scurried through the sludge to a narrow path between two-storied wood houses. The walls tilted awkwardly, shadowing their path, and the shadows made it almost as dim as twilight as they sidestepped refuse left lying in the cracked mud. Because it was cold, it did not stink, but it would, when spring brought warm weather.

"I'll never get used to cities," muttered Ivar.

"It's not so bad," said Erkanwulf. "A man's freer here, where he can get rid of his past. And safer too, inside walls."

"Only if those who are guarding you are trustworthy."

His companion chuckled. "True enough. Wait here." He left Ivar.

The side street debouched into a square at whose center stood a post where men could be tied for whipping. Beyond that lay the barracks; Ivar recognized them from his brief visit to Autun two years back. It was getting dark in truth. An aura of red lined the western sky, what he could discern of it beyond buildings and in the shadow of the clouds. Erkanwulf's cloaked figure skulking at the barracks door, and vanishing inside, was rather like that of the shades they'd encountered in the forest that awful night last autumn. Ivar shuddered and wrapped his cloak more tightly around his torso as the chill of night crept into his bones. He'd been cold for a long time, and when he stood still he felt it most of all.

No one moved in the deserted square. Now and again dogs barked. Wheels squeaked as a wagon passed down a distant street. Someone coughed, and a moment later a man came out of a house, stopped to look at Ivar, and strode away past the barracks, soon lost as night concealed his tracks. With so many people crammed all into one small space, surely there should be more noise, like the pastures and fields and compound of his father's estate which had always been busy with coming and going except in the worst winter and spring storms.

He shivered and stamped his feet. They had agreed that if Erkanwulf was gone too long, then Ivar would retreat back to the cottage in the woods, but just as he was beginning to get really anxious the side door to the barracks cracked open and a figure slipped out and hurried across to him. Ivar groped for his short sword and began to draw it, but relaxed as Erkanwulf trotted up, breath steaming.

"Come on! Captain's here, off duty, and willing to hear us out. Hurry!"

They ran across the square and were ushered into a lamplit room at the end of the barracks hall where Captain Ulric slept and ate. The captain was sitting on a bench beside two of his sergeants, all three picking at the remains of a chicken.

Ivar's eyes watered, but he forced himself to look at the captain instead, trying desperately to ignore the trickle of moist juices. He was so hungry.

"I didn't expect to see you again, Brother Ivar," said the captain, although his tone wasn't unfriendly. He meant what he said.

"With your help, Captain, we were able to reach Princess Theophanu."

"So Erkanwulf led me to understand. What news?"

"None. Her Highness sorrows to hear of her aunt's plight, but she has no army and no treasury and cannot act against Lady Sabella and Duke Conrad. She offered us coin, fresh horses, good cloaks, and such weapons as we might use to defend ourselves, but nothing more than that. She bides in Osterburg at the seat of the duchy of Saony. That is all."

"The Wendish king, the first Henry, was duke of Saony before he became king." Ulric pushed the chicken away but paused with a hand on the wooden platter as he caught the desperation of Ivar's gaze. "You two look hungry."

He shoved the carcass toward them, then engaged his sergeants in conversation while the two young men stripped every last scrap of meat and fat from the bones. Ale was brought, and the cup refilled after they had drained it. That, and the warmth and smoky draft from the lamps, made Ivar so tired that he forgot his rehearsed arguments.

"Do you mean to support Biscop Constance, or not?" he demanded. "If you do, I have a plan that may allow us to free her. If not, then I pray you will let me go my way without hindering me, and let Erkanwulf remain here with no punishment. He's been a loyal soldier."

"Oh, I know it," said Ulric without looking at Erkanwulf, but Erkanwulf grinned at hearing those words and his shoulders lifted as he self-consciously rubbed the dirty stubble of a beard grown along his jaw. "But if you free Biscop Constance, what then? She has no loyal soldiers and no treasury. She is in no wise different than her niece in Saony. Better she remain safe in Queen's Grave. If she escapes, Lady Sabella will hunt her down and this time kill her."

"We must move quickly. I will need your help, horses, provisions, men to escort us. A special seat built onto a saddle so that the biscop can ride, because she is crippled."

"If all this comes to pass, then what?"

"We will ride to Wendar, to the town of Kassel. That way, Lady Sabella holds no noble Wendish hostage in Varre. Once the biscop reaches the duchy of Fesse, she can choose herself whether to ride to Osterburg."

Ulric was a cautious man. They both spoke in low voices. His sergeants, cool, stalwart men who spoke no word but only listened, sat so still and alert that a mouse could not have crept through that tiny chamber without being caught. Ivar wasn't sure whether they were listening to the conversation or listening for sounds from outside, in the barracks where the last conversations of men making ready for rest played out, and out of doors beyond the single closed shutter.

"A large guard protects the palisade and gates enclosing Queen's Grave. How are they to be suborned?"

"Not at all. They will believe they are only following Lady Sabella's orders."

For the first time, Ulric looked surprised. One of the sergeants rolled his eyes and tapped a foot thrice on the ground, as though impatient with this nonsense.

"Nay, hear me out." Ivar hadn't known how passionate he had become about this idea over the last few weeks. He had a debt to pay twice over, and perhaps, if he were honest, he could admit that it was as much for himself as for the biscop that he wanted so badly to succeed. "I know someone in Sabella's retinue. I hope to persuade him to steal what we need."

Once Captain Ulric had heard the whole thing, he sat for a while in thought with his bearded chin propped on a hand, then stood. "Very well. I'll give you cover until dawn. After that, you must leave Autun, and Arconia, and never come back. Or, at the least, never be caught. If you come into my custody, I will be forced to treat you as a criminal and hand you over to Lady Sabella. I can assure you, she will not be merciful."

3

IN the end he needed no particular disguise, only a cap drawn down over his head to cover his red hair. Any lowly servant could be found wearing such a thing to keep his ears warm in this cold winter weather. His robes, although cut for riding, were dirty and patched enough to pass as those of a laboring man, and the months of labor at Queen's Grave had given his chapped hands something of the look of those of a man born and bred to labor. He was hidden in plain sight with his gaze cast down and a slump in his shoulders to minimize his height; the sons of noble houses had a tendency to grow tall. Count Harl had always noted this with a certain arrogance, sure of God's favor manifest in the straight limbs and handsome faces of his children, but after so long on the road Ivar had begun to think it was more likely that he had simply gone hungry less often as a child than folk like Erkanwulf and frail Sigfrid.

Captain Ulric had friends among the servants. One of these, an amiable woman with dark hair and pale blue eyes, took him with her when she made her evening rounds carrying buckets of coal to fill the braziers in the lady's suite. He staggered under a pole laid over his shoulders as she weighted it down with two full buckets on either side, their handles hooked into notches cut into the wood. A cover hid the hot coals, but heat radiated off the bronze buckets, warming him.

"Come along," she said, "but say nothing." She carried only the empty buckets, tongs, and shovel, so he was sweating and his legs shaking by the time they climbed the steps that led up to the old palace, once the imperial winter residence of Emperor Taillefer.

They passed by the broad porch of the famous octagonal chapel where lay the emperor's tomb. A pair of bored guards stood on watch, chatting as they chafed hands and stamped feet to keep warm.

"Yes, the lad would have been whipped to death, I'm thinking, and all for a loaf of bread, but the lord cleric intervened and got him sent to the church as a servant instead. Hoo! That was a stroke of fortune."

"Or God's work done through man's hands."

"Truth rises with the phoenix! Here, now, did you hear about—"

"Come!" whispered his guide, seeing how Ivar had slowed to listen. He hurried after her.

The central palace, built all of wood, was an echoing hall and terrifically cold within, but they passed through to a separate wing where the lady and her personal retainers made their home. Like Count Harl, but unlike her brother the regnant, Sabella had planted herself in one place and traveled only brief circuits of the countryside when the mood took her or a pocket of discontent needed quelling.

Beyond the smaller audience chamber lay a series of rooms that housed her attendants and clerics. They passed through the tiny room set aside for her schola, dark and empty now. The sloped writing desks were veiled by shadows, and chests and cabinets sealed tight against vermin. Beyond that lay a handsome chapel, lit at this hour by a dozen lamps molded into the shape of guivres. Quietly, they set down the buckets next to a trio of braziers. A woman knelt on cold stone although there were carpets aplenty to cushion her knees. Her wheat-colored hair was braided back from her face and covered with a mesh of gold wire threaded with pearls, held in place with a golden coronet. Because her back was to them, Ivar could not see her face, but he did not need to see her face. He had stared at her back, at her profile, at her pale, drawn features through that hole in the fence in Quedlinhame often enough that he would know her anywhere and instantly. It wasn't only her rich burgundy underrobe and fur-lined overtunic that betrayed her as a woman of highest station. It wasn't only the heavy golden torque shackling her slender neck that announced her royal status.

He recognized as well that particular way she had of clasping her hands, perfected in those days when it had hurt her to press her palms together because of the weeping sores, her stigmata, the mark of her holiness and the sign of the Lady's favor. The ones she had inflicted herself, by digging at her skin with a nail, so Hathumod claimed.

If Tallia had been lying about the sores, then was it possible she had lied about the heresy as well? What if the phoenix was a lie?

Nay, God had sent Tallia to test their faith. She was the flawed vessel that leaked God's word but could never hold it. They had seen the truth when the phoenix rose and healed Sigfrid.

She prayed all in a rush, words crammed together.

> *"Let them be chaff in the wind.*
> *Let their path be dark and precipitous.*
> *Let the unworthy fall to their deaths.*
> *They hid a net to trap me.*
> *They dug a pit to swallow me.*
> *Let that net trap them, and the pit swallow them!"*

Meanwhile, Johanna, the servant, transferred ash into the empty buckets and hot coals into the braziers.

"Are we done?" asked a childish voice.

"Do not disturb me!" Tallia exploded. Leaning back, she exposed a small child kneeling on bare floor in a position that had, previously, concealed her existence from Ivar. She cracked the little girl across the cheek, her own expression suffused with rage. By the movement of her body under her robes, it was obvious she was hugely pregnant. "How many times have I told you!"

"I don't want to pray so many times. Papa said—"

"You'll fall into the Abyss with the others! You'll do as I say, Berengaria!"

The girl had pinched, unattractive features. Her skin was blotchy, neither dark nor pale, and she seemed all mismatched somehow, nose too small, lips too large, nothing quite right on her. Her sullen expression only exaggerated her sour looks.

"Must you make so much noise!" cried the lady, turning to glare at Ivar and Johanna. "Aren't you finished yet, bumbling around like cattle?"

"Yes, my lady. I pray pardon, Your Highness," said Johanna in a mild voice. "But I am always taken by the holy whisper of God when I pause here. It's as if I hear Her voice, whenever you pray."

Tallia's expression softened, although she still had a tight grip on her daughter's tiny wrist. The child whimpered as the princess frowned. "That's right. I've seen you before. I remember you. What is your name?"

"I'm called Johanna, Your Highness. After the discipla who was martyred in such a cruel way, yet loving God and professing Her worship and Her Unity, now and forever."

Horribly, that fervid gaze turned on Ivar, and he ducked his head but not before seeing how her eyes narrowed and a cunning, frightened look came to her face. "Who is this, then? He looks familiar, but I don't know . . ."

"He's my cousin from the countryside, Your Highness, come new to town. He was here some months back helping out but had to go back to aid his ill mother, who passed up to the Chamber of Light after many months of agonizing sickness, may God grant her peace now that she is well shut of the world." Johanna was a babbler, and it was obvious she had learned long since how to lie to avoid the lady's ill temper.

Ivar kept his shoulders bowed and his face cast down, hoping Tallia would not recognize him.

"Does he believe in the Redemption? I'll have no servant toiling in my house who is a heretic!"

"Oh, he believes, indeed, Your Highness!"

"He must say so himself! He must! People lie to me. They say they're dead and then they're alive again. They say I will rule, but then they keep the reins in their own hands. They babble about the phoenix, when the phoenix doesn't matter, and only because of his handsome face and pretty ways—"

Into this tirade clattered the duke, emerging out of a different door with an older and extremely handsome daughter in tow. He was dressed for riding, as was the girl, and he slapped his gloves against his thigh to announce his arrival.

Tallia ceased speaking as though he had struck her.

"Where's Berry?" he roared.

The girl shrieked, leaped away from her mother, and pelted across the floor to throw herself into her father's arms. In that instant, her face was transformed. "I wanted to go! I wanted to go!" she cried.

"For the sake of God and peace, Tallia, you told me she was too sick to go riding!"

"She is ill in her soul, my lord," she said, shuddering, a hand on her belly.

"Too sick! Puling and moping will kill her, not keep her healthy! Do you want her to die as did the two others?"

"You can't talk to me like this!"

The older girl, just broaching puberty, rolled her eyes in a way that reminded Ivar strikingly of the sergeant with Captain Ulric. Indeed, she had a martial stance that suggested she trained and rode and knew how to handle weapons.

"I told you," repeated Conrad. "I told you to let the child have done with all this praying. That's what clerics are for. Twice a day is enough. She needs exercise and a good appetite."

Tallia was white with anger, but the little girl held onto her father with an unshakable grip.

"Let me stay with you, Papa. Let me stay with you!"

"Of course you'll stay with me, as you should."

"I hate you!" Tallia whispered.

He laughed. "That's not what you said last time you came crawling to my bed."

Tallia sobbed, then cast a glance of pure loathing at the older daughter and throttled her own tears.

Johanna tugged at Ivar's sleeve. "Let's go."

He set his neck under the yoke and lifted the buckets. He sidled sideways through the door and trudged after Johanna as they walked down a corridor that ended in a set of double doors.

"It's like poison," she said in a low voice. "Most of the time, thank the Lady, they stay in Wayland where they belong, but Lady Sabella will have her daughter in Autun to give birth with her own midwives attending."

"Why? Hasn't Wayland any midwives?"

"It's agreed between them. If the young queen gives birth to a boy, Lady Sabella gets him to raise. If a girl, naturally, the duke takes her. The last two died before they were weaned. Only the eldest has survived so long, and her not yet seen five summers."

"Lady Tallia doesn't want to raise her own sons?"

Johanna paused before the doors with a hand on one latch. "Lady Tallia has no say in any decision, for all that she's the last descendant of the royal house of Varre and they call her queen. She's a frightened, petty, mean-hearted creature. For all that, I do pity her, caught between the stallion and the guivre." She flicked a glance at the closed door, as if she could be heard by listening ears. "Have a care, Brother Ivar. The stallion is hot-tempered and hotheaded yet honest in its passions and will kick and bite to protect its fillies. It's the guivre's cold glare that will kill you."

She lifted the latch and opened the door for him to slide through, careful as he balanced the pole on his shoulders so that the buckets would not clang against the walls.

In this fine chamber a middle-aged man with attractive features strummed a lute and sang a cheerful song about the fox that devoured the chickens despite the farmer's efforts to hold it at bay. Tapestries covered the walls, and a dozen or more lamps, fearsome guivres with flame spouting from their eye sockets, gave light to the pleasant company collected around Lady Sabella. Her hair was half gone to gray, but she seemed otherwise vigorous and alert as she reclined on a couch and chatted with a circle of companions: several noblewomen, two men in cleric's robes, and a blond man who sat with his back to Ivar. Two stewards waited beside the hearth next to a table laden with platters of meat and bowls of sweets and fruits, lightly picked over but otherwise ignored. They watched for any sign or gesture from their mistress. One marked the entry of the two servants and nodded at them briskly, a signal to get on with their work.

A third cleric sat at a writing desk, intent on his calligraphy, head bowed and pen scratching easily on parchment. Ivar skipped over him and fixed his gaze on the back of the blond man seated beside Sabella. There was something wrong about his shoulders. They were too broad, and his hands, when he gestured, were as wide as paddles, the hands of a man comfortable wielding a great sword with little thought for its weight and the thickness of the pommel.

Definitely not Baldwin.

"Hsst!" Johanna nudged Ivar toward the brazier placed beside the writing desk.

Obviously Sabella kept Baldwin sequestered. Perhaps after they had replenished the coals in this chamber, they would move on to the noble duchess' most intimate inner chambers.

He set down the buckets and looked up into the confounded gaze of the cleric who had, until an instant before, been so busy writing that his face had been concealed.

Writing!

His fingers were stained with smudges of ink. The parchment was virgin; no one had written on it before. Ivar had just enough experience of the cloister to know that the knife had seen little use in scraping away mistakes, although half the page was covered with flowing, handsome letters.

The cleric's pale skin flushed pink, and a single tear trembled at the lower rim of his right eye. Snapping his mouth shut, he fixed his gaze back on his quill, checked the tip, dipped it in ink, and set back to work. The letters poured out of his hand fluidly, fluently. He wasn't even copying from an exemplar, but writing from memory.

Even the masters at Quedlinhame, who had spoiled him because of his handsome face and pliant manners, had agreed that Baldwin was too stupid to learn to read and write beyond the simplest colloquies meant to teach ten year olds.

Johanna appeared at Ivar's elbow, nudging his foot. He winced, and aided her as she stoked up this brazier and moved on to the rest placed around the chamber to warm Lady Sabella and her entourage where they lounged at their ease.

"As dreary as this winter has been, at least the Eika have not raided," the blond warrior was saying.

"Nay, Amalfred, all last year they confined their raids to Salia," remarked one of the women. "Easy pickings there."

"If Salia falls, then why not strike at us?" he retorted.

"We shall see. The merchants say it's too early to sail yet, that the tides and winds aren't favorable. They say some kind of enchantment has troubled the seas. We'll be safe if the winds keep the Eika from our shores."

"Perhaps." Lady Sabella's gaze flicked incuriously over the two servants as they went about their task in silence. She glanced toward the cleric, who was bent again over his writing.

Ivar could not interpret the way her lips flattened into a thin line that might betoken suppressed passion, or disgust. The two emotions were, perhaps, related, he supposed as he kept his face canted away from her. He had himself swung wildly between those feelings, back in the days when restraint had been the least of his concerns, when he and Baldwin had run away with Prince Ekkehard and his companions. Right now, however, he was as flushed and out of breath as if he'd been running. Who could have thought he had missed Baldwin so very dearly?

"Perhaps?" asked the warrior. He was a man boasting perhaps thirty years. He spoke with the accent of the west and was most likely a border lord. "Pray enlighten us with your wisdom, Your Highness."

"Perhaps," she repeated, her gaze sliding smoothly away from

Baldwin, as if he were of no account. "The Eika are not all that threaten us, although it is true they raided all along the Salian shore last summer and autumn. According to reports."

"My lands are overrun with Salians," said one of the women.

"With our stores low, their presence threatens us," answered Sabella. "We must act in concert to drive them back to their homes."

"What of those who accept the truth?" asked the lord. "The heresy of the Translatus is still accepted by the apostate clergy in Salia. If the refugees who have accepted the truth return home, they will be executed."

"Then their blood will be on the hands of their masters. God will judge. But the winter has been cold. Our stores are low. Strange portents trouble us. Nothing has been the same since that terrible storm that struck last autumn. I have refugees of my own from within my duchy to feed. I cannot feed Salians as well. Let the Eika conquer them—and feed them! To the fishes, if necessary."

"Ha! They say there are people in the sea who eat human flesh."

"They say some in the west who are starving eat human flesh, Lord Amalfred," observed Sabella.

"Brixians, perhaps. They're the only Salians who would degrade themselves in such a way."

"My lord," said one of the clerics sternly, "if such folk are starving, then God enjoins us to give them aid and compassion."

"Well," continued Amalfred boldly, "if Lady Sabella grants me those stores, then I can feed my restless soldiers who mutter about rebellion."

"I pray you, Your Highness," said Baldwin without looking up from his writing desk. How pleasing his voice was, compared to the coarser voices of Sabella's companions. "Those rations of grain are meant to go to the poor in Autun, Your Highness. There are so many who haven't enough to eat."

"The poor of Autun cannot aid me," said Sabella, "but Lord Amalfred's hungry soldiers can fight to protect the Varren borderlands."

"And gain a little territory in Salia for themselves," added one of her companions.

Sabella laughed, but she looked again, frowning, at the pair of servants. "Haven't you done? What slow pair of fools has been foisted on me now? What are your names?"

"I pray you, Your Highness," said Baldwin sweetly without looking up from his writing desk. "I have forgotten again whether it is the monastery of Firsebarg or that of Felden which desires a new abbot to rule over them, now that their lord father has been absent so long."

"Firsebarg, Baldwin! Why won't you attend the first time I tell you these My sister Rotrudis' useless whelp, Reginar, has gone missing since last year. Must I remember everything for you?"

Johanna tugged on Ivar's sleeve, and he hastily followed her out of the chamber by a side door. They came into a narrow courtyard abutting the wall.

"Wait here a moment, I pray you," Johanna said, indicating he should set down the buckets. "I must use the necessary. Then we'll get on with our work."

She had lit a taper from one of the braziers and by its light slipped into one of the closed stalls built out from the wall.

Up here on the height it was cold and the wind bit hard. He blew on his hands and stared about him, but there wasn't much to see. A pair of torches lit a distant gate. He could not see the town below but felt the expanse of air. All other souls slept. Only Lady Sabella had riches enough to burn oil at night.

He stared at the door, and at last it creaked open and creaked shut. A light appeared, and a pale head loomed before him. Without speaking, he grabbed the cap that covered Ivar's head and ripped it off, then held the lamp close to see the color of his hair. With a muttered oath more like a moan than words, he grabbed Ivar's left hand first, released it, and grasped the right one. There winked the lapis lazuli ring, gleaming in lamplight.

He shut his beautiful eyes and his legs gave out as he sank onto the stone in an attitude of prayer. His hands shook, and Ivar pulled the lamp from his grasp before he dropped it.

"Ai, God. How can it be? You were dead. I saw you myself. I touched you. I pressed that ring onto your cold hand. You were dead."

"It was a ruse, Baldwin. I am sorry you had to suffer, not knowing the truth." He set down the lamp and, hesitantly, placed a hand on Baldwin's shoulder. "I was never dead, only drugged. I escaped from Queen's Grave to take a message to Princess Theophanu."

Baldwin surged up and embraced Ivar tightly, bursting into tears.

Ivar was at first too choked up to speak, but he understood how little time they had. "Surely your absence will be noted."

"Yes, yes," murmured Baldwin into his shoulder. "I came out to use the necessarium, but she'll wonder and suspect. She keeps me prisoner. You can't imagine how awful she is, always watching me."

"You saved our lives."

"I know." He said the words not with anger or accusation, but simply because they were the truth.

He released Ivar, then grasped his hands in his own and stared keenly at him. There was a look in Baldwin's handsome face that had never been there before, but Ivar could not identify what it was. The light from the lamp, shining up from below, highlighted the perfect curve of his cheekbones and lent sparks to his lovely eyes. The midnight blue of his robes blended into the night, making him appear almost as an apparition, not a real human being at all. He had lost none of his unfortunate beauty.

"Why are you here, Ivar? I knew you wouldn't abandon me."

"Will you escape with me, tonight?"

"Yes."

"I need one thing."

"What?"

"Parchment, ink and quill, Lady Sabella's ducal seal, and a person who can write in the manner of her schola. We'll need a letter to the guard at Queen's Grave, an order to release Biscop Constance and her retinue."

"I can get those things by midnight," said Baldwin.

"Even the seal?"

"Even the seal. I can write whatever you want."

"I saw that—I saw—Baldwin, how did you learn to write so well? Can you read now, too?" He grimaced, hearing how he sounded, but Baldwin neither smiled nor frowned.

"She doesn't like it when I pray and act the cleric," he said softly. "It reminds her of her daughter, so it gives her a disgust of me. That's why I prayed so much, and practiced my letters so hard. Once I learned, I found I was good at it. Everyone says I have a beautiful hand for letters. They all praise me. I know every word in every capitulary and cartulary that comes out of her schola. I have the seal of Arconia, Ivar. I am the seal. That's what she calls me. See?"

From the folds of his robe he pulled a small object tied to his belt. Ivar fondled it, feeling the ridges and depressions of a tiny carving impressed into stone. He hadn't enough light to read its features, but it felt like the sigil of a prince by which that prince set her approval and authority onto every letter and document that left her schola.

"I'll come as soon as all have gone to their beds. She won't want me tonight because she's in her blood. Meet me at the river gate. We'll need horses."

"That's taken care of, Baldwin. But if you can slip away so easily, why haven't you done so before?"

"Why would I? What have I to live for, if I am alone? Here, I had some hope of finding a way to free the others. I saw them." His voice trembled at the edge of tears. "I saw them in Queen's Grave, but we were never allowed to speak. I must go."

He released Ivar's hand, gave him a last, searching look, took the lamp, and hurried back inside. The door shut.

Ivar simply stood there, dumbfounded. His thoughts were all tumbled. He gasped in a breath that was also a cry.

"Hoo!" Johanna came up beside him so quietly that Ivar hissed in surprise. "That one! Some say he's a saint."

"A saint?" He was flushed, and trembling, and, truth to tell, a little irritated. Since when did Baldwin tell *him* what to do with so much cool assurance?

"He's so even tempered, despite the way she treats him."

"Does she abuse him?"

"She's got a bad temper. She despises those she has no respect for, and treats them worse. She hates herself for loving his beauty so much. Duke Conrad's the better prince. All know that. But Lord Baldwin slips food to the starving and a kind word to the weary, behind her back. No natural person can be so beautiful. That's why he must be favored by God. Now, come. We've one more chamber, and then I'm to take you back to the barracks."

He pulled his cap back over his hair and followed her. His thoughts rolled all over each other in a confusing jumble that he just could not sort out. Nor had he managed it when at last Johanna delivered him to Captain Ulric and he gave his report to the captain and his companions.

"Very well," said Ulric, who like most experienced military men knew how to act quickly. "Erkanwulf, you'll ride south with the cleric after he has delivered the seal and the order."

"Won't he ride to Queen's Grave with me?" asked Ivar.

"She'll be after him. He'll have to lead her on a chase while we rescue Biscop Constance. If they escape, they'll meet up with us later. If that meets with your approval, my lord."

When they had escaped the Quman, the others had looked to Ivar to lead them, but here it was different: he could only follow as the captain told him what they were going to do and only afterward asked permission as a courtesy, given the difference in their ranks.

Yet there was hope. He agreed to everything Captain Ulric said.

Quietly and in shadows, the war band left their barracks by ones and twos. Slowly, the stables were emptied out. Ivar walked with Erkanwulf through deserted streets with a taper to light their way, leading four horses whose hooves clopped hollowly on the pavement of stone.

They waited for hours and hours at the river gate although, in truth, it wasn't longer than it would take to sing the morning mass. The gurgle of the river serenaded them. The wind brought the smell of refuse. It was otherwise silent and dark. He could barely distinguish the walls of Autun behind him where he stood huddling at their base on the broad strand between gate and river's edge. A score of boats had been drawn up onto the shore. The wharves were farther downstream, by the northern gate. A rat scuttled into the wavering, smoky light given off by the taper, froze, and vanished when Erkanwulf threw a knife at it. The blade stuck in the ground, and he leaned down to pull it free.

"Where are the others?" Ivar asked.

"Most of them will remain behind to join the force that hunts for us. They'll join us later. A dozen men wait for you past the ferry. Here is Captain Ulric."

The captain emerged from the river gate, spoke tersely and in a low voice with the pair of guards who had let them all through, and stepped back to allow Baldwin to pass through. Baldwin paused with a hand half raised in the air, as if touching something he had not seen for years. He turned, searching, and found Ivar.

"They say I'm to ride south, so that she'll follow me and not suspect what's happening. Is that right?"

"That's right, Baldwin. That's the plan. She'll follow the light that shines brightest to her."

Baldwin reached into his sleeve and withdrew a rolled parchment bound with leather. "Here it is. A letter calling for the biscop's release and stating that as long as she departs Varre and never returns she is free to go, otherwise her life is forfeit. I thought it was most believable done that way. She's not merciful."

He offered it. Hand shaking, Ivar took it from him. He was hot and cold at once. Words had abandoned him. He tugged the lapis lazuli ring off his finger and pressed it into Baldwin's warm palm.

Baldwin slipped the ring onto his own finger, held Ivar's gaze a moment longer, and turned to the captain. "I'm ready."

"Erkanwulf will guide you," said the captain.

The pair moved away into the night, although the taper's light was visible for an interminable interval as they made their way up the strand.

The parchment Ivar held paralyzed him. That quickly, Baldwin was gone, torn from him again. And anyway, he was so unaccustomed to succeeding that it seemed impossible he just had.

"I'll ride with you to the ferry," said the captain. "Sergeant Hugo will accompany you to Queen's Grave. The rest of us will meet you as soon as we can on the road to Kassel. Go then. Go with God. May She watch over you."

Only later, after he had crossed the river and felt its swirl and spray against his face, did he realize that Captain Ulric had spoken those last words without a trace of self-consciousness.

May She *watch over you.*

In Autun, at any rate, belief in the Redemption had triumphed, and he had to wonder: was it Lady Tallia's example, or Baldwin's, that had won the most converts?

4

WITH his hair concealed under a dirty coif and a boiled leather helmet on his head, Ivar stood among the dozen soldiers who acted as his cover and watched as Sergeant Hugo delivered the false order to Captain Tammus.

"Being sent into exile?" demanded the scarred captain after the deacon who presided over the camp's chapel read the missive out loud.

"I just does as I'm told," said Sergeant Hugo with a shrug. "Still, there's troubles along the Salian borders worse these days than ever. I hear tell of famine. Lady Sabella needs all her troops for other business. Best to be rid of them. They can starve in Wendar as well as here."

"Easier to kill them." Tammus had a way of squinting that made his scars twist and pucker. He was an evil-looking man, with a vile temper to match, but he wasn't stupid. Ivar was careful to keep his head lowered. Tammus might remember his face. There had been only three young men interred in Queen's Grave, and his "death" had been so very public and unexpected and dramatic. His hands felt clammy. Despite the chill, he was sweating.

"No orders about killing," said Hugo without expression. "We're to escort them to the border with Fesse and let them go on their own. That's all I know."

Tammus grunted. He took the parchment from the deacon and sniffed at the seal, then licked it, spat, and handed it back to the woman.

"It is genuine," said the deacon, sure of her ground but hesitant as she eyed him fearfully. She had, Ivar saw, a fading bruise on her right cheek. "The seal is that of the duchess, which she keeps on her person. The calligraphy is in an exceptionally fine hand. I recognize it from other letters she has sent this past year."

He wiped his nose with the back of his hand as he surveyed the dozen men-at-arms waiting beside horses, two carts, and a dozen donkeys and mules. They had tracked down Captain Tammus easily enough in the camp that lay outside the palisade. His was the largest house, two whole rooms, and the only one whose walls were freshly whitewashed. The camp looked unkempt and half deserted. Mud slopped the pathways. Ivar heard no clucking of chickens, although the guardsmen had once held a significant flock, taxed out of the nearby villages. Bored and surly-looking soldiers had gathered, but there were only a dozen of them, of whom half scratched at rashes blistering their faces and two limped. They looked to be no match for Hugo's troop, who were healthier and had, in addition, a strength of purpose that lent iron to their resolve.

Why did we not think to do this sooner?

It was a foolish thought. Until his escape, no one in Queen's Grave had opportunity to speak freely to those outside.

"You have until nightfall," Tammus growled at last.

Hugo hesitated, as if to argue, but did not. He snapped his fingers, and his men mounted and rode briskly to the gates, which were opened at Tammus' order. After they rode through, the gates were shoved shut behind them.

"Something's wrong," said Ivar.

He dismounted. The bare ground, covered with a sheen of ice, crackled beneath his boots as he walked forward. He knew this landscape well enough. He had had many months to learn its contours. He had lost track of the time since he had escaped, but it had been nine or ten months, early summer then and the end of winter now. In that time the tidy gardens, fields, and orchards had gone untended, so it appeared. Worst, a dozen new graves marked the cemetery plot north of the infirmary. He recognized them because of the heaps of earth, yet not one bore a wooden Circle staked into the ground or a crude headstone.

It was deadly quiet. Not a soul stirred, not even come to see what the noise was or to investigate the whickering of horses and the sound of armed men.

He dropped his reins and ran for the compound, past the abandoned sheep pasture and the wildly overgrown bramble where once goats had feasted. The front door was stuck, canted sideways because of broken hinges. He yanked it open, grunting and swearing and crying, and tumbled into the vacant entry hall, sprinted, shouting, into the biscop's audience chamber, but it, too, lay empty. Even her writing desk was gone. He bolted out into the courtyard. Sister Bona's grave lay bare, untended except for a dandelion.

Abandoned.

Were they all dead? But if so, wouldn't Captain Tammus have known? Or had he simply ceased to care?

"Ivar?"

He spun, hearing that gentle voice but seeing no one. "Hathumod? Ai, God!" He was weeping with frustration and fear. "Where are you? Where is everyone?"

Forever ago, or so it seemed because it was a moment he preferred not to recall, pretty young Sister Bona had crawled out of the courtyard past a loose board. It jiggled now, and he grabbed it and wrenched it to one side, then cursed, because he'd gotten a splinter deep in his palm.

Hathumod's face blinked at him out of the shadows.

"What are you *doing* in there?" he demanded.

"Ivar! Oh, Ivar." She was weeping. "I thought you were dead."

"I pray you, Hathumod. Come out! What are you doing in there?"

She shoved the loose board aside and clambered out. Once, she would have been too stout to squeeze through, but she was so thin now that it hurt to look at her, all skin stretched over knobby bones. She had lost that rabbity look, although her protruding front teeth stood out more starkly than ever with no plump cheeks to give harmony to her features.

"We have stores hidden in here that we don't want the guards to know about."

"Where is everyone?"

"We had to retreat to the amphitheater, at the head of the valley. It was too dangerous to stay here."

"Why?"

She stared at him as if he had said something particularly stupid. "Because of the sickness, of course!" Her lips quivered. She burst into tears. "So many dead we couldn't bury them decently. And we were all feared we would die, too."

"Who still lives? What of Sigfrid and Ermanrich? What of the biscop?"

"Th–they live. Th–they aren't the ones. . . . It's been so awful." She tried to gulp down her sobs. She rubbed angrily at her face, but she could not stop crying. His intense relief at discovering that some still lived made him furious.

"Take me to them! We have only until nightfall."

"F–for what?"

"To free you."

She wailed, bawling.

He grabbed her shoulders and shook her. "Hathumod! We must go quickly!"

"I–if only you'd come last autumn. Half our number are dead."

"Hurry!"

He grabbed her wrist and she followed him meekly outside. Hugo's men had fanned out to explore the compound, but Ivar called them back.

"There are stores hidden behind a loose board in the courtyard. Get those, and abandon the rest. There was a terrible sickness here. The demons who cause it might still be lurking. Sergeant, stay here and make ready. Half your men and the mounts come with us."

They rode down the path that led past the vegetable garden and the grain fields. Hathumod wept, unable to stop herself.

"Who feeds them?" asked one of the soldiers. "Ground's not been broken up or even ploughed."

"The guards are feared to come in," Hathumod sobbed, "on account of the sickness."

They had built a pair of huts within the hollow of the amphitheater, protected somewhat by the high ridgeline. Four scrawny goats grazed in brambles at the limit of their tethers. Six sheep mowed the amphitheater slope; none had lambed or were even pregnant. Ivar did not see the community's ram.

The monastics had heard the sound of horses and were waiting, clustered around the seated biscop. Like the others, Constance had grown thin, and thinness made her look old, frail, and weary. No more than a dozen huddled fearfully with the forest at their back. Ivar recognized Sigfrid's impossibly petite form at once, but Ermanrich seemed to be missing. Nay, that was him standing next to Sigfrid, only he was shrunken in girth, a stick looking none the healthier for having lost his energetic stoutness. His face was pale and his chin scumbled with a half grown beard, but it was his features that lit first.

"Ivar! It's Ivar! I knew he would come back!" He hobbled forward; something was wrong with his right foot, and as soon as Ivar dismounted he flung his arms around him in a warm embrace.

"No time." Ivar pushed him away. He gauged the heavens and the shifting light that marked the waning afternoon. "We must leave now, while we have the chance. We have an order, sealed by Lady Sabella's seal and thereby binding. You are exiled from Varre, free to go as long as you cross into Wendar and do not return."

Some wept, but Biscop Constance in her calm way asked the first, and only, question. "Who has written this false command, knowing themselves a rebel against Lady Sabella? Such an act is treason, punishable by death. Was it one of the clerics I trained? I thought them all exiled from her court."

"It was Baldwin."

"Baldwin!" cried Ermanrich.

"Baldwin can't write," objected Hathumod from behind him.

"That is enough," said Constance. "I will need assistance. I cannot ride."

Ivar nodded. "We have a cart and two mules to draw it. We have mounts for everyone. How are there so few left?"

"There are three out in the woods gathering," said Constance, "but it is true we are few in number. Sister Nanthild was first to die of the illness. It struck after the night of the wind. We lost half our number. It is only since we left the compound and came to live here that the deaths have ceased. I believe that the well is poisoned. You see how weak we are. If you had not come, Brother Ivar, I fear we would all have perished by summer from starvation. The guards refused to cross the gate or even bring us baskets of grain. The ram died, and the only pregnant ewe miscarried. We have not seen the sun for so many months we have forgotten what it feels like to enjoy its brilliant lamp. Plants cannot flourish without sun. Likewise, rainfall is erratic. God is angry, so I am convinced."

"We must hurry." He did not like to think that it might all be for naught, that he might rescue them and yet still fail. The world had so changed that he no longer recognized it. Like a cloudy day, it had gone all shadowed and dim. "Let us go."

The three gone into the woods to forage were found. The rest had to bundle up their valuable possessions, to fold them into saddlebags and cloth sacks and or toss them into the back of the second cart or over the withers of their mules: blankets, cloaks, tunics, weed hooks, shovels, sickles, and scythes as well as awls, knives, kitchen implements, and a salt cellar; a silver ewer and four copper basins; needles, skeins of yarn, three spindles, and six fleeces also used for bedding; a leather chest containing the biscop's scribal tools; two psalters, three Holy Verses, and four other books, one of them a scroll of St. Augustina's *Confessions* and another a history of Varren princes. What remained of their stock of dried herbs taken from the infirmary and stored in a small wooden chest. An ivory-and-gold reliquary containing the bones of the left hand of the founder, Queen Gertruda.

They met up with Sergeant Hugo at the gates with daylight to spare and rumbled out through the guards' encampment in a silent line of riders with the two carts positioned in the middle of the procession. Captain Tammus stared. He seemed ready to spit, but like them, he said nothing. No one, apparently, wanted to risk touching them. Before they'd rolled out of sight, a half dozen guards ran through the open gates to see what they could loot. The last Ivar saw of the gate was the men running back out again with nothing in their hands, scared off, no doubt, by the sight of those forbidding graves.

Then the curve of the road cut off the view, as it always did. Each path drew its own landscape. He understood that now. Something always got left behind, and sometimes it was even something you wanted to lose, but mostly the things you wanted to lose stayed with you.

He laughed, and Sigfrid, riding awkwardly astride a donkey, turned to look at him.

"How are you come to us, Ivar?"

"Let us ride until nightfall. Then I'll tell the tale."

They rode in silence, despite their joy, for it appeared Constance's schola were too weary and exhausted to sing. Their pace was killingly slow, burdened by the grind of the two carts and the awkward seats of several of the monastics who, like Sigfrid, had never learned to ride and yet were too weak to walk far. Through stubbornness and God's will they turned east onto a half hidden trail into the deeper forest and made it as far as that same clearing where Ivar had met Erkanwulf the previous summer. The thatched roof that covered the old stone chapel still held. They settled Biscop Constance and the weakest nuns in its shelter while the soldiers set up a half dozen traveling tents for the rest of them, in case it rained. The sergeant set out sentries and ordered a big fire built in front of the chapel. There was plenty of deadwood to be gathered and split for burning. Wind soughed through the leaves of the giant oak.

"Erkanwulf and I saw shades here," said Ivar, chafing his hands as he stood before the fire. "They killed some of the men pursuing us and drove the rest away, but they didn't touch us. I don't know why."

"We heard no news of that," said Sigfrid. "Do you mean to say Captain Tammus suspected all along and sent soldiers to fetch you back?"

"I must believe so. Did no one confront the biscop?"

They turned. She had come forward, leaning on her stick and supported by Sister Eligia, one of the survivors.

"We have heard nothing, no news at all from the outside world for the last nine months, Brother Ivar," she said. A pair of soldiers rolled a log up behind her as a bench, and she sank down and thanked them graciously. "Sabella passed by to gloat that same day you left us, but she did little more than inform me of Tallia's latest stillborn child as well as rumor from the south that the Wendish army had been lost in the east and that a cabal of malefici meant to cast a spell to drown the world in water. I could not make sense of her report. There came a night soon after when unnatural lightning coursed through the skies and a powerful wind ripped past us. Poor Brother Felix was crushed by a falling tree limb. Sister Gregoria broke her leg so badly that it festered and even Sister Nanthild's medicines could not heal her. That was a grim omen, for soon after, the sickness struck us down one by one. Give us your report, I pray you, Brother Ivar. Did you reach my niece, Theophanu? Is it she who has sent you to aid us now?"

Except for the sentries, every soul there drew close to hear.

"Princess Theophanu sent word that she has no army and no treasure and cannot aid you, Your Grace."

Sister Eligia cried out, but Constance touched her forearm to quiet her. "Go on. How do you come to us now, then, with Lady Sabella's seal?"

"We took matters into our own hands, Erkanwulf and I." He told the story at length, and was interrupted often. The soldiers who knew somewhat more of the matter offered comments at intervals. The sergeant brought around ale and cheese and days-old bread, and they drank and ate with a will, and gratefully, for they were all so hungry. When Ivar had finished his story, Constance nodded. She lifted both hands in the manner of a biscop calling her flock to prayers.

"Let us sing in thanksgiving, Brothers and Sisters." She had a light soprano, clear and true, and the others followed easily, accustomed to her lead.

> *"Exalted be God, our deliverer,*
> *Who has rescued me from my enemies*
> *And saved me from lawless men."*

But not delivered yet. Ivar brooded as the others settled down to sleep on blankets and furs. Having been cast out into the wilderness, they were content to be free. Ivar sat with knees drawn up and chin on knees. Beside him, Ermanrich snored softly.

"You are troubled, Ivar," murmured Sigfrid.

"We must wait for Captain Ulric. It could all come undone if Lady Sabella suspects and sends another troop after us. If Captain Tammus rides quickly to Autun and discovers the truth."

"A journey of some days. We are safe for the moment. That isn't what troubles you."

Ivar frowned, but it was Sigfrid asking: so frail in his body and so strong in his mind, a curious vessel for God's favor but a precious and holy one nonetheless. "I wonder if I could have acted otherwise. I should have insisted that Hanna go with me when my father sent me south to Quedlinhame. I shouldn't have spoken so harshly to her when we next met. What if Hanna won't forgive me? Why was I so unfair to Liath as to think she might love me in the same way I loved her? Was I blind? And what of Baldwin?"

"Are you afraid of Baldwin?"

He shrugged off the question by turning it. "We would all be dead without his sacrifice."

"Yes," agreed Sigfrid calmly, "but he was only following the example of the blessed Daisan, was he not? Not every person is given the blessing of sacrifice, Ivar. We have reason to hope that he will escape and reunite with us, do we not? God has rewarded Baldwin for thinking of others before himself."

"Is that meant as a rebuke to me?"

"Only if you hear it that way." Sigfrid chuckled. "I missed you, Ivar. No one else frets in quite the way you do."

The words cut through the knot that had for many days been stuck in his throat. Before he knew it, he was weeping, tears streaming down his cheeks as he struggled not to sob out loud and wake Ermanrich and the two soldiers who were crowded into the tent with them and sleeping soundly.

After a while, Sigfrid asked, "What do you fear, Ivar?"

"I fear I lost something but I don't know what it is. That I'll only recognize it when it's too late."

"Two days," said Sergeant Hugo. It was agreed they dared wait so long in the clearing before moving east again through the forest. The first day passed quietly enough. Constance rested, yet was never alone. By turns, and as if by accident, each soldier approached her and spoke privately to her as a man might to his deacon when he had a trouble to confess. Some spoke at length, others more briefly.

Hunters returned with two wasted and sickly deer, which they ate anyway because their food stores were so low, and a grouse, whose meat was shared among the monastics. The nuns gathered morels and blewits, and Hathumod found an old stand of couch grass in a nearby clearing and dug up the now-bitter roots. With these victuals they ate well enough, although they had to drink water from a nearby stream and many developed a flux.

Sergeant Hugo and his soldiers went through all their tack, greasing and repairing it. They carved arrows out of stout shoots in case they ran out of metal-tipped ones. The nuns scoured the woods for anything edible that might be dried or boiled for carrying.

The second day Ivar spent most of his time with Constance recounting again and again the story of his travels with Erkanwulf, repeating details or, on occasion, recalling ones he had forgotten or overlooked. Every utterance made by Theophanu, Rotrudis' children, or their courtiers had to be reexamined. Had he been Liath, he would have recalled every word he had heard, but he was not Liath. He was the flawed vessel, and he worried that he had forgotten something important.

"Of the walls, again. There was building going on?"

"No, but there was one scaffolding. That would have been on the western wall, I think. I remember the light shining on it as we rode out. No one was working there."

"Within the hall, was there any new work being done? Any repairs? Were the walls freshly whitewashed?"

A whistle shrilled from the woods, down along the trail where the string of sentries ran out farthest.

Sergeant Hugo jumped to his feet. Soldiers grabbed spears, swords, and bows. A bird's trill rang out, and several among them whooped and clapped.

Captain Ulric rode at the head of his troop, his usually pleasant features creased with anxiety and a certain grim relief at seeing them. The rest of his men spread out so as not to overwhelm the clearing. Soon there were almost threescore folk gathered around the ancient chapel: Hugo's dozen, the fifteen monastics, and about thirty men at arms, all mounted, with the captain. It was strange, though, since Ivar had thought that the captain commanded almost a century of men.

"We are at your service, Your Grace," Ulric said after he dismounted and knelt before her. She extended a hand. He kissed her ring. "I pray pardon for coming so late."

"That you have done this much was beyond my expectation, Captain. I know all among you have kinfolk. A few have wives and children of your own. What will become of them? My half sister Sabella is known to wreak her revenge on the helpless when she cannot find those who angered her."

"This we knew, Your Grace. It is why we waited so long to act."

"Why act now?" she asked him, but glanced at Ivar as the words faded and Ulric did not immediately reply. "Brother Ivar convinced you?"

"He gave me the means, but it was not his argument that convinced me. In truth—" He paused to grin at Ivar with a look that seemed half apologetic. "—there have been other portents and omens. Dissatisfactions and fears."

"Stories of grace," she said, "as I have been hearing these two days."

He nodded. "Stories of God's grace. Of the phoenix. We all know them, Your Grace. We know they are true. But the lady is reckless. She punishes those who work the land and shows mercy to those who are most cruel and greedy. The wars to the west have taken the lives of a score of my militia, but their families gained no bounty for their sacrifice, not even payment for each lost man, as is traditional. The weather is wrong, Your Grace. I am no farmer, but I know the way of the seasons. First came that unnatural wind that blew down houses and smashed trees throughout the woodlands.

We've had no sun for months, not since the autumn. We had untimely rain last summer and little enough this winter. The stores in
Autun grow low. The lady has not husbanded them wisely, not as
you would have done, seeing that each family received a ration to
last them through the lean months and seed corn if they lost their
store to wind and bad weather. Lady Sabella has lost God's favor, so
I believe. She has usurped what does not belong to her. Thus we are
come. This one—Brother Ivar." He nodded toward Ivar. "I took his
plea as a sign that it was time to act. We have gathered our families
and left behind our homes to follow you, Your Grace."

"Where is Baldwin?" demanded Ivar. "Didn't you find him? Is he
lost?"

"Nay, nay, he is with the others, he and Erkanwulf, a few hours
behind us. We rode ahead to find you. We must move rapidly, Your
Grace. Our desertion will be known too soon. Because we are so
many, and laden with carts and children, we will not move as
swiftly as Lady Sabella's mounted cavalry when they ride on our
trail. We have done what we can to cast doubt upon our road, but
they will discover it."

"I see." All this time, Constance had held his hand. She let go, and
he pressed it briefly to his forehead, gaze cast down. "You have
stepped onto a path from which there is no turning back."

"Yes, Your Grace."

"You have put yourself into my hands."

"Yes, Your Grace."

She was used to command. She had been born into the royal family, and had been younger than Ivar was now when the biscop's
staff had been placed in her right hand.

"I must ask of you and your company that you ride a more difficult and thorny path even than the one you have embarked on
now. I have interviewed Brother Ivar at length. It seems clear to me
that my niece Theophanu cannot aid me, perhaps will not aid me,
and may not even have the means to feed and house my growing
retinue. She may even see me as a threat, and certainly as a re-
minder of her weakness. Avaria is too far. While it is true I might
find refuge in Fesse, I am determined to take the harder path."

The captain blanched, as might a man preparing himself for
worse news than what he has just heard. "Your Grace." He bowed
his head and thereby accepted his fate.

"Sabella usurped my place and imprisoned me because she rightly
feared to murder me outright, although I am sure she hoped my in-

juries would kill me. They did not. Now I am free to act as I was not before. I will not ride into exile in Wendar. Henry set me as steward over the duchy of Arconia. No more would I trust a steward of my own who fled in time of trouble. I cannot act in a way I would myself condemn. We must rouse the countryside and fight to restore what is ours."

Ivar was too stunned to speak, and yet his heart thrilled to hear her impassioned words. She was crippled by her injuries, but she was not weak. Examining her proud face and brilliant eyes, he saw that she was in some measure stronger than she had been before her fall.

"Your Grace." Ulric clenched one hand. The other rested on his sword hilt.

The men murmured, their voices like the rush of wind through leaves. Farther away, a hawk *skreed*, and Ivar glanced up to see the bird glide away over the treetops. The fire popped loudly as a stick, burned almost to ash, broke into pieces. Sister Eligia coughed.

"I can offer nothing but uncertainty," said Constance, "but this I promise: We will win Arconia back."

Every man and woman knelt, and some sighing and some with a grin and one weeping and several with expressions of grim fatalism, promised to serve her and her cause.

Even Ivar knelt. How could he do otherwise? Still, he was a little disgusted that he had planned so well and now had to watch the arrow curve off target.

"Where must we go?" he demanded.

She nodded. "That, too, I have considered. We must circle north to avoid capture, and then west to a place where we will find support and refuge. We will ride to Lavas County and seek aid and comfort from Lord Geoffrey."

"Best to travel as one group," said Captain Ulric as they waited for the baggage train to arrive. "We might split into many smaller groups and hope to reach Lavas County undetected, but every small group will therefore be more vulnerable. Our trail is easily followed if we travel together, but we are also protected by our numbers. Lady Sabella will have to hear of our journey, and our road, and raise a large enough force to meet us without fear of being defeated by our numbers. That will take time and forethought, and may give us the advantage we need. Yet we must also consider, Your Grace, what we will do once we reach Lavas County. Of a certainty, Lady Sabella or Duke Conrad will send an army to drive us out."

"As we travel, we will discuss what choices we have," Constance agreed. She paused and turned her head as though seeking something.

The soft light cast its muted glamour over the clearing. Horses grazed at the sparse grass. They were being led in groups to water at the nearby stream, heard as a quiet laughter beneath the constant noise of men walking, talking, hammering a stronger axle into one of the carts, and, here and there, singing.

> *"I woke at midnight in the deep wood*
> *I woke at midnight when the moon was new*
> *There I saw a kindling fire*
> *A bright fire!*
> *Truth rises with the phoenix.*
> *So spoke the holy one:*
> *Truth rises with the phoenix."*

"What song is this?" Ivar whispered to Sigfrid, who sat cross-legged beside him with his bony hands folded in his lap and his thin face composed and calm.

"I've not heard those words before," said Sigfrid, "but I know the melody well enough." He hummed along, picking up the refrain at once.

"Truth rises with the phoenix," echoed Ivar. Wind rippled, bringing a spatter of rain. He wiped his eyes as the mizzle shushed away into the trees. Above the chatter of men and the clatter of branches, he heard the tramp and rumble of an approaching procession.

Naturally, Baldwin rode at the front on a handsome roan mare. His seat was matchless. Even his clerical robes, cut for riding, fell in pleasing folds and layers about his legs and was swept up in back to cover his mount's flanks. A well-dressed girl of about fourteen rode beside him on a sturdy gelding. She was so dazzled by Baldwin's attention to her that she did not notice the captain approaching with a frown on his face.

"Louisa! Come at once to pay your respects to the holy biscop."

Her eyes widened. She startled and touched the linen scarf that mostly covered her dark hair. "Yes, Father. I pray you, Brother Baldwin, excuse me."

He smiled at her, and she flushed.

"Shameless!" muttered Ivar.

Beside him, Sigfrid chuckled. "You are no different than any of us. Poor Baldwin. Do we truly love him, or only his beauty? Yet he looks well."

He looked well. He cast his gaze anxiously over the multitude, found what he sought, and smiled so brilliantly at Ivar and Sigfrid that Ivar actually heard murmurs from the followers who with their carts and donkeys and bundles were moving in a sluggish flow into the clearing. Many faces turned to watch the young cleric as he dismounted and pressed through the crowd. Hands reached out to touch his robe, and seemingly unconsciously he brushed his fingers across the foreheads of small children pushed into his path.

Ermanrich whistled under his breath. "You'd think he was a saint the way they treat him."

"Ivar!" Baldwin surged forward to embrace him, weeping with happiness. "Ai, God! Sigfrid! Ermanrich! Hathumod!" He kissed each of them, tears streaming in a flood of joy.

"You must greet Biscop Constance," said Ivar, whose temper had sparked with unfathomable annoyance.

"It worked?" Baldwin asked as guilelessly as a child inquires about the ineffable mystery of God. "She is free?"

Biscop Constance approached them, leaning on her staff and assisted by Sister Eligia. "I am free, Brother Baldwin, in no small measure because of the risk you took in Sabella's court."

"Baldwin!" Ivar tried to keep his voice to a whisper, but his irritation kept pushing it louder. "It's not right to make the holy biscop approach *you*. You should have gone to her first!"

Baldwin dropped to his knees before the biscop. When she extended her hand, he pressed her ring to his lips. His tears wet her hand. Remarkably, she also had tears on her face.

She, too, was blinded by his beauty.

Ivar found himself wiping rain off his face, only it had stopped raining and he had already dried his face once.

"Are you the one?" she asked Baldwin.

"I am Lady Sabella's seal. I admit to worse things I did. I was her concubine, it's true, but I'm not proud of my sins, Your Grace." His face was so open and innocent that it appeared that whatever he had done he had done without malice or forethought.

"We have all done that which displeases God."

"And God's mercy has saved us. I have sworn an oath to God, that I will serve Her alone and for the rest of my days, as penance for my sins and in service of Her glory, which has come down to us out of the heavens and casts its brilliance across the Earth."

Constance examined him closely. "Are you that one I have heard whispers of? The rose among thorns?"

He shook his head, bewildered by her comment. The captain's daughter had come as close as she dared to stare at Baldwin, but her father drew her back with a look that might scar.

"Truth rises with the phoenix," said Constance.

He blushed. "Oh. That. It's true I made up words to pass the time, and set them to a melody I liked to sing. It was an easy way to help folk remember the phoenix."

"Then it's true, for surely you have a form most like to the angels." She bowed her head.

Baldwin looked up at Ivar and mouthed the words, *"What's true?"*

Ivar could only shrug.

She raised a hand and by this means brought silence to the assembly crowded around to hear. "A great evil has fallen upon us. Famine, sickness, war, and dissension plague us. God is angry, yet She has not forsaken us as we have feared. Many here have heard the stories of God's grace."

"Truth rises with the phoenix!" cried a woman from the back, and other voices echoed her.

"Do not fear the days to come," said the biscop as folk around her knelt. "Her glory has come down to us out of the heavens and casts its brilliance over the Earth. If we will only believe, then we will be safe. God will answer us in our time of trouble, grant our every desire, fulfill our every plan. She sends us help from her sanctuary." She raised Baldwin to his feet as he smiled pliantly with that look of beautiful incomprehension that in Quedlinhame had so charmed his praeceptors. "A holy one walks among us."

Behind Ivar, Hathumod burst into tears.

5

"YOUR Excellency! I pray you, forgive us for disturbing you. Come quickly, Your Excellency!"

The servant's voice was shrill with a panic that roused Antonia out of a restful sleep. She grunted and slapped a hand over her eyes to shut out the flicker of lamplight as the clumsy servant leaned over her and the sting of oily smoke made her cough.

"Your Excellency!"

"I have woken."

The fool woman remained poised there, as stupid as a cow. "Come quickly."

In the adjoining room, little Berengaria began to wail as Mathilda's shrieks filled the air. The servant groaned and fled, leaving Antonia to rise in her shift and grope her way through the dark room to the opened door that led from one chamber into the other. There was, mercifully, lamplight, and a trio of servants hastily shoving a heavy table out of the way.

Young Mathilda was spinning, arms straight out and rigid, hands in fists. "Get away, you beast! It has red eyes! Why can't anyone else see them?" She sobbed gustily.

"Your Highness, if you will only sit down—"

"Shan't! You're trying to kill me! Just like Mama and Papa! They're never coming! You did it! You did it!"

She swung wildly, battering her attendants. They skittered back to circle as nervously as a pack of dogs waiting to have a stone thrown at them.

One of the double doors leading out into the courtyard creaked open and Captain Falco slipped in. He was dressed, armed, and alert. He slept athwart the doors on the pavement outside, but despite his constant faithful presence and the quiet surroundings in Novomo where they had bided many weeks now, Mathilda still suffered from night terrors.

"I hate you! I hate you!" she shouted, but it was not clear whom she hated, or what she feared.

"Your Highness," ventured Captain Falco.

"Go away! Go! Go!" She stamped her feet over and over, drumming them on the floor, and flailed with her arms as she screamed and screamed. It was as if she was possessed by a demon.

"Your Highness!" said Antonia sternly.

A nursemaid had caught up Berengaria, who could not cry for long before starting to cough, and bent her efforts to soothing the little one.

"Take her into my chamber," said Antonia. "Get her away from her sister! You should have done it at once, when you saw the fit coming on."

The nursemaid whimpered, and started for the other door, but Mathilda leaped forward and grabbed at her shift.

"No! You shan't steal her away! She's mine!"

Berengaria set up a wail that at once broke into racking coughs, and the child was wheezing and gasping for breath as Mathilda began to jump up and down shrieking with each leap, completely out of control.

"Captain Falco! You must restrain her!"

He hesitated. He hated to do it. He knew the princess fought him, and despised him, although he had never done one thing to harm her. Indeed, his softness had done the most damage, no doubt. A stern hand must control a hysterical child.

"Captain!"

She would not do it herself. Last time, Mathilda had bitten her.

He turned his head, caught by a new sound. Out in the courtyard, torchlight gleamed. She heard a cacophony of voices and the clatter of many feet advancing on them. Falco drew his sword and stepped into the doorway, calling for his men. Mathilda was still screaming. The hapless nursemaid scuttled to the safety of Antonia's chamber.

There came a slap, like an arrow thumping into wood. Falco fell to his knees and cried out. The second door slammed open, and an apparition appeared—gaunt, filthy, and ragged but entirely alive.

"Mama!"

Mathilda flung herself forward and hit her mother so hard that the queen would have tumbled over if so many attendants were not already pressing up behind her. All of the princess' hysteria collapsed into noisy, grieving, frightened sobs. She clung to her mother for what seemed an hour while no one spoke and Adelheid grasped her, dry-eyed, until at last the girl cried herself to sleep.

By this time the nursemaid had crept back into the room with her mouth gaping open like a simpleton's and Berengaria silent and slack in her arms.

"Captain," said Adelheid in a low voice.

He had by now recovered from his shock and joy. At her direction, he took Princess Mathilda out of her arms and carried her to her bed. The child was so heavily asleep that she did not even stir. Adelheid beckoned to the nursemaid, who brought Berengaria to her. The toddler was still awake but now too weak after her fit of coughing to do more than gaze blankly at her mother.

"What is wrong with her?" The hoarse quality of Adelheid's voice did not change. She did not weep, or storm, or show any sign of anger or joy.

"It's the cough, Your Majesty," said the nursemaid, stumbling over the words. "She's had that cough since the storm that overset us all."

"Demons were set loose in the world," said Antonia briskly. "They have found a way in to where weakness and innocence offer ripe pickings."

Adelheid glanced at her, but Antonia could not interpret what feelings, if any, stormed beneath her pinched features. It was not that the young queen was no longer pretty, although certainly she had lost her bloom. It was as if the light that animated her had been snuffed out. She was cold and hard, like a woman who would never laugh again.

"Have you no honey for her throat?" asked the queen, speaking sternly to the nursemaid. "Ground up with chestnut meat, it might soothe her. She has always suffered these fits, as I'm sure you have not forgotten." She noted each of the other attendants with her gaze. "I would have a bath, although I am sorry to disturb you all from your rest."

Lady Lavinia pushed forward out of the throng. "Let us only be thankful you have survived, Your Majesty. Anything in my power to give you is yours."

"You have endured the storm better than many," observed Adelheid. As servants scurried off to haul and heat water and lay out clothing, she walked forward into the chamber to stand beside the bed shared by her daughters.

"The wind caused much damage, Your Majesty," said Lavinia, "but my people have set to work with a will to repair roofs and fences and walls with winter coming on. For a few days afterward there was some ash fall, but not so much that we could not sweep it off the streets and dig out the few ditches and pits that it disturbed. Still, there has been no sun for many months. It has been a hard winter."

For a long while Adelheid watched her daughters. Berengaria, too, had fallen asleep, but her thin face was pale and she whistled with each exhalation. A steward brought in cracked chestnuts, and the nursemaid sat down at the table to grind them into a paste she could mix into honey.

Beyond, in the courtyard, torches and lamps were lit and servants scurried to and fro. Captain Falco had vanished, replaced by two solemn guardsmen. Lavinia yawned silently and rubbed her eyes, but did not stray by one step from Adelheid's elbow. The lady of Novomo was worn and worried but steadfast. She had lost less than most: her daughter had been sent north soon after Adelheid's departure for Dalmiaka, and so had weathered the storm in her mother's hall. Of her close kin, all were accounted for; all were alive.

Soon it would be dawn, such as dawn was these days without any sight of the sun's disk ever appearing to promise that the light of God's truth would soon illuminate all of humankind. God had clouded the heavens as a sign of Their disapproval.

"I have seen such things. . . ." murmured Adelheid, more breath than speech. She did not weep, although her tone harrowed her listeners.

"What have you seen, Your Majesty?" asked Lavinia, wiping a tear from her own face.

"God's wrath. I was spared only because I prayed to God that I might see my daughters once more. That they are safe is the best I could hope for. Henry is dead, murdered by his own son."

"Patricide!"

The servants whispered together, and this rush of conversation, like the press of wind through trees, flowed outside into the court-yard from whence it would no doubt be blown throughout the entire palace and town.

Henry is dead, murdered by his own son.

Adelheid turned. "What must I do, Sister Venia? I had this report from an Aostan lord who saw Henry fall. Prince Sanglant has claimed the Wendish throne for himself although he is only a bastard and thereby has no right to take it. The Wendish folk have deserted us. The Aostan lords and ladies have fled to their castles, those who survived. The plain of Dar has been swallowed by the Enemy. Darre itself is a ruin. No one can live there. The western coast has burst into flame. The mountains spew fire. So we are punished for our sins. The nobles will strike against me. Already they blame me for what they term 'the Wendish folly.' Those who were once my allies have deserted me."

Antonia smiled. At long last, God had answered her, as she had always expected Them to do. "Do not fear, Your Majesty. God are testing us. Through our actions, we will reveal our true natures. Then They will separate the wicked from the righteous. Anoint me as skopos, and I will set all to right."

"How can I anoint you, Sister," the queen asked bitterly, "when I have no allies and no army and you have no chair?"

"It is true I have no chair, but I possess the skopos' robes and scepter, which were abandoned by Holy Mother Anne. She did not respect God as she ought. Earthly concerns stained her, so she forgot what was due her position as God's shepherd on Earth."

"Perhaps. But all fell out as she predicted. The Lost Ones have had their revenge, and we survive in the ruins of their triumph."

"We are not yet ruined, Your Majesty. Be strong. I have one other thing Anne left behind." She crossed into her chamber. After a servingwoman helped her into a robe, she waved the woman out of the room and turned to her wooden storage chest. She had bound a burning spell into the lock in the form of an amulet identical to that Anne had used in the palace in Darre: wolfsbane, lavender, and thistle. Tracing a sign, she murmured the words of unbinding and protection before teasing apart the amulet and unlocking and opening the chest. She dug beneath layers of silk and linen and returned to the other room.

Adelheid had not moved, although by now day was rising and the servants had extinguished the lamps.

Two stewards entered, the second waiting as the first whispered to Lady Lavinia, who nodded.

"Very good, Veralia. Have the guards bring the prisoners to the courtyard. I'll be out in a moment." As the first steward hurried out, Lavinia bent her head to hear the message brought by the second, then turned to Adelheid. "Your Majesty, if you will attend me, there is water now for a bath and clean robes to change into. A meal to be served and wine to drink."

Adelheid did not move.

"I must go out for a moment, Your Highness," Lavinia continued, looking anxious when Adelheid did not respond. "My soldiers scout the countryside every day, seeking refugees. Enemies. Allies. We cast a wide net, and now and again catch a handsome fish. Few march as boldly to our walls as you did."

Lavinia faltered as Antonia shook her head, enjoining silence. Mathilda's attendants had shoved the big table out of the way and up against a tapestry depicting the trials of triumphs of St. Agnes, the virgin whom fire refused to burn. Antonia set her burden down on this table and unwrapped the cloth covering. It gleamed in lamplight, polished and bright.

"That is Emperor Taillefer's crown," said Adelheid. Her expression sharpened. The fire that had refused to touch St. Agnes, tied to the stake for refusing to offer incense to pagan gods, had leaped into Adelheid's heart and caught there.

"Henry may be dead, Your Majesty, but his daughters live. You are still Empress, crowned and anointed."

"I am still Empress," she whispered, nodding.

God grant a certain light to some people that causes them therefore to draw the eye. As one watches a flame ignite in oil, Antonia watched Adelheid burn once more. The trials she had suffered had seared away her soft prettiness, but even this could not touch the core of her, which was iron.

"We must bide our time and make our plans carefully," the queen went on. "We must seek what advantage we can. We must act quickly to build a base of support. News must go out at once that there is a new skopos. Then folk must come to us to receive your blessing."

Perhaps she had underestimated Adelheid. Anger and suffering had honed her into a fitting weapon.

"Many will seek God's guidance," Antonia agreed.

"It's true I still have an army, if Lady Lavinia can feed and house us. There are other allies who will be desperate for guidance—as you say—in this time of trouble. Frightened people seek a strong leader." She touched each gem fixed to the seven points on the massive crown: gleaming pearl, lapis lazuli, pale sapphire, carnelian, ruby, emerald, and last of all banded orange-brown sardonyx, which represented God's hierarchy on Earth: God, noble, commoner.

"My lady!" The first steward reappeared at the door. Veralia was stout and brisk, a good captain of the hall. "The guards have brought the new prisoners, as you instructed. They are armed, but have offered no resistance, so Captain Oswalo deemed it best not to provoke a fight. They are heavily guarded."

Adelheid stepped forward. "What have you found, Lavinia?"

"A small band of Wendish folk, so I am told. I have already given instructions that any Wendish refugees are to be brought to me. We know not what jewels we may find among them. Veralia?"

"They were arrested by our soldiers yesterday, on the road that leads down out of the north."

"Wendish refugees should be fleeing *to* the north," said Adelheid.

"Captain Oswalo wondered at first if they might be spies, but—well—you will see, my lady. Your Majesty. There is a young Wendish lord and his attendant, a cleric, a servingwoman, two barbarians, and a girl who claims to be the descendant of Emperor Taillefer."

Indeed, a piercing, immature voice was suddenly audible to every soul in the chamber, driven in from outside by powerful lungs and delivered in Wendish.

"I *said* I don't want to come here! I *said* it. Why does no one listen to me?"

"Perhaps because your voice is too loud," remarked a second voice, that of a youth. Its timbre caused Antonia's heart to race; she flushed, heat speeding to her skin.

"It has to be loud if no one can hear me!"

"Everyone can hear you, brat."

"I'm *not* a brat. I'm not! We need to keep going south, to Darre. I have to find my father, you know that. He's supposed to be in Darre, so that's where we're going. If we'd fought them to begin with, we wouldn't be prisoners now!"

"That's right. Because we'd all be dead. They outnumber us three to one."

"That never stopped my father! Did it, Heribert? Did it?"

The sound of that name made her dizzy. She thought she might collapse, but she forced herself to totter forward in the wake of Lavinia and Adelheid as they sallied out the door, their curiosity piqued by the childish outburst. Adelheid began to laugh, almost sobbing.

"How came this prize to me?" she asked Lady Lavinia.

"Do you know these folk?" Lavinia asked.

Antonia caught herself on the door's frame as she stared past Adelheid's shoulder.

"I know the one who is most important to me," said Adelheid.

Even Antonia, who had only seen her as an infant, recognized Sanglant's daughter in the lanky, furious girl straining to break free of a stolid young servant woman who held her by the shoulders. Whether the girl meant to kick the youth who stood with arms crossed in front of her, alternately making irritated faces at her and measuring his captors, or whether she meant to throw herself onto Lavinia's guards like a wild lion cub, Antonia could not tell. The servingwoman had a queer cast of skin but looked otherwise normal. There were, indeed, two barbarians, one man and one woman with dark complexions, slanted eyes, and outlandish tunics fashioned out of stiffened cloth nothing like woven wool. The woman wore an elaborate headdress. The man carried a quiver and a strung bow and seemed only to be biding his time, waiting for a signal. There was a youthful servingman as well, a callow lordling of a kind she recognized from her days as biscop in

Mainni, some minor noble's youngest son sent off to serve a higher born man.

She recognized the youth who was arguing with the princess. He had his father's look about him; no one could mistake him for another man's son.

But what bent her back and made her sag against the frame was the seventh in their party, dressed in well-worn cleric's robes. A careful observer might remark on a certain resemblance between the noble youth and the once elegant cleric, but few bothered to look closely in a place where they had no expectation of reward.

The princess broke free of her servant and marched right up to Adelheid.

"Who are *you?*" she demanded, planting fists on hips as she jutted out her chin. She looked to be about twelve or thirteen years of age, which was manifestly impossible, but her behavior suggested that of a much younger child. "You're *dirty!*"

The empress looked down on the child, not kindly. "I am the one who holds you hostage."

"You do not!"

The barbarian archer twitched and slid a hand toward his quiver.

"Put it down, Odei," said young Villam. "Best to see what they want before we get ourselves killed in a hopeless fight."

The man glanced at Princess Blessing, then nodded. He served the girl, but obeyed the youth, who already possessed his father's calm habit of command. Yet hadn't this boy died years ago? She had a vague memory of a tale told of Villam's youngest son vanishing beneath a stone crown. And hadn't Sanglant's and Liath's baby been born only five years past? This could not be the same infant she remembered.

There was one among the prisoners who could answer her questions. One who watched without expression as the other six looked, each according to her nature, alarmed, angry, rebellious, puzzled, thoughtful, or scared.

"Now we have something Henry's bastard son wants," said Adelheid. "If you will, Lavinia, lock them away, but do not neglect them. These are a fine treasure. This will serve us well."

"Yes, Your Majesty. Captain, place guards in the North Tower and install them there."

"Yes, my lady. At once."

"Will you ransom us?" asked the youth boldly.

"If it serves my purpose," replied Adelheid, looking him over. She nodded. "You must be Helmut Villam's son. The resemblance is re-markable. Are you one of his by-blows? I understood he had no le-gitimate sons still living."

The lad smiled, reminding Antonia even more of Villam, who had known how to use his charm to advantage. "That mystery must remain unanswered." His pause was not quite insolent, not quite proud. "Your Majesty."

She laughed, amused by him, liking his face and his manners, al-though he was still a youth and she long since a woman. Still, the gap in years was not that great. Stranger matches had happened. "Take them. I'll have that bath, Lavinia, with thanks."

"Go," said Lavinia to her captain.

Antonia stumbled forward and grabbed the cleric's sleeve as, in the confusion, he hesitated while the guards pressed the others into the courtyard. He turned and looked at her, not appearing at all sur-prised to see her. In the solemn morning light, his eyes appeared more blue than hazel. A trio of guards waited to escort him while the rest dispersed. The child had begun to complain again in that ir-ritating voice.

"I don't want to go to the tower! I want to go to—"

"You deserted me," Antonia said, keeping her voice low so others would not hear. Long had it festered. Until this moment, she hadn't realized how angry he had made her. "You disobeyed me! I never gave you permission to leave me."

"I remember you," said Heribert in a voice not his own. "He never liked you."

"What do I care if he liked me or not! He is a bastard, no better than a dog! It is your desertion of the one to whom you owe alle-giance that offends God."

"I acted because of what was in my heart. I loved him, but he is lost to me and I can love no other."

She slapped him.

His face, so finely bred and once so familiar, seemed that of a stranger as he carefully drew his sleeve out of her grasp and turned to the guards. "I would follow them I know," he said with his back to her as if she were no better than a servant. No one to whom he owed fealty. No one who mattered one whit to him.

She fell, and fell, into the Pit, into a fit of coughing furious sick-ening rage, but he was already beyond her and she would not make a scene with servants walking past and Captain Falco watching be-side the door with rebuking curiosity.

"Are you well, Your Excellency? I pray you are not ill."

Falco did not so pray. He distrusted her. Few could love the righteous. They envied and hated them instead.

But her son. Her own son, for whom she had sacrificed so much!

Heribert would be punished, of course. Did it not state in the Holy
Verses that children were commanded to respect and honor their
mothers and fathers, or else be stoned to death?

Yet Heribert was weak. She knew that because she had raised him
to be weak and compliant. It was the bastard, the false one, the
enemy—Prince Sanglant—who had corrupted him.

Therefore, it was Sanglant who had to fall.

PART THREE

ADVENTUS

IX
WELL MET

1

THE adventus of Sanglant, son of Henry, into the ancient citadel
of Quedlinhame at the head of his victorious army would be com-
memorated in poetry and song, Liath supposed, but no doubt the
poets would sing of fine silken banners rippling in the breeze and
gaily caparisoned horses prancing under the rein of their
magnificently-garbed riders, a host splendid and brilliant beyond description, shining in the light of the sun. That's what poets did. This
ragged army and dreary day offered no fodder for song, so song
would make of them something they were not.

But march they did along the road, silent, weary, hungry, but not
beaten. On this gray, late winter day, the view before them was
dominated by the hill and its ancient fortress, now the cloister ruled
by Sanglant's aunt, Mother Scholastica. The fields on one side of the
road lay in stubble, and on the other a field of winter wheat had
sprouted mostly weeds.

Scouts had ridden ahead to inform the abbess of their arrival, and
that wise woman had sent her novices and nuns and monks out to
line the road as a way of greeting the man who claimed the regnancy and who possessed, more importantly, the corpus of the dead

king. Townspeople stood back, staring rather than cheering. They looked thin and pale. Like the wheat, they hadn't had much to subsist on over the winter. As the army trudged between the rows of robed novices and sturdy monks, Liath peered into those faces, although she knew Ivar was long gone from Quedlinhame.

On that other adventus, so well remembered, Henry's troops and clerics had sung triumphant hymns as a processional. That so many of Sanglant's still breathed was a testament to his leadership, but certainly their arrival stirred no festive mood and no songs. Not yet. The songs would be written later.

No one in Wendar had heard Henry, with his dying breath, name Sanglant as his heir. In Wendar, Sanglant would have to fight with intrigue, diplomacy, and force of personality. These weapons, which he liked least, he would of necessity wield most.

It was not going to be easy.

That, certainly, became clear as soon as they saw the welcoming party arrayed in the middle of the road: two men and two women in cleric's robes and a woman wearing the key and chain of the mayor. Liath sorted faces, and turned her attention inward in order to race through her palace of memory, marking names and features.

Sanglant was ahead of her in thought although he rode at her left hand on his gelding, Fest. She heard him mutter under his breath. The words escaped her, but the tone was sour.

"Ha!" said Duchess Liutgard, who rode to his left and was never shy of speaking her mind. "Now the game starts in earnest, Cousin. Where is your aunt? She has snubbed you by not coming out to greet you herself."

"Is the insult worse to me, or to my father?" asked Sanglant grimly. "He deserves better state than this trifling welcome."

A monk whose face seemed familiar to Liath came forward from the group and bowed his head. "Your Highness. You are welcome here to Quedlinhame, ancient home of your father's grandfather's maternal lineage. I pray you, Your Highness, let me lead your horse into the town as befits your rank."

"You are the prior?" asked Sanglant.

"I am."

Sanglant looked at his cousin Liutgard, and for an instant Liath felt insulted in her turn, that Sanglant shouldn't look to her first, who came first in his heart. Yet Liutgard's understanding of court politics so far surpassed Liath's as Liath's understanding of sorcery exceeded Liutgard's knowledge of the magical arts. Sanglant, being a good commander, called for spears when he needed spears and swords when he needed swords.

"Where is Mother Scholastica?" Liutgard asked. "I am surprised she has not come to greet the regnant, as is fitting."

"Has he been anointed and crowned, my lady?" The prior did not appear cowed by the ranks of soldiers. "What of his siblings, Henry's other children? What transpires on the field of battle—of which we have not yet heard a full accounting—may be reexamined by clearer heads."

"As if you can possibly comprehend what we faced!" cried Liutgard, half rising in the saddle. Her horse danced sideways in response to her mood.

"We also suffered many losses in the storm. Your own heir—"

It was a cruel blow. Sanglant caught Liutgard's horse as her hands went slack on the reins. She was felled, speechless, and he must speak for her.

"What of Duchess Liutgard's heir?"

"Killed in last autumn's tempest by a falling branch when she was out riding," the prior said primly, as if some fault accrued to the girl.

"There is another daughter. Ermengard. Destined for the church, if I recall rightly."

The prior nodded. "Mother Scholastica did all that was proper. She brought the child to Kassel to take up her sister's place."

Liutgard jerked the reins out of Sanglant's hands and pressed her horse forward until it almost trampled the prior, who took several steps back as his own people crowded forward to protect him. She was hoarse with fury. "Mother Scholastica could bear these tidings to me herself, as would have been *proper.* Instead she allows me to come to this grief through your careless chatter!"

Sanglant turned to his captain and spoke quietly. "Fulk. We'll set up camp."

Fulk gave the order, and one of the sergeants blew the signal that marked the day's end to the march. Townsfolk scattered out of the way as soldiers rolled out wagons and dismounted from their horses.

A *skree* reverberated from the heavens as the griffins returned. At first glance, they might appear as eagles. Within moments, however, their true nature became apparent, and the townsfolk who had lingered to chat or trade with the soldiers screamed and ran for the safety of the walls. To his credit, the prior stood his ground as the two griffins landed with a whuff of wings and a resounding thump on the ground. The poor mayor, gone corpse white, knotted her hands and began to weep.

Liutgard reined her horse aside, her face white and her hands shaking.

"Prior Methodius, my tent flies the black dragon." Sanglant gestured casually toward the griffins. "You will also know where I camp by the presence of my attendants."

"Have we your permission to retreat, Your Highness?" asked Prior Methodius, voice hoarse with fear.

"You may go."

They retreated slowly, like honey oozing down a slope. They were afraid to run despite wanting badly to do so. Sanglant dismounted on the road, holding himself under a tighter rein than he did his gelding.

"I wish the griffins had torn them to bits!" cried Liutgard. "She is challenging your authority, and mine! That was a good answer to their impertinence."

He smiled, although not with any pleasure. "I did not call the griffins. They always return about this time of day."

"It will be taken as a sign. There is no telling what alliances your aunt has formed in the last few years. King Henry was gone from Wendar for too long. Half of the Wendish folk beg us for aid, and the other half curse at us for abandoning them. We can never trust her now. She scorns us, who served Henry best!"

"What do you say, Burchard?" Sanglant asked, seeing that Liutgard was caught up in a passion.

Duke Burchard rode at Liutgard's left. His hands shook with a palsy, and he was always exhausted, at the end, so the poets would say, of his rope. He was not a warm man, Liath had discovered, but she respected him.

He turned his weary gaze to Liutgard. The duchess had the stamina to adjust to reversals and hardships. She had lost one husband, and must at this moment be too stunned to really absorb the news the prior had brought her.

"I will see you anointed and recognized, Your Majesty. Then I mean to go home, set my duchy in order, and die. I have seen too much." One of his stewards helped him down from his horse and led him away to a tent, the first up, where he could lie down.

So they went, some time later, into the royal tent salvaged out of the ruins of Henry's army. On the center pole, the red silk banner with eagle, dragon, and lion stitched in gold flew above the black dragon.

Inside, Liath sat on a stool as Sanglant paced, while his stewards and captains came and went on errands she could not keep track of. Now and again he glanced at her, as if to mark that she had not escaped him, but he listened, considered, gave orders, and countermanded two of these commands when new information was brought to him. He knew what to do. She was superfluous. Lamps were lit, and when she stepped outside to take in the texture of the chill winter air, she saw that it was almost dark.

On the road, a score of folk carrying torches approached. They halted when Argent coughed a warning cry and raised his crest.

She walked over to him. He bent his head and allowed her to scratch the spot where forearm met shoulder that he had a hard time reaching with beak or claws. His breath was meaty, and his huge eyes blinked once, twice, then cleared as the inner membrane flicked back. She should fear him; she knew that; but since Anne's death, her reunion with Sanglant, and the departure of the Horse people, nothing seemed to scare her, not even when it should. She watched, and she listened, but she spoke little and offered less advice.

"In some ways," she said idly to Argent as he rumbled in his throat, "it's as if all Da's training to be invisible has flowered. Do beasts know what their purpose is? Or do they simply exist?"

A voice raised in protest. "I pray you, Holy Mother, do not venture forward. The beasts could tear you to pieces."

"God will watch over me."

Liath remembered that pragmatic voice well enough; she watched from the anonymity of Argent's shoulder as Mother Scholastica dismounted from a skittish white mule. The torchlight illuminated her. Her stern face had grown lean and lined in the manner of a woman who has had to make many difficult, distressing decisions, but her back was still straight and her stride measured and confident as she approached the tent with her attendants scuttling behind. She did not glance even once at the griffins, although her attendants could not stop looking. The entrance flap swept open and Sanglant emerged to wait for her beneath the awning.

"Aunt," he said graciously. "You honor me."

"Where is Henry?"

He gestured toward the interior of the tent, but certainly he turned and went inside first, and she allowed him to do so, giving him precedence. A trio of clerics scurried in after her. Others waited outside, huddled under the awning as they whispered and, at intervals, cast glances into the night where the griffins waited. After a moment Liath realized that naturally they could see only shadows; she could see them because of the pair of lit lamps hanging from the awning and, of course, because of her salamander eyes.

She gave Argent a last vigorous scratch and went back to the tent. The clerics stared at her, but the guardsmen nodded and made no comment as she slipped past them.

"I bring unwelcome tidings, Liutgard," Scholastica was saying.

"You bring no tidings at all," replied Liutgard caustically. "I have already heard the news."

Even this disrespectful greeting did not jolt Scholastica's composure. Sanglant indicated that the abbess should sit in the camp chair to his left normally reserved for Liutgard. The stool to his right sat empty. He noted Liath's entrance with a glance, but otherwise kept his attention on his aunt.

"Where did Henry's death take place? In what manner did you find him? How can you verify that he was in thrall to this daimone? What of Queen Adelheid? Whose blow killed him? Where is his corpus now?"

"We brought his heart and bones from the south."

"His remains must be buried at Quedlinhame beside his mother."

"Naturally. Why else would I have come here, Aunt?"

"To be anointed as regnant. Do not trifle with me, Sanglant. Liutgard and Burchard support you. Yet rumor has it that you abandoned Sapientia in the wilderness."

"Never did any sour soul deserve that fate more!" laughed Wichman from the corner.

"Silence!"

It was startling to see Wichman cowed as he ducked his head and murmured, "I pray for your pardon, Aunt."

"Do not mock. I will not tolerate it. What of Sapientia, Sanglant? Are you responsible for her death?"

"We do not know if she lives, or is dead."

"Among the Quman savages, living is surely like death. We are not like the Salians or the Aostans or the Arethousans. We Wendish do not kill our relatives in our quest for power."

"I do not seek power, Aunt. I seek order, where it seems there is no other who can grant it. You witnessed the events of last autumn. We felt its effects most bluntly. I have soldiers who are scarred from burns they suffered in that wind and others who died coughing with ash in their lungs. I did what had to be done. That it is not worse with Wendar's army is due to my efforts. I will not have it said otherwise."

"So I witnessed." Liutgard stood with shoulders locked back, arms and neck rigid. "So I will swear, as will all of my soldiers and attendants."

"So I will swear," said Burchard wearily, "although my own daughter perished." He paused to touch Liutgard on the arm before continuing. "What became of Princess Sapientia I do not know, only what reports have been spoken of, but she could not have held the army together. Henry willed the kingdom to Sanglant on his dying breath. This I witnessed. This I swear."

Liath had by this time crept around the wall of the tent as nobles and guardsmen shifted to make way for her, not betraying her by giving her more notice than they would to a faithful hound seeking its master. She wasn't sure whether their deference annoyed her or placated her. She would never become used to this life. Never. But as Scholastica examined Burchard's seamed face, Liath slipped onto the stool beside Sanglant and hoped no one would call attention to her arrival, which no one did. There were five sturdy traveling lamps placed on tripods and another four hanging from the cross poles. The light gave every face a waxy quality, too bright, but there also gleamed on one wall the unfurled imperial banner. Gold-and-silver thread glinted in the crown of stars, which was embroidered on cloth and stained with tracks of soot that no one had been given permission to wash out. Even the rents and tears in the fabric had been left. The Wendish banner had been washed and repaired, but not the imperial one.

"It is not part of our law for the bastard child to inherit," said Scholastica, "but I have observed that laws are silent in the presence of arms. That Liutgard and Burchard speak for you gives strength to your case." She looked at each duke in turn, as if her disapproval could change their minds, but Burchard merely sighed and Liutgard glared back at her. "Let Theophanu and Ekkehard agree, and it will be done."

"I have already sent Eagles to Osterburg."

"I sent Eagles and messengers out as well, when I heard rumor of your coming. While you wait for their arrival, you must disperse your army. I cannot feed so many for more than three days. Our stores are already low. The weather bodes ill for the spring."

"I will keep my army beside me."

"Will you take by force that which you can only win with God's favor, and the agreement of your peers?"

His frown was quick but marked. Unlike his father, Sanglant did not rage easily, and a few men muttered to see him brush the edge of anger. "I did not seek this position. I am my father's obedient son. I have done only what he wished."

"A man may turn away from a platter of meat when he has just eaten, only to crave it when he hungers. We are not unchanging creatures, Nephew. We wax and wane like the moon, and at times we change our minds about what it is we want. Although, I see, some things have not changed." She gestured toward Liath. "The last, if not the first, or so your grandmother divined. Your concubine?"

"My wife," he said, his irritation even more pronounced.

"An Eagle is your wife?" she asked, as if he had claimed to have married a leper.

"Liathano is of noble birth out of Bodfeld."

"A minor family which can bring no worthwhile alliance to your position. Surely it would be wiser to seek a more advantageous match. Duke Conrad's daughter, or Margrave Gerberga of Austra's youngest sister, Theucinda. Margrave Waltharia herself, if it is true that her husband died on your expedition, leaving her free. There was some interest there before, between the two of you, I believe."

"I have what I need."

Scholastica turned her gaze and examined Liath with a look meant to intimidate. Strangely, Liath found herself caught between an intense boredom at the prospect of having to endure much more of this sparring and at the same time a feeling of being wrung so tight that like Sanglant she could not sit restfully but kept tapping one foot on the carpet.

"Your mother was a heathen?" asked Scholastica at last.

"No, not really, Holy Mother," said Liath, aware of how disrespectful she sounded and, for this instant, just not caring.

"A Daisanite woman of black complexion whom your father impregnated?"

"My mother was a daimone of the upper air, imprisoned by the woman who later made herself skopos. My father loved her. I am the result of that passion."

Was that a smile that shifted the lines in that grim expression, even for an instant? Liath had no idea, but she saw that such a bald statement did not confound the abbess although her three clerics made little noises of astonishment. In some cases, a smile is a sword.

"Do you have a soul?" the abbess asked kindly.

Half the people in the tent gasped, while the other half, shocked into silence, stared. Sanglant shifted, ready to rise and confront this challenge, but Liath set a hand on his forearm and he quieted, although she could feel the tension in his muscles, a hound barely leashed and poised to lunge.

"Are not all creatures created by God? I am no different than you, Mother Scholastica."

Her eyes narrowed and her mouth thinned, but it was impossible tell if she were offended or intrigued. "So you say. I understand that you are educated."

"Yes, I am educated as well as my father was able to teach me. I can read and write in three languages."

"You were condemned as a maleficus."

"I am not one. I was educated as a mathematicus."

"You admit it publicly, knowing that the church condemned such sorcery at the Council of Narvone? That you were excommunicated in absentia by a council at Autun?"

"I am not afraid of the church, Mother Scholastica." She was surprised, more than anything, at how weary she felt in defending herself, and how peculiar it was to be shed at long last of the fear that had so long hunted her. Da had taught her to fear; it was the only defense he had known. "I believe in God, just as you do. I pray to God, just as you do. I am no heretic or infidel. You cannot harm me if my companions refuse to shun me, and the skopos and her mages are dead."

As soon as she spoke the words, she knew them ill said. The abbess stiffened and turned deliberately away from her.

"I am not accustomed to being spoken to in this manner, Sanglant," said Mother Scholastica. "Especially not by one who was excommunicated. I have heard tales of this woman. She is infamous for seducing and discarding men."

"So you believe," said Sanglant. "I know otherwise."

"Even your father was not immune."

"My father was betrayed by his second wife, a pretty woman of impeccable noble lineage."

"Will your fate run likewise, Nephew?"

He laughed curtly. "Liathano has already made her choice, and I had no say in it. I will not beg her to stay, nor can I prevent her from leaving."

"Then why do you stay?" the abbess asked Liath, carefully not using her name, as if she were a creature that could not possess a name and therefore a human existence.

"Because I love him."

"Love is trifling compared to obligation, faith, and duty. Passion waxes and wanes like the moon of which we have spoken. It is more fragile than a petal torn from a rose. You may even believe that your motives spring from disinterested love, but you have not answered my question. What do you want?"

Liath had no answer.

2

"I pray you, Sanglant, forgive me. I haven't the patience for court life."

"No," he agreed.

She sat on the pallet they shared, watching him where he sat cross-legged at the tent's entrance. He twitched the flap open and looked away from her to stare out into the camp. The ring of sentry fires burned steadily; a few shapes paced, as he wished he could. In the royal tent he had room to pace, but he had acceded to Liath's wishes weeks ago and set aside a smaller tent where they could sleep alone.

Even in Gent he hadn't slept alone but rather with a pack of dogs as his attendants.

She coughed, bent slightly to scratch her thigh. He glanced at her. She had stripped down to a light linen shift so worn it was translucent. A lamp hung from the crossbeam of the tent, and by its flame he admired how the fabric curved and layered around breast and thigh and hip.

"No," he repeated. "When you were an Eagle, you had no power and had to endure what was cast before you. Now, you have defeated Anne and her Sleepers. Nothing keeps you here except the memory of Blessing—and your love for me. Otherwise, I have nothing you want, as my aunt suspects."

"Does she?"

"Perhaps not. She is the third child, after Henry and Rotrudis. She was placed in the convent early and invested as abbess by the time she was fourteen. Obligation and duty are the milk she has drunk all her life. She must believe you seek power or advancement. She may not be able to believe otherwise."

"What do you believe?"

He shrugged. "I have nothing you want, Liath. Therefore, I believe you."

She smiled, so sweetly that he laughed, although the sight of her pained him now that he was so close to bearing the full weight of the burden his father had thrust on him.

"With Da, I learned to run from place to place. Fugitives only want never to be caught. They never think beyond their next escape route. I set myself against Anne, and I defeated her—if what we have seen these past months can be called a triumph. What is left to me? I have outrun those who sought to capture me. I have lost my daughter."

"As have Liutgard and Burchard lost theirs." He sighed. "And I will become regnant, as my father wished. Will you leave me? It is true you haven't the patience for court life."

From this angle he could see, also, the hill on which the fortress and convent of Quedlinhame stood, ancient seat of his great great grandmother's inheritance. Lucienna of Attomar had brought lands and wealth to the first Henry, together with allies enough to assure him of support when he reached for and took the throne of Wendar. Without Lucienna and her kin, the first Henry would not have become regnant. In honor of that connection, the old fortress had been turned into the most favored and wealthiest monastery in the land, shepherded always by a girl born into the royal line. Like young Richardis, his aunt, who had renamed herself Scholastica when she entered the church as a youthful abbess three decades ago. She was accustomed to wielding power, and to passing judgment. Henry had trusted her. But she did not trust Sanglant or his half-human wife.

A torch shone on the distant wall, marking the gate. Otherwise, it was dark. As usual, clouds obscured the sky. He let the canvas fall and turned to look at his wife. She remained outwardly as calm as a pool undisturbed by wind or debris. Like the stars, she was veiled. But he no longer believed she was hiding anything from him. All artifice and concealment had been burned away, first in her journey into the aether and then, finally, in the cataclysm itself.

"You said once—" To his surprise, he faltered with the words catching in his throat, but he drove himself onward. "You said that what you saw and experienced in the heavens, with your mother's kin, gave you peace."

She nodded. "Yes, peace. More than that. I found joy."

Jealousy gnawed like a worm, as the poets would say, and poets had a knack for speaking truth. "Joy," he said hoarsely, hating the sound of the word, hating the sound of his voice because he knew that on this field he was helpless. He had no weapons and no strategy.

She caught his elbow and drew him close. "I did not stay there." She pressed her lips into the curve of his neck.

Once, this alone would have driven all thought of trouble from his mind. Now, there were many things he wanted to say, but he let them go.

3

FOR three days they remained encamped outside of Quedlin-hame, waiting. Liutgard went into seclusion. By the second day folk came down from the town to trade with the soldiers, not that the soldiers had much to trade with. The men cleaned and repaired their gear, hunted in the woodlands despite the dearth of game, and herded the horses into meadowlands to graze and rest.

With so much time on her hands, Liath flew with the Eagles, al-though she was no longer truly one of their nest. The twenty who had survived the trek north out of Aosta had gained another fifteen comrades, coming piecemeal into their ranks once the army reached Wendar. Most recently a very young Eagle named Ernst who had been chafing at Quedlinhame for several months had arrived at camp, proclaiming himself eager to be out of that cage. Now, in the afternoon, a dozen Eagles sat together under an awning that pro-tected them from a drizzle. The sky had a grayer cast than usual. The fortress hill seemed colorless, set against the dreary sky. The soft light cast a glamour over the oak forest, while to the east the heavens had brightened to a pearllike gleam where the rain stopped and the clouds lightened. The sun never broke through.

"Not much snow in the mountains when we were crossing," Hathui was saying to Ernst. "Maybe more came after we crossed. But if there isn't snow, then the melt won't swell the rivers come spring."

"If spring ever comes," said Ernst. "We had no snow at all. It was uncanny warm all winter. First, there was so much rain the fields flooded. In parts of Osterburg, streets and houses both ran underwater, all the way up to my knees! Nay, wait, that flood came in Askulavre. The bad rainstorms were earlier, back in the autumn. But now there's only a bit of rain like this. And yet always cloud."

"My granddad said there was one winter when he was a lad they never saw sun, and all spring, too," said another Eagle, a southerner out of Avaria with curly dark hair and big, callused hands. "He lost two of his brothers that next winter. It was worse the year after for they'd eaten most of their seed corn. He used to talk about that time a lot when he was blind and bedridden. I'd sit with him, just to hear the tale, for he liked telling it. Still, I wonder." He gestured toward the heavens. "Crops can't grow without sun and rain in the right measure."

"Too warm all winter," said Hathui. "Too dry in the south last year, when we were down there. A terrible drought, so bad every blade of grass was brittle. Up here, everything is soggy. I've got mold on my feet!"

Everyone laughed, and for a while they talked about how their feet itched and how their clothes and tents stank of mildew. Everyone had mold on their feet except Liath, who was never sick and never plagued by fleas or lice or rashes. She sat as usual in the back. The other Eagles were accustomed to her presence in a way no one else could be. They ignored her. For her part, she braided fiber into rope as Eldest Uncle had taught her. At intervals she played surreptitiously at setting twigs to burn, honing her ability to call fire into smaller and smaller targets. Mostly, she listened to their news and their gossip and their conclusions as well as the information they had gleaned speaking to the locals. She listened to Ernst's earnest report of conditions in Wendar over the last six months or more, ever since that windstorm had swept over them. Folk even so far north as Wendar had felt and feared and marked this unnatural tempest, although they had no way of knowing the truth.

The Eagles with Henry's army had seen, and witnessed. Yet even they did not know the whole.

"I wonder," she said aloud, and noted how they all stilled and started and turned, then waited for her to speak. She smiled as she realized in what manner she fooled herself, wanting to believe they did not scrutinize her every least movement and word for hidden meanings. She was no longer an Eagle. That part of her life was gone.

"I'm just wondering," she said into their silence, "if the strange weather is an artifact of Anne's spell. It might even be an effect of the spell woven in ancient times under the Bwr shaman's supervision that rebounded on us. The Bwr shaman are tempestari, so the legends say."

"So we observed ourselves," said Hathui. "It was her magic that stemmed the blizzard that swept over us when we were in the east."

"Or created that blizzard."

Because she had power over the weather.

In a still forest, an unexpected wind may agitate the leaf litter, unearthing hidden depths and items long concealed by layer upon layer of detritus. She rose, tucking fiber and the short length of rope into a pouch. Thoughts skittered like mice fleeing across a church floor suddenly illuminated by a lamp. There was a pattern there, a plan, a potential action. All at once she was too restless to sit, troubled and stimulated by a hundred threads any one of which, teased out to its end, might give her an answer.

"I'll come with you," said Hathui.

Liath laughed as they crossed out into the drizzle, which was already fading into spits and kisses. "Did Sanglant set you on me, to be my guard?"

"Something like that."

"Walk with me. Let me think."

They walked.

Time had passed unnaturally for her. It was strange to be walking in the Wendish countryside after she had traveled to such distant lands. A damp breeze stiffened her hands until she tucked them inside her sleeves and promptly stumbled on uneven ground, tripped, and had to flatten her palm on the ground to avoid pitching headlong into a mire of slimy grass and mud. She swore as she wiped her hand off. Hathui laughed.

They had set up camp beyond the fields that ringed the hilltop fortress, in scrub country used sometimes for cultivation and sometimes for pasture and sometimes left fallow. Stands of young beech grew in neat copses that had recently been trimmed back by woodcutters. Sapling ash grew in soggy hollows, everywhere surrounded by honeysuckle or fescue. She knelt beside a tangle of raspberry vines and brushed a hand over its thornlike hairs. Too tiny to light. She could not focus that tightly.

Yet.

From out in the woodland cover, they heard a horn.

"They've caught a scent," said Hathui. "Why didn't you go with him?"

"It reminds me too much of my life with Da. Look. There are the griffins."

They glided so far above that for a moment Liath imagined them no larger than eagles.

"They must be very high," said Hathui. "There they go."

The specks vanished into the south, toward hills and wilder forest lands.

Crashing sounded in the brush and they turned just as a dozen riders emerged laughing and shouting excitedly, a pack of hunters separated from the main group. She recognized Sanglant among their number. He rode over to them.

So often in these last months he had looked worn by the burden of ruling, but this moment he had that same reckless, carefree attractiveness she had fallen in love with back at Gent so many years ago. Not so long ago in her memory, not nearly as long as in his.

"What are you hunting?" he asked. "You have that look on your face." He nodded at Hathui, marking her presence, and she inclined her head in answer to his unspoken message.

"I am thinking," Liath said, "about the weather."

He regarded her curiously before turning in his saddle to give a signal to his retinue. They rode back toward camp. He dismounted and handed the reins of his horse to Hathui.

"What?" he asked.

"Even the sages and the church mothers did not understand the vagaries of the weather. Only God know why there is drought, or why fine growing weather. Why famine strikes, or plenty waxes and wanes across the years. But what if this weather—" She gestured toward the sky. "—is not natural weather, rather than another pattern in the unknowable pattern woven by God? What if these are unnatural clouds caused by the spell and the cataclysm? By the return of the Ashioi land? When a rock is flung into the sky and falls to earth, a puff of dust may rise where it strikes. Volcanos blast smoke and ash into the air. So many rivers of fire ran deep in the earth on that day. So much was shaken loose. What if we made this ourselves?"

He considered, then shrugged. "If we did so? What then?"

"There are tempestari."

"Ah." He tilted back his head to look for a long while at the sky. Then he began to pace. "If only you had ridden east to Blessing. Li'at'dano might have helped you. If she lives."

"I think she does live. I'm sure of it. It's as if she speaks to me."

"Can you ask her, then?"

"I don't know how to speak in dreams." She shrugged, impatient with this train of thought. "Anyway, had I ridden east, I wouldn't necessarily have realized how badly the weather is affected here in Wendar. We can't dwell on 'if onlys.' God know I regret losing Sorgatani. She could help me. Without Eagle's Sight, I can only wonder and wait."

Fest bent his head and snuffled among the raspberries, but finding no fodder to his liking he tugged toward greener pastures, and after a sign from Sanglant, Hathui let him lead her away.

"It's possible," he said. "I have myself considered how far the ripples of this spell will spread. That the Ashioi land has returned is, I fear, the least of our troubles."

"I'm thinking . . ." She trailed to a halt.

He smiled at her, touched her cheek, and she leaned against his palm for a few breaths. With that touch, she might imagine herself in a place where troubles did not wind around her and weigh so terribly on them all. She might imagine peace and a quiet chamber furnished with an orrery brought north out of Andalla. She might imagine forest and fields and the brilliant dome of heaven with stars as distinct as the flowers in a spring meadow and as numerous as the sand on a pale shoreline.

Of a wonder, he did not move, content to stand with her as she dreamed.

At last she sighed. "Sister Rosvita once spoke to me of a convent dedicated to St. Valeria, under the rule of Mother Rothgard. In that place they kept certain forbidden records of the sorcerous arts. If I went there—it isn't that far from here—they might have the answers I seek."

"To make of yourself a tempestari? Do you mean to shake the winds loose and unveil the heavens?" He withdrew his hand, but he was laughing at her with such sweetness and pride that she felt tears fill her eyes, although they did not spill.

"If I must. If I can. It is what I can do."

"It is," he agreed, "if anyone can."

"I was named after her, the greatest sorcerer known to humankind."

"Who is not human."

"Perhaps that's why."

"When will you go? Should I escort you?"

"I don't know. I haven't thought beyond wondering."

"Then favor me in this way, Liath. Wait until this matter with my aunt is resolved. Let me be crowned and anointed and you beside me as my queen. After that you will command a retinue of your own. It will be a simpler matter to send you to this convent on your own progress."

She shook her head, smiling. "In this way, we're well matched, Sanglant."

"In what way?" he asked, shifting as might a hound that suddenly distrusts its master as she waves it toward a tub of bathwater.

"Where I am ignorant, you are wise."

"And in like manner, in the other direction?"

She laughed and kissed him. The day seemed at once hotter, brighter, brilliant, but she knew how fragile happiness could be and how swiftly it could pass, veiled by clouds.

4

THEY heard the horn midmorning the next day. Soon after, an Eagle cantered up to the royal tent, dismounted, and knelt before Sanglant. He was sitting, hearing the morning reports, but he waved the others away and they stepped back to make room for the Eagle.

"You are Gilly, sent to Osterburg."

She nodded. She was at least a dozen years older than he was, and slighter than most of the women who became Eagles, but she was tough like a whipcord. "I have returned in the retinue of Princess Theophanu, Your Majesty. I rode ahead to tell you this news."

"What message from my sister?"

She looked at Hathui, then back at the king. "She sends no message, Your Majesty. She herself rides to Quedlinhame. She'll be here today."

*   *   *

Because of the way the camp was sited, set back about a league from the town wall and surrounded by a blend of scrub trees and open ground, they heard a flurry of horns at midday but saw nothing. Soon afterward, Lewenhardt noted a trio of banners flying over the tower next to the owl standard marking the presence of Mother Scholastica, but it was too far away for him to make out their markings.

Near dusk, with a wind whipping up out of the southeast, a sentry came running to announce that a party approached from town.

"Let the men assemble." Sanglant took his place in the chair that his father had used while traveling. He drew his fingers over the carved arms: here an eagle's sharp beak, there a lion's rugged mane running smooth under his skin, and under this the hollows and ridges of its paws. He set his feet square on the ground in front of him, although he had to tap his right foot.

A host came, led by Mother Scholastica on her white mule who, as abbess of the venerable and holy institution of Quedlinhame, was as powerful as any duke. Four monks and four nuns walked with lamps held high, lighting her way.

Behind her rode Theophanu on a gray mare. His sister wore a fine gown that appeared silver in the fading light, stitched with gold thread. There were other women with her. One he knew immediately, even with the lowering twilight and the distance, and he flushed and glanced at Liath, who sat frowning beside him, obviously uncomfortable but brave enough to stick it out. She was squinting, head tilted to one side, trying to see something. Her hands tightened. She took in a sharp breath.

Waltharia, margrave of the Villams, had ridden to Osterburg and now come to Quedlinhame, no doubt because she had heard the news of his return. She wore a cloak. What she wore beneath he could not discern, but he knew well enough the feel of her, that old and pleasurable memory. Desire stirred, and he shut his eyes briefly to fight it. He was a little embarrassed, in truth, because he still felt an abiding affection for her, and he knew that while it was all very well for Liath to accept and dismiss the existence of women who no longer had any chance to get close to him, it was a different matter entirely to have to dine and laugh with a woman who had been his first and most famous lover. Whom he had, not two years ago— well, never mind that. Perhaps Waltharia would hate him because her husband Druthmar had died in the south, fighting in his army. Perhaps, but he doubted it. She would grieve, and then find another husband; that was the way of the world.

He could not help anyway but be glad to see her, because he knew she would support him. He hoped she would support him. He needed her support.

Theophanu had come armored with other great nobles of the realm besides Waltharia: Wichman's twin sisters, Sophie and Imma, Biscop Suplicia of Gent, Biscop Alberada of Handelburg, two other women in biscop's surplices whose names he did not know, and three abbots. Margrave Judith's heir, named Gerberga, rode at Theophanu's right hand. He did not know her well. Beside her rode his younger half brother, Prince Ekkehard, dressed as a noble, not as a cleric, and in any case easy to overlook among the rest.

They were handsome women, each in her own way, splendid and terrible, a phalanx that could help him or harm him depending on their wishes and their whims. These were the powers of the realm in whose hands he must place his father's body and in whose eyes he must prove his worthiness to rule as regnant.

Three ranks of lesser nobles and courtiers rode behind them, all come to confront or placate the man who claimed Henry's throne. Belatedly, he noticed that it was one of these, in the second rank, who had caught Liath's attention. She stared, her expression fixed and cold and unreadable.

"I will not," she whispered, so low it was clear she meant no man or woman to hear her, but he had a dog's hearing, keener than that of humankind. "I have climbed the ladder of the mages. I have walked through fire and lived. That which harmed me can harm me now only if I allow it to, and I will not."

A cold shock ran through him. He ought to have noticed. He had not. But Liath had. She had seen his beautiful face first of all:

Hugh.

5

IT was a shock, but she let the anger and fear burn off her. A part of her would always remember; a part of her would always cringe. But not the greater part, not anymore. She could face what she had once feared without shrinking back from the expected blow.

Still, it was hard to wait beside Sanglant when she did not feel
comfortable acting as his consort, a person whose power and authority must be seen and felt at all times in public, with so many
faces watching her, measuring her, judging her.

The riders drew up on the road. Mother Scholastica raised a hand
to halt the others. She surveyed Sanglant with an expression Liath
could not interpret. At length, Princess Theophanu dismounted and
assisted her aunt to dismount. After Mother Scholastica had both
feet on the ground, the rest of the front rank dismounted in their
turn. Liath did not know them all, but she was sure from their bearing, their pride, and their rich tunics and cloaks that they were nobles of the first rank, the equals whose support the regnant must
obtain if he wanted the throne and crown of Wendar.

There were few men among them—so many men had died fighting in the wars—and she was reminded of Sanglant's confrontation
with Li'at'dano and the centaurs, female all. He did not look in the
least discomfited, but then, nothing about women made him uncomfortable. He neither feared nor exalted them, although it was
certainly true that the Bwr shaman had annoyed him because of her
lack of respect.

"Well met, Brother," said Theophanu, coming forward beside her
aunt. She turned to Liutgard and spoke polite words of regret,
which Liutgard accepted with a bitter glance for the silent abbess.

"I pray you, Theophanu, Aunt, sit beside me." He rose and invited them to step in under the awning where two stools had been
set up to his right, but Mother Scholastica halted at the edge of the
carpet, coming no farther, and Theophanu had perforce to stop
beside her.

Silence reigned. Sanglant sat back down while they remained
standing.

"Let us dispense with pleasantries," Mother Scholastica said.
"Theophanu has ridden far. Let her speak plainly."

"So I will," said Theophanu in her cool way, "for I am weary, having ridden far. You have made a claim for our father's throne. You
have in your possession his corpus, awaiting decent burial. These
things I acknowledge. Know this also: I have no army to fight you.
I have a century of stout Lions, a hundred cavalry of my own retinue, and what levies we can raise out of Saony. Fesse and Avaria
stand with you, I see."

"We do," said Liutgard.

"We do," said Burchard, "and we witnessed Henry's last words, when he named Prince Sanglant as his heir. We witnessed much else, but it is too much to tell here." He ran a hand over his hair and staggered. Behind him, a steward steadied the old duke with a hand under the elbow.

"Others mean to stand with you as well," said Theophanu as one of the noblewomen in her entourage crossed the gap to approach Sanglant.

He stood and extended his hands, and this woman placed her folded hands in his as a sign of allegiance. Liath did not know the woman, but she had heard stories, and there were only so many women who wore the margrave's key and might exchange a glance as intimate as that with Sanglant.

"You are well come back to Wendar, Sanglant."

"I pray for your forgiveness, Waltharia. You will have heard the news. I did not even find Druthmar's body."

She was serious and sorrowful, wiping away tears, but not angry. She did not take the news too lightly, but she did not beat her breast and moan and wail. "I have wept, and will weep again," she said gravely. She and Liutgard exchanged a knowing glance. "He knew the risk, and served as he was able."

"He was a good man," said Sanglant.

"Yes." She looked past him to Liath, smiled with a strange expression, and spoke in a tone that balanced amused regret and sincere interest. "This is your bride, the one you spoke of?"

"It is."

"Well met, Liathano."

"Well met," Liath echoed, but she had a horrible, disorienting moment as she met Waltharia's honest gaze.

I will like her.

Waltharia smiled slightly, withdrew her hands from his, and moved to stand beside Liutgard and Burchard. Liath felt the other woman's presence like fire. It almost made her forget about Hugh, waiting with apparent humility in the second rank.

Beautiful Hugh.

He was not looking at her, and because of that, she kept glancing at him to see if he was looking.

"It is no surprise that Villam is loyal to Sanglant," said Theophanu. "Where is our sister Sapientia, Brother?"

Sanglant sat down. "She may be dead. Certainly she is lost."

"It was your doing," said Theophanu calmly, where another woman might rage or accuse.

"I do not deny that I took control of the army from her. She was not fit to lead, Theophanu. I did not kill her."

Liath could not help but think of Helmut Villam, and perhaps Sanglant did as well, because he chose that moment to look toward Hugh. The other man had his gaze fixed modestly on the ground.

Two noblewomen standing beside Theophanu spoke up.

"No loss. She was always foolish."

"You would say that! Knowing foolishness as well as you do!"

"I pray you, Sophie. Imma." Theophanu did not raise her voice, but the two women fell silent. "Let us have neither quarreling nor levity. It is a serious matter to accuse one in our family of responsibility in the death of a sibling."

"We are not Salians or Aostans," remarked Mother Scholastica, "to murder our kinfolk in order to gain preference or advantage for ourselves."

"Or Arethousans, for that matter, happy to sell a sister into slavery or death if it means wealth and title for oneself." Wichman's comment came unexpectedly, for he had loitered quietly to the left of Duke Burchard this entire time.

"Have you a complaint, Wichman?" asked Sanglant.

"Not at all. Sapientia was weak, and a fool. She's better dead, if she's dead. Henry named her as heir only after he thought you were dead. I don't care if you're a bastard, Cousin. Although certainly I know you are!" He laughed. "I care if you can win the war and hold the kingdom together. If you will, grant me the duchy of Saony. I'll hold it honorably and support you."

Liath realized that Sophie and Imma were sisters, as they got red in the face and burst into nasty, passionate speech.

"And pass over the elder—!"

"You snake! You are a viper to strike so at our heels!"

"I pray you, silence!" said Sanglant. "Let me think on it, Wichman. I must consult with my sister, Theophanu. She has served ably as regent in my absence. Your sisters, as well, have a legal claim. My aunt's counsel must also be heard."

"But you will still decide," said Wichman with a sneer. "You have the army, and the strength, to do as you will."

"So be it," said Theophanu. "Spoken crudely, but with truth. I cannot stop you from becoming regnant, Sanglant, and I am not sure I wish to. I have struggled to maintain order in Saony and not lose our family's ancestral lands. In this way I have remained loyal to our father."

She paused, and Liath thought she meant to go on in this vein, to say something rash. But Theophanu did not possess a rash temperament.

"So you have," agreed Sanglant. "You have done well."

"I have done what I can. You will find that we are weak, and that the Enemy's minions are powerful. They have brought fear, famine, plague, strife, hunger, and heresy in their army. This is the battle you must fight now, Your Majesty." A hint of emotion had crept into her voice. Liath thought her tone sarcastic, but it was difficult to tell because her expression did not change and her tone remained even, except for that edge that made each word sharp and cold. "You will not find it as easy a war to win."

"No battle is easy, Theophanu," he said wearily. "I have seen too many of my trusted companions die. Our father died in my arms. What we won came at a great cost. Not just men at arms. The devastation I saw in Aosta was . . ." He struggled for words, and finally shrugged. "Aosta lies in ruins. We saw entire forests set ablaze, or flattened by the tempest. We saw a town swamped by a great wave off the sea. I have among my army some few clerics who escaped the holy city of Darre. They say that a volcano erupted to the west. That cracks opened in the earth throughout the plain of Dar and that poisonous fumes, the breath of the Enemy, foul the air so that no one can live there. Wendar has been spared such horrors, at least."

"Do you think so? We have suffered while you and our father abandoned us for other adventures, Sanglant. Do you not recall the Quman invasion? The endless bickering wars between Sabella and Henry? Plague in Avaria? The Eika assault on Gent? Drought and famine?"

"So you see," he agreed. "If we do not have order, then we will all perish."

"If you will." Mother Scholastica lifted her staff, and they stopped talking. "If you will give Henry's corpus to me, Sanglant, then those among my clerics who are trained in preparing the body for burial will do what is fitting. Let him be laid to rest now that he has returned to Wendar. After that, we will hold council in the church where Queen Mathilda is buried. Let us pray that the memory of his wisdom guides us to do what is right."

"Very well," said Sanglant. "There is much to tell that you will not have heard."

"Much to tell." Theophanu looked at their brother, Ekkehard, but he remained standing passively beside his wife, Gerberga, who was now the margrave of Austra and Olsatia because she was Judith's eldest legitimate child.

No love lost between those two, she thought, for Ekkehard's stand suggested a coolness between him and his older wife. Hugh's silence suggested volumes, which Liath could not yet read.

How had Hugh come here? Where had he been? She had seen him briefly in the interstices of the great weaving, but he had vanished. Unlike the others, he had not died.

Of course not.

He shifted so slightly that no one who was not held by a taut thread to his presence would have noticed. She noticed. In the manner of a young woman who does not mean to inflame male desire by glancing up, just *so*, from under half-lowered lashes that suggest both desire and modesty, he looked up to meet her gaze.

It was all there to be seen, all that he wished for, everything he remembered. He had not changed.

But she had.

Sanglant muttered a curse under his breath. His sword hand tightened on the arm of the chair. He rose, and Hugh looked away from Liath.

"How soon can the funeral be held?" asked Sanglant.

"We will need an entire day to prepare the body," said the abbess. "The day after tomorrow is the Feast of St. Johanna the Messenger. It would be an auspicious day to commend his soul to God."

"So be it. I will bring his body to you at first light."

6

HE rose before dawn. Barefoot, wearing only a simple shift, he walked beside the cart as it creaked up the road to the gates of Quedlinhame. The grind of the wheels on dirt sang a counterpoint to the multitudes who had gathered along the road to mourn the passing of their king. Folk of every station cried out loud, or tore their hair, or wept psalms: ragged beggars and sturdy farmers, craftsmen and women with callused hands, silk-clad merchants, and simple laborers. They sobbed as the cart rolled past, although in truth there was nothing to see except a chest padded by sacks of grain so it would not shift when the cart lurched in potholes and ruts.

He wept, too, because it was expected of him but also because he grieved for his father, whom he had loved.

He had lost so much, including his schola, Heribert and Breschius, but he had gained the remnants of Henry's schola, and it was these who walked behind the cart carrying the Wendish crown and the Wendish banner to display to the crowd. They sang, in their sweet voices, the lament for the dead, although the wailing of the crowd almost drowned them out.

> "Put not your trust in the great.
> Not in humankind, who are mortal.
> A person's breath departs.
> She returns to the dust.
> On that day her plans come to nothing."

At intervals he glanced back to be sure that Hathui was close by, guarded by Captain Fulk and his trusted soldiers. The others he did not fear for, but he knew Hathui might be in danger. Keep her close, he had told Fulk, and Fulk, unsmilingly, had agreed.

They toiled up the slope and halted before the gates of the town. The bell rang for Lauds, and with a shout from the guard and the squeal of gears, the gates were opened.

The townsfolk of Quedlinhame thronged the streets, falling back as Sanglant advanced in all his penitent splendor. The burden lay heavy. Soon he would be crowned and anointed, and after that day he would no longer be free. Duty would chain him as thoroughly as Bloodheart ever had, but duty had always chained him. Henry had known him better than anyone else. He had known that, in the end, the rebellious son would give way to the obedient one. He dared not blame his father. Henry had loved him best of all his children, though it might have been wiser not to have a favorite. No doubt Sapientia, Theophanu, and Ekkehard had suffered for getting less, although by birth and legitimacy they should have had more. As each step took him closer to the church and the royal funeral, he wondered what had become of Mathilda and Berengaria, his youngest half siblings. Was Adelheid dead, or had she somehow, impossibly, survived?

Ai, God. What had become of Blessing? Would he ever know?

The crowd pressed in behind the clerics, giving no right of way to the soldiers and noble captains who accompanied him, but Fulk pushed past them with Hathui in train. Keeping her close. A dozen beggars wearing the white rags of professional mourners raised such a cry of shrieking and yelping that he could no longer hear the clerics' sweet song.

He set his face forward and trudged up the hill to the convent, where his aunt, his sister, and his noble brethren waited on the broad porch of Quedlinhame's church. He knew them for what they were: the dogs who would nip at his heels, just as Bloodheart had long ago predicted.

X
A VIGIL

1

LONG after the crowd of mourners and courtiers had left, deep into the night, he remained kneeling on the cold stone floor of the church, at the center of the apse. Sometimes he wept; sometimes he prayed; sometimes he breathed in the sweetness of God's presence. Why did one man live while another died? Why did God allow suffering? Why did the wicked flourish and remain so damned handsome, standing within the shield of their powerful relatives? As usual, he had no answers.

He heard the door scrape and soft footfalls. At first he thought it was the guard changing at the door, perhaps Captain Fulk checking on him, and on Hathui, who knelt silently about ten paces behind him.

Theophanu knelt beside him. She was accompanied by her faithful companion Leoba, who knelt with head bowed a little in front of the Eagle.

Theophanu set a candle, in its holder, on the floor.

"You mourn late," she said in her bland voice.

"Should I not?"

Instead of answering, she rested her head on clasped hands and murmured a lengthy prayer.

He remained silent, listening for God, but heard nothing except the sigh of wind through the upper arcades that housed the bells. Shadows hid the aisles and the painted ceiling. Even the ornamentation on the pillars was colorless, washed gray by night. Did God exist equally in the shadows and in the light?

"He loved you better," she said suddenly.

"I know. I am sorry for your sake, Theo. You didn't deserve to have less of his love."

She shrugged. "I became accustomed to it."

She was so frustrating. It was impossible to know what she was thinking. That was why folk didn't quite trust her. He just didn't have the patience, not anymore, but he held his tongue, waiting for her to continue.

She wasn't looking at him. Her gaze was fixed on the coffin that rested before the altar, draped by Wendar's banner. The mass had been sung. The hymns had gone on for hours. At dawn, Henry's remains would be laid in the crypt beside those of his beloved mother, Queen Mathilda.

After a while, she moved the candle two finger's breadths to the right.

"Do not forget me, Sanglant. Our father did, and I was patient. Do not believe that I will be as patient for you."

Sometimes in battle an opening appears that must be seized in the instant or forever lost. "I have need of you now, where you can serve Wendar most ably."

"Where is that, Brother?"

"Saony."

"As regent?"

"No, as Rotrudis' successor. As duchess in your own right." There it was, the merest crack seen in the lift of her chin and the crinkling of her eyes: he had amused her. "It is the obvious choice, Sanglant. Her daughters are fools and her son is a rutting beast. How better to placate me, who might challenge your claim to our father's throne, than by offering me a duchy?"

"You have administered Saony ably these last few years."

"So I have," she agreed coolly. "It is the least I deserve. But, I suppose, the most I can hope for."

"Is that a warning, or are you accepting the duchy?"

The dim light revealed an unlooked for glimpse of emotion as she glanced at him with eyes wide. Almost he thought she might chuckle, but she did not. "I'm tempted to see it given to Wichman, just to see those two harpies claw themselves to death with jealousy."

Leoba choked down a laugh.

He snorted. "Wichman isn't temperate enough to be a good steward. Saony is the heart of Wendar and always will be."

"What of Sophie and Imma and Wichman? They cannot be so easily dismissed."

He shrugged. "Wichman will complain, as he has always done, but he will not challenge your right to the ducal seat or mine to place you there. As for the other two—in truth, Theo, what does it matter what they say?"

"They will run to Conrad for his support. They've threatened to before."

"Let them. How can those two help Conrad? Can you imagine him suffering their bickering and whining?"

"If he sees advantage in it, yes."

"A prince without a retinue is no prince," he countered. "Sophie and Imma bring him nothing."

"Except a claim—an excuse—to restore them to the place you have usurped from them. An excuse to march his army into Wendar."

"Is Conrad so ambitious?"

"Yes. He married Tallia. She has a claim to Wendar as well as to Varre. A claim as strong as yours, now that I think on it. Stronger, many would say."

"I can fill up an army with weak-minded fools and whining cowards, but that doesn't mean I can win a battle with them. Let Sophie and Imma run to Conrad if they wish. He is welcome to them. I suppose Wichman is too closely related for the church to approve of a marriage between you and him."

"Wichman! Spare me that! He's a beast."

He was taken aback by her anger, which flooded forth so unexpectedly. "Nay, I meant it only as a jest—"

"I know. But you have spoken a truth despite yourself. The wars have killed all our men, and the rest are married."

"It's true the matter of a husband is a difficult one, but there must be a man sufficient to your needs and of suitable birth who can be found."

"A faint promise," she observed. "More whisper than shout."

He shrugged. "A realistic one. Do you accept, Theophanu?"

She fell silent, lips closed, eyes cast down, that veil of secrecy smoothing her features once again. Behind the altar, each set on a tripod, three lamps burned steadily: one in the guise of a lion with flame flaring from its eyes and mane, one in the form of an eagle with fire snapping out of holes opening along the sweep of its wings, and the third in the shape of a dragon with head flung back and fire breathing from its jaws.

"Saony," she said, tasting the word, testing its flavor. "Yes. I will be duchess of Saony. That, at least, is something."

2

LIATH knew Sanglant would pray until dawn. He had told her he meant to do so. Sleep eluded her. She did not wish to return to the distant tent out where the woods would creak and rattle all night. Not even the company of Eagles tempted her. This night, Sanglant wanted to be alone as he prayed for his father's soul, and she did not want to stray far from him.

She stuffed two unlit candles into her sleeve as she left in procession with the rest of the mob, whose noise was for once muted by the solemnity of the occasion. Long ago she had learned how to fade into the background so others did not notice her. She slid smoothly from one group of mourners to the next until she came around past the necessarium and found a solitary path that led back into Quedlinhame's compound. She remembered the ground plan of the institution perfectly, of course. It was easy to find a shadowed corner and wait there for an hour or more as folk went to their beds and the readers settled to their night's round of prayer in the Lady's chapel. When she was sure she was alone, she lit one candle, which she would not have needed had there been even a slip of moon visible, and made her way to the library.

The library hall was as silent as the tumulus in which they had laid Blessing. Nothing stirred. Shadows filled the distant corners, obscured the ceiling, and cloaked the tidy carrels and the latched cabinets set against the walls. She halted at the lectern and ran her fingers over the catalog as she listened, but she heard no noise at all from the hall, the neighboring scriptorium, or the warren of rooms behind her that housed the rest of the cabinets.

The catalog was latched shut but not locked. She popped the latch and opened it, turning each page as she sought the entry to Isidora of Seviya's famous *Etymologies*. Isidora's encyclopedic work would certainly contain information on tempestari. Da's book, so painstakingly compiled over years of wandering, had contained few references to the art of weather workers. It had been too crude a form of sorcery, something dabbled in by hedge witches and ignorant hearth wives, and he scorned it. He had reserved his attention for the secrets of the mathematici and the sciences of astronomy and astrology, although it seemed strange that he would name his daughter after a legendary weather witch whose power he had in no way comprehended. Li'at'dano had not woven trifling spells to make incantations against another farmer's crop, or with the blowing of conch shells and the shouts of revelers drive away a storm that threatened to disrupt a wedding or feast day. She was no fulgutari to divine the future by interpreting the strokes of lightning and the sound and direction of thunder. She was something altogether more powerful and more dangerous. Anne had learned enough to force the clouds to move north and away from the stone crowns so that weather would not impede her spell, and some glamour from that vast working remained to this day, shrouding the sun and chilling the Earth.

There. The entry listed the cabinet in which the *Etymologies* could be found. She began to close the book, but her eye caught on another entry, and a third, and more and more of them as she turned another page. It felt so good to feel the texture of parchment against her skin. It eased her heart to see each book and scroll listed in neat array, each one cataloged, each one accessible. So much set down over the long years. Folk would try to discover what they did not know. They would seek into the dark of mysteries and try to answer or explain. God had made humankind curious in that way, although at times it brought good and at times ill.

Perhaps it was his foot brushing the stone floor. Perhaps a brief cessation of the wind, barely heard where it moaned through the outer eaves. Perhaps he had taken in his breath at the wrong moment, in that hollow space where she inadvertently held hers. Perhaps it was only the scratching of a hungry mouse oblivious to the dangers awaiting it in the library hall.

She was not alone in the hall and had never been alone. He had been waiting in the shadows all along. She looked, and looking betrayed her.

"I knew you would come here," he said.

She started. She had been looking to her right, but his voice came from the shadows to the left, near one of the entrances to the tiny rooms in which the rest of the library collection rested in cabinets. She might have walked through that archway all unknowing, within reach of his hands.

Yet she had always been within his reach. She had never quite shaken him off.

"What is it you seek?" he asked her, and at last she saw his shape against the wall, just standing there to watch her.

Anger is a refuge when one is taken by surprise.

"Where is my father's book?" she demanded.

"It is safe."

I can immolate him. Her heart beat like a fury battering against its cage. Reach deep into him and burn him until he was nothing but cinders, like those poor soldiers she had killed, all of whom had screamed and screamed as the agony ate them from the inside out.

"Better a clean death," she said, hearing how her voice shook and knowing he would interpret it as fear of him, when it was herself she feared. She would not be a monster, not even toward the one who had earned her hatred.

"You are right to be angry with me," he said in his beautiful voice, "because I wronged you."

"You abused me! Do not think to turn my heart now or ask me to forgive you."

"You are all that matters," he said, and she knew, horribly, that he was telling the truth as he understood it. Some things are true whether you want them to be or not. "I thought otherwise before, but I have seen things I cannot forget, terrible things. I regret what I have done in the past. I pray you, Liath, forgive me."

"I am not a saint."

"No, you are fire!" He moved, but only to lean against a table as though he would otherwise have fallen to his knees. "Can you not see it yourself, in this dark room? You are ablaze."

So easily he unsettled her. This was not the battle she had anticipated.

"I want Da's book," she said, grimly sticking to the weapons at hand.

" 'God becomes what you are out of mercy.' "

"What are you saying?" He was only trying to knock her off-balance, as if he had not already.

He straightened. "Do you know what is in Bernard's book?"

Don't get angry. Don't flare up. *Don't set the library on fire!* She took a deep breath before she answered. She thrust aside the easy retort and kept her voice even.

"I know what is in Bernard's book. The florilegia he compiled over many years—all the quotes and excerpts he copied out relating to the art of the mathematici. There is also a copy of al Haithan's *On the Configuration of the World*, which Da obtained in Andalla."

"And one other text."

"In a language I don't recognize, glossed in places in Arethousan, which I also cannot read."

"I can read Arethousan. 'God was born in the flesh so that you will also be born in the spirit.' "

She had expected many things, guessing that she and Hugh would one day meet and that on that day she would have to remember her strength. But this so shook her that at first she could not speak.

He waited, always patient.

"That's a heresy! The church condemned the belief in the Redemption."

"At the Great Council of Addai. Yet what if the Redemption is the truth? What if the holy mothers were lying?"

"Why would they?"

"Who can know what was in their hearts? What if the blessed Daisan allowed himself to be martyred in expiation for the sins of humankind? What if the account bound into Bernard's book is true, the very words of St. Thecla the Witnesser herself? I have studied. The text your father hid in his book is an account of the redemption of the blessed Daisan, son of God. It is the witness of St. Thecla herself, and glossed by an unknown hand in Arethousan—because the original text is written in the tongue of Saïs, as was spoken in ancient days. As was spoken by the blessed Daisan. It was his mother's tongue."

"It can't be."

"Perhaps not. Where did Bernard find this book and why did he bind it with the others?"

"I don't know. He never spoke of it. He must have found it in the east. It could be a forgery. Arethousa is rotten with heresy."

"So the Dariyan church says. But it could also be the truth. Here." He stepped back from the table. "Judge for yourself."

It was impossible to stop herself from picking up the candle and approaching him, to see that in truth and indeed a book lay on the table. Was it Da's old, familiar, beloved book? That book was the last thing she had that linked her to Da except his love and his teaching, except his blood and his crime against the creature that had become her mother, whom he had killed all unwittingly and out of love.

Da's book.

She halted before she got into sword range. "What do you mean to do?"

"It's yours. I'm giving it back to you."

She tried to speak, but only a hoarse "ah" "ah" got out of her throat. She struggled against tears, against anger, against grief, against such a cascade of emotions that he moved before she understood he meant to and glided away through one of the archways and vanished into the shadows, just like that.

She bolted forward, sure that the book would vanish, too, become like mist and evaporate as under the glare of the sun, but when she reached to touch it, it was solid and so very very dear to her. She could still smell Da's scent on it, even though she knew that fragrance was only a memory in her mind. She grasped it, the heft of it, its weight. Metal clasps held the book together. The leather binding was grayed with age, but it had been oiled and lovingly cared for, and the brass roses adorning the metal clasps had been polished to a fine gleam. She ran her fingers down the spine, reading with her touch the embossed letters: *The Book of Secrets.*

A masking name, Da had often said, *to hide the true name of the book within.*

She crushed the book against her chest, and wept.

3

VERY late in the night Ekkehard appeared in the church, looking tousled and sleepy with only a simple linen tunic thrown on over his shift. Yawning, he knelt to Sanglant's left. A pair of Austran guardsmen loitered a moment at the back, as if checking to make sure he didn't bolt out a side door, before retreating onto the church porch to pass the time chatting with Sanglant's soldiers.

"Where did you come from?" asked Theophanu. "Your wife's bed?"

Ekkehard had a way of hunching his shoulders to express discomfort that had always annoyed Sanglant. He was the kind of rash personality who either leaped before looking or looked away in order to pretend trouble wasn't there.

"I pray you, Theo," Sanglant said, "do not tease him. Let us honor our father's memory in peace."

"If only Sapientia were here," added Theophanu, "we might be in harmony again, just as Father always wished."

The tart comment surprised a laugh out of Sanglant. "I am not accustomed to this much bitterness from you, Theo."

"Forgive me, Brother. I forget myself."

"You sold me to the Austrans," said Ekkehard suddenly. "Like you'd sell a horse."

"For stud," commented Theophanu. "About all you're worth at this point. You betrayed Wendar by aiding the Quman and showed disrespect to our father's memory by leaving Gent when you were meant to watch over it as a holy steward. Sanglant was merciful. Toward you, at least. Perhaps not so merciful toward Sapientia."

"Sapientia sent me to my death," muttered Ekkehard. "I don't care if she's dead. Anyway, Gerberga's not so bad. She's not like her mother. Better married to her than trapped as abbot in Gent."

"I am glad you approve of your marriage," said Sanglant wryly, "since you had no choice in it. Will Gerberga support me?"

"Yes." Ekkehard scratched the light beard covering his chin, and yawned again. "That's what she sent me to tell you."

"At what price?" asked Theophanu.

"Didn't she tell you already?" Sanglant asked. "You rode with her from Osterburg, did you not?"

"She is closemouthed, like her mother was, but a better companion. I like her well enough. She is a good steward for Austra and Olsatia."

"Why do neither of you ever listen to me?" said Ekkehard. "I have something to say."

"Why did Gerberga not approach me herself?" Sanglant asked. "Why send you in the middle of the night?"

"Because we can speak privately, and no one will mark it."

"Everyone marks it," said Sanglant. "How else did Gerberga know I was here?"

"Yes, but no one is surprised that the children of Henry should pray through the night to mourn him. He did the same for our grandmother."

"In truth," said Theophanu, "I'm surprised you did not come sooner, Ekkehard. It is fitting for a child to mourn his beloved father with a vigil."

Ekkehard had not once looked toward the coffin. He had shed no tears that Sanglant had seen during the lengthy mass and reading of psalms. "Do you want to hear, or not?"

"Go on. What does Gerberga want?"

"The marchlands of Westfall and Eastfall suffer because their margraves are dead in the wars. You must appoint a new margrave for each one, to bring order. She would prefer that you listen to her desires in this matter, as she has suitable candidates in mind, but she will accept any reasonable lord of good family who will act in concert with her and agree to marry Theucinda."

"Theucinda must be fifteen or eighteen by now."

"She is only a little younger than I am. Gerberga says this, also: If Bertha lives, then she might become margrave of Eastfall, and you could let Theucinda marry the new margrave of Westfall."

"Ooof!" exclaimed Theophanu with an ironic smile. "A great deal of territory falls therefore into Austra's hands and that of her descendants. I would not recommend it. Make Wichman lord of Eastfall and marry poor Theucinda to him! He'll fight the barbarians and rape the local girls, and be happy, although his wife might not be."

"That's not funny," said Ekkehard savagely. "Wichman is a beast! Theucinda doesn't deserve to be forced to marry him!"

Ah. For the first time, there was real passion in Ekkehard's voice.

"How much older is Gerberga than you?" Sanglant asked. "I trust she never leaves you alone with her younger sister."

"I would never!" he cried in a tone of voice that betrayed he had thought often of just what it was he would never do. "It's just she's a third child, like me. She knows what it's like . . ." He bit a lip and glanced sideways at his brother and sister, gauging their reaction. Like all of Henry's children, he was a good-looking young man, although he would have been more attractive had his features not been marred by a perpetual expression of sullen grievance. ". . . to be a third child."

"You are fourth," said Theophanu.

"Third, if one counts only legitimate children!" he retorted.

Even in the dim light, Sanglant could see how his younger

brother's cheeks were flushed. His eyes had narrowed with anger, or resentment; in Ekkehard, it was hard to tell the difference.

"Do not forget," Sanglant said in his mildest tone, "that you were shown mercy, Ekkehard. You fought and killed your own country-men."

"As did you! You rebelled against our father! Some say you killed him yourself and now pretend otherwise."

The thrust had no force in it, not for Sanglant, so he wasn't pre-pared when Theophanu slapped Ekkehard so hard that the blow brought tears to his eyes as he gasped. Leoba choked down an ex-clamation.

"I will have no fighting here to demean the memory of our fa-ther!" said Sanglant.

"Is this some poison Gerberga has been feeding you?" Theophanu demanded. "Who has said it?"

"No one." He wiped his eyes, trembling. "No one. Gerberga doesn't believe it. She told him so. She said only a fool would believe you killed Henry, and anyway, Liutgard and Burchard would never support you if you had, and they were there and they saw it all. It's true about the daimone, isn't it? It's true?"

"It's true," he said, glancing toward Hathui, who despite her ap-pearance of contrite prayer was no doubt listening closely. "Being true, as it is, I wonder that the margrave of Austra shelters the man who truly betrayed Henry."

Ekkehard sniffed and wiped his nose with the back of a hand.

Waiting for his brother to speak, Sanglant realized that he, too, was trembling, that he had in him reserves of hatred he hadn't known he possessed. Bloodheart was dead, and any power he had left to harm Sanglant resided in Sanglant's heart and head alone. He had other enemies, of course, some of whom had not yet declared themselves. But he had only one man he truly hated.

"That's the other thing she wants," said Ekkehard, his voice shaky. He glared at Theophanu. Her expression was cool and dis-tant, without trace of the anger that had flared.

"That who wants?" asked Sanglant, who had now stuck in his head the image of his enemy, to whom God had given exceptional beauty. Why did the wicked flourish and the innocent suffer? Why did God allow beauty to grow in a vat of poison?

"That Gerberga wants," said Ekkehard irritably, "in exchange for her support of your claim to the throne and crown of Wendar."

"Of course. Eastfall and Westfall must have strong margraves in these times. I am agreed to this, and I see no reason not to marry Lady Theucinda to a worthy man, a younger son, perhaps, who has not yet been claimed as another woman's husband."

"Or been killed in Henry's wars!"

"Enough, Theo! What is the second request, Ekkehard?"

He smiled, but it wasn't a kind smile. "There is something Gerberga wants very much, that she cannot have because of a promise she made to her mother when she was named as Judith's heir. She can't go against a promise sworn to her mother, surely you see that."

"I see that. What is it she wants?"

Through the open doors, the graying of shadows heralded the approaching dawn. Birds cooed sociably. A creature scrabbled in the rafters. Then, once again, it was silent. Even the guards had ceased speaking in that undertone that had drifted at the edge of Sanglant's hearing all night.

"She wants to be rid of Hugh," whispered Ekkehard. "She hates him, but she promised her mother never to harm him, no matter what, and to give him shelter when he needed it. Margrave Judith loved him best of all. Just as our father loved you, the bastard, the least deserving."

An explosion of pigeons burst out of the arcade, fluttering away into the twilight sky. The sound of their passage faded swiftly as they flew over the town and out past the walls. Sanglant's senses were strung so tautly that he imagined them skimming over the fields. He felt he could actually hear the pressure of wing beats against the air as their flight took them over woodland and farther yet, racing south into the uncut forest lands where beasts roamed and lawless men hid from justice.

Theophanu clutched his hand, pressed tightly. "Beware. Hugh is the most dangerous of all."

A certain pleasant, malicious warmth suffused Sanglant. " 'Nor will any wound inflicted by any creature male or female cause his death.' Was I not so cursed? Hugh can't kill me."

"Perhaps not," said Theophanu, "but he can strike at your kinfolk. At your Eagle. At your wife."

As if her words were an incantation, a shape appeared at the door, limned by the pallor of dawn. Hathui was already on her feet, ready to move.

"Liath!" He started forward to meet her, but he had not gone halfway down the nave when he halted, seeing what she carried.

Memory struck hard.

*She thrust the bundle she carried into his arms. "Keep it safe for me,
I beg you," she said to him before she rode away to carry the king's word
to Weraushausen, to Ekkehard and the king's schola. Years ago.*

The book had been the talisman that had linked him to her in
those days when he had thought of nothing except her, because the
memory of her had been the only thing that had kept him sane
when he suffered as Bloodheart's prisoner in Gent. The book had
brought her back to him. He had kept it safe, and she had married
him because she trusted him where she trusted no one else.

She thrust it into his arms.

"See here, Sanglant! Touch it! Look! It's Da's book."

"Where did you get it?" he said hoarsely, and even Theophanu exhaled at the anger that made his voice tight. "*Hugh* had this. Have
you seen Hugh?"

Her expression was bemused, not frightened. She should be frightened and angry! "Not really. He saw me. He *gave* the book to me."

"Did he speak to you?"

She hesitated, seeing Theophanu and Ekkehard recoil at his tone.
She saw Hathui but not with any indication that she understood the
danger the Eagle was in. "I must speak to your aunt, Sanglant."

"Did he harm you?"

"Me? He can't harm me. I would have killed him if he'd tried to
touch me."

Hugh *had* touched her somehow. Her mind was filled with him,
or with what he had said to her, words she would not repeat to her
own loving husband who thought at this moment that he was likely
to batter himself bloody with jealousy.

"If he gave the book back to you, it's because he has some plot in
mind."

"He might have copied it out. He's had it long enough. It's what
I would have done." She spoke the words distractedly. She wasn't
really listening. He knew how she fell away from the world when
her mind started churning and turning, caught by the wheel of the
heavens and the mysteries of the cosmos.

"He wants something he thinks he can get by disarming you in
this way."

"He didn't disarm me!" she retorted indignantly, then frowned.
"Well. It's true he took me by surprise."

"No doubt he hopes we're quarreling over it now. Sow discord.
Plant doubts. Reap the harvest. I expect he's grown more subtle."

The comment made her fall back to earth and actually *see* him. She leaned against him, ignoring Theophanu and Ekkehard's stares, and with the book crushed between them she smiled so dazzlingly up at him that he got dizzy all over again. "Just as you have?" she asked him.

He laughed. "So easily I'm disarmed!"

"I pray you, Sanglant," said Theophanu, "if you will not have people say that she has wrapped you in a spell, then you ought not to act in public like a besotted fool. Even our father once asked this woman to become his mistress."

Ekkehard was staring with mouth agape and eyes wide. "Ivar of North Mark was in love with her, too," he murmured. "She was condemned as a sorcerer at Autun, at Hugh of Austra's trial, don't you remember? She was named as a maleficus. She was excommunicated by Constance and a council of biscops and presbyters! Henry raised no objection!"

"I wasn't there," said Sanglant, "or it wouldn't have happened."

Liath pushed away from him, but she left the book in his hands. "It's true enough, everything they say."

"Let us not have this argument again, Liath. You are my wife, and will be my queen."

"I pray you, Your Majesty," said Hathui. "Listen."

Footsteps drummed on the church's porch as with the flowering dawn came the many nuns and monks and clerics to sing the morning service. Mother Scholastica walked at their head, attended by the great nobles of the realm: Duchess Liutgard, Duke Burchard leaning on a staff, Margrave Gerberga, Margrave Waltharia, the children of Duchess Rotrudis, the four biscops, three abbots, and many more. Hugh was not among them.

Yesterday the assembly had sung the mass while, beneath, workers had prepared a place in the crypt beside Queen Mathilda. This morning Henry would be laid to rest, and the world would go on.

"Sanglant," said his aunt as she halted in front of him. He kissed her ring. She turned to his siblings. "Theophanu. Ekkehard." They kissed her ring in like manner as the monastics filed forward along the aisles on either side as a stream of bowed heads and folded hands.

"There is much yet to be discussed," said Mother Scholastica. She looked at Liath but did not, precisely, acknowledge her. "But that must wait. Who will carry Henry's bones into the crypt?"

"The great princes," said Sanglant, "as is fitting."

He stepped aside to allow Mother Scholastica to move forward into the apse and up to the holy altar. Hathui retreated into the shelter granted by Fulk and his soldiers. The great princes crowded up behind Sanglant as he knelt on the lowest step, Theophanu to his right and Ekkehard to his left. They were silent as Mother Scholastica raised both hands and the assembled monastics sang the morning service.

"Let us praise and glorify God, who are Eternal."

Sanglant could not keep his thoughts on the psalms, which flowed past him as might boats on a river spilling onward toward the eternal sea that is God. Memories of his father spun into view and then receded from sight: setting him on the back of his first pony, giving him his first set of arms, teaching him the names of birds, sending him out to his first battle arrayed in the Dragon's plumage, explaining somberly to him why he could not marry Waltharia, laughing over mead, repudiating and exiling Wolfhere, weeping at his injured voice, demanding that he accept his place as Henry's heir. Henry often said that it was necessary for the regnant to give in order to get what he wanted; he had given Sanglant everything, and in the end he had gained what he wished, although he had died to obtain it. His empire was shattered, but Wendar had not fallen. His son would not let it fall.

As the others stood, Sanglant realized he still held the book. He thrust it into Liath's hands, ensuring that all there saw the exchange and wondered at it. This, too, his aunt would mark now and question later. With his siblings and his cousins, he hoisted the box, and with incense trailing around them and the steady prayers of the monastics muffling the sound of so many footsteps, they carried the coffin down stone steps into the crypt. Down here the bones of his Dragons had rotted until they gleamed.

No. He shook his head, sloughing off the memory. That had been Gent, and this was Quedlinhame. This weight was that of his beloved father, not his faithful Dragons, but they had all died regardless. They were not protected by the curse that left him, in the end, safe from a death that could capture others but never his own self.

Lamps shone in splendor around the open tomb into which they placed the coffin, a glass vial of holy water, the neatly-folded but still bloody clothing in which Henry had died, and a dried bouquet of red dog roses, always Henry's favorites. There were none in bloom in Mother Scholastica's famous rose garden, so they had pillaged the herbarium for a suitable tribute. Later, a stone monument would be carved and placed upon the marble bier, but for now a slab of cedar carved with curling acanthus and stylized dog roses was slid into place. The stone made a hoarse scraping sound, as though it, too, grieved. There were more prayers, and the lamps, one by one, were extinguished.

Before the last lamp went out, he marked Hathui's position, close by him, in case there was trouble.

For a long while they breathed in the silence of the crypt. He rested with hands on the slab, but it was cold and dead. How deep did fire smolder within marble, he wondered? Could this dead tomb erupt into flame through Liath's perilous gift? For an instant, shuddering, he feared her, who might kill any of them and burn down the entire town around their corpses if it pleased her. If she were angry enough. If she were wicked and listened to the Enemy's lies.

In darkness, doubts crept into the heart.

"Enough," he said roughly, pushing away from the tomb.

Someone at the back of the crowd snapped fire to a wick. He hoped it was done naturally and not by Liath's sorcery, but no one muttered in surprise or made a sign against the Enemy. He saw the faces of his companions surrounding him. Liutgard of Fesse was frowning and pensive, lines graven deep around her mouth, and he supposed she was thinking of her daughters. Burchard of Avaria had his eyes shut, while Waltharia watched Sanglant expectantly. Theophanu seemed cast of the same marble as the effigies around her; Ekkehard looked bored. Gerberga, like Waltharia, studied Sanglant; meeting his gaze, she nodded to acknowledge him, to show that she had received his answer via Ekkehard. She had very much the look of her mother about her but without the cruel line of mouth that had betrayed Judith's essential nature: every creature under her power would do exactly as she wished or be punished for disobedience. Yet Henry had often said that Judith was a good steward for Austra and Olsatia; those who obeyed her, flourished.

Wichman was scratching his neck and eyeing Leoba, who was drawn tight against the shelter of Theophanu's presence. Wichman's sisters, Imma and Sophie, spoke together in whispers, a miniature conspiracy caught out by the unexpected light. The church folk stood together as a united group behind the formidable presence of his aunt.

Hathui, marking his scrutiny, nodded.

Liath stood behind him and to his left. He could feel her but not see her. It was as if she did not want to be seen.

"Nephew," said Mother Scholastica. "If you will assist me."

She did not need his aid to ascend the steps, but she desired to show the assembly that they acted in concert. In the church they remained for the brief service of Terce, and when the monastics had filed out to return to their duties about the cloister, he retired with his aunt and his most intimate noble companions and kinfolk, just a few, not more than a dozen or so, to her study.

She sat in her chair. The traveling chair, the royal seat carried into Aosta and back again, was unfolded for Sanglant, and benches drawn up in ranks for the rest. He was only prime inter pares, first among equals. Yet Liath remained standing behind him after the others sat. She still held the book. One of its corners pressed into his back. Hathui took up a position by the door. Fulk and the rest of the guard had places outside, guarding all the entrances.

Mother Scholastica lifted an owl feather from her desk. The point had been trimmed to make a quill. She wore clothing rich not by ornamentation but because of the quality of the dye and fineness of the weave. The golden torque that signified her royal kinship shone at her throat; the golden Circle of Unity that marked her status as a holy abbess hung from a golden chain; she displayed only two gold rings on her hands, needing no greater treasure to advertise her high rank both as the daughter of a regnant and as God's holy servant, shepherd over the most holy and important cloister founded and endowed by the Wendish royal house. She controlled so many estates and manor houses spread across so wide a region that half of Saony might be said to be under her rule.

"Very well, Nephew," she said. "You have the support you desire. None here will speak against you, and your army. You have brought Henry's remains home to be buried, which is the action of an obedient son and, perhaps, of a righteous ruler who has served God and his regnant honestly. In three days' time I will anoint you. Then you will commence your king's progress through Saony, Fesse, and Avaria so that the lords and clerics and common folk can see that order has returned to our land."

He said nothing. She had not attacked yet. He was waiting for the first strike.

"You have proved your fertility at least twice over, according to reliable reports," she continued, "although we know that one child is deceased and the other most likely so."

The book, against his back, shifted so that a corner dug painfully in against one shoulder. He wasn't sure if Liath was only startled, or if she'd done it on purpose. *Twice over.* He did not look at Waltharia.

"Yet there must be heirs. Among the Wendish only those who wear the gold ring—" She touched the torque that wrapped her neck. "—may become regnant. It's true you wear the gold ring, but before this no bastard child has contested for the right to rule. Many protest that an illegitimately-born child has no right to the throne. Custom argues in their favor. Yet I have studied certain histories in the last two days. One alternative is to allow you to rule as long as you designate as your heir a child legitimately born to one of your siblings."

Margrave Gerberga smiled and glanced at her young husband.

"I have no husband," said Theophanu, "and Sapientia is lost."

"Sapientia does have a child," said Gerberga. "Hippolyta. A girl not more than six or eight years of age now."

"And related to you as well," said Waltharia with a sharp smile.

"Hippolyta is unsuitable," said Mother Scholastica. "She is a bastard, like Sanglant, and born for another purpose. She has been installed in a convent and will remain there. Do not argue this point further, I pray you. As for you, Theophanu, husbands can be found."

"So they tell me, but I have seen no evidence of it yet."

"Henry's children are not the only ones descended from the royal line," said Liutgard. "I have one daughter left to me. Ermengard is legitimately born."

Scholastica nodded. "It is something to consider. There is another course. That Sanglant marry a noblewoman whose rank and lineage will bring luster to his court, and support to his kingship. Waltharia of Villam, for instance."

"Impossible," said Gerberga. "Such an alliance would give the Villams too much power. However, I have a young sister, still a maiden, who has sufficient rank and lineage on both her mother's and father's side to become queen."

"I might then raise the same objection," said Waltharia. "But be assured, Gerberga, that I do not wish to marry Sanglant."

"I would object to either alliance," said Liutgard.

"I am already married," said Sanglant, who was growing tired of this maneuvering. They were like dogs circling and growling around a fresh carcass.

"If you must put her aside in order to gain the throne, I'll gladly take her into my own bed," said Wichman.

Liath coughed, and someone in the chamber tittered.

"I was just joking," said Wichman suddenly, sounding strangely nervous.

Waltharia, whose face Sanglant could see, looked ready to laugh.

"I am already married," he repeated.

His aunt was not done. "Married under the old custom of bedding as a wedding, a union not even blessed by a simple deacon. Married to a woman born into a lineage whose highest aspiration was to install one of its sons in the Dragons. She brings no noble connections, no treasure, no dowry, no lands—"

"She—"

"I am not finished, Nephew! *And* she is excommunicated. She cannot become queen in this state. If she does, all of Wendar will be placed under anathema."

Each of the biscops nodded in turn. Scholastica had arrayed her allies carefully.

"Is this what you wish, Sanglant?" asked Henry's half sister, Biscop Alberada. "That no mass may be sung? That no soul receive burial in holy ground? All for the sake of one woman?"

"Who will enforce this anathema?" he demanded, knowing that his temper was fraying and that he was pressing forward recklessly. "The skopos is dead."

Scholastica set the owl feather onto the desk and folded her hands to rest on that surface. She had relaxed, he saw, believing the fight won.

"The skopos is never *dead*. St. Thecla lives in every skopos. God still rule, Sanglant, or had you forgotten that? It is true I am abbess here because your grandfather Arnulf the Younger placed me in this position, as befit my birth. These good abbots rule their institutions because of their good names and righteous ways. But each of these holy biscops received her mantle with the blessing of the skopos in Darre. They are her representatives here in the north, and there are others, besides, who have not had time or opportunity to meet with you yet. We—all of us—will enforce the anathema if you disobey us."

He fumed, but he was outarmed and outnumbered, and while it was all very well to live with Liath and ride with his army and ignore that distant excommunication brought down years ago in Autun, it was quite another thing to condemn the entire realm to spiritual exile.

"The accusation and sentence were unjust," he said at last. "She is innocent."

"The excommunication is valid until lifted."

"Then lift it!"

They watched him. One abbess, four biscops, and three abbots, most considerably older than he was and well versed in the intrigues of courtly power, presented a daunting force. As Mother Scholastica had so kindly pointed out, these were only the ones who had arrived here in time. More would come, and it was likely they would bow to Scholastica's authority, not his.

"There is a second, and greater, objection," continued Mother Scholastica, "brought recently to our attention. She is accused of being a heretic as well. It is said that she is concealing secret texts which teach the most wicked heresy of the Sacrifice and Redemption. Even now the church struggles against the Enemy's minions, whose whispers have infected the countryside and towns with this infection. We have long wondered how the plague of heresy first came into our land. It has been suggested that this woman has possession of a book, a forgery out of the east, that is the source of the disease. As you can imagine, this is a serious charge."

"Hugh," muttered Liath. She moved the book, not to hide it, but to fix it more firmly against his back in case anyone tried to pull it out of her arms.

"Who has said these things?" demanded Sanglant. "Let him come forward and speak these accusations in public. The Enemy uses whispers murmured in darkness in order to cast doubt. I believe such matters must be examined in the light."

That he could damage Hugh's credibility he did not doubt, but he had already made his biggest mistake. He didn't realize it until Liath stepped out from behind him and walked right up to Mother Scholastica's desk without ceremony or any particular respect for the holy abbess' rank and preeminence.

First, make sure every commander knows their part in the plan.

"Liath," he said, warning her off, but she set the book on the table and opened it.

"Here," she said in that infuriating way she had, oblivious to the well gaping open at her feet as she stared up at the heavens. "The very question I meant to ask you, Mother Scholastica. This book I inherited from my father, but I do not read Arethousan. You see how the ancient language of Saïs is glossed in Arethousan by a second hand."

The biscops and abbots crowded forward. Alberada's eyes narrowed; Suplicia of Gent's eyes grew wide. Others grimaced, and one old churchman set his lips together so tightly that the pressure wrinkled his clean-shaven chin.

Scholastica unclenched her hands, which had suddenly and painfully tightened, and touched the ancient parchment as though it were crawling with vermin. " 'Krypte!' " she said in the voice of a woman condemning souls to the Pit for disobedience. " 'Hide this!' " She traced her finger along the path of words, translating slowly. Like all church folk of her generation, she had learned Arethousan from Queen Sophia and her foreign retinue. " 'Many around have been fulfilled among us . . . these miraculous signs and omens, all the things from the heavens. I write for you an orderly account, most excellent Theophilus, so you may know the truth regarding this thing in which you have been instructed by word of mouth.' "

"Who is Theophilus?" asked Liath.

"Silence!" Scholastica turned the page, searching among the letters, none of which had any meaning to Sanglant. Some she was able to read; others she skipped over. He could not tell the difference. " 'God is born in the flesh . . .' This is the heresy of dual nature!" She turned from white to red as she turned another page, and another. No one spoke or moved except Biscop Alberada, who wiped her brow and shuddered. " 'Then came the blessed Daisan before the judgment of the Empress Thaissania, She of the Mask. And when he would not bow before her but spoke the truth of the Mother of Life and the Divine Logos, the Holy Word, then she announced the sentence of death. This he met joyfully, for he embraced the promise of the Chamber of Light. But his disciples with him wept bitterly. So was he taken away and put to the flaying knife and his heart was cut out of his breast . . .' "

Her voice, ragged and chill, grew several degrees colder on these words, and her gaze, startlingly hot, lifted to sear Sanglant where he sat rigid, not knowing what to do, entirely at a loss, routed from the field. She was incandescent with anger, but she went on in a tone like a bell tolling for the dead.

" 'And a darkness fell over the whole land . . .' "

She broke off and rose. Even the church folk shrank back from her righteous wrath. The great princes tensed.

"A darkness, indeed! This is the source of the storm that has afflicted us! This is the heresy of the Redemption, and that of the dual nature! Brought into this realm, we now see, by a renegade monastic who strayed from the church and forgot his vows, and passed the poison on into his daughter."

The words dropped like iron, more damaging than a spear thrust or a sword's cut.

Only Liath did not appear to notice. She was too busy gazing in wonder at the open page. "Do you suppose it is a forgery, or the truth? How could one tell? It looks old, but the parchment might have been scraped clean and reused. It could have been discolored to appear old. Or it might be as it seems, centuries old. Is the Arethousan gloss written contemporaneously with the original, or was it glossed later? How can we know the truth of something that happened so long ago? One would have to gather evidence from many sources . . ."

She looked up expectantly. Only then did she falter, and he saw her bewilderment and the slow dawn of understanding.

As he understood, too late.

Hugh knows her better than I do.

Hugh had guessed she would betray herself, once the book's existence was revealed, because she could not stop asking questions. Because she wanted to know the truth, whether the Earth rotated or the sun rotated, or if the winds were born in vast bellows or set in motion by the turning spheres, or why and how arrows shot into the heavens returned to a particular spot on the Earth. If an ancient manuscript was truth, or lie. She cared nothing for the politics of the situation or the church's traditions of orthodoxy.

In that way, of course, she *was* a heretic, just not in the way they imagined.

"I don't know where my father came by this text," she said. "As I already told you, I can't read it. I only knew a little Arethousan. It was taught to me by Father Hugh."

"You have already condemned yourself," said Mother Scholastica. "You admit twice over this is your father's book." She turned pages. "Here, a florilegia of sorcery, the arts of the mathematici which were condemned at the Council of Narvone. And here—what language is this?"

"It's Jinna. This is a copy of the astronomical text *On the Configuration of the World*—"

"An infidel's black sorcery!"

"No, it's just a description of the workings of the heavens, based in part on Ptolomaia's *Tetrabiblos*. There's nothing heretical in that!"

"It must be burned."

"It will not be burned!" Liath grabbed the book right out of the Mother Scholastica's grasp, clapped it shut, and hugged it to her chest.

Sanglant shut his eyes momentarily, unable to bear the looks cast his way: some gasped, some gloated, some were genuinely shocked, and Wichman, at least, was enjoying the spectacle as he scratched at his crotch.

Liath tried reason, although she must see by now that reason would fail. "I had hoped, Mother Scholastica, that you and your scholars could examine this text . . ."

"It must be burned."

"But don't you want to *know*?" She was indignant. "If it's true, then the church mothers lied to us. If it is a forgery, then the heresy is discredited. It never serves any purpose to burn what you fear."

How passionately she spoke! Only he, among those in this chamber, understood how literally she meant those words.

Mother Scholastica turned away from her to Sanglant. "You cannot hide, Nephew, from the poison you have brought into the court. Do you see, now, how she seduced you?"

It was true that he could not hide. He opened his eyes to face them, all gazing expectantly at him. Was Theophanu happy to see Liath discredited, or was she merely puzzled? Ekkehard looked bored. The margraves and dukes were waiting, as soldiers in battle, to see what command he would give, by which they would judge his worth. That Scholastica and the church folk held their line was evident to all.

He shifted ground.

"I demand that Hugh of Austra be brought before me. I charge him with Henry's murder, in collaboration with Adelheid of Aosta. I charge him also with the murder of Helmut Villam." He gestured toward the door. "I have with me this Eagle, called Hathui, known to many of you as Henry's loyal servant, a particular favorite of my father's. She is my witness. She saw both deeds committed with her own eyes and will swear that Hugh is the murderer."

Gerberga smiled tightly but said nothing, neither to support or to challenge him.

"That is a serious charge," said Mother Scholastica, "especially since it is known that you bear a long-standing grudge against Hugh of Austra, in part relating to the conduct of this woman." She indicated Liath without looking at her.

"That is not all." He was determined to press the attack on the only flank that hadn't collapsed. "Hugh of Austra was accused and found guilty of sorcery at a trial in Autun. In that same trial, Liathano was excommunicated although she was not present to defend herself nor had she any folk at that assembly to speak in her favor. I demand that those who presided at that council be brought together a second time to reconsider the evidence."

"How will you manage that, Brother?" asked Theophanu. "Constance has been shut away by Sabella. She is a prisoner in Arconia in a place called Queen's Grave, so I am given to understand. You would have to invade Arconia to get her back."

"I am regnant of Wendar *and* Varre, am I not? I am Henry's heir. It is no invasion if my king's progress takes me to Autun to visit my aunt."

Mother Scholastica looked at each of the biscops in turn, and they nodded one by one. "It is a fair request. The matter of heresy must never be treated lightly, since heresy is punishable by death. But be clear on this. I will not anoint and give the church's blessing to any soul who is an excommunicate."

He looked at Liath. She met his gaze, lifting one eyebrow as if his expression surprised or troubled her, and she nodded, just once. The exchange annoyed him. She knew what he had to do, and she didn't really care. She had never wanted to be his queen; she had only gone along with it for reasons even he did not truly understand. He would never understand her well enough to trap her as Hugh had done so easily.

Well. Liath had given up more than anyone here knew. He trusted her.

"My quarrel is not with God, whose servant I am. Let me be anointed and crowned here in Quedlinhame. After this, the king's progress will ride to Gent."

"Why to Gent?" asked Ekkehard. "I don't want to go to Gent."

"Gent is the birthplace of the first Henry, Duke of Saony and later king of Wendar. It is well to honor the founder of our royal line. In Gent's cathedral, Arnulf the Elder married the last of Varre's royal heirs to his own children. On that day, Varre's noble house and its right to rule Varre passed into Wendish hands. The holy biscop of Gent can anoint and crown me again in Gent, before the multitudes who live there and in the neighboring counties. Then the king's progress will ride west through Saony and into Fesse, and from there into Arconia. Into Varre."

"A wise choice," said Mother Scholastica. "I approve."

"And yet another reason," he added. "Many there will attest to the miracle of St. Kristine, who appeared to a young Eagle on the day that the Eika horde led by Bloodheart attacked the city. That any of Gent's townsfolk survived the sack of Gent is due to that miracle,

and to that Eagle who led some of the population to safety along a
secret path revealed to her by the saint. Let the deed be remembered.
I know there are witnesses in Gent who will recall that day."

Mother Scholastica frowned. "I've heard such a tale, but I don't
see—" But she did see. She almost laughed, her mouth twisted up in
an expression that wasn't a smile. "So be it. God wish justice to be
done. Let it not be said that any trial was decided before all the evidence was weighed. Is there more, Sanglant?"

"That is all for now."

"I am not your enemy, Sanglant."

"In this matter?" He shrugged. "We are not enemies, Aunt. We
both wish what is best for Wendar and our royal lineage. I am my
father's obedient son, and you are God's obedient servant. So be it."

"So be it," she echoed. "Let Hugh of Austra be found. As for the
rest, we will make ready. In three days' time, Prince Sanglant will be
crowned and anointed as king."

4

"HE gave you the book to make you look guilty!" said Sanglant
later that day, when they returned to the relative peace of their encampment beyond the town.

She sat on a bench with Da's book on her legs. It was comforting
to stroke the cover, the brass fittings, the cool leather binding that
was, in this one corner, flaking from age. It needed to be oiled.

"This book condemns you by its existence. That's why they want
it burned."

"I will never let them burn this book, or indeed, any book!"

"You're being stubborn!"

She met his gaze calmly. "I am right."

He sighed, pacing, rubbing his head. "Maybe you are. I don't
know."

"But they're right," she added, "that another woman, one trained
to court, would be a more suitable queen."

He looked at her with disgust and left the tent. She heard his voice
rise outside. "Fulk! Fulk! Is there any news of the fugitive yet?"

Moments of peace were not easily discovered on the king's progress. For once, remarkably, there was not a single soul in the tent with her. Only a thread of light filtered through the smoke hole at the center of the scaffolding that held up the canvas, but because she had salamander eyes she had light enough to read the beloved words. She knew them all by heart, of course, but it gave her such intense pleasure to touch each letter, each word, and let the meaning flower before her eyes.

Astronomy concerns itself with the revolutions of the heavens, the rising and setting of the constellations, their movements and names, the motions of the stars and planets, Sun and Moon, and the laws governing these motions and all their variations.

"Are you reading? Your lips aren't moving."

Liath was so startled she almost overset the bench, and then was so embarrassed that she laughed nervously as she identified the tall woman who had slipped quietly into the tent and stood examining the furnishings with interest: a bed, a table, two chairs, two chests, two benches, and a half dozen carpets overlapping each other.

"It is true, then. The servants must all sleep outside. I heard that in Arethousa the emperor dines in solitude at the high table, not sharing his platter or his conversation with his companions. It must be an eastern custom."

"Margrave Waltharia." She rose. "Pray, be seated."

"Thank you." She sat on the bench next to Liath, very close, and Liath had to sit down right next to her or risk insulting her offer of intimacy. She was dressed in skirts cut for riding, and she smelled of horses. "So, it transpires that you are not the great granddaughter of Emperor Taillefer."

"I was misled," said Liath cautiously, "by the woman who claimed to be my mother."

"You could have lied. No one would know differently, since according to all reports it is certain that the Holy Mother Anne—who claimed to be your mother—is now dead."

"It isn't the truth, so it would be wrong to say it was. Anyway, I never desired to be born to such a position."

"Yet you carry yourself as if it is already understood." The words were said without rancor. Waltharia was not angry or suspicious, only blunt. "You are a puzzle. And you do gleam a little, in this dim light."

"Do I?" she asked, genuinely surprised. She looked at her hands but could see nothing unusual.

"Did you not before?"

"I don't know. No one ever said anything." No one but Hugh, but that was too intimate a confession to make to a woman she did not know, and one who had been, in times past, her husband's most famous lover. "Would you marry him, if you could?" Liath asked. "Mother Scholastica suggested it."

Waltharia shook her head without any sign that the question irritated her. "She's a canny tactician. She was only saying that to draw out a reaction from the others. She'd no more wish me wed to Sanglant than Gerberga or Theophanu would."

"But would you?"

She smiled. She was not a beautiful woman, the kind who turns heads, but she was attractive, and strong, and healthy, and her gaze was clean and clear. She had power and knew how to wield it. "No, I would not, although you are right to wonder, because I am powerfully attracted to him. I might have when I was young and my dear father was still alive—years ago—but what I wish for has changed. I am margrave of the Villam lands. There is much to be gained for a family who can hold on in the marchlands. I take the long view. Marriage to Sanglant would not substantially aid my house in any way that my loyalty to the Wendish throne does not already do. And it would restrict my power. No, I have in mind to marry Lord Wichman."

"Wichman! You can't be serious! He's a beast . . ."

Waltharia was already chuckling.

Liath smiled awkwardly. "Ah. You were only joking."

"It would be more tempting if he were not quite so coarse. To marry a son of the royal house would bring an important alliance to my family. Still, I have in mind some lord out of Varre, one who will be grateful for a measure of distance between him and his older siblings. Sanglant promises to bring one back for me when the progress returns from Varre."

"Will he know what you would like?" Liath felt herself bit as she said it, wondering how Sanglant might understand a woman like Waltharia so well that she would trust him to find her a husband.

Waltharia's mood turned somber with startling ease. Her face remained calm, but her hands twisted up the fabric of her riding skirt. "Druthmar was a good man. My father chose him for me. I mourn him. You know, they never found his body. I must believe he is dead, but it is hard not to hope and pray that he is still alive and may somehow find his way back to me."

"I'm sorry for your loss."

Waltharia looked at her for a long moment, then smiled softly and sadly. "So you are. I thank you for it."

Liath traced one end of the book compulsively, not knowing what to say next. The situation seemed so odd to her. At last, she blurted out, "I don't know why you're here. What do you want?"

"Your measure. You are a puzzle, and in a way you are an obstacle. I believe that Sanglant will be a better regnant for Wendar than any of his legitimate siblings. Wendar needs a strong regnant in these dark days."

"That's true. I know why you think I am an obstacle."

"Do you? Sanglant is so companionable and amiable and competent that it is easy to forget he is also like a dog in refusing to give up the things he craves. His father spoiled him. Even Queen Sophia—a very fine and strong-minded woman who was particular about her prerogatives—let the boy run wild in her chambers. He means to become regnant, despite being a bastard. He means to have you as his queen, despite the objections of most of the noble lords and clerics in this realm, who quite rightly object to your lack of rank, your suspicious heritage, and the evident fact that you know sorcery. That's leaving aside the charge of heresy, and the excommunication. How these two desires can be reconciled is the question. I admit he has wrung victory out of defeat in terrible situations, but this battlefield is not the one he is accustomed to. Do you aspire to be queen, to rule beside him?"

"No, in truth, I do not. But I won't leave him."

"Ah. And if a compliant young woman of suitable rank can be found—God help her!—who would agree to be queen and accept you as his concubine? Would you accept such an arrangement?"

Liath frowned, but she owed him this much, that she truly consider such a course of action. Waltharia waited, perfectly at ease as the light from outside faded and the space within the tent darkened until every shape was only a deeper cast of shadow, even her own. From beyond the walls of the tent came the many noises of the camp settling down as twilight fell over them: horses stomping and blowing, men singing or calling out orders, a wagon's creaking rumble as objects were moved, a dog's bark, the distant piercing cry of the golden griffin as it soared above. Liath felt herself caught within the inner heart of the camp, unseen but measured as the outer seeming went about its public life.

"No, I couldn't live with such an arrangement."

Waltharia nodded. "So be it." Nothing in her tone revealed whether she approved or disapproved of Liath's answer. "It can be done, but it will not be easy. You must agree to be patient and to work at this one step at a time."

"I can be patient. There is a thing he lacks, Lady Waltharia."

"Is there?" she said with a laugh. "I have not yet discovered it, then. No, I pray you, I am only jesting. What do you need?"

"You see in what manner we are dressed. Sanglant's road has been a difficult one. He and his army escaped the cataclysm with little more than their weapons and horses and the clothes on their backs. A regnant cannot be anointed and crowned without vestments appropriate to such a ceremony."

"Yes, it's well you warned me. I will see that suitable robes are brought, although it will be difficult with his height. Still, it can be managed." Unexpectedly, she reached out and took Liath's hand in hers. "Ah. Your skin is warm. Do you have a fever?"

"No. I'm never sick with such things."

"Is it true?" she whispered. "That your mother was a daimone of the upper air? A creature of fire?"

"It's true."

"What does it mean? Do you have a soul?"

"All creatures created by God have souls."

"Can you fly, as it is said daimones can?"

All at once, grief choked her as she remembered what she had lost. Barely, she was able to rasp out the words, although she didn't know why she should confess something so dangerous, so terrible, and so private to a woman she scarcely knew. Her rival. Possibly her ally.

"Once I could, but not on Earth. Only in the heavens."

"Have you walked in the heavens? Have you seen the Chamber of Light?"

"No. Only souls unchained by death can walk there. But I have climbed through the armature of the spheres, I have climbed the ladder of the heavens. I have seen . . . such things that I weep to recall them. So much light."

"As in the prophet's vision. Yet you are here."

She nodded, unable to speak.

"You were forced to return?"

She shook her head.

"Did you come back of your own volition, for *him?*"

"For him," she said hoarsely. "For the child."

"Ah." She turned Liath's hand over and placed the tip of a finger in the middle of Liath's palm, as if reading something from that touch. "That was a great sacrifice. I think even Mother Scholastica does not understand this."

"Why are you here, Lady Waltharia?"

"Do you think I mean to curry favor for my family by befriending you?"

"I admit . . . I don't know what I was thinking."

"I have already told you. Wendar suffers, and Sanglant will be a strong regnant. To support him, I will support you. But you must help me. No more scenes like the one played today in Mother Scholastica's study. Do not hand them the weapon they can use to pierce you with."

"Yes, I understand that. I thought she would be my ally. She is a scholar! She ought to want to know the truth!"

"She is a daughter of the royal line and the most powerful abbess in the land. Scholarship is not her first consideration."

"No, perhaps not."

"Have you taken thought to what you will do when Sanglant goes to the church to be crowned and anointed?"

"Not yet. A little."

Waltharia nodded. "If there is aught else you wish to ask me, if you desire my counsel, send the Eagle with a message. My stewards know that she is allowed into my presence at any hour of day or night."

"The Eagle?"

Waltharia released her hand and stood. "The one who witnessed my father's murder."

She left as precipitously as she had come. In her wake, a woman entered bearing a lantern whose commonplace flame illuminated her familiar face and wry smile.

"Hathui! Were you outside all this time?"

"I brought the margrave here."

"Ah. It would make sense that you must speak with the margrave about her father, and what you saw."

"Yes, for my own part. For yours, however, she is only the first."

"The first?"

Hathui hung the lamp from one of the horizontal poles that supported the canvas ceiling. Then she turned, still smiling, and shook her head as she might at a child who refuses to go to bed when she's told. "Who will approach you, to gain your favor and your notice."

"There are others?"

"Oh, yes," said Hathui wickedly. "But I've put off the rest until tomorrow."

Liath laughed helplessly, angrily, and wiped tears from her eyes. "Books are easier to understand."

"For some."

"Ai, God, Hathui. What am I to do?"

"Learn quickly."

Hathui's scarlet-trimmed Eagle's cloak was certainly the worse for so much wear, and it had been mended in a dozen spots. Her brass Eagle's badge glowed in the lamplight.

"It was easier riding as an Eagle," said Liath. "I remember when I first saw you and Manfred. And Wolfhere."

"I remember," said Hathui in a low voice, frowning.

"Do you think Wolfhere is dead?"

"No."

"Do you know where he is?"

"No."

"I didn't see him through the crown. He wasn't one of those weaving the spell. But Hugh was. It's strange, now that I reflect on it. It was only a touch, at the end, but he was thinking of you."

"Hugh of Austra was thinking of me?" Hathui's voice shook, and real fear creased her lips and eyes.

That expression made Liath recall that day back in Heart's Rest when Wolfhere had rescued her from Hugh. She had been so weak then, not in body so much as in spirit. As skittish as a calf, Hanna had once said. Hathui hadn't seemed frightened then. In fact, she had seemed as clever and strong as any woman can be who knows herself and her power and her place in the world and is satisfied with all of these things.

"The one who thought of you was with Hugh. Hugh was using him to absorb the power of the backlash that comes at the tail of such a powerful spell. Hugh must have known that the people who wove the spell would die, so he sacrificed this other man in his place."

"Who are you speaking about? I already know Hugh is a murderer twice over."

"Three times, then. This other man thought—that he would never see you again unless you met on the other side."

"The other side?"

"I don't know where that is."

"I know," Hathui whispered hoarsely. Even in lamplight, with shadows thrown helter-skelter by the sway of the lamp, it was easy to see how the blood had drained from her face. "My grandmother was an unrepentant heathen. Even after she professed to enter the Circle of Unity she still set out offerings for the Old Ones. You said Hugh is a murderer three times. What did you mean?"

"It was no one I had ever met, but I felt a kinship with him. He was seeking the same thing I seek. The heart of the universe. His name . . ." So much had happened so quickly; the spell had overwhelmed her. She had grasped his name, but she could not remember it.

"It must have been Zacharias!" murmured Hathui, weeping. "Is he dead, then? Truly dead?"

"Yes. I felt him die, through the spell. Who is he?"

Hathui sank to the carpet as she sobbed. Liath knelt beside her, resting a hand on her shoulder, but she was helpless to comfort her.

"M-my brother. Ai, God. How? *How?*"

"Hugh of Austra was part of Anne's weaving."

"You destroyed the spell by killing Holy Mother Anne."

"No. I killed Anne, it's true. I did my part. But I had allies, whose names I do not know. It was the plan made by the ancient ones. I was only the final weapon they unleashed. Zacharias did his part as well. How they came in contact with him I do not know, but in the end he cast himself into the crown that Hugh was weaving. Northeast of here, somewhere out beyond the marchlands. Because of what he did, the entire northern span of the weaving was knotted and tangled and thereby ruined."

"Zacharias did that?" Hathui gasped through her tears.

Not alone, Liath thought, but she hesitated. Others had done their part. Pale creatures erupting out of paler sands had consumed Brother Severus. An Eika prince had killed the pair of clerics weaving the crown in Alba.

"Zacharias accepted death, to save what he loved most."

For a long time they remained without moving, Hathui weeping, Liath beside her, wishing she knew what words of comfort would ease Hathui's grief but keeping silence, because silence was all she had to offer. A gust of wind rocked the tent, and long after it had departed the lantern's metal handle squeaked softly against the wooden pole as it swung back and forth, back and forth, the light cresting and troughing in the corners until at last the motion stilled.

"Ai, God," Hathui breathed. "So he is gone. Truly gone. Oh, Zacharias. He was probably afraid."

"We're all afraid. What lies within us can be as fearful a thing as all those terrors that lie without. He had courage when he needed it."

"That is enough," said Hathui through her tears. She sat back on her heels and placed a hand over Liath's. "I'll stand by you, Liath, whatever comes."

"Will you stand by Sanglant?"

"He has already won my loyalty."

"Then I accept your offer gladly, Hathui, and I'll tell you, there is none I value more."

Hathui's gaze narrowed as she examined Liath's face. "Did you know your eyes shine when it's dark? I never noticed that before. It's like a touch of blue fire. What lies within you, truly, Liath?"

"Power enough," said Liath softly, "that I am afraid of what it can do if let go unchecked."

"No!" said Sanglant from outside, clearly annoyed, "but let word be brought to me at once if there is any news."

Liath stood. Sanglant entered, and indeed he looked mightily irritated. Then he saw Hathui. He knelt at once to set a hand on her shoulder.

"What is this? Have you come to some hurt?"

"No, Your Majesty. Liath recalled a vision she had. She knows what became of my brother."

"Brother Zacharias?"

"Yes. He is dead."

"Ah." He glanced at Liath. She nodded, and briefly told him the tale. "I am sorry. Brother Zacharias was a troubled man, but a brave one. In his own fashion. This is yet one more crime to add to Hugh of Austra's list."

"There is no sign of him, I take it," said Liath.

"None. I've heard more of the tale now. He arrived in Austra out of the east but would not say where he had come from, only that he needed shelter. Gerberga brought him with her when she came west to visit Theophanu in Osterburg. Now Hugh has vanished. He must have plotted it all along. Give you the damning book, and fly away so that the taint could not touch him."

"Where can he fly?" Liath asked. "His sister's lands are closed to him. He must guess she has turned against him. Burchard and Liutgard will turn him over to you if they find him in Fesse or Avaria. No one in the North Mark will trust him, if he even wanted to return to such a benighted place. Where can he go? Who will take him in?"

"I've sent riders south and west. He might go to Varre, to offer his services to Sabella or Conrad, but Conrad never liked him either and Sabella has nothing to offer him. Where else can he go, then, except back to the poisonous nest where he gained so much power?"

"He'll elude your searchers," said Liath, shaking her head.

"So be it. If he flees to Varre, we'll catch up to him. If he flies to Aosta, then he cannot trouble us here in Wendar, can he?"

"So we can pray," said Hathui grimly, "for I would like to sleep soundly at night. I have a boon to ask of you, Your Majesty."

"What is that?"

"If he's caught, I want recompense for the harm he's done to me and my kinfolk. A grant of land, perhaps, to add to what they already claim."

Sanglant smiled. "I so swear, Hathui. You will have satisfaction."

"Your Majesty," she said, head bowed, and kissed the royal seal ring on his right hand, the one he had taken off his father's body.

He stood in unusual stillness for a long time, unwilling to break into her grief, but at last she shook her head and rose.

"There is wine," he said. "Captain Fulk will see you get anything you wish. We'll keep a close watch, but I expect Hugh is gone. And that you are safe from him for the time being. Still, we must be cautious."

"Your Majesty," she said. She nodded at Liath, and left the tent.

He remained still for a shockingly long time, and she watched him, curious and also not at all recovered from the unexpected memory of the weaving that had risen like a tide to engulf her. It had troubled her. It had roiled the waters.

"What is it?" she asked him finally.

"Did you touch him? In the library?" His voice was hoarse, but then, he always sounded like that.

"Are you jealous of him, Sanglant?"

"Of *course* I'm jealous of him! I know he—" He faltered, grimacing. "I know he . . . possessed your body."

"He took what he wanted. I didn't go to him willingly."

"I know! I know! It just . . . gripes me to think of him touching you. That isn't all of it. He has all the skills you treasure. He can read and write and puzzle over the mysteries of the heavens, just as you do." He waved toward the walls, the ceiling, the lantern. "He knows sorcery. He's more like you than I am."

"That's true," she agreed, smiling as he got to looking more agitated. "It's a terrible thing to imagine that a man as evil as Hugh can be compared to me in so many ways."

"That's not what I meant!" he answered, laughing but still worrying at it. "He's just so damned beautiful."

"That's true," she agreed.

"How can the outer seeming so ill match the inner heart?"

"I don't know. Yet in the end even his beauty has failed him. His
own half siblings ought to trust and embrace him, but they hate
and distrust him instead. He betrayed those who did trust him. He
is a fugitive, a man without kinfolk or retinue to aid him. Perhaps
God have set him before us as a lesson."

"What sort of lesson? I am not well versed in these clerical
riddles."

He was amused, and no doubt a little relieved, but in her own
heart laughter had fled. " 'Chaos in the world is the result of disorder in the human soul.' I didn't say it," she added. "I'm just quot-
ing. I read it in a book."

"Which doesn't make it any less true. Did you touch him?"

She thought of Waltharia, a nice enough woman, someone she
had liked perfectly well. Someone who had shown her a moment's
surprising, and genuine, compassion.

"Why should I tell you?" she asked him, and when he winced, she
was glad of seeing him pained. She hadn't known she harbored so
sharp a sting in her inner heart. Flame trembled. She had learned
how to contain it, but maybe she was more like Hugh than she
knew, wanting to hurt what she could not control.

"Nay," he said raggedly, "I have no right to question you on such
matters, God know. I trust you. Let's leave it at that."

"I would as soon touch Hugh as lie in a bed of maggots," she said,
relenting. "Let's leave it at that. There's much to be considered these
next two days and not least of them is what royal garments can be
found for your investiture. Waltharia has said she will help me in
finding suitable clothing."

"Waltharia?"

"Oh, indeed, we are quite close, she and I."

She was doubly pleased, and ashamed of the pleasure she took in
it, to see him look askance at her, and frown, and scratch one shoulder in a way that showed he was quite discomfited by these tidings,
wondering what they meant and what the two women might have
said to each other. He took refuge in pacing, and she let him pace as
she allowed the turmoil in her heart to simmer in an alarmingly
smug manner.

In time, he came to rest beside the bench. He picked up the book, opened it with the exaggerated care of a man who rarely touches such things, and shook his head as he stared at one of the pages. From this angle, she could not see which one.

"I haven't the patience for this," he muttered at last as he closed and set it down with proper reverence.

"I haven't the patience for court life."

"No," he agreed. "You will always say the wrong thing at the wrong time."

"Even if I'm right!"

"Especially if you're right," he said, laughing. "But court is a battlefield, nothing different. You must choose not just how you arrange your forces but when and in what order you attack, when to make a strategic retreat, when to make a flanking action, when to stand your ground."

"Its own form of scholarship."

"Perhaps. I would not say so."

"We each received training in our youth. That can't be changed. I wouldn't have it otherwise. Because of that, there is much we can learn each from the other. I've been thinking about Gent, and strategy, and excommunication."

"The nobles support me. As long as they support me, the church is limited in how far its influence can reach."

"That may be, but *I* do not wish to remain an excommunicate in the eyes or heart of the church. Of course it didn't affect me at Verna or when I was with the Ashioi because I didn't even know of it. In the final march against Anne it mattered little. Now it matters a great deal. I know what I must do."

"What is that?"

"You won't like it."

"Is that meant to encourage me to dissuade you?"

"I mean to do it, because I know it's right."

"So am I threatened! I pray you, if we are to be allies, we must know what the other intends."

"Very well," she said. "You are not the only one who must hold a vigil."

XI
SHADOWS AND LIGHT

1

"I don't like you," said Blessing, "so go away."

Although Lady Lavinia's enclosed garden had not yet begun to bloom, Antonia found a measure of peace there when she was not tutoring Princess Mathilda or receiving petitioners and penitents in the great hall beside Queen Adelheid. She had been sitting in solitude on a stone bench considering the nature of evil and the punishments and penance most fitting for oath breakers. Hearing the shrill voice of her enemy's child, she leaned forward to peer through the foliage that concealed her. A screen of clematis grew alongside the pictur-esque ruins of a tiny octagonal chapel, a remnant from the old Dariyan palace that had once stood here. Beneath her feet a mosaic floor, swept clean, displayed an antique tale involving two hounds, a huntress, and a half naked man. She had often encouraged Lady Lavinia to destroy the floor, but while the lady was otherwise all compliance, in this matter she refused most obstinately.

"You can't make me go. You're my mother's prisoner."

"I can punch you in the face."

"Bastard of a bastard!"

"Am not!"

"Are so!"

"Brat! Leave off!" A masculine voice entered the fray. Antonia parted the leaves with her hands so she could see. She had succumbed once to a man of that line. It was a bitter failing to know that a youthful face and laughing, generous features might warm her still, although he was young enough to be her grandson. Berthold Villam sauntered up from the far end of the garden along the paved pathway that paralleled the irrigation channel. He was conversing amiably with his Aostan guards.

The two girls faced each other like two young furies, although Blessing looked years older. Yet their expressions and stances were remarkably similar. It was difficult to remember, seeing a woman budding out of the girl, that Blessing was very young despite the age of her body. She looked ready to spit or bite, as little hellions may do, but Berthold's command fixed her to one spot where she fumed and got red and then white as her temper flared.

Princess Mathilda spat at Blessing's feet before bolting for the safety of the colonnaded porch where two of her servingwomen waited in the shadows. As they led the girl away, their chatter faded out of earshot.

". . . and Meto said what? Here, now, Your Highness, your mother said you weren't to speak to the child for she's not of your station and a wild thing indeed. Let's go in. So, go on. What did Meto say to her when he found out she meant to marry Liutbold?"

"Marry Liutbold! Is that what that was about? That's the first I heard of it. What can she have been thinking?"

"She's stupid," said Blessing.

Berthold halted beside the girl, scratching at the peach fuzz he had been growing for the last three months. "Princess Mathilda is a royal princess just as you are, Your Highness. You'd do better to make her an ally than an enemy." He had switched to Wendish, which the guards did not, perhaps, understand.

"She's an enemy."

"Perhaps. But she keeps stumbling into you when she isn't supposed to see you at all."

"That's because she hates me."

"She might. Or she might wish for a child her own age to play with. She might want to like you, and act like this because she doesn't know how else to get your attention."

How had this youth come to be so wise?

"She's not my own age! I'm older!"

"You look older, brat. But you don't act it!"

"I do!" She bit her lip. She pouted. But she shut up and fixed a stare on Berthold that would have eaten another man alive.

"Come, brat," he said more fondly, extending a hand.

She laid her head against his arm as a dog rests its muzzle lovingly along its master's thigh.

"Here is Brother Heribert. He's found you a green apple left over from last season. Isn't that amazing?"

"It'll make me puke!"

"Anna can stew it up with herbs and make it all tasty. He found some flowers, too, a kind I've never seen before. Maybe you can dry them and press them to make something pretty."

"I don't want to. Papa let me fight with swords. I want to fight with swords!"

One of the guards made a noise halfway between a hiccup and a cough.

"I can so! I can so!"

"Blessing!"

She shut her eyes and to Antonia's amazement did not burst into tears, as she would have done just two months ago. She struggled, that dusky face mobile in all its expressions, flashing quickly from thwarted anger through innocent bewilderment into a determination that showed itself by the way she jutted out her jaw.

"Your Highness, I have found you an apple."

Antonia looked away, letting the branches ease back into place. It was bad enough to hear his voice. She could not bear to look at him as well.

"Thank you, Brother Heribert."

"Properly spoken, brat," said Berthold with a laugh. "We'll teach you manners yet."

"I hate you," said Blessing in a tone that meant exactly the opposite. "Come, Brother Heribert," she added grandly. "We'll go up to Anna. We don't need *him* anymore."

"It's time for your lessons," he said in the voice that sounded like Heribert but not like him.

"I hate books!"

"You must learn. It is what he wanted."

"Go on, brat. Learning is a weapon as sharp as steel."

"You'll come too, Berthold?" she asked plaintively.

"In a bit."

Her sigh seemed loud enough to rattle the leaves. She tromped off.

Antonia from her concealment saw the pair as they climbed the steps onto the long porch that looked over the enclosed garden. A trio of bored guards dogged their heels. One held the chain bound to Blessing's left wrist, a necessary precaution after her first two escape attempts. On the third step Heribert paused and glanced back over the garden, and for an instant Antonia thought he looked right at her, although surely she was safely hidden in the bower.

"That child has a terrible liking for you, my lord," said the older of the two guards attending Berthold. He spoke in Dariyan.

"Do you think so?" Berthold had taken to Dariyan so easily that it was likely he had some prior knowledge of the language, although nothing Antonia knew of the Villam clan suggested an earlier link to Aosta.

"Surely enough, for I've two daughters close to her in age and I know the look they gave those lads they took a liking to."

"Poor thing," said Berthold.

"Think you so?" asked the younger guard. "She is a brat. Princess Mathilda is a nobler child."

"I pray you, Philo, I will not hear Princess Blessing spoken of in that way." The tone was gentle enough to make the older guard chuckle and the younger one truckle.

"I beg pardon, my lord. I meant nothing disrespectful. Yet it's her father killed our lord, the queen's husband. His own father! Surely the stain of his patricide marks her somehow. She hasn't the look of proper people. What if that's the influence of the Enemy?"

"I'm no cleric to answer such troubling questions. Princess Mathilda is a fine young lady, indeed, as she must be with such royal parents. What say you we go find those pastries you were speaking about?"

"Is it the pastries you lads are wanting a closer look at, or the cook's helpers?" said the elder, and the younger two chortled.

They walked away in good charity with each other. Queen Adelheid had no idea how thoroughly Lord Berthold had cozened his guards and what freedom they allowed him, none of which she had approved. He had the run of the castle, as long as he kept out of the way of those who would get his guards in trouble. Antonia watched the three men retreat down the length of the garden between the serried ranks of fruit trees only now leafing and budding as the warmth of spring tried to penetrate the clouds. There was a brilliance in the sky today that gave her hope that the sun would break through soon. If not now, when?

Berthold could have escaped a hundred times in the last three months, but he had not, because Blessing could not. Like Villam, he was loyal to Wendar and, despite Mathilda's superior claims, it was obvious to Antonia that Berthold had made his choice. Adelheid might believe otherwise, but she had allowed herself to be blinded by his youthful charm.

Nay, Heribert was the cause of it all. He had turned Berthold's heart, although it wasn't clear with what inducements. Blessing, too, had a hand in it, however unwitting. Mathilda had many fine qualities, including Henry's infamous temper and openhanded generosity and Adelheid's devious mind, but she did not shine, not as Blessing did. The child was without question an abomination, intermingling the blood of three races, but she had power that could be molded and used as a tool, either by the Enemy or by the righteous.

Adelheid knew that. It was the only reason she hadn't killed Blessing in revenge for Henry's death.

Antonia sat down on the bench to resume her meditations, but peace had fled. It was dry and cool and the air had a dusty bite to it. No breath of wind rustled leaves. Even the poplars that lined the far wall stood in silence, although normally any least breeze caused them to murmur. There hadn't been rain for a month although usually the dry season commenced much later in the year. These signs seemed bad omens.

Worse yet to come, as the holy prophets said, although how anything could be worse than what she had seen and the reports that filtered in from the provinces of Adelheid's blasted realm she could not imagine.

When she rose, her knees popped, and her back hurt. These days she was always out of breath and battling a nagging cough. By the dry fountain, two clerics and one attendant waited for her. Few had survived the destruction in Darre, but that was just as well.

"Your Grace," said young John.

"Your Holiness," said elderly Johanna.

The servingwoman, Felicita, took her arm and assisted her up the steps, which had gotten steeper in the last month.

"We will go first to the queen's chamber and then to my audience hall for the afternoon's petitioners."

"Yes, Your Holiness."

At midday, Adelheid usually sat for an hour beside Berengaria, but she was not in the nursery today. Antonia sank down on the couch beside the bed where the tiny child tossed and turned in fitful sleep. Her face, normally pale, would turn red when she coughed. She had not spoken a word for three weeks now, and it was supposed by everyone except Adelheid that she was dying.

Had Berengaria been innocent, or guilty? It seemed she had been guilty, although it was difficult to know how a child so small could have offended God. Perhaps she was being punished for her mother's sins, as in the ancient days of the prophets when God smote the unrighteous for their failings, great and small, old and young, female and male, and even the cattle.

So be it.

"Poor thing," murmured Felicita. Antonia smoothed sweat-soaked hair back from the child's face as the nurse looked on with resignation.

"Has the queen been in to see her daughter today?" Antonia asked.

"No, Your Holiness," said the nurse. "I heard her in the corridor with her attendants, but then Captain Falco came with some news and they went away again."

"What news?"

"I'm not sure, Your Holiness. There was some talk of prisoners, but you know how the guard do bring in all kinds of folk these days, most of them beggars wanting a loaf of bread and nothing more."

Antonia went into the sitting room where Mathilda sat at a table and laboriously formed her letters. The girl looked up, hearing footsteps, and smiled.

"Your Holiness! Come see, I pray you. I know every one!"

She was a cunning girl, and eager to display her skill on the wax tablet although generally in the church novices were not taught their letters this young.

After every letter had undergone scrutiny and approval, and been done again, the child peeped up at her. She had big eyes and long lashes, but she wasn't sweet, not anymore, not since the days before. As it had in the greater world, the cataclysm had shaken loose the many lesser evils that cut into a soul and thereby in those gouges gave purchase for the Enemy's minions to claw their way inside.

"I'm better at my letters than *she* is, aren't I?"

"You are very skilled at your letters, Your Highness."

"Better than her?"

"My child, do not seek to be compared to that you do not wish to become."

"She doesn't like me."

"She doesn't like herself. She is very young."

"She's older than me. She can't make letters like I can. Will Berengaria die?"

"We will all die, child. We will all come to dust someday."

"But our souls will live."

"Those that do not fall into the Pit."

She shivered. "I saw it."

"You saw what?"

"The Pit. There was a big wind. There was fire. The earth split apart. It swallowed people. All that poison poured out. Wasn't that from the Pit? It was stinky."

"Maybe so, child. Do not vex yourself. You were not punished."

She bit her lip and stared at the letters, then with a sharp movement wiped the slate clean. "I'll do them again," she said. "I'll be perfect so God won't punish me."

2

ANTONIA meant to stop in her audience chamber—there was so much work to be done—but her steps led her to the North Tower. This time of day, all the prisoners would be within. Blessing was allowed into the courtyard only in the morning, under guard, and her attendants had leave to exercise only in the afternoon, so none would be able to attempt escape without leaving the others behind.

"Holy Mother." The guards dropped to one knee, bowing heads, then rose and opened the door.

The lowest room of the North Tower was now a barracks. Pallets and rope beds filled half the floor, benches and three tables the rest. Men knelt as she entered. At least two dozen were barracked here.

"Holy Mother." A sergeant—she'd forgotten his name—came forward. "The queen is above with Captain Falco. Have you come to see the new prisoners? They were brought in at dawn."

"Yes. I'll go up."

A stone staircase curved along the outer wall of the tower, leading up to the next level. Here, the three servants slept on pallets laid out on the plank floor. Two of them, the barbarians, sat here now. The young male was binding hemp into rope. He looked up at her, his gaze impassive, and without the least interest in her rank and exalted status he went back to his work. The female had her eyes shut and, although she was sitting, seemed to be asleep. What coarse hands she had! They were large and callused, and she had the unattractive, flat-faced features of the Quman, although Antonia had been told she was born to a different tribe entirely. It made no difference. They were both doomed to the Pit, because they were heathens who refused to accept the Circle of Unity. Except for a single chest, the rest of the circular room was empty and the shutters barred. A pair of guards sat on the wooden steps that had been lowered from the level above, fastened with ropes and a pulley. The stone staircase, continuing upward, had been blocked off with planks.

"Holy Mother! Will you go up to see the prisoners? Let us help you, if you will."

A brawny and gratifyingly polite young soldier lent her a steadying hand. It was not as easy as it had once been to climb stairs that were almost as steep as a ladder, but she got to the second floor without incident. In this chamber Lord Berthold and his attendant slept on decent beds, and therefore good tapestries were hung from the walls and two braziers, now cold, hung from tripods. Carved benches flanked a good table. There was even a chair set beside an open window.

He sat there, staring out over Novomo with an expression on his face that made her shiver because it was so inhuman in its lack of emotion.

"Brother Heribert," she said, that thrill of rage and helpless expectation flooding her weary bones. Ought not a child to love its parent? Didn't the Holy Book enjoin obedience? He did not turn or even acknowledge that she had spoken. She might as well have been invisible, and mute.

"Heribert!"

He roused, startled, and looked at her, but did not rise to greet her, as any natural child would have. He should love her and be grateful to her. He had been a great burden to her, after all, since it was expected she would be celibate. That his father had seduced her—well, that was the work of the Enemy, and no doubt those seeds sown had sprouted and corrupted Heribert in a most improper way to make him so rebellious and ungrateful.

Before she could speak to tell him so, Captain Falco spoke, his voice heard through the open trap cut into the ceiling. "I will ask you again, where have you come from? Who is this young woman who accompanies you?"

He got no answer.

She walked to stand under the trap. The stone staircase here had also been blocked off, and the ladder that offered access to the third floor rested against one of the benches.

"Can I help you with that, Holy Mother?" asked the guard, who had followed her up. "Can you climb the ladder?"

"I can," she said grimly.

The man set the ladder up through the trap. Heribert rose. From the chamber below, she heard voices.

"Let me up, I pray you!"

"My lord, you weren't to have gone out! The queen was very angry. We told her you were ill with a terrible flux. Lord Jonas threw a hood over his head to pretend he was you and let Paulinus and Tedwin escort him out to the pits. He rowled like a cat hung out on a hook."

Berthold's laugh rang merrily. "After all those pastries, I may yet wish I were that cat—"

Above, the queen said, "Hit him. Make him talk."

A slap fell hard on flesh.

"Stop it! Stop it, you bitch!"

"Shit!" swore Berthold, from below. "Who is that?"

"The other prisoner, my lord. Dark as honey, that one, and I'm sure she tastes as sweet. I didn't know Wendish women came so dark, like Jinna. But she carries herself like a duchess and she's Wendish, all right, the bitch."

A second slap cracked, from above. From below, feet scrambled on the steps. Heribert's brow furrowed as he considered Antonia's face, or the bright tapestry depicting a hunting scene, or the air itself, perhaps, where the sunlight caught the drifting of dust motes. His gaze was focused on no single thing.

She set foot on the lowest rung as Berthold's head appeared in the open trap.

Above, a scuffle broke out. There came another slap, a muffled shriek, and a woman's sharp curse. Blessing screamed.

"Sit down!" roared Captain Falco.

"You'll not treat me in this manner! Get your hands off me, you pig!"

"I pray you, child," said a new voice, a man's voice. "Sit down."

Antonia recognized *that* voice. She climbed as Berthold dashed across the floor and, seeing her on the ladder, hopped from one foot to the other because he was too well bred to demand she hurry up.

She had trouble clambering out onto the floor above. By the time she got to her feet, Berthold had swarmed up the ladder behind her, and he stood there, skin flushed, eyes wide, and mouth open as he stared.

The queen was furious; spots of color burned in her cheeks. This kind of unrestrained anger never made her prettier.

The servant girl, Anna, had Blessing clasped in a tight embrace. The princess looked ready to kick, but did not.

A white-haired man was bound to a chair. Two guards stood behind him. Captain Falco, looking as angry as Antonia had ever seen him and bearing a fresh scratch on his face, had his big hands clamped around the wrists of a dusky young woman who appeared to be about the same age as Berthold.

"Elene!" young Villam cried, in the Wendish manner, dragging out each syllable: *Ehl-leh-ney.* "Elene of Wayland!"

Captain Falco released her. The newcomer turned to look at the elderly man, who nodded at her before looking toward Berthold.

"You look like Berthold, Villam's youngest son," said the one called Elene. "I remember you from the king's schola, where I was held hostage."

"You remember *me?*" said Berthold in the tone of a man who has just fallen heels over head in love.

"Of course. The others weren't kind to me, not as you were. They called me names. They were jealous of my father, of course."

"Elene of Wayland," said Adelheid. She folded her hands and tucked them close against her belly as might a child who has been warned not to snatch at a piece of sweet cake it particularly wants. "Are you Conrad's daughter?"

The girl looked at her, just that, then turned her back most insultingly and crossed to kneel beside the elderly man. "Have they hurt you, Wolfhere?"

"Hush!" hissed Anna in a too-loud voice as Blessing squirmed in her arms. "Hush, my lady!"

"I want to go to Berthold!"

Anna let her go, and Blessing bolted across the room and flung herself so hard against Berthold that he staggered and almost plunged down through the trap.

"Brat! Hold, there! I can't breathe."

But he didn't look at her. He had not once taken his gaze from Duke Conrad's beautiful daughter, who had, against all expectation, turned up in Aosta under the protection of Brother Lupus, known as Wolfhere, the last of Anne's cabal.

How very interesting.

"Enough!" Adelheid tugged pointlessly at her sleeves as she struggled to recover her composure. "Let the Eagle stew in the hole until he is willing to tell us why he travels north through Aosta without a retinue and with a duke's heir in his talons. Conrad's daughter may remain with her royal cousin for now."

"I don't want her!" retorted Blessing, who was still clinging to Berthold. "I don't like her."

"I'll show you, you little beast!" said Elene, with a spark of gleeful spite as she spun to face Blessing. "You think I don't know how to discipline nasty little sisters?"

"Hush, Blessing!" scolded Berthold. "Duke Conrad is your father's cousin. You'll treat Lady Elene with respect."

"I won't!"

Wolfhere spoke for the second time. "Princess Blessing. Be good, as your father—and Brother Heribert—would wish you to."

The words silenced her. She sniveled, but kept her mouth shut.

Elene smiled. She looked at Wolfhere, and he at her, and some message passed between them that Antonia could not read, but she understood its import. Prisoners as they were, fallen into the hands of enemies, they were not scared in the least.

They have a plan already.

"Captain, take him quickly, before I lose my temper," said Adelheid. She turned toward the trap. "Holy Mother! Why have you come?"

"To see the prisoners, Your Majesty. How are they come here, in these terrible days?"

"They were found walking north. How can a pair of travelers with but one sorry mare between them have survived the journey through southern Aosta? Yet neither deigns to speak. We will have to torture the Eagle to extract a confession. Captain!"

Falco untied Wolfhere from the chair. The old man's hands were still bound, and he was bundled away down the ladder while Elene stared after him. Adelheid followed.

"Here, now, brat," said Berthold, "let go."

"Won't."

"How have you come here, Lord Berthold?" asked Elene.

"I pray you, Holy Mother," said Berthold sweetly. "Will you lead us in prayer?"

The girl started, then lifted her chin to acknowledge the blow. She was not subtle, but it was clear that, like her infamous father, she was stubborn and strong. And hiding something. There was a perfume, if not quite a smell, about her that reminded Antonia of Anne and the tower in Verna: the stink of sorcery, that she knew so well herself.

"You are Meriam's granddaughter," Antonia said.

The girl looked at her, surprised. That youthful face had a great deal of pride, but she was also wary, guarded, watchful. She was thinking, plotting, planning.

"Who are you?" she asked imperiously.

"I am the Holy Mother of the faithful, child."

"You are the skopos? Holy Mother Anne's successor?" she asked. "Yet you speak Wendish. You're not Dariyan-born. Did Holy Mother Anne choose you to succeed her?"

"God have chosen me to do their work on Earth."

Elene giggled, her expression touched so slightly with hysteria that Antonia almost missed it. Beneath the noble arrogance inherited from her father, she was fragile. The strength she had shown in front of Wolfhere had no deep roots. "I pray you, Holy Mother, intercede with the queen. Do not let them harm Wolfhere. He saved my life!"

There was a secret here, but she would have to probe carefully to uncover it. "How did he save you, child?"

"I can't tell you."

"I pray you, Holy Mother," broke in Berthold, "can't you see she is exhausted? Let her rest. Surely you can interview her later."

"Wolfhere must not be harmed!" Elene dropped to the floor, weeping.

"Let go, brat!" Berthold shook off Blessing. He crossed to Elene, grasped her hands, and knelt beside her. "I pray you, lady, do not despair. I won't let Wolfhere be harmed."

She lifted her face to stare up at him through her tears. Such a handsome couple! So young and so emotional, as the young were.

"Stop it!" said Blessing furiously. She stomped forward and tried to shove herself between Berthold and Elene.

"That's enough, brat!" said Berthold sternly.

"Stop it, yourself!" Elene pinched the girl so hard on her backside that Blessing shrieked, leaped away, and flung herself into Anna's arms, sobbing noisily.

"No one loves me! I hate all of you!"

Elene's tears had dried. She looked at Berthold, measuring him, and he stared at her with all the intelligence of a young man who has fallen hard and helplessly into the snare of infatuation. She did not remove her hand from his. Tremulously, she smiled.

"No! No! No! He loves me, not her!"

"Your Highness," said the servant girl, clutching the writhing child so tightly against her that the strain showed on her face, "I pray you, do not make a scene. Of course Lord Berthold loves you. We all do."

"Even Papa got rid of me! No one loves me! No one! No one! No one!" She fell into a sobbing temper tantrum that took all the servant girl's strength to contain.

Antonia smiled. "Lady Elene. What is it you wish?"

She released Berthold's hands and stood. His concern had given her an infusion of strength. "I wish for Wolfhere to be released so he and I can continue north. I want to go home!"

"Queen Adelheid will not be so easily persuaded."

"I have other—" She cut herself off, remembering prudence.

"I expect your grandmother has taught you some of her arts, child. I am not ignorant of Anne and her sorcery. I know Meriam. Is she dead?"

Elene's shoulders curled. Her tense stance slackened. "Yes," she whispered. "She's dead. Anne knew it would kill them all, and she didn't *care!* That's what Wolfhere said."

"Wolfhere would know, would he not, for he was Anne's most loyal servant."

Elene tilted her head sideways as a measuring smile teased her lips. "That's right," she said in a mocking tone.

Impertinent child!

"I don't know what Wolfhere told you to convince you to travel with him. I stood among their number, once, before Anne tried to betray me. I saw what was coming. I saw who supported Anne, but I also saw that I would be sacrificed, so I chose a different path. That is why I survived."

"What are you talking about?" asked Berthold.

Blessing sobbed on and on. "No one! No–o–o one!" The child had remarkable stamina, which was, no doubt, some unnatural inheritance from her parents.

"Of course you are right," said Elene quietly. "I pray you, Holy Mother, do not let them harm Wolfhere."

"I am sworn to God's service, not to the trivial quarrels of humankind. Yet I hate to see suffering. It is possible that you and Wolfhere have information that may be of value to me."

"I'll tell you everything, if you'll let us go."

"Were you not already planning to escape? What manner of sorcery did your grandmother teach you?"

Elene twisted one hand within the curve of the other. She bit her lip.

"I know something of sorcery, Lady Elene. I am not without weapons of my own, cruel ones, more dangerous than you can know. Ones whose reach flies farther than that of arrows or spears. Ones whose touch is deadly, and whose heart cannot be turned aside by any manner of plea or bribe. My servants are not of this world, and nothing on this Earth—nothing you have—can stop them."

Blessing stopped crying, but she shuddered against her servant.

Elene hid her face in her hands. "I know who you are. My grandmother spoke of you. You're the one who controls the galla."

"That I am. Now do you see it is better to cooperate with me? Even if you used magic to escape, my servants can still hunt you down no matter where you run."

"What are galla?" asked Berthold, his face twisted with nervousness and confusion and a touch of proud Villam outrage.

"Something very bad," said Elene so faintly that her voice faded and was lost as, below, a bench scraped and a guard's yell drifted up from the lowest level. She lowered her hands. "What do you want from us, Holy Mother?"

"I want the truth. Tell me everything you know, Lady Elene. I cannot allow you or Wolfhere to leave, but I will see that you are well treated and that Queen Adelheid does not harm you."

"Yes." Groping, Elene found a chair and sank into it with Berthold supporting her. Once she was sitting, he kept a hand protectively on her shoulder as she told her tale in a halting voice, backtracking often, repeating herself, and without question obfuscating where she could.

She was terrified, that was easy to see, and humiliated because she knew she was afraid. She made mistakes and revealed more than she meant to: how Meriam had demanded that her son sacrifice his eldest daughter to Anne's cabal; how they had been shipwrecked but rescued by Brother Marcus; how Wolfhere had vanished in Qurtubah, near the ruins of Kartiako, because the others suspected he had turned against them; how a simple, illiterate brother called Zacharias had saved her from the monstrous akreva, taking the poison meant for her; how she and Meriam and their tiny retinue had crossed through the crown into the deserts of Saïs, into a trackless waste where no creature lived or breathed; how Meriam had woven the great spell with Elene's assistance, on that terrible night.

"She died." Elene's voice was more croak than human and her body shuddered as Berthold patted her shoulder. She did not cry. "She needed my strength, but she sent me back at the last moment. She had planned it with Wolfhere all along."

"With Wolfhere? Planned what?"

"That he would follow us and return me to my father. She fulfilled her vow to Anne. She knew it was right, what they did. But the Seven Sleepers failed. The Lost Ones have returned. They will kill all of humankind if they can. In Jinna lands they still tell tales of the ancient war with the Aoi. My grandmother heard those stories when she was a child. You know what Anne meant to do—to banish the Lost Ones forever, so they would never trouble us again. Why did you abandon Mother Anne, knowing that her cause was just and necessary?"

"I saw no reason to sacrifice myself when I could serve God better by surviving. Did Anne know that she and all the others would die? That the weaving would extract its own cost? Did Sister Meriam know she was doomed? Did all of them die?"

By the way Elene lowered her eyes and sagged against Berthold, Antonia guessed she was about to lie. "I could not see into the weaving. I only know . . ." She wept.

Berthold shot Antonia an indignant glance. "Is this necessary?" He looked so much like his father that Antonia had a momentary sense of dislocation, as if she had been thrown by means of a spell back to the days of her youth. But she had to press on.

"What do you know, Lady Elene?"

"Something terrible happened. I don't know who fought the spell, but it broke down in the north, and then something terrible happened. White fire, and a river of burning rock. My grandmother was . . ." Her lips twisted as she struggled not to sob out loud. "She was gone, engulfed utterly in a blast of light. Later, a wind flattened our camp. Our servants were killed, smothered in sand. There came . . . a creature that dug out of the sands." She covered her eyes with a hand. "A huge lion, but it had wings, and the face of a woman. It was going to kill me. Wolfhere came, and we escaped."

"The ancient messengers of God." A fire of excitement burned in Antonia's heart. The rush of heady discovery made her giddy. "The oldest stories come to life! Is this true, that you have seen such things? One of the lion queens, the holy messengers of God?"

"I saw them."

"What did Wolfhere do that allowed you to escape their just wrath?"

Elene grimaced and wiped her cheeks as she calmed herself. "Ask him. I fainted from loss of blood."

"Can you mean they struck, and yet you survived?"

"Do you not believe me?"

Elene pulled her tunic up to display a length of bare thigh, supple and comely. Berthold flushed bright red and looked away, but Antonia saw the whitened scars from three cruel cuts that had torn the flesh and healed cleanly. A cat might leave such a mark, if it were very, very large.

"Very well," said Antonia. "I believe you, Lady Elene. You will remain here in the custody of Queen Adelheid. Do not forget the galla."

She left them, but it was difficult to concentrate on the discrete rungs of the ladder with her thoughts in a tumult. *What power did Wolfhere have?* He seemed the least powerful of Anne's cabal, the one who wandered in the world to give reports back to the others because it was the only thing he *could* do. Yet he and Antonia were apparently the only ones who had survived out of Anne's cabal. There might be others of Anne's schola who had received some training in the arts of sorcery, but it was likely they had perished in Darre or cowered in fear in some hiding place. Without a strong leader, they were no more than boats set adrift without oars or rudder.

On the lower floor, Heribert still stood by the window. By all appearances he hadn't moved at all since she had gone upstairs. His glance touched her, then flicked away.

His disinterest infuriated her. She struck with the only weapon she had. "If Prince Sanglant loved you, he would not have abandoned you."

That caught his attention. He regarded her first with puzzlement, then with faint comprehension. "That's what the other one said. If he loved me, he would not have abandoned me." He tried out the words, considering the concept. It was not like Heribert to be so slow. "Where did he go? I look and look, but I cannot find him."

"North, so it is said! Back to Wendar in search of the one he loves more than you. He never loved you."

He shook his head as might a child, trying to shake off a hurt that would never go away. "That can't be. He loved me. But he abandoned me to follow the other one. It's the other one who stole him."

His ponderous maundering annoyed her. She had done so much for him, and this was how she was repaid. She continued down to the guardroom, eager to depart the North Tower now that she had so much to think about. How far did Elene's sorcerous abilities extend? Impossible to know.

"Be sure that none of those here leave the tower until I give further orders," she said to the sergeant. "Not even Lord Berthold. I know he is a favorite among you for his amiability, but he must remain confined to the tower for the time being."

"Yes, Holy Mother. But there are certain chores and tasks that my men don't wish to be involved in. Who is to do those?"

"The servant girl can continue to run errands for you in such matters. She will not attempt to escape. Where has the old man been placed?"

"In the dungeon, Holy Mother."

"Make sure he is chained, so he has no chance of escape. He is dangerous, although he may appear inoffensive and weak."

"Yes, Holy Mother."

As a mark of favor, she allowed him to kiss her ring.

Her attendants escorted her through Novomo's gardens and open corridors to her audience chamber. The day's supplicants had been waiting, crowded outside the chamber. Inside, Antonia stood with arms outstretched as her servants arrayed her in the holy vestments. She settled in the high-backed chair with the Holy Lance of St. Perpetua laid on a table, on cloth, beside her. The golden cup was filled with wine and placed on an embroidered tablecloth draped over a table behind her. A dozen scribes sat at a table to her right, prepared to record the petitions, the litigants, and her decisions.

Clerics opened the doors. The petitioners crept forward on their knees and one by one pleaded, begged, and made excuses.

"I pray you, Holy Mother, I have in my possession this letter granting me the benefice of St. Asklepia in Noria, but without an escort of twenty armed men I cannot risk the journey south along the coast. Without my presence, there is no accounting for the riot and ruin that may afflict the land. I cannot pay taxes into your treasury if I am not there to supervise. Pray delegate soldiers for this task. . . ."

"Lord Atto has set his own bastard son as abbot over our monastery, Holy Mother, and this scoundrel keeps three concubines in his chamber and a pack of dogs in the chapel. We pray you, let our good Brother Sylvester be raised to become Father over the cloister of St. Justinian. Have this evil man turned out as he deserves. . . ."

"I pray you, Holy Mother, every last stand of ripe grain was burned and all our vineyards destroyed last autumn. I have no stores and the people in my parish are starving. . . ."

"It's true we are obligated to provide thirty armed and provisioned soldiers and their mounts for the skopal palace. We are hard-pressed in our own county at this time and need all those men to hold off brigands and outlaws. . . ."

"Our biscop died last autumn, Holy Mother. We pray you, appoint a worthy successor. . . ."

Every day except Ladysday she heard such cases, or ones so similar that without the record of the clerks she might have gotten confused when a competing group of brothers from the same monastery of St. Justinian arrived to press a claim for the very bastard son whom they said had been slandered by evil men and who was in truth a most pious and learned shepherd who would be happy to offer a generous donation to the papal treasury to prove his worth. Folk would shirk their tithe, and then turn around and beg her to take various foundlings and wastrels into foundations she controlled, but she knew it was only an attempt to fob off extra mouths onto others more willing to feed them. Still, she did not turn away the unwanted. They could always be put to work, and they would be grateful to be alive. The cleverest among them could be trained to act as servants in her growing schola, the least could clean out stables and sweep streets, and the queen always had need of the wicked to toil in the mines. The strong would survive; the rest would smother under the weight of their sins.

For now, she and Adelheid had to rule carefully to gain that measure of authority which would allow them to expand their sphere of influence. That Darre had fallen confused the multitude. Daily, refugees staggered in from the south with tales that scalded a man's ears—rapine, devastation, looting, buildings torn apart down to the last foundation stone by desperate folk seeking to rebuild elsewhere, pirates along the shore, robbers along the road, and children dying with flies crawling over their eyes and mouths. It was necessary to act ruthlessly to establish preeminence against the many forces rumbling and boiling throughout the stricken Aostan lands. She had no authority save that of God, but of course the authority conferred on her by God's will was higher than all others.

Every day, therefore, when the last of the petitioners had been heard, when all were gathered in the hall to gain her blessing before setting out on their journeys back to their own lands, when Queen Adelheid arrived from her own audience chamber to share a final benediction and prayer, a statement was read out. Antonia had compiled it herself from such writings as had been rescued from the skopal palace in Darre and from her own understanding of necessity and truth. The assembly would hear, and they would carry news of it back to their homes.

The skopos can be judged by no one;
The Dariyan church has never erred and never will err until the
   end of time;
The Dariyan church was founded by the blessed Daisan alone;
St. Thecla the Witnesser was the first skopos;
The skopos alone can depose and restore biscops;
She alone can call councils and authorize holy law;
She alone can revise her judgments;
She alone can depose emperors;
She alone can absolve subjects from their allegiance;
All princes and noble vassals must kiss her feet;
Her legates, however humble, have precedence over all biscops;
An appeal to the skopal court supercedes any other legal appeal;
The skopos is undoubtedly made a saint by the merits of St.
   Thecla.

Every day Adelheid, queen and empress, bent her head and listened in apparent humility. Like Antonia, she knew they had nothing but God's authority on which to rebuild what had been lost. Therefore, God would succor them, and they would do what was right by God. Wicked folk would hate Antonia for her fidelity to God, but she knew that the Lord and Lady had brought her to this position because They wished all those who stood in the Circle of

Unity to obey her. St. Thecla had risked all to witness. Antonia could do no less.

"There will be more tomorrow," said Adelheid when the audience hall had cleared and they sat in a pleasant silence with only the scratching of pens and the gossiping of Adelheid's servants to distract them. Lamps were lit. Lady Lavinia excused herself to attend to four relatives, one a holy presbyter, who needed to be settled in before the evening's feast.

"There will always be more, Your Majesty." Antonia admired her clerics as they worked industriously on codicils, grants, and letters. "As we govern wisely, our influence increases."

"Yes. More come every week."

"They fear the Enemy. Therefore, they come to us for rescue. Soon we go in to supper, Your Majesty. It is necessary we discuss Duke Conrad's daughter and the Eagle. The girl is a sorcerer, trained by her grandmother. She is dangerous."

"Because she is a sorcerer, or because she is not loyal to us?"

"I recommend you kill her at once. Be certain to strike when she least expects it, or while she sleeps. She may have weapons at her disposal that will make her difficult to kill."

Adelheid regarded her in silence. One by one, lamps were lit in the hall, casting shadow and light according to God's will: skopos and empress in pools of light, and the rest in the growing shadows each depending on their nature.

"What of the Eagle? Henry never trusted him."

"Kill him, too, if you wish it, but he may yet be of use to you. He knows the secrets of Anne's power. He knew her longer than anyone. He has power of his own that I do not yet understand."

"Where have they come from? Why are they here? Is it not important we learn these things?"

"I have possession of her story. Anne is dead."

"How can the girl know this for certain? Where did they come from?"

"From the deserts of Saïs. I will tell you the whole later, after we have eaten."

"How could they have crossed the Middle Sea when such monstrous waves destroyed every shoreline?"

"How and where they crossed I do not know. Only the Eagle can tell us that tale."

Adelheid's gaze skimmed the audience hall, noting each person and what they were doing or to whom they were speaking, noting what soldiers guarded the door and which shutters were open and which closed. "What power have I here, Holy Mother? I have your power, as skopos. It has served us well. So far."

"Do you not trust in God, Adelheid?"

Her expression was wary, and her tone sharp. "It is men I do not trust. A powerful lord—and there are still some in Aosta, especially in the west where they were spared the worst of the cataclysm— may choose to raise another biscop or holy deacon to high office. She may claim the skopos' throne, and that family will therefore gain support for their own faction."

"Their claims would be false."

"So we would argue."

"You have seen God's hands at work here on Earth. How can you doubt Their power?"

"I have seen destruction raised by a great working, raised by human hands. All I know of God's power is that They chose to spare me from death while killing Henry. I have one child who lives, and another who will soon die." The shadows had touched her, but she went on without faltering. "I have few supporters from the noble clans who rode south and east to support Henry's empire. Darre is in ruins, uninhabitable. What remains of southern Aosta I do not know. I have marched through the eastern lands myself. They are devastated. Must I go to the Arethousans for help? Sanglant will not aid me. He intends to become regnant in Henry's place. Yet now Elene of Wayland falls into my hands. With her, I might buy coop- eration from Duke Conrad. He has ambitions of his own. She is more valuable to me alive than dead."

"She is dangerous."

"Are you not more dangerous still, Holy Mother? 'The skopos can be judged by no one.' This is a powerful spell."

"It is no spell! The skopos is obliged to govern all peoples who re- side in the Circle of Unity."

"Then is the emperor, or empress, your servant?"

Antonia nodded. "As above, so below."

"You have other servants, scourges whose touch is death."

"I have the tools I need."

"You are well armed for the coming war. Let me keep Lady Elene alive, as a hostage, a companion piece to Princess Blessing. As for the Eagle, I care not. Do with him as you wish. If his death would save my daughter's life, I would tear out his heart with my own hands!"

"A heathen desire, Your Majesty. And yet," she added kindly, seeing how Adelheid set her jaw and clenched her hands upon the arms of her royal chair, "spoken out of a mother's desperation. I have no healing powers of that kind. My gift is to restore God's realm on this Earth."

"So I pray," murmured Adelheid.

Antonia smiled, knowing that her first battle had been won.

XII
WHERE THEIR
FLIGHT TOOK THEM

1

HE did not like it at Quedlinhame, and he liked it less so many days later at Gent when, for the second time, she rose before dawn and drew on a penitent's robe.

"It dishonors you," he said, watching her.

"It does not dishonor me to pray. It does not dishonor me to ask forgiveness for my sins. I am stained with the blood of many men."

"As am I!"

She was dressed like any humble pilgrim in a robe of coarse, undyed linen, with head and feet bare despite the cool spring weather and damp ground. "You killed them cleanly. I did not."

"We can all pray in the church for forgiveness, Liath. This . . ."

"This shows the church mothers that I am not afraid to stand barefoot before God even though I am a mathematicus and—the manner of creature I am. I am not a heretic. I am not afraid to be humble before Them. It's the proud who won't kneel before God's truth. It's those who fear to question who are the ones who don't truly believe. God do not fear our questions. Otherwise why would They have made the world with so many mysteries?"

"I can't argue with you!"

"Not in these matters."

He paced, but his protests and his discomfort did nothing to alter the pace of her preparations. She would go, as she had at Quedlinhame, much to the surprise of Mother Scholastica. In truth, he had to admire it as a good tactic, unexpected and effective as a counterblow.

"How long will this go on?" he asked. "Will we ride the breadth of Wendar and Varre with you kneeling on the church steps at every stop?"

"If I must. Until the excommunication is lifted."

His own splendid clothing had not yet been unpacked from its chest. He would not approach Gent's cathedral until after midday. It took time to ready his retinue.

"You'll continue to ride with me on my progress! You'll not go into hiding! Or into a convent!"

Though somber, she smiled. "Be assured that every soul in this army is aware that you bed me every night without the sanction of the church. That you married me despite your father forbidding the match."

"That you use your sorcery to seduce me and keep me as your prisoner. I know. I know."

"I do not fear what others may say of me or think of me. They can't harm me. Let me do this without having to struggle against you as well, Sanglant."

She did not wait for his answer. After she left the chamber, he surveyed the room. In this same chamber he had resided for many weeks when he had last bided in Gent about two years ago. It was hard to keep track of the time, although he recalled that it had been a cold winter when he and his retinue had arrived. The tapestries on the wall depicting a hunt, a feast, and an assembly of dour clerics and biscops were the same ones he had gazed on before. The handsome Arethousan carpet that covered the floor had the same bright red-and-yellow flowers and green vines as the one he remembered. No reason for the mayor to have changed it, since Arethousan carpets were treasured for their rarity and quality. A copper basin and pitcher rested on a side table. Whatever chests had rested against the wall had been replaced by those he traveled with. Years ago, Liath had appeared to him in this very chamber through an aetherical gate, and she had stolen Jerna, and vanished.

God, he had been so angry. He began, again, to pace.

The latch jiggled. The door opened a handspan.

"Your Majesty?"

"Come in, Hathui."

She entered, followed by his crowd of intimate attendants. Captain Fulk and Captain Istvan the Ungrian represented his guard. To create ties of kinship between the great lords of the realm and his personal guard he had taken in a quintet of young lords, one each from the retinues of Liutgard, Burchard, Gerberga, Waltharia, and a cousin related by marriage to the deceased Duchess Rotrudis. A trio of clerics from his schola were led by Sister Elsebet, and she had with her a young monk named Brother Ernoul whom Mother Scholastica had attached to his household so that Sanglant might offer the worthy, clever, and affable youth advancement in the world. He had also acquired four honest servingmen, sons of stewards, chatelaines, or castellans, each one a relative of one of his soldiers who had died. Den's younger brother swept dust from around the braziers and refilled them with hot coals, while Malbert's cousin and Johannes' uncle laid out his robes and finery on the bed so that the seamstresses could repair any last moment's snags or frays. Chustaffus' older brother brought a covered pitcher of hot water which he placed beside the basin, waiting until his services were needed.

"Your Majesty," said Hathui, "there is a cousin of Lord Hrodik whom Biscop Suplicia wishes you to interview. She believes that this lady, a widow without surviving children, would serve you well as chatelaine of your progress."

"The biscop comes out of that same lineage, does she not?"

"So I hear, Your Majesty."

"She is putting forward her own kinswoman in hope of gaining influence."

"Of course, Your Majesty. Yet you must have a chatelaine and stewards in the same way an army needs soldiers and captains. Duchess Liutgard will leave you in Fesse. Duke Burchard is already gone. Their capable servants cannot serve you forever."

"Let me interview her, then. But I pray you, Hathui, continue asking among the other noble lords for worthy candidates. Alas that so many of Henry's court died in Aosta."

Prayers were murmured among the assembled. In their wake, he heard a slight noise from outside the chamber whose direction he could not fix.

"Where is Lord Wichman?" he asked.

They looked around. Hathui answered. "He was with us a moment before, Your Majesty."

He went to the door, which Fulk opened. "Don't follow me."

The palace at Gent was famous for its circuitous corridors, made more confusing by layers of rebuilding over the last hundred years. The most recent spate of building had occurred after King Henry's defeat of Bloodheart's army, and, except for the unseasonably cool and cloudy weather, it was clear Gent had suffered less than most parts of the country over the last few years. No children begged on the streets. The outlying countryside was well populated and adequately housed, and the road through Steleshame and down into the river valley was particularly well kept.

Many alcoves offered a place to sit beside an open shutter. Here and there a burned-out corridor had simply been closed off with bricks or boards to become a blind alley. What couldn't be seen by the casual passerby might be heard to one seeking the sound of a struggle.

"No . . . uh . . . my lord . . . I pray you, let me go! I'll scream!"

"I think not, you little bitch! Now, just. . . ."

"Wichman."

Halting at the mouth of one of these dark corners, he saw two shapes caught in an intimate embrace, one pressing hard against the other, trapping her against a boarded-off back wall.

"Oh, Lord, Sanglant! Can't you let me be?"

"Let the woman say she prefers to remain of her own free will, and I'll walk on."

She was breathless, straining against groping hands, and desperate. "I pray you, Your Majesty. Grant me your protection. He's trying to rape me."

Wichman slapped her.

Sanglant grabbed his shoulder and yanked him back. The other man, turning, came at him with a punch that landed on Sanglant's chin and slammed him into the other wall. Wichman was in a rage, and pushed in cursing and pummeling fists against his body. God, Wichman was strong. Each slug staggered Sanglant. Most he caught on his arms, but one got under his guard and punched up right under his ribs, making him grunt.

Sanglant hooked a leg around Wichman's, shoved against him with his hip, and upended him, then came down with both knees on his chest.

Wichman coughed and swore. "One isn't enough for you? You have to have all of them?"

Three servants and two guards appeared, looking anxious.

"Go on," said Sanglant, and they looked at his expression and scurried away.

"Perhaps you have to force women to get them in bed with you, Wichman, and perhaps you mind not that they hate and fear you for it, or perhaps you even enjoy it, but I won't tolerate it."

"What will you do to me, Your Majesty?" he said with a sneer. "What can you do?"

Sanglant wiped a bit of blood from his lip. It would swell later. "Marry you to Bertha of Austra."

"She's dead! Your wife lost her!"

"She may not be dead. If she lives, she'll find her way back to Wendar. What would you think of that?"

"You don't scare me, Cousin. I'll take the puling maiden that's Bertha's little sister. I hear she's comely enough. And Westfall in the bargain. Or make me duke of Saony. That will make my sisters croak and bark! Too late for that, isn't it! You gave Saony to your sister like a bone to a bitch, for she'll never have the throne. What's left for me, eh? I found me a tight sheath for my sword, as my consolation, so leave me be, you damned prick!"

He was wild, and aroused, no better than a dog that has scented a bitch in heat. Impossible to reason with.

"Do not touch this woman again." Sanglant stood, and he braced himself as Wichman rose, brushed off his clothing, and laughed.

"Saving her for yourself? She's handsome enough, if not as bright a jewel as your soulless wife."

Sanglant punched him hard, and Wichman went down again, and this time rose afterward with more caution, rubbing his chin.

"I'm not angry, Wichman. Nothing you say about my wife can harm her, but it's necessary for you to understand that on my progress you must curb your tongue."

"I meant to curb my tongue in this warm creature's lips. Why are you so stingy?" He took a half step toward Sanglant, but thought better of it. "Kings ought to be generous, not close-fisted, hoarding all the gold for themselves." He walked away.

"My lord," she said from the darkness where she hid. "Your Majesty. I thank you."

He knew who it was. He'd known all along. "Have you any boon to ask of me, Frederun?" he asked her.

"Nothing you can grant me, Your Majesty." She moved forward enough that he could see her shadowed face and the curve of her breasts and hip beneath her linen gown but not so close that he could touch her without taking a step toward her to claim her. "What I most desire I can never have."

"Have you any need of a dowry to make your way? For a marriage, perhaps? To be released from your service in the palace?"

"I need nothing, Your Majesty. Only to be left in peace. I like my service here well enough and the company of the other women who are my companions. It is only men who trouble me." A tremor afflicted her voice, and he knew he was partly the cause of it but that she could never say so.

"Are you content?"

She did not answer, but he heard her begin to weep.

"If there is anything, apply to one of my stewards."

Her voice was hoarse and barely audible. "Yes, Your Majesty."

Weary, he returned to his chamber, where Hathui had kept them waiting, just as he'd ordered.

"Is all well, Your Majesty?" she asked him as he entered. She had a way of squinting as she examined his face that made him feel quite naked, not in body but in soul.

"Only reflecting on my sins. Let us go to the chapel for the morning service. Then we'll make ready."

She nodded. It was impossible to know how much anyone had heard, but he understood well enough that there was little secrecy and less privacy on the king's progress. He had known that all his life. This was the first time it chafed him.

2

ON the first day of the new year, 736, King Sanglant of Wendar and Varre, son of Henry, approached the cathedral on horseback with his magnificent entourage behind him, each one splendid and terrible in rich robes and gold or silver coronets, depending on their rank. Behind them rode the twoscore soldiers out of his personal guard who had survived the cataclysm in Aosta as well as another score newly brought into his service. Down the widest avenue in Gent they rode four abreast. There was just room on either side for folk to press back against buildings, to stare and call out and sing praises and weep as he rode past. When they came into the square, he saw that the entire expanse was filled with a multitude, the people who lived in Gent and those who had walked a day or even three days to the city in order to witness the anointing and crowning of the new king and to receive the bread that would be distributed in the wake of the ceremony.

The steps rose before him. He halted his horse at their foot and handed the reins to Wichman, who as his cousin had the right to the office of king's groom and insisted on taking his place at Sanglant's right hand. Sibold eased forward along the side. He would hold Fest during the actual ceremony.

Sanglant dismounted. How strange to set his foot on these cold stairs where he had died—only of course he could not die. Here Adela and Sturm had fallen. Here the last of his faithful, bold Dragons had met their deaths. Up by the doors the brave Eagle, Manfred, had been cut down. This much he owed them: that where they had died he could honor them by his own triumph, if there was honor in surviving when all those around him perished.

He ought to have died, too, but he had no power over the geas laid on him at birth.

A crowd of beggars knelt on the first few steps; they would feast at a special table tonight. Above them waited the great princes of the realm in their finest clothing, his peers, who had acquiesced to his elevation because there was no one stronger and more fit to reign after Henry. He noted them: Theophanu and Ekkehard, Duchess Liutgard, Rotrudis' sullen daughters, the powerful margraves, and a handful of important counts and nobles. Beside them stood an intimidation of biscops, abbesses, abbots, presbyters, and noble clerics. All these would witness.

All these, but there was one more who amazingly had space to herself halfway up the steps.

Liath knelt with head bowed. Her golden-dark hair, uncovered and unbound, spilled gloriously down to her rump. It curled wildly, dampened by an earlier misting rain that had ceased at midday. She had, apparently, brushed ashes over it, although only a few traces remained. Bouquets of flowers—violets, white heal-all, late primroses, and an abundance of starry woodruff—lay at her bare feet, gifts from unknown hands. There were even two wreaths woven of pale green bracken. No one looked at her, but everyone knew she was there. He moved sideways and, without speaking to her, picked up one of the frail bouquets of woodruff and carried it with him the rest of the way up the steps. Behind, the crowd quieted.

Mother Scholastica came forward to meet him and, together with the most noble biscops, escorted him into the cathedral.

In the years since the defeat of Bloodheart, Gent had prospered. The stone cathedral had survived better than many of the wooden buildings. All the broken windows had been repaired and the interior restored, repainted, and refurnished with holy vessels on the Hearth. Only the stone pillars still bore the scars of the Eika occupation. Stone angels lacked a wing; gargoyles leered out of a single eye; beakless eagles flew silently. He paused in front of the altar beside the chain fixed into the stone with an iron spike. Here, in this spot, he had been chained. As the company gathered about him, he stared at those heavy links, but they no longer had power to disturb him. He placed the fragile bouquet on the chain to remind him of Count Lavastine, who had freed him from his prison, and the nameless Eika prince who had let them go without a fight.

When everyone was in place and as much quiet as could be expected in such an assembly was gathered, he knelt. The rush of their kneeling was like the thunder of wings, echoing up into the vault.

Mother Scholastica produced from her sleeve an ivory comb studded with gold and gems. With this, she combed out his newly cut hair. The biscop of Gent brought forward a vial of holy oil. His aunt anointed him with a touch: on the right ear, from forehead to left ear, and on the crown of his head. The oil's scent swamped him. The humble oil of olives had been liberally mixed with frankincense and myrrh to produce a profound aroma.

"May Our Lord and Lady crown you with the crown of glory," his aunt intoned, "may They anoint you with the oil of Their favor."

Theophanu and Ekkehard draped a cloak trimmed with ermine over his shoulders. The dragon of Saony, the eagle of Fesse, and the lion of Avaria graced its expanse, embroidered in gold thread. This cloak had been worn by the first Henry and put aside into storage by Arnulf when he took Varre's royal family into his own house. It still reeked of cloves, having been stored with great care for all these years. Henry's royal cloak had vanished in the south.

"The borders of this cloak trailing on the ground shall remind you that you are to be zealous in the faith and to keep peace. Let it remind you of the royal lineage out of which you spring."

She gave into his hands Henry's battered and scarred scepter. "Receive this staff of virtue. May you rule wisely and well. Crown him, God, with justice, glory, honor, and strong deeds."

As a wind sweeps across a forest as with a voice, a murmur greeted this pronouncement. Out of the assembly, all the way back by the doors, a man's voice rose.

"May the King live forever!"

A shiver of foreboding made tears rise in Sanglant's eyes, but the crowd had already raised its voice to acclaim him, and those in the square and streets beyond shouted and sang as well, heard as a distant echo.

Right behind him someone coughed.

Ekkehard muttered, "My feet hurt. I've been standing for hours."

Psalms must be sung. Each biscop and prince and noble must come before him to kiss his ring and make known that they, each one, accepted his authority to rule. So it would go in every important town his progress stopped at as they rode west into Varre. So it would go for the rest of his life. Time, at least, was neither male or female. He did not desire death. He could wait, truly, for a good long time before he must embrace it, as every mortal creature must. But he hoped that Time would not abandon him. Yet if it was the Lord and Lady's will that each soul spin out a certain length of thread upon Earth, had his mother's curse then shielded him from Their touch? Surely not. His mother was not as powerful as God's will, even if she did not believe in Them.

That thought struck him all at once as he spoke words and greeted and nodded and looked each person in the eye to mark the honesty of their gaze. What did his mother believe in? How did the Ashioi explain the existence of the world? What did they worship?

Surely Liath knew.

"Your Majesty." Waltharia knelt before him, her expression solemn. She nodded to show her approval. The gesture reminded him uncannily of her father, who had a habit of nodding in just such a way, with a slight twist to the chin.

Shouts and frantic cries drifted in from outside. They lifted into screams, a chaos of fear that rolled into the church.

"Your Majesty! Come quickly!"

"Save us, Your Majesty!"

He leaped up. Wearing robe and crown and still carrying the staff, he strode down the nave. The train of the robe swept the floor behind him. The crowd parted to let him through, although there was a bottleneck at the doors where terrified people from outside tried to press into the sanctuary.

"Make way! Make way!" cried his soldiers.

He knew their voices. They did not sound afraid.

He had glimpsed them sporadically on the march east. They spent most of their time hunting. Now they circled low, waiting for the square to clear before they swooped down to land next to the steps. Liath had risen. Folk scattered into the avenues and alleys of Gent, fleeing the monsters. A few foolhardy youths wavered at the edge of the square, measuring the response of his soldiers, who instead of fleeing had merely moved back to leave room for the griffins. Others crowded onto the porch of the church. Many cowered inside.

He strode out onto the steps.

The griffins hit hard and not particularly gracefully. Argent *whuffed* and spread his wings discontentedly. A handful of sharp wing feathers drifted down. Domina raised and lowered her gleaming head, bobbing up and down, stalking back and then forward. Her movements had the quality of a dance. At intervals she shrieked, and when she had done, she crouched and sprang into flight. The backdraft of her flight stirred his robes. Liath's hair was swept back, then settled, as the two griffins circled once, twice, rising higher, before they caught an updraft and rose dizzyingly. Soon they were only specks climbing toward the clouds.

"They'll talk about this ever after," remarked Waltharia, coming up beside him. Her voice trembled. Like the others, she had never become easy around the griffins, even though usually they kept their distance from all large habitations of humankind.

The others surged out after her, chattering as they stared and pointed. Because of his presence on the steps, the townsfolk crept back into the square to see him standing before them robed and crowned in the vestments of kingship.

"You have powerful allies," said Mother Scholastica, who let no earthly creature frighten her. "The griffin is a heavenly creature that partakes of the nature of an eagle, a lion, and the serpent, who is sometimes also called a dragon. In this way, it reminds us of Wendar. Yet I wonder what this display portends?" She looked up at the sky, squinting as she attempted to trace the dwindling figures.

"What do you think it portends, Aunt?"

She measured him. "Some will say that this is a sign of God's favor."

"And what will others say?"

"That you are ruled by sorcery. Your legitimacy will always be in question, Sanglant. Do not believe otherwise."

"You crowned and anointed me."

"So the griffins remind me. Yet they may not always remain with you." She looked toward Liath. "Choose your alliances wisely."

Gent's biscop, Suplicia, came up beside them, shaking her head in wonderment. "Griffins! It is a sign of God's favor."

A woman broke free of the gathering crowd and climbed the steps to kneel before Biscop Suplicia.

"I pray you, Your Grace, let me speak. I am an honest and loyal merchant in this town."

"I know who you are, Mistress Weaver," said the biscop kindly. "You are bold to throw yourself forward at such a solemn time. Remember, this is the king."

Robes and crown were a fine thing because they allowed him to remain silent and keep his distance, shielded by the aura of majesty.

She looked at him but only nodded. What had once passed between them had left nothing more than a fleeting memory in her expression. She had moved on. Indeed, she looked indignant as she bent her head humbly and spoke before the church women.

"I pray you, Holy Mother. Your Grace. Your Majesty. Many among us have wondered this day why a woman who has served God so well must kneel outside this holy place as a penitent. I speak of this woman, the Eagle. Know this, there are many here who were themselves saved or who have children or cousins or kinfolk who were saved because St. Kristine of the Knives chose to appear before that one. The blessed saint chose that woman to lead the children of Gent to a place of safekeeping. Why is she dishonored and humbled in this way?"

"You trouble me with your bold speaking, Mistress," said Mother Scholastica sternly. "What means this?"

"Nay, it is true, although I did not witness the event myself," said Biscop Suplicia. "It is a story told throughout the city by those who survived the Eika. If this is that same Eagle, then there must be many here who will be willing to speak. If you allow it, Your Majesty."

"I see the strategy unfold," said Mother Scholastica, glancing at her nephew and again at Liath, who had not moved since the departure of the griffins. "You knew this would happen."

"I hoped it would," he replied.

The handsome Suzanne kept her gaze lowered, but she heard him. "Many will speak if they are allowed, Your Majesty," she said without looking at him. "Your Holiness, I beg you." She lifted her right hand. A dozen worthy and prosperous-looking people ventured forward from the crowd and knelt on the steps below her.

"I am called Gerhard, of the tanners, Your Holiness. I know of fourteen young people whose lives were saved by this woman."

"I am called Gisela, of Steleshame, Your Holiness. I witness that many took refuge in my steading who were saved by the intervention of the saint through this woman."

"I am called Karl, Your Holiness. I am a blacksmith . . ."

So they went on, a solemn procession of sober-minded responsible folk who, by the work of their hands, had caused Gent to prosper in the years after the Eika invasion. The most noble abbess and biscops and church folk heard them out. As they spoke, one by one, others, more humble, crept forward from the crowd to place flowers and wreaths at Liath's feet before scuttling away as though they feared lightning might strike. They spoke softly to her, but he could hear them because his hearing was as keen as a dog's.

"Do you remember me?" they would whisper.

"This is my brother. He and I—we remember you, Eagle."

"God praise you, Eagle."

"I followed you out through the crypt. Lady save you, Eagle."

It was this crowd, more than that of the prosperous merchants and artisans, that attracted Sanglant's notice, a tide of common laborers and craftsmen, most of them very young. Fully half of them wore at their necks crudely fashioned necklaces from which hung two charms: the Circle of Unity and a flowering bird. He knew the symbol. He had seen representations of it elsewhere, carved in similar manner.

It was a phoenix.

3

IT was late. The feast had ground on for hours, pleasantly enough. The beggars had eaten a most noble portion. Bread had been passed out to the multitudes waiting outside the mayor's palace. Sanglant retired after the singing, but he could not sleep and so pulled on his tunic, laced up his sandals, and slipped back into the great hall with Hathui and Fulk padding at his heels.

Dogs slept in the rushes. Beggars snored beneath trestle tables. What else stank in the hall he did not care to identify. It would be swept out at dawn in preparation for tomorrow's second feast.

"Where do you mean to go, Your Majesty?"

He threw his cloak over his shoulders.

Hathui did not ask again after he did not reply, but a look was exchanged between her and the captain. Four soldiers appeared, two bearing lamps, and followed him as he went outside. As always, the sky was dark. No moon or stars shone down on them. The light of the lanterns rippled over the courtyard as he walked to the palace gates, once shattered and now rebuilt. Gent would always haunt him. He had suffered too much here. Like the buildings, he had scars, but he had prospered nevertheless.

Beyond the palace gates he walked the cold streets. It was dark and dank, and his feet slopped in mud. In the handful of years since Bloodheart's ouster there had been time to rebuild walls and residences but not yet the plank walkways that had once kept men's feet out of the muck.

Wind moaned through eaves. A smattering of rain kissed his face. All the smells of the city drifted on that night air: offal and sewage, fermenting barley and rancid chicken broth, the rank savor of the tannery and the slumbering iron tang of the blacksmith's forge. The old marketplace had been reconstructed as a row of artisan compounds. The old mint was still a ruin, a jumble of charred pilings and shards of lumber too badly burned and broken to be scavenged for other buildings. Eyes shone in lamplight, and feral dogs growled as he and his escort passed. He growled back. They slunk away into the shelter of overhangs and collapsed walls.

"Amazing they haven't been killed," said Fulk. "I'd think it would be good sport for the lads in the town to hunt them out, vermin like that."

"No doubt they've tried," replied Hathui. "It's hard to kill them all."

The central square of Gent opened before them. The soldiers swept the lantern light in swathes across the stones, but the square was empty. Everyone had gone home or found lodging. They mounted the steps, but these, too, were deserted. A single flower petal lay forgotten on stone. Otherwise, every wreath and bouquet brought here earlier had vanished.

"Where is Liath?" He took a lantern. "Wait here."

"Yes, Your Majesty," said Fulk, but he looked at Hathui as with a question, and she nodded back at him, and abruptly Sanglant wondered if there was some deeper intimacy going on between those two.

Never mind it. He was not the right person to judge.

Folk slept restlessly in the nave. Once, years ago, refugees had gathered here. This group were commoners who, having walked in from outlying areas to witness the anointing and crowning of the regnant, had no other place to stay before they set out for the journey back to their homes in the morning. He kept the lantern held low so none would mark him, and made his way to the stairs that led down to the crypt.

The stairs took a sharp corner, *here*, which he remembered as clearly as if it had been yesterday. A spiderweb glistened, spun into a gap in the stones. He halted at the bottom of the stairs. A field of tombs faded into darkness. Beyond the halo of lantern light, it was utterly black.

"Liath?" he said softly, but there was no answer.

He waited, listening, but heard nothing. He smelled the aroma of clay and lime but no scent of oats. Instead, the fragrance of drying flowers brushed him. The bones of his Dragons had been thrown down into this holy place. In a way his old life, that of the King's Dragon, Henry's obedient son, had died here, too. The old Sanglant could not have taken on the regnant's mantle despite Henry's desire to raise him to that exalted state. It was Bloodheart's captivity that had changed him. How strange were God's ways!

" 'Be bound as I am by the fate others have determined for you,' " she said.

"Liath!" He shifted the lantern, but he still could not see her. The pit of darkness had swallowed her.

"Do you remember?" she asked. "That's what you said to me, that day."

"I don't remember saying it. I remember following you down here. God know I remember the day well enough. I died that day, or would have, if my mother hadn't cursed me. And you lived."

"I remember something else you said," she added, and he heard amusement in her tone. She was laughing at him.

"What is that?"

" 'Down that road I dare not walk.' "

He laughed. "Not here among the holy dead, at least. But there is a cold bed waiting to be warmed if you'll come with me."

"Not tonight, beloved. It wouldn't be right."

"So you say. I'll not ask again if it displeases you."

"Nay, don't scold me, Sanglant. I'm still reflecting on my sins. What do you think happened to Wolfhere?"

"What has that to do with your sins?"

"I'm not sure, but I feel sure there is a connection. Do you think he's dead?"

"If he is, I will not mourn him overmuch, considering he tried to murder me when I was an infant. He was taken with Blessing, though. So much so that he tried to kidnap her."

"Blessing said otherwise, so you also said."

"That he protested against her being taken? She can't be expected to have understood the whole."

"Brother Zacharias ended up with Hugh. So I must wonder, where did Wolfhere end up? Will we ever know?"

"A mystery," he agreed, but he was getting restless again. His legs had a way of getting twitchy when he needed to move. "Do you mean to stay down here all night?"

"The griffins have left."

"What?"

"So I believe. They made their farewells, and flew east."

"Why would they desert me now?" he demanded, thinking of Mother Scholastica's words.

"Spring is come. They'll want to rebuild their nest and mate."

"So do all creatures! This one not least among them!"

She laughed but, infuriatingly, did not move forward to where he could see her. He thought he caught the fine scent of her now. He smelled the bouquets and wreaths that had surrounded her before: a tincture of violet, the earthy aroma of bracken, the comfort of woodruff and heal-all. She liked to wash her hair in water scented with lavender, to make it shine, and she had always a clean, dry smell about her that reminded him of the way stones smelled on a hot summer's afternoon when the sun's light has glared down on them all day. It was a good scent, an arousing scent.

"Go on, Sanglant," she said, as if she could feel his desire through the air, which perhaps she could. "I'm trying to find the tomb of St. Kristine of the Knives. I want to place all the offerings there, in thanks."

"That was a miracle. She rose in a time of great need. You won't find it tonight."

"Maybe not. But I have to look."

He knew enough of her now to know when she could not be swayed, and he respected her well enough to let it be as she wished. Even if it irritated him a little. Even if it made him think.

"God be with you on your search," he said, and turned away to climb up the steps.

Outside, his escort waited. He caught them yawning.

"Your Majesty!"

"I have a wish to see the river gate." He did not offer to let them return to their beds. He knew they would not go back to the palace without him.

"Yes, Your Majesty," said Fulk, who seemed amused. Hathui hid another yawn behind a hand. The soldiers—tonight it was Sibold, Surly, Lewenhardt, and one of the new men, Maurits—set out with lanterns raised to illuminate their road.

Here in the square he had mounted for that last ride with his Dragons. Now he walked, like a penitent, along the path he and his soldiers had taken that day. Then, hooves had rapped. Tonight, footsteps tapped. The main avenue that led to the gate was still intact, paved entirely with stone. Then, the city had breathed with fear. Tonight, only the wind stirred. All slept, sated with feasting or exhausted by standing in the streets for hours waiting to see the king and his fine procession and the grand ladies and lords and their entourages, so many visiting Gent that it must seem like a plague of nobles to the humble folk who must open their larders to feed them all.

Would the crops grow this season if there was no sun?

Could Liath learn the art of the tempestari in order to aid the kingdom?

If sorcery had created this disaster, then wasn't it necessary for sorcery to be wielded to correct it? Surely that would be no sin. Surely it were better for the church to lift the prohibition against weather-working than for people to suffer and die. And yet, once begun, where did it end?

The avenue debouched into an open space before the eastern gate. When they had rebuilt the wall walk, they had put in steep wooden stairs in new locations, so it took them a little while, searching, to find their way up.

A lookout was built out over the gate. Two milites, guardsmen from Gent, turned to challenge him, then recoiled in surprise.

"Your Majesty!"

"Begging your pardon, Your Majesty!"

"Never mind it. It's well you're alert." They moved back to let him look over the river and the eastern shore, although he saw only darkness.

"That is the future," he said softly. "That which we cannot discern."

Had he listened to Liath, that day when Bloodheart's army struck, none of this would have happened. It was difficult to know which decisions were God's will and which merely human choice, a mistake made in this case because he knew too little of her to trust that she might be able to see what others could not: that is, what is truth, and what the lie. In a way, he saw as little now as he had then on that day the Eika had used magic to deceive their human foes into opening the gates to their own destruction.

He wondered, sometimes, if Li'at'dano had known how vast a cataclysm the great weaving would create. If she had known that it would harm humankind as much as the Ashioi. Had she encouraged the mages of ancient days to open the gates to their own destruction? To weave the tides that would overwhelm them?

He tasted the moisture of the river purling along below. Its tang tickled his nose.

"There's more salt," he said. "I can smell the tides."

"Have you not taken a tour of the land hereabouts, Your Majesty?" asked the older guard.

"I have not. What would I see?"

"Terrible things," muttered the lad.

"Here, now, boy, be quiet! Begging your pardon, Your Majesty."

"Nay, you must tell me what you know and what you yourself witnessed."

"Yes, Your Majesty."

"It was terrible!" exclaimed the lad. He shifted restlessly, mail rustling like the wind in dry leaves. "A great wave struck the shoreline. A score of fishing villages were wiped out, just like that, swept into the sea never to be seen again! I hadn't any kinfolk there, but a fellow I know—he lost his entire family! Never saw them again! For seven days after the tempest, the river ran backward. It flooded fields all around the city."

"With seawater?"

"With evil things—! Ow!"

The older man clipped the younger one on the head to silence him. "Nay, Your Majesty. He'll tell you all manner of wild tales. This is what happened. The tempest made the land shake and the shoreline fall away. Or the sea fall. I don't know which. You'll see by daylight that there's no seagoing boats drawn up on the strand below, as there used to be."

"Indeed. Gent is known for its trade and its many workshops. The river seems to be flowing well enough."

"So it appears, but the course changed."

"It's a league farther to the sea than it was before!" said the lad.

"How can that be?"

"Not a league, Your Majesty, but a good long way. There were two channels before. One wasn't deep enough before to take seagoing vessels. Now even the deeper channel dried up. Not even silted, just went dry. Boats couldn't come through, it was a swamp, no more than an elbow deep. After the winter, the river cut a new path to the sea, many fingers but none of them deep. There's talk of building a new port out by the shore where ships can put in, mayhap carting goods overland to Gent. Digging a canal. Yet if we lose our trade, I don't know how the city will thrive."

"There's been no ships anyway," said the lad. "None at all, and winter's over and sailing season ought to have begun. The fishermen—those who survived—say the tides have changed and the winds are fierce out there. That it isn't safe to be on the water. That creatures swim there that will tear boats into pieces with their claws and eat the men who fall into the water."

"Whsst! Stop telling stories, boy!"

"Nay, let him speak, Grandfather. Stories may hold a grain of truth. Yet Gent seems prosperous."

"As long as the stores hold out, Your Majesty. Biscop Suplicia and Lady Leoba are good stewards. I pray Lady Leoba will not go riding after the princess again, God save her, for she watched over us well enough and with the biscop's aid set aside grain against famine. That's what's held us. Yet if there's no crop and no trade this year . . ."

He could not go on.

"It would be God's will," muttered the lad. "Punishment for turning away from the truth of the phoenix."

"Hush!" The old fellow slapped him in the head again.

"I did not know," murmured Sanglant.

The wind came up suddenly out of the north, spilling over the parapet, rattling along the rooftops.

"Like that," the old guard said. "A north wind like that, it never used to come this time of year. Weather's changed. The winds aren't the same as they was used to be, in the days before."

"Everything's changed," whispered the lad, then hunched his shoulders, waiting for a blow that did not come.

"I did not realize the tides of destruction had washed so high." Sanglant leaned out over the wall, breathing in the murmur of the air. The night's presence poured over him. The whole wide world lay beyond. It stretched to every horizon, covered in darkness, unseen and unknowable without moon or stars to light the land.

A battle might be fought and won in a day, but the ebb and flow of the sea and the heavens never ceased. What had been set in motion might not trough, or peak, for weeks or months or years. The riptide might already be dragging them under while they never knew they were drowning.

Out of the night a deep hoot trembled. Grit slipped under his sandals as he turned, trying to pinpoint the sound.

"Whsst!" said the old guard. "That's an owl! Did you hear it?"

"Is that a good omen?" asked the lad plaintively. "Or an evil one?"

"I've not seen feather or beak of a bird these last months," the old man said, then shrieked and ducked as a huge owl skimmed out of the darkness right over their heads and with a graceful plummet came to roost on the wall. Its massive claws dug into the wood. By lantern light, its amber eyes gleamed boldly, seeming lit from within. The light set off the streaks of white on its breast and the tufted ears.

"What is this?" asked Sanglant.

It blinked.

"Where is your mistress?" he demanded.

But all he heard was the wind.

PART FOUR

THE MOUNTAIN OF THE WORLD'S BEGINNING

XIII
BLOOD

1

WHEN winter turned to spring and the village deacon sang the mass in honor of St. Thecla's witnessing of the Ekstasis and Translatus of the blessed Daisan, the folk of Osna village met after mass to discuss the summer's journeying to other ports.

For months Alain had been ill and weak and weary, unable to do more than sleep, eat the gruel Aunt Bel cooked him, and sit beside the hearth dozing with Sorrow and Rage stretched out on either side. He had suffered from the lung fever; a terrible infection had inflamed his right foot; he had battled recurring headaches.

In the end, Aunt Bel's nursing defeated these afflictions.

Now he walked with only a slight limp as he accompanied Henri to the church in the afternoon. It was cold and, as usual, cloudy.

"We haven't seen the sun for months," remarked Henri. "The winter wheat never sprouted. I fear the spring planting won't get sun and warmth enough to grow if the weather doesn't change. There'll be famine."

"There already is."

Henri glanced at him but made no comment.

Sorrow and Rage had gamboled ahead. They rushed back, nipping at each other and running in circles. Aunt Bel and her daughter Stancy walked in front of them. Bel's other surviving children, Julien and Bruno and Agnes, trailed behind, laughing over the antics of Julien's younger child, a chubby toddler named Conrad but called Pig by one and all for his love of mud.

"Eeuw!" squealed Pig's older sister, Blanche, now eight or nine. "Eeuw. Pig's throwing it at me again, Papa! Make him stop! I hate him! He's awful!"

"Don't you touch him!" cried the baby's mother. "If you will provoke him, it's no wonder he throws mud at you!"

"Do stop, Blanche," agreed Agnes. "He's just a baby."

"Come walk with me, Blanche." Alain held out his hand, and she ran to him and clutched his fingers. She was a pale, frightened, resentful creature, motherless since birth. The wife Julien had brought home from Varingia did not like her, and Blanche returned the favor.

"I hate that pig stinker," she muttered, eyeing Alain sidelong to see if he would respond. "And *her*, too. I hate everyone, and they all hate me."

He did not respond, although her unhappiness gave him pain. In truth, she was an unlikable girl who struck out at others and bullied younger children. It seemed to be the only way she knew to battle her wounded heart.

He sighed, and she sniffled but kept silent, unwilling to offend the only person who offered her more than perfunctory kindness. His attention strayed. Aunt Bel's scarf hadn't lost that particular twist she gave to the knot that made it hang somewhat to the left. Stancy was pregnant again, tired but hale. Her husband Artald was already at the church door talking with several men from the village. Their agitated voices rose as a local woodsman regaled them with a tale.

"It was so quiet all autumn and winter I thought we'd done with these refugees plaguing us," exclaimed old Gilles Fisher, cutting the other man off. "Yet now they come. We haven't enough to feed them. I say we gather staves and drive them out."

"Fotho says it's mostly women and children and old folk," objected Artald. "It doesn't seem right."

"It was women and children and old folk last year and the year before, too, what with the Salian war going on and on and before that Eika raids."

"Nay, it was better last year," said Artald. "Not so many came north, and then only in early summer. They were caught down there in the border country."

Agnes stifled a sob.

"What's this?" asked Aunt Bel. "I smell a drizzle coming on. Let's go inside so we don't get wet."

In they all marched. Sister Corinthia presided because the old deacon had died two years ago and the count's father had sent no one to replace her. That Aunt Bel had had the foresight to keep a cleric in her house to educate her grandchildren had given her immense prestige in Osna village now that Sister Corinthia led all the services. The cleric had even picked out two village children bright enough to be educated at St. Thierry.

The young cleric led them in a dozen psalms before stepping aside to let Bel stand up.

"Have you some news for all of us, Fotho? I pray you, speak loudly and clearly so we can all hear. Hilde, take the children outside and watch them."

Hilde was Stancy's eldest, a stout, well grown girl about the same age as Blanche but of an entirely opposite disposition. She herded out a score of mewling, giggling, restless children, some older than she was. Silence descended as the score of adults regarded first each other and then the quiet woodsman who shuffled forward to stand on the first step of the dais where they could all see and hear him. Everyone was sitting on fine benches built in Aunt Bel's workshop. Blanche clung to Alain, and he let her crawl up onto his lap, the only child who hadn't gone outside.

"Refugees," said Fotho. "Come up the coast road. Not a man over twelve or under forty among 'em. They're wearing nothing but rags—if they have clothes at all, which most of the children don't. They're starving. They come up out of Salia. They say there's fighting along the border again. No food to be had."

"Is it Eika?" asked Agnes tremulously.

"They're not out of Medemelacha way, if that's what you're asking, lass," said Fotho kindly, and with some warmth. He was a decent-looking young man a few years older than Agnes. He had a yen for her, as everyone knew, but it was a hopeless case even though Agnes was now considered to be a widow after only a year of marriage.

"Is it even safe to sail to Medemelacha?" asked Gilles Fisher. He was too crippled with arthritis to sail or even to build ships, but his keen mind and store of knowledge were precious to the community.

"That's one of the questions we must ask and answer," said Henri. "It was safe last year, even with the emporium under the rule of that Eika lord."

Agnes wiped away a tear, glanced at Fotho, and dropped her gaze to the ground.

"It doesn't sound as if these refugees will give us any trouble," said Artald. "I say we let them move on. They can beg at Lavas Holding."

"Hah! As if Lord Geoffrey has aught to give them, or as if he would!" It was Mistress Garia's truculent son who spoke, but he had the decency to blush as every person there looked at Alain and away as quickly. "We've not heard a word from Lavas Holding for six months. Hung us out to dry, the lord has."

"What do you suggest, then?" asked Stancy. "We haven't enough to feed every soul who comes begging."

"If you turn no one away, there will be enough," said Alain.

They fell silent. Blanche sucked a dirty thumb, eyes wide and expression fierce. The light through the glass window washed the floor in five colors, according to the panes: there was red, and a pale green, as well as yellow, blue, and smoky violet. Because the bay of the church faced east, the sun shone through the glass window in the morning. Now, at midday, there was no direct light, but it was still bright enough with the doors flung wide to see the murals painted along each side of the nave. There, the blessed Daisan at the fire where he first encountered the vision of the Circle of Unity. And again, the blessed Daisan with his followers refusing to kneel and worship before the Dariyan empress Thaissania, she of the mask. The seven miracles, each depicted in loving detail. Last of all the eye might rest upon the blessed Daisan lying dead at the Hearth from which his spirit was lifted up through the seven spheres to the Chamber of Light. Beside him, St. Thecla the Witnesser wept, her tears feeding the sanctified cup.

Once he had seen brave scenes of battle hiding beneath the lamp-lit murals, but now he saw only suffering and it made him angry, and it made him sad.

Sister Corinthia cleared her throat. "Spiritually, you speak what we all know to be true, Friend Alain. The church mothers teach that every heart is a rose, and that to turn away from those in need when you could aid them causes the rose to wither. In this same way, plants need water to live, and we need breath. But in truth . . ." She faltered and looked to Aunt Bel for help.

"One loaf cannot feed one hundred starving beggars," said Aunt Bel. "Wishing does not make it so."

"Which one will you refuse?" he asked Bel. "Let it be your choice. And if not yours, then whose? Who will volunteer to be the one who chooses which supplicant lives and which dies?"

No one answered him.

"Yet your Aunt Bel is right," said Henri later as they readied the boats for sailing. "If we give all our stores away, we'll starve, too. That seems not just foolish but stubborn."

Below the house, workshops, and gardens lay a narrow trail that led to the boat shed, built two years ago. They rolled the new boat down to the tiny beach and pushed it out onto the water. Julien and Bruno set the sail and put out into the bay to test the waters while Henri and Alain remained behind to look over the old boat, always in need of repairs. Alain slid under the boat, which was propped up on logs. The work came easily to his hands. The smell of sheep's wool greased with tar made memories swim in his mind of the days long before when Henri had taught him the skills of shore and boat.

Inspecting his work, Henri grunted. "Well, Son, you haven't forgotten how to fasten a loose plank. Here. There's another spot."

They worked in companionable silence. Alain ran his hands over each fingerbreadth of the hull while Henri replaced the leather lining and hemp rope that secured the rudder to the boss. A gull screeked. Water slurped among the rocks.

From the boat shed, angled to take advantage of the view, they could see north over the sound. The eastern islands floated on gray waters. The distant promontory shielding Osna village gleamed darkly, and beyond it to the northwest lay ragged shoreline and white breakers where once the vast Dragonback Ridge had vaulted. A flash of sail skimmed the bay to the north.

"Rain," said Henri, pausing, hands still, to stare across the waters.

The smell of salt and tar and wet wool caught in Alain's mind, and he was swept as by the tide into memory.

Two slender ships skim up onto the strand. Scale-skinned creatures pour out of them. They cannot be called men, and their fierce, horrible dogs cannot be called dogs, but there are no other words to describe them. They burn as they go, destroying the monastery and the hapless brothers.

There is one who watches with him, her gaze sharp and merciless. "It is too late for them," she says.

*   *   *

"No!" He jerked back, slamming his head against the boat.

"Alain?"

"She is the enemy," he said raggedly. His head pounded. Stabs of pain afflicted him, waking that old headache that had caused his blindness and muteness.

"Who is the enemy?"

"The one who says, 'This is as it must be, we can't do anything else even if we want to.' "

"Do you speak so of your aunt?"

"No, no." He rubbed his head. Spots and flurries of light blurred his vision. "Of the one I met on the road."

"What one?"

"The Lady of Battles."

"Who is the Lady of Battles? Are you well, Alain? Is your headache back? Maybe we'd better go back to the hall and let you rest."

"What was my mother like?"

There came a silence from Henri and only the answer of the land around them: the hiss of surf, the wind in leaves, a branch snapping under the weight of Rage's paw, a distant shout of laughter, a bird's warble, quickly hushed. The ache in his head faded as he breathed, waiting.

After a bit, he felt Henri move, then heard the noise of the file as Henri worked to shave the curve of a wooden plug to the exact fit for its oar port, to replace one eaten away by dry rot. Alain leaned back against the boat, recalling the familiar comfort of familiar patterns. Henri had always had a habit of thinking as he worked, or perhaps it was better to say that working helped him think, that the motion of hands teased patterns of thought into symmetry.

The hounds snuffled into the woods. The sea sighed.

"Is that what drove you?" Henri asked at last. "Seeking your mother?"

"I admit I have always wondered."

The file scraped at the wood.

"Not so much about my mother," Alain continued. "What she might have been like, of course I always wondered that. Yet if a birth is witnessed, and the witnesses tell the truth, there's no doubt of a mother's identity. It was wondering who my father was that drove me."

The file stilled. "Do you wonder that still?"

Alain shifted to look into Henri's face. He took Henri's seamed, callused hand in his own and held it tightly. "No. I know who my father is. He is the one who raised me and cherished me."

Tears fell, although Henri wept silently. One coursed down his cheek to land softly on the back of Alain's hand, a warm salty drop followed by

"No good song is ever sung of a traitor," he says to Deacon Ursuline.

"It is not treachery. It is an alliance," she objects.

He sits and she stands in the hall built by his Alban carpenters to re-place the one that burned in last year's assault on Hefenfelthe. Most of his court have retired to their beds for the night, but he is, as always, wakeful, and Deacon Ursuline is persistent.

Torches burn in sconces bracketed every three strides along the wall. The tang of smoke licks at him, reminding him of scorched timbers and dying men. His dogs whine from their corner. No doubt they dream of the slaughter which feeds them.

"That is the point in keeping the old royal lineage alive now that the rest are dead," she continues mercilessly. "If you marry the eldest princess, then it will bind the Alban people closer to you."

"She will have turned against her ancestors, the queens, if she agrees to such an arrangement. She was to be the sacrifice to death, not to life."

"The queens made such alliances in plenty when they ruled. It is the way of noble houses to marry this daughter to that son, this lady widow to that lord's unmarried brother, to make peace or expand influ-ence or consolidate fortunes. Among humankind, it is not considered treason but wisdom and expedience."

It is a cool night, cloudy and dark as always these days. Through the open doors and shutters he hears the footsteps of guards on the wall that surrounds the rebuilt hall and repaired stone tower, the heart of Hefenfelthe. Beneath the light of one of the torches, two Eika warriors dice, a game they learned from human comrades. Their human pack brothers doze restlessly beside them, twitching and, now and again, moaning in sleep as they chase dreams. Other Eika guards stand in that strange half dream and half waking stupor that humans mistake for sleep. Even Trueheart, grasping the standard, sways on his feet.

Over the long autumn and this interminable winter and seemingly endless spring, the winds and tides have conspired to confine him to Alba's shores. Yet while the sea's caprice chafes him, it has also given him time to consolidate his victory in Alba. The central and southern plains are now quiet. The last of the resistance has been forced into the northern and western hill country, too rugged to pacify easily but possible to contain through judicious use of forts, raids, bribes, and the resettlement of former slaves on those lands closest to the rebels.

"Among humankind such alliances lead to offspring," he adds. "Should I marry the Alban princess, we could not breed."

"No, I suppose not. It would be a political alliance only. This, too, you must consider, Lord Stronghand. If you do not make plans for succession, then your empire of Eika and Alba will fall apart when you die."

"That is true, Deacon Ursuline. I have considered the question more than once over this long winter. All things die in the end. We are only flies compared to the life of stone. We sons of OldMother are shorter-lived even than humankind. Yet this hall—" He indicates the rafters, the plank floor, the steps leading up to the tower. "—will survive me, and it will even survive you."

"As long as war or tempest do not destroy it. You must build an edifice that will survive despite war and tempest."

"Using what materials? I have stone, steel, and flesh."

"You have mercy and justice."

"I have my wits."

"With all respect, Lord Stronghand, your wit will not survive you."

"What if I care nothing for what passes in the world once I am gone?"

"Do you not?"

He laughs. "If I cared nothing, I would not be sitting here."

In the distance, too faint for the deacon to hear, guards call out a challenge. He cocks his head, listening, and identifies the lilt of voice and rhythm of hurried stride as that of Lord Erling. Strange that Erling should be here in Hefenfelthe instead of tending to his own earldom. Trueheart shakes himself alert.

"Is someone come?" asks the deacon belatedly, turning to look. "It's so late . . ."

The young Alban sweeps through the door as if on a gust of wind, hair blown in disarray and cloak streaming back as he approaches the dais. Four soldiers, two Eika and two Albans, follow him. Stronghand's Eika guards shift into readiness, axes and spears raised, but Erling halts and drops to one knee. Stronghand lifts his hand and, given permission by this gesture, the young man rises.

"I did not expect to see you," says Stronghand.

"News!" He is flushed with news. His skin is red.

"How fares the middle country?"

"Well enough considering we've not yet had sun this year. Folk fear it is a sign of the gods' displeasure."

"Do you think it so?"

Erling has taken to wearing a Circle of Unity. His is silver, finely made, and incised with leaves as if to recall the old religion he left behind. He touches it now. "It might be. I am no priest to name God's will. Still, the folk who have lost what they once had might have reason to suppose God displeased with them. I worry for the summer's growing season if the weather remains so damp and cloudy."

"As do we all," says Deacon Ursuline.

"What brings you south, Erling?" Stronghand asks.

The young man nods. "I wished to observe the anniversary of my mother's death at Briden Manor, south of the river. I rode south to plant a tree at her grave."

"So the tree priests would have you do," scolds the deacon, although her tone is benign, not harsh. "Better to pray for her soul and dedicate a convent in her memory."

"Can I do that?"

"Surely you can, and endow a dozen novices to pray for your mother's soul each and every day of the year."

"I like that idea! But I would need a priestess—a mother—to watch over them and guide them."

"I can make sure that such a woman, we call her an abbess, is available to you, Lord Erling. You need only ask."

"As must I," says Stronghand, tapping one foot. "What news do you bring me so late at night and in such a rush as if on the wings of a storm?"

"Ah! Just that, Lord! An omen has been seen in the south! A dragon! Seen flying by the sea."

The Eika murmur among themselves at this astounding news.

Dragons! Have the First Mothers risen out of the wake of the sorcery that altered the world? Have things changed so greatly?

"Come." Stronghand rises. He leads them up the stairs, into the tower, and by ladders and steep steps to the roof. It is a stiff night, cuttingly cold up so high with the wind's bite on hands and face. The men shiver and rub their hands, but he leans into the wind and listens.

After a while, he speaks.

"It was long told among my people that the FirstMothers bred in ancient days with the living spirits of earth and in that time gave birth to the RockChildren. It's said that in Wintertide, in the Western Sea, one may hear them calling . . ."

"Listen!" cries Erling.

Yes!

They all lean south, many pressed against the stone battlements as though likely to hurl themselves over if only that would bring them closer to what they seek. The call thrums through the air, its vibration so low that he feels it through the stone.

A sun rises in the southeast.

"Look!" cries Trueheart.

There are two of them, seen first simply as a bending, twisting aurora of light far off but approaching fast. Their bellies gleam. Their tails lash like lightning. They are coming up the river, following the course of the water as they fly inland on what errand he cannot guess. Alarm bells clang, and he hears a clamor as folk rush out of their halls and hovels.

They grow in size; they near; they are huge, impossibly vast. A hot stream of stinging wind pours over Hefenfelthe and in their wake the clouds churn and the forest roars.

"Look!" cries Erling. "The stars!"

Above, the clouds have parted to reveal those pinpricks, the most ancient ones, the eternal stars. But as the dragons course northwest, as the heat and wind falter and the cold night air sweeps back, mist shrouds that glimpse of the heavens and soon all is concealed again.

"It's time to move," says Stronghand, when all is silent. They stare northwest, but there is nothing to see. Night veils all things. "That is an omen, indeed, Lord Erling. You were right to bring news of it so quickly."

"Yes, my lord," the young man says, but he is barely breathing. He is still in shock, staring fixedly northwest as if turned to stone.

"We must make ready," continues Stronghand. "Trueheart, you'll remain here as my governor. Stores must be set aside for next winter. Seed corn hoarded, as much as possible. Plant fields. Hunt and trap, raid our enemies in the north and west and take their grain and seed corn for ourselves and our loyal servants. If they starve, so much the better. Lord Erling, you and the other lords I have raised will remain secure if your people have enough to eat. Be prepared for anything."

"So have we seen!" Erling whispered, still staring after the vanished dragons.

"In six months I will return to make an accounting."

"Where do you go, Stronghand?" Trueheart asks. "Will you fight again in Salia?"

He looks at Deacon Ursuline. She nods. "I must consult with the Wise-Mothers. I believe they have much they can tell me."

"Should they choose to do so," she says.

"Should they choose to do so. There is much I desire to know. This war is only beginning."

another tear.

The tears were only beginning.

Dizzied, he shaded his eyes with a hand, but he had to concentrate, to fix on this moment, this Earth, this place—not the other one—because Henri was still talking.

"She was strong-willed but weak in her heart. Desperate, and beautiful. She used her beauty to feed herself, to get what she wanted. It was the only way she knew, Alain. Had she not been so desperately poor, she might have been otherwise. I do not know what she endured before she came to Lavas Holding. She would never speak of it. Pregnancy killed her. It's the war women fight. Just as men die in battle, so some women are fated to die in childbed, wrestling with life. You survived it. She did not, though she wished to live. Fought to live. Sometimes beauty is like a candle flame—it shines because it burns. I would have married her, but she wanted something else."

"What did she want?"

Henri shrugged with one shoulder, a movement so constrained that if Alain had not lowered his hand at that instant he would have missed it. "I don't know. She wished to be something she was not."

"As I did."

"No, Son. No. Well, perhaps." He laughed weakly. "That comes of her, I suppose." He set down the file, scratched his beard, scratched his hair, and picked up the file again. "After all this, who do you think your father is? I mean, the one whose seed watered her garden."

"It doesn't matter," he said. "I know who I am now because I know what I must do."

Henri frowned. "You will leave us."

"I must." Sorrow barked, and he heard the hounds thrashing back through the undergrowth. He rose and stepped to see around the boat and up the trail. "Here comes Artald."

Stancy's husband waved to get their attention as he strode up. He was local born and local bred, a man without much imagination but levelheaded and generous, and a hard worker whose labor had helped Aunt Bel's workshop prosper. He wasn't puffing at all although he'd come in haste.

"Where's Jul and Bruno?" he asked as his gaze skimmed the sound, seeking their sail. "Well, no use waiting for them."

"What news?" asked Henri.

"A runner from t'village. They say Chatelaine Dhuoda has come with a small company."

"Lord Geoffrey with her?"

"Nay, nothing like that. She's looking for Alain, here. Best if he goes, don't you think?"

"Best if I go," agreed Alain, looking at Henri.

Henri frowned and absently patted the head of Sorrow as he nodded. "Just so, if she's asking particular for him. Is she come to take young folk to Lavas Holding for their year of service?"

Artald shrugged. "Runner spoke nothing of that, Uncle. I'll go with Alain."

"Best we all go," said Henri, "considering in what state we found him."

"Ah!" Artald stroked his beard. "Hadn't thought of that, truly. They might be wishing him mischief, after all is said and done."

"They won't harm me," said Alain. He whistled, and Rage padded in from the woods, worrying at one paw.

"Still," said Henri, "we'll all come. Best to sound the horn and call Julien back, if he can hear. He's the only one among us who has any real training at arms."

The horn was slung up under the low rafters of the boathouse. Artald unfastened it and walked down to the edge of the water before lifting it to his lips. The low moan trembled across the waters. Alain bade Rage sit, then pulled three burrs out of the fur in and around a paw. After this, he gathered up tools and supplies and headed up the trail with the hounds panting along behind him. A second call chased him, then faded, and he paused on the trail to let Henri catch up.

"In so much hurry to leave us?" asked Henri.

"I pray you, forgive me, Father. It's just I've been expecting this."

"That the Counts of Lavas will come seeking you?"

"No. Only that there would be a sign that this time of peace had come to an end."

That evening he packed such things as he thought he would need: a spare tunic; a pair of soft boots that Aunt Bel absolutely insisted he take along; rope braided by Bruno; a pouch of silver sceattas out of Medemelacha; a collection of small tools from the workshop rolled up in a leather belt that Artald felt were indispensable to a man wanting to make his way in the world; a strong staff carved by Julien; gloves Stancy had sewn out of calf leather; a heavy wool cloak woven by Agnes; and a bowl, cup, and spoon carved by Henri, each one with a hound's head incised into the concave base.

The household had their own taxes to gather and make ready to deliver to the chatelaine, but Bel made sure they ate well and drank well that night.

He slept easily, although others fretted at his leaving. The pallet he slept on in the hall was not the one he had grown up sleeping on, back in the village. The estate, however fine it was, had no hold on him because these surroundings were only a way station. He had left Osna village years ago. That leave-taking could not take place a second time.

In the morning, a dozen accompanied him to Osna: Henri, Bel, Stancy, Artald, Agnes, Julien with his Varingian spear, five of the workers armed with staves and shovels, and little Blanche because she refused to remain behind. Bruno was left at the workshop with the rest of the household, just in case, in these difficult times, some cunning soul had planned a ruse in order to loot or burn the estate while it was undefended. Aunt Bel was famous for her careful and farsighted ways, and many would suspect that her storehouses remained well stocked, as indeed they did.

"We ought to put up a palisade," said Artald as he swung along beside Stancy. He steadied her at the elbow as she picked her way over a series of ruts worn into the path. "I've been speaking of it for three years now. Past time we started."

"Have a care," called Julien from the front. They came up behind a score of ragged folk who, seeing them, shrank back into the trees. A child wailed and was hushed. All of the children had sunken eyes and swollen bellies. The adults, all women except two toothless old men, drew the little ones back and ducked their heads.

"I pray you, good folk," said one of the women, creeping forward on her knees. "A scrap of bread, if you have it. Pray God." One of her eyes was crusted shut with dried pus.

Behind her, others coughed, or scratched sores and pustules. One woman had a scaly rash splattered down the right side of her face and ringing her neck like a strangling cord.

Alain stepped forward, still holding Blanche's hand.

"They're dirty!" she cried. "I hate them!"

He pulled two loaves of bread from the pouch on his back and gave one to the child. "Here."

"That's your waybread, Alain!" objected Aunt Bel. "You'll go hungry!"

"Pray do not worry on my account, Aunt." He turned back to Blanche. "This is your offering to make, and you must make it."

"Can't! I'm scared!" she whined. "I hate them."

"Blanche," he said kindly, looking her in the face.

Weeping, she shuffled forward, shoved the bread into the hands of the creeping woman, then bolted back to the safety of the hounds, pulling on their ears until Rage nipped gently at her to get her to let go.

"Do not fight among yourselves," said Alain as the other refugees converged on the woman, who clutched the loaf to her chest. He marked among them a girl no more than Agnes' age whose cheeks were so hollow that you could trace the skull beneath stretched skin. He gave her the other loaf. "Listen! Let all be satisfied that you have each dealt fairly with the others. Otherwise you will never know peace."

All were silent as they walked on, leaving the beggars behind. At last, as the woodlands were cut with the fields and clearings that signaled the advent of village lands, Agnes spoke.

"How could you understand them, Alain?"

"They were Salians," said Henri. "I know enough of that language to trade in Medemelacha." He glanced at the girl, who paled when he said the name, and reached out to squeeze her hand. "There, there, lass. He may yet be alive. That report I heard might have been wrong."

"It would be easier if I knew," she murmured as she wiped her eyes.

"True enough," agreed Henri. "Poor child."

"God must hate them, too," said Blanche. "Otherwise why would they be sick? Only bad people suffer. If they did a bad thing, they'll be punished."

"That being so," snapped Agnes, "why are you not covered with weeping sores and white scales? Why hasn't your nose fallen off?" Her face got red, and she began to cry.

"Enough!" said Aunt Bel. "I'll not come walking into the village with the pair of you snarling like dogs fighting over a bone! For shame!"

"It's a long way to walk," said Artald. "From the border with Salia all the way up to here. Days and days walking, a month maybe. They must have been right desperate to leave their home."

"They looked desperate to me," said Stancy. "Poor creatures. Who knows how many they started with and how many lost along the way. It's the fault of those Eika raiders."

"Mayhap not," said Henri, "for it seemed to me there was peace in Medemelacha, and order, too. I saw no beggars on those streets."

"Driven out or murdered," suggested Aunt Bel, "so as not to bother them who didn't wish to share. Who stole all good things for themselves."

"Perhaps," said Henri, "but I saw Eika and human folk working side by side. None of them looked like they were starving. I don't know. What do you think, Alain?"

Alain had been staring at the clouds, wondering if the light had changed, heralding a change in the dense layer and perhaps promising sunshine. The talk had flowed past him, although he heard it all. "War brings hunger in its wake. What is this now, these clouds, these sickly fields, this fear and these portents, if not echoes of an ancient war?"

"It's God's will if the sun don't shine, or the rains don't fall," said Artald. "So Deacon teaches."

"That storm last autumn was not made by God," said Alain. "That was made by human hands, in ancient days."

They looked at him, as they always did, as if they did not know if he were a madman or a prophet, and then looked at each other and away again, at the trees, at the clouds, at the startling appearance of a robin hopping along the ground under the skeletal branches of an oak.

"Look there!" cried Stancy. "Look at that!"

"Mayhap spring will come after all," said Henri.

The others kept walking, but Alain halted and with a gesture commanded the hounds to move away down the road. Blanche hovered beside him as he moved slowly forward until he was close enough to kneel and stretch out his hand. He breathed, finding the rhythm of the wind in the weeds and the respiration of the tree. The bird hopped toward him, then onto his palm, turning its head to stare at him first with the right eye, then the left. That gaze was black and bright, touched with a shine.

"Come quietly and slowly, Blanche, and kneel beside me. No fast movements."

Scarcely breathing, she crouched next to him and held out her hand. After a moment, the robin hopped onto her fingers, gave her that same piercing examination, and abruptly spread its wings and flew away.

She burst into tears. "How do you *do* that?"

"Just be patient, little one. If you find what is quiet within yourself, even the wild creatures will trust you."

"No one trusts me."

"That robin did."

She sniffed, wiping eyes and nose.

"Best come now," he said. "Let's hope we see more birds this spring, for it's an ill portent to have them all vanish like that." He tilted his head back to look up into the bare trees. "For so it was then. An ill portent."

"Here, lad, are you having another headache?" Henri had returned, leaving the others waiting up the road. "Let me help you up if you're not feeling well. No need to go on today if you've a mind to go back home."

"No, no, Father. I'm well enough. Just remembering a forest once where all the birds had fled. But there was a terrible black heart alive in that place. That was why they fled. They feared evil."

Henri looked around nervously as Blanche whimpered. "Think you we're haunted?"

"Here?" He patted Blanche tenderly on the head. "Nay, I think it was the wind blew the poor creatures so far that it's taken them this long, those that survived, to find their way back home."

"So it may be," said Henri, still holding his arm and gazing at him. "So it may be. A poor creature may be blown a far way indeed before it turns its gaze toward home."

They caught up to the others, who set on their way without question or comment. They smelled the tannery before they saw it, and marked the square steeple of the village church rising above trees. In the common ground and meadow in front of the church, an assembly had gathered by the chair and table where the count's chatelaine held court to choose young folk to serve for a year at Lavas Holding and to receive the tithes and taxes the village paid to the count in exchange for his protection in times of war. Alain did not at first recognize the old woman who sat at the table. It was not until she looked up and saw *him* walking among his kinfolk, and turned her face away in shame, that he realized this woman was Chatelaine Dhuoda, but so aged with white hair and wrinkled face that anyone might be excused for mistaking her for a woman twenty years older.

She rose and, bracing herself on a cane, came around the table. As the crowd parted to let him through, she dropped to her knees.

"I beg you, my lord, return to Lavas Holding. Forgive us our sins. Come back."

Henri whistled under his breath. Sorrow barked. The chatelaine, noticing the two black hounds, wept quietly.

"Does Lord Geoffrey know you are here?" Alain asked.

"He does not, my lord. He is the false one. He lied to gain the county for his daughter."

"Did he? Is he not descended legitimately from the brother of the old count, Lavastina, she who was mother of the first Charles Lavastine and great grandmother of Lavastine?"

"He is, my lord."

"How has he lied?"

"If he had not lied, then why do we suffer? He abused you, my lord, because he feared you. Why would he fear you if he did not believe that you were, in truth, Lavastine's rightful heir?"

He nodded. "I'll go, Mistress Dhuoda."

"To Lavas Holding?"

"I'll go, because I must. But I pray you, do not address me as 'my lord.' It isn't fitting. I am not the heir to Lavas County."

"Yet the hounds, my lord!" Angry, she gestured toward the hounds, who sat one to his right and one to his left. "The hounds are proof! They never obeyed any man but the Lavas heir!"

"Is that the truth?" he asked her. "Or are you only looking at it from the wrong side? Any man but the Lavas heir, or any man but the heir of the elder Charles?"

"I don't understand you, my lord. The hounds themselves are the proof."

"I am ready to leave," he said, "as soon as you are able to go."

It took her only until midday to collect what little Osna village could afford this year in taxes, and as Lavas Holding hadn't the wherewithal, so she said, to feed any more mouths, she took no young folk out of the village to serve the count for the customary year. The cleric with her filled in the account book that listed payments and shortfalls, and there were far more of the latter than the former.

"It seems you will leave us again," said Aunt Bel to Alain. "and it grieves me that you go. I do not know when we will see you."

"I do not know," he told her. "My path has been a strange one. I know only that our way must part here."

She wept, but only a little. "There is always a place for you with us, Alain, though I think you are not really ours."

He kissed her, and she hugged him. The others, too, gave him in turn a parting wish and a kiss or an embrace, depending on their nature.

"I pray you," he said to Stancy and Artald, "stay strong, and keep the others well. Do not let the family splinter."

"Be temperate," he said to Julien, and to Agnes, "Don't wait forever. Marry again in another year, if you've had no word of your lost husband."

"I should go to Medemelacha myself!" she said fiercely, but in an undertone, so the others wouldn't hear. "But Uncle won't let me. He says it's the place of women to guard the hearth and men to do the dangerous traveling, as it says in the Holy Verses. Everyone says I should just marry Fotho, but I don't want to! I want to go to Medemelacha and see if there's any news of Guy."

"Then make a bargain. If they let you go this spring, when the sea is passable, and if you find no word of him, you'll make no objection to marrying as Aunt Bel wishes."

All this time Blanche clung to his arm, lips pinched together and expression so curdled that it would turn sweet milk to sour.

He came to Henri last of all.

"I am sorry to see you leaving, Son. But I know you must go. You were never ours, only a gift we held for a time until it was reclaimed."

At last, what calm had sustained him shattered. Alain could not speak as he embraced the man who had raised him. Blanche began to wail.

"No! No! I won't let you go!"

Henri looked both amused and annoyed, as they all did when dealing with Blanche. "You'll have a hard time scraping that barnacle off."

"Perhaps." Alain did not try to dislodge her, although the others came swarming to scold at her and tug at her. "Perhaps best not to," he said, which made them all regard him in surprise.

"What do you mean?" Aunt Bel asked.

Julien was flushed, looking ashamed, and Agnes rolled her eyes in disgust.

"She doesn't thrive," said Alain. "She's like a tree growing all twisted, and not straight. Let me take her with me as far as Lavas Holding."

"Who will care for her?" demanded Agnes. "Who would show kindness to a creature as unlikable as she is?"

"They'd as like turn her out with the chickens as keep her in the house," said Stancy. "Poor mite." She looked at Julien, who only ducked his head. "If you'd speak up for her more, Jul, and scold her when she's deserved it, then she might not be what she is."

"No! I won't let you leave!" Blanche shrieked, too caught up in her tantrum to listen.

"I can see that she is taken care of."

"I don't like it," said Aunt Bel. "Lavas Holding hasn't enough to take in young folk for their year of service, the chatelaine said so herself. I won't have it said I turned out my own grandchild and sent her to scratch with the chickens."

"Do you trust me, Aunt Bel?"

"Well, truly, lad, I do."

"Let me see what can be made of her in fresh soil." That they none of them liked the child made them too ashamed to agree. "Blanche! Hush!"

She quieted, but kept her arms locked around his waist. Tears streaked her dirty face as she looked first up at him and then at the others.

Aunt Bel looked at each member of her family in turn, but they only frowned or shrugged. "Very well, Alain. It may be for the best."

"What for the best?" muttered Blanche, with a distrusting sniff.

"You will come with me as far as Lavas Holding," he said to her, "as long as you behave and do exactly as I say. Which you will."

The words stunned her. She stuck her thumb in her mouth and frowned around it.

"But she's no clothing, nothing. I'll not send a pauper—!"

"It will be well, Aunt Bel. Best we go now, and let it be swift. The chatelaine is packing up."

They wept, as did he. Blanche did not weep, not even when her father kissed her, not even when Agnes gave her the fine blue cloak off her own back that had been part of her wedding clothes.

It was hardest for Alain to let go of Henri, and in the end it was Henri who broke their embrace and set a hand on Alain's shoulder to look him in the eye. "Go on, then, Son. You'll do what's right." He brushed a finger over the blemish. "Do not forget us."

"You are always with me, Father."

Alain kissed him one last time. He slung his pack over his back and, with Blanche clutching his left hand, he followed Chatelaine Dhuoda and her skeletal retinue out of Osna village and back into the world beyond.

2

AT first, Anna wasn't sure what noise had startled her out of sleep. Blessing breathed beside her, as still as a mouse and all curled up with head practically touching bent knees. There was a serving-woman called Julia, a spy of the queen's, who slept on a pallet laid over the closed trap, but her soft snoring kept on steadily. Then the scuff sounded again, and after that a single rap of wood against stone.

Anna raised up on one elbow to see Lady Elene leaning out the window, looking ready to throw herself to her death. Anna heaved herself up and stumbled over to her, stubbing a toe on the bench, cursing.

"Look!" said Elene. As Anna moved up beside her, Elena's hair brushed her skin, a feather's touch, and Anna shivered and gulped down a sob for thinking so abruptly of Thiemo and Matto, whose hair might have brushed her in such a way.

"What lies off there?" Elene pointed. "See those lights?"

From this vantage, in daylight, one might gaze south over countryside falling away into rolling hills. Not a single candle burned in Novomo. The town was as dark as the Pit. Closer at hand, Anna inhaled the strong scent of piss from that spot along the curve of the tower where the soldiers commonly relieved themselves.

But distantly, like a show of lightning along an approaching storm front, she saw a shower of sparks and an arc of light so radiant that her breath caught as she stared.

"What is that, my lady?"

"There must be a crown out there, although Wolfhere never spoke of it. Someone is weaving in that crown. Yet how could they do so, with no stars to guide them?"

"Why do you need stars, my lady?"

"It's the secret of the mathematici, Anna. I can't tell you. But I can say that it is weaving, of a kind. You must have stars in sight to guide your hand and eye."

Anna liked the way Lady Elene talked easily to her. She was proud, but not foolish, and she had taken Anna's measure and measured her loyalties and while it was true that the daughter of a duke did not confide in a common servant girl, she did not scorn her either. Indeed, the more it annoyed Blessing when Lady Elene paid attention to her particular attendant, the more Lady Elene showed her favor to Anna, which Anna supposed was ill done of her, but in truth it was nice to have a mature companion who did not sulk and shriek and throw tantrums at every least provocation. It was pleasant to speak to a person whose understanding was well formed and who had a great deal of wit, which she did not always let show to those she did not trust.

"Yet look!" She was more shadow than shape, but with a sharp breath she shifted and Anna felt the pressure of her hips against her own as Elene stretched out her hand again. "That's someone come through the crown from elsewhere. Who could it be? Who might have survived?"

Anna shivered again, mostly from the cold. "Who else knows the secrets of the crowns, my lady?"

"Marcus and Holy Mother Anne and my grandmother are dead, as is that other woman out of the south. Sister Abelia, they called her."

"How do you know they are dead?"

"I wish to God I had not witnessed, but I did. *They are dead.* Yet one of the others might have survived. The ones in the north I could not see after the weaving was tangled."

"If it's true, could you trust them, my lady?"

"Not one of them, so Wolfhere says."

"Can you trust Wolfhere, my lady?"

"So you have asked before!" Elene laughed, although her amusement was as bitter as her tone. "He is the only one I would trust. Well, him, and my grandmother, and my poor dead mother, may she rest in the Chamber of Light, but she can't help me now."

"What of your father, the duke, my lady?"

She shrugged, shoulder moving against Anna's arm. "He gave me up, knowing I would die. He did as his mother asked, and I obeyed."

Daring greatly, Anna placed a hand over Elene's as comfort, and Elene did not draw her hand away. They watched until the spit and spark of light vanished, and for a long time after that they continued watching, although there was nothing to see.

"Holy Mother! I pray you. Wake up."

Antonia had the habit of waking swiftly. "What is it, Sister Mara?"

"Come quickly, I pray you, Holy Mother. The queen has sent for you."

She allowed her servants to dress her in a light robe and a cloak. For so late in spring it was yet cool as winter when it should have been growing steadily warmer as each day led them closer to summer. Lamps lit her way, although a predawn glamour limned the arches and corners of the palace.

A score of folk blundered about on the open porch before the queen's chambers. They parted to let her through, and she made her way inside to find another score of them cluttering the chamber and all of them dead silent, even those who were weeping. Within, Mathilda slept. Adelheid sat on her own bed with Berengaria limp in her arms.

Only the dead know such peace.

Adelheid looked up. "So it has come, Holy Mother. She has breathed her last." Her eyes were dry, her expression composed but fixed with an inner fury caged and contained.

"Poor child." Antonia pressed her hand on the cold brow, and spoke a prayer. The tiny child had lost almost all flesh during its long illness. With its spirit fled, it seemed little more than a skeletal doll, its skin dull and its hair tangled with the last of the sweating fever that had consumed it. "Even now she climbs the ladder that leads to the Chamber of Light, Your Majesty. You must rejoice for her, for her suffering has ended."

"Mathilda is all I have."

Antonia found this shift disconcerting, although she admired a woman who had already thought through the practicalities of her situation. "You are yet young, Your Majesty. You may make another marriage."

"With what man? There is no one I can trust, and none whose rank is worthy of me."

"That may be, but you will have to marry again."

"I must. Or Mathilda must be betrothed, to make an advantageous alliance."

"Mathilda!"

"Hush, I pray you, Holy Mother. I do not want her to wake."

"If no suitable alliance exists for you, how should it exist for her, Your Majesty?"

She did not answer. From the other chamber they heard the ring of a soldier's footsteps. A woman came running in.

"Captain Falco has urgent news, Your Majesty."

"I'll come." Adelheid handed the dead child to the nurse, who accepted the burden gravely but without any of the tears that afflicted the rest of them. Her eyes were hollow with exhaustion, that was all.

Adelheid rose and shook out her gown. Strange to think of her dressed when she ought to have been sleeping, but she often watched over the child at night these latter days since everyone knew that the angel of God came most often in the hour before dawn to carry away the souls of the innocent.

Captain Falco waited in the outer chamber. He was alert, his broad face remarkably lively. "You will not believe it, Your Majesty! Come quickly, I pray you."

Only one fountain in Novomo's palace still played, with a splash of water running through its cunning mechanism. In this courtyard, where there was also a shaded arbor and a fine expanse of lavender and a once splendid garden of sage and chrysanthemums, Lady Lavinia hovered under the arcade and wrung her hands, looking flustered as she stared at a man washing face and hands in the pool.

Antonia caught up short, stricken and breathless, but Adelheid did not falter. She strode out to him as eager as a lover, and as he rose and turned, obviously surprised to see her, she slapped him right across the cheek. Half her retinue gasped. The rest choked down exclamations. She did not notice. Fury burned in her. She looked ready to spit.

"You killed Henry!"

He touched his cheek. He did not bow to her nor make any homage, yet neither did he scorn her. "We were allies once, Your Majesty."

"No! You seduced me with your poisonous arguments. It's your fault that Henry is dead!"

"Surely it is the fault of his son, who killed him. And, if we must, the fault of Anne, who would have killed Henry had you and I not saved him by our intervention." He spoke in a calm voice, not shouting, yet clearly enough that everyone crowding about the courtyard heard his reasoned words and his harmonious voice. "I beg you, Your Majesty! I pray you! Do not forget that we wept and sorrowed over what had to be done. But we agreed it together. We saved him. It was his son who killed him."

"If you are not gone from Novomo by nightfall, I will have you executed for treason."

She swept her skirts away so the cloth would not brush against him, and walked off. In a flood, her retainers followed her, leaving Antonia with a stricken Lady Lavinia and a dozen serving folk who by their muttering and shifting did not know what to do or where to go.

"Is your daughter well, Lady Lavinia?" Hugh asked her kindly.

She stifled a sob, and said, only, "Yes, Lord Hugh. She survived the storm, which is more than I can say for many."

"God has favored you, then. I am gladdened to hear it."

She sobbed, and forced it back, and wavered, not knowing what to do. Perhaps she loved him better than she loved Adelheid. It would be easy to do so.

"Lady Lavinia," said Antonia. "If you will. I shall set matters right. The queen is distraught, as you know, because of her grief."

"Yes! Poor mite. Yes, indeed."

"Then be at rest, and do what you must. Lord Hugh, come with me, if you please."

He bowed his head most humbly and with that grace of manner that marked him, and with his boots still dusty from whatever road he had recently walked, he went with her to her chambers. There she sat him down on a bench and had the servants bring spiced wine. A cleric unpinned his brooch and set his cloak aside.

"What is this?" he asked, observing the room. "There hang the vestments belonging to the skopos."

"I am now mother of the church, Lord Hugh. Be aware of that."

The news startled him, but he absorbed it, sipping at the wine not greedily but thoughtfully. "Much has changed. I have heard in this hour fearful stories. The guards at Novomo's gate told me that Darre is a wasteland."

"So it is, as terrible as the pit. Stinking with sulfur and completely uninhabitable. Now. Listen. You have done me a favor in the past, and I shall return it, although I am not sure you are what I had at first hoped."

He smiled, but she could not tell what he was thinking. He was beautiful, indeed, and weary, and she did not yet know where he had come from and what story he would tell her, but it did not hurt her eyes to watch him as she related all that had happened in the last six months and the plight confronting this remnant of Aosta's royal court. He never once flinched or exclaimed or cried out in horror. Little surprised him, and that only when she revealed what prisoners they had in hand.

"Truly?" he asked her, and repeated himself. "The daughter of Sanglant and Liath? Truly?" He flushed.

"Be careful, Lord Hugh, else you reveal yourself too boldly."

"What do you mean?"

"Do not think I do not know."

That caught him, because exhaustion made him vulnerable.

"I have an idea," she added, "but it will take time, and plotting, and patience."

He lifted a hand most elegantly to show that he heard her, and that he was willing to let her proceed.

"What prospects have you, Lord Hugh? Why are you come here, to Aosta, when you were sent north by Anne into the land of your ancestors to work your part in the weaving?"

He smiled, but did not answer.

"Where have you come from?"

"From Wendar. I survived Anne's sorcery, as you have surely already understood. I set another in my place and in this manner I am living and he is dead."

"In this manner," she noted dryly, "did Sister Meriam sacrifice herself in favor of keeping her granddaughter alive."

"I am not Sister Meriam."

"Indeed, you are not, Lord Hugh."

"What do you want of me?"

"Queen Adelheid needs a husband. Why should it not be you?"

He rocked back, almost oversetting the bench, then steadied it. "I am a presbyter, as you see me, Holy Mother. It would be impossible. I cannot marry."

"If I gave you dispensation to leave the church, you could marry. There was often talk among the servants and the populace about what a handsome couple you and Adelheid made. Henry being older, and you so young and beautiful and beloved by the Aostans of Darre."

"I am faithful to God, Your Holiness. I do not seek marriage."

"You lust. Can you say otherwise?"

His lips thinned. His hands curled into fists. His eyes were a cold blue, as brittle as ice. "I am faithful, Your Holiness."

"To God?"

He shut his eyes.

"To a woman you can never have."

That fierce gaze startled, when he opened his eyes so abruptly. "I had her once!" He slammed a fist into the bench, then set his jaw and shut his eyes again and took in three trembling breaths before he quieted himself. "I am faithful to her. To no one but her. And after her, to God. And after God, to Henry."

"Who is dead."

"I did my best to save him!"

"I do not doubt it," she said, to mollify him. "What of Henry's son? Is she with Prince Sanglant?"

He could not speak. He was shaken, and tired, and so gnawed through with jealousy that he had become fragile with it, ready to fall to pieces but not yet shattered.

"This is too much and too quickly," she said more gently. "You are only arrived after a long and undoubtedly arduous journey. How came you here?"

"I journeyed by horse southwest from Quedlinhame until I found a crown. With my astrolabe it was a simple enough thing to measure precisely my route to Novomo. This I have taught myself that Anne did not know and had not mastered. I can go anywhere whose destination is known and measured. Two weeks only I lost in the crossing. Soon I shall have it down to a handful of days."

"And all alone, no retinue at all."

"None, except the beast, who resides in the lady's stables now. I have fled those who do not trust me. Even my own kinfolk were turned against me by poisonous words." Weary, indeed, to admit so much so honestly.

"I do not trust you, Lord Hugh. Why should I?"

"Trust that I have no power save my knowledge of the arts of the mathematici. My mother is dead, and my sisters hate me. Queen Adelheid wishes me gone. That bastard who calls himself king has the power to banish me."

"And he holds the woman you desire close to his heart."

"Damn him!"

He wept tears of rage.

The sight so astounded her that she could not move except to wave away the servants who had come into the room, hearing his distress. Her amazement allowed her the patience to wait him out and to explore the lineaments of his anger, shown in the curl of his hands, the stiffness of his jaw, and the way his lower lip trembled like that of a thwarted child. She had never seen him lose control so nakedly.

So might an angel cry, hearing of an insult to God which Their creature was powerless to avenge.

When he had calmed a little, she touched his hand. "I will speak with the queen. You will rest. Later we will speak again. There is a pallet in the outer chamber. No one will disturb you. Ask for food and drink, anything you desire."

"You cannot give me what I desire," he said, voice still hoarse with tears.

"You ought to desire God's favor, Lord Hugh, not a mere woman. Mere flesh."

"You do not know what she is."

"But I do know. I saw what she is, and a fearful thing it was to see. You forget I was there at Verna. I think even my galla might not touch one such as she. She is very dangerous, and no doubt that makes her sweeter and brighter in your eyes. I think she is too dangerous to let live."

"No!"

"Then chained. Dead, or chained.'

He had not dried his eyes, but the tears lingering on his face did not mar his beauty. "I will do anything to get her back."

"Will you? Will you even marry Adelheid?"

With his chin dipped down, his gaze up at her had an almost flirtatious quality. "How will that aid Adelheid's cause, or my own? Or yours, Your Holiness?"

"In no possible way, if Adelheid does not forgive you and take you back into her counsel. As for the rest, consider who is Adelheid's heir—younger by far and easier to steer on a proper course."

That made him think. He sat in silence, gaze drawn in as at an image she could not touch, although she could guess it: Antonia as skopos and Hugh as the deceased queen's consort, ruling Mathilda as regents.

"Best to rest, Lord Hugh," she added kindly, "and see if sleep and food ease this trouble that disturbs your mind."

"It never will," he whispered to himself.

She nodded, humoring him, but he was far gone, and indeed when he was taken aside to the waiting pallet, hidden behind a curtain, he slept at once and heavily, dead to the world, as it was said by the poets, who knew from sordid experience how cravings make a man pregnable who might otherwise be fortified with temperance.

He slept all day and all night while the queen was caught up in her sorrow, seeing her younger daughter wrapped in a shroud and carried in a box to the crypt in Novomo's fine church, the only suitable place to lay a princess to rest. The bell tolled seven times, to ring the dead child's soul up through the spheres. A posset laced with valerian helped the queen to sleep as well, that same night.

The next morning dawned peacefully, as Lady Lavinia had cause to remark when Antonia met her by the fountain after Prime.

"I've had word that a train of merchants will reach Novomo by midday. They have ridden all the way from the eastern provinces. One is said to have come as far as from Arethousa! The queen, even in her grief, is sensible of their long journey and wishes to see them feasted properly this afternoon."

"She is wise. If there is no entertainment, then I think a prudent feast cannot be seen as improper despite her sorrow. The child was not yet two, after all. We cannot be surprised when infants die, as so many do. I do not object."

Lavinia put a hand into the water and, after a while, looked up. "I pray you, Holy Mother. Will the queen forgive him? He was always faithful to her, and most especially to Henry. I never heard an ill word spoken of him, never a whisper."

"What do you mean, Lady Lavinia?"

"I do not think it right he should be banished, but I cannot go against the queen's wishes."

"What if he should marry the queen?"

"He is a holy presbyter! He is wed to God's service. It would pollute him to marry!" She faltered. Her cheeks were stained red, as if the sun had pinked them, but of course there was no sun, only the monotony of another cloudy day.

"It would be a shame to stain the beauty of a man as beautiful as he is."

"I do not know if it would be right, Holy Mother."

"It is not your place to interpret God's wishes."

"No, Holy Mother."

"Still, there is something in what you say. He might not be the right one. Yet the queen must marry again."

"She mourns her dead husband, Holy Mother."

"Henry?"

"Indeed, Holy Mother. She held a great affection for the emperor in her heart."

A strange way Adelheid had taken, thought Antonia, to show her fondness, but perhaps it was true that she had believed, or convinced herself to believe, that she had no other choice. Hugh, naturally, would fall into any scheme that offered him power, but it wasn't as clear to Antonia what he felt he would gain by wielding such malevolent sorcery. *Possessed by a daimone!* Still, perhaps he, too, had done it only out of loyalty to Henry and Wendar. She doubted it. Henry, through the daimone, would have given him anything he wanted. Anything.

Was it actually possible that a man with as much beauty and intelligence as Hugh was so very . . . *small* when all else came to be measured? That he was himself chained by being fixed on one thing? Who was slave, and who was master, then? One had escaped while the other still polished his shackles.

"You are a practical woman, Lady Lavinia. Have you a recommendation?"

She sighed and looked toward the fountain. Water wept into the circular pool at the base. "Many nights such thoughts have troubled me, Holy Mother. I am a widow, and have not remarried. I find there is a lack of men whose lineage and temperament please me. In these cruel days, the queen must choose wisely or not at all."

"Has she spoken to you of such matters?"

Lavinia's hesitation was her answer.

"What passes in private between you and the queen I will not intrude upon, but remember that God know all your secrets, Lady Lavinia. If you must unburden yourself, do so to me."

"I am your obedient servant, Holy Mother."

Perhaps. It was difficult to know whom Lavinia served. She was an ordinary woman, devoted to her lands, which she administered prudently, and to her children and kinfolk, whom she protected as well as she could. She remained loyal to Adelheid in part, Antonia supposed, because she thought Adelheid's regnancy would serve her and her estates best compared to that of another overlord. But if her heart stirred, it stirred in defense of Lord Hugh.

Thoughtful, Antonia returned to her chambers only to find that the servants had fed him a hearty portion of cheese and bread when he had woken, and afterward gotten him a cloak.

"Where has he gone?"

"Holy Mother!" They stared at the floor. "Did we do ill, Holy Mother? He went as he wished. It was just after you departed these rooms, Your Holiness, to sing the dawn prayers. Was it meant otherwise? Had it been better had we kept him beside us?"

"No. No. Do not think me angry. Have you any notion of where he meant to go?" For his actions would reveal his thoughts.

Why, to pray, they assured her, and she believed them. That is, she believed that they believed that was where he had gone. Why should he tell them the truth?

She knew where he intended to go. What would attract him first, beyond anything. He must have power to get what he wanted. Antonia had merely shown him the path.

"Come, Felicita. Give me my audience robes . . . no, not the heavy ones, for I mean to walk some while afterward in them. Send for Brother Petrus. He's gone? Very well. You will attend me, Sister Mara. No, no hurry. Let me rest my feet a moment. I must see the queen. It is likely she will wake late, out of her grief."

And, waking late, would leave Hugh waiting in her antechamber to see her and to beg her forgiveness. No need to rush there to interrupt his pleading. He would plead so very beautifully, after all. Not even Adelheid would be able to resist him.

But after all, Adelheid slept in a stupor all morning. There passed an interlude of alarm around midday during which Antonia hurried to the prisoners' tower to make sure that the captives had not been disturbed. Yes, the sergeant told her, the holy presbyter had indeed come by, but after hearing that the princess was afflicted with a mild sickness in her stomach, he had ventured only into the dungeon.

It was a chilly, nasty, dirty place. She had to lean on the arm of a guardsman to make sure she did not slip on the steps, which had no railing. The large open chamber had been fitted with three smaller cells built with mortared brick. In the darkest of these, Wolfhere sat on straw with his hands in his lap and his manacles resting along his legs. He blinked as the lamp lit him and regarded her with a bored resignation that irritated her. Despite the burns on his face and neck, he had never told her anything secret, only commonplace tales that helped her not at all. In time he would. It was only a matter of patience. Eventually the solitude and the rats would drive him insane, and he would tell her everything in exchange for a glimpse of sky.

"Your Holiness," he said in that bland way that made her twitch and wish to hit him.

"What did he want?" she demanded.

"He wanted to know who the father of the esteemed cleric Heribert might be."

She would have burned him then had she any fiery implements on hand, but she had to content herself with a gentle smile. "A strange question to ask of a lowly Eagle."

He shrugged. His nails had gotten so long they curved, and his beard was matted and filthy. In fact, he reeked. "Perhaps not so strange a question to ask of a man who knows the Wendish court well."

Almost, she slapped him, but she tweaked the sleeve of her robe instead, smile fixed. "To what purpose do you seek to annoy me? You have not answered my question."

"He also asked me how I was come here, and where I had been, so I suppose that means he is himself newly come to Novomo."

"What did you tell him?"

"Nothing more than I have told you, Your Holiness. I think he came more to gloat at my ill fortune. But you may ask him yourself. I am sure he will tell you, as he and I are old enemies."

"Are you so, and on what ground?"

His smile was keen, and it reminded her of how tough a man he was to be able to smile with such strength after so long in captivity. "I had twice the great pleasure of rescuing a young woman from his grasp. I suppose he will never forgive me."

"Liathano. This is an old story."

"It is a story that will never get old for Hugh of Austra."

That flash startled her. "Is it possible you are more clever than you seem, Wolfhere?"

"What answer can I give that will satisfy you? God are my witness, that I am only myself, and nothing more."

"So you say. I am not done with you, Wolfhere."

He winced, the first sign of weakness she had surprised from him. "I am the obedient servant of God and regnant, Your Holiness."

"Servant of Anne."

"Of God and regnant, Your Holiness. Then, now, and always. Nothing more." He spoke with such finality that, for an instant, she believed him.

Hugh was discovered walking in Lavinia's enclosed garden beside the poplars, chatting amiably with Brother Petrus, whom he had known in the skopos' palace.

"Holy Mother," he said, bowing in the manner of presbyters as she approached. "I beg your pardon, Your Holiness. I was restless, thinking on those things we spoke of yesterday."

She was flushed from the annoyance of having wondered where Hugh had gone, and perhaps for this reason, Brother Petrus bowed and retreated hastily, leaving them to their talk.

"I have taken some trouble to find you, Lord Hugh."

"Gardens give me solace, Your Holiness. Forgive me."

"Did you not fear that Queen Adelheid would make true her threat to see you executed?"

"I was told that she slept, Your Holiness. Lady Lavinia gave me leave to walk in the garden."

"And leave to go to the prisoners' tower, and interview the Eagle?"

"I admit I was greatly surprised to discover Wolfhere in Novomo. What can it mean that he is here?"

"What did you hope to learn from him?"

"I'm not sure," he admitted. "He was Anne's servant. Surely he knows something of Anne—her plans, her sorcery, her history, her books—things that might be of value to us."

"If he does, I have not yet discovered it! Despite my best efforts. He is a stubborn man!"

"He made some pact with Sister Meriam, it appears," he mused. "Why?"

"As yet, that mystery remains unanswered. We can discuss it later, Lord Hugh. I must go to my audience chamber for the afternoon. Many supplicants appear before me. There is a great deal of trouble in the world that wants fixing, now that God's wrath has fallen upon us."

"Just so," he agreed. "I feel myself weighted by trouble, as though the Enemy had gotten a claw into my heart."

"Do as I ask, Lord Hugh, and you will gain that which you seek."

It was cloudy, as always, but seemed brighter in this corner of the garden where he walked. He paused beside a clump of carefully tended vervain to run a hand over its pale spurs. "It is so difficult," he murmured, "to gain that which one seeks. Have you ever wondered, Your Holiness, about these tales of a heresy sprung up in western lands. The tale of the phoenix—have you heard it?"

"Lies whispered by the Enemy's minions! No doubt such calumnies are but one among many misdeeds that have brought God's hand down upon us."

"Truly, many speak who know nothing. Still, one wonders where such tales came from and why they arose."

"I do not wonder! The Arethousans cast them at us, hoping they would fly among us like a plague. Let ten thousand fall to the contagion! In this manner they hope to weaken us, but it will not happen. We will remain strong as long as we remain in God's favor."

"And when I have cast away my vows and am wed to Adelheid,

what then? Is she to be killed, Your Holiness, so that Mathilda may rule in her place and we as regents over her?"

"Even the walls may have ears, Lord Hugh! Be more discreet, I pray you!"

"I crave your pardon, Your Holiness. But I am confused as to the manner of the plan, its working out, and its fulfillment. Must I lie with her?"

"Is she not desirable? Other men call her so. She is deemed very pretty."

"So is a rock polished by the river, before it is set beside a sapphire."

"You will persist in your obsession."

"How will my marrying Adelheid gain me what I seek?"

"Is that your only objection? I cannot promise you the thing you want, but earthly power may grant you weapons you do not currently have. What kinfolk will aid you?"

"None."

"What princes will assist you?"

"None."

"You have only me. I can use you, and if you aid me, then I will reward you. So God command us. Those who serve will be given what they deserve."

He nodded, having wandered by this time to a stand of skullcap. He twisted off a leaf. "The queen trusted me once. She may not do so again, even though I gave her no reason to distrust me. Yet if she refuses to trust me, there are ways to encourage her."

The garden was still in its ragged spring garments; a few violets bloomed late; deep blue peeped from close stalks of rosemary. "So there are, but cautiously, Hugh. Cautiously."

"I am ever so," he agreed humbly, gaze cast down.

Satisfied, she beckoned for her attendants. "I will call for you later. Do not come to the feast tonight. We shall begin our persuasion of the queen tomorrow."

3

LADY Elene always woke before dawn to pray. Because she had taken a liking to Brother Heribert's strange manners, she insisted he climb the ladder to pray beside her every morning. Of course if Elene would pray, then Lord Berthold would come up with Heribert to pray also, Lord Jonas trailing at his heels. Blessing sulked on her pallet. Anna always dressed and knelt behind the nobles. Because she did not know the verses and psalms by heart, she must repeat them after the others had finished. Elene always remembered, as a courtesy, to ask the cleric who attended them to allow time for Anna's response. In fact, to include Brother Heribert she had to, because he had not been quite right in the mind ever since the collapse of the hill on top of him and could scarcely recall his own verses and prayers, which he had once known better than anyone.

The others knelt on soft carpet. Anna knelt on the hard plank floor with her hands covering her face, the better to concentrate on God's will. The better to disguise her words when she spoke "She" for "They." No one knew that the phoenix had touched her heart. No one but Blessing, who had learned to keep silent about this one thing after that time when Prince Sanglant had punished his daughter's servants for exposing her to heretical words. Blessing hated to see her servants punished, knowing she would never be punished herself. It was the one thing about her that gave Anna hope.

"Blessed be You, Mother and Father of Life," said Lady Elene.

"Blessed be You, Holy Mother," whispered Anna into her hands.

"Blessed be You," repeated Brother Heribert in his awkward voice.

Lord Berthold yawned.

Lord Jonas made no sound. He often fell asleep kneeling, eyes open.

Blessing gulped down a false sob, stifled under her blankets.

On the floor below, the trap thumped open, landing hard. Anna flinched, hands coming down. Berthold rose, and Blessing's sniveling ceased.

"Blessed is the Country of the Mother and Father of Life, and of the Holy Word revealed within the Circle of Unity," continued Elene stubbornly, ignoring the clatter of feet beneath, "now and ever and unto ages of ages."

A cleric's cowl appeared in the open trap. The woman climbed higher and revealed herself as Sister Mara, one of the Holy Mother's faithful attendants. She looked around the room. After a moment, she climbed all the way up and spoke in whispers to Julia, who shook her head. They walked around the room and opened up both chests while Lady Elene kept praying as if they weren't there. At last, Sister Mara left.

When prayers came to an end, Berthold said, "What was that all about?"

"Begging your pardon, my lady. My lord." Julia rubbed her brow with the back of a hand, looking nervous. Normally she had a robust confidence, but she seemed tired after speaking with Sister Mara. "You're to stay within today, all day. No garden."

Elene raised an eyebrow and looked at Berthold, who shrugged.

Blessing popped up from the bed, unaware and unashamed of her nakedness, although by now she showed the signs of blossoming womanhood. "I don't *want* to stay in."

"Shut up, brat," said Berthold gently. "Please cover yourself."

"I don't *want*—"

"Do shut up!" snapped Elene.

"I hate you!"

"I hate *you*, you evil creature! I'll pinch your ears if you don't stop whining."

Blessing clapped hands over ears and huddled under the blankets until, sometime later, after the others had gone down to the lower floor to entertain themselves with chess and reading, Anna was able to coax her out.

"I don't feel good," whimpered the girl. "I got a cut on my leg."

"How could have you gotten—" But it was no cut, of course. "Princess Blessing. Your Highness. Oh, dear."

"Is anything amiss, Anna?" asked the servingwoman, Julia, from the window, where she sat and sewed.

"Sit down," Anna said sternly, and Blessing sat cross-legged. A few drops of blood stained the bedding, but it wasn't too bad. "I pray you, Julia, Princess Blessing is feeling poorly. Might you go down and ask the sergeant if we can have a posset, something to settle her stomach? It must be what she ate last night."

Julia glanced sharply at her. Perhaps she suspected. Perhaps she had overheard, although Blessing had whispered. But she went, leaving Anna and the child alone.

"Now, Your Highness, listen closely and listen well."

"My tummy hurts."

"I know it does. And so it will do, about once every month, for a good long while now."

"Why?"

"You know a woman's courses."

"That you get?"

"Yes, as you've seen, the Lady favored women by giving them the power of life, while men have only the power of death. That is why we can bleed every month and survive it. Now you have started bleeding."

"What does that mean?"

She bit her lip, worried it, then plunged on. "It means you must be secret, Blessing." How difficult a thing this was to get across to a child who had the understanding of a five or six year old but the body of a budding adolescent! "Among my people, a girl isn't likely to be wed until she's older and she and her betrothed have the wherewithal to set up a household. But among noble families sometimes girls are married as soon as they begin bleeding."

"Why?"

"Why marry? To form alliances. To make treaties. To consolidate an inheritance."

"Why not when they're little, like me?"

"Girls are betrothed all the time when they're children. But no man will bed a wife until that girl is a woman and can grow a baby inside her."

"Is Lady Elene old enough? Why can't she get married and leave us? I hate her!"

"We are all prisoners, Your Highness. Our captors may do with us as they wish, even kill us. That's why you must be silent and secret."

For as long a while as Anna had ever seen Blessing sit and think, the child frowned and considered. She was a lovely girl, with a complexion neither light nor dark and with shining thick dark hair falling halfway down her back that must be combed and braided and pinned up. Her eyes seemed sometimes green and sometimes blue and sometimes a hazel shading toward brown, a blend of her father and mother. Like both father and mother, she drew the eye; folk watched her; even the soldiers did, sneaking a look while pretending not to. Beauty is dangerous among the innocent, who might be ravaged when they least expect it.

"If I were Queen Adelheid," Anna said at last, "I would use you, Your Highness, as a pawn in a game of chess."

"I am the great granddaughter of the Emperor Taillefer! She can't do anything without my permission!"

"She can do anything she wants, Your Highness! How will you stop her? If Queen Adelheid knows you are bleeding, she may think it worth her while to marry you off and be rid of you that way. Right now she thinks you're still a child."

Blessing stared at her hands, then drew a finger along her inner thigh and stared at the blood painting her nail.

"Think what a prize you are, Your Highness. Many men might desire to take you for a wife only because of who your parents are. Some may hope to reward themselves. Others might hope to punish your father or mother."

Tears slipped down the girl's face. "Why does my father never come, Anna?"

"He does not know where you are. We haven't any way to let him know. If any of us escape, Holy Mother Antonia will hear of it and send horrible demons after us to eat us alive. That's what Lady Elene says."

"I don't believe her! I hate her!"

"You should! You must! You will! She is like your mother, trained as a sorcerer. She knows. We are trapped, Your Highness. And you are more vulnerable than ever now! Do you understand me? Lady Elene is our friend. So is Lord Berthold and Brother Heribert. And Lord Jonas. And our servants, Berda and Odei. But *no one else*. We can trust no one else."

Footsteps rattled on the ladder. Blessing folded her hands over her loins as soon as Julia's head appeared and sat there stubbornly, refusing to budge, until Anna wrestled a shift on over her bare shoulders. A moment later, the healer appeared.

"Berda, come here!" said Anna.

"Small queen sick in her belly?" The healer knelt by the pallet.

Anna turned her back to Julia and lifted two fingers to seal her lips. The healer nodded. Blessing, still sitting cross-legged, pulled her shift up to her hips to show the blood streaking her thighs.

Berda nodded. "A drink calms the belly," she said in her odd voice. Her broad hands smoothed the shift back over the girl's legs. She touched the girl's forehead, throat, and her collarbone on each side.

"Some sickness in the food," she said. "Have you piss this morning?"

Blessing shook her head.

"Come, small queen."

They went to the corner, where the chamber pot was tucked away behind a bench, and Blessing did her business. Julia came over to look, but after Blessing rose, Berda squatted quickly with her heavy felt skirt concealing this complicated maneuver, since the steppe women, Anna had seen, wore both skirts and trousers. She then peed in her turn, and rose with a grimace.

"Moon turns," she said. "I am bleeding. Must move my bed to upstairs."

It was a habit of the Kerayit healer to sleep downstairs with the men most of the month, and upstairs with the women during her bleeding, although it seemed to Anna that it had not been more than two weeks since her last sojourn upstairs. Never mind it. They would burn that bridge after they had crossed it. She looked at Berda, and the healer nodded, covered the pan, and offered it to Julia to dispose of, as was her duty.

"I fetch drink of herbs for the small queen. She rest this day."

Rest she did. Berda found clean rags for her, to catch the blood, and pretended they were her own. It was not so difficult, once the ruse was begun; Julia, like the other Aostans, found the healer so peculiar that she didn't like to get close to her.

Afterward, they went about their usual routine. Water must be brought up for washing, and the buckets taken downstairs and emptied and rinsed out. The morning chores broke up the monotony of the day, so Anna eked out each least errand, dawdling where she could. She didn't even mind it when, after the upstairs was tidied and washed, she was sent down to empty the dungeon bucket. The old man didn't scare her, although the stink was bad. After the first few weeks, the soldiers simply stopped going down with her because they hated the pit, and she was free to make quick conversation with the Eagle, mostly a detailed account from her of yesterday's doings, and perhaps a few oblique sentences passed back and forth between him and Lady Elene.

This morning, though, the soldiers loitered nervously by the outer door, as if keeping an eye out for someone they expected to come along at any moment. Anna had a clean bucket in one hand as she reached the head of the steps that cut down into the gloom. The sergeant on duty glanced back into the chamber and saw her.

"Here, now," he said, lifting a hand to get her attention.

But she was already descending along the curve of the stair with the cold stone wall brushing her shoulder and the bucket dangling over air as soon as she cleared the plank flooring. It was quite dark, but she knew the feel of the wall and the angle of each step by now. She could have gone down with her eyes closed, and indeed she paused partway down, in the shadows, and closed her eyes, because she heard voices.

The tower rose in levels, with the deepest chamber dug out of the earth and markedly colder than the ground floor and the other rooms stacked above. The space below was used to store beans and onions, and here also three small cells had been bricked in. From her place on the stairs, with the dampening of sound and the lack of any footsteps clomping above, she heard them speaking in low voices. One of those voices was familiar to her; the other had a strange, enchanting timbre that seemed to stick her feet right where they were so that she didn't dare, or want, to move.

"You cannot escape because Antonia controls the galla."

"I do not fear the galla."

"You should."

"Perhaps."

"Then why do you not escape? If you can, why don't you?"

"Is that not obvious? I have those to whom I am responsible. If they cannot run, then I cannot run."

"Thus meaning, you cannot protect them from the galla. Is it Princess Blessing, or Conrad's daughter, who holds you here?"

"Why can it not be both?"

"I heard the story once that you tried to drown Prince Sanglant, when he was an infant."

"It's a story that has been told many times, and on occasion in my hearing."

"An interesting tale, and if true, a shame you did not succeed. Although it might make a man wonder what allegiance holds you to Princess Blessing. Is it her father you seek to serve? Her mother? Anne's tangled weaving, still to be obeyed? Or do you merely have a weakness for these caged birds?"

"It's true I do not like to see such bright creatures imprisoned by cruel masters." Wolfhere sounded bored beyond measure, tired of the game. "What do you want, Lord Hugh?"

"Where did you come from? How did you get here?"

Wolfhere sighed.

"You were seen last in the company of Brother Marcus and Sister Meriam. You ran from them. Yet now you appear here, with Meriam's granddaughter in your care. Where were you? How did you escape the cataclysm?"

"Fortune favored us," said the old man dryly.

"You were least among the Seven Sleepers. Cauda draconis, the tail of the dragon. They told me that you were too ignorant to weave the crowns. Is that true?"

"Yes, it's true. I was never taught the art of the mathematici. Mine was the gift of Eagle's Sight, and of the skills necessary to a messenger who spends his life on the road. Thus, I am peculiarly situated to survive long journeys through hostile lands."

"Why should I believe you?"

"It matters little to me if you believe me or not, Lord Hugh. Why should it? The battle is lost, and Anne is dead."

"Thus your purpose for being."

"Thus my purpose for being," said Wolfhere in a flat voice. "What is it you want? Or are you merely here to gloat?"

"It's true I have no liking for you, Eagle. You stole from me the thing that is rightly mine. I mean to have it back."

"How will you accomplish that? Liath is dead, is she not? Like the others."

She heard the other man take in a raggedly drawn breath, sharp and sweet. "Not dead. Not dead."

Abruptly, the old man's tone became edged. "Where have you seen her? How do you know?"

"Where have I seen her? In Wendar, my friend. Standing beside the bastard who calls himself king."

"I have heard the tale of Henry's passing. I wasn't sure it was true."

"Oh, true it is, and the prince of dogs crowned and anointed by Mother Scholastica herself, although I think she was not best pleased in the doing."

"So it is true. And Liath has survived, so you say." No doubt he was eager to hear these tidings, but he kept his voice low and even.

"Can you not see her yourself, with your vaunted Eagle's Sight? Have you not spoken with your discipla, Hathui, who has gained the protection of the new king and stands in his very shadow?"

There was a long pause, and a quiet shuffling of feet above her. Anna glanced up to see a shadowed form bent over the trap, looking down toward her, but it was obvious that his eyes had not yet adjusted to the darkness below.

"You may as well know that I am blind," said Wolfhere. "Since the cataclysm."

"Blinded? Useless and helpless, then. Master of nothing, servant to no one. Yet why tell me so? Why confess as much to me, Eagle?"

"Because I hurt, Lord Hugh. If I tell you that you can gain nothing from torturing me, then perhaps you will not do so."

"Ah. I suppose it is the Holy Mother—or the queen—who sees you used so ill. What do they want to know?"

"Nothing I would tell you, if I would also not tell them. Leave us be, Lord Hugh. I do not know what is your purpose here. I ask you only for this favor: leave us be."

"What will you give me in return?"

"In return for what?"

"For leaving you be."

"So we come around again to my first question: what do you want?"

"Who is Liath's father?"

"Bernard."

"And her mother?"

"A daimone of the upper spheres. I am surprised to hear you ask."

"It was once a closely guarded secret."

"Yes, once it was. Back when we still held some measure of control over her. Anne took you into the Seven Sleepers. I am not surprised that you lived, when others died, but I am surprised you ask me questions you must already have heard the answers to."

"Folk may lie."

"I am shocked to hear it."

Lord Hugh chuckled. "Is it safe to let you live, Eagle?"

"Oh, indeed it is. I would even call it necessary."

"Think you so?"

"Of course I must. Leave us be, Lord Hugh. We have nothing you want."

"No, no," said the other man musingly. "I'm not sure you do have anything I want."

She felt warm breath on her neck and heard the merest croak of the step just above the one she stood on, where it had a wobble.

"Hsst!" said the sergeant in her ear. "Up out of here, girl, or we'll all be in trouble."

They fled up, and just in time, for the sergeant had just shoved her out the door and over to the pits to pretend she was at some kind of filthy work with her head bent down to hide her face when she heard all the soldiers with bowing and scraping in their voices as some august presence departed the tower and went on his way.

"Idiot," said the sergeant, coming over to her and yanking the pail out of her hand. "No one was to disturb them! I'll take care of the prisoner today. You go back up, and keep your mouth shut and your feet where they belong."

"How was I to know?" she said, and he slapped her.

Later, as the cloistered hours passed without incident, the sergeant relented and came up himself to gossip with Lord Berthold, his favorite. The queen's younger daughter had died the day before, which explained the tolling of the bell. There was anyway to be a feast that night, if a solemn one, because an envoy had come from a distant land, but he wasn't sure where, maybe Arethousa, come to parley with the grieving queen. So that was why it was that Berthold and his retinue could not leave the upper chambers for any possible reason this day.

Therefore they expected no visitors late in that afternoon with the courtyard gone quiet and a murmur rising from the great hall whose roof could be seen from the east facing windows. There, most of those who lived in the palace had gathered to feast or to serve. The smells rising from the kitchens made Anna's stomach hurt and her mouth water.

Berthold and Elene played another game of chess by the window, glancing at each other in a way that Anna recognized as dangerous and that, mercifully, Blessing did not see for what it was. Two attractive young people thrown together for hours and days and weeks on end. How well Anna knew where such intimacy led! She wiped her eyes, but there weren't any tears left for Thiemo and Matto. They had vanished under the hill with Berthold's companions, with their old life, with all that had transpired before the storm.

Heribert sat beside Blessing, who for once was frowning at tablet and stylus and with awkward strokes getting some of her letters right. Anna sat down on the carpet near Blessing's feet, and went back to mending a tear in Blessing's other shift. Julia sat on the bench, embroidering. Lord Jonas was downstairs playing dice with Odei; those two could go at it for hours, and the spill of dice across the floor was, like a poet's song at a feast, a steady accompaniment to other labors. Berda sat in a shadowed corner grinding a root into powder. The light came gloomy through the open windows, and it was cool, but no one wanted to shutter themselves in.

Elene sniffed, wiped her nose, and looked up, holding a lion in one hand. "Do you smell that?"

Berthold stifled a yawn. "Smell what? I hate sitting indoors all day."

Berda glanced up as well. "It is sharp," she said, touching her nose.

The lady frowned. She did not set down the lion. "Now it's gone. I thought. . . ." She, too, yawned, and caught herself.

Even Anna yawned and almost pricked herself with her needle. Her grunt of frustration set off an avalanche of yawns among all of them, except Heribert.

"The curve here, Your Highness. It is uneven."

"I'm just tired! I can do better!"

"Yes," he agreed. "So it appears from the way you are yawning. There is a sharp glamour in the air. It tingles in the bones."

Berthold pushed the chess pieces aside and pillowed his head on his arms. "Just a nap, and we'll start again."

Elene's head lolled back. The lion fell out of her hand, and when it struck the floor she jerked upright. "What is that?" she demanded. "A glamour . . . a spell . . ."

Anna was so tired. The languor smothered her. The walls spoke in whispers, reminding her of the peace of the sleep which awaits every soul, the crossing into death. . . .

Soft footsteps mounted the stair-step ladder. A middle-aged man appeared in the opened trap. He was named Brother Petrus, one of the holy clerics who served the Holy Mother.

"Up here, my lord," he said as he clambered out.

She pricked herself with the needle, and the pain woke her. A drop of blood swelled.

Blessing had fallen asleep against Heribert's shoulder. Berthold roused dully, lifting his head. Elene struggled, reaching for the lion she had dropped on the floor. Berda snored softly, head lolling back against the wall, her throat exposed.

An angel climbed out of the trap and paused to regard the chess table and the pair of young nobles fighting sleep.

"Well," he said in a melodious voice so soothing Anna was sure he tamed wild beasts with it. She recognized it immediately as the voice of the man who had been talking to Wolfhere. "Conrad's doomed daughter and Villam's lost son. How unexpected this is. How handsome they look together, dark and fair!"

Elene grunted, got hold of the lion, and dug it into her palm. Her eyes flared. "Who are you? What sorcery . . . ?"

The chess piece rolled out of her hand, landed on a corner of carpet, and tumbled off that onto the plank floor. Her eyes fluttered as she fought to keep awake.

"You know tricks, Lady Elene, but you are inexperienced."

Anna thrust the needle into her hand again, and the pain burst like fire and focused her mind, but it was so hard to fight. It was so much easier to sleep.

He turned and saw Blessing. "Ah," he said, voice catching. "So old already. Just as I'd hoped. . . ."

From this angle, seated crosswise to Blessing and slightly behind her, Anna saw his expression darken.

"How can it be that you still wake?" he asked.

Before she could answer, Brother Heribert said, quite clearly, "Who are you?"

"Better I should ask, who are you? You are Brother Heribert, a particular intimate counselor of the prince, guardian of his daughter. Before that you were a cleric in the schola of the biscop of Mainni, rumored to be her—" He laughed. Anna ducked her head and, feeling the dizzy drag of exhaustion pulling her down, jabbed the needle in. "God in Heaven! Look at your eyes! How comes this? I thought I was the only one who knew this secret. Why are you here?"

"I am looking for the one I love. They say it is the other one who stole him. The one called Sanglant."

"Who *stole* him?" The angel shifted back on his heels as might a man who has been struck, then rolled forward to his toes, and regained his balance. "Who stole who?"

"Lord Hugh?" asked Brother Petrus, who was fingering an amulet looped at his neck. "Ought we not hurry, my lord? It will be dark soon."

"Yes." The angel nodded, but he looked only at Heribert, not at Brother Petrus. "Who is lost, and who is blind?" he said to himself. "Can it be? Tell me, friend, if the other one stole him, then do you want to get back this one you seek?"

"I don't know where he is."

"Gone utterly, I fear, if what my eyes tell me is true, and I think it must be. But I know who killed him."

"What does that mean?"

"It means that his soul is fled from Earth."

"How do I find him?"

"Seek you his killer and get your revenge. Kill the one who killed him."

"Will it bring him back, if I kill the one who killed him?"

The angel's smile would brighten a hall shrouded in darkness. "Oh, yes. Certainly. Delve deep, and seek him at his heart. Drive out the soul you find there. That will kill the one who killed him. The one called Sanglant."

"But he loved him! He trusted him!"

"Alas," the angel said in a gentling voice, as a mother might soothe a weeping child. "So it happens among humankind, that the ones we love most are quickest to betray us."

"How will I go?"

"Come with me now. I will set you on your way. Brother Petrus, there is an attendant who serves the princess. Find her, and place an amulet around her neck . . . Ah!"

Elene grunted, struggling against the spell, lips moving as she murmured an incantation.

"Petrus, the knife."

"Your hands, my lord. Let me do it, if it must be done."

"I'll not let others stain their hands so mine may remain clean. This is my decision, not yours." He took a common kitchen knife, good sharp iron, out of Petrus' shaking hands, and went to the table. Grasping Elene by the hair, he set the knife to her pulsing throat.

Elene tried to struggle, but she could not.

Anna shrieked, but the only noise that escaped her was a moan. She staggered up, but she was too slow with that lethargy weighing her down. She was too slow, and it was already too late.

He cut.

Elene's blood spurted over the board, spattering Berthold's sleeve and hair, although he was too fast asleep to stir. Blood flowed. A Dragon and a Queen toppled sideways in the first gush. The rest of the pieces were soon awash, islands in a red sea.

Hugh braced her body in the chair and dropped the bloody knife onto the carpet. He walked over to Anna and grasped her. She sagged against him; she could not help herself.

"Is this another so afflicted?" He raised her hand, smoothed a finger over the three spots of blood, and teased the needle out of her fingers. She was helpless to resist. Only his strong arm held her up.

"Quickly, Brother Petrus!"

A movement, an arm sweeping past her face, and a sweet smelling fragrance wafted into her nostrils. She came alert to see a smoky mist dimming her sight through which she saw all those sleeping and heard an uncanny hush drawn over the palace grounds as though every living creature had been muzzled and shod in wool.

His eyes were so very blue that she thought she should drown in them. "I am taking Princess Blessing. You have now a choice. You may come with me, to attend her, or you may stay behind."

Her mouth worked, but she got no words out.

He smiled sadly.

Oh, that smile. She might die hoping for another taste of that smile. She had never seen a man as beautiful as he was.

"What is your name?"

"Anna, Your Grace," she whispered.

"Anna," he said, making music of her name. "Carry the princess. We must make haste."

"If I won't, Your Grace? If I refuse to go?"

"Then a more faithful servant will carry her," he said in the most kindly voice imaginable, and it chilled her to hear it, because he did not raise his voice or look angry. He was no Bulkezu, to howl and rage. He did not look like a man who had just cut the throat of a defenseless young woman. "And you will wake later, hoping she is well cared for but never knowing if she will be."

Weeping, she gathered up Blessing, although the girl had grown enough to weigh heavily in her arms. It took all her courage to look at him again, and all her courage to speak words he might not want to hear. "There are some things we need, Your Grace—"

"There is nothing you shall need that has not already been prepared. We have taken everything from this town that we want. Brother Petrus, let us go swiftly, as you advise."

"Yes, Lord Hugh."

So they went, leaving the chamber and the dead girl and her sleeping companions behind. Below, four soldiers waited; they also wore amulets. Lord Jonas and Odei sprawled on the floor among a scattering of dice. Brother Heribert followed like a dog, hesitant, twitchy, but determined.

"Unchain the Eagle," said Lord Hugh to two of the soldiers. "Make sure there is blood on his hands, and the knife in his possession. Then meet us at the appointed place."

In the barracks below soldiers slept, draped over benches or snoring on pallets. Two sat on either side of the door, slumped against the stone wall. One had his mouth open, and the way drool trickled out scared her.

Their feet crunched on gravel as they crossed along a wing of the palace, moving swiftly. Guards slept on benches and on paving stones. One had an arm slung somewhat around a pillar as though embracing it. In the courtyard facing the great hall a dozen servants had dropped platters of food and flagons of drink. A pair of dogs had fallen down asleep in the act of filching a fine haunch of beef intended for the queen's table. From the hall itself, glimpsed through open doors, came only silence. One of the soldiers grabbed a pair of plump roasted chickens and tied them up into a handkerchief which he fastened to his belt. The scent of all that good, warm food made Anna's stomach grumble, and she hated herself for feeling a hunger that Lady Elene would never again know. Blessing stirred, whimpering, but did not wake.

Five more soldiers waited by the barracks, holding the reins of fourteen horses, four of them laden with packs. Every wakeful creature there wore an amulet around its neck like to the one Anna wore. By the horses, Lord Hugh nodded at Brother Petrus.

"All the rest is done as I commanded?"

"It is all arranged, Lord Hugh. All will be done as you have ordered. Yet I am not sure, my lord. Was there some other fate that you intend for Lord Berthold? Villam's son is tainted with Villam's treachery in plotting against Emperor Henry, may he rest at peace in the Chamber of Light."

"Villam's son means nothing, although there is, I think, some mystery regarding his disappearance and reappearance. Leave him as he is. Find out his secret, if you can. He may trust you if you befriend him after we are gone."

Petrus hesitated.

"Go on, Brother. You must not fear to speak freely to me."

"Why the young lady, Your Grace? She was beautiful. Proud, it's true, but lovely. It's like trampling a flower in bloom."

"Some flowers will be trampled when an army marches to lift a siege, Brother. No one rejoices in destruction, yet at times it is the only way. Her grandmother taught her things she must not be allowed to use. We cannot take the chance. I will do penance for the deed."

"Yes, Your Grace. Still . . . if you think her a risk, why leave alive the old man?"

"He is too weak and ignorant to threaten us. He'll serve us by diverting suspicion. No doubt her death was more merciful than his will be."

"Yes, Your Grace."

"Do not douse the sleeping fire until the lights on the hill have vanished. Do as you have been instructed. Let no one chance upon you in the tombs. All depends on timing and where you place the decoy."

"I will not fail you, Lord Hugh."

"I trust not. Afterward, await my return."

"Yes, Lord Hugh. God go with you, Lord Hugh."

The angel's smile had something of irony in it. "So we may hope."

He beckoned. A soldier took Blessing out of Anna's arms and lifted her up to one of his companions, already mounted. Another took Anna up behind him. The rest made ready, and they rode out of the palace by the spies' gate, a triple-guarded gate set into the palace's outer wall that led to an escarpment and a steep trail carved into the northeastern face of the hill on which the town of Novomo had been built. Shale littered the hillside. They picked their way down. None spoke; only the rattle of rock broke the silence.

How far did the spell extend? Had he cast his web of sorcery across the entire town?

How could any person be so beautiful and so wicked?

At the base of the hill they stopped beside a vineyard, which lay quiet under the late afternoon sky. Nothing stirred except a single honeybee, searching for nectar.

"Brother Heribert," said Lord Hugh. "Take such provisions as you can carry. Walk north, over St. Barnaria's Pass. Do you know the way?"

"The way we walked when we came south?"

"Rumor has it you came down from the mountains. Return there, and follow the path north into Wendar."

"Who will guide me?"

"You must guide yourself. You seek Sanglant, who calls himself regnant. When last I saw him, he was at Quedlinhame. Seek him, and do what you must."

Without answering, the cleric collected a sack of provisions offered to him by one of the soldiers. He paused beside Blessing's limp body to touch her knee, then went on his way through the vineyards, soon lost to view. The rest circled south to join the main road leading out of town. Twice Anna saw folk in the distance, laborers or farmers about their tasks. Once she saw a wagon at rest behind a tree, but she saw no sign of its occupant, only a mule with its head down, cropping grass. Twice she heard a dog bark. A large party had passed this way before them; she saw their dust ahead on the road, moving south.

As dusk lowered, they paused beside a chalky path that split off from the main road and climbed a nearby hill. Here they paused.

"Two riding up behind," said the guardsman who rode as rear guard. "That'll be Liudbold and Theodore. They're late coming."

"We'll wait here," said Hugh, and soon enough the two soldiers who had been left behind at the tower reached them.

"Theodore. Liudbold." Hugh looked at them each in turn. "What is your report? I expected you sooner."

"Begging your pardon, my lord," said the one addressed as Theodore. "It were trickier than we thought. The old man had life in him. He was wakeful and struggling, and he got a fist in on Liudbold's jaw here."

Some of the other soldiers coughed and snickered as Liudbold touched a hand to the bruise forming on his face, but they fell silent when Hugh raised a hand.

"Yes, he fought the spell, with some success. That shouldn't surprise me, I suppose. What did you do?"

"Well, at first we thought of tying him up, but then we recalled that he was meant to look as if he'd freed himself. So we knocked him cold, hauled him upstairs, then rolled him in the blood and left him with the knife in his hand."

"It will do," Lord Hugh said kindly. "You kept your heads about you. Well done."

Such praise would melt stone! The soldiers murmured, but Lord Hugh turned his horse onto the path and led the others away from the road. Behind, the pair of men riding in the rear guard swept their path to hide their tracks. Ahead, tall figures awaited them, stones arranged in a circle.

She said nothing, but by asking no questions caused Lord Hugh to notice her silence.

"How came you to Novomo, Anna? How did Princess Blessing and her party reach Aosta, and why? Where did you come from? How came you to lose her father and mother?"

She shrugged, pretending ignorance, as he studied her. She was sick at heart. It seemed beneath that mild gaze that he saw everything and knew everything.

"My lord presbyter," said one of the soldiers, a man with a scar on his chin. "I can make her talk, if that's what you're wishing."

He turned away. "Think nothing of it, John. I already know much of the tale. When I have need of the rest, I'll get it."

"I just don't like to see you treated with such disrespect, my lord presbyter. It gripes me to think of the queen refusing to see you, after all you done for her and the common folk in Darre."

"The queen is grieved by the loss of her daughter. It is to be expected."

"Only you would be so forgiving, my lord."

The other soldiers murmured agreement.

"Like that cleric you released to walk north. I think that one has lost his wits!"

Hugh nodded without smiling. "And so he has, poor soul."

They came up to a flat space of ground, bare of vegetation, situated in front of the standing stones.

"Dismount quickly, all except the one with the servant and you, Frigo," said Hugh, gesturing toward the man who carried Blessing. "Move when I give the command. Do not hesitate."

Blessing slept. Anna could not go to her, sitting as she was in the grasp of a man much bigger and stronger than she was, but she saw that Blessing wore about her neck an amulet as well, only this one was woven with sprigs of lavender and a twisted knot that looked ready to strangle any unsuspecting neck caught in its grasp. It looked different than all the others.

Hugh gave his reins to one of the men. He placed his feet on a circle of pale ground, white with dust, and drew from his sleeve a strange golden implement like a wheel embedded within a wheel. This he raised to sight along the horizon. Then he turned to gaze toward Novomo, hazy in the fading light.

"We must be ready," he said to his soldiers. "Make sure the supplies I mentioned are at hand. Her devils can follow us no matter how far we travel, so when I speak, you must obey exactly as I say."

They murmured assent.

Anna laughed. "We can't go!" she crowed. "You can't weave a spell from the heavens when it is cloudy! You're trapped here!"

He looked back at her. She clapped a hand over her mouth. Was that a knife, winking in the hand of one of the soldiers?

"Wise, after all," said Lord Hugh. "But I possess an instrument that tells me where every star will rise and set. The music of the spheres reaches through the clouds. It is only our weak eyesight that stymies us for, unlike the angels and daimones, we cannot see past that which blinds. With this instrument, I do not have to see what I have already measured in order to know it is there. I can weave even when clouds shroud the heavens. I can weave even in daylight, although I must not let my enemies guess that I can do so."

As night fell, he wove, drawing light out of the heavens although no stars shone where any human eye could see. He wove an archway of light and, at his command—for who would refuse him?—they walked through it into another place.

XIV
THE GUIVRE'S STARE

1

TO walk from Osna village to Lavas Holding was normally a journey of five or six days. Years ago, when Alain had walked with Chatelaine Dhuoda's company, the trip had taken fifteen days because she had stopped in every village and steading along the way to accept taxes and rents or the service of some of the young people in the village. Now, although they stopped only at night for shelter, the roads had taken so much damage in last autumn's storm that they were ten days traveling. Tangles of fallen trees barred the track. In two places streams had changed course and cut a channel right through the beaten path where wagons once rolled.

"God help us," said the chatelaine in the late afternoon on the seventh day. She was the only one mounted. The rest walked. "What's that?"

Alain went forward with five of the men at arms to discover a wagon toppled onto its side. The remains of several people lay scattered across the roadway and into the woodland on either side, disturbed by animals.

"How long have they lain here, are you thinking?" asked one of the lads, a fellow called "Fetch" by his comrades.

Mostly bone was all that was left of them, with bits of hair and patches of woven tunic ground into the earth and a leather vest half buried beneath dirt and leaf litter. It was impossible to tell how many had died here or how far wolves and foxes had dragged pieces of corpse.

"Months." Alain wrenched loose an arrow fixed into the spokes of one of the wheels. "Bandits. Look at this fletching."

The soldiers were young men, no one he knew from his time as Lavastine's heir, although it seemed strange to him that so many new milites would have come into service in such a short time. They were all lads from villages owing allegiance to Lady Aldegund's family, and had a lilting curl to their "r's" when they spoke. They looked nervous as they scanned the trees and open clearings.

One shrieked. "What's that? What's that?"

It was only a white skull, caught in brambles, staring out at them.

"Go get it, Fetch," said the eldest.

"I won't. It might be cursed!"

"Have we a shovel or anything to dig with?" asked Alain. "Best we dig what grave we can and let these poor dead rest. It's all we can do." He looked at each of his companions in turn and shook his head. "Come now. Their souls have ascended to the Chamber of Light. They can't hurt you. If it were your own brother lying here, wouldn't you want him laid to rest so that animals would stop chewing on his bones?"

They had in their party only one shovel, but another man had an antler horn he used as a pick and the rest sharpened stout sticks and by this means and some with their bare hands they dug swiftly and deep. Blanche watched silently, sucking her thumb, and it was she who was first to help pick up bones that had been dragged away into the bushes and she who brought the skull and laid it on the heap collected in the pit. She wiped her hand on her skirt and sighed.

"Will I be just bones like that one day?" she asked.

"The part of you which is flesh will die, it's true, and rot away to bone, but see how white and strong bone is. It's to remind us of the strength of our souls, which lie hidden beneath flesh as well."

She frowned at him but said nothing more. The chatelaine's cleric said a prayer over the dead, and they filled in the hole. One of the lads shook out the leather vest and rolled it up; the leather only needed a bit of cleaning and oiling to restore it and there was no sense in letting such good leather go to waste.

"It's getting late," said Alain to the chatelaine. "We'd best think of camping for the night."

"I don't like to camp in a place of death," she said. "We'll go on a way."

"Think you there are bandits still lurking?" Fetch asked Alain as they walked along at the front of the group.

"There might be."

A branch snapped in the trees, and all the milites flinched and spun to look, only to see a doe spring away into the forest. They laughed and called each other cowards but hurried forward anyway to where the woodland dropped back into an open countryside marked by low, marshy ground and thickets of dense brush where the earth rose into hillocks. The road had been raised to cross this swamp, and it was out on the road they found themselves at dusk with nothing but mosquitoes and gnats and marsh flies for company.

"Light fires," said the chatelaine. "We can see anyone coming from either side if thieves have a wish to attack us. The smoke will drive off the bugs."

It was difficult to find dry wood, but enough was found that they breathed in smoke half the night and were bitten up anyway. The wind came steady out of the northeast. Late, very late, Alain woke and, startled, found himself staring up at the heavens. Blanche snored softly beside him.

Stars winked, and then were covered again by cloud.

"Ah!" he said, although he hadn't meant to speak.

"Do you see?"

"I pray you, Chatelaine. Can you not sleep?"

"I cannot sleep, my lord. But I saw there a glimpse of hope. God smile on my journey. It is right that I sought you out. For months we have seen no sign of the sky. But now . . . now I have."

"Any spell must ease in time."

"You persist in believing that these clouds are the residue of a vast spell woven by human hands?"

"I know they are."

"Not God's displeasure?"

"It is true that some evils fall upon us without warning or cause. Yet so many of the evils that plague us we bring about by our own actions. Why should we blame God? Surely God weep to see their children act against what is natural and right. So the blessed Daisan would say. So Count Lavastine said. We aren't made guilty by those things that lie outside our power, but we aren't justified by them either. Evil is the work of the Enemy. It is easier to do what is right."

"Think you so, my lord? It seems to me that humankind have in them a creeping, sniggering impulse to do what is wrong."

"Yet none say it is right. Those who do wrong make excuses and tell stories to excuse themselves or even blame their folly on God, but their hearts are not free of guilt. That guilt drives a man to do worse things, out of pain and fear. It is a hard road to walk and more difficult still to turn back once you've begun the journey."

She chuckled scornfully. "Many folk say they are doing right and believe it. The Enemy blinds them."

"They blind themselves."

"Who is to say that the wicked don't flourish and the innocent fall by the wayside? Where is God's justice when it is needed?"

He peered at her, but it was difficult to make out her face with the cloud cover cast again over the heavens. "It is in our hands, Mistress Dhuoda. We have the liberty to choose our own actions."

"What if we choose wrong?"

He sighed, thinking of Adica. The wind sighed, echoing his breathing. Reeds rustled out in the marsh. A man rolled over, making a scraping noise against the ground as he turned in his sleep. Blanche snorted, seemed about to rouse, and settled back into slumber.

"Why didn't God fashion us so we could do only what is right, and never what is sinful?" she continued.

"Then we would be no different than the tools we ourselves carry. If we did what is right, we would receive no merit from it, not if we had no choice. We would be slaves, not human beings."

"It might be better so," she murmured.

"Do you think so?"

"Sometimes I do," she said, and after that nothing more.

At length he fell asleep.

2

THEY came to Lavas Holding on St. Abraames' Day. From a distance, the settlement looked little different than the place he had first seen seven years ago—or was it eight? It was difficult to keep track.

The high timber palisade surrounded the count's fortress with its wooden hall and stone bailey. Beyond the wall the village spilled down a leisurely slope to the banks of the river. Now, however, a fosse and earthen embankment circled the village and the innermost fields, orchards, and pasturage, cut in two spots by the course of the river. Many of the locals looked familiar to Alain, but all of the men at arms were new and by the sound of their words not Lavas born and bred but from farther east.

"Where is Sergeant Fell?" Alain asked the chatelaine as folk pressed close to stare.

"He was given leave to retire back to his home village, with no more than ten sceattas for all his years of service. And likewise, the others, with little enough or nothing, turned off because Lord Geoffrey feels safer with milites brought from his wife's kin's lands to protect him. It's brought grumbling, and rightly so."

"Who is this, Mistress Dhuoda?" demanded one of the soldiers, coming out of the hall with a spear in one hand and a mug of ale in the other.

"Captain, I pray you, where is Lord Geoffrey?"

"He's ridden out with the lady's brother, to take a look at a bull."

"The one belonging to Master Smith of Ferhold? He's already said he won't part with that one for any amount of sceattas."

"He'll part with it," said the captain with a sneer, "if Lord Geoffrey wants to add it to his herd. Who's this?" He squinted as if against bright sun and pointed toward Alain with his spear.

Servants edged closer to whisper and stare. There was Cook, looking thinner and older, and an astounded Master Rodlin with a pair of sleek whippets at his heel. The whippets lowered their heads, whining, and cowered behind the stable master, but Sorrow and Rage sat peaceably with their faithful gazes turned on Alain, waiting to see what he wanted them to do.

"Those are big dogs," added the captain, and in his look and in the suppressed hiss of murmured voices there was a tense air as of a storm brewing.

Alain fixed his gaze on Cook and, taking Blanche's hand, led the girl over to the old woman.

"My lord," Cook murmured, with a glance toward the suspicious captain. Her hands were chapped and dappled with age marks, and her left hand had a kind of palsy, but her eye was still keen.

"I pray you, Cook," he said quietly, "do not call me by a title that does not belong to me. I have a favor to ask of you."

She nodded, dumbstruck. The captain coughed and looked around to mark the position of his soldiers, but only five or six were in view, loitering by the stables or at the corner of the hall.

"Keep watch on this child for me, if you will. She is the daughter of a man I called brother."

Cook regarded him, nodded, and extended a hand.

"Go on, Blanche. Do as I say."

She bit her lip, she looked up at him with a frown, but she placed her grimy hand in Cook's aged one without protest.

"I pray you, Lord Alain," said Dhuoda, coming up behind him. "We must not stand here in the courtyard like suppliants, else he'll take action." She indicated the restless captain.

"I'll wait in the church."

"Nay, my lord! You'll wait in the lord's audience chamber. It would be fitting!"

"I pray you, Mistress Dhuoda," he said in a softer voice. "Make no trouble for the innocent souls standing here around. I prefer to wait in the church, if you don't mind it. I wish to pray beside the count's bier."

"Of course!" She flushed red. "Of course, my lord!"

"Who is this man?" demanded the captain, stepping off the porch that fronted the hall. "He's not welcome here!"

Somehow or other the servants got moving right away and impeded his path, leaving Alain and Dhuoda to walk in solitude out to the stone church set apart from the other buildings beyond the palisade.

"What does Lord Geoffrey fear?" asked Alain, indicating the new earthworks.

"He fears justice, my lord. He fears Lady Sabella."

"Why should he fear her? Is she not in the custody of Biscop Constance in Autun?"

"Not for many years, my lord. Lady Sabella usurped her old seat. She holds Biscop Constance prisoner and rules Arconia again. Lord Geoffrey offered his allegiance to Biscop Constance, but it's likely the noble biscop cannot help us. There are bandits roaming the lands. Have you not heard of our troubles?"

"What particular injuries has Lavas Holding sustained?"

"Ravnholt Manor was burned to the ground last autumn a few weeks after the great storm. Eight people were murdered, and perhaps more, because it was hard to discover remains within the ruins of the hall. A dozen or more we found later hiding in the woods, but four girls were never accounted for although witnesses had seen them alive and running from the conflagration. They were not little ones but youths, and one recently wed. You will have no doubt about what the bandits wanted with them, poor things."

"Did no one seek them out? What happened to the bandits?"

"There was a single skirmish, my lord, two days later. Then the bandits vanished, or so Lord Geoffrey's scouts said. I don't know the truth of it."

"Do you not believe them?"

She shrugged, reluctant to say more. After the silence grew thick, she went on. "The girls who were taken were only servants' daughters. Two were slaves—their parents had sold them into service to discharge the debts they owed Ravnholt's steward."

"Did Ravnholt's steward not seek to recover those lost souls?"

"The steward was killed in the raid."

"Who is in charge there now?"

Her dark look matched the dreary day and the ominous swell of wind in distant trees. "Lord Geoffrey left the land fallow. Said he'd see to it later. Yet we've desperate need of planting. Surely you know . . . it's hard to think of planting with frosts still coming hard every night. There is a blight in the apple trees here and eastward. There may be no apple crop at all this year. In the south a black rot has gotten into the rye . . ." She looked sideways at him, blushing again. "Yet you must know, for that's where you were found, wasn't it? In the south, by a mill."

"Mad, so they tell me," he said as they came up to the church and its narrow porch. He stepped into the shadow and turned to look at her, who stood yet in the muted daylight.

"Not mad," she said, but she didn't mean it. "You had the dancing sickness, my lord."

"And much else besides, I am thinking. I sustained an injury to my head. For a long while I wandered without my faithful hounds. I was lost and blind." He snapped his fingers, and the hounds waggled up to him and licked his hands. He patted them affectionately and rubbed his knuckles into their great heads, just how they liked it, and scratched them behind their ears.

She wrung her hands together, gaze fixed on the dirt. "Now you are come back to us, my lord."

"No," he said kindly. "I am only passing through. I will not stay."

She wept silently, nothing more than tears running down her cheeks.

"Do not despair," he said. "The one you seek will come."

He went inside into the gloomy nave, so shadowed that he had to stop four steps in and stand there for a while to let his eyes adjust. The hounds panted beside him.

"Come," he said at last.

They walked forward to the bier set halfway along the nave, flanked by benches. Rage and Sorrow sat at the foot of the bier, below Terror, and Alain knelt at Lavastine's right hand. The statue had been "dressed" in a long white linen shift overlaid with a wool tunic dyed to the blue that had always been Lavastine's preferred color. The cloth looked well brushed, though a little dusty. An embroidered border of leaping black hounds encircled half the hem, the kind of painstaking work that revealed the hand of an experienced needleworker. He wondered if the embroidery was work begun recently and as yet unfinished or if some woman's heartfelt task had been interrupted. Lavastine's feet were vulnerably bare, and his sharp features were as familiar as ever, with his beard neat and trim and eyes shut. No doubt folk new to the holding believed this a masterful piece of stone carving. Who would believe this was the man himself?

Bowing his head, Alain rested his brow against that cool cheek.

"I pray you," he whispered, "forgive me for the lie. I gave it up in order to enter the land of the meadow flowers, but now I am come home to this Earth and I must confess it to you. I said Tallia was pregnant only to spare you heartbreak, knowing you were slipping away. I do not regret sparing you pain on your deathbed. I regret only that I failed in the one task you set me. Still, it was not to be. God made it so. They knew I was not your rightful heir. If Tallia had gotten pregnant, then the threads would have tangled even more. No good rule can be based on a lie. And, God help me, Father, had Tallia not betrayed me, I would never have met Adica. I'm sorry I could not be the son you desired, but that does not change the love I cherish for you."

When he ceased speaking, a quiet so profound settled into the church that he thought he could hear the earth's slow respiration, the breath of stone. Pale daylight gleamed on the altar and the golden vessel and the *Book of Verses*, left lying open as if the deacon had been interrupted in the midst of her prayers. Behind him lay the side chapel dedicated to St. Lavrentius, who had died before the time of the Emperor Taillefer while bringing the Circle of Unity to the Varrish tribes.

It is here, he thought, that it began. He had met the Lady of Battles on the Dragonback Ridge, but he wondered now whether that was coincidence or fate or free will? Was it in her nature to ride that path when a storm blew in off the sea? Had it only been accident that they had converged there? Or had she ridden that way on purpose, knowing she would meet him and in such an hour when he would have no choice but to save those he loved by pledging himself to her cause?

It was here, in this shadowed nave, that the answer lay. Beneath him lay the crypt where the counts of Lavas slumbered in death, although their souls had surely ascended to the Chamber of Light. Here in the aisle of the nave rested the last of the line of the elder Charles.

What had he been hiding?

Sorrow whoofed softly, and in answer Alain heard the skittering of mice near St. Lavrentius' altar as they scattered into their hidey-holes. Once he and Lackling had knelt in that chapel at this very same time of year; Lackling had wept when one trusting little creature had crept into his hand and let him stroke its soft coat. Now, all rustling and scratching ceased.

The door opened, and a man—face shadowed by the daylight behind him—entered alone.

"You are come," the man said, more in sadness than in anger, yet there was anger as well, throttled by the stink of fear. The door closed behind him, and he halted. "Take it! Take it! It has rotted in my hands!"

"I pray you, Lord Geoffrey. Sit, if you will. I have not come here to take anything from you that is yours by right."

Geoffrey choked down a sob of fury, but he did not move. "You have outwitted me at every turn! Was it nothing but a dumb show that you turned up here babbling and dancing? Did you mean to tempt me to do what I did, and thus discredit myself by making me seem a cruel and bitter man? By making me seem afraid of you?"

"Are you afraid?"

"I am always afraid!" he roared. The hounds barked, first Sorrow and then Rage, and he took a step back. "They still guard you, then, those beasts."

"Sorrow and Rage are my faithful companions."

"What do you want? Why have you come back?"

"I came because Chatelaine Dhuoda asked me to return to Lavas Holding with her. Before that, I lived quietly over the winter by

Osna Sound, recovering from the injuries that plagued me and the wound in my heart."

"Dhuoda is a traitor!"

"Is she?"

"No! No!" He began to pace along the entryway, falling out of sight behind a square pillar only to reappear at the wall, where he spun and strode back the other way. The walls trapped him. He could only turn, and turn again. "She told me straight out she meant to go. She is my kinswoman. She has the right to question me."

He halted, facing the aisle. His face was pale and anguished, his hands clenched.

"Was Lavastine your father?" His voice scraped out the question. He bowed his head an instant, then raised it defiantly.

Rage turned to face him but did not otherwise move. Sorrow remained seated, snuffling at Terror's stone hindquarters as if seeking a scent.

Alain rose as well. He kept one hand on Lavastine's quiet hand, feeling the swell and hollow of knuckles and the intricate ridge of a petrified ring caught forever on the right forefinger. The gem, too, had gone to stone. He could not recall what color it had been.

Geoffrey went on in an enraged, triumphant rush. "Cook said your mother traded her body for food. They called her 'Rose' for her beauty. She was beautiful enough that every man desired her. Cook said any man who lived here and was old enough to thrust his bucket into her well could have been your father, for many did. She turned no one away. All but Lavastine. He wouldn't take what other men had used. He never slept with her, not for want of her trying. That's what Cook told me. She kept silence when my cousin raised you up for fear of offending him. For fear he'd have her silenced!"

He was panting like a man who had been running.

"What do you say to that?" he finished.

"In truth," Alain said, "I believe that the halfwit boy Lackling was Lavastine's bastard son."

Geoffrey hissed out his breath but made no retort.

"I do not believe I was Lavastine's son by the laws that rule succession, those of blood. Yet I called him 'Father' and he called me 'Son.' I cannot tell you now that those words meant nothing."

"They mean nothing legal!"

"What they mean matters only to me, and mattered to him. That is all."

"What do you want, damn you?"

"Let me see you," said Alain.

After a hesitation, Geoffrey came forward. In the filtering of light that illuminated the Hearth, Alain could see the other man's features. Geoffrey was changed. He had once looked far younger and more carefree, a good enough looking man, but now his face was scored with lines and fear haunted his gaze. His mouth furrowed his face in a frown that seemed set there, as in stone. Despair marked his forehead in a dozen deep wrinkles.

"You are troubled, Lord Geoffrey."

"This county is troubled! One thing after the next! I even rode east—but there was no help for it! Laws are silent in the presence of arms, so the church mothers say. Those who ought to rule are set aside, and those who rule turn their gaze away from the plagues that beset us, seeking only their own advancement and enrichment and pleasure."

He shook a fist although not, it seemed, at Alain, but rather at Fate, or at God, or at some unknown individual whom Alain could not see and did not know. Rage growled, and Geoffrey lowered his hand quickly to his side but did not unclench it.

"So I am served, a taste of the supper I served to you! Have you come to gloat?"

"I am here for another reason," Alain said, smiling faintly, because he knew pain lifted that smile as well as an appreciation of its irony. "Strange that it took me so long and over such a road to see it. I pray you, Lord Geoffrey, sit down."

"I will not!"

Alain sighed. Where his hand lay on Lavastine's, he had a wild and momentary illusion that the dead count's stone skin warmed; he breathed, in that instant, the pulse of another, as slow as the pulse of the earth but no less steady. Down, deep in the earth, the rivers of fire that burn in the heart of the mortal world flow on their mighty course, and behind them, so distant that it is like reaching to touch the stars, dwells an old intelligence, weighty but not dim. Down he fell, remembering the touch of those ancient minds on that day when the bandits had brought him to Father Benignus' foul camp. That day Alain had killed Father Benignus by revealing to his followers that he was nothing but a shell that sustained its own life by feeding on the souls of those he had murdered.

Only his skeleton remained, darkening where sunlight soaked into bone. The stench of putrefaction faded as anger boiled up and men

snarled and shouted, closing in. Rage leaped, growling furiously. A
sharp blow cracked into the side of his head.

Gasping, he came up for air and found himself after all in the silence of the church, with Geoffrey standing stiff and arrogant before
him and the hounds quiescent, not moving at all, ears down.

He steadied himself on Lavastine's cold arm. "One boon I ask you,
Lord Geoffrey."

"What is that?"

"I have brought a child with me, a girl seven or eight years of age.
She is the eldest child of one I once called 'brother,' a good man who
has now a wife and child. Although he was betrothed to the girl's
mother, they never wed. Let her serve, I pray you, in your retinue.
Honor her as the granddaughter of one of your faithful householders in Osna Sound. Treat her well. Let her serve Chatelaine Dhuoda.
If she has the wit to learn to mark accounts and learn to write and
read, let her do so. If she has not such wit, let her serve in the
kitchens under Cook's tutelage."

For a while Geoffrey said nothing. At last, as if puzzled, he
scratched his beard. "What means this girl to you? Why do you
bring her here?"

"Nothing good will come of leaving her where she was. Best she
make a new start, if she can."

"That's all? Is she pretty? Is she meant to tempt me, or some other
man? Is she your by-blow, meant to twist my daughter's heart and
loyalty if she grows up beside her?"

"None of these things. A tree will grow twisted if the wind rakes
it incessantly. Better she grow true, if she can. I hope it may be possible for her to do so here at Lavas, away from an otherwise good
family that does not like her. That is all."

"You always had a care for the unfortunate!"

"Do not mock the unfortunate, Lord Geoffrey. They suffer more
than the rest of us do."

"For their sins!"

"Do you think so? Rather they suffer for our sins. Is it not a sin
to look the other way when you might extend a hand to one who is
drowning? Is it not a sin to eat two loaves of bread when you might
share one with those who are starving? Suffering is the task God set
us. We choose whether to take action or turn away. Thus are we
judged."

Geoffrey broke down and wept. "It is all gone wrong! My daughter—lamed in a fall from her pony! My dear wife dead in childbirth days after the terrible storm. Our sons held as hostages in Autun. Bandits afflict the forest and prey on the farmers. Plague eats at our borders. Hoof rot strikes down our sheep and cattle. All the birds are fled as if we live in a desert. And more besides. Far more! Too much to tell! How have I offended God?"

"You know that answer better than I do, Lord Geoffrey. Better to ask what you can do to set things right. Do you believe that your daughter is the rightful heir to Lavas County?"

"There is no other that I know of."

"If one such should appear, would you offer your loyalty to that one?"

"There cannot be another claimant! Count Lavastina had but two sons, Charles and, eighteen years later, my grandfather, the first Geoffrey. There my cousin lies." He pointed at the bier. "He is the last of the elder lineage. I am the only surviving descendant of the younger. Who else could there be?"

"Have you never wondered how the elder Charles acquired his fearsome hounds?"

Geoffrey shrugged.

"I do not know the answer," continued Alain, "but I wonder. Fear left me to seek another. And there was one person the hounds feared. Is there a connection between them?"

"You speak in riddles to torment me!"

"I pray you, forgive me. Something was set wrong long ago, in Lavas County. If we set it right, then it may be like a rock thrown into a still pool. Its ripples may spread to wash over the entire pond."

"These are mysteries! Conjecture! If you do not claim Lavas County, then what matters it to you who does?"

"Justice matters."

Geoffrey shrugged impatiently. "There is something more to this! Who is your father?"

Alain shook his head, distracted from his thoughts and, in truth, a little annoyed, but he let the irritation go. "My father? Henri of Osna is my father. As is Count Lavastine. As might be the shade of the lost prince in the ruins up on the hill. As might be the man who was also my grandfather, if he shared his own daughter. Or another man never named and never known. This is the truth." He lifted his hand from Lavastine's arm and stepped forward to stand between the hounds, so close to Geoffrey that he might reach out to touch him. "My path was marked the day the Lady of Battles challenged me. I know to whom I owe a son's love. Beyond that, I care not because it matters not."

"It makes no sense to me. You say you do not wish to contest my authority as regent for my daughter, or her claim, unless one comes who has a better claim than ours to the county of Lavas. You say that, knowing there are no other surviving descendants of the elder Charles and the first Geoffrey."

"I have no reason to suppose there are descendants of those men, besides yourself and your daughter and young sons."

"Then how—? What—? You are saying you believe there is another surviving descendant of my great great grandmother, Count Lavastina. She had no surviving siblings, no nieces or nephews to contest the elder Charles' portion. The family lineage is written carefully by the Lavas clerics, but there is no record of it!" He grinned, the gesture more rictus than smile.

"If it could be proved that a rightful claimant existed, would you step aside?"

"My daughter inherits nothing except Lavas County."

"If it could be proved that there exists a person whose claim supersedes hers, would you withdraw her claim?"

Geoffrey gestured recklessly, a broad swipe. Sorrow barked at the abrupt movement but at a word from Alain held still. "Why not? You're a fool to speak so! If you'll give your pledge to make no claim yourself, to reject the claim Lavastine made on your behalf, then I'll pledge in my turn to accept that claim which supersedes that of my daughter. But it must withstand scrutiny! Biscop Constance herself, or a council of church folk with equal authority, must certify the truth of the claim. You can't pass off some girl—is that it? Is that the story of the child you want to leave here?"

"No. She is the unwanted granddaughter of a householder from Osna Sound, nothing more."

"Very well, then! We'll make these pledges publicly and have them written down. You'll depart, and leave me and my daughter in peace!"

Alain smiled sadly. "Beware of making such a pledge lightly, Lord Geoffrey, and only because you believe it will not turn around to bite you."

"I just want you gone before the sun sets!"

"So be it."

3

GEOFFREY had a guard waiting outside, and these dozen sullen men escorted them back to the hall with Mistress Dhuoda. The chatelaine twisted her hands fretfully as they walked.

"Sit here until the folk hereabouts can be assembled, enough to swear to what they see and hear," said Geoffrey brusquely once they had come into the hall. He took his captain aside and gave him orders, and sent Dhuoda to fetch his daughter from the upper rooms.

Alain sat on a bench in the corner of the hall. The hounds lay down at his feet. He sat there so quietly that after a while, when most of the guards went out to round up an assembly, it seemed they had forgotten him. On this cold spring afternoon no one used the hall. It appeared, by the arrangement of tables, that no feast had entertained the rafters for a good long time. The high table was pushed up against the wall of the dais; neither chairs nor benches rested beside it. A pair of tables and benches sat end to end by the wide hearth, where a fire burned, although it did not warm the corner where he waited. In the good days, under Lavastine, fully four or five score people might crowd into the hall for a grand feast. Now it appeared that a dozen ate by the fire, perhaps on warmer days, and that otherwise folk ate in their own chambers or houses, or in the barracks and kitchen. The floor was recently swept clean except for a spattering of bird droppings just to the left of where the entrance doors opened wide to the porch.

Alain gazed at the rafters by the door. A pair of swallows had been used to build their nest there, tolerated because swallows were thought to bring good luck, but he saw no activity.

Voices buzzed from outside, but no one came in past the two guards standing on the long porch, whose backs he could see. Once, long ago, he had sat in the high seat and presided over Lavas county, her lands and her people. He did not regret what he had lost. Those days seemed like a dream, something glimpsed but never really held. Once Tallia had sat beside him as his wife. How he had loved her! Yet what had he loved, truly? A dream. A wish. An illusion. She was not the person he had made her to be in his mind. Perhaps we can only be betrayed where we have allowed ourselves to be blinded. If we know a man is evil or untrustworthy, then we cannot be surprised if he acts dishonestly or in a way that harms others. If we see clearly, we cannot be surprised.

It was easy now to recall those days and see Tallia for what she truly was: weak in spirit, petty, frightened, cruel in a small-minded way, and intent on getting her own way, without regard to others. The broken vessel, Hathumod had called her, too fragile to hold the weight of the heresy she claimed with the authority of one who has witnessed. She had lied about the nail, but in fact when he thought back through his sad marriage, she had not lied about wanting to marry him. Her uncle had forced her to marry. She had stated openly from the beginning that she prayed every day and every night for a chaste marriage and perpetual virginity.

He had wanted to believe otherwise so badly that in the end he had betrayed Lavastine by lying to a man he respected and loved. Ah, well. It was done and could not be undone.

Dust filtered down around him. Sorrow's tail thumped on the floor. A horse neighed outside, challenging another. A door creaked behind him, being opened. He wondered if he had dreamed that second betrayal, the one at the mines. Those months were as a puzzle to him, seen in glimpses all hacked into parts that could not be sewn back into a complete tapestry.

Tallia had been pregnant, and she had ordered her steward to cast him into the pit because she had recognized him and feared he would recognize her and harm her. Which betrayal burned worst? That she had tried to have him killed, or that she had given another man the thing she had refused to him?

Desire is a fiend that devours its victims while they still live and breathe.

And still. What she had refused him, Adica had offered freely and with the sweetness of meadow flowers. Who could say which woman valued herself more highly? The one who gave that which was precious to her, or the one who lied to hold it all to herself?

"I pray you, I beg your pardon, my lord. Forgive me."

He almost overset the bench because he was so startled by the familiar voice. The hounds remained still. Rage's tail thumped once. Cook bent into an awkward bow before him. Arthritis stiffened her back.

He wiped his forehead, shook his head to cast off his thoughts, and took her hand as he stood. "Do not bow, Cook. I pray you. Ah! Here is Blanche!"

The girl squeezed up against him, hugging his side.

"I must speak before the rest come in," Cook continued, wheezing. "They're holding them all outside. I snuck in the back way."

"Sit, I pray you."

"It's easier for me to stand with my aching bones, my lord. Let me just say my piece, and I won't bother you more."

"Go on."

She had lost several teeth, which made her cheeks sunken, but her gaze remained firm and intelligent. "I beg your pardon, my lord. I did not mean for Lord Geoffrey to discredit you. Last year I told him what I did know, because he asked me for the truth."

"You said nothing but what you knew to be true. You have no need to apologize for it."

"Yet I'm sorry. I never believed he would treat you so cruelly. I wouldn't treat a dog so, chained and caged like that! So I told him!"

"Then you did me a service for speaking when you might have kept silent. Never mind it." He patted Blanche on the head. "What of the girl?"

"Oh! This one?" The pinched look left her face. She gave a grand smile and tweaked the girl's ear fondly. "What a hard-working little creature she is, isn't she, then? She stuck beside me all this time and did everything I asked of her. Good with a knife! Very careful handed, which you don't often see in a child this age. I can't trust just any lass with peeling and cutting. Washed me up turnips and parsnips, cutting out the soft spots, of which there are plenty, for these are the end of our winter store and some of them mostly mush by now."

Blanche blushed, face half hidden against Alain's tunic, but she was smiling proudly.

"Will you keep her in the kitchens, then, as your helper? And keep care of her? Can you do that?"

"For you, my lord? Willingly. I swear to you I will do by her as I would for my own granddaughter."

"You'll stay here, Blanche."

"I want to go with you, Uncle," she said into the cloth.

"You can't." He only needed to say it once. "Here you'll stay. Tell me you understand."

She spoke in a muted voice while her arms clutched him. "I stay with Cook."

A dozen soldiers tromped onto the porch and came into the hall, placing themselves to either side of the dais. A pair of servants carried the count's chair in from another chamber and set it in front of the high table. Folk moved cautiously into the hall behind the soldiers, their movement like the eddying of river currents caught in a backwater. A few crept close to him and knelt furtively, whispering words he could not really hear because of the shifting of feet and murmur of voices.

A door banged—open or closed. The assembly quieted as Lord Geoffrey entered with his young daughter. It was difficult to tell her age. She had a childish face and was short and slender and in addition walked with a pronounced limp, but despite her pallor she kept her chin high and gaze steady as she looked first at Alain and then over the assembled soldiers and local people for whom she was responsible as Count of Lavas. The hounds growled, a rumble in their throats too soft for anyone but him, and perhaps Blanche, to hear.

Lavrentia alone sat. Even her father remained standing.

"Let me hear your pledge," she said in a high, clear voice. She lifted a hand to give him permission to approach, and Alain smiled to see the gesture, which echoed Lavastine's decisive ways.

He set Blanche aside, giving her into Cook's arms, and mounted both steps to stand on the same level as the lady. He did not approach her chair nor kneel before her. Instead, he turned to face the crowd. The hounds stood side by side on the first step, and the soldiers nearby shrank back from them.

"I pray you, listen!"

As though a spell had been cast over the multitude, they fell quiet and listened. Not a murmur teased the silence, although one person coughed.

"I make this statement freely, not coerced in any way. I came here of my own accord under the escort of Chatelaine Dhuoda. You know who I am. I am called Alain. I was born here in Lavas Holding and grew up in fosterage in Osna village. Count Lavastine of blessed memory believed I was his illegitimate son and named me as his heir. I sat in the count's chair for some months before King Henry himself gave the county into the hands of Lavrentia, daughter of Geoffrey. This you know."

Geoffrey was white, shaking, and strangely it was his young daughter who brushed her small fingers over her father's clenched fist to calm him.

"This is what I must say to you now, so you can hear, and remember, and speak of it to others who are not here today. I am not Lavastine's heir. I am not the rightful Count of Lavas."

"Nay! Nay! Say not so, my lord!"

"We won't believe such lies—!"

"I knew he was a grasping imposter."

"What of the testimony of the hounds?"

"I pray you!" said Alain. "Grant me silence, if you will."

They did so. There was another cough, a shuffling of feet as folk shifted position, a handful of murmurs cut off by sibilant hisses as neighbors shushed those who whispered, and, from outside, a chorus of barking, quickly hushed.

"I will depart this place by sunset with nothing more than what I came with, all but this one thing: this pledge made by Lord Geoffrey. That his daughter, Lavrentia, will rule as Count of Lavas but will stand aside if one comes forward with a claim that supersedes hers and is validated by a council of respected church folk or by Biscop Constance of Autun."

"I swear it," growled Geoffrey. The hounds growled, in unison, as if in answer or in challenge.

Geoffrey wiped his brow. The girl bit her lip but did not shift or otherwise show any fear in the face of the fearsome black hounds. Pens scratched as a cleric, seated by the fire, made a record of the proceedings on vellum.

Alain descended from the dais and went over to the bench where his pack lay. He hoisted it, whistled to the hounds, and before any person there could react, he kissed Blanche, made his farewells to Cook, and walked to the door. He came outside past the brace of guards and was out into the courtyard and practically to the gates before he heard the rush of sound, a great exhalation, as the folk inside the hall rushed outward to see where he was going.

They crowded to the gate and some trailed after him to the break in the fosse that met with the eastbound road. A handful kept walking behind him all the way into the woodland until it was almost dark and at last he turned and asked them kindly to go back before it was too dark for them to see.

There was a lad, weeping, who sidled forward, grasped his hand, and kissed it.

"I pray you, be well," said Alain. "Do not weep."

There was Master Rodlin, without the whippets, who stared at him and said, "What of the hounds? They follow you still. Is that not the mark of Lavas blood? And if not, then what is it?"

"They cannot answer, for they do not have human speech," said Alain. "They chose to follow me long ago to help me on my path.

Serve the rightful heir, Master Rodlin, as faithfully as you did Count Lavastine."

"When will that one come?" he demanded.

"Like the hounds, I cannot answer. If Lavrentia is the rightful heir, you must serve her with the same loyalty you showed to Count Lavastine."

Rodlin frowned but grabbed the lad's hand and led him away. The holding was hidden by the trees and the stone tower by a twilight that caused colors to wash into one dim background.

One remained, wringing her hands. "Do you remember me?" she said. "Will you curse me, for teasing you when you first were come here? Do you hate me for it?"

Her eyes were still as startling a blue as when he had met her years ago. She had a well-fed look to her and her belly curved her skirts in such a way that he supposed she was in the middle months of pregnancy.

"Did you ever meet the prince in the ruins?" he asked her.

Her lips twisted into a resigned smile. "Did you lie to me that night when we both went up to the ruins?"

"No, I did not. I saw him."

"Then you saw more than I did! I looked, but I saw nothing. Or maybe that's just how it goes when a girl is young and stupid. I married a good man who works hard and can feed me and my younger sisters and our child. There are only shadows in those ruins now."

"Have you walked there since?"

"I went there at midwinter, just a few month back. Because I thought of you, in truth. Because we saw you in the cage. I didn't think that was right. It was Heric done it, and I cursed him for it."

She paused, waiting.

"What do you want?" he asked her. "You did no wrong to me, and I none to you, I think."

"I just wanted to see you in the dusk," she said, "to see if the shadows made you look like they say that prince did. To see if you might be his by-blow, as some whispered. Shadow-born. Demon's get."

"Do you think I am?" She puzzled him. She was cleaner and prettier than she had been before, better cared for in both dress and manner, and while she did not seem precisely friendly, neither did she seem spiteful.

"You're not what you seem," she said, turning away. She took three steps before turning back to look at him. "There was nothing in those ruins, not even shadows, because there was no moon to make shades. But if you want to hear the weeping of ghosts, go to Ravnholt Manor."

Because of the cool weather and the clouds, the abandoned path leading to Ravnholt Manor was not at all overgrown or difficult to pass except for some fallen branches and a thick cushion of leaf litter. He came into the clearing at midday two days after his departure from Lavas. He discovered eight graves dug beside a chapel that was just big enough to seat a half dozen worshipers beside its miniature Hearth. From a distance, the mounded graves still looked fresh, but that was only because so few weeds had grown in the dirt. It wasn't until he came up close that he saw how the earth had settled and compacted. A deer's track, its sides crumbling, marked the corner of one mound. A rat sprinted away through the ruined main house, whip tail vanishing into a hole in the rubble. Otherwise it was silent.

No. There. He heard a faint honking and, looking up, saw a straggling "v" of geese headed north, not more than a dozen. He put a hand to his face, feeling tears of joy welling there, and he smiled. Rage and Sorrow snuffled around the fallen outbuildings. There was a weaving shed, a privy, two low storage huts, and a trio of cottages. The byre hadn't burned, but its thatched roof had fallen in. Alain poked through the rubble of the longhouse with his staff, but he found nothing except broken pots, a pair of half eaten baskets, and the remains of two straw beds dissolving into the ash-covered ground.

A twig snapped.

"What do you want?" asked a voice from the woods, a man hidden among the trees. The voice seemed familiar, but he couldn't place it.

"Just looking for the four women who were taken from this place by bandits."

He felt a breath, an intake of air, and threw himself flat. An arrow passed over his head and thunked into a charred post behind him. Barking wildly, the hounds charged into the trees. By the time Alain scrambled to his feet, he heard a man shrieking in terror.

"Nay! Nay! Call them off! I beg you! Anything! Anything!"

Alain pushed through the brush to find Sorrow standing on top of a man. His right wrist bled where Rage had bitten him. A bow carved of oak lay on the ground atop a fallen arrow. The man writhed, moaning and whimpering, as Sorrow nosed his throat.

A ragged wool tunic covered his torso. It had been patched with the overlarge stitches that betray an inexperienced hand. His hands were red from cold. He was also barefoot; his feet were chapped, heavily and recently callused, and the big toe of his right foot was swollen, cracked, and oozing pus and blood.

Alain picked up the arrow and broke it over his knee, then unstrung the bow and tied it onto his pack.

"Mercy! Mercy! It was my sin! I am the guilty one!"

"Sorrow! Sit!"

Sorrow sat on the man's left arm, pinning him, and panted, drooling a little, as Alain stepped forward to look the man in the face.

"I know you. You're called Heric. You were a man-at-arms in Lavas Holding seven or eight years back."

The pungent smell of urine flooded as the man wet himself.

"I'm sorry! I'm sorry! I pray you, forgive me!"

"For trying to kill me just now?"

Heric kept babbling. "It was my sin! Mine!"

Although it made his head ache a little, Alain remembered. "You were the one who put me in the cage."

"Don't kill me! Don't kill me!"

"What of the reward you received for bringing me in to Geoffrey? Surely he gave you something? How after all that do you come to be hiding in the woods wearing such rags?"

"Don't let them chop off my hand! I didn't steal anything!"

"Only my freedom!"

Heric screamed and jerked his leg, but Rage was only licking at the swollen toe. "I had to! You were an outlaw! You were a thief, the worst of all! You took what wasn't yours to have. So they all said!"

"Roll over onto your stomach."

"The beast'll bite me!" But he did so, easing his arm out from under Sorrow as the hound looked up at Alain for direction.

Heric had been a big man once, but hunger had worn him down. He hadn't a belt for the tunic, and a crude cord woven out of reeds tied back his unruly hair. This man had betrayed him. But Alain could find no indignation on his own behalf for this pathetic creature who had no shoes, no gloves, and only two arrows, one now broken, with which to kill himself some supper. He hadn't even a knife.

"Why are you here at Ravnholt Manor?"

"Heard deer and rats seen roundabout," Heric replied, head twisted to one side so he could speak without choking on dirt. "I'm hungry."

"Do you know what happened to those four women?"

"No."

"Ah." Centuries ago, as humankind measured time, Alain had been bitten by a blind snake hiding in the lair of a phoenix. The effects of that venom still coursed through his blood, and where the poison burned, he burned with outrage. "You're lying, Heric. I pray you, do not lie. God know the truth. How can you hide from Them?"

"I didn't kill anyone! It was the others. It was them who are guilty! Even here at Ravnholt. I just stood watch, I never hurt anyone! After you escaped the cage, after that storm and that monster—ai, God! Then all those who were so friendly to me before, all them turned on me and cast me out! What was I to do? The woodsmen—that's what they call themselves—they're not so particular!"

"Although an honest woodsman might object to a pack of bandits calling themselves by an honest name."

"We was hungry, just like others. Did what we had to do to get a scrap to eat."

"Murdered folk here at Ravnholt Manor? Where are the four girls who were taken?"

He sobbed helplessly into the dirt, nose running. He stank with fear. "I left them after they done it. I wasn't guilty. I didn't do it!"

"After they done what?"

"*Killed* them! Raped them and killed them. Said they might try to escape. I said they ought to spare 'em. But no."

"You touched none of those girls?"

"I didn't kill them!"

"But you raped them! Isn't that harm enough? And stood by and let them die after! Doesn't that stain your hands with their blood? The one who refuses to act to save the innocent is as guilty as the one whose hand strikes the blow!"

These words set Heric caterwauling and writhing on the earth like a man having a fit.

"Roll over and sit up."

Heric's sobs ceased and, cautiously, he rolled onto his back, then sat, not even brushing off the leaf litter and dirt and twigs that smeared his rags. He eyed first Rage, who wanted to get back to licking the infected toe, then Sorrow, who yawned hugely to display his teeth.

Alain took a few breaths to clear his anger. "I believe you are telling the truth about those poor girls, but I'll see those graves."

"There aren't no graves! The others slit their throats and cast them into the brush, that's all."

"Then you'll bury their corpses. Lead me there."

"Won't! It's close by the hidey-hole. We'll be killed, you and me. Twenty of them agin' two of us. I have no weapon, not now you took mine . . . unless you want to give me back my bow."

"No, I don't want to. Come, then."

"We're not going there, are we?" His voice rose in panic. "I don't want to die."

"Did those girls want to die? Did they cry and plead, Heric? Did you hear them begging while you stood by and watched?"

"I turned my back!" he said indignantly. "I'm not a monster, to watch murder done!"

"If turning your back is not a monstrous deed, then what is?" He signaled with a hand. Tails lashing, the hounds waited for his command.

"Where are we going?"

"To Lavas Holding."

"Not there, I beg you! They'll hang me! They'll chop off my hands and then my head."

"If you're not guilty, why do you fear their justice?"

Heric spat into the dirt. Rage growled.

"Are you so wise?" he sneered. "What justice is there for a man like me? I served the old count faithfully, and what did I get for my good service? I got turned out by the new lord without even a thanks! An old hunting dog is treated better than I was! Lord Geoffrey will hang me just to be rid of another mouth to feed. He was happy enough to offer boots and clothes and a handful of sceattas when I brought you to him, for him to parade around the county. Because he thought folk would stop their whispering. And after— hsst!" He spat again. "After that storm, after you escaped, those who cheered most to see you mad and chained slapped me and spat on me and called me an evil man. Because they feared it was God sent the storm to free you. Why should I not fear their justice? They'll be glad to hang me to make the shame pass from their own sinful hearts."

"I'll see you get justice."

Heric laughed hysterically. "How can you do that? How can you? What are you? Where are you come from? What happened to the madness that ate at you?"

After all, Alain found that spite still lived in his heart. "A little late to ask those questions, isn't it?" he said with a sour grin. He turned his back and began walking.

After a sharp rustle came a thump and a yelp of pain. Alain turned to see Sorrow sitting on Heric's chest again. With a growl the hound opened his mouth and gently closed his jaws right over Heric's face.

"Come," said Alain firmly. Sorrow eased back, scratched an ear as though he didn't know what for, and padded after Alain.

Blubbering, Heric rose and limped after, Rage bringing up the rear.

"One will always be awake," said Alain. "One, or the other."

"I'll come! I'll come!" He staggered along like a man walking to his death.

And, Alain reflected, it must seem so to him. It might even be true. Yet, however little Heric deserved mercy for his cowardice and his rapine, he must at least be judged only for the sins he had committed, not made into a sacrificial beast by those who wished to assuage their own shame with the blood of someone else.

They walked in a silence broken only by the wind's passage through branches still bare of spring buds. Except where evergreens gave cover, it was possible to glimpse vistas into the forest, a place of muted colors and a profound solitude. Now and again a clearing opened up; here and there coppices filled a well-husbanded section of woodland. They passed an old charcoal pit, two or three seasons in disuse, with leaves and dirt scattered in damp mounds and a half burned log laced with clinging vine. Human hands had teased a streamside clearing into an orchard made proud by a dozen trees, not yet far gone in neglect. Farther on, a wide meadow boasted a sturdy shelter suitable for a flock of sheep on summer pasture.

"This was a peaceful place once," said Alain. "Well tended and well loved."

"Maybe so," muttered Heric, "but they still kept a girl from Salia to serve the steward's son in whatever manner he wished."

"How do you know?"

"She got free and come to the bandits, that's why. It was she made the plan, and give the signal. She knew the ways and times of the household, that's why. The others said she killed that one herself, the one who used her, but I didn't see it."

"Made she no protest when four girls were taken to be used in the same rough manner she was? And worse, for they were killed after?"

"What did she care for them? She wanted revenge, and took it. It was she argued loudest that they were a nuisance and ought to go. I think it was for that she was jealous of the attention they got. She liked keeping the men on a string, you know how it is. That girl at Lavas, called Withi, I liked her well, but she did do that to me, curse her. Went off in the end with a man who could keep her fed." His tone was self-pitying. "The Salian girl, she said also those other girls cursed her ill with words and slaps, back when she was only a concubine. So it was revenge twice over."

"Might she have been lying?"

"About what? Being taken to bed each night by a man she hated? The other girls slapping her and calling her a Salian whore? How would I know?"

Alain tramped on, unable to speak for the bitterness lodged in his throat. It seemed that injustice was woven through the world in inexplicable patterns, impossible to tease apart without unraveling the entire web.

"Seems like God are blind and deaf and mute," continued Heric, having gotten a good wind to fill the sails of his complaining. "But I heard a story about a phoenix. You heard it? They say a phoenix descended from heaven and tore the heart out of the blessed Daisan to make him suffer just like the rest of us. I wonder if it's true."

"I think that story was twisted in the telling."

"Huh. 'Truth flies with the phoenix.' That's what one of those girls cried out as they was cutting her throat. Well, she flew, anyway, right up to the light, or into the Pit."

"Don't mock!"

Rage barked and Sorrow growled. Heric fell into a sullen muttering that was not audible enough to fashion into words.

They went on, and soon a second murmuring noise caught Alain's hearing. He lifted a hand and halted on the path just before it curved left. He recognized this place from his morning's passage along this way. In another twoscore or so steps they would come to the main road. As they listened, they heard the sound of a cavalcade moving along the as-yet-unseen track: harness jingling, wheels scraping along dirt, voices chattering, and a dog's bark. Sorrow whined but did not answer.

Heric whimpered. Alain looked back to see that Rage had gotten hold of the man's leggings as he tried to creep back the way they had come.

"That's a big party," he whined. "Listen! A hundred or more, Lord Geoffrey riding to war. Maybe come to have you killed!"

Alain shook his head. "They're riding *toward* Lavas Holding." He turned to the hounds. "Rage. Sorrow. Stay. Guard."

He picked his way past fallen branches, more numerous close to the joining with the road as though the bandits had pulled down obstacles to cover their tracks. Soon he heard the procession in full spate but marked also with the giggling of children and an unexpected snatch of hymn from a voice he had heard before but could not quite place.

> ". . .who made a road to the sea
> And a path through the mighty waters."

He came to the last turning, where the path hitched around a massive oak that served as a towering landmark. He recalled it from earlier years. The autumn storm had half torn it from the ground. Its vast trunk had fallen westward to leave roots thrust like daggers across the path. He used these as cover as he examined the road.

There were soldiers riding in pairs or marching in fours while between their ranks trundled carts and wagons filled with household goods and children and elders and caged chickens. Youths and sturdy looking women walked alongside, most of them carrying a bundle or two. A pair of clerics walked beside a wagon containing several fine chests. He saw—

Hathumod!

She sat on a wagon next to a white-haired woman placed among pillows. Another, older woman dressed in cleric's robes made up the third in the bed of the wagon. Her back was to Alain, but by the movements of her shoulders and hands she seemed to be talking in a lively way while the others listened, the white-haired woman with a smile of patient interest despite the pain etched into her face, and Hathumod with a scarcely concealed look of boredom.

The wagon passed and was gone beyond his line of sight through the trees before he realized who he had just seen. And where she must be going: Lavas Holding was about three days' journey west, and there was no crossroads that came sooner on the road than the holding itself.

Soon it would be dark. The cavalcade must camp for the night, most likely on the road itself. Soldiers scanned the woodland as though they expected attack, but the upturned oak hid him because he did not move. What strange company was this? It was like an entire village on the move, not like a noblewoman's royal progress.

When the last ranks of infantry had passed, he waited a while longer, and at length a trio of silent outriders ambled by. He waited even longer until one last pair of men rode past with hands easy on the reins, their gazes keen and penetrating, and a bow and a sword, respectively, laid across their thighs.

It was one of these who saw him, although he hadn't meant to be seen.

"Whsst!" The young man's chin jerked around fast. He had his bow up and arrow ready, holding his horse with tightened knees, before Alain could take a second breath. The other man reined his horse around to face back the way they'd come, sword raised.

"I'll come out," said Alain in an even voice. "I've been waiting for you. What business has Biscop Constance in these parts? I heard she was a prisoner of Lady Sabella in Autun."

"Come out," said the archer. "What think you, Captain? Are there more? Should we shoot him?"

The other man's horse took one side step. "Let him come free if he moves slowly. Let's see what he knows first. Better the battle come sooner when we're ready for it than later when we're not."

Alain put his hands out with palms raised and turned toward them, and walked onto the road.

The captain narrowed his eyes, examining him. "I've seen you before."

"Gent!" said the young one. "In Count Lavastine's company. Wasn't he—?"

The captain hissed sharply between gritted teeth. "You're Lavastine's heir—the very one. Your claim was put aside in favor of Lord Geoffrey's daughter." He extended his sword as a threat. "What brings you here? I heard you had marched east as a Lion."

"So I did. Now I am come back."

"To challenge Lord Geoffrey?"

"No. I have another purpose."

"What might that be?" asked the captain in a genial tone that made it clear he demanded an explanation.

In that woodland, sound carried far. The progress of the cavalcade had faded westward. With the promise of nightfall, the wind sighed to a halt.

A jingle of harness out of the east rang brightly in warning.

"Damn," said the captain. They had all heard it. "As I feared."

"What are we to do, Captain?" asked the young man, looking exceedingly nervous but also determined and angry. "If they catch us . . ."

"Who follows you?" Alain asked.

"Lady Sabella's soldiers," said the captain.

"If I can turn them back," said Alain, "will you take me to Biscop Constance? I ask only to speak with her briefly. Then I'll be on my way."

"Turn them back!" scoffed the young man.

"Hush, Erkanwulf! We must get the biscop to Lavas Holding. You ride and alert the rest. Form up with all soldiers to the rear and flanks, out into the forest. I'll stay here."

"No, Captain. Begging your pardon, Captain. It's you they need, more than me. I can wait behind and catch up. If I don't come, it's because I'm dead."

The captain considered. He was a thoughtful man, Alain saw, one who was neither too eager nor too cautious; a good commander. His features triggered an old memory, but if he'd seen this man at Gent, and he surely had done so, it was in passing. Many men rode in the war parties of other nobles. A lord might note faces and go on, not marking them because he had no authority over them.

With regret, the captain nodded. "So be it." He turned his measuring gaze on Alain. "If Erkanwulf brings me news that the ones who follow us turned back, then I'll see you have an audience with the holy biscop."

He sheathed his sword, gave a hard look at Erkanwulf, and rode on. He looked back twice before vanishing around a bend in the road.

"Best if I do this alone," said Alain.

"I'd rather die than betray my captain!"

"If you take the horse down that path, you can tie him up and then watch without being seen."

"And without hearing! You might tell them anything, the disposition of our forces, our numbers, our destination if they haven't guessed it already. You might be a spy in league with Lady Sabella."

"I might be, it's true, although I'm not."

Erkanwulf scratched his head. "I'm minded to believe you, although I don't know why. How will you stop them?"

A second jangle of noise rang closer. The first had been a trick of air and leaf, but this grew steadily in volume.

"Go," said Alain.

Erkanwulf hesitated only a moment, biting his lip, before he dismounted and lead his horse down the track that cut off toward Ravnholt Manor.

Alain set himself in the middle of the road with a hand on his staff and the other hanging loose at his side. He waited, breathing in the loamy air. The battered roadbed gave beneath his right foot where a trickle of groundwater seeped up to dampen the leather of his boots and creep in through the seams. A fly buzzed around his left ear. A bee wandered into the shadow of a copse of withered honeysuckle grown up along a patch of open ground. He waited, content to let the time pass. He felt the barest glimmer of sun above, like the kiss of a mouth through cloth. If the weather didn't change, then crops wouldn't grow or would grow weakly. The thought stuck with him and gave him courage.

In time, the first outriders appeared out of the east as shadows lengthened on the road. It was a good long straight stretch of track, open enough that he soon saw most of the company moving along. He faced about threescore riders. Half were mounted, dressed in surcoats bearing the sigil of the guivre of Arconia. A dozen of the infantry wore a tower sigil that he did not recognize. The others wore any kind of leather coat or tough jacket, men brought quickly into service for a specific task but not serving in the duke's milites on a permanent basis.

Their captain rode in the third rank behind a double line of anxious-looking younger men bearing small shields and short spears. He was a fearsome-looking man, grim with anger and horribly scarred. He was missing an eye, healed as a mass of white scar tissue, and old gashes scored his forehead and jaw. Now and again a man in the first rank would lift an arm to point out yet another mark of the passage of a significant cavalcade. They knew what they followed. They could not be turned aside through misdirection. They had marked Alain already and now sent scouts on foot into the underbrush, seeking to forestall an ambush. The *shing* of swords leaving sheaths cut the air. Shields were raised, and spears wavered. Some had bows, and these men set arrow to string and scanned the woodland for movement.

"Tammus!" shouted Alain. "Keeper!"

The captain started, and around him his men muttered. Slowly, the war band moved toward Alain as toward a trap they must spring.

"I am alone except for one witness, hidden in the trees," continued Alain, "and farther back two hounds guarding a criminal who consorted with bandits."

"A likely story," said the captain. "How do you know my name? Are you one of the biscop's men?"

"I am not."

"To what lord or lady do you owe allegiance?"

"I serve God, Captain Tammus. Whom do you serve, God or the Enemy?"

They murmured angrily at that, like bees stirred up by smoke, and one rash fellow actually rode out ahead of the front rank brandishing his sword.

"Fall back!" snapped the captain.

The man obeyed. The rest halted an easy spear's toss from Alain. A branch snapped in the woods.

"What do you want?" asked the captain. "I've no patience. We're close to our quarry and you're in our way."

Alain was close enough to see Tammus' eye flare as he reacted to a bold stare. The captain had but one hand. The other arm ended in a stump at the wrist, seared by fire.

"To pass, you must kill me, keeper."

One among the guard sniggered.

"Hush! Why do you call me that? How do you know my name?"

"You kept the guivre for Lady Sabella. I saw you feed a living man to it, once. That's how you kept it alive. I think you might have called yourself by a different name, then."

Tammus' gaze flickered, losing touch with Alain's as he traced the reaction of his men. Soldiers looked one at the other; hands fluttered as in sign language; a murmuring passed back through the ranks.

"Hush!" said the keeper. "I am Lady Sabella's servant. I do as she bids me. You are in my way. We'll ride right over you. You have no weapon."

Alain caught his gaze again and held it. He challenged him as a hound might, with a stare from which one must back down and the other emerge triumphant.

"With your own hand you must kill me," he said, "or with your own voice you must command one of your men to slay me because you refuse to spill my blood with your own weapon. Either way, your hands are stained."

"I am the lady's servant," growled Tammus. "I do as she bids me." He could not now look away without losing face, not with every man among his company watching him.

Alain said nothing, only kept his gaze locked on the captain's. He remembered the night he had stumbled upon the guivre's cage, how it had been shrouded in canvas to conceal the monster within. He recalled the slack body of the drugged man who woke up too late to the fate that would consume him. He knew in his heart and in his limbs the touch of the guivre's gaze, which struck like the sword of God, for he had felt it that night. So did the creatures of God teach humankind what they needed to know.

"I've killed lots of men and in worse ways than cutting a man down on the road," muttered Tammus hoarsely.

"I know," said Alain, remembering that great eye and its power. "For I am the one who aided Brother Agius in killing that poor beast at Kassel. With a sword I killed it, and Lady Sabella's army was routed. Do you think you can kill me?"

A breath was the only sign; lips parted. Wind curled in leafless branches.

Tammus lost his nerve. He froze. Every man there felt it, heard it, saw it, *knew* it with the same instinct hounds have for weakness. It took only that one breath for the advantage to shift, for the battle to be lost.

Alain did not move. It was they who fled back the way they had come.

4

"YOUR Grace."

Alain knelt in the spot indicated by Captain Ulric.

"I don't *know* how he did it!" Erkanwulf was saying off to one side. Because of his mounting exasperation, his voice carried. "He just *looked* at them. They turned tail and ran. That was before I saw those monstrous black hounds!"

"I know who you are, or who you once were." Biscop Constance had aged horribly. Lines marked her face as deeply, in their own way, as Tammus' scars had disfigured him, and she favored her right side over the left as though it was agony to shift her left hip at all. But her gaze was calm and her voice was mild. "Beyond what

I witnessed myself, and what I learned when I ruled Arconia, I have heard just these last few moments such tales as make my head spin. You are a count's bastard son. A count yourself. A cheat and a liar and thief. A whore's son. A faithful Lion who died in the east in battle. You are, it appears, a man who commands the loyalty of fierce beasts. Who can turn back a war band on a forest lane with his gaze alone."

"I am the son of a Salian refugee, Your Grace. I was raised in an honest household of merchants out of Osna Sound. That is all that matters."

"Perhaps. Why are you come, Alain of Osna? What do you want from me?"

"I ask you to bring justice to the folk murdered at Ravnholt Manor, including four young women who were raped and murdered. Find their bodies, and bury them. Bring to trial the bandits who killed them."

As many as could crowd in around her shelter had come to see; everyone surely had heard the tale of the encounter on the road by now. They were silent, but their stares had an unexpected force, as powerful as that of the guivre.

"Is that all? I think there is more."

"I am looking for a woman."

She smiled, misunderstanding him. Hathumod touched the back of a hand to her mouth, repressing a sound. She stared at Alain with a remorseful gaze. There were others behind her whom Alain recognized from court, and from his sojourn at Hersford Monastery: among them the handsome young man who had once been Margrave Judith's husband. How long ago it seemed that he had walked up on that porch to interrupt a fight between Prior Ratbold and a ragtag collection of five clerics and two Lions! How these heretics had fetched up in Biscop Constance's train he did not yet know.

"The woman I am looking for was an Eagle," he continued, "and then afterward I heard a story that she ran off with Prince Sanglant."

"Liath!" A red-haired young man stepped forward so angrily it seemed he meant to strike.

"Brother Ivar!" Constance's tone was a reproof. Ivan shrugged a shoulder, shifted his feet, but did not move back to his former place beside the beautiful bridegroom whose name, Alain abruptly recalled, was Baldwin. The beauty was now, incongruously, dressed as a cleric. His eyes were wide, and his right hand fingered a gold Circle of Unity whose surface was chased with filigree. He wore a ring, bright blue lapis lazuli.

Alain's breath caught; words vanished. He knew that ring, once most precious to him.

"Go on," said the biscop.

"I pray you," he said, finding his voice. "Where did you get that ring, Brother?"

There was a moment of confusion. Then Baldwin looked toward the red-haired Brother Ivar, who answered.

"In a tomb buried deep in a hillside, a heathen grave far east of here. What matters it to you?"

"Ivar," said the biscop softly, "I will suffer no disrespect toward those who come honestly before me."

"It was the same place we got the nail," said Hathumod, "and the Lion's tabard and weapons. How came these things there, to such an ancient grave?"

To touch again the gift she had given him! The thought coincided with a curious look on the handsome cleric's face as the man clutched his other hand possessively around the one on which he wore the ring.

Fingers may brush, and yet after all two people may be separated by a gulf that cannot be bridged. "Never mind it," Alain murmured. Adica was gone. Taking the ring from a man who cherished it would not bring her back. Yet it was nevertheless difficult to speak through the pain in his heart.

"Liathano is indeed the one I seek. Have you news of her whereabouts?"

"Why do you wish to know? What business do you have with her?" demanded the redhead.

"Hush, Ivar!" Hathumod punched his arm. He shot a glance at her that pierced, but she only made a face at him.

"I would know the answers to these questions likewise," said Constance, "although I must tell you, in truth, Alain of Osna, that I do not know what has become of the Eagle. I have been held as a prisoner by my half sister Sabella for over five years. What news we have is scant, gathered by Brother Ivar and young Erkanwulf. King Henry has lingered many years in Aosta seeking an imperial crown. Sabella and Conrad between them have usurped the governance of Varre. Who can blame them, when Henry abandons his people? Princess Theophanu bides in Osterburg, protecting Saony, which is the ancient seat of my family's power. Prince Sanglant defeated a Quman army at the Veser River and afterward rode east seeking

griffins and sorcerers with which to battle a mysterious cabal of sorcerers who he claimed intended to destroy the world. He is said to
have ridden south to Aosta in pursuit of his father and the sorcerers. More than that I do not know."

"Ah," said Alain. "Some knew, then, of the coming storm. It was
not in vain that the Old Ones spoke to me."

"The storm? The one that swept over us last autumn?"

"It was the final closing of a spell set in motion centuries ago."

He surprised her, who was a woman not easily startled. She
touched her left ear as if she were not at all sure she had heard those
words spoken. "What mystery is this you speak of? Have you some
hidden knowledge of events lost in the past in the time of the blessed
Daisan?"

"This took place long before the time of the blessed Daisan. They
are hidden from us only by the passage of years. Only by death,
which hides us all in the end. I pray you, have you any news of the
one called Liathano?"

"Of her, no. She was lost in a haze of fire."

"Truth rises with the phoenix," murmured the beauty, and Alain
felt the pinch of those words in his heart as though some unnoticed
hand were trying to get his attention.

"What did you say?" he asked him.

" 'Truth rises with the phoenix,' " the young man repeated patiently, and his smile made the folk nearby murmur and point as if
he had just done something extraordinary. "We who believe in the
truth and the word speak so, to acknowledge the sacrifice made by
the blessed Daisan, who died so that our sins might be forgiven."

"Agius' words are seeds grown in fertile soil," said Alain.

Constance shut her eyes, touched a finger to her own lips as she
might touch the mouth of a lover.

" 'His heart's blood fell to Earth and bloomed as roses,' " Alain
added.

She looked at him, just a look, that was all. That gaze, met and
answered, nothing more, until her expression shifted, grew puzzled,
almost intimate, and she extended a hand and beckoned him closer.
She sat in a chair at the rear of the wagon in which he had earlier
seen her riding. Her breath fogged the cold air. When he stood next
to her, she touched his cheek.

"You are marked as with a rose," she said. "A curious birthmark.
I've never seen such a one before."

"It is not a birthmark but the memory of a false oath," he said.

"It serves to remind me of my obligation, something I cannot see except in the faces of other human beings."

"Who are you?" she asked him, and looked at Baldwin as if for an answer, but Baldwin did not speak. He was staring at the sky and he raised a hand and pointed.

"Is that the sun? See there. It's almost gone below the trees, but it has a bluish cast. As though haze screens it, not clouds."

First a soldier turned, then an elderly woman. Others, facing west like the biscop and Lord Baldwin, raised hands in supplication. A flood of crying and rejoicing lifted from the assembled cavalcade as a covey of quails flush in a rush of wings up from the brush.

"The sun! It shines!"

It was more a shimmer than the actual disk of the sun. No person could stare at the sun without going blind. Everyone knew that. But along the western sky the cloud cover had altered in some manner to reveal the sun's long hidden shape as if veiled behind only one layer of cheesecloth, not ten.

"A miracle!"

"This is the work of the Holy One!"

"Truth rises with the phoenix!"

They cried and pointed and stared, all shaken into such a tumult of excitement that Alain walked away, slipping from one gap to the next as he squeezed out of the crowd with no one paying him any mind. *They* stared at the western horizon. *He* walked east to the edge of the camp strung out along the road and into the trees. Close to the eastern end of the camp, three soldiers had been set to guard Heric.

Alain whistled softly, but no one noticed him. Word had raced more swiftly than he could walk and they were all gazing westward. Some began to sing a song he had never heard before.

> *"Truth rises with the phoenix,*
> *Truth rises like the sun."*

Sorrow and Rage bounded up and trotted alongside as he settled into a long stride, heading east along the road. He hadn't much light left. He'd need to make good time, to get far enough that no one would come after him.

But after all, just as he got out of sight of the trailing end of the cavalcade's encampment, he heard slip-slapping footsteps and labored breathing.

"My lord! My lord Alain!"

He paused and turned halfway back, waiting. Sorrow whined. Rage yawned to show teeth. She did not run, precisely, but loped in an awkward, determined way, then stumbled to halt a few steps away. The hounds made her nervous, but she was brave enough to come close despite her fear.

"Where are you going?" she asked.

"East on the trail of Prince Sanglant. If any know where she is, he will."

"Do you love her, my lord?" Tears streamed down her face.

"I hope that God have taught me to love all of humankind. But the kind of love you mean—no."

"If I could go with you. . . . Will you take me with you?"

He shook his head. "I pray you, Sister. Serve where you are needed most. Every storm leaves destruction in its wake. There is much to do."

"Yes," she said, bowing her head obediently. "I will do as you say." The words were thin, spoken through tears.

"You are brave and good, Hathumod. Your hands will do God's work if you let them."

She choked down a sob as she nodded. She had gone beyond speech and now could only stare as he gave a sign of farewell and walked away down the road. Where the road curved, he paused to look back. Eager to get on, the hounds wagged their tails.

She still stood there, fading into the twilight. She hadn't moved at all, as if caught in the guivre's stare.

XV
THE IMPATIENT ONE

1

BECAUSE she was Feather Cloak, the blood knives insisted that she be carried in a litter when she traveled. The sacred energy coiled within her body must not be allowed to escape through the soles of her feet by touching the earth.

She did not like the blood knives. They were officious and grasping, set in their ways and bloated with self-importance, and it was obvious to her that they liked her less than she liked them. She did not follow the ancient laws in the manner to which they were accustomed.

Yet she was Feather Cloak. She had been elected, according to the custom of the land. Let them chew on that gristle!

For the time being, however, she thought it best to humor them in ceremonial ways. Thus she found herself on the road in a jolting litter carried by four men, with another eight walking in front or behind to take a turn when the current group needed a rest. They traveled in procession from the Heart-of-the-World's-Beginning to the city on the lake, called We-Have-No-More-Tears by the exiles but Belly-Of-The-Land resting on the Lake of Gold by those who had lived in the shadows, because that was the name they had called it in the days before exile. The turning wheel spun at the front, announcing her presence. Her son had come with them as well. He was ripe for adventure but not yet old enough to "put on the mask." He had the other baby slung to him, but he had dropped back to talk to one of the mask warriors, a young woman he fancied might see him as older than he was. In addition, she was accompanied by mask warriors, merchants, and judges come to witness the opening of the market, and a "bundle" of blood knives wearing scarlet tunics and the bright blue feathers of the death bird in their hair. Twenty of those blood knives in one place seemed like a lot.

"I am not accustomed to this," said Feather Cloak to her companion, White Feather, who was walking alongside the litter carrying one of the infants in a drop-back sling.

"No, neither am I," said White Feather.

"All the blood knives were gone by the time I was born."

"Yes," agreed White Feather with a flutter of her lips that resembled a grim smile. It was as much as she ever said on the matter. "So they were."

For the past two days they had been walking through an area of dispersed settlements, most of them lying off the main road. Now, as the raised roadway curved around a field of sap cactus, they came into a community abandoned during the exile but repopulated over the winter by those who had returned from the shadows. A large residence was raised on an earth platform. Small houses were set in groups around central patios. A remarkable number of people came out to greet them, more bundles than she could estimate easily. She could not get used to the crowds. They had no doubt been alerted to her arrival by the runners sent ahead to announce the procession.

Those in the back of the crowd craned their necks to get a glimpse of her. These were all folk who had returned from the shadows. They stood differently, wore their hair differently, tilted their chins differently, and they hadn't the stick-thin wiriness common to those who had survived exile, who had never ever in their lives gotten enough to eat except now in the days of the return when the exiles wallowed in the riches that those returned from the shadows called dearth.

"We'll stop here for the night," she said, suddenly wanting to talk to the ones gathered here, who stared at her but kept silent for fear of their voices polluting her.

The blood knives began to protest that they were less than a third of a day's journey from the city on the lake, enough to make it by nightfall, but already the men who carried her heeded her command and bore her up to the residence while householders scattered to make room. The chief of the town was a man and a woman. Despite both being of middle years, they were newly married to judge by the blackened remains of wedding torches stuck in the ground on either side of the residence gateway.

They welcomed her easily, and with an efficient manner born of practice. A mat was brought and placed on the chief's seat. Here she settled, relieved to be out of the sway and lurch of the litter. The blood knives swarmed, always wanting to control her least action, but White Feather swept them out ruthlessly so that Feather Cloak could nurse the babies.

After this, the chief brought sharp beer and sweet cactus fruit, gruel, toasted grubs, and fowl dressed in wild herbs and sweetened with sap. She still could not get used to the sight of so much food. Yet when at last she addressed the chief to thank them for the food, they apologized for the impoverished feast, which they said was nothing compared to what was due to her eminence.

"Let me speak to your council to hear how life goes for you here," she said.

The council was called hastily, elders, folk who had distinguished themselves, someone to represent each clan.

"We have no Rabbit Clan in our town," said the chief. "Nor Lizard Clan."

The blood knives stirred. "None out of the Rabbit Clan survived in exile," they said. "No one kept their House, as is proper."

Folk whispered, looking frightened. It was a dangerous thing to let the world slip out of balance.

"But there were so many before," said the lady chief. "We were the few, who walked out into the barbarian lands. Those who remained behind to tend to the land were multitudes. Yet now we are the many, and you, those who came out of exile, are the few."

White Feather seemed about to speak angry words, so Feather Cloak raised a hand, and all fell silent.

"The tale of our time in exile has already been told." She looked directly at the blood knives. "Has an almanac yet been painted to record the tale of our struggle?"

"We have much ordering to do, to restore the Houses and the lines and the proper measure of tribute. We must recover and restore the ritual almanacs first."

"I would not like to see the tale lost," she said mildly, but as a warning. Let them chew on that! She gestured to the council, inviting them to speak. "Is this the town you came from originally?"

They told their stories. The husband chief had been born here, even if raised in the barbarian lands. He had come to this home, because it was the only one he knew. A scattering of people who had claims that allowed them to labor in the surrounding lands had brought in other unlanded folk. Mostly, people worked the fields, but despite this, the community was sparsely settled compared to the days before exile.

"Not enough men to clear the fields," complained the lady chief. "We women are behind on our tribute offers of cloth. We can't harvest the fiber quickly enough. The fields are still green. We have no thread for weaving."

"What is your measure of tribute?" Feather Cloak asked them.

The list, reeled off from memory, seemed to her a staggering sum: feathers, paper, cloth in the form of short capes, incense from the smoke tree, and a range of agricultural goods for the temple and palace in the nearby city. But of course the birds were gone, the trees dead and any new growth yet seedlings, and the fields only newly sprouted with what little seed those who had survived the shadows had carried with them.

"The tribute lists must be redrawn," said Feather Cloak, as she said every day. "Until the people are healthy and the granaries are full, until there is seed corn in plenty, we must put all our effort into restoring our fields and our population."

"Tribute is necessary to maintain the universe," said the blood knives, as they said every day. "To keep the balance, we must pray, we must bleed, we must keep our oaths, burn incense, and offer sacrifices."

"So it must be done," she agreed, "but not to the measure in the days before exile, or we will be drained dry again!"

"All your blood knives are dead," they said, coming back to this point as they did every day. "It is no wonder the land was drained dry, that the balance was lost."

"You know nothing!" cried White Feather.

"Silence!" said Feather Cloak, and they gave her silence.

The council was made uncomfortable by this dispute. They feared the blood knives. They prayed to the gods. They followed the example of the one who was elected from among the elite to become Feather Cloak, meant to be a mature woman, pious, virtuous, generous, of an invincible spirit as well as possessing the unquenchable power of life, granted to her by the gods.

"I will set a measure of tribute for this year, and the next. The year after, a census will be taken and a new measure allotted."

It always struck her as strange that, while some in the communities welcomed this relief, others were made uneasy by it. When she called an end to the council, she saw the blood knives circulate out among the gathered council, whispering and plotting. All left her, so she was alone in the chamber, with a mat for sleeping and four strips of cloth hung from the post and lintel doorframe to give her privacy. The walls had been recently plastered and a painting begun on one wall, depicting the long march through the shadows with the sacred animals standing guard overhead.

"You must rest," said White Feather, bringing the babies back for another feeding.

Feather Cloak's son played the flute in a restful way, and out in the courtyard an unseen woman was grinding grain into flour in a soothing rhythm, but Feather Cloak could not find calm in her heart.

"Most of the blood knives must have stayed behind in the land, while these few walked out into the world," she mused. "Yet I never knew any blood knives. They were all gone by the time I was a child. And you, my elders, never speak of them."

White Feather looked at the mural, the images picked out with charcoal but only a few places colored in. The room was dim because night was coming. "They were weaker than our enemies. They could not help us. They cried to the gods and wanted to follow the old ways in exile, when it was obvious to everyone by then that the old ways would kill us." Her voice grew tight and her jaw rigid. "That the old ways did kill us."

"We no longer live in exile," said Feather Cloak.

"It is difficult to leave exile. Even when you have come home. Especially when you have come home."

For all of Feather Cloak's life, the city on the lake had lain deserted although in the days before exile it had been the greatest city in the land which was at that time called Abundance-Is-Ours-If-The-Gods-Do-Not-Change-Their-Minds. When she was a young child, there had still been a few marshy areas through which a girl and her age mates might search for scrumptious frogs and crunchy insects, but by the time she had given birth to her first child even these wet depressions had dried out and the lakebed become a haven for nothing except a few inedible weeds and precious stands of hardy sap cactus.

Now, of course, after winter rains and spring rains, the lake had disgorged its share of the returning waters. She asked her bearers to halt on the causeway. From the height of the litter, she gazed over stretches of unbroken water rimmed by brilliant bursts of green where reeds and grasses burgeoned along the current shoreline. Vast flocks of birds of every description, most of them kinds she had never seen, ranged on the waters, clucking and wheedling and croaking and whistling each in their own tongue, and insects buzzed and chirred and in general made a nuisance of themselves. She-Who-Creates was busy!

The farmers had dug their canals out beyond that shoreline, figuring that the lake would continue to grow, although naturally no one had any idea if it would ever refill the old basin, or grow beyond it. Most of the adult population was out there today building more fields out of dirt and mud, or tending to young plants waxing in earth planted and tended over the last few months.

He-Who-Burns showed his face intermittently. Those who had walked in the shadows told her that in the days before there came for certain months of the year a time with rain, and after that a time when He-Who-Burns baked the Earth with his blazing fire. There were two seasons, together with the passages between them, tied to the equinox. It was still early in the year, in the time of rains when all things grew, watered both within and without in the field that is Earth. Although the city had lost its abundance during the time of exile, it seemed that after all, having returned to Earth, that the gods had not changed their minds. They still wanted their children to flourish, to make a new home all over again.

"Feather Cloak! You are too bold!"

"Feather Cloak! You must not let the noonday sun touch you!"

"Feather Cloak! You were to approach on the eastern causeway. This is the causeway for merchants and artisans!"

"Feather Cloak! Have you come to begin work on restoring the temples? All else means nothing if the proper rituals are not observed!"

"How are you come to leave the sacred precinct in the Heart-of-the-World's-Beginning? Who allowed this to happen, in this month? It was not the proper time!"

The blood knives, the ones who had set up residence in the temple in the center of the city on the lake, had seen her coming. They swarmed like wasps out along the causeway to meet her, and to castigate her. She fanned herself with a fan built of green-and-gold feathers, the mark of the most holy bird sacred to She-Who-Creates, and because of this gesture they fell silent according to their own laws and their own customs.

"It is time to see the market opened," she said to them, and to her bearers she said, "We will move on."

The causeway was not yet surrounded by water, and there were some children off to one side digging in the mud for roots or seeking tadpoles, young frogs, grubs, crickets, or other such treats. They gaped to see the litter pass, and the blood knives shouted at them for their lack of respect and modesty.

"Why are they not at their study in the house of youth?" Feather Cloak asked them, and after that they considered her words more thoughtfully.

The procession entered the city through the gate of skulls and moved on toward the central precinct. Many folk had returned to the city, but in any case only one house out of twenty was inhabited. In the days before, according to the census undertaken in the days before by the blood knives, the city had been organized into five bundles of wards, and each ward had been organized into a bundle of neighborhoods each populated by forty households of ten to twenty people each. It was difficult for her to imagine so many people, but the empty quarters told their own story.

Even the palace where she must stay, with its forgotten rooms and echoing reaches, must remind her of how many had died, how many had been lost.

A suite of rooms had been prepared in haste for her coming. The blood knives complained about the poor furnishings, the deterioration of the wall paintings, faded from their years in exile, the lack of a sumptuous feast. Nothing was good enough. The balance had been lost in exile.

"Enough!" she said. "Bring the judges to me, and the scribes. Word has gone out through the land at my order. Just as Belly-Of-The-Land lies at the center of the land, so will the central market be opened by official decree, so that all of the people will know that we Cursed Ones have taken possession of all of our land. As before, so again."

Folk began arriving that afternoon. By the next morning, as her bearers carried her to the market plaza, she could actually hear the steady hum of so many voices raised in common conversation that the sound seemed to permeate the entire city. The procession passed the temple plaza, marked off by walls and undulating stone serpents. Smoke rose from the house of He-Who-Burns, sited at the top of the great temple in the very heart of the city. Looking through the wide gate, she saw a bundle of young women dancing in their serpent skirts before the altar of She-Who-Will-Not-Have-A-Husband, calling, and clapping, and keeping time with the stamp of their feet. Runners passed in through the gates to the temple plaza, carrying cages with quail.

"The sacrifices must be made at sunset," said the blood knives. "The first day of the month of Winds must be sanctified by blood."

They never stopped.

"It would be best if you remained at the Heart-Of-The-World's Beginning," they said. "Our runners can bring you news of all that transpires in the land."

But could she trust the news they brought her? She did not voice these doubts aloud, and they went on.

"We insult the gods by not bringing in work gangs to whitewash and paint, to refurbish the house of the gods."

"Let the fields be raised and planted first," she said.

The oldest among them leaned in close, his breath sharp with the smell of pepper. "If you who were cursed to die in exile had not stopped performing the sacrifices, then you would not have lost the gods' favor."

She bent her head to look him in the eye, a look that would have quelled dissent among her own people, but he came from a different world. He feared the cloak, but he did not respect her.

"How do you know what we suffered in exile?" she asked him. "You walked between the worlds for the course of a Great Year, fifty-two cycles of fifty-two years, yet according to all reports I have heard, it seemed to those of you that you walked in the shadows for only some months. We lingered in exile for generations. The world you live in—in your heart—has not changed, but the world you come to is not the one you left."

"What we owe the gods does not change," he said. "If we remember the offerings, then the rain will fall at the proper time and the sun will shine at the proper time."

There is no arguing with a man who cannot see the world as it is around him. It was human sorcerers who had woven the spell that had exiled them, and human sorcery that had poisoned the lands beyond. She remained silent, and he mumbled complaints under his breath, tallying up his list.

But her brooding could not last. A market in her life in exile was any patch of ground where folk spread a blanket on which to display a handful of precious nuts or bruised tubers or reed mats or a wooden staff with a carved spear point. This plaza was only the entryway; the market took up the entire district, and even if it was by no means fully tenanted, it was truly overwhelming, more people than she had ever seen together at one time in her entire life.

Beyond stone-and-brick arcades lay streets and alleys where all different categories of merchandise were sold. There were grinding stones, bricks, tiles, wood hewn and shaped, shells, bones, and feathers. There was copper and tin, and bronze tools and weapons, and all manner of ornaments molded from gold and silver. There were spines from the sap cactus for needles for punches, and for sacrifice. There were mantles and tunics woven from its thread as well as tough cord and rope, and also its sweet sap for a syrup and a fermented sap strong enough to kick you. There were arrowheads of wood and others of stone or bronze, even a few brought from human lands, forged of iron.

There was too much. And she barely glimpsed the streets where foodstuffs were sold: cactus fruit and delicate squash flowers just starting to wilt, birds plucked and hung while others fluttered in cages, rabbits, dogs, bees, eggs, and so many fish of such variegated types that she was amazed so many existed.

And all this seen and gawked at before they brought her to the central square of the market house where this mass of commerce was overseen by a bundle of judges, each in their own cubicle. In fact, the market came under the jurisdiction of a local authority, but her presence was acknowledged and feted with a series of speeches and poems deemed appropriate to the occasion. The sacrifices, all those delicious quail, would come later.

Yet she wished she could set foot on the earth and just walk through the market, taking her time, taking in smells and sounds. She wept a little, to see such riches, although the judges assured her with the greatest embarrassment that if only the gods favored them, then in a few years the terrible poverty of today's fledgling market would be replaced by a decent selection as in the days before, and folk would have cacao beans and folded cloth with which to trade properly.

How could they not recognize how life flourished here, even if it seemed poor to them. There were so many people. There were so many children!

It was hard to concentrate, and doubly so when a parade of mask warriors chivvied a mixed herd of sheep and goats into view.

This was too much! She got to her knees, rocking the litter so that her bearers staggered. As the blood knives cried complaint, she swung down, let fall, and walked over to examine the beasts, who bawled and ba'aahed from the shelter of a makeshift corral over against the arcade leading to the street of live animals. Many folk gathered to stare, and especially she noted among them the wasted bodies and thin faces of those who had survived exile, yet they were only a few compared to their brethren who had come out of the shadows.

White Feather accompanied her, to protect her from the nattering of the blood knives, and a pair of judges came up quickly to ascertain what manner of trading was to go on.

It was Cat Mask, after all, who was leader of the group. He had a fresh scar on his left thigh but looked otherwise entirely pleased with himself.

"We have been tracking beyond the White Road," he explained to the market judges, "and brought these here, our prizes, to the market."

"For sacrifice!" cried the blood knives.

"Two of them," said Feather Cloak. "Let two suffice, two males. The rest must be sold for breeding stock."

Oh, they did not like to hear it, and some of the folk gathered to stare murmured in favor of the blood knives, while others murmured in favor of her decree.

"If we do not maintain the balance," said the blood knives, "then He-Who-Burns will darken."

"Clouds cover the sun in the north," said Cat Mask. "But He-Who-Burns shines on us here in our own country. It is the fault of the human sorcerers. Everyone knows that they are the ones who wove the spell. Now it has rebounded against them."

"You babble like a Pale Dog," cried the blood knives. "How long will our good fortune, if that is what you call it, last, if we do not restore order. How soon will He-Who-Burns turn his bright face away from us in anger and despair?"

"Two is enough, until there is plenty," said Feather Cloak, but they muttered and scowled to hear her speak. They were fighting her now for no other reason than to test her authority; she did not know how to counter them.

"See what else we brought," said Cat Mask, dismissing this as he might the whine of a mosquito. Like all the young adults who had grown up in exile, he had never seen or conversed with one of the blood knives. "See, what we have brought from the lands beyond!" He and his mask warriors preened, being proud of themselves. "This herd is not the only one we captured."

There came in a line, dressed in wooden slave collars, a bundle of children: four infants, eight of toddling age, seven very young, and one older girl of nine or ten years of age who looked glassy-eyed with shock, staring only straight ahead. They looked nothing like the Bright One, having a different complexion and broader features and black hair more like to that of the Ashioi than Liathano's mass of fire-gold hair. They were not handsome children, not like those of her kind, but they were very young and there were so many in that one group. After so long in exile, she was still astonished by the sight of children.

"Brought you no captives?" asked the blood knives. "No warriors taken in honorable combat?"

Cat Mask shrugged. "The adults we killed were not warriors. It was too much trouble to bring them, so we killed them." He looked at his companions, and they shared winks and nods. "And we were very hungry, so we ate them."

Everyone laughed, since it was disgusting to think of eating a stranger, and one with sour flesh, at that.

"We thought it worthwhile to bring these children. A bundle plus two."

"I only count a bundle," said the eldest of the blood knives.

"Oh, that's right," remarked Cat Mask, scratching his chin. "When we came through High-Hill we met with Lizard Mask's sister, who has settled there. She just lost her little son to the coughing sickness, so she took a pair of little boys thinking that, if she raised them, she might forget her grief over the other one."

"Very well," said the blood knives. "A bundle will be enough. But you who raid into the lands beyond the White Road must bring us strong captives as tribute for the gods."

"If we can find any!" said Cat Mask with another laugh. "They looked pretty scrawny and weak. We had to fatten these little ones up on goat's milk."

"It is their blood we need," said the blood knives, "not their flesh."

They stepped forward to take the children, but before they could lay hands on them White Feather pushed past them and scooped up one of the toddlers.

"I claim this one for mine, to raise as my own!"

Her voice was loud, and her tone harsh, and the child hiccuped and sniveled into the growing silence as the blood knives opened and closed their hands and folk pressed forward to see what was going on.

Before three breaths had passed, a man with the delicate frame of an exile stepped out of the crowd and pulled an infant out of the arms of one of the mask warriors. "And I claim this one, to replace the child my wife could never have."

"And I!" said a woman, coming forward to put her hands on one of the little walking ones. "For I lost my child and my husband when the Pale Dogs raided our settlement, just before the shadows fell over us. I want this child to raise."

In her wake, other people in the market shoved forward—women and men both—and claimed children until only the oldest girl remained with her vacant stare and her vacant, terrified expression.

The blood knives raged, but they were few, and the crowd was many, and the folk who had a grip on the children looked very determined.

"These are the children of dogs! They are not our kind," the blood knives protested.

"How will they know anything different," asked White Feather boldly, "if they are raised among us?"

"It goes against our laws."

"It does not!" she retorted. "In the days before, some among humankind walked together with our people and painted the clan marks on their bodies. In this way, they became part of the clans, and their blood and our blood mixed."

"Yes! Yes!" cried the blood knives triumphantly. "And that turned the balance. You see what came of it!"

White Feather was burning with anger now. She was as bright as the sun. "I will not listen to you!" she said in a voice that carried like sunlight over the market square, where all commerce had come to a stop. "I listened once, when the last of you still ruled us in exile. What fools we were!"

"You were fools to allow your blood knives to die without training up those who could succeed them."

"You know nothing, you who walked in the shadows while we struggled, while the land died around us! Hu-ah! Hu-ah! Let my words be pleasing to She-Who-Creates, who sustains us!"

Now she could not be interrupted.

"In those days as the land died and we died, the blood knives still ruled. Many had already died because there was not enough to eat. But in those days, when I was a child, there was a great sickness and most of the remaining people died. Dogs feasted on corpses, for there were none to prepare them for the death rites. Vultures grew fat on lean flesh. Bones lay everywhere. And still we died. After this, we abandoned the cities. The few of us who still lived scattered to the villages. There we lived as the fields withered and the birds laid fewer and fewer eggs. The lakes dried up, there were no more fish, and the rivers leaked away until they ran no more than a trickle of water. And still we died.

"At last the remaining blood knives decreed that in order to restore the balance and placate the angry gods we must offer to the gods the thing we valued most. I was young then, a young woman newly married. I had just given birth to my first child, a daughter.

"The blood knives took her from me and sacrificed her. They said I was young, I would have another, and that the blood of this one would save us.

"But my womb was parched. Like the land, it was dying. I had no other child. They sacrificed the only one I bore, and the sacrifice was for nothing. The land died because it was uprooted from Earth through the magic of the human dogs. This reason, and no other. We died, and we had no more children. Don't you see? The blood knives were wrong. And in the end they died, too."

She balanced the first child on her thin hip and grasped the wrist of the older girl as well, drawing her close. "I will take these two girls to replace the one I lost. They are mine, now. I claim them, according to the law, as is my right. I will not let the blood knives sacrifice any child of mine. Not again."

The blood knives turned to Feather Cloak, who had set her feet on the dusty earth of the marketplace.

They said, "There must be a sacrifice."

"Two goats from that herd," she said, "and captives of war, strong warriors. But not these children."

The eldest leaned close, his breath sharp with the smell of pepper, and he whispered, "You will regret this."

2

AT the Heart-of-the-World, peace seemed to reign. In all the wide land that lay south of the great pyramid, called the Mountain of the World's Beginning, the Lost Ones had come home and made themselves busy in a hundred ways: building, sweeping, gossiping, mating, planting, fishing, hunting, trading, digging, bathing, carving, plaiting, weaving, grinding, sewing, minding the children, and all the rest besides.

But in the council chamber of the exiles, two brothers argued, while Feather Cloak and half a bundle of trusted councillors watched.

"How can you have managed so quickly, in no more than half a year," Zuangua was saying, "to make the priests so angry?"

"You were always first to complain of the power hoarded by the sky counters," said Eldest Uncle with a crooked smile.

"Yes, but I did so where they couldn't hear me! Yet the Feather Cloak must go to the marketplace, and you do not even counsel her in the proper way to observe the authority held by the priests. Now their knives are raised against you! They make no secret of it."

"Have you come here only to scold us?" asked Eldest Uncle.

Feather Cloak sighed. The journey back from the city on the lake had wearied her mostly because she could see what was coming. She had hoped for a respite, but hard on her heels had come Zuangua carrying a mantle-load of arrogant anger. She had refused to speak to him until Eldest Uncle could be fetched from the watchtower on the border where he made his home. Now, she listened as he shook his head impatiently at his twin brother's words.

"I came here to warn you! I speak up for you exiles as much as I am able, because of what binds us, my heart and your heart, but those of us who survived in the shadows have many complaints!"

"Complaints!" cried White Feather.

The others—Green Skirt, Skull Earrings, and seven others, all of them from those who had endured exile together—echoed her outrage.

"How can you have complaints?" asked Eldest Uncle in a milder tone, seeming half amused and half exasperated.

Zuangua held up a fist, showing its back to his aged brother.

"One." He lifted the little finger. "How have so many died? So many! We who walked beyond the White Road to fight the Pale Dogs and protect our homeland were less than a quarter of the people. Coming home, we discover we outnumber you twentyfold! How have so many died? How has the land fallen empty in a span that is no more than your life?"

"A very few among us saw great grandchildren born," said Eldest Uncle with the patience of the old. "That is a long time."

He was not angry, although the accusation was insulting. Even Feather Cloak, normally the most placid of souls, found herself flushed, cheeks hot. She tucked her infant more tightly against her. Those who had returned from the shadows could not possibly understand how precious each child had become. Green Skirt held the other baby with the fond attention of a besotted aunt, although the two women were not related by blood ties. White Feather had her own children to care for; the toddler was sleeping in a sling tied around the older woman's torso, and the girl was crouched by the wall, arms hugging her knees, eyes closed, rocking slightly on her feet.

"How long?" asked Zuangua. "How many years?"

"We could not count the round of years accurately. We had no sun and no stars by which to measure the calendar."

Zuangua had brought with him a pair of followers, a tough-looking woman wearing a fox mask and an older man with a merchant's sash slung around his torso. Fox Mask stood with arms crossed and feet braced aggressively. The merchant sat cross-legged and with a cold stare examined Feather Cloak's council members as though he would have liked to spit on each one.

"Very well," he said grudgingly. "It may be impossible to determine."

"So have we told the sky counters," murmured Eldest Uncle. "Many times over. But it appears they do not believe us."

"So it does. That brings us to my second point." Zuangua raised the next finger beside the little. "What of the priests? No land can survive without order, for we see that it did not. Yet how can it be that every one of the blood knives died?"

None of the elders replied, and most looked at the ground. White Feather's baby stirred, made restless by the tension, and the infant Green Skirt was holding gave a single, flustered cry before the old woman shushed her gently.

This was a subject no one had ever spoken of, even during exile.

"I wait," said Zuangua.

Eldest Uncle rubbed his chin. He did not look at the others. "When the famine came, during the first generation, and we died in great numbers, the blood knives offered us no solution, only problems. And when the great sickness came, still they refused to change. They could not count the measure of the sky in that place, but all they spoke of was the way things used to be done. We worship the gods still, and properly, giving of our own blood in tribute, but those who used the power of the blood knife to keep themselves raised high above others are all gone. It is true. They are all gone."

The merchant coughed, for something in Eldest Uncle's tone made everyone uncomfortable.

Zuangua frowned. "It is difficult for me to know which of those words I like least, and which I dislike most." He still held up his hand, and now he raised the middle finger to stand beside little and next. "Three. Two of the twenty clans have vanished from among the exiles."

"And ten of the remaining clans number less than five bundles in their lineage. Yes. We know how many we lost."

"How can this be?" The merchant slapped his own chest three times. "I am born into Rabbit Clan. Here in the land I find no house to welcome me!"

"There are others of the Rabbit Clan among those who survived in the shadows," said Eldest Uncle, "or so I am told."

"How could you let the clans die?" the man roared.

Eldest Uncle smiled sadly. "How can you know how it felt to watch the people die of hunger and thirst as the land failed? To smell the stench of the sickness that afflicted us? To watch fathers sing the death rites over their only child, and then fall themselves as their strength failed? What do you know of bones left to bleach on the hillside? Hu-ah! What could you have done better than what we did!"

Age gave a man power. Eldest Uncle, as well, was known as a sorcerer. He was a seeker after the grains of truth hidden in the mantle thrown over the universe which most folk call the world, for what most folk call the world is really only the things we can touch and smell and taste and hear and see.

"My apologies," said the merchant. He set hands on knees and inclined his head, just a pinch, toward the old man. "You must see how it appears to us, to wander in the shadows for so long, watching the Pale Dogs swarm over the Earth we love. To return at last to find our homeland . . ." He wiped away a tear, and this show of emotion seemed so unforced and genuine that Feather Cloak found her throat choked and her own eyes filling. "It is a land of bones."

"So it became," said Eldest Uncle. "So many died. We struggled to stay alive."

"I am not finished." Zuangua raised his forefinger, and showed the back of his hand to his brother, to all of them, open now except for the folded thumb. "Four. In the days I remember, the Feathered Cloak rose from the high lineages marked out by the gods from the heirs of Obsidian Snake, who led us over the seas."

For the first time, he looked at Feather Cloak directly. His regard distracted Feather Cloak for a moment, as it always did. His features were attractive, his bronzed complexion a handsome shade. He wore his long black hair unbound so its glossy fall would dazzle women's eyes. Yet one might admire in this same fashion Cat Mask and other warriors she had known all her life. There was this difference: Zuangua had the look of a well-made sword already whetted in battle. Compared to him, the others had no shine and no edge.

His smile was a challenge. She lifted a brow in response, refusing to be baited, not by his challenge and not by his sexuality. Still, it did her no harm to let him see she found him handsome. Some men, receiving women's regard, puffed up until their vanity made them foolish. It would be interesting to see if Zuangua would succumb to that fault.

"He believes me unworthy of the Eagle Seat," she said without dropping her gaze, yet the words were directed not at Zuangua but to Eldest Uncle and her faithful councillors.

In Zuangua, doubt held no purchase, but she recognized by the flicker of his eyes that he had not expected her to meet his challenge.

"Are you finished?" she asked him. The infant stirred, smacking and searching, and without breaking her gaze from his she helped it find the nipple. Its suck calmed her.

He said nothing.

"War will come soon," she continued, still looking at Zuangua. "Today, it comes."

"Have you seen this in a vision, Feather Cloak?" asked Eldest Uncle.

"I do not need sorcery to see what stands right before my eyes. Choose now, councillors. I can argue one way, but my voice will soon be drowned out."

"Five," said Zuangua.

Abruptly he broke the gaze, gestured to his followers, and vanished up the tunnel leading to the entrance.

"Five objections," commented Green Skirt with the sardonic tone mastered only by women who have reached a certain age. "Did he speak 'five'? And leave the words unsaid? Or were we meant to understand him by his actions?"

White Feather sighed as she rocked her baby in her arms, the child fussing, getting hungry. "I do not remember the days before, except in the stories told by the grandparents. Now it seems I am sick of hearing about them. The land in exile is the one I know. Yet I am glad we have come home." She patted the child's back, and it murmured baby syllables, content to be held. The older girl had opened her eyes, gaze fixed on the woman who was now her mother.

"Everything has changed," said Feather Cloak. "It must, and it will. But the qualities and objects we valued in exile will not be valued here on Earth. As one strand straightens, so twists the other. That is the way of the world."

They nodded. Eldest Uncle regarded her with a fond smile, Green Skirt with the savor of regret. White Feather wore an exasperated frown and Skull Earrings looked tired, jowls drooping in the fashion of men who have finally hit their decline. The others sighed and murmured soft words meant to cheer her, but no one sounded cheerful. Above, wind moaned through the hole, and roots stirred as dust danced in the changeable light.

"I have one more question," she said as they looked at her. "What happened to the last of the blood knives?"

At first there was silence, a form of speaking measured only by gazes shifting between them, words left unspoken. At length White Feather's lips twitched in that flutter smile that suggested a grim sort of laughter, or a laughing kind of anger, or maybe a joke.

"We were very hungry," she said, "so we ate them."

3

FIVE days only, hardly any time at all. The horn was blown to summon a council at which Feather Cloak must preside.

Kansi-a-lari entered the underground chamber accompanied by bells and by Zuangua and a dozen of his adherents. Behind them, remarkably, walked the joined forces of Cat Mask and Lizard Mask. Many, warriors and craftsmen, female and male alike, walked in via the tunnel to stand in the cavernous council grounds facing the Eagle Seat where Feather Cloak presided. Blood knives huddled in clusters. More people waited outside who had walked all the way from their scattered settlements and newly populated towns. The cavern was jammed to bursting and could fit no more than those standing shoulder to shoulder. All had, of course, left their weapons outside, according to the law.

All but one.

Kansi-a-lari strode forward with a stone-tipped spear in her right hand. She halted five paces from the Eagle Seat, set the haft against the ground, and raised her left hand toward the ceiling and the distant sky, visible through the jagged gap in the roof. Dust motes painted the air with a red-gold haze.

"Say what you have to say," said Feather Cloak, repeating the ritual words.

"I challenge your right to sit on the Eagle Seat and preside over the councils of our people," said The Impatient One. "In the past six turnings of the moon we have rested and made offerings of our own blood. We have planted our fields. We have built and repaired our houses. We have numbered our craftsmen and our warriors and made an accounting of spears and swords. We must strike while humankind struggles."

"They outnumber us," said Feather Cloak.

"Yes! We must strike first, and swiftly."

"Just as you have done today."

Kansi glanced back at Zuangua, who shook his head, looking impatient and bored. "We have waited long enough," Kansi-a-lari said. "We have waited too long!"

Like her uncle, The Impatient One attracted the eye. Hers was the beauty of the jaguar, deadly and fascinating. She prowled among men, and few had the strength of will to resist her. With women, though, Kansi-a-lari behaved differently, knowing she could not sway them with a hard stare or a provocative hand placed on her hip. She liked men better, because she found them easier to control.

"If we strike," Feather Cloak asked, "to what purpose do our warriors fight and die?"

"To test the strength of humankind. I have sent scouts east and west. West is wasteland, but there is a great city northeast of here that we may profitably strike. They are rebuilding. They will not be ready for us."

"So you have said, but what do you intend?"

"Kill those who resist. Bring worthy captives home to offer to the gods. Fill our storehouses with their grain and their treasures. Set in place a governor to rule their farmers and merchants. That way their taxes will serve us, not our enemies."

Feather Cloak waited while the assembly discussed this proposition in low voices, among themselves, all the blood knives who remind silent, as if they had already known what she was going to say. In the cavern, no wind blew, and despite the cool weather it had gotten stuffy. The great golden wheel of the assembly, resting behind her, remained still. Only in the wind did it turn. In this way it represented the people: each discrete emerald feather was visible at rest, but when in motion the many individual parts blended to become one bright whole, indivisible to the eye's sight.

She sighed, seeing that she must speak although she knew it would do no good. "So soon you will press past the White Road? It is better to rebuild our own cities and till our own fields until our feet are firmly planted in the roots of this Earth."

Kansi-a-lari shrugged. "Human slaves can plant and build for us. With their labor, we leave more of our own people free to fight. So it was done in the days before."

"In the days before," said Feather Cloak, knowing her words clipped and short and irritated and knowing as well that to show annoyance was to weaken her own argument, "we made enemies who worked in concert to cast us out of Earth entirely! Have we learned nothing from the past?"

"Yes!" Kansi had that jaguar's grin that made men wonder and sweat. "They hate us. They fear us. But we have to learned to strike while they are weakened so they cannot attack us again! It is time to leave the ways of exile behind and embrace what is ours, this world we were sundered from for so long!"

"No. It is too soon. Let the young ones grow. Let us rebuild and make ourselves strong first."

Kansi turned in a circle, marking each person standing in the council chamber: the elders and the younger leaders, the warriors and the craftsmen, those born in exile and those so recently returned from the limbo of the shadows. The blood knives watched her hungrily.

"I have walked among humankind, those who live in *these* days, not the ones you remember from the past. I was born in exile, but I have not waited in exile and lost my spirit and my anger."

Eldest Uncle tugged on an ear, perhaps only to hide his irritation with his only child.

"Do you insult us, who have endured exile with you?" demanded White Feather.

"I say what I have to say. Listen! I have seen that humankind cannot be trusted. Especially not those who call themselves the mathematici. They are the ones who know the secret of the crowns. They are the ones who could harm us again. Therefore: strike now! If she who sits as Feather Cloak will not lead us, *then I will.*"

Among the warriors came a general stamping of feet and pounding of spear butts on the ground, but Feather Cloak shushed this rumble by raising a hand.

White Feather stepped forward. They had prepared for this.

"I say what I have to say!" White Feather displayed Feather Cloak's twin daughters, one in each arm. Their black hair peeped out of the striped cloth wrapped around those plump baby bodies. The little ones were alert, watchful, quiet. "Those of you who walked in the shadows do not truly understand what became of this land in exile. We endured a great drought. Of water. Of *life*. We died! The carcasses of our mothers and aunts and fathers and uncles littered the land because none had the strength to send them to the gods!"

She swept her gaze around the chamber, challenging any to interrupt her. None did. "Know this! Feather Cloak bore a son and now twin daughters, although most of our people became barren. Even The Impatient One had to couple with a man born of humankind in order to conceive a son!"

"Done at the urging of the council!" cried Cat Mask, out of turn. "Not out of lust for power!"

"Do not throw sharp words at me, young one!" said White Feather. She was old enough to be his aunt, and he frowned, head twitching sideways just once, as he suppressed his annoyance. "We must not ignore how powerful Feather Cloak's magic is, that she retained her fertility when the rest of us ran dry. There is wisdom in choosing as leaders those who seek life, not death." She stepped one pace back. "I am done speaking."

Kansi-a-lari smiled.

Feather Cloak felt a cold current in her blood as at ice released into a summer stream. That was a predator's smile, having seen that its prey is now cornered.

"I have no argument against White Feather. Feather Cloak's magic and power served us well in exile. But we do not stand in exile any longer. I say what I have to say: I have walked in both worlds. Humankind is a threat. They outnumber us. We must move swiftly or be overrun. Our sorcery is stronger than theirs. I battled their strongest warrior, and I defeated him because I possess magic and he had only brute force. Our scouts suggest there is great destruction in their land. If they are in disorder, leaderless, and struggling to rebuild, even to survive, then now is our best chance. We may not get another."

Feather Cloak stood. The heavy feather cloak fastened over her shoulders spilled around her body, whispering in the tones of conspirators. She had regained her physical strength since the birth of her daughters, but as she faced her rival she knew that The Impatient One had chosen the right time to attack. Her resolve still suffered. She had not yet adjusted to what it meant to be home, on Earth, a place she knew only in story.

She raised both palms. The assembly stilled, not even a foot shifting on dirt, not even a hand scratching an arm. She still had that power.

"Let it be put to the vote," she said coolly. "Let each household delegate a speaker to cast their stone into the black basket or the white, as the gods decreed at the beginning of time. The assembly will meet on an auspicious day as chosen by the blood knives, at the Heart-of-the-World's-Beginning. I have spoken."

4

ANNA tasted dry grass as they rode through an archway of light into dawn. Chaff coated her moist lips. A smear of red lit hills and she stared, wondering what that light might signify.

"The sun!" murmured scarred John, who rode ahead of her. As her ears cleared, popping, she heard the other soldiers exclaiming at their first glimpse of the sun in months. Above, clouds obscured the night sky, but the eastern dawn rose with a startling glow as though the far hills were on fire.

Blessing snorted and, kicking, came awake. "Put me down!"

Anna twisted. "Your Highness! I pray you! Keep still, Your Highness! I am with you."

"Don't fight," said the one called Frigo, getting hold of the girl's ear and pinching.

She shrieked, a sound that ought to have woken the dead and certainly made every man there clap a hand over an ear as she sucked in air to shriek again. Without the slightest expression of anger or pleasure, Frigo tweaked her ear a little farther and she subsided into coughing and mewling. He let go, and she stayed quiet.

The archway of light sprayed fountains of sparks as Lord Hugh strode out of the circle of stones. Twilight shrouded him, but it was lightening quickly. He counted his party, nine soldiers and two prisoners, before turning to survey the crown. It had ten stones standing in eerily perfect order, as if recently raised.

"Where are we, my lord?" asked Frigo as Blessing sucked on her little finger and stared at Hugh with a look meant to slay.

"According to my map, we are many days east and somewhat north of Darre, but south of the latitude of Novomo." He consulted his memory; Anna could tell by the way his gaze went vacant as though he were looking at something inside himself. " 'Four leagues beyond Siliga, eleven stones.' "

He marked each stone and gestured toward a vast tangle of bramble that lay a stone's toss east of the circle just where the hillside had collapsed. Beyond, the land sloped down into a coastal plain. Anna thought she could see water to the south beyond a desiccated landscape of pale grass and stands of paler bush, which were almost white, like stalks of slender finger bones.

"There must be a stone there," Hugh said.

Scarred John dismounted to investigate. The presbyter lifted the golden disk. He fussed with it, moving one circle on top of another, turned a crooked bar on the back, sighted toward the eastern horizon, read—lips moving—from the back, then shook his head. After this, he fished in the pack he wore, withdrew a square of waxed canvas, wrapped the disk up inside, and returned it to the pouch.

"Are we lost, my lord?" asked Frigo.

"I hope so," muttered Blessing.

"My lord! There is a stone under these brambles!" shouted John, withdrawing his spear from the mass of vines and thorns.

"We are not lost," said Hugh. "We are exactly where I hoped to be. I only wish to know what day. According to my earlier calculations we should have lost three days in the passage. Yet I can't be sure. So be it. From here we ride east."

They nodded.

"Where are we going?" Blessing demanded.

Hugh looked at her, nothing more. Anna shivered, not liking the weight of his gaze. He was capable of anything. Blessing hadn't seen Elene murdered. Better, for now, not to mention it to the girl. It was hard to know how Blessing would react.

"Let me be precise," Hugh continued, catching each man's gaze to make sure he had their attention. "We will be pursued."

"My lord," said John, "if we've come so far as you say, how can any catch up to us?"

"I do not fear human pursuit." Hugh smiled patiently, as though he had heard this question a hundred times and would happily answer it a hundred more times without losing his temper. His amiable demeanor was what scared Anna most about him. "When the alarm is raised, you must retreat immediately within the circle. I cannot protect those who remain outside." He nodded to one of the other men, a sturdy fellow with broad shoulders and spatulate hands. "It is then that we rely on you, Theodore. We have but one arrow for each man in the party."

Theodore nodded. "Eleven in all, like the stones, my lord."

"But there are twelve of us!" said Anna.

Hugh's gaze was like ice, yet his smile remained. "You are expendable, Anna. If you are marked, then you will be killed. You must hope that Antonia does not think of you at all when she sends her pursuers." His gaze moved away from her. She was not, she saw, important enough to linger on. The red dazzle of dawn faded as the sun moved up into the sky, not visible as a disk but seen as a bluish glow behind a blanketing haze.

"Theodore? Do you understand your part?"

"I do, my lord," said the man stoutly. "I will not fail you."

"No," he said, with a nod that made the archer sit up straighter. "I believe you shall not."

Beyond the standing stones lay a village, a substantial settlement with a score of roofs surrounded by a livestock palisade and a ditch. No guard manned the watchtower now. They rode across the earthen bridge that spanned the ditch and pulled up before closed gates.

Theodore shouted a few times, but there was no answer. The silence made Anna nervous. The horses flattened ears and shifted anxiously. She did not hear anything except the wind, not even a dog's bark. Finally, scarred John volunteered to get inside. He dismounted and offered his reins to Liudbold, then tested the gate. It was, indeed, barred from inside. He tested the palisade, moved off around until he found a listing post that offered a place to fix rope. Soon he clambered up the side with bare feet braced against wood and hands advancing up the joined rope. They watched him keenly. His soft grunts were audible because it was so deathly quiet. Once, a few oddly shaped fields had been tended by farmers. There was a vineyard and a stand of twoscore olive trees scattered along a nearby slope. The road east cut up into a defile, quickly lost to view. From here they could not see the coastal plain.

John reached the top and balanced himself there on his belly as he scanned the village. His mouth opened. He jerked, as at a blow, and slipped backward. Anna shrieked, thinking he would fall, but he caught himself awkwardly and hand over hand rappelled down, hitched the rope off with a flip and a yank, and ran back. He didn't reach them before he bent to one knee and retched, although he hadn't much in his stomach to cough up.

"Move the men back, Captain," said Hugh to Frigo. He took the reins from Liudbold and waited while the rest turned their horses and moved off.

"Plague," said John when he came over with Lord Hugh. "Got the dogs, too, them that had eaten the dead folk left lying in the street. Good thing that gate is closed."

"We must be cautious," said Hugh. "Let's leave this blighted place. Frigo, set your scouts. We can't be sure we won't stumble across bandits. We've few enough in our party that a smaller group taking us unaware could do great damage."

"Yes, my lord."

They rode east through a land so dry that the vegetation snapped under the hooves of their horses. There was little grass for grazing. The grain went faster, obviously, than Lord Hugh had planned, so he adjusted the rations. Where they passed the remains of juniper or olive groves all the trees had been felled in the same direction, shattered by wind. Of spring greens she saw only thistle and creeping vine.

This was rugged country, the kind of scrub-infested land that in Wendar would have been left to the shepherds as summer pasture. Along their path they passed three more silent villages before midday. Once, folk had lived and traded here. Anna wondered if they had all died or if some had escaped. She imagined children herding goats and sheep along those slopes. She imagined women walking to market with babies bundled on their backs and wheelbarrows heaped with onions and parsnips, or whatever strange food folk ate in these parts. Nothing tasty, she supposed.

It was so quiet, as though death had eaten the world and moved on, leaving only the stones and the empty buildings and the whitened grass. Now and again as they rode along a narrow passage with ridges rising steep on both sides, she imagined that refugees peered at her from the rocks above, but in truth she felt nothing. She felt that even the animals had fled, that nothing lived here anymore and that the clouds would never part and only dust would be her companion evermore. Certainly, her tongue was sticky with dirt, but she didn't dare ask for more water. Therefore it was a surprise to her when scarred John came riding back from forward scout with the news that he had sighted a column of armed riders.

"Fourscore at least, my lord," he reported. "Not Aostan, by the look of them."

"Are these the ones you've been expecting to meet?" asked Captain Frigo. Blessing sat behind him, wrists tied, fingers gripping the back of his saddle. She tried to get a look around him, as if hoping to see a saint come to rescue her.

"It's hard to say without a look at them," said Hugh. He nodded at John.

"There's an abandoned village ahead, my lord. If we hide there, we might see them pass by without being seen ourselves."

"Is there no other cover?" Hugh asked. "I'd rather not ride in haste into a village that might be harboring the plague."

"Forest up along the hills," said Theodore, who had been riding inland for part of the morning and only recently returned, "but the trees are downed, just as we've seen everywhere else."

"Some rocks," said John, "this side of the village. Very rugged. As like to cut your hands as give you shelter. But enough to hide our party and give a little defensive protection. They're within view of the road."

"We'll go there. Hasten."

"They'll see our tracks," said Frigo.

"Drag sticks behind us, if you must, but we've little choice as we're badly outnumbered. We've ridden single file thus far. We must hope they believe us only a pair or three of riders."

Soon they saw the thread of dust rising far to the east that marked the passage of many mounted men. From her position in the middle of their group, it was difficult for Anna to tell how much of a flag they themselves raised. She had her own horse now, a stolid creature that moved along with the herd sniffing bottoms now and again but otherwise lacking curiosity and initiative. Not the kind of horse to escape on, even if she had anywhere to go and food and drink to run with. Even if she might hope for shelter from an unknown band of soldiers.

The rock formation erupted out of the ground in the midst of dry plain. The sloping ground hid the village from sight, but scarred John assured them it was right over the crest, situated to have a commanding view of the road, which was the main east-west thoroughfare in this region. The red-brown rock spilled down the slope in a series of ragged ribbons, pooling into hummocks high enough to hide horses and men. Once they crossed into the formation, they had to move carefully on the rock. Two men cut their hands. One of the horses got a gash on his right foreleg. The rock was striated and quite rugged, oddly warm to the touch despite the lack of direct sunlight. It seemed freshly deposited, but naturally that was impossible.

Theodore trotted out to the road to survey the rocks and after a few minutes jogged back to say that they were well hidden. Two men had gone out on foot with sticks to brush away their tracks. The rest drank sips of warm, sour ale as they waited. No one spoke.

"Gag the girl," said Lord Hugh suddenly. Blessing did not struggle as Frigo tied a linen cloth over her mouth and hobbled her ankles as a secondary precaution. Hugh examined Anna as well, then nodded, and the captain got another cloth and another rope. Blessing watched, gaze burning, as Anna was gagged. The cloth bit into the corners of Anna's mouth and she choked, then steadied her breathing. He hooked her hands up into the small of her back and made a knot, something easy for him to get her out of should they have to move quickly. After that, he ignored her.

She sat down, but the rock cut into her buttocks, so she stood up again, wishing for sturdier shoes. The captain fingered his sword's hilt. Certain of the soldiers soothed the more restive horses. Hugh climbed up beside scarred John to a ledge that allowed them a view over the landscape. He bent his head as if praying.

They waited. After a while, the pair of soldiers returned and squatted down with the rest, wiping sweat from their foreheads. A spiderweb trembled between two spines of rock. In a shadowed crevice, moss flourished where moist, hot air steamed up from a crack in the ground, stinking of rotten eggs.

The wind caught up puffs of dust at intervals but died as quickly. A brown seam appeared in the eastward sky above the rocks. Hugh's shoulders grew taut; he bent forward and pointed at a sight Anna could not see. Other men stationed in clefts and crevices within the fountain of rock saw it as well, and made gestures each to the other. Theodore set an arrow to his string.

Frigo handed Blessing's leash to Liudbold and climbed up to crouch beside Lord Hugh. Anna edged forward to listen.

"That's a general's banner," muttered scarred John. "What's such a lord doing with a century of men riding into Aosta?"

"So it's true," said Hugh. "Adelheid hopes to make an Arethousan marriage for Princess Mathilda. Why else would an Arethousan lord general ride into his enemy's lands in times such as these and with no greater force than that, if not to negotiate an alliance?"

"Hand her own daughter over to *them?*" Captain Frigo spat. "Their mothers are sows and their fathers asses."

"So it is said. But alliance with the north is closed to her, or so she believes. Her country is devastated. I know not how Arethousa fares. It would be a pragmatic decision."

"But *Arethousans*, my lord!" continued Frigo.

"Do not despair, Captain. Perhaps they mean to hand over a young princeling to Adelheid who can then be Mathilda's consort. Who is bold, and who is desperate?"

"They can't be trusted. They don't even believe in the true faith!" He hesitated. "But perhaps you know otherwise. Are these the ones we have ridden here to meet?"

Anna yawned, stretching her face, trying to ease the cloth jammed into her mouth. Frigo hadn't hobbled her. If she ran, would the lord general's party give her shelter? Or would Theodore plant an arrow in her back before she could reach them?

Did she want to return to Queen Adelheid? And how did they know Lord Hugh was right? The Arethousans might be going anywhere or just on a scouting expedition. They might be riding west to kill any foreigner they stumbled across.

"Look," said scarred John with a grunted laugh. "The one in the gold tabard. He's got but the one eye. Can you see it? Bet some Aostan captain got a taste of him!"

His companions sniggered.

"How can you tell, John?" demanded Theodore. "He's too far to see his eyes."

"Just 'cause I'm not blind like you! And you, the archer!"

"Quiet, now." Hugh lifted a hand as a signal to the men behind him. "Let them pass."

"What do you make of it, my lord?" asked Frigo. "What if they see our tracks?"

Hugh gave no reply. He was murmuring under his breath. A strange, sharp scent soaked the air, making Anna want to sneeze. A wind came up out of nowhere, blowing dust across the plain, obscuring the view. Hugh's men covered their faces with cloth. Grit stung Anna's skin, but all she could do was turn her face away and shut her eyes.

At length, the wind died as suddenly as it had come. They rose and shook dust out of the creases and crevices of their clothing, unbound their captives, and moved on. The rest of the troop set their faces forward, but Lord Hugh continually looked back, watching and listening, as if he expected a storm to sweep down on them out of the west.

5

IN the days before, less than four generations ago according to the estimate of the exiles but over two thousand seven hundred turnings of the year measured by the calendar of Earth, the first city built by those who sailed out of the west rested atop the Heart-of-the-World's-Beginning. This was a vast and sacred cavern whose mysteries could not be plumbed except by the gods' acolytes, the sky counters, who were also known as the blood knives. In the earliest times, so legend said, a plaza adorned with serpent-masked sculpted heads marked this holy chamber. Later a pyramid rose in a series of incarnations on the central plaza, dedicated to She-Who-Creates, who alone understands the secret heart of the universe.

The city grew out from this hub by means of two broad avenues. The Sun's Avenue woke to the east and lay down to sleep in the west, anchored at either end by a temple dedicated to He-Who-

Burns in his rising and setting aspects. A second great avenue bisected the Sun's Avenue, this one along the north-south axis dedicated to She-Who-Will-Not-Have-A-Husband. By this means the avenues divided the city into quarters, according to the instructions of the most ancient elders who had undertaken to construct the city in obedience to the dictates of the gods.

So it had been, until the day the great weaving had severed the city, cut it as with a knife in a line that ran right through the huge pyramid sacred to She-Who-Creates. Now, at dawn, Feather Cloak ascended the staircase of the great pyramid and halted about a quarter of the way up on a wide terrace. Here rested a pair of stone benches, shaded by recently built thatch shelters, and from this isolated way station she surveyed the city and the crowd. The Impatient One climbed the steps behind her and took her place on the other bench. They did not speak.

It was possible from the height to see clearly the gash that separated what had been exiled from what had never left Earth.

Brilliantly painted serpent masks flanked the steep stairs. Below, color flooded the long stretches of wall demarcating the plazas that lined the south and east avenues. As was the custom, murals covered every wall to remind the people of their ancient lineages: black eagles, golden phoenix, red serpents clutching arrows in their jaws, howling red dogs, white spider women with their wisdom nets, hawks and lynx and tawny spotted cats. Lizards and rabbits and the graceful, deadly jaguar, and all the others besides.

Yet on the northwestern side, as sharp as any line drawn in sand, lay that portion of the city that had been left behind in the wake of the great weaving. It was a city of bones, stone scoured to gray, roofs lost to time and wind and rain, the open shells of buildings, and grains of sand coating the ancient roadway. The contrast disoriented her each time she tried to view the whole. It was impossible for the gaze to flash from ancient past to vibrant present so quickly, just as it is impossible to see a crone standing beside her own child self.

It was strange to think that, just as she stood between peak and base, she also balanced between the ancient past and the unexpected present. Below, as many of her people as could make the journey had gathered in the plaza. They were a multitude without number: twenty multiplied by twenty, and by twenty yet again and once more.

She had lived all her life in a dry and dusty world, sparsely inhabited with a dry and dusty people, thin, weary, and withered. But the exiles made up no more than one in twenty of the multitude below. So many had returned out of the interstices of time, still plump and fiery, inflamed with anger at an ancient war she knew only from Eldest Uncle's stories and those of her old grandparents and great-aunts and -uncles, now dead. Their fury was palpable, like the buzzing of bees, something felt in the air, through the stone, and in the motion of bodies gesticulating and swaying or standing in rigid stillness. They had walked in the shadows for fifty-two passages of fifty-two years, caught betwixt and between, neither living creature nor yet a ghost. They had not forgiven, and why should they?

They lacked the calm-minded clarity that allowed folk to make good decisions, she knew this, yet it still heartened her to see her people whole and living and strong. There were so many children, squirming and giggling and wiggling, held up to watch as the ceremony began.

The blood knives sang down the gods to witness, according to the law. Elders chosen from the clans, including Eldest Uncle, came forward to oversee that stones were cast fairly, and none cast twice. In lots of five, the household leaders came forward to cast their household's vote in the black baskets or in the white.

Black represented the dark face of She-Who-Will-Not-Have-A-Husband. In this way, she turned her back on her petitioners. White represented her bright face, and in truth her regard was nothing to be hoped for. If the white baskets ran full, then Kansi-a-lari's petition would be granted and the Eagle Seat and the feather cloak would pass to a new leader.

So came warriors wearing the mask of their lineage: a hawk, a lizard, a spotted cat, a long-snouted tepesquintli. Others were craftsmen with a feather headdress or short mantle or sash displaying their mastery at leatherwork or obsidian-knapping, weaving or paper making or carving, ceramics or surveying or mural painting or incense grinding. Farming households voted, as did the scribes who served the gods and the merchants who kept the blood of trade moving between towns. All those who tended to the life of the people had a voice, as the gods intended, but only one could lead—else chaos would reign as it had in the days of legend before the gods ordered all things to foster peace among the tribes.

It had not been so, not exactly like this, in the days before exile. According to Eldest Uncle, the priests who wielded the blood knives had in those days wielded more power than they ought, and it seemed that their time in the shadows had not changed their outlook. They were not bold enough to tear the cloak off her shoulders, but it was obvious they had only been biding their time.

The day lengthened, although the sun never grew hard and bright as it was said to have done in the days before. It was traditional to fast, although she could drink sap wine and spring water.

The stone reaches of the northern avenue and a segment of the western road remained for the most part deserted. No one wanted to walk where the hand of time lay starkly, just as no person wished to sleep beside the skeletons of her forebears. Better they be sealed away behind the brilliant paint of life. Wind teased along the deserted avenue, moaning faintly in the stones, causing a thin veil of grit to rise and, then, settle. The wind spread among the assembly. It rippled through feathers, tugged at the ends of capes and tunics, and tangled in children's unruly hair.

She tasted the sour burned smell of the lands to the northwest where molten fire had destroyed a wide swathe of land and everything that lived there. Through this wasteland their enemies would have to ride to reach them; through this wasteland their soldiers would have to journey to strike humankind. The country itself shielded them, or caged them. Marching straight inland, it was as yet impassable, and it was barely manageable going right along the shore.

The voting lasted all day and through the night, lit by torchlight. Her legs ached. At intervals she sat. On occasion she dozed.

Dawn blossomed, a new day. In the days before, the ceremony had normally lasted three days, but by midmorning the presiding elders raised their staffs to declare the vote finished.

Twenty baskets had been set out for each color, and now the contents of all must be consolidated into a few and any stray stones of the wrong color removed. She knew what the outcome would be, but she waited along with everyone else.

Close by the steps she saw Rain, the artisan who had fathered her twin daughters although not her son. He was a slender man, not at all impressive in the width of his shoulders; he had no belligerent lift to his chin. He had trained with weapons as all children must but followed a different path, and if one had clear sight one might see the humor that twisted up his lips and the intensity of intelligence in his gaze and the wiry strength of his arms and the clever skill in his hands. He was holding one of the infants, lashed in a sling against his body. From this distance she could not, in fact, tell which one it was, the elder or the younger, and she could not recall who had the other child. Any one of ten or twenty aunts or uncles might have claimed the precious bundle. In the six moons since their birth, she thought it possible that they had never once been set down.

Rain was speaking to one of the refugees, the newcomers, as she thought of them, although they were so old that across the duration of their shadowy exile the stones of the city had been scoured clean of the bright murals that gave the city its vigor. For an instant, seeing it was a young woman, a mask warrior, she felt the sting of jealousy. Then he happened to look up at her and, seeing her head turned his way, made a gesture with his free hand to show he was with her in spirit. The young woman turned and addressed a remark to a person who had up to this time been hidden behind a cluster of onlookers, and she saw it was her son. He was an upright boy, respectful and clever, but one look at his face told her that it was *he* who had a hankering to speak to this mysterious newcomer. He smiled and flirted in the manner of youths caught in a fever they did not yet understand and were not quite yet old enough to act on.

He was growing up. In this matter, at least, the world did not change.

She looked sideways, at last, to examine her rival. The Impatient One had her eyes closed, but her right foot tapped the stone to a brisk rhythm, like a racing heart.

The baskets were dragged out and set on the lowest step of the pyramid. Three baskets held white stones close to the brim with a fourth for the overflow. Only one black basket was lifted out, and it was not even half full.

No announcement was made. They all knew, even those who had, despite everything, cast their vote for her rule, that had sufficed for a rule in exile, but sufficed no more.

The Impatient One opened her eyes and lifted a hand to point toward the height of the pyramid. Feather Cloak pressed the back of her hand to her forehead, for strength, and without replying began the ascent.

It was an exhausting climb. The steps were narrow, and the risers high, and when the platform that crowned the height opened at last before them she was dizzied. Clouds piled into stormy risers to the east. She thought she heard the growl of thunder, but it faded. The Impatient One, with a frown and a lift of the elbow, waited for her to begin the ritual.

First, the circuit of the platform, paced west to north to east to south. She wept to see the city laid whole around her, so long desired and now fulfilled. On the western face of the pyramid the lower stairs had crumbled away into a dangerous slope of loose shards and the weathered, broken remains of what once were stairs. It was possible to actually see the ragged joining where new met old, but it was disorienting. She felt she might fall and fall, tumbling down the slope into the forgotten past now yanked unexpectedly into line with the present.

Farther down, at the northwestern corner along the base, lay a field of impressive rubble jamming what had once been the sacred entrance to the Heart-of-the-Universe, the cavern beneath the temple.

She licked away a tear from the corner of her mouth as she returned from her circuit and walked to the center. She halted beside the blood stone and removed from the hem of the feather cloak a pair of sap cactus spines. One she handed to Kansi-a-lari.

"Will you cease work on the rockfall?" she asked the other woman. "If we could unearth the entrance to the Heart-of-the-Universe . . ."

The Impatient One wiped sweat from the back of her neck. "Then what? Will the gods blast our enemies? Will the earth open up and swallow them? Will we gain the ability to see what they are doing without them knowing, or to move faster than they can move themselves between their weaving crowns?"

"Respect the gods," said Feather Cloak, shocked at such talk even from The Impatient One. "We have survived, and suffered. Let us seek peace, not confrontation."

"As you did, with the blood knives?" mocked the Impatient One.

"Do you think they are your allies? Do you think you can control them?"

The Impatient One smiled cruelly. "Blood will sate them."

She stuck out her tongue and held its tip with thumb and two fingers. Raising the spine, she touched its pointed end to the pink flesh.

Feather Cloak sighed. "With this blood," she said, "I let authority pass from my hand into the hand of the one who is chosen."

She settled down cross-legged on the blood stone, leaning over the shallow basin that marked its center. She held her own tongue and pierced it smoothly. The pain flashed like fire, and it throbbed, but sharp red blood dropped into the basin made by the blood stone.

Kansi-a-lari did the same. Where blood melded and mixed, it

smoked, bubbling for the space of one breath before it dissipated into the air with a scent so acrid that both sneezed.

"With this blood, I accept authority into my hands from the one who came before."

Kansi held out her hands, palms up, and waited. At least she did not gloat, but she was, obviously, restraining her impatience with the leisurely pace of the ritual. She wanted to get on with it, get moving, make decisions, push forward.

The time for careful steps is done. The world she knew and understood was passing out of her hands. Fled, like a kiss stolen from a man who doesn't really want you.

The headdress. The rustling cloak. The spines. All these were transferred. These sigils of the authority released her, and she was only what she had been before, called Secha by her family and named The-One-Who-Looks-Hard-at-the-Heart as a child for her habit of staring at her playmates with a level gaze when she found their antics distasteful or mean-spirited.

She-Who-Sits-in-the-Eagle-Seat rose, hands raised heavenward to show her palms to the sight of the gods, who through the hands can see into the heart. She might stand at the height of the temple dedicated to She-Who-Creates for a day or a year, waiting for the gods to speak to her, although Secha doubted that The Impatient One could stand still for more than twenty breaths.

And indeed, not twenty breaths later, Feather Cloak grunted, wiped away the sweat beading her forehead, and set off to descend the steps.

In that moment of solitude granted her, Secha touched chin and forehead to acknowledge the gods. The sky had lightened. The clouds shone like the underside of a pearl, and she glimpsed the shimmering disk of the sun high above and tasted its heat on her bloody tongue and in the sticky hot dust kicked up by the feet of the multitude below.

At length she stood and followed Feather Cloak down the steep stairs.

Feather Cloak was met on the lower terrace by a swarm of people who wore emblems of rank not seen in Secha's lifetime: the marks of high lineage, of privilege, of priestly sanction and a warrior's prestige. Sashes; a blood knife banner; a beaded neckpiece; bright feather headdresses; long, clay-red mantles; gauntlets of precious shells strung together on a net.

Secha passed around them like a shadow, forgotten and unseen.

She was free, although the wound in her tongue burned and the taste of blood reminded her of the sharpness of defeat. No weight bowed her shoulders. She was only herself now, a woman with certain skills who must find her way in the new world whose landscape was still unexplored. The exiles and the ones who had walked in the shadows must build together.

It would not be easy.

XVI
A TEMPTING OFFER

1

"ARE you sure he is dead?" asked Adelheid.

"There is no escape from the galla."

"Are you sure?"

When Antonia thought about Hugh of Austra, her gut burned and her heart hammered, and she had to murmur psalms until she calmed herself. "They are not mortal creatures, as we are. They desire only a return to the pit out of which they sprang. They will pursue those whose names they carry because when that soul is extinguished, the bond that binds them to Earth is broken."

"The world is a large place!"

"They do not seek as would a human scout. If he walks on Earth, they will find him by other means than the five senses. Had he vanished out of this plane of existence, they would return to me seeking release. Only I, or the death of that soul, can release them. They did not. Thus, he must be dead."

She and Adelheid walked through the enclosed garden beside the clematis. A few brave flowers budded among the leaves, but none had opened. Like her anger, they remained closed tight, waiting for more auspicious weather.

"What if he has a defense against them?" Adelheid worried at it, as a dog keeps chewing a bone long since shed of all its flecks of tasty fat and flesh. "Prince Sanglant did, with griffin feathers."

"Prince Sanglant is in the north. He is Hugh's sworn enemy. Think you Sanglant gave the man he most despises a dozen griffin feathers as a precaution?"

"Hugh might have stolen such feathers. He said he was at the Wendish court before he was exiled."

"It might be true he was at the Wendish court. Or he might have lied to us. Perhaps you believe Hugh stole Princess Blessing to return her to her father in exchange for peace between them? Or that the old Eagle is the one who murdered Lady Elene?"

"He was covered in her blood. And caught in the stables, trying to saddle a horse and make his escape."

"A crude ploy on Lord Hugh's part, I imagine, to distract us. The old man has no reason to murder the girl."

"Why would Lord Hugh want her dead?"

"She is his rival. She was educated by a formidable mathematicus."

"Then why not kill the old man at the same time?"

"He knows nothing important. Anne said so. His skills are trifles compared to what the rest knew. He is no threat."

"Yet you had him returned to the dungeon, in chains. If we do not mean to kill him, and if he is no threat, then why not let him bide in the tower with Lord Berthold?"

"As Berthold has requested? No, I think not. The soldiers hate him, believing he murdered the young lady. They would believe themselves ill used if he did not suffer. In any case, it serves me to keep him in chains. I still have a use for him."

Adelheid shook her head, her face pale as she pinched tiny buds off a branch with nervous anger. "These are wheels within wheels, like a toy from Arethousa. Easily broken. Difficult to fix. How can you be sure that Hugh is dead?"

Adelheid feared Hugh! That was the root of her displeasure.

"Do not despair, Your Majesty," said Antonia in a soothing tone. "Once the galla swarm, a man possessing griffin feathers must move quickly to save himself. To save all of his troop would be beyond his capacity. There is no way to shield oneself from their power, there is no ancient spell of warding. It is impossible—unlikely—nay, it is impossible."

"You cannot be sure! And the child, too! If she is dead, then

Mathilda has no rivals in the second generation. I should have slit her throat myself. Now I will never know if she perished."

Almost, Antonia lost her temper, but fortunately soldiers appeared under the archway that led into the palace.

"Your Majesty! Holy Mother!"

Captain Falco hurried forward, and Adelheid paused beside the mosaic floor. He knelt before her.

The queen touched a finger to her own lips, hissed a breath, and spoke. "What news, Captain?"

"Your Majesty," he said, for he always put Adelheid first, although it was wrong of him to do so. Afterward, he inclined his head toward Antonia. "Holy Mother. When we searched more carefully, we found where they had left the road."

"Did they go to the crown?" Antonia asked.

"It's true there was some disturbance by that path, but it appears they decided not to go that way."

"Because of the clouds, they could not weave," said Antonia. "God stymied them."

"Go on," said Adelheid impatiently. "What did you find?"

"Two days' ride down the road we found where they scattered into the woodland. They must have been fleeing from—" He broke off, and glanced nervously at Antonia; it was good that he feared her. "We brought the remains back in wagons, Your Majesty, although I admit we found no stray horses living or dead."

"What manner of remains?" Antonia asked.

"A tumble of bone, hard to sort out because cast here and there along the ground and amid bushes. We found twelve skulls. Two of them were somewhat smaller than the rest. Belt buckles, metal bits, such things. This as well, among the bones." He offered her a silver brooch molded in the shape of a panther grappling with a hapless antelope.

"Austra's sigil," said Antonia.

"He was wearing that when he arrived," said Adelheid breathlessly. Her cheeks became red as she took the brooch from the captain and weighed it in her palm. "Still, why ride south? Why not ride north?"

"He claimed to have been exiled from Wendar," said Antonia. "So he could not hope to find refuge there. Yet I, too, wonder what they hoped to find in the south."

"Twelve skulls," mused Adelheid, "but thirteen went missing."

She gave Antonia such a look, but Antonia refused to be drawn. There had been no reason to raise a galla to pursue Heribert.

"I left men behind to continue searching, Your Majesty," said the captain, "knowing you would wish to account for everyone."

"What if it was Hugh who survived?" Adelheid asked, still studying the brooch. "How can we know? Bones do not speak."

"Do you wish Lord Hugh dead? Or alive? Your Majesty." It was said sharply, but Antonia had tired of this conversation which they had repeated a dozen times since the morning four days ago when they had woken to find Lady Elene murdered, and Hugh, Princess Blessing, and Brother Heribert vanished together with nine soldiers including one of Adelheid's loyal captains.

"I wish Henry still lived," said Adelheid. She wiped an eye as though it stung. "He was a good man. None better."

She sank down on the stone bench and rested her elbow on her knee and her forehead on her palm, the very image of a woman mourning a lost lover. Her gaze strayed over the ancient mosaic, and her eyes glittered, washed with tears.

"So it went in the old story," she said, indicating the mosaic on which Antonia stood. The man was draped only in a length of cloth that did a poor job of covering his shapely body. The huntress' hair was as dark as Adelheid's, braided and looped atop her head in the antique style, common to Dariyans and depicted in mosaics, painted walls and vases, and sculpture. She had a bold nose and black mica eyes and the faintest memory of Prince Sanglant in tawny features.

"I do not know the story," said Antonia impatiently, "nor am I sure I wish to know it."

Adelheid raised a startled face to look at her. "Surely you must know it! It is the first tale I was told as a child."

"The story of the blessed Daisan?"

The Aostans were tainted by their past, as everyone knew. Despite the loving and firm hand of God directing them to all that is right and proper, they persisted in remembering and exalting the indecent tales of ancient days.

"The story of Helen. When she was shipwrecked on the shores of Kartiako, she went hunting but found instead this man, here." She indicated the male figure who held a staff, and was standing beside an innocent lamb. The image of the lamb had sustained damage about the head, stones chipped away. "She thought he was only a common herdsman, but he was the prince of Kartiako, the son of the regnant. She did not discover his worth until it was too late. Thus we are reminded each time we walk in this garden not to let appearances deceive us. Not to reject too swiftly, lest we regret later."

"Are you speaking of Lord Hugh's return to Novomo, Your Majesty? Certainly you rejected him swiftly enough."

Adelheid looked at her without answering, expression twisted between annoyance and tears, and turned away to break off a twig of clematis. She rolled the leaves against her fingers until they were mashed to pulp.

"I was thinking of Conrad's daughter," she said reluctantly. "I regret she was killed in such a cowardly way. She did nothing to deserve it."

"Your Majesty!" Brother Petrus hurried down the steps with a pair of stewards at his heels. "The envoys have come, Your Majesty! They'll be here by day's end."

Adelheid rose and flicked away the last tear. "We must grant them a splendid reception. Captain Falco, muster all the guardsmen and soldiers. Let them line the streets and array themselves about the palace and the courtyard and the audience hall. Brother Petrus, let my schola assemble, every one. Send Veralia to me. She will supervise my stewards. She must consult with Lady Lavinia. I will go crowned and robed. Afterward, there must be a feast, as fine a meal as can be assembled at short notice." She recalled her company and belatedly nodded toward Antonia. "What do you wish, Holy Mother?"

Antonia hid her irritation. It was good to see Adelheid so lively, even if it was for a distasteful cause. "Surely you cannot mean to go through with this, Your Majesty?"

"What choice have I?"

"But your own daughter!"

"What choice have I?"

It had come to this. Hugh had come to them, and Adelheid had foolishly driven him off. Now his power was lost forever, and in addition they had lost two excellent hostages.

Worse, he had stolen Heribert, that faithless whore. But she could not let Adelheid know how cruelly this blow struck at her heart. She could never show weakness. She must forget Heribert, consider him dead, slice the cord herself. She should have severed the tie the day he ran away at Sanglant's order. In this matter, Hugh was blameless. It was Sanglant who had corrupted Heribert.

And in any case, once the searchers found him and returned him to Novomo, she could devise a suitable punishment.

"Holy Mother? Is there aught that ails you?"

"Nay, nothing. I am only reflecting that you are right. What choice have we?"

But after all, Hugh was the treacherous one, doubly so, with plans afoot she could not fathom.

Knowing that they must appear in greatest state before the arriving delegation so that no one would suspect their weakness, Antonia went to the chest sealed with sorcery to fetch Taillefer's magnificent crown of empire to place upon Adelheid's brow.

The amulet was sealed properly; yet after all when she opened the chest, she found an empty silk wrapping. Hugh had stolen it, no doubt to crown Sanglant's daughter as a puppet queen. And now it was lost in the woods, on the back of a panicked horse.

She could only rage while her servants cowered.

2

IN the afternoon of the third day, Lord Hugh and his party came down out of the hilly country closer to the sea's shore and found an abandoned town that looked as if it had been swept clean by a towering wave. Cautiously, John scouted in through the broken gates and afterward they all followed him. They found the bones of a dog scattered beneath a fallen beam in a ruined house but no sign of recent life. A stream spilled seaward, overflowing its banks where it met the wide waters. Its water had a brackish, oily taste, but they drank anyway and filled up their leather bladders so they wouldn't have to break open their spare cask of ale.

Lord Hugh prowled the town, seeking signs.

"See here," he would say, where spars had lodged in the gapped teeth of the ruined palisade. "A wave caused this. Yet inland the pattern of disturbance suggested a wind out of the east southeast. There must have been two storms of destruction, one after the next. As ripples run in ponds, the second following the first."

The town had not been large, and the shattered remains of pilings suggested it had once boasted a wharf. Farther up the strand, fish had rotted, their bones strewn like twigs along the shore. The sea lapped the strand placidly. John tried fishing but had no luck. Blessing tried to run away and after had a rope tied to her waist and had to follow along behind Frigo like a dog on a lead. He was neither cruel nor kind to her but dispassionately amused. Hugh rarely looked at the girl at all, and when he did, he would frown and set his lips in an expression Anna could not interpret. A man might look so at a two-headed calf, or at the child sprung from the union of his bitterest rival and the woman he desired most in the world but could never have.

"Should we camp in the town, my lord?" asked Captain Frigo.

"What do the men say?" Hugh asked him. "I think the shelter will do us some good, but if they prefer a more open site, if they fear plague, that is as well with me."

Frigo nodded, scratching his beard. "They're muttering that it's well enough to walk a town like this in daylight, when night might bring ghosts, and devils carrying sickness. I think otherwise. There's no sign of dogs or corpses. Deserted as we are here, it's best to have a defensible position. They'll see the wisdom of staying within walls if anything attacks us by night. Wolves or bandits. Those other things."

"Wisely spoken, Captain. Set up camp."

John and Theodore found a campsite that suited the nervous men. They planted their backs against the broken wall of a merchant's compound with a long storehouse along one side and a stable along another. The courtyard gave them space to set up a couple of lean-tos for shelter without having to camp right within the ruins where scorpions might scuttle and ghosts poke their knuckles into a man's ribs while he slept.

Scarred John unfolded a leather-and-wood tripod stool. Lord Hugh unrolled a map on top of the small traveling chest. He pinned the corners with an oil lamp, a heavy silver chain mounded up over a silver Circle of Unity, his knife, and his left hand. He studied the map, twisting a wick between thumb and middle finger but not yet lighting it.

"We escape tonight," Blessing whispered to Anna as the girl trotted past in Captain Frigo's wake. The big man glanced at her. Anna wasn't sure how much Wendish he understood, but she guessed he couldn't follow her conversations with the princess as

well as she could follow the Dariyan spoken between soldiers and
master.

Under the shelter of sloped canvas, she unrolled the blankets she
and Blessing shared, and there she sat to watch Lord Hugh as he
stared at the parchment. The canvas ceiling rose and fell as a twilight wind gusted out of the east.

The men chatted companionably as they got the horses settled in
the stables and sentries up onto the walls. Liudbold and scarred
John set to work splitting wood from the abandoned houses to fuel
the fire. Frigo sat on his saddle and, with Blessing trussed tight beside him, set to work dressing a sapling trunk with an adze.

Lord Hugh had that ability to build trust between himself and
those who served him. In this same manner, Prince Sanglant led his
men, knowing all their names, their home villages, their sense of
humor, and which man needed a coarse joke or which a kind word
to keep his spirits up. In this wilderness, Hugh's entourage was
nervous and watchful but not terrified, because they trusted him.

In her mind's eye, she saw Elene's blood leaking over the chess-
board and pooling around Berthold's slack fingers. She could not
shake off the memory.

He glanced up, noted her regard, and dismissed it. Scarred John
brought him a cup of ale. He thanked him, drained it, and handed
back the empty cup. Bringing out flint and tinder, he made ready to
light the wick.

A strange sound rang over the ordinary moan of the wind along
the deserted walls. Every man quieted and froze in position, as
though spelled. She saw their shapes like pillars, arranged out of all
symmetry. For ten breaths at least, no one spoke or moved. The
wind turned abruptly, and grew cold as winter's blast, swelling out
of the northwest. The sound rang down on that wind.

"Sounds like bells," said Theodore in a low voice.

A horse snorted and sidestepped.

A man yelped and cursed. "Ah! Ah! Right on my foot!"

"More fool you for standing there!" retorted his companion.

Lord Hugh moved his right foot to the ground, set the oil lamp
beside it, and slipped the Circle and chain over his head. As he rolled
up the map and stowed it in the chest, he spoke.

"All must retreat within the circle I draw. Bring the horses, too."

He took a bulging pouch out of the chest, closed it, and secured
the hasp. His hands were steady as he spilled a line of flour in a circle big enough to contain men and horses together. A stench like the

breath of the forge swept over them. Horses shied. Men shouted in alarm, and the three who had not yet crowded into the circle raced out of the dusk to join them. At their backs a dark storm advanced out of the heavens.

One skittish gelding broke and bolted.

"Let it go!" Lord Hugh shouted. "Come. Come. Are all within?" His gaze caught Anna, and as if struck she gasped and covered her mouth with a hand. "Not you. You must take your chances outside."

Scarred John drew his sword.

Blessing screamed and began to kick and pummel Captain Frigo. "No! No! No! I'll hurt you! Let her stay!"

He slapped her, but the pain meant nothing.

John's sword poked Anna's hip. She edged sideways, seeing one curve in the circle not yet sealed by flour. He poked her again. The edge bit into her flesh, and she sobbed and skipped out beyond the sword's reach.

"No! No!"

"Stop it!" warned the captain.

"Won't! Let her come back!" Blessing squirmed. She kicked him again, almost got her knee into his groin.

Frigo took out his horsewhip and, swearing, slashed the girl across the chest, but the pain did not daunt her.

Anna started to cry with terror as a stinging wind poured over them. It was not quite utterly dark; they had not yet crossed the boundary into night past which there is no returning. But what fell out of the heavens was blacker than night, towers of darkness that stank of iron and muttered like bells heard down a vast distance. She heard them speaking. She heard *names*.

Hugh of Austra. John of Vennaci. Frigo of Darre. Theodore of Darre. Liudbold of Tivura. Each of them named and marked.

Blessing of Wendar and Varre, daughter of Sanglant.

The only name that was missing was Anna's.

"Let her come back! Let her!" shrieked Blessing, writhing, slamming her fists into air as Frigo twisted away from her blows. He slugged her on her jaw, and she went limp just like that.

"As I thought," said Hugh conversationally to Anna as he bent to pour the last of the line into place, to seal the circle, "you were not deemed of sufficient interest that anyone could recall your name and birthplace, if they ever knew it. You are more likely to survive if you move away from us. Follow the horse."

Flour streamed onto the earth. Hugh was speaking words she did not recognize or understand, and as night and monsters crashed over them, the thread of flour met itself and between one heartbeat and the next the men and horses huddled inside vanished.

She screamed, choked, wept. Moaned.

A breath of stinking cold horrible air rushed past her, soaking her in a chill that stabbed all the way to the bone. Death! Death! She wet herself, but the hot urine soaking her leg jarred her wits into life. Darkness swept down as on a gale, and she fled, running as the horse had, but tripped over her own feet and hit herself hard. Elbows bled. She scrambled forward as a dark shape skimmed over her.

The horse had run itself into a corner. Kicking, it lashed out at the creature. Her vision hazed. The horse screamed as a black pillar engulfed it.

Sparks spit golden above her. An arrow fletched with a shimmering tail pierced the creature, and it vanished with a loud *snap.* Bones rattled to earth where the horse had been. Its flesh had been flensed and consumed. She scrabbled forward as another *thing* swirled into view above her. Its cold presence burned her. She sobbed. A second arrow bloomed as a splash of brilliance in the heart of shadow. With a hiss, it snapped out of existence.

The hardest thing she had ever done was in that moment to look back over her shoulder. Better not to see what would devour her, but she had to know. A haze of mist marked the spell in which Hugh had contained his retinue. Most of the galla swarmed about it, as if confused. Bells tolled in her ears. She choked on bile. She got to her knees and crawled, thinking she might not draw their attention if she remained low to the ground.

A third hiss, followed in a steady measure by two more; nothing careless, not in Theodore's aim. She reached the scattering of steaming bones and fell among them. The clatter resounded into the heavens. A sixth bright arrow burned, and a seventh.

"Eight. Nine," she whispered, pressed among the bones, hoping death would shield her.

Hugh of Austra. So it murmured as it circled the sealed earth, seeking its prey but confused by the mist that concealed him. An arrow blossomed in darkness off to her right. With a snap and a roar of brilliance the tenth flicked out. A line like silver wire spun in an eddy of air before drifting to the ground.

If the galla had intelligence beyond that of hunting hounds, she could not see it in them.

Eleven. The last shadow pushed at the haze. *Blessing.*

The fire that bloomed within its insubstantial black form almost blinded her, like the flash of the sun.

In the silence, her ears rang with bells, and after a while she heard herself sniveling. She stank of piss. The bones in which she lay stank of hot iron. Her eyes stung as she wept. She could not stop herself. She just could not stop, not even when the spell he had raised dissolved and his soldiers broke out cheering. Not even when flame sprang from the oil lamp and they set about their encampment, each one as merry as if he had faced down his own death and laughed to escape it.

She could not stop, especially when Lord Hugh came into view, carrying the burning lamp. He paused to study the bones with more interest than he studied her, a touch of that ice-blue gaze. The kiss of a winter blizzard would have been more welcome.

He was a monster, no different than the monsters that stalked him. Hate flowered, but she lowered her eyes so as not to betray herself.

"A cup of ale in celebration, my lord?" asked scarred John. She glanced up to see the soldier arrive with a cup in each hand.

Hugh smiled. Strange to think how beautiful he was. Impossible not to be swayed by beauty, by light, by an arrogance that, softened, seems like benevolence. All of it illusion.

So might the Enemy smile, seeing a soul ripe for the Abyss.

So might the Enemy soothe with soft words and a kindly manner: *Come this way. Just a little farther.*

They drank.

"Here, now," said scarred John, sounding surprised. "The girl survived! Yet see—is that the horse?" He made a retching sound. He shook with that rush which comes after the worst is over. "That would have been us! Sucked clean of flesh!" He clutched his stomach, looking queasy.

"So would we all have been," agreed Hugh. "The Holy Mother Antonia controls many wicked creatures. She is a servant of the Enemy. Now you see why we must oppose her and Queen Adelheid, whom she holds on a tight leash."

The others gathered where Anna lay, humiliated. She did not know what to do except let them stare at her and pick through the bones around her as though she were deaf and mute. At last, she crawled sideways to get away from them. None stopped her or offered her a hand up. Her leggings were soaked through, and a couple of the men waved hands before noses and commented on the stink.

"Is it safe now?" they asked Hugh, kicking the remains of the horse. "Can we sleep?"

"It is safe. Before we left, I instructed Brother Petrus to scatter skulls and bones in the woodland a day's ride south of Novomo. After some fruitless searching, a loyal soldier will by seeming happenstance lead the searchers to these bones, and Mother Antonia will believe we are all dead, killed by those black demons, her galla."

They all stared at him.

He nodded to acknowledge their amazement. "I knew the plan would work because Antonia remains ignorant of the extent of my knowledge. I know a shield—this spell I called—that would hide us from the sight of the galla. I had in my possession griffin feathers to send them back to their foul pit."

"How did you come by such things, my lord?" asked scarred John, always curious. "It was said of the Wendish prince, the one who killed Emperor Henry, it was said he led a pair of griffins around like horses hitched to a wagon. But I never believed it."

Captain Frigo stood with Princess Blessing draped over his shoulders like a lumpy sack of wheat, but she was breathing. "Hush! It is not our part to question Lord Hugh."

Hugh's smile was the most beautiful thing on Earth, no doubt. If only he had been flensed instead of the poor horse.

"Questions betray a thoughtful mind, Captain. Do not scold him." He nodded toward John, who beamed in the light offered by the lamp's flame, content in his master's praise. Above, no stars shone. In the gray darkness, men settled restlessly into camp, still unnerved by their brush with death and sorcery. "I was brought up in the manner of clerics, John, to love God and to read those things written down by the holy church folk who have come before us. I had a book . . . I have it still, since I copied it out both on paper and in my mind. In it are told many secrets. As for the griffin feathers. Well."

Anna clamped her mouth shut over the words she wanted to speak. Prince Sanglant had captured griffins. Had Lord Hugh done so as well? Had he, like Bulkezu, stalked and killed one of the beasts?

He twitched his head sideways, as at an amusing thought known only to himself. "Does it not say in the Holy Verses: 'He who lays in stores in the summer is a capable son?' I took what I found when the harvest was upon me."

"And in the morning, my lord?" asked scarred John.

"At dawn," he said, "we ride east."

At midday the wind that had been dogging them all day died. Dust kicked up by the horses spattered right back down to the earth. No trees stood, although here and there hardy bushes sprouted pale shoots. The rolling countryside looked as dead as if a giant's flaming hand had swept across it, knocking down all things and scorching the hills.

Blessing rode in silence behind Frigo. She had not spoken since he had knocked her unconscious, only stared stubbornly at the land ahead. Because Anna was watching her anxiously, fearful that she'd sustained some damage in her mind, she saw the girl's aspect change. Her expression altered. Her body tensed. She saw something that shocked her.

"God save us," said Frigo as the slope of the land fell away before them to expose a new landscape.

Now Anna saw it, too.

East, the country broke suddenly from normal ground into a ragged, rocky plain whose brownish-red surfaces bled an ominous color into the milky sky. Nothing grew there at all. It was a wasteland of rock.

"That's not proper land," muttered scarred John. "That's demon work, that is."

"I've never heard of such a thing," said Theodore, "never in all the stories of the eastern frontier, and I've been a soldier for fifteen years and fought in Dalmiaka with the Emperor Henry and the good queen." He glanced at Hugh. "As she was then."

Hugh had not heard him. He, too, stared at this wilderness with the barest of smiles. "This is the power that killed Anne," he said.

"What is it, my lord?" asked the captain. "Is it the Enemy's work?"

" 'There will come to you a great calamity. The rivers will run uphill and the wind will become as a whirlpool. The mountains will become the sea and the sea become mountains. The sun shall be turned to darkness and the moon to blood.' "

Every man there looked up at the cloudy heavens as if seeking the hidden sun.

" 'All that is lost will be reborn on this Earth,' " he added.

They stared, hesitant to go forward.

Theodore broke their silence. "What's that, my lord?" he said, pointing east into the wasteland of rock. "I thought I saw an animal moving out there."

Hugh shook his head. "How can any creature traverse that? We'll have to move down toward the sea."

Although they did this, and although it was just possible to keep moving east by sticking to the strand, they rode anyway always with one eye twisted toward desolation. It was so cheerless and barren and frightening that Anna wept.

3

HE came with his entourage of treacherous Arethousans from whose lips fell lies, false jewels each one, because their ears had heard nothing but the teachings of the Patriarch, the apostate whose stubborn greed broke apart the True Church.

Adelheid's soldiers waited in ranks beside the gate and along the avenues. Servants swarmed like galla, each dressed in what best clothing they could muster. All must appear formidable, the court of queen and empress. The court of the skopos, the only true intermediary between God and humankind.

Adelheid did not rise to greet him as his retinue reached the court before the audience hall. She sent Lady Lavinia outside to escort him in, while Captain Falco hurried inside to report.

"This must be, indeed, the fabled one-eyed general, Lord Alexandros."

"The one we heard tales of when we marched in Dalmiaka?"

"The same, so it appears. It's said he became a lord by winning many victories for the emperor, who rewarded him with a noble wife and a fine title. He rides a handsome chestnut gelding and has a string of equally fine mounts, all chestnut. That suggests a man with vanity in his disposition."

"Well observed, Captain."

Adelheid wore a fine coronet of gold, but it looked a paltry thing to Antonia's eyes compared to the imperial crown she should have been wearing. Still, Adelheid herself, robed in ermine, with face shining, looked impressive enough to stop any man in his tracks and distract him from such tedious details as the richness of her ornaments.

The queen's gaze sharpened as movement darkened the opened double doors that led onto the colonnade fronting the hall. Antonia was seated to her right but at an equal height on the dais. From the doors, they would be seen side by side, neither given pride of place: the secular hand in hand with the sacred, as God had ordered the world below.

General Lord Alexandros entered with a brace of men to either side. Three carried decorated boxes in their hands and the fourth an object long and round and wrapped in cloth. All were dressed in red tabards belted over armor, except for the general himself. He wore a gold silk robe belted up and cut away for riding but still marked at the neck and under the arms and around the hips with the discolorations of the armor he'd been wearing over it. He had just come from the saddle, had only taken time to haul off his armor, but Adelheid had wished for this advantage: that he not be allowed any time to prepare himself but would be thrown headlong in all his travel dirt fresh into the melee.

The empress did not rise. Naturally, neither did Antonia.

He paused to survey the hall and the folk crowded there. That half were servants and commoners he would not know just from looking; all were handsomely dressed, and the lords and ladies who attended stood at the front of the assembly. He had, indeed, but one eye, that one a startling blue. The other was covered with a black patch. He was swarthy, in the manner of Arethousans, not particularly tall but powerfully built through the shoulders and chest, a man confident of his prowess in battle.

"Now we will discover," murmured Adelheid, "whether his wits are as well honed as his sword is said to be."

She raised a hand. He strode forward, his men coming up behind. He alone was armed, with a sword sheathed in a plain leather scabbard. Of the rest of his men, none entered the hall.

He stopped before the dais, snapped his fingers, and mounted the steps as the attendant carrying the long object unfolded the cloth and opened it into a sturdy stool. As the general reached the second step, the man quickly placed the stool to the left of Adelheid's throne and scurried back to kneel with the others.

General Lord Alexandros sat down.

Such audacity! Antonia found herself speechless. Indignant!

In the hall, folk caught their breath. Every gaze turned to the young empress.

Adelheid lifted one brow and measured him, and waited.

He snapped his fingers again. One by one the other men came forward, set their boxes at her feet, and opened them by means of cunning mechanisms fitted into the inlay decorating their exteriors.

From the first emerged a songbird, painted bright gold. It sang a pretty tune and turned back and forth, bobbing up and down as though alive. Adelheid forget herself so much that she clapped her hands in delight.

The second box revealed a rope of pearls of indescribable beauty. Each one was beyond price, and yet here were strung a thousand together. Light melted in their curves. Adelheid lifted up the rope, not without some effort, and let them slide across her lap.

General Lord Alexandros lifted two fingers, and the third man opened a jeweled box and displayed its contents to Antonia.

On a bed of finest gray silk lay the complete bones of a hand, fastened with gold wire.

"A song, to entertain," he said in Dariyan, indicating the cunning songbird with a gesture of his hand. His accent was coarse, but Antonia expected no fine words out of a lying Arethousan. "Pearls, of beauty and richness. For the Holy Mother of your people," he finished, pointing at the skeletal hand, "a precious relic."

"A relic?" Antonia examined the bones. They had no shine to them, nothing to indicate their special holiness. "Any man may sell a finger bone and say it is the relic of a holy saint."

He shrugged, and it angered Antonia to see that her comment amused him. "So I am thinking. Perhaps it is only the bone of a cow herder. But it come from the most holy sanctuary of the Patriarch of the True Church. This is the hand of the St. Johanna the Messenger, a holy discipla of the blessed Daisan. Still, if you think it a fake, I will take it away."

Adelheid's eyes widened. She still held the pearls, but her gaze fixed on the hand. "A precious relic, indeed!" she breathed. "How came you to have it, General? Why bring it to us?"

He gestured. His four attendants touched their heads to the floor in the servile eastern style, backed away, and knelt at the foot of the dais.

"Your Majesty," he said. "Holy Mother. I have no fine words. I am only a soldier. I speak with plain words, if you please."

Antonia began to reply, knowing him impertinent and proud, but Adelheid forestalled her. The young empress was of that type of woman who is susceptible to the appearance of physical strength in a man, thinking that strong arms are preferable to strong faith and a righteous heart.

"Go on, General. I am listening."

When he met Antonia's gaze, it was clear he knew she did not approve of him. He judged her, as a man sizes up his opponent before opening battle, and made his attack.

"I ride a long road to come to Aosta. Many bad things I see. There is wasteland, a land of smoking rock. There is drought, dry land, sickness. There is empty land, all the people run away. There is starving. Above, we see no birds but one time a great beast which has brightness like gold. We are attacked three times by beasts, these who have the form of men but the faces of animals. They are wearing armor which I see in the ancient paintings in the halls of Arethousa. The Cursed Ones are returned to Earth. Now they stalk us."

"These are evil tidings," agreed Adelheid. "Yet much of this we know ourselves, here in Aosta."

"This we suffer together." He nodded.

"What do you want?" demanded Antonia. "You are a heretic, apostate, an Arethousan who lies as easily as breathes and who, like the fox, will steal eggs from a mother's nest to feed your own kits."

Adelheid's hands clenched on the pearls as she rounded on Antonia. "I pray you! Holy Mother, let him speak. I sent envoys to inquire about an alliance. I did not expect the lord general himself to answer my call."

"What lordship has he?" Antonia inquired sweetly. "Your proud lineage is known to all, Your Majesty. I am a daughter of the royal house of Karrone. What is he?"

He flexed his arms a little. By the breadth and thickness of his hands, one could read his lineage: a man of the sword, grown with the sword, risen by the sword, a general who had fought his entire life. "I married a noble wife," he said. "Born into the house of Theophanes Dasenia. She is cousin of the last emperor. Also, she is cousin two times removed to the Princess Sophia who marries your King Henry in early days. A clever, industrious woman, proud, a giver of alms. Noble in all ways."

His breath caught. The assembly was quiet, hearing in his voice a grief that made Antonia, for a moment, feel an inconvenient thread of sympathy wrap her heart. Quickly severed.

"Dead, now." He was pale. Adelheid, too, had lost her color, and yet in all ways her looks had changed utterly since the general had entered the hall. His interest made her seem younger.

He looked at the empress, but what he saw Antonia could not read in his expression. "Arethousa is fallen, Your Majesty. The city is destroyed. Its people are exiles, those who live. Many more are dead. Even the great church is ruins."

Adelheid nodded, as if this did not surprise her. Why should it? She had seen Darre.

"What of the young emperor, General Lord Alexandros?" Antonia asked. "Does Lord Niko live?"

He nodded, but his gaze remained fixed on the queen as on the spear of his enemy, which might pierce him at any unguarded moment. "The emperor lives under the skirt of his aunt, Lady Eudokia. She and I were allies once."

"Once?" Adelheid asked quickly. "No longer?"

He smiled, as if Adelheid's question were suggestive of brilliance. How easily men of a certain age were dazzled by young, pretty women. Henry had fallen in just such a manner, it was said.

"This is what I say," he continued. "Lady Eudokia prefers blindness. She walks in the ruins and calls them a palace. I cannot be blind to what I see."

"What do you want, General?" Antonia asked, seeing it was wise to intercede before the conversation ran out of her control. "I believe that the Empress Queen Adelheid has made a rash suggestion that her daughter might marry the boy who is now Emperor of Arethousa. Is that what you have come to speak of? If so, let us move directly to the point. Speak bluntly, as you soldiers phrase it!"

That one good eye fixed on her briefly and disconcertingly, and he marked her and acknowledged her, but he shifted his attention back to Adelheid.

They always did! Men were fools, not to see where the true power lay. They were unbelievers, not placing their trust in God's servants first. Not reaching for faith before earthly lusts. Always humankind failed, and it irritated her so much!

"This I hear also on my journey," he said. "Darre, this great city, also lies in ruins. Poison smoke kills the people who live there. Every person must flee. The city is dead."

Adelheid did not move, not to nod, not to shake her head. She had grown tense. The pearls pooled in her lap, but she was no longer touching them but rather the arms of her throne as she glared at him.

"What do you want, General? Have you come to mock me?"

"I want to live." He patted his chest. "I—and you, Your Majesty—stand atop these ruins. Two great cities. Two noble and ancient empires. All ruins."

She nodded but did not trust herself to speak. Tears filled the queen's eyes. She had seen so much and lost so much, and his words affected her deeply. All there, in that assembly, strained to listen. He had that capacity, as did Adelheid: that he could draw to him those willing to follow. Like the pearls, he had luster, difficult to see when one first looked at his stocky body, bushy black beard, and terribly scarred face.

"Ruins, yours and mine. To the north, these Ungrians and Wendish, perhaps not so badly harmed. To the east, the heathen Jinna and their fire god. These also, perhaps, have not suffered so badly as we do, but it is hard to say. Last, heed me. Listen well. To the south, the Cursed Ones return. There is land where once there is sea. Already they raid into the north. When they gather an army and move in force . . . we will be helpless."

So silent was it in the hall that Antonia heard horses stamping outside. So silent was it that when someone coughed, half a dozen courtiers started as at a thunderclap. It was almost dark now and in this silence a score of servants began lighting lamps.

"This I know," said Adelheid at last. "There is long enmity between your people and mine, General. There is the matter of church doctrine, not easily put aside. But these are things, now, that matter less than the evils that besiege us. This is why I sent my envoys to ask for an alliance."

He nodded again, as if to seal a bargain. "For myself, I admit I care little what the priests and deacons sing. I care little whether the blessed Daisan is a man such as myself or mixed with the substance of God."

Before Antonia could speak, Adelheid reached to fasten a hand over the skopos' wrist. Such a tiny, petite hand, to have such an iron grasp. Antonia did not like this man, but she knew that to object now would destroy her tenuous alliance with Adelheid. How bitter it was to rely on earthly power! If only God had given her the means to smite her enemies more comprehensively than with individual galla, she would take to the task with a vengeance.

The general nodded as if to show he understood Antonia's disgust. He indicated her with an open palm, showing respect in a way that won her grudging admiration. "Here are those who will fight for God. Let them battle where they can do good. As for me, I will use my sword where I can and my wits where I must. Are you agreed to the marriage?"

It was a swift thrust, but it did not take Adelheid by surprise. "My daughter Mathilda, to be betrothed to the young Emperor Niko. Yes. She is young yet, not more than five, but she will grow."

His good eye narrowed. Where the scar damaged his face, he had no expression. It appeared that the muscles were somehow paralyzed. "Your daughter is of no use to me. She is a child. *You* are a woman."

That fast, everything changed. Just as a wind will overset the careful preparations of a farmer who has not yet bundled his hay, so the plans agreed between Antonia and Adelheid flew away to nothing.

The empress laughed. Her nearest courtiers, seeing and hearing the words not spoken, set hands to faces, or hid their eyes, or chortled, or exclaimed, each according to their nature.

Antonia fumed. She must remain silent or lose all. She saw her own power eroding so quickly that she knew she must cling to the shoreline before the entire sandy cliff collapsed beneath her. It was no good to protest that the queen must not trust Arethousans or that her beloved Aostans would never trust her again should she marry one, because she had already considered and approved the idea of marrying her young daughter to one of them. To a foreigner! A heretic!

Here he sat as if he already ruled by Adelheid's side.

"Betroth your daughter to the young emperor if need be," he went on. "This is also good. But the power of yours and of mine— the power to keep our empires alive—must be joined. Otherwise we will die and our empires will die. Do you want this, Your Majesty?"

Antonia seethed with a rage she could never express.

"No," said the empress. "I do not want my empire to die. Yet if I make an Arethousan king beside me, my people may turn their backs on me."

" 'King' is only a title. I will be your consort, a simple lord. Call me what you will. What you must. But only you and only I, joined together, can save our empires."

She took hold of his callused hand, hers so slight and his so large but surprisingly gentle as he touched her small fingers and smiled. By this simple means, they were betrothed in the sight of humankind.

But not of God.

He rose, and Adelheid rose with him. None spoke. The court was too stunned to speak, seeing what no one had ever expected: the empress of Aosta binding herself to a crafty Arethousan who by guile and wit and no doubt worse means had raised himself to become general and lord among that heretical people.

"Holy Mother," he said, "I pray you, we throw ourselves on your mercy. Without your blessing, we are done. Without your blessing, the empires will fall, these two, who hold the ancient and true ways up as a light for all humankind."

She was silent and stubborn. She could wait him out.

He had not done yet.

"Yours is the most power of all, Holy Mother. Yours, the right to strike first."

Still raging, while displaying a calm face, she succumbed to curiosity. "What do you mean?"

"We are vulnerable to those who live in the north, if they choose to invade us while we are weak. You can weaken them. You alone have that power."

A clever man, but naturally, he must be, because all Arethousans were clever, lying, unscrupulous creatures who drank bathwater and ate too much garlic and onions and dressed improperly, men like women and women like men, and pretended a false humility that was in truth nothing but pride. Yet she could not help herself. He had piqued her interest.

"What do you mean?"

"You are the Holy Mother. She commands the obedience of all children of God. Is that not so?"

"That is so. I am delighted that you, a heretic, can recognize my authority."

He nodded, not *quite* bowing his head. He was a dangerous man as he had himself confessed. He did not truly believe; to him, the church was merely a tool.

A weapon.

"Those who are disobedient, what comes of them?"

"They are censured. They must do penance."

"And after this? If they still disobey? I think you have the power to place them under a ban."

"Ah!" breathed Adelheid, cheeks flushed and eyes bright as she understood him.

As Antonia did. "I could place them under anathema, if they deserved such an excommunication, but how does this help Aosta? How does this help Arethousa? How does it help the holy church, which must be my sole concern?"

Because he was a dangerous man, he smiled. He shrugged. "One time, when I am young, I stand on duty at night. I hear a noise in the bush. It might be anything, but I thrust with my spear. I stab a man in the leg. So we discover this one I catch is a spy. He tells us where the enemy camps and what they intend. So we take the enemy by surprise. This is my first victory. It comes sometimes that a man must thrust his spear into the dark where there may be nothing but a rat. In this way, we strike even if we do not know what we will hit. It is better than nothing. It is better to do something than to stand and wait."

"I am tired of being helpless," said Adelheid. "I am tired of standing and waiting while others take action."

"You believe I should place all of Wendar and Varre under anathema. If I do so, none may be blessed at birth or marriage. None may receive last rites. The deacons may not lead mass, and the biscops may not ordain deacons. This is a terrible thing, General."

"They have acclaimed as regnant a man who killed his own father," said Adelheid. "Is that not a terrible thing? Does it not go against God's own Word? If we on Earth do not love, respect, and obey our own mother and father, how can we then love, respect, and obey the Mother and Father of Life?"

"I see," murmured Antonia, and she did see. "There is merit in this plan. If they send word that a more worthy contender has been raised to the throne, then I will consider lifting the ban. If they persist in giving their loyalty to a half-breed bastard who murdered his own father, then I cannot."

"You see," added Adelheid triumphantly. "There might be more than one reason why Lord Hugh murdered Lady Elene. She is Conrad's daughter. She had a claim to the throne, just as her father does. One that would have superseded any claim Lord Hugh might have hoped to put forward for Princess Blessing."

Alexandros listened but said nothing.

"Let us go one step farther," Antonia added. "All except the Duchy of Wayland will fall under the ban. Conrad may be persuaded to ally with us. He is ambitious. He has other children."

"Sons?" asked Adelheid, then caught herself and glanced at the general. How fickle she was! She had pledged Mathilda on the one hand yet was already plotting a new alliance on the other.

The general seemed not to hear, or to understand, or else he chose to ignore the question.

Antonia could not. Did Conrad have sons? Might young Mathilda marry into the Wendish royal house, or were she and Conrad's children too closely related? There was also Berthold, Villam's child, who might yet serve them. Indeed, now that she thought on it, he and Wolfhere were exactly the right people to serve her in this.

Hugh of Austra was a fool, and a dead fool, just as he deserved, his bones tumbled in the woodland. Never kill the children of noble houses. They were always more use alive than dead.

"So be it," she said, raising her staff so that the assembly would listen and would hear. There is more than one way to fight a war. There is more than one way to win a battle.

4

TO haul stone you must walk to the quarry, hoping it is close by, and load what weight you can carry into a sling woven of tough fiber, whose burden rests on the band that crosses your forehead. Men wearing nothing except a kirtle that barely covers their loins work at the rock face with pickaxes, wedges, and sledgehammers. The air is heavy with the dust of stone. Everyone is sweating even though the sun remains hidden behind a high veil of clouds.

Secha paused to take a sip of cleansing water and then stacked three stones in her sling, hoisted it, balanced it across her forehead and back, and trudged away on the path that snaked down a hillside to the White Road. Here, she turned west along the broad path, returning to the watchtower. She had one baby caught close to her chest; the other was with Rain, who had set up a temporary workshop with the building crew who were shaping stone for the repair and reconstruction of this watchtower.

All along the White Road, folk were building and repairing the fallen watchtowers. She had been at this work for five days now. It gave her something to do as she adjusted to her new life.

She passed an older man who was returning with an empty sling. He acknowledged her without quite looking her in the eye. Like all of those who had walked in the shadows, he was eager to move on, to stay away from her.

They feared her, because she had worn the feathered cloak. They feared standing close beside her, because she had won the enmity of the blood knives.

There came another thin, old man down the path toward her, and she brightened, seeing him and the pair of young mask warriors who walked a few steps behind him.

"Here you are," said Eldest Uncle as he turned and fell in beside her, matching her pace. He carried nothing except a skin bloated with liquid.

She greeted the young ones with a nod, and they fell back to let their elders speak privately.

"That's a new mantle," she observed.

"A fine gift from my daughter, so I am meant to understand." He folded back the corners of his hip-length mantle so she could admire the short kirtle tied around his hips.

"New cloth, and new sandals, as well."

"I am well taken care of," he said with a chuckle. "It's like feeding a dog so it doesn't bark untimely."

She laughed. The baby stirred, and she halted to let him lift the infant out of the sling and fix it to his own scrawny hip. The baby was awake, eager to look at faces and trees, although the wasteland to the north was too jumbled a sight to interest her infant gaze.

They set out again, settling into a swinging pace.

After a time, she said, "You have news."

"So I do."

They walked a while, passing another two returning with empty slings, who greeted Eldest Uncle with open smiles and Secha with guarded ones.

"They fear me," she said.

"It was the custom in the days before that she who challenged for the feathered cloak, and lost, gave herself as an offering to the gods."

"What of she who was challenged, and lost?"

He shrugged. "Challenges were rare. Usually a vote was called only when the Feather Cloak passed into death and a new one must be chosen. Then a pair of candidates would be picked by the warriors and the blood knives, and set before the baskets. Even so, the outcome was usually determined in advance."

She snorted. "Then little has changed."

"You did not fight hard enough, Secha," chided Eldest Uncle. "Where is that look you used as a child when my daughter bullied the other children? You were younger than her, but wiser in your mind!"

"I am not the right leader, Uncle. Not for this day. Not for this war. It is better that I stepped aside in favor of others."

He frowned. "Even if they are wrong?"

"Are they wrong? I do not know."

"Ah!" Such a sound a man might make when he is told that his beloved has left him. "She has persuaded even you with her arguments."

"No, but I am not persuaded by my own. I am a good magistrate, Uncle. I can judge disputes and oversee labor and distribution. I can see who lies to me and who tells the truth, who seeks selfish favor and who wants to do what they think best for their clan. In exile, I could raise my hands and know that my decisions allowed every person in the tribes a chance to live that could not be stolen from them by another's greed or anger. That does not make me the right person to stand at the head of an army. That does not make me the right person to raise my hands to the gods now that we have returned home."

He grunted. The baby babbled and tried to touch his chin, which distracted him for a bit.

She saved her breath for walking, although she had become accustomed to the balance and strain of the load.

After a while, he said, "Feather Cloak wishes me to attend her on a matter of grave importance. I ask you to come with me."

A pair of mask warriors came striding along toward them, on patrol.

"Uncle!" Almost in unison, the young men touched the tips of their left fingers to their right shoulders. "Any help you need, Uncle? Aunt?"

"We are well," said Eldest Uncle, and the men touched their shoulders again and continued past at a brisk pace, trading jocular salutes with the warriors who attended Eldest Uncle.

"I feel that I am torn in half," said Eldest Uncle, glancing after them. "So it was in my youth that we greeted elders in such a manner. How came it that such simple signs of respect failed us in exile?"

"So many died," she said, "although I do not remember those days myself when corpses filled the streets. Many things were lost that were once treasured."

The baby fussed a little, and Eldest Uncle bounced her on his hip in time to his stride, to soothe her. "We should not have let it happen."

"It is past now. We must let go of what we were in exile, and face what we will become."

His eyes were crinkled with a kind of amusement, but his lips had a set, conservative mood to them. "I fear."

"What do you fear?"

"I fear that you are right. Secha, will you come with me? I rely on your strong eyes to see what I might miss."

"I'll come." She laughed. "Only I will need attendants to bring along the babies."

"You don't ask what matter calls us."

"That you ask is reason enough."

The watchtower and its scaffolding came into view atop the steep slope. Here, for many months, Eldest Uncle had made his home. During their exile, he had spent more of his time in a clearing nearby, where the burning stone that marked a gateway between the aether and the world they had lost burned into existence at intervals. What he was waiting for she could never quite fathom. Maybe he had just been waiting to go home.

"Anyway," she added, "I find I am already tired of hauling rock. I am ready to see what comes next."

5

FOR many days they were forced to camp at the edge of a wasteland still steaming from vents and pits, a desolation so complete that no life grew there, not even the tiniest spear of grass or fleck of mottled lichen. Farther away to the southwest the sea sighed and sobbed on an unseen shore, heard mostly at night when the sound of the wind died away. In this direction lay open ground patched with grass and low-lying shrubs that had miraculously escaped the burning.

Here, within a ring of head-sized stones rolled and levered into place by their captors, they were allowed to set up their tents. Water arrived during the night, carried in leather buckets by unseen hands. Lord Hugh rationed their stores carefully, but already they had been forced to slaughter two of the horses and soon—in another ten or so days—they would run out of grain.

Along the southeast boundary of the campsite, a chalky road ran more-or-less west to east. South of the road lay land that appeared magnificently lush to Anna's eyes, although compared to the fields and woodland around Gent it looked dusty and parched, with dry pine, prickly juniper shrubs, and waxy myrtle, and the ubiquitous layer of pale grasses. It wasn't lush at all; it only seemed so because they had ridden through a wilderness of rock for so many days that any land untouched by destruction seemed beautiful in comparison. Yet there were tiny yellow flowers blooming on vines growing low to the ground. A spray of cornflowers brightened an open meadow. She hadn't seen flowers for so long. It was hard to believe it was spring.

"If they haven't killed us yet," Hugh was saying to one of the men for the hundredth time, "it is because they are waiting for someone."

"It was well you knew the secret of their parley language," said Captain Frigo, "and that talisman name. Otherwise we'd all be dead."

Hugh nodded thoughtfully. "Never scorn any mine of information, Captain. What seems crude rock may turn out to have gold hidden away in deeper veins. Who would have thought that unfortunate frater would possess such an intimate knowledge of the very noblewoman we are here to negotiate with?"

Their captors remained hidden. Anna wasn't sure they were even human. They emerged only at night to retrieve the empty water buckets and return them full. They had animal faces, not human ones. But Lord Hugh said those animal faces were actually masks and that behind the masks the Lost Ones looked just like Prince Sanglant, with bronze-colored skin, dark eyes, and proud faces.

Maybe so.

Princess Blessing sat in the middle of the clearing with hands and feet bound. She stared into the foliage day and night, when she wasn't sleeping. She hadn't spoken a word for days, but now and again Anna caught her muttering to herself the way clerics and deacons murmured verses as a way to calm their minds.

Late one afternoon, Anna sat beside her and wiped her brow. Grit came off on her fingers. The breeze off the wasteland carried dust, and it had filtered into every crevice of their baggage. No matter how much she combed her hair, or Blessing's hair, the coarse dust never came out.

A twig snapped.

"Hey!" Theodore, standing sentry, raised his bow with an arrow set to the string. In the forest, humanlike figures scattered into the trees.

Anna scrambled to her feet, staring. This was as close as she had seen any of the masked figures during the day, but already they vanished into the landscape as would animals fleeing from the noise and smell of humankind.

"Hold!" said Hugh. "Be calm, Theodore."

In the distance, a cry like that of a horn rose and stretched on, and on, before arcing into silence. Within the foliage, green and gold spun into view before disappearing behind a denser copse of pine. Anna placed herself between Blessing and the threat, but the girl pushed at her knees.

"I want to see!" she whispered.

"Put your weapons down," said Hugh to the soldiers. "They outnumber us. These rocks are too low to create a defensive perimeter. Let us use our best and only shield."

He crossed to Blessing, took her by the arm, and invited her to stand with a gesture. She looked sideways up at him, glanced back toward the company moving nearer through the forest, then got to her feet with a remarkable show of cooperation. Anna did not trust the stubborn set of the girl's mouth, but she merely took two steps sideways and kept her own mouth shut, ready for anything, hands in fists.

The foreigners appeared at the bend where the chalk-white road curved away out of sight. The shadow of the trees lay across the wide path. These formidable creatures were after all not cursed with animal heads. A few wore painted masks: a fox-faced woman, a man with the spotted face of a leopardlike cat, a green and scaly lizard. There were also a half dozen who possessed no mask. One of them was a man so old and wizened that he might have seen a hundred years pass. He wore only a short cape, a kirtle, and sandals. A younger woman, scarcely better clothed, stood beside him with a hand cupped unobtrusively under his elbow. Other figures sheltered within the trees, half concealed. Anna thought she heard a baby's belch, but if there was a baby, it remained hidden.

A man strode at the front rank whose proud, arrogant features reminded Anna forcibly of Prince Sanglant, although he had a cold gaze that made her nervous. He surveyed the humans in the same manner that a handsome cat examines a nest of helpless baby mice it has just uncovered.

Yet even he could not match the woman who led them. She was short, sturdy without being either fat or slender: sleek and well fed, a leopard stalking in lush hunting grounds. Her hair was lighter than that of her kinfolk although her complexion was the same: bronzed, almost gleaming. She wore a startling cloak sewn entirely of brilliant feathers. A pair of young people behind her carried a huge golden wheel trimmed with bright green feathers. It was this wheel Anna had seen whirling and flashing in the trees. The richness of its gold stunned Anna. Indeed, every one of the folk facing them wore gold necklaces and gold-beaded armbands and wristlets and anklets and thin gold plates shaped to cover the breastbone, as rich as noble princes arrayed for a court feast. Yet their dress was that of barbarians, plain linen kirtles cut above the knee, feathered and beaded guards on arms and legs. Some of the men, like the old one, wore little more than a white breechclout, the kind such as farmers and fishermen donned in the heat of the summer while out working in marshland and mud. All wore short capes.

There was silence as the foreigners came to a halt on the other side of the rock corral and the two groups examined each other. Hugh moved first, tugging Blessing forward.

"I seek the one known as Uapeani-kazonkansi-a-lari. This is her granddaughter."

The fox-masked woman barked words Anna could not understand. Half the company laughed. The old man frowned. The woman in the feathered cloak raised a hand to silence them, but she appeared neither pleased nor offended.

Still, no one replied, so Hugh went on.

"This is the child of Prince Sanglant, your kinsman. I am called Hugh, born of Austra, named lord and presbyter by the right of my noble lineage and God's blessing. I claim right of speech with your leader."

"I speak," said the one wearing the feathered cloak. She spoke in comprehensible Wendish, tinged with a Salian flavor. "Few among humankind know the name of Uapeani-kazonkansi-a-lari. So I told the scouts, who came to me and reported that a group of warriors led by a man with hair the color of sun had come to our border and asked to speak to the woman who chose that name. The priests wish to see you all brought at once for sacrifice. But I said differently. I told them, better to hear what the one with hair the color of sun has to say and kill him after, than to kill him first and never hear his words."

"Indeed," agreed Hugh affably. "It is foolish to throw away perfectly good knowledge out of spite."

She flicked her palm in a dismissive gesture. "Say what you have come to say."

"I speak to the mother of Prince Sanglant." It wasn't a question.

Now Anna saw the resemblance not so much in features as in the way a smile creased that woman's face. The prince's smile bore more honest amusement—her smile was cold—but nevertheless the expression was the same.

Hugh nodded, as if in acknowledgment of that smile. "I am come here to offer you an alliance, Uapeani-kazonkansi-a-lari."

That startled them!

They broke out talking between themselves, commenting and arguing, but when she raised the back of her hand to them they quieted.

"How do you know that name?" she asked, her tone more like a threat than curiosity. "Did my son tell you?"

"No. A man became known to me who had knowledge of you, whom he called Kansi-a-lari. He was called Zacharias."

This smile was softer and more genuine. "The-One-Who-Is-More-Clever-Than-He-Looks. Still, your pronunciation is almost as good as his. Where is he now?"

"He is dead, caught within the spell on the night the Crown of Stars crowned the heavens. On the night your people and this land returned to Earth."

"Perhaps not as clever as I thought, then," she remarked in a careless way.

Dead! This was the first news Anna had heard of Brother Zacharias since he had fled the prince's retinue at Sordaia. So he *was* a traitor! He had fled directly to Lord Hugh. Her heart burned with anger, and she was glad—*glad*—that he was dead. He deserved it for betraying them!

"Clever enough," said Hugh with a wry smile.

"Why will you, our enemy, offer us an alliance?"

"In what way am I your enemy?" he asked amiably. "The war you speak of took place so long ago it has passed out of human memory. I know nothing of the exiles. I am not at war with you. Nor are any of my people."

She shook her head. "My uncle says that your people invaded the woodlands where his people bided for long years."

"How can that be? No Ashioi survived on Earth."

"They survived in the shadows."

"In the shadows?" He considered, eyes almost closing as if he was thinking hard. With a slight nod, he went on. "If the memory is still fresh in your eyes, let me say that nevertheless I offer you an alliance."

"What have you to offer us?"

Hugh still held onto Blessing, who had not moved. Strangely the woman who was Sanglant's mother had glanced at the child only once and by no other sign showed any interest in her. Not the rest, though. Anna was accustomed to observing without being herself observed, because she was not important enough that noble folk took notice of her. Both the handsome man and the old man studied Blessing with alert interest. The woman standing at the side of the old man studied each person in Hugh's party. Indeed, that woman caught Anna's gaze and, for a moment, examined her so closely that Anna felt a fluttering sense of dread in her own stomach. She had a sudden horrible feeling that if their shadows grew long enough to touch those of the human party, they would gobble them up and swallow them alive. She clutched her hands together to stop herself from trembling.

"I can offer a weapon to you, if you are still bent on war."

She laughed. "Your words make no sense, Golden One. First you say there cannot be war between your kind and mine because too many generations have passed. Then you say that you will offer us a sword with which to gain an advantage over our enemies. Which is it?"

"You came to Henry's court in later days, only a few years ago, and warned him of a great cataclysm. Is it not true that you offered him at that time an alliance, while he stood in a position of strength?"

"Now he is dead," she observed. "You know a great deal, Pale Sun. I like you."

Blessing grunted. The sound was so quiet that it went unremarked by everyone except Anna.

"It's true I made that offer to Henry," she continued. "Because that was the will of the council. But those who wished for an alliance no longer lead the people."

"Who leads?"

"I lead. I am Feather Cloak."

"Is this the same position your son claims among the Wendish? He calls himself king."

"Does he?" she asked, but it was obvious by her expression that she already knew. "Something like, in your eyes, I suppose. What is your offer? What sword do you bring to us?"

He shrugged, a movement that might have been designed to dislodge an annoying fly. "First of all, I have information. The Aostans are weak and divided."

"The Aostans?"

"Those who live in the south. The Arethousans, too, have suffered grievously and are weak."

"The Arethousans?"

"Let me proceed in a different manner. I have with me a map, which I can read, that shows the lay of the land."

"Such a *map* would save us time and trouble, it is true. *If* we meant to march to war. But it is a long journey from these southern lands to those in the east, and the west, and the north. There is a great deal of wasteland to cross. It is an even longer road to Wendar."

"So it is. There are shorter paths."

"Ah." She smiled in the manner of a warrior who has humbled his worst enemy. "You speak of the crowns. I know the secret of the crowns."

"So you do, according to Brother Zacharias. Still, you were forced to walk across the breadth of the country through many lands in both winter and summer. I need not do so. I can walk where I will. I can cross between any crown and any other crown in the space of no more than three days. I can cross great distances in a short time. Who else has this power? Do you, Uapeani-kazonkansi-a-lari?"

Anna thought her legs would collapse, but she held steady. Disbelief choked her, and it was just as well, lest she cry out.

Traitor! Would you sell your own people to the enemy?

"This offer tempts," said the woman coolly. Her tongue flicked between her lips, as though she began to lick her lips for a taste of what she desired, but stopped herself. "So I ask myself: what do you want? In the marketplace, no one trades without asking a thing in return."

He nodded, but he was tense now, eager, held taut. He teased his lower lip with his teeth, caught himself doing so it seemed, and licked his lips instead, in an echo of her, blinking quickly and taking a deep breath. "I want only one thing. One thing, in exchange."

The faces of the Ashioi were masks, their expression impenetrable, even those whose features were not concealed by the painted snarls and open maws of animals.

"I want the half daimone woman called Liathano."

Blessing twisted in his grip and bit him on the hand.

He shouted in pain, shook loose his hand, and slapped her so hard backhanded that the blow sent her tumbling to the dirt.

"Little beast!"

She lay there, breathing hard. Anna hesitated, hating herself for her fear, before sidling forward to kneel beside her. The girl's hair concealed her face, but as Anna smoothed it back she saw the mark of Hugh's ring, which had cut the skin, and the deep purple red welt that would spread and hurt.

Blessing grinned at her through tears of pain. "I've been waiting to do that," she said triumphantly.

All around them, the Ashioi laughed.

6

THE pale ones had little to recommend them by the standards of civilized folk. They were not a beautiful race; they were too hairy, too pallid, too big. Of course they smelled bad. Yet the wealth of metal they bore was staggering. Each of the warriors carried a metal-pointed spear and a strong metal sword. All were armed with such riches. They stank of cold iron. Even the captive girl was shackled in iron chains as she stared fixedly with her eagle's glare at Zuangua, as though she recognized him. She lay with one hand propping herself up and the other gingerly exploring the pattern of cut and bruise on her face. Her expression was a mirror of her emotions, and it took no great cunning to see the thoughts filter by the way she frowned, then smiled one-sidedly to spare the bruised cheek, then winced and cocked a shoulder as though shutting off a nagging voice.

Secha knew that to clad prisoners in iron was to be wealthy beyond imagining. It would be difficult to defeat an enemy whose soldiers fought with such weapons. The Ashioi possessed only stone and bronze, but they had captured a few iron implements in recent months. They knew what power iron held and how difficult it would be to learn to forge in the manner known to humankind. There was a kind of magic to it.

No one willingly gave up such secrets, not unless they wanted something very badly in return.

After the girl bit their leader and the laughter died down, Feather Cloak turned to her people.

"Enough!" she said. "We will talk in council and decide what is best to do now that we understand the bargain that has been offered to us."

Folk scurried away to scrape out a fire pit and rake dry grass back away from the rim, while additional mask warriors took up guard stations around the rock corral that fenced in the prisoners.

Fox Mask strutted up and down along the fence, making jokes to her companions about the leader. "The color of root paste, his skin! Might as well marry a mealworm! Hair as fine as spider's silk! Imagine how nasty that must be to touch!"

Secha could not laugh. Inside that fence, the leader was giving his men directions. They secured their shelters, heated porridge over a small campfire, fed and watered their horses, shared out food and drink, and took themselves off to pits where excrement and piss were immediately covered with a thin layer of dirt. Not entirely uncivilized, then. The servant tidied the girl, blotted blood off her face, and made her comfortable on blankets. As twilight drew over them, the warriors settled down in a defensive ring that would allow some to rest while others kept watch.

Fox Mask could say what she wanted, but their leader carried himself as do men who are accustomed to admiration. He had poise, a trait Secha respected. Despite knowing he faced an overwhelmingly superior force that could kill him and his warriors easily, he showed no sign of fear without, however, blustering in the manner of warriors such as Cat Mask and Lizard Mask who relied on muscle more than brain to win their skirmishes.

Behind her, flames crackled, eating through the latticework of kindling sticks, and bigger branches were stacked on the fire to let it blaze. Feather Cloak took her place within the aura of light as the council gathered in a ring, facing the light.

"Speak," said Feather Cloak. "Let me hear your words."

"Let us take them as an offering and be done with it," said the blood knives.

"No," said Feather Cloak. "It is foolish to throw away such a powerful weapon."

"How can this spell he speaks of be used as a weapon?" asked the blood knives.

"Why fight at all?" asked Eldest Uncle. "If humankind is so weakened, it is best to parley. We can rebuild if we are at peace. We cannot rebuild if we are at war."

Zuangua smirked, regarding his twin. Old rivalry existed between the siblings, twined together with long affection. "You have forgotten, Brother, that most of our people are those who were caught in shadow, betwixt and between. For us the war is yesterday, not three or four generations ago. For us, there can be no peace!"

"War is better." Fox Mask's statement ran like an echo back through those assembled. Only in the trees behind Secha was there silence, where waited her mate and her son and her infant daughters.

"War," said the others.

"War!" they cried.

She looked toward the fence, feeling that they were being watched. Indeed, the man with sun hair had walked without fear up to the rock wall. He stood there, listening and watching and able, most likely, to understand the meat of the debate without understanding the skin that was its surface of words. Secha admired him for his exotic beauty, but also for a self-possession untroubled by any ripple of uncertainty. It meant a lot to hold firm in the face of the unknown.

For this reason, she knew she must speak, as was her right.

"Listen," she said. "I have something to say. Why should we trust this golden one? He means to betray his own kind. Why not betray us in turn? He is brave and bold, it is true. Is he brave and bold enough to pretend to be our ally while leading us into death?"

"It's true that all he claims to want is that woman," said Feather Cloak. She did not bother to hide her disgust. "It doesn't seem like much."

" 'That' woman is a great deal," said Eldest Uncle. "She will be hard to defeat, and difficult to capture and hold."

"But a fine armful to hold, so they say!" said Zuangua with a laugh.

Feather Cloak pulled a mighty grimace. Her indignation made her young uncle laugh again.

"Jealousy is a sharp spear," Zuangua retorted, and Secha supposed it was so. He was cleverer than he acted, that one.

"I am not jealous!"

"You may not be, if you say so, but the Pale Sun Dog is. He is jealous of your son for having what he wants for himself."

Feather Cloak seemed ready to burst with anger, so Secha cut in. "What man can help himself when faced with a creature born half of fire? Moths will die in flames. So might men, unable to resist that brilliance."

"That is true, at least," said Feather Cloak, mollified, "for I traveled for a time with my son in human lands. There was some head butting as men will do, over that woman. Yet even so, as Secha says, why should we trust this Pale Dog? Even my own son has turned against us and cast his loyalty in with his father's people."

"Is it certain your son means to fight us?" asked Secha. "When was this news known? The Bright One did not harm us. She aided our cause."

"If any can convince him, it would be his wife," said Eldest Uncle, taking hold of Secha's line of argument. "She is not against us. She is not our enemy."

Feather Cloak shook her head decisively. "She is too powerful and must be killed. That judgment was passed on her in exile, was it not? By the one who wore the feathered cloak before me?"

"Since your words are true, there is no answer to them," said Eldest Uncle. "But we no longer live in exile. Everything has changed. Our strategy must change as well."

"She walked the spheres!"

"As did you, Daughter! Think of this: the rope that bound us to the aether is severed. No one can ascend that ladder again. She is not our enemy."

"Who is blinded by brilliance now?" demanded Feather Cloak. "I say, capture her, and give her to the blood knives."

The priests nodded eagerly.

"Let us defeat all of humankind and then I'll *eat* the Pale Sun Dog for supper," said Fox Mask with a coarse laugh that made half of her companions chortle and slap the backs of their hands together to show their appreciation for her wit.

Secha did not find her amusing. "Revenge, like jealousy, makes slaves of those who cling to it."

Zuangua stepped forward to cut off the eruption of commentary. "Then what do we bargain with, since she is the only thing this Pale Dog wants?"

"Is it worth bargaining at all?" asked the blood knives. "How can this spell he speaks of be used as a weapon?"

The warriors laughed. They already knew.

Zuangua shook his head, frowning at the blood knives as if he could not understand their ignorance. "If it is true that he knows how to move where he wills and when he wills, this is a sword as powerful as the mystery of iron."

Cat Mask stepped forward. "Strike quickly and decisively! I said so all along!"

"Strike in small groups!" said Lizard Mask as he stepped up alongside his rival. "I said so all along!

"My question is not answered," said Secha, watching the pale sun man watch his enemies and thereby learn. She thought that he was probably learning far more about them than they had so far learned about him. "How can we trust him? He might send our war bands to the bottom of the sea or into the heart of a mountain to be entombed in stone."

"Is that possible?" asked Zuangua, interested. "A good tactic!"

"I don't think it is possible," said Feather Cloak. "The weaving links the crowns, nothing else."

Secha went on stubbornly. "He might weave us so we are lost in these days and months that pass within the crowns. The tide of days could ebb and flow around our warriors and they would be lost, just as we were lost in exile."

"You can weave the crowns, Feather Cloak," said Cat Mask to Feather Cloak. "Why do we need him?"

Kansi shook her head. Each time, Secha saw her speak in a different way as the angle of her head and the tilt of her neck and the frown on her lips revealed a new emotion. "I could walk between Earth and exile because I could call the burning stone, which was a gateway. Yet I have not seen the burning stone since we returned to Earth. My father is right. That ladder is broken, as far as I know. As for the other, I do not know the secret of weaving between the crowns on Earth."

"Let his skill be tested before we make any bargain," said Zuangua. "I'll go, with the pick of my warriors. You can keep the child and his other servants as hostage against our safe return."

Above, the thin veil of clouds that had shielded the sky parted. Stars shone through in ragged patches. Wind chased chaff into the flames, where it flashed and died.

Eldest Uncle shut his eyes and bowed his head.

"It is risky," said Feather Cloak.

"Yes," agreed Zuangua, showing his teeth.

His warriors, led by Fox Mask, crowded up behind him, all grinning with that same reckless smile. They were restless, shoulders twitching, heels bouncing, elbows shifting as though they were about to burst into a run.

"We have waited long enough. We are ready to go to war."

7

UNDER guard, Lord Hugh's company marched into the land of the Cursed Ones. Anna stuck close to Blessing in case Lord Hugh meant to hit the child again. She stuck close because she feared the way the girl stared admiringly, hungrily, at the Ashioi.

"Do you hear what they're talking about?" the girl asked her, but all that streamed from those foreign mouths sounded to Anna no different than the chirping of birds and the howling of dogs. Blessing understood it all. It seemed that her father's blood, or her mother's sorcery, or the aetherical milk she had suckled as a child, or all of these combined, had opened her ears to the Ashioi language.

Anna envied her.

The child had learned from her abduction. She kept silent about her unexpected skill. She let no one except Anna know, because she wasn't sure who was her friend and who her enemy. After several days they were delivered to a prison. It had a high stone wall and raised towers where guards stood watch. Through the gate lay a dusty courtyard and a dozen shelters. They were only stone platforms raised above the level of the earth. Posts set in the ground supported crude roofs. There were no walls. It was an awful place.

It made her want to cry, but she could not cry, because she had to take care of Blessing.

At the gate, Feather Cloak waited with her entourage. Inside, lord Hugh called them together. "I must leave," he said to them. Their expressions were anxious, but they listened obediently. "I have sworn to these Ashioi that I will not teach them or aid them if any of you are harmed. I stand by that. You will be protected." He smiled gently. "Yet make yourselves useful. If you have marketable skills, let yourselves be coaxed into sharing."

"Any chance we can share with the women?" asked Theodore. "They sure look at us invitingly, if I must say so."

"And them wearing almost nothing but the skin they were born in," said Scarred John appreciatively.

The others chuckled, and then looked downcast.

"Would it be going against God, my lord?" asked Theodore. "They're heathens. It might be wrong."

"Yes, they are heathens. Therefore we are enjoined to bring them into the Circle of Unity. Do not fear to associate with them. But only if they ask first, lest you unwittingly break their laws."

This command the soldiers liked well enough, but Anna clutched Blessing's arm and wished only to be allowed to sit down in the shade. The heat made her dizzy.

Lord Hugh departed, but as the men spread out to explore the courtyard, the handsome man appeared at the gate. Anna had figured out that the man was Blessing's great-great-uncle. Like Prince Sanglant, he was restless, even impatient. His gaze roved, and he spotted Blessing. He called out, "Come!"

Anna knew that word well enough! "What does he want?" she asked Blessing.

The girl considered her uncle with an eagle's brooding gaze. She bit her lip. She grasped Anna's wrist and tugged her closer to the gate. He scared Anna. He was fierce and he looked unkind, but Blessing walked right up to him and spoke in the language of the Ashioi. He laughed, and it was obvious even to Anna that these fluent words did not surprise him; he had guessed all along. When he spoke, replying, Blessing gasped out loud. She yelped with joy. She released Anna's arm and hopped in a circle.

"He says he'll take me, he'll train me in arms to be a mask warrior, like the others. Right now! So I can kill bad people. He won't make me wait, not like my daddy did."

"You can't go with them, Your Highness!"

"Why not? I can go! I hate it here. He's given me a new name, and I like it better!"

"What name?" she asked, as her voice was throttled by fear. The uncle did not even look at her, because she didn't matter to him. He only looked at Blessing, with a cruel smile.

"He calls me 'Little Beast.' I like that name!" She danced over to his side, and he was so delighted that he tousled her dark hair as if with affection.

"You're too young!" cried Anna.

The girl took her uncle's hand and, without a backward glance, walked through the gate.

"Then let me come with you!"

But Blessing was already gone, and the masked warriors pushed Anna back into her prison and shut the gate.

8

"WE have waited long enough," said the blood knives. "We marched out here into the wilderness, Feather Cloak. We are exposed, we might be attacked, we risked contagion through contact with the corpses of the Pale Dogs. Now we have waited six nights and a day. Those who crossed through the loom have not returned."

Feather Cloak was drawing with a stick in the dirt, as she had been for the last six days, trying to understand the threads and angles by which the Pale Sun Dog had woven a gateway through the standing stones. The blood knives drew off to one side and began muttering together.

Secha dropped into a crouch beside Feather Cloak. "The sky counters are displeased with you, Feather Cloak."

"What do you think?" The other woman paused with the stick hovering above the earth. "Is the angle there sharp enough?"

Secha had already drawn the pattern; she had seen its measure at once, watching the sorcerer draw the bright threads down off the stars. It amused her that Feather Cloak struggled even though she had proved herself strong in the deep magic known to those who walked the spheres. Feather Cloak could reach into a thing and draw its qualities out of it, twist them and turn them. She could cause fog to rise out of the ground, or earth to crack, or vines to curl around the limbs of her enemy. When they had lived in exile, she had called the burning stone out of the aether and walked through it onto Earth. But angles and numbers defeated her. She looked very annoyed.

"What are you come here for?" she demanded, when Secha made no answer.

"To tell you that the work crew has cleared the bodies out of the village and cleansed them. The pit where the dead flesh is buried is ringed with death stones. Their spirits can't walk, to haunt us."

They had set up camp on level ground outside the ditch that ringed the deserted human village. It was a bare landscape that reminded her of exile, pale grass, brittle shrubs, and the long sweep of hills. On the seven days' march here they had seen no sign of human life, but birds flocked in great numbers out of the south where they had taken refuge in the Ashioi country. Small animals abounded, and they feasted on the little spitted creatures every night.

She rose. The grave site lay almost out of the site to the west, just off the trail that led onward into the enemy's lands. A few mask warriors were still piling stones on the mound, but it was well sealed according to the old custom.

"I think the stones are unnecessary," Secha commented.

Feather Cloak stood. She was not, in fact, wearing the feathered cloak; on the march out here she had set it aside as too cumbersome, despite the sky counters' protest. "Let them have their ceremonies," she said dismissively.

"If you do not show them respect, they will come to hate you."

Feather Cloak looked sidelong at her, and that intense gaze sharpened. She had a way of tightening her jaw that made her look very threatening. "Why this concern, Secha? You've never liked me. Not even when we were children together."

"You do not know me very well."

"That is your answer, then. The blood knives do not know me very well." She ran a dusty foot over the dirt to erase the crooked hatch work she had drawn.

"The priests told me that the soles of the feet must never touch the ground, lest the sacred energy coiled within be released into the earth."

"My power is greater than the priests' ignorance. They know that, so they do not challenge me."

"Not yet."

"If you cannot help, then leave me alone."

"As you command, Feather Cloak."

She walked down the path to the village, crossed the bridge of logs laid across the ditch, and passed through the open gate. A third of the company was resting in camp, a third was on guard, and the rest were roaming through the abandoned houses and sheds, looking for anything valuable. The biggest crowd had gathered around one long stone building set a little ways away from the others, with a monstrous stone hearth at the back. Here she found her daughters, one carried by her son and the other by their father.

Her son saw her immediately, and he ran over to her. He was such a good-looking boy, and although he was short and slender because of the years of deprivation, he was clever, and he was eating a lot these days and putting on weight.

The baby was awake. She reached for her mother as soon as she came close. Secha took her and settled her on her hip as the youth circled, unable to stand still.

"The mask warriors are saying that according to the old custom, I'm old enough to be shield carrier now."

"That's what you want?" she asked him, although she already knew his answer, and he only grinned, knowing she knew. "It's important to choose carefully who you bind yourself to as an apprentice," she added. "You want the best training, and a chance to prove yourself when you're ready, but not before."

But he was already dashing off, no doubt to spill the good news to that young mask warrior he had been following around. Well. She would make sure that he wasn't put in *that* unit. He would need a trustworthy mentor, someone steady and experienced.

The warriors parted respectfully to let her through into the stone building. It had a stone floor, and a tile roof that had collapsed in one corner. All the windows had lost their shutters. The stones were blackened along one wall, heavy roof beams scorched. Charcoal and other debris littered the floor. It looked as though the place had burned. On the side opposite the massive hearth, shelves had collapsed, and broken pottery made the footing tricky. A pair of mask warriors were picking through the debris by the shelves, although she had no idea what they hoped to find.

Rain had the other baby slung on his back. He was scavenging through the tools near the stone hearth, which was built rather like a little house, open on one side. In some cases these metal implements were merely rims of metal whose bodies of wood had burned away. But there was a massive hammerhead with a hole for a haft, a pair of black iron spears no longer than his arm, tongs and rings, and a spray of spear points and ax and adze heads scattered on the stone floor beside heaps of slag and crumbling charcoal dust.

Seeing her, he smiled.

"This was a forge," he said, displaying a lump of melted bronze on his palm. He set it back down and picked up three wedges in turn, each one bigger than the one before. "Look at the strength of this metal. This must be iron! My master always said iron was impossible to work, yet here it's been done. There's a quarry a short walk from here, and I think they were mining up in the hills. We could make an outpost here, start a mining operation of our own. There's trees enough for charcoal. If we only had the smithing magic." He hefted the massive hammerhead in both hands. "To be able to forge iron like this . . . well, they say the raiding parties in the east are looking for blacksmiths."

She settled down cross-legged and in those ruins nursed the babies as he babbled on, showing her each tool and speculating on its purpose, and in this manner fell into a reminiscence about the man he had apprenticed to when he was very young. He'd learned a few things, enough to appreciate the craft and the sorcery, but the old smith had died too early and the knowledge had been lost. That was when Rain had turned to flint-knapping and gained respect for skills honed over many years of practice.

So many had died.

But the days in exile were over, although the taste of dust was still fresh in her mouth. The suck of life is powerful. The babies were strong and sturdy, dark and fat. They were beautiful, and so was this world with its sere hills and secret winds, its changeable sky and restless sea. Even the breath of ancient burning had brought new life to this small corner, where bugs scurried in the cracks and a dusky green vine had grown in through the open window and announced its presence with a pair of perfect white flowers.

Every window is a gateway onto another place. She thought of the doorway woven by the Pale Sun Dog, and she wept a little, remembering the beauty of those glittering threads.

"It'll be dusk soon," he said, interrupting himself. "You'll want to go back to the stones." He took the sleeping babies from her and let her go.

Dawn and dusk were gateways, a passage between night and day.

So was each footstep, which brought you farther from the place you started but closer to the place you hoped to reach.

The youngest of the blood knives was lurking by the village gate, and she fell in beside Secha, looking around with all the furtive nonsensicalness of a child playing at hide-and-seek. She was not much older than Secha's own son, but she was a sleek and fine young woman who seemed years older, honed to a cutting edge that made young men stare. She was not at all the kind of woman Secha had any wish for a sweet lad like her own dear son to fall into lust with, but otherwise she liked her far better than any of the older blood knives.

"They're sour and bitter," said the girl with a smirk, as if she had tasted Secha's thoughts. "They want to go back to the temples and lick blood off their tongues. But I know you understood the magic of weaving, didn't you?"

"No. But I could. If someone taught me its secrets."

They crossed the ditch in silence except for the creak of planks beneath their feet.

"In the house of youth I was best in my cohort at calculating numbers," the girl confessed without humility. "It was a great honor to my household when the sky counters brought a serpent skirt to the chief of our village. They tied the sash of apprenticeship over my shoulder and sent me out to serve with the army. But now I see something I want more."

Secha nodded, and the girl looked at her and nodded, and that was all that needed to be said.

A pair of brawny mask warriors walked past, going toward the village, and the young woman tilted her chin and canted her shoulders and twitched a hip so that they flushed dark and pulled on their ears and hurried on, too intimidated to look back after her.

"Why do you do that?" Secha asked.

"Because I can." Then she started, like a young hare. "Best they not see me with you," she murmured, and shied off into the camp as swiftly as she could without running and drawing more attention to herself.

The blood knives were preparing to depart the camp in the company of Feather Cloak and a number of mask warriors, so Secha fell in at the end of the procession, unnoticed and undisturbed. Just beyond the encampment a path split off from the main road and curled up over a slope. Within a cradle of shallow hills stood the eleven stones that marked this circle. Ten stood as though newly raised while the eleventh had fallen off to one side where the hillside had caved in under it. The brambles and vines that had covered it had been cleared away in the last few days.

They waited somewhat back from the circle, since no one wanted to get too close. No one knew quite what to expect, even though the dawns and dusks of the last six days had passed uneventfully. The young serpent skirt sidled out of the gathering shadows to join the other sky counters. She did not look once at Secha; her gaze was fixed on the dark stones.

The wind died. Twilight settled. Out here beyond the White Road, they rarely saw the sun, and tonight the entire sky was covered with a mantle of pale cloud. It was chilly. A pair of warriors breathed into their hands. Feather Cloak was tapping her foot, looking irritated and impatient. She had brought Little Beast with her—the rest of the hostages had been left behind in a pen—and her granddaughter stood perfectly still. The contrast was almost amusing. She was waiting. They all were waiting. Each in their own way.

It was entirely quiet. Distant sounds drifted on the wind: a goat's complaint, chiming laughter, a snatch of song.

A faint melody ringing as out of the heavens tingled through her, seeping into flesh and bone. She gasped.

The crown flowered into a blossom of brilliant light, threads weaving and crossing, caught in the warp of the unseen stars and wefted through the stones. Led by Fox Mask, the mask warriors burst out of the gateway. They were laughing and howling and chattering and singing, burdened with tools and sacks and an iron kettle and a pair of cows and four horses and a herd of terrified sheep and one interested dog that everyone seemed to ignore although the animal was busily keeping the sheep in a tight group.

The blood knives cried out a brief poem, a song of praise, because there were six prisoners as well, bound and under close guard, one woman in long robes and five men, all struggling against the ropes that restrained them.

Last came Zuangua. He held an iron sword drawn behind the Pale Sun Dog, whose face was pale with weariness. Threads dissolved into a shower of sparks. These flares died, and suddenly it was dark.

"Silence!" cried Feather Cloak.

"Success!" barked Fox Mask in answer, and in reply they heard the weeping and curses of the prisoners.

Sparks bit, and oil lamps and reed tapers were lit. Light and shadow wove through the assembly.

Zuangua said, "Where is my Little Beast?"

Little Beast sprang forward and barreled into him. He patted her on the head as he might a favored dog. "Can I go with you next time, Uncle?" she demanded. "I'm old enough to be a shield bearer."

Her speech was fluid and fluent, shockingly so, but they had gotten used to it; everyone agreed it was some gift of the blood or the taint of sorcery, inherited from her mother. Maybe she had been bitten by snakes.

"Old enough," he agreed carelessly, and he looked at the blood knives as if daring them to try to wrest her from him.

But the priests stared avidly at the prisoners. The woman in long robes had begun chanting in a singsong voice that reminded Secha of the sky counters' praying. It seemed she had power, because the other prisoners calmed and steadied, although by their flaring eyes and gritted teeth they were still as terrified as the bleating sheep. There was a short man with thick arms and massive shoulders; there was a youth little older than her own son; there was a man with blood on his tunic and another who limped from a wound, and the last was white-faced with shock although he was the tallest and plumpest among them.

"You can't have all of them," said Zuangua to the priests. "Those two—" He indicated the burly man and the youth. "—we took from their forging house. They're blacksmiths."

The priest-woman in her long robes looked toward the stone circle. The Pale Dog was leaning against one of the stones as though exhausted, his eyes closed and his breathing shallow. His mouth was parted, and his chin and jaw and lips moved ever so slightly, as if he were talking to himself in an undertone. Everything was pale in him, fair hair, fair skin, undyed linen tunic pallid against the night, and a gold circle hung on a necklace at his fair throat. The dark stone framed him, highlighting his beauty and his cunning power, his strength and his shine.

The priest-woman cursed him. You didn't need to understand the words to hear the power of her speech.

But if he heard her, he gave no sign. His eyes remained closed. He might have been sleeping, mumbling as dreamers do, except for the twitching of one little finger.

Zuangua had a mask after all, one tipped up on his head: he wore the visage of a dragon, proud and golden, just as he was.

"I have something to say," he began, and Feather Cloak raised a hand to allow him to continue.

"He is a very evil man," observed Zuangua as his warriors waved their hands in agreement. "He has lost even the love and loyalty for kinfolk that every person ought to have! He betrayed them all, without mercy."

"Thus will humankind fall," said Feather Cloak. "They are faithless each to the other."

Secha spoke up. "Not all of them are. Liathano kept faith with your son, Sanglant."

At the mention of those names, the Pale Dog's jaw tightened, but he did not open his eyes. He had very good hearing.

"Your son kept faith with his father," said Zuangua to Feather Cloak, "which I saw with my own eyes." He grinned wickedly. "Even this 'little beast' who stands at my side seems to love me."

The girl glanced at him, surprised at his words, then grinned. "You'll teach me to fight!" she exclaimed.

"Beware the beast does not bite you in your time," said Feather Cloak.

"I'd never bite him! I like him, and I *hate* you."

Feather Cloak studied the girl. In truth, thought Secha, her disinterest in her only grandchild was no more unnatural than the pale sun hair's disavowal of his kin. "I thought you hated this one called 'Lord Hugh.' "

"I hate him! He's a very bad man. He'll cheat you if he can. He'll kill you."

Feather Cloak smiled, amused, perhaps, by the piping voice and passionate expression of the girl. "A fair warning, Little Beast. He may try. He is not as strong or as clever as he thinks he is. What of the raid, Uncle?"

He indicated everything they had captured. "We walked between this crown and one that Sun Hair told us was far in the north. He called the place *Thersa*. We took the villagers by surprise. They could not fight us. It may be true that the Pale Dogs are many, that they have multitudes, and that we are few. But I tell you, it will be difficult for them to protect themselves against this manner of warfare."

She raised both hands.

The wind came up just then, as though she had called it, and possibly she had. Or maybe it was just the night wind rising off the cooling ground. There was a hint of salt in that air, a fine hissing spray carried in from the sea. And another scent as well, a witching smell that made her ears itch.

The prisoners fell silent. The blood knives covered their faces and prayed. With a puzzled frown, Feather Cloak lowered her hands.

The Pale Sun Dog opened his eyes and, without letting his gaze rest even for an instant on the other Pale Dogs, he scanned the heavens and then the surrounding slopes, the tender grass in its pale splendor and the thorny shrubs that lay along the slopes as strands of darkness. A nightjar whirred. An owl who-whooed.

The night breeze was cool, teasing her hair, kissing her cheeks. That salt breath of the sea faded, and now after all it was only a common night, cloudy, cool, and filled with the crickling of nocturnal insects.

Feather Cloak spoke. "Among the Wendish there is a saying: 'the *luck* of the *king*.' If the *king*'s fortunes fail him, then no warrior will follow him. *'A prince without a retinue is no prince,'* which means that without followers, he cannot rule. If we are not strong enough to defeat Sanglant and shatter his army, then we need only cause such devastation in his country that his people cry for a new feathered cloak—a new *regnant*—to save them. There are others who claim the right to lead. It matters not which one leads, or which one claims. Best if they fight among themselves, because that will weaken them. Destroy Sanglant's support, destroy the trust his people have in him, and you have destroyed him even if you have not killed him."

"He is your son," said Zuangua, looking a little disgusted.

"He turned his back on his mother's kinfolk. He swore allegiance to the Pale Dogs. He can't be trusted."

Zuangua shrugged. "No one distrusts the Pale Dogs more than I do. Yet if your son can't be trusted, then neither can this one. For it seems to me that he has done worse by turning his back on his kin and his kind, all and together. At least your son keeps faith with those he has sworn community with. This one is no kind of trustworthy ally."

"I did not say I trusted him. But what he offers, we can use. We will learn as much as we can from him, and after we are done, we will kill him. We will let the blood knives have him, if they can bind him. We will kill all of the human sorcerers, those who know the secret of the crowns. Then the sorcery of the looms can never again be used against us. For this reason, I will accept his alliance."

The blood knives nodded eagerly. The mask warriors stamped their feet and barked and howled and shrieked approval. The prisoners huddled close to the priest-woman her long robes, and even she with her words of power looked afraid. The flickering light made a golden mask of Feather Cloak's face.

Zuangua nodded thoughtfully. "Yes. We must kill all the human sorcerers. They are the most dangerous of all."

Feather Cloak raised both hands, palms facing heaven, to allow the gods a glimpse into her soul. "I accept his offer of alliance. I offer him in turn the woman called Liathano."

"What of a powerful offering for the gods?" demanded the blood knives. "What of your promise to us?"

"You can have her afterward," said Feather Cloak, and she smiled mockingly at them. "If you can bind her."

"This is a bad thing," muttered Secha.

"To protect ourselves is a bad thing?"

"To seal an agreement on a lie is a bad thing."

But Kansi-a-lari, The Impatient One, was Feather Cloak now.

"I have spoken," she said irritably.

She beckoned to Sun Hair. She let him approach her. The prisoners watched in dread and anger, and her company watched with an intense excitement so palpable that it seemed to Secha that the ground trembled beneath the soles of her feet, shaken by their eagerness.

These were the tokens they exchanged: He gave to Feather Cloak an iron feather whose essence was so pure that it gleamed with a light all its own. She gave to him a folded mantle, a humble item, to be sure, but he pressed the cloth to his face as though it were the end of his desire.

Thus was the bargain sealed, and their path chosen.

9

MIDNIGHT—or as close to midnight as they could estimate, since no stars were visible to measure out time. They measured by psalms instead, and when they finished singing "Vindicate me, God, for I have walked without blame," all quieted.

Because the church in Novomo had been built in the waning years of the Dariyan Empire, it boasted an impressive processional frieze worked into both walls of the nave above the twin rows of columns that separated the nave from the aisles on either side. In those shadowed aisles waited courtiers and servants, their faces unseen except as pale washes marked by the dark stones that were their eyes and the occasional flash of a ring or gold necklace catching candlelight. Above the waiting masses, the frieze marked the ascent of saints and martyrs toward the Hearth. Each held a saint's crown to place before God. The colored stones in the mosaic shimmered to mark their holy robes and their holy crowns. Even their eyes shone; in this way the saints differ from the guilty who live and suffer on Earth, whose eyes are only pits in whose depths the righteous can discern the black stain of the Enemy.

Candlelight alone lit the church except for a single oil lamp placed on the Hearth itself and burning with the confidence and constancy of the just. By the smoky flames of threescore slender candles the ancient faces of the holy saints and martyrs watched and judged, their serene expressions caught forever in mosaics so cunningly worked that they almost appeared to be a painting. In the empty nave, threescore clerics lined up in two rows. Each cleric carried a taper in cupped hands. Back by the portico, Empress Adelheid and her consort waited under a mosaic rendering of the old palace that had once stood in Novomo; that structure was now half buried within the new palace, which had been erected about a hundred years ago and restored and remodeled several times since then.

So it was with the world: The skopos stood closest to God, beside the altar, and her clerics faced her with the light of truth in their hands. Secular power must wait at the doors of the church, because it could not enter fully. As for the rest, they must huddle in the shadows and pray.

Antonia raised her hands although she had already commanded silence. To her right Lord Berthold knelt on one knee, an arm braced against his thigh. His companion, Lord Jonas, stared at the ground, cowed and frightened, but Berthold studied the scene with the expression of a man who has seen the loveliest rose on Earth trampled and shredded before his eyes. He had grown up well loved and well protected by his father's affection and by his high rank. No doubt the youth had never before understood how cruel and ugly the world was in truth. He did now. You could see it in the way he stared as if he wasn't seeing, in the way he heard and saw without showing the least color of feeling, as if all emotion had been drained out of him with one sharp, deep cut. As it had been, because weeks ago he had woken to find Lady Elene dead beside him and her blood coagulating around his fingers and sleeves and in the tips of his hair.

That was the truth of the world. It was long past time he discovered it for himself, although unfortunately it had not seemed to bring him to prayer service more often, as it should have. She had offered him a position in her schola—in time a youth of his lineage could hope to rise to become presbyter—but he had refused her so tonelessly that she had known at once that his soul had already fallen into the Pit and was spinning and tumbling in the darkness.

"It is written in the Holy Verses that we will love God, who are Mother and Father of Life for us all, at rest in the Circle of Unity which binds us. How then can the holy church recognize as regnant a man who murdered his own father? How can the holy church bless those who allow such a man to raise himself to power after such an unjust deed? To bless those who have turned against the church and the skopos?"

The halo of light scarcely brushed Adelheid, but Antonia knew her well enough to see by the cant of her shoulders and the tilt of her pale chin that the empress was smiling. The general shifted restlessly. He could speak Dariyan but not so well that he easily understood the words of clerics and scholars, the words of the church whose tenets his kinfolk rejected.

It still galled her, but she knew that even a crude tool may suffice. Must suffice. General Lord Alexandros was, in fact, correct: if Arethousa and Aosta were to survive, they must protect each other against attacks from all sides.

Therefore.

"Let those who aid this patricide be cursed. May they be cursed in their towns and in their fields. May they be cursed in their cattle and in their flocks. May they be cursed in their children and in their graveyards, in their granaries and in the work of their hands. Those who do not obey this decree, those who offer aid and comfort, will disappear from the Earth. They will be swallowed by fire and swept away by the sea. In waking and sleeping, in eating and drinking, in both bread and wine will they be cursed. They are bound by the chains of anathema. They are exiled from the Circle of Unity."

She extended a hand. Brother Petrus, standing at her left, handed her the trio of scrolls on each one of which the ban was recorded. These she offered to Lord Berthold, who took them without a word of comment and without any change in his mask of stone.

"As these tapers are extinguished, so shall the light of those who disobey us be extinguished and cast into the darkness."

Each cleric knelt and ground out the flame against the floor. The church drowned in darkness, but for the single lamp burning behind the holy mother who rules over all, skopos and guardian of God's Truth.

The Abyss must be dark like this. Black and empty to the eye but swarming with the pitiful breath of souls who wonder, hopelessly, what will come next. Because, of course, nothing will come next. They are doomed to fall forever. That is the true meaning of the curse.

She savored the silence. Every soul there was cowed, as they should be, wondering what power she had that she might raise. The skopos was most powerful of all, and it was necessary for them to remember that.

"Come, Jonas," said Berthold quietly behind her. "Wolfhere and the others should have come now with the horses from the stable. Let's go."

Something about the tone of his voice bothered her. "You will deliver the decree, Lord Berthold," she said in a low voice, not wanting her words to carry. "Others will follow on your trail, in case you do not survive the journey. Lest you think to shirk your duty to the skopos."

Out in the nave and aisles, no one had yet gained enough nerve to act or speak.

"I will survive the journey. The Eagle will guide us."

"So he will. He was spared for that purpose. As were you."

"Think you so?" he asked defiantly, and she would have had him scourged for his disrespect, but then it would be all to do over again. No one else had heard. This one time, she would have to let it go.

He rose and, with Jonas following at his heels like a dog, walked down the center of the nave until he and his companion faded into the gloom between the ranks of clerics. She heard the door open, but not close. As they waited they all of them heard a few distant comments, the cheerful ring of harness, and caught a glimpse of a lantern raised high and moving out of sight as the riders left the courtyard on the first stage of their long journey.

All the foreigners were, at long last, gone. Even the cremated remains and pickled heart of Lady Elene had been packed into a box and sent with Berthold. The skulls of Hugh's party, though, had long since been cast out onto the trash heap.

After a long silence came the *snick* of flint on metal and the flare of a wick catching a spark as one of Adelheid's servants lit a lamp. Down the nave Antonia faced that other flame, placed behind the empress and her consort. What is holy and what is profane must ever be at odds, and yet they must work together as well, because the world is imperfect, stained by darkness.

"Come, Holy Mother," said the empress. "We have rid ourselves of the Wendish at last. In the morning, we will rise free of the taint of northerners. Let them rot without God's blessing, so I pray."

With so many soldiers accompanying the general, Antonia could not mention that the easterners plagued them still.

And yet.

At least the Arethousans knew civilization of a kind, unlike the raw barbarians out of the north who had learned only a hundred years ago to dress in decent clothing instead of a patchwork of skins. The Arethousans were heretics, of course, but at least they had known the name of the blessed Daisan for as many centuries as had the noble Aostans. The northerners had worshiped hills and stones and graves and trees until a generation ago, and some still did in secret, hoarding their heathen ways despite knowing that such falsehoods would bring disaster down on their heads.

Well. Her knees hurt, and her back had a twinge. The robes weighed on her shoulders, and she would be sore tomorrow from standing for so long. She signaled, and folk hustled out of the church in unseemly haste, as if the ceremony had disturbed them when it should have bolstered their determination. Her attendants rushed to help her, bringing a chair. They carried her under the dome decorated with stars and heavenly creatures: a dragon, a griffin, a serpent with a woman's body and face, and a sphinx. A private door was nestled behind a curtain, concealing a small room to one side of the apse. Here, in private, they helped her out of the mantle and vestments. They offered her a couch and wine to rest on. Here, empress and general settled side by side on a second couch, then sipped wine out of golden cups.

"Is there more we can do?" Adelheid asked. "What of the galla, Holy Mother? Surely they could be sent hunting. A Wendish biscop here, a Varren lord there. That would frighten them, would it not?"

"And might rebound against us, if we are accused of harboring malefici, Your Majesty."

"Sorcery is a weapon, like a sword is a weapon," said Alexandros. "If you can thrust, then thrust."

"The ruling of the Council of Narvone has never been superseded," said Antonia patiently. "In western lands it is specifically forbidden to use black sorcery."

"What is this Council of Narvone?" the general asked. "In the east there is only one council that speaks on sorcery. In the holy year of The Word, the year 327, the Council at Kellai did not prohibit magic. Magic is allowed if it is supervised by the church. This ruling we follow in Arethousa. When is—was—this Council at Narvone?"

Antonia examined him thoughtfully. "I did not know you followed church affairs so closely, Lord Alexandros. The Council of Narvone did not take place until after the death of the Emperor Taillefer. In the kingdom of Salia, women are not allowed to take the throne. Since Taillefer died leaving no sons but only daughters, the lords and church folk feared that one of his daughters would usurp power where she had no right to take any. Specifically, they feared his daughter Tallia, who was biscop of Autun. They confirmed the ruling of Kellai, but they condemned the arts of the mathematici, tempestari, augures, haroli, sortelegi, and the malefici, as well as any sorcery performed outside the auspices of the church."

"You rule the church, Holy Mother." Adelheid set down her cup. She had barely touched her wine, although the general called for a second cup for himself. Brother Petrus poured, then retreated to stand by the other servants. Lady Lavinia directed a servant to light a third lamp.

"God rule the church, Your Majesty. Do not forget this, I pray. If we choose to use sorcery, we must tread carefully. Anne did not, and she is dead. My powers are not as great as hers were."

Adelheid shrugged. "So you say, but I never saw her perform more than illusion. It was Hugh's magic that bound the daimone into Henry. Everyone says she was powerful, but in that case, why is she dead, and why did she fail?"

"I have no skill in the arts of the tempestari," said Antonia. "I cannot read the future out of the movements of birds and the placement of entrails, a power some claim. I am no mathematicus, to weave within the crowns. That skill remains beyond me."

"Then what can you do?" Adelheid demanded.

"I know the art of bindings and workings."

" 'Bindings and workings,' " repeated Alexandros, each syllable precise because he did not, quite, understand what she meant by the phrase. "This 'bindings and workings' is not mentioned at your Council of Taillefer, is it?"

"No, indeed, it is not."

They sat in a simple room at odds with the elaborate decoration in the church beyond. Here were only whitewashed bricks but no mosaic work. A pair of couches, covered with wine-colored fabric and stitched with gold thread, faced each other in the middle of the room. An unexceptional table was pushed up against one wall; it held a burning lamp, a vase filled with dried stalks of lavender and a single red rose, a pair of lectionaries, and a forgotten goose quill caught in that slight groove between the curved edge of the table and the wall. Not one tapestry adorned the walls. These walls were as blameless as an unblemished calf being led to the slaughter. A lamp molded in the shape of a griffin hung from a hook sunk into a dark beam overhead. A brass lamp molded in the shape of a dragon remained unlit. A lamp burned over the door, flame twisting behind glass like the soul of a daimone bound into the body of a mortal man. Just so had Henry lived and died.

Hugh and Anne had both used her, of course. They had sought to manipulate her to do their dirty work for them without teaching her the sorcery they themselves knew. With knowledge comes power. But she had outlived them both—as long, that is, as Hugh was really dead. Anne's demise she rarely doubted, but she still wondered about Hugh. They had never found the thirteenth skull.

Sanglant had escaped death at the hands of the galla. That meant it was possible to survive where the galla stalked.

"He is dead," she murmured, trying the word on her tongue, savoring it but finding it bitter and unreliable.

Alexandros' good eye studied her, then examined the chamber, the servants, the walls, and the lamps, each in turn, as if marking the position of his enemy before battle is joined. His gaze halted on the empress. The taut line of his mouth softened. Adelheid's crown gleamed under lamp light. The gauzy glamour of the light made her look young again, particularly handsome this night, a gentle, pretty woman in need of a strong arm to hold her upright in stormy weather.

Like Henry, Alexandros was a fool. So were all men.

All but Hugh, now that she thought on it. Hugh had never desired Adelheid. Yet Hugh had been a fool like all the others; he had only fixed on other prey.

As she must.

Alexandros spoke. "Who is most dangerous to us, in the north? It must be Sanglant, the king. If Wendar is strong, then Wendar threatens us. If Wendar is weak, they will not attack us. Already we must guard on our south against the Cursed Ones. On our east, against the Jinna. I say: kill Sanglant, and we are safe a while from Wendar."

"It's said he can't be killed," said Antonia, "although I've never believed it."

"Henry believed it," said Adelheid. "He spoke of it often. He *bragged* of it. How could he have loved that one more than the others? Well. Maybe it's true, but we must still try. And what of his wife? The sorcerer, Liathano? Isn't she dangerous?"

"Liathano!" Alexandros nodded vigorously. "The prince's concubine. She who is named after the Horse woman who cannot die."

"How comes it you have heard of her?" asked Antonia.

He smiled, taking his time, and answered. "We are allies for a time with King Geza of Ungria. He took Princess Sapientia as his wife."

"She was married to Geza's brother, Prince Bayan," cried Adelheid. "Henry would not have liked that! A naked grab for power!"

Alexandros chuckled. "We are all naked, Your Majesty," he said in a way that made Antonia wonder if she ought to trust him less, or trust him more.

The words made Adelheid laugh. She drank her wine.

"This one, called Liathano," continued Alexandros. "At her we strike, if the man stands beyond our reach."

"Tempting," mused Antonia. "She is powerful. It isn't likely we can harm her."

"What harm to try?" demanded Adelheid. "Strike there, and you weaken Sanglant. It is only a few galla."

"What harm except to the men whose blood must be spilled to call the creatures out of the Pit," said Antonia with a frown, not liking the empress' levity. "If we kill heedlessly, our own people may turn against us."

"There are guilty aplenty who have earned death," said Adelheid.

"And many innocent who deserve life," said Alexandros, "but are dead."

The fool believed in innocence, no doubt because he must believe his wife and children stainless although every Arethousan was stained by their heretical beliefs. It was only remarkable that God had waited so long to castigate them.

"Your Majesty. Lord General. I am willing to act against the one called Liathano. But what does it benefit us to kill her, beyond the satisfaction of revenge?"

Adelheid shook her head. "Revenge is satisfaction enough! Reason enough! If Sanglant cannot be killed, then kill what he loves best. Send galla. Send spies. Send what you will. But if she is dead, then he will suffer as I have suffered. That is good enough for me."

EPILOGUE

FROM Gent, the king and his retinue rode to the northern sea. Just as the young guardsman had reported, the shoreline was substantially altered. The river had lost its path to the sea and now spilled into a vast expanse of marsh where once it had pushed through in a double channel emptying into the wide northern waters. The shoreline, according to a pair of locals who guided them, had actually receded, leaving the seabed exposed and sandy flats scoured by the winter winds, casting sand inland in great stinging storms.

"After the tempest," said the spry crone whose commentary Sanglant found most reliable, "the river ran backward, and eddied, for a fortnight. There was flooding upstream. Yet water will flow north out of the southern hills. Now, you see," she pointed at the expanse of flat ground cut by ribbons of trickling water, "how it is clawing a hundred finger tracks to the sea."

They stood on a bluff overlooking what had once been the deeper, western channel. Its exposed troughs had only a trickle of water pushing through them. The rest of the ground was slick with rocks and water weed, and littered with the skeletons of a half dozen sunken, battered ships. Here and there he glimpsed what might be bones tumbled every which way. A vast, rusted chain snaked across the old channel.

Liath was exploring through the muck below with Sibold and Lewenhardt in attendance. They were laughing at something Sibold had pried up from a muddy hole, but he couldn't see what it was. Liath straightened and looked up toward him, lifted a hand to acknowledge him, and went back to her excavations.

Sanglant wandered along the bluff, marking where unknown folk had built and later abandoned two ballistae.

"I wonder," said Hathui, who remained always at his side, "if these are the catapults used by Count Lavastine to break the Eika fleet as it escaped out to sea."

"Lavastine? This is not his county."

"He was with King Henry, Your Majesty, when the king brought an army to retake Gent."

"Of course. I recall it now. His heir . . ."

He paused, remembering with unexpected clarity that awful moment at the feast held to celebrate King Henry's victory at Gent over the Eika chieftain, Bloodheart. After gorging on food laid out before him, he had had to bolt into the darkness to empty his stomach. He had been, in those days, little better than a prince among dogs, half wild, barely conscious of his human mind. Lavastine's son had come to him at the edge of camp, and Lord Alain had treated him gently, with respect and kindness, so that he did not feel shame at his condition. He touched the gold torque at his neck, where once an iron collar had chafed him. *"As long as you wear the collar at your neck, then surely you will not be free of Bloodheart's hand on you,"* the young man had said to him.

True words, although he hadn't understood them then.

"What happened to him?" he asked.

"Lavastine's heir? It transpired that he was not after all Lavastine's son, bastard or otherwise. Lord Geoffrey's daughter was named as heir. The one called Alain might have been punished more severely, but it wasn't possible to prove that he had had a deliberate hand in the deception. Some declared that Lavastine had forced the youth to accept his position as son. Most in the county praised his stewardship. The king chose to be merciful and allow the lad to serve him another way. He marched as a Lion into the east. After that, I do not know."

"He showed me kindness. I can't forget that."

He returned to the locals, who had obviously explored this site before and in the intervening years scavenged what they could from the wreckage. On the highest windswept curve of the bluff he stood knee-deep in windblown grass as he surveyed the land.

Liath and her companions had struck out across the old channel, following the path made by the massive chain. Beyond the riverbed, to the east, lay rockier ground, and beyond that a delta of reeds and drowned grass. In the other direction, to the west, had once lain pastureland and broken woodland, but these had turned to marsh, and now the scrub and trees soaked their feet in water. North, the old tidal flats that had once surfaced only at low tide gleamed in barren splendor, completely exposed. The sea shone in the distance, visible as a shimmer of silver running below the pale horizon of cloud.

"Snowmelt," said the crone. "Floods from the melt cut those little channels through the flats. There was plenty of snow last winter and too much rain in the autumn, before the great storm. But we've had no rain for planting season."

"It's like the heavens closed right up," said her cousin, who was quieter but more inclined to fancy. "Like they was a wineskin run dry." He nodded to himself, and grinned, liking his comparison.

"You're quite the poet!" retorted his skeptical cousin. She was steward at a royal estate and had, as a child, spoken once to King Arnulf the Younger himself, so she had no hesitation in addressing a new king young enough to be her grandson. "What it means to us, Your Majesty, is that we've had no planting season, what with this frost and every night so cold. Will these clouds ever leave?"

Sanglant had no answer. The tides of destruction had reached farther than he had ever dreamed possible. He could only assess the changes in the land and, with his progress, ride on through a world transformed.

CAST OF CHARACTERS

Historical characters are not listed as deceased.

Characters listed as deceased are those who died within fifteen years (or so) **before** the action in **King's Dragon** begins. Characters who die during the course of the series are not listed as deceased in this list.

Wendar and Varre:

King Henry (son of Arnulf the Younger and Mathilda of Karrone)(king regnant)
his bastard son by Alia (Kansi-a-lari):
    Sanglant
his children by Sophia of Arethousa (first wife):
    Sapientia
    Theophanu
    Ekkehard
his children by Adelheid of Aosta (second wife):
    Mathilda
    Berengaria

Henry's brothers and sisters:
Richildis (renamed Scholastica, abbess of Quedlinhame)
Rotrudis (duchess of Saony)
Benedict (married to Marozia of Karrone)
Constance (biscop of Autun and later duchess of Arconia)
Bruno

various other children who died in infancy

Alberada (Henry's illegitimate half sister, daughter of Arnulf the Younger, now biscop of Handelburg)

Sabella (half sister, daughter of Arnulf the Younger and Berengaria of Varre)

the Regnant's Progress:

His Schola:

Rosvita

  Her Clerics:

  Amabilia

  Constantine

  Fortunatus

  Gerwita

  Heriberg

  Jehan

  Jerome

  Ruoda

  Aurea (a servant)

  Other Clerics:

  Elsebet

  Eudes

  Monica

His Lions:

Thiadbold (a captain)

Artur

Dedi

Folquin

Gerulf

Gotfrid (a sergeant)

Ingo

Karl

Leo

Stephen

Fridesuenda (Dedi's betrothed)

His Eagles:
Ernst
Hanna
Hathui
Manfred
Rufus
Wolfhere

Sanglant's Retinue:
  m. to Liathano
    Blessing (their daughter)

His Schola:
Breschius
Heribert

His Personal Guard:
Captain Fulk
Captain Istvan
Anshelm
Arnulf
Berro
Chustaffus
Cobbo
Den
Ditmar
Everwin
Fremen
Johannes
Lewenhardt
Liutbald
Malbert
Maurits
Sibold
Surly
Wracwulf

Blessing's Retinue:
Heribert (see also schola, above)
Anna

Berda
Matto
Odei
Thiemo

Jerna (a daimone)

personal servants:
Ambrose
Johannes
Robert
Theodulf

other retainers:
Gyasi (a Quman shaman)
  his nephews, including Odei

Gnat (a Jinna)
Mosquito (a Jinna)

Argent (a male griffin)
Domina (a female griffin)

royal households:
Henry's servants:
Wito (a steward)

Sapientia's companions:
Everelda

Theophanu's companions:
Gutta (a serving woman)
Leoba

Ekkehard's companions:
Benedict
Frithuric
Lothar
Manegold
Milo
Thiemo
Welf

The Duchies:

Saony
Duchess Rotrudis
her children:
    Imma
    Sophie
    Wichman
    Zwentibold
    Reginar (abbot of Firsebarg)

Marcovefa (a Salian concubine)
Rowena (a deacon)

Fesse
Duchess Liutgard
m. to Frederic of Avaria (her husband, deceased)
their children:
    older daughter
    Ermengard

Avaria
Burchard and Ida
their children:
    Wendilgard
    Agius (a frater)
    Frederic (m. to Liutgard of Fesse, deceased)

Ucco (a mountain guide)

Arconia
Berengar and Sabella
their daughter:
    Tallia

Amalfred (a Salian lord)
Tammus (a captain, known also as Ulric, keeper of the guivre)

Wayland
Conrad (called "The Black")
m. to Eadgifu of Alba (first wife)

their children:
   Elene
   Aelfwyn
m. to Tallia of Varre (second wife)
their children:
   Berengaria
   two daughters (died in infancy)

Foucher (a foreman at the mines)
Robert (a criminal)
Walker (a slave at the mines)
Will (a slave at the mines)

Varingia
Duchess Yolanda (daughter of Rodulf the Elder and Ida)
Rodulf the Younger
Erchanger

Towns & Counties:

Autun:
Ulric (a captain)
Erkanwulf (a soldier)
Louisa (daughter of Captain Ulric)

Gent:
Amalia (lady of Gent)
Autgar (an apprentice to Suzanne)
Ernust (a guard)
Fastrada (a serving woman at the mayor's palace)
Frederun (a serving woman at the mayor's palace)
Gisela (mistress of Steleshame, a nearby village)
Hano (a saddler)
Helen (a foundling)
Hildegard (count of Gent)
Hrodik (lord of Gent)
Humilicus (a prior)
Matthias (Anna's brother)
Miriam (a child)
Raimar (Suzanne's betrothed)

Suzanne (a weaver)
Uota (a servant)
Werner (mayor)

Lavas Holding:
Lavastine (count, turned to stone by an Eika spell)
Lavastina (his great-grandmother)
Charles Lavastine (son of Lavastina)
Charles the Younger (son of Charles Lavastine, father of Lavastine)

Geoffrey (Lavastine's cousin, descendent of the younger brother
of Lavastina)
m. to unnamed lady (deceased)
Lavrentia (the current count)
m. to Aldegund (second wife)
two sons

Cook (a servant)
Dhuoda (a chatelaine)
Fell (a sergeant)
Heric (a servant)
Lackling (a servant)
Raimond (a servant)
Robert (a servant)
Rodlin (stable-master)
Rose (deceased, a refugee)
Ulric (a carter)
Waldrada (a deacon)
Withi (a woman)

Meginher, Aldegund's brother

North Mark:
Harl, count of the North Mark
married various women
his children:
Rosvita (a cleric)
Gero (heir and later count)
various children
Ivar

Dorit (a hired woman)
Fortensia (deacon in Heart's Rest)
Lars (a hired man)
Liudolf (a marshal)

Birta (an innkeeper)
m. to Hansal
their children:
    Thancmar
    Inga
    Hanna
    Karl

Osna:
Bel (a householder)
m. to Ado (deceased)
their children:
    Stancy
    m. to Artald
        various children
    Julien
        Blanche (illegitimate daughter)
    m. to Julia
        Conrad
    Bruno
    Agnes
    m. to Guy
Henri (Bel's brother)

Corinthia (a deacon)
Fotho (a woodsman)
Garia (a householder in Osna)
Giles Fisher (a boatbuilder)
Miria (a deacon)

The Bretwald:
Martin (a boy saved from Gent)
Flora (Martin's wife)
Balt
Baltia
Bruno

Nan
Ulf
Uta

Others:
Dietrich (a lord)

Church-folk:
Biscop Alberada of Handelburg
Biscop Antonia of Mainz (later removed from office)
Biscop Suplicia of Gent
Biscop Thierra
Deacon Adalwif (in the marchlands)
Methodius (prior at Quedlinhame)
Mother Otta (abbess of Korvei)
Mother Rothgard (abbess of St. Valeria)
Mother Scholastica (abbess of Quedlinhame)
Willibrod (a cleric in the service of Antonia)
Zacharias (a frater)

Hersford Monastery:
Adso (a monk)
Bardo (abbot)
Beatrix (cousin to Ortulfus)
Egbert (a monk)
Felicitus (gatekeeper)
Fidelus (a monk)
Hosed (a farmer whose land is tithed to the monastery)
Iso (a lay brother)
Lallo (monk in charge of the lay brothers)
Mangod (a lay brother)
Ortulfus (abbot)
Ratbold (prior)

Queen's Grave:
Ivar, son of Harl & Herlinde
Baldwin
Ermanrich
Hathumod
Sigfrid

Biscop Constance
her retinue:
Bona (a nun)
Eligia (a nun)
Frotharia (a nun, assistant to Nanthild)
Nanthild (the infirmarian)

Maynard (a villager)

The Marchlands

Austra and Olsatia
Judith
her children:
   Hugh (illegitimate)
   Gerberga (current margrave)
      m. to Ekkehard of Wendar
   Bertha
   Theucinda

Adelinde (companion to Judith)
Eigio (servant to Hugh)
Hemma (a serving woman)
Vindicadus (a servant in the employ of Hugh)

March of the Villams
Helmut Villam
his children by various wives:
   Waltharia, margrave
      m. to Druthmar
     several children
   Berthold

Hedwig (a former Eagle)
Humbert (a steward)
Jonas (comrade to Berthold Villam)
Waldhar (a servant)

Westfall
Werinhar (margrave of Westfall, deceased)

Eastfall
currently without a margrave

The Lands Beyond

Salia:
Clothilde (a deacon, attendant to Tallia)
St. Radegundis (the last queen of Taillefer)
Tallia (a biscop, daughter of Taillefer)
Taillefer (the emperor)

Arethousa:
Lady Eudokia
Lord Nikolas (nephew of Eudokia, putative emperor)

Basil (a chamberlain)

General Lord Alexandros
Sergeant Bysantius

Ungria:
King Geza
Prince Bayan
Lady Ilona (a widow)

Aosta:
Queen Adelheid
m. to unnamed lord (her first husband)(deceased)
m. to Henry of Wendar (her second husband)
   their children
   Mathilda
   Berengaria

her servants and soldiers and allies:
Lady Lavinia of Novomo
Captain Falco
Captain Rikard
Gerbert (a soldier)
Milo (a soldier)

the office of the skopos:
Clementia

Abelia (a cleric)
Hatto (a presbyter)
Ismundus (a presbyter)
Petrus (a presbyter)

others:
Arcod (a factor traveling with Brother Severus)
Ildoin (a monk traveling with Brother Severus)
John Ironhand (pretender to the Aostan throne)

St. Ekatarina's Convent:
Mother Aurica (abbess before Obligatia)(deceased)
Mother Obligatia
Carita
Diocletia
Hilaria
Lucida
Paloma (a lay sister)
Petra
Sindula
Teuda (a lay sister)

The Ashioi:
Eldest Uncle (twin of Zuangua) (father of Kansi)
Green Skirt
Kansi-a-lari, aka Uapeani-kazonkansi-a-lari,
   The Impatient One (Sanglant's mother)
Rain (a flintknapper)
Secha
Sharp Edge
Skull Earrings
White Feather
Zuangua (twin of Eldest Uncle)

warriors:
Buzzard Mask
Cat Mask

Falcon Mask
Fox Mask
Lizard Mask

The Eika:
the WiseMothers (the most ancient ones)
OldMother (the one who leads each tribe)
YoungMother (the next OldMother)
SwiftDaughters (those females who will not breed)

Rikin Fjord:
Stronghand
Bloodheart (Stronghand's father)

Rikin slaves:
Otto
Ursuline (a deacon)

other chiefs and individuals:
Dogkiller (Vitningsey's chief)
Flint (Hakonin's chief)
Grimstroke
Ironclaw (Isa's chief)
Nokvi (Moerin's chief)

Stronghand's army:
Aestan (an Alba soldier)
Eagor (aka Tiderunner)
Far-runner (friend of Yeshu)
Fellstroke
Last Son
Longnose
Quickdeath (of Hakonin)
Sharpspear
Tiderunner (friend to Aestan, aka Eagor)
Trueheart
Walker
Will
Yeshu (a Hessi interpreter)

Albans:
Eadig (earl of the Middle Country)
Ediki (of Weorod)
Elafi of the Isle (a sorcerer)
Erling (earl of the Middle Country)
Ki of the Isle
Manda of the Isle (Eel Tribe)

the Horse People:
Li'at'dano (a shaman, the Holy One)

Capi'ra (a warrior)

Sorgatani (a Kerayit shaman)
Berda (a Kerayit healer)

the Quman:
Bulkezu (a chief)
Cherbu (brother of Bulkezu, a shaman)
Gyasi (a shaman)
Odei (nephew of Gyasi)

Agnetha (a prisoner)
Boso (an interpreter)

the skrolin:
Gold-skin
Pale-skin
Pewter-skin

The Seven Sleepers:
Clothilde (founder)
Anne
Bernard (a frater)
   Liathano (called Liath) (his daughter)
Hiltrudis (deceased)
Marcus
Meriam (mother of Conrad the Black)
Rothaide (deceased)
Severus
Theoderada (deceased)

Venia (replaced by Reginar)
Wolfhere (replaced by Abelia)
Zoe (replaced by Hugh)

In The Past:
Abidi (Urtan's mate)
Adica (a shaman at Queen's Grave)
Agalleos (of the Copper people, uncle to Maklos and Shevros)
Agda (the healer at Queen's Grave)
Beor (war captain at Queen's Grave)
Dorren (a Walking One—a messenger)
Etora (Beor's sister)
Getsi (a granddaughter of Orla)
Hani (a young man of Kartia)
Hehoyanah (a young woman of Kartia)
Kel (a young man at Queen's Grave)
Kerayi (Weiwara's infant, aka Blue-bud)
Laoina (Walking One of the Akka people)
Maklos (of the Copper people, twin to Shevros)
Nahumia (leader at Old Fort)
Ni'at (of the Horse people)
Orla (leader of Queen's Grave)
Oshidos (of the Copper people)
Pur (a stone knapper at Queen's Grave)
Shevros (of the Copper people, twin to Maklos)
Sos'ka (of the Horse people)
Tosti (a young man at Queen's Grave)
Ulfrega (war captain at Four Houses)
Urta (child of Urtan)
Urtan (Adica's cousin)
Useti (Weiwara's older child)
Weiwara (a woman at Queen's Grave)
Wren (mate of Dorren)
Wrinkled-old-man (the younger twin born to Weiwara)

the weavers:
Adica (Queen's Grave)
Brightness-Hears-Me (the tribe of Essit)
Falling-down (the fens)
Hehoyanah (apprentice to Two Fingers)
Horn (dying)(replaced by Two Fingers)

Shuashaana (Shu-sha, of the Copper people)
Spits-last (Tanioinin of the Akka people)
Two Fingers (of Kartia)

the Three Queens:
Arrow Bright
Golden Sow
Toothless